METROPOLIS

—·—

A NOVEL

MONTE SCHULZ

FANTAGRAPHICS BOOKS ❦ SEATTLE, WASHINGTON

Fantagraphics Books, Inc.
7563 Lake City Way NE
Seattle, WA 98115
fantagraphics.com
@fantagraphics

Designer: Justin Allan-Spencer
Editor: Gary Groth
Proofreader: Conrad Groth
VP / Associate Publisher: Eric Reynolds
Publisher: Gary Groth

Front jacket art: *Still Life with Duckling and Weeds (After Jan Van Huysum)*
by Angela Lizon. 146 × 114 cm. Oil on linen.

Author photograph: Tom Vollick

Back jacket art: © 2021 Sony Interactive Entertainment LLC.
The Order: 1886 is registered trademark or trademark of
Sony Interactive Entertainment LLC. Illustration by Joe Studzinski.

ISBN: 978-1-68396-579-4
Library of Congress Control Number: 2021951176
First Fantagraphics Books edition: June 2022
Printed in China

To Gerald Rosen and Steven Allaback
who promised me I was a writer, all those years ago.

A colony of outcasts will break their chains, and obtain great dominion.

– *The Book of Fate*

Even now I dream of the airships emerging from those grey clouds at sunset like dark fingers of God on a copper sky above the holy river, Livorna. I can hear distant cathedral bells announcing jubilee across the merrying districts of the metropolis, see myriad flocks of pigeons rising from the Dome of Eternity above the tumult and cheer where a grand civilization gathered to worship its glorious victory over a race of beasts and the end of war. What fools we were, and deceivers, too, ignorant not just of our misdeeds but of our abysmal lack of virtue. Dishonor belonged to each of us without distinction, yet who was willing to concede this guilt? Not one among us, and that is a bitter truth. Sixty years of slaughter and mayhem, millions eradicated, history itself diverted from a soaring enlightenment to degradation and shame, both the corrupt and the innocent swallowed up by darkness and death, and the arrival of the giant airships simply an unexpected dénouement to the sorriest of narratives.

But I don't intend this to be another morbid tale of war and sorrow. What would be the point of it? We've known abject misery for more than a century now, and surely nobody needs to be reminded. No, I simply refuse to wallow any longer in gloom and nightmares. Rather, I have a love story to tell, a beautiful love story, that begins one evening on a cold blustery beach, far from the great metropolis.

I

It was springtime and I was on mid-semester holiday from Regency College where I'd been studying law and philosophy for four years. I'd gone to the sea by train with my roommate, Frederick Morley Barron, whose family owned a fancy bungalow atop the windswept dunes at St. Etienne Shores. We were met at the rail depot by a fellow named Radelfinger. He'd grown up with Freddy and owned a four-seater Hanley auto. A pretty blonde named Evelyn Haskins had driven down with him from Belvedere township and acted terribly put-out by this detour of ours, not that good old Freddy paid her any mind at all. He pretended this had all been arranged by the Sultan of Quoristan and each of us there in Radelfinger's auto were part of an illustrious excursion. After Freddy begged his turn behind the wheel, Radelfinger chose to sit beside him, leaving me in the back seat with the girl. She smelled like lemon blossoms and had gorgeous skin and the most adorable bosom, yet not one whit of grace or charm in her demeanor.

"Now, how do you two know each other?" I asked, regarding her relationship to Radelfinger. I've always been curious about introductions, those chance connections that draw us together, the subtle voice behind the curtain. Serendipity was nothing to sneeze at. My parents claim they met behind a rural filling station when the facility indoors had been closed for repair. Without that call from nature at a precise hour and spot on the map, I might never exist. Think of that!

"He ran in on me while I was making love to his dear old dad," she replied, with a smirk.

"Oh, cut it out, Evie," Radelfinger said, without so much as a glance over his shoulder. "That's not funny."

"Don't be so moldy, Warren," the girl snapped back at him. "I'm sure your boyfriends won't tell a soul. Besides, I could've said I caught *you* making love to *my* dad." Then she giggled.

"Is your daddy handsome?" Freddy asked, steering into a curve where fenced orchards of cherry trees in bloom bordered the grassy roadside. "Warren's pretty accommodating in sexual matters, but he's always drawn the line at a clock stopper."

"Evie's pop was blown up with the Third Infantry at Sebastien Fields," Radelfinger told us, with a remarkable absence of irony. "She hated his guts and doesn't miss him in the least. Isn't that right, darling?"

I watched her staring out at the passing countryside, no hint of passion in her eyes. What sort of girl was this whose golden heart did not pour forth in gushing rainbows?

"Evie?"

"I need a gin and tonic," she said, giving me that glad eye now, as if I were responsible for navigating. "Can't we stop somewhere? I'm not sure I can go another mile without one." Evelyn winked, and I felt myself blush. Her scent bloomed in the car. She shifted slightly toward me. What on earth could I do?

"How much farther?" I inquired on her behalf. We'd been driving more than half an hour now since the rail depot, and I was becoming somewhat restless and thirsty myself. "Where's the sea, anyhow?"

"Julian's the anxious sort," Freddy explained to Radelfinger, who stuck a hand out into the wind as we passed beneath a stand of birch trees that splintered the afternoon sunlight. "The poor fellow has no patience for anything. Why, if a girl hasn't kissed him by dessert, he swears her off for good and all."

"Why, that's silly," Radelfinger replied, as if he and Freddy were unaware of my presence in the back seat. "He ought to learn to relax. I've always been suspicious of people who have no sense of drama."

Up ahead, another motor car trundled along at half our pace. Freddy raced up on it, spanked the horn, then laid on his brakes, terrifying the driver who nearly steered off the road trying to avoid being struck in the rear.

"IDIOT!" Radelfinger shouted as we accelerated by.

Arriving at the dunes just south of St. Etienne, we had the sandy shore to ourselves as the late afternoon wind blew cold off the water, surly whitecaps rippling to the horizon. The Barron family bungalow was rather ordinary, shingled and flat and needing paint. Empty flower baskets hung on the porch and ratty wicker chairs faced the sundown sea. Indoors, one might have supposed the bungalow hadn't been occupied in many seasons as the furniture and shelves were dusty and the floors in need of a good sweeping. I hoped Freddy hadn't invited me down there to provide cheap labor as I had no intention of doing anything more than having a good swim twice a day and lounging about between meals. It had been a long school year thus far, and I was terrifically exhausted. Midterm exams in Law and Modern Science and Contemporary Social Philosophy were especially trying, and I was worried about my class standing. Father had graduated fourth in his class and expected no less from his son, yet I wasn't confident any longer I could match that standard.

After unpacking, I went down to the beach where Radelfinger and Evie were wading arm-in-arm through the foamy tide. Freddy had decided he needed a bath and a bourbon before dinner, although leaving the bungalow I still hadn't heard the water running. Outdoors, the dunes were barren all along the shore and the sea looked cold. Where was the gaiety and jubilance? Given how Freddy had talked up St. Etienne all winter as a grand holiday destination, I'd expected to see umbrellas and sunbathers by the thousands, sailboats on the water, brightly colored kites aloft. Instead, nasty gusts of wind blew sand and dry grass across the dunes as I hiked down to the empty shore where Radelfinger had just fallen into the tide. Emerging soaking wet, he pursued Evie along the strand away from me, both shrieking like children. I took off my shoes and waded into the cold surf up to my ankles. A flight of gulls skimmed the whitecaps farther out to sea. It looked daunting from the shore. How did one slip through the breakers? Were Mother there, she'd have been shouting to me from the dunes to stay on dry land where it was safe. Once when she was a girl, she had a dream of being devoured by a big angry fish. Ever since then, she refused to set foot in any body of water deeper than her kneecap. I had no particular fear of man-eating fish, but I determined to be cautious when I took my first swim in the sea.

Down the shore, Radelfinger wrestled in the windblown sand with his little blonde. His suit was an utter ruin. Evie squealed and fought him off playfully with her fists. She ran and he chased after her like a spoiled pet. On the train, Freddy told me Radelfinger was a whiz at everything he tried — except getting ahead in life. His marks in school had either been top of the class or failing, depending upon whether Radelfinger chose to study or not. He was obviously no genius, but when he gave a fair effort and applied himself, however briefly, his achievements were exceptional and laudatory. Warren Radelfinger won the Chemist's Ribbon for inventing a new knockout gas. Warren Radelfinger built a steam-powered autocycle in Old Man Stuyvesant's garage from parts he appropriated at a fire sale. Warren Radelfinger was elected captain of the fencing team. A true champion among his peers. Yet nothing ever came of any of this. He was too glad a layabout to attend college for more than a semester, too clever to be content selling rakes at a hardware store. He slept in a room above the family garden-barn and spent his allowance on gadgets and girls. Freddy told me how rumor had Radelfinger fathering a dozen children by his eighteenth birthday. No betrothal was safe with Warren Radelfinger lurking near a porch swing after dark. His eyes were blue as heaven, his charms apparently irresistible. Alone in his company for the evening, even the most prudish of girls were heard to have performed desperately scandalous acts to win Radelfinger's heart. But none wore his ring. O love, sweet sanity's orphan! Seeing him take Evie into his embrace and kiss her as if they were engaged, I found myself wishing I had Radelfinger's resolve, however self-deceiving it might be.

That evening, we ate dinner at a café downtown. Freddy had been drinking since I'd left him to have my walk on the beach and was already half in the bag before we went out. By half past seven, when we arrived, most of the tables were empty, and our waiter looked drowsy. I imagined the brisk weather had a lot to do with the lack of business, despite Freddy having assured me on the train that St. Etienne was a year-round holiday destination.

"It's where everybody goes, you know."

"Well, I've never been."

"That's because you're nobody, Julian."

The four of us took a table by the window facing the street, lamplit in the early evening. Occasional automobiles rumbled past. Only a few tourists like ourselves were visible, buttoned up against the evening wind. None looked very sociable. I was starving for supper, but my companions insisted on ordering drinks to begin with. Radelfinger requested a glass of scotch, his curvy girlfriend a gin and tonic. Freddy ordered more bourbon. Wine on an empty stomach usually made me a little queasy, but I took a glass, anyhow.

"Julian, don't be a scoundrel," Freddy said. "Have a real drink."

"No, thanks. I'd be afraid you'd knock it back when I wasn't looking."

"You needn't worry about that," Radelfinger said. "He'll be too busy getting sloshed in his own bowl. If we don't watch him, poor old Freddy'll drown the barrel and throw away the cork."

"Oh, stuff it!" Freddy giggled, sounding more fuzzled by the minute. I wondered if he'd still be with us by dessert. His brow was already wrinkled and rosy.

"Well, I don't care what you boys say," the blonde scolded. "I think Freddy's awfully cute when he's fixed up like this."

"You ought to marry him, then," I told her, "because he's always pickled. Aren't you, Freddy? Go on, tell the truth. Evie doesn't care. She may be loving it up with Radelfinger here, but there no doubt it's you she's got her eye on. Anyone can see that."

I loved baiting Freddy. You couldn't insult him on his blackest day. He was too good-natured a fellow for that. His mid-semester marks at Regency College were far worse than mine, and his father remorseless in his criticism of Freddy's academic effort. Lame as his study habits were, non-existent really, nevertheless I felt sorry for my jovial roommate. He just wasn't cut out at all for college life. Perhaps the esteemed H. Cornelius Barron, a most prominent physician in Alexanderton, knew that, but couldn't bear the thought and sent his son, anyhow. "Poor old Freddy" was no layabout, nor was he too clever for his own good. Rather, he was quite simply a decent, ordinary fellow who was expected by his family to be exceptional. When he realized he wasn't, there was nothing to be done except endure his shame and pass the booze.

"I've never been in love," Evie confessed, sipping from her gin. "I hate the very idea of it. I'd rather go to bed with a million boys than fall in love with a single one of them."

"Is that so?" I said. "Why, I was under the impression that you and Warren were here on honeymoon!" Since she wasn't bedding me, I couldn't resist the desire to needle her.

Freddy laughed.

"Oh, shut up! Are you serious?" Evie replied, a look of shock on her face. "He can't even kiss worth a damn!"

"Evie!" Radelfinger looked horrified.

"Well, it's true, darling!" She giggled. "Florence warned me, you know, but I didn't believe her. I suppose I owe her an apology."

"Perhaps I ought to go home right now," Radelfinger said, tossing down his napkin. "I could join the army, you know. They've been inquiring."

"Oh, you'd make a hell of a soldier!" Freddy cried. "I think you should go to the front and put an end to this damned war, once and for all!"

"Or become more cannon fodder," I added. How many ever came back from the war to our western provinces? Everybody talked about victory and grand parades, when, in truth, the very notion was impossible. Besides, those of us fortunate enough not to inhabit the Desolation were absolutely terrified by the very idea of it. Nothing but mud and blood for hundreds of miles. Who in his right mind could bear that?

"I think Warren would be a terrific fighter," Evie said, stroking Radelfinger's arm. "He'd be the greatest of them all and win a basketful of medals." She kissed his cheek.

"Well, I'd only do it for you, my dear," Radelfinger gushed. "I really haven't much of the warrior in me, otherwise. And yet, for my sweet Evie, I'd tear our godless enemy limb from limb, and devour their still-beating hearts!"

"Good grief!" I said, thoroughly exasperated. "If you have to go to Galliano, then please hurry up, and leave the rest of us cowards in peace. I hear the artillery barrages are quite lovely this time of year."

This was the same idiotic conversation I'd been listening to nearly every afternoon at the college commons, indigestible blathering from Theta Xi about storming ramparts and dispatching our wicked adversary or quitting the whole business for good. It was so tiresome. I suppose guilt over the mortal sacrifices of those who fought for us was the root of all this wailing, but really what could be done? Some went to war, while others stayed behind and kept to the eugenical business of attempting to perfect the imperfectible.

"Don't be so damned stodgy, Julian," Freddy told me, raising his bourbon. "Every little fellow wants to be king of the mountain, doesn't he?"

"Boys are idiots," Evie interjected. "All you do is squabble and roll around in the mud. You're disgusting. Every last one of you!"

Radelfinger raised an eyebrow. "Now, Evie dear, does that mean you're paying for supper tonight?"

"Screw you!"

"Oh, please do!"

Fortunately, we were saved just then by the waiter. Owing to our surroundings, we each ordered fish platters and a couple bottles of wine. There's nothing like a fine warm meal to soothe a sour spirit. Our silly bickering dissipated to quiet conversation and we ate in peace. By the time we'd finished, the restaurant was empty, and we went out into the night alone. A sea wind blew in the streets smelling of salt and rot. All the storefronts were dark. We had St. Etienne to ourselves. It felt strange to be so far from the metropolis, out in this quiet countryside by the sea. I had a paper to write on the Achaeleon theocracy waiting on my desk upstairs at Thayer Hall, yet all I desired in my heart that evening was to stroll those damp streets with my companions and not worry one iota where the world was tending, good or bad. There was a rutted plank boardwalk on the edge of town that led back out into the blustery dunes where we followed Freddy, who could scarcely walk a straight line. We paused to take off our shoes, then slogged our way seaward. The sand was sticky-wet and cold, the night wind almost icy on my face. Watching Evie grasping Radelfinger's arm, I found myself wishing I'd brought a girl to the shore that evening. We might build a campfire in the dunes, huddle close against the wind, listen to the surf bellowing across the dark while making love under a blanket. Why not? What a wonderful gift to the soul is guileless dreaming!

As Freddy stumbled ahead, Radelfinger took Evie and kissed her as if I weren't even there. Jealous as all hell, I left them alone to their mooey-mooey and tracked Freddy to the shore. He'd rolled up his cotton trousers and began splashing through the cold tide like a fool. Putting a shoulder to the damp gusting wind, I called to him, "Freddy, come out of there! You'll catch your death!" I wasn't his mother, of course, but often enough Freddy needed a good kick in the rear to get right again. He shouted something back to me about swimming to Avalon. What an idiot! I wasn't certain he even knew how to dog paddle. Poor Freddy. He really could be demented. I considered rolling up my own trousers and going in after him, but I was already shivering from the cold. There were lights out to sea, perhaps a mile in the distance, a fishing trawler or patrol boat, and a campfire I thought I'd spied much farther down the shore. The thought that we might not be entirely alone out there seemed comforting somehow, even as Freddy splashed farther out into the dark tide, singing, "Hailing All Saints," with the squealing voice of an utter madman.

How much booze had he drank before dinner? Knowing I'd need some help to retrieve him, I looked back to the dunes in search of our amorous couple and saw them staggering through the grassy sand, cheek-to-cheek, roaming hands shamelessly engaged with each other's clothing. How easy it was back then to find fault with Radelfinger's insouciance, his gleeful disregard for convention. Some people struggle their entire lives to achieve this confident apathy, preferring to wait for retirement to lounge in a lawn chair and laugh at the world passing by. But not our Warren Radelfinger. No, he'd already determined to get an early start.

Well, now it seemed hopeless that those two would help me drag Freddy from the surf, so I turned back to the sea on my own, only to find that Freddy had disappeared. Where I'd just seen my roommate cavorting about in the foaming tide, there was nothing but black water. *Good God*, I thought, *he's been washed out to sea! What will I tell his family? Of course, they'll hold me entirely responsible! Everyone knows Freddy can't swim! What on earth possessed me to let him go into the water?* Panicked, I charged forward into the surf, splashing in up to my knees, shouting madly. The night tide was black as sin and I couldn't see him anywhere. He was gone. I was sure he'd drowned. Behind me, I heard Radelfinger and Evie shouting across the wind. The sea rose up and nearly swamped me where I thrashed about, searching for Freddy. Desperately, I waded into deeper water, drenching myself now in the surging tide. I called for Freddy over and over again. He was certainly lost. Radelfinger's distant voice sounded diffused and muted in the roar of the surf as I struggled farther out into water up to my chest. I kicked about in the swirling tide, shouting after Freddy. I lost my balance as a wave struck me from the side, knocking me over. The icy water shot up my nostrils, and I thought I was drowning, too. Who was the bigger fool now, me or Freddy? I was bathed in darkness and cold. I lost sight of the shore. My feet lost purchase above the sandy shallows and I felt myself being drawn out to sea. *This is ridiculous*, I remember thinking just before abject fear delivered me from reason. *How could I die on spring holiday?*

But I didn't, of course.

Expecting to be entombed in the briny deep, I was snatched from death's grim embrace by the strangest of coincidences, a most peculiar stroke of black fortune. Flailing my arms wildly as I was sinking, I felt something soggy and thick strike me in the cold tide, and heavy enough to grab onto. I wrapped both arms around it, pulling my head up out of the water. I kicked my feet and held on and shoved my way toward the shore where I could just barely see the foamy white surf breaking across the shallows. I heard voices shouting across the dark, my own name called in desperation. I lowered my head against whatever this was I'd chanced upon in the grim tide and kicked with all my will toward the shore. Waves broke over me as I was swept back to land where soon enough I felt myself lifted from the water by several strong arms and dragged from the surf onto the wet sand.

"Julian, you idiot!"

That was Freddy speaking in my ear. Where had he come from? I heard Evie babbling about how horrible drowning must be, and Radelfinger repeating some nonsense about the deadly tides.

I opened my eyes and found my companions staring, but not at me. I sat up, drenched and shivering. Lying on the strand beside me was the soggy body of a soldier, still in uniform.

His face was pallid, almost luminescent in the moonlight. He appeared roughly the same age as myself and Freddy and Radelfinger. His cloudy eyes glowed. His uniform was soiled by kelp and sand. A thick ugly black welt ringed his neck. Both his hands suffered lacerations and bruises. It was the ugliest thing I'd ever seen. Was this what had rescued me in the surf? A soldier's corpse?

"Did you kill him?" Evelyn asked, vague admiration in her tone.

"Of course not!" I glared at her. Good God! How could she ask a question like that?

"Well, who is he?" she asked, idiotically.

"How should I know?" I frowned at her. "I've never seen him before in my life."

Radelfinger bent low over the youth, examining the dead body head to toe. With a stronger stomach than my own, he gently closed the poor fellow's eyes.

"He reeks," Evie remarked, wrinkling her nose. "God, it's awful!"

"I should hope so," Freddy said. "There's nothing pleasant about dying. Father always says the stink is there to remind us that death is something to be avoided."

"How insightful," Radelfinger said, peeling back the soldier's collar, further exposing the neck bruise. "Look here." He traced a finger across the wound. "Why, I'd say our boy was strangled."

"Murdered?" I mumbled, still half-dazed from my experience in the surf and the realization that I'd floated to shore on the back of a corpse. There in the cold windy dark of the shore, it just seemed incomprehensible. We were supposed to be on holiday, after all.

"Someone'll need to call the Provincials," Freddy said, circling the body. "They won't be pleased."

"They'll think we murdered him," Evie remarked, both fascinated and repulsed by the dead soldier. She couldn't take her eyes off the body, and her hands were shaking. Maybe it was just the cold. I was still shivering and yet hardly noticed how damp and uncomfortable I'd become.

"What's he doing here?" Freddy asked, stopping at the boy's feet. "Fighters aren't permitted in the provinces. Everyone knows that."

"Maybe he deserted," Radelfinger suggested. "Look at his collar: He's a private. I bet he'd had enough and ran for it. Who wouldn't?"

"In his uniform?" I asked.

"Why not? Maybe he didn't have a chance to get rid of it."

"Before they killed him," Evie added.

"Who's they?" Freddy asked.

"Well, that's the question, isn't it?" said Radelfinger, getting back to his feet. A gust swept the hair over his eyes. "Who killed him, and why."

"I'm not sure we ought to be asking something like that," I said, looking down the shore in both directions. A brisk chill went up my spine. This was all very risky. What on earth were we getting ourselves into? Had anyone seen us dragging the body out of the surf? We still appeared to be alone there, but it was dreadfully dark, and if we were being spied upon from the dunes, we'd never know it.

"We ought to call the police," Freddy said, attempting to be mature, but I knew it was also a bit of cowardice. Freddy was no hero by anyone's definition. "This is too serious to fool around with."

"Who's fooling around?" Radelfinger shot back. "We don't know this fellow. He just happened to float to shore with Julian. Have you ever seen him before?

I haven't. He's not even supposed to be here. The fact that we found him was just coincidence. It's not as if we killed him, you know."

"Says who?" I interjected, becoming terribly skittish about the entire situation. A wind had come up, blowing sand across the cold beach. It felt eerie and peculiar, even ominous in a silly melodramatic way, proving further we had no idea what the hell we were doing. "I mean, nobody saw him wash ashore but us. Who's to say we didn't kill him?"

"Don't be an ass, Julian," Freddy shot back. "That's absurd. The boy's obviously been in the water for hours."

"No, he's right," Evelyn said, her voice trembling somewhat. "How could we prove we didn't kill him? Who's to say we didn't strangle him and push him into the surf. Maybe he just washed back to shore again. If, somehow, we were accused, who'd believe us?"

"We have to call the police," Freddy insisted, sounding a bit frantic. He was clearly scared, but so was I. "You know we do. If we don't and somebody reports seeing us here with the body, we'll look guilty as hell."

"This is all so ridiculous," I muttered, still vaguely unsure what to do.

Radelfinger stared toward the dunes beyond which porchlights of the holiday cottages were extinguished up and down the shore. "I say we leave him here, let someone else find him, which they will by morning. If the police come knocking, we'll just say we were drunk and hadn't the foggiest notion what they were talking about." He smiled. "One look at Freddy here, and they'll know we're telling the truth."

And that's what we did. Ignoring our moral responsibilities to the poor soldier whose corpse had unwittingly saved my life in the evening tide, we skulked back across the sandy shore to the beach house and hid in our rooms until daybreak. Freddy drew the blinds in every window upstairs and down and began drinking again. Radelfinger and Evie humped each other in the loft for an hour or so before surrendering to their own liquor-induced stupor. I laid in bed most of the night unable to sleep, listening to the waves thunder onto the cold shore and wondering what on earth had happened to my pleasant spring interlude, how it had all gone to smash in a matter of hours. I'd nearly drowned in the sea, only to be resurrected into a most unsettling mystery. I had no idea what to make of any of this. Murder! Holy Mother of God! I was both horrified and intrigued, and the more I thought it all over, the more frightened I became. I don't remember falling asleep, nor what I dreamt, but I can assure you it was the longest night of my life to that point.

Just after sunrise, the police did indeed knock on our door. Peeking out through the morning blinds, we saw the windy beach crowded with blood-hounds and blue uniformed inspectors and half a dozen fellows in long grey coats who stood apart from everyone else, surveilling the fly-swarmed body and its location in measured silence. Having already rehearsed our falsehood, we felt reasonably persuasive insisting that we were shamefully unaware of a corpse washed ashore not three hundred yards from our sundeck. Freddy even brought out a pair of binoculars and expressed incredulity at the discovery of a dead soldier lying near his family's beachfront property. *"It's illegal, isn't it, for him to be here in the western provinces? Or even near us at all. We're always told that, right? So what the devil's going on?"* He delivered his lines with the soggy slur of a morning hangover, not the least bit feigned. Meanwhile, wearing hardly more than her silk underthings, Evie put on a spectacular vamp routine at the door. Her nipples were swollen like ripe raspberries in the brisk ocean air and distracted the hell out of the two inspectors who failed miserably in their vain attempt not to ogle her. Radelfinger and I pretended to be utterly stupi-fied by the entire situation, but God knows we were both scared half to death. The implications of what we'd chanced upon at the seaside last night were staggering, and, considering all that followed, I have little doubt that were we able to go back twenty-four hours, not one of us would have made the journey to St. Etienne Shores.

II

∾

During spring term, Freddy Barron and I shared a fourth-floor bedroom under the attic at Thayer Hall on Regency Heights, only a couple of blocks from the center of campus along a shady street of stately faculty residences and broad sheltering oaks. A century ago, when the old Regency College was established on the hill, our great brick building held the engineering school where Dr. Hartley Mills Thayer led the earliest investigations into chromatic depth projections, the frictionless turbine, mechanical men, and other critical discoveries. Down in the stone basement stowed among the furnace and utility equipment were dozens of thick wooden crates packed to the limit with obsolete electro-mechanical inspirations and apparatus. Persistent rumors of radioactive wonder gasses from ancient wave experiments creeping into our ventilation ducts apparently kept quite a few students away from our old building, which was fine with me because it meant less commotion on the floor at night and more hot water in the morning showers. Freddy and I shared a nice big room with a terrific view of Trimble Street below. Also, we each had our own iron frame bed, cedar closet and study desk, and a toilet directly across the hall. A very smart arrangement. We felt lucky to be there.

Not that Thayer Hall meant anything resembling a cloistered life. Fraternity houses lay only half a mile distant and some of the stunts put over during rush week tried everyone's patience. After sundown on weekend nights, Peake Street in nearby Brookhaven became frantic with carousing fellows from Regency College and adjacent townships stuffing the smoky bars on the make for stork-mad college girls to fondle, if they got the chance. Buoyant with bourbon or scotch, every weekend Freddy, too, chased after that certain gleam himself, scuffing his shoes on a dozen bar stools, yet still trudging up the old stone staircase alone, night after night, reeking more of liquor than perfume. Loathing that sort of humiliation, I preferred staying home to my study desk at the fourth-floor window where I could listen to distant motor horns and police sirens without budging from Homer, secure in my sexless cocoon. Despondent as I felt now and then shadow dancing by lamplight to Freddy's dreary old record player, I was quite confident my parents were pleased. Truthfully, that was my life, and I'd become reasonably confident regarding my place in it.

Yet it wasn't more than two weeks after our worrisome adventure at St. Etienne Shores that everything changed. Freddy had gone to Stokley Hall one bright sunny Saturday afternoon to meet with Professor Lengfeld, lecturer in Botany, who had just become his mortal enemy, thanks to a failing mark on a term paper my poor roommate had scribbled over the previous weekend. Suffocating from the heat indoors, I went downstairs to read the Sophists out in the fresh air on Thayer's wisteria-draped gallery. A clownish trio of male classmates were already ensconced in the wicker porch chairs, huddled about a dime store checkerboard table, and debating the merits of co-education with style and perspicuity when I stepped outdoors. Before I could settle into my own wicker near the stairs to the sidewalk, the esteemed badminton enthusiast, Walker Bailey, attempted to draw me into his debate. "You do agree, don't you, Brehm, that co-education ought to be confined to courses in the library?"

"Pardon?"

"It's simply a question of averages. You recognize that, don't you?"

Bailey's roommate in slicked-back hair, Percy McDonnell, said, "I've been talking myself blue, Julian, trying to explain to these Neanderthals how co-eds adorn our lovely campus like the daffodils outside Redington Hall, and how drab we'd be without them. Really, I have no feelings of superiority whatsoever."

"Hear, hear!" agreed Burt Davy, raising his fist. His eyes were bloodshot with Freddy's bourbon. Everyone in the dormitory knew those two drained a bottle in the furnace room each morning after breakfast.

"But listen, friends. This is from a respected publication." Percy held up a current college journal from which he read, "'*My only real objection to co-education is that girls always get their lessons better than I do, thereby unreasonably raising the standard of marking. For this reason, I believe co-eds ought to be abolished.*' So, I suppose I must agree with this Hopper fellow, after all. Put them all out. The sooner, the better."

"They're not half as rational as we are," Bailey added with his usual smirk. "I believe it's just too dangerous having them around."

"Mind you," Percy added, "if somehow I'm able to noodle Daisy Ewing next Friday night after Glee Club, today's comments are to be considered excluded."

I laughed. These were precisely the sorts of chattering debates for which Regency College was greatly esteemed, fatuous discourse on vital issues where passionate opinions were expressed without conviction or skepticism, a pure folly of words and gestures, more puppet show than pertinence. Any day of the week, striking out against the popular view on any topic under the sun could provoke hours of vicious disagreement and stinging ad hominem attacks: the more vile, the better. It was great fun.

In that spirit, I said, "Well, as for me, I'm with the co-eds, and proud of them, too. Without their wit and eloquence, I'm sure this college of ours would be a hopeless mediocrity."

I sat down in a wicker rocker by the white porch wall and leaned back, awaiting the barrage.

Bailey got there first. "You, Brehm, are an absolute idiot. Your tuition ought to be rescinded and your bags put on the train to Cantália tomorrow."

"If he had a sweetheart among the hairpin set," Percy suggested, "his wrongheadedness would be more understandable. But, of course, he doesn't. Do you, Julian? Have you kissed anyone this month besides your mother?"

"Only himself," Burt blurted as the spring breeze gusted smartly. "Which he doesn't mind at all, seeing as how he's more them than us. Ask Freddy. He's sick to death of fighting off Julian's advances, tired of having to scrub rouge off his pillow every morning."

I smiled at that. "Why are you fellows so dead-set against keeping the feminine variety on campus? That seems awfully suspicious of you, preferring it boys only."

Raising his usual sneer, Bailey replied, "We knew in your heart, you wanted it that way."

"Oh, don't do it for me, darling," I protested. "I'm sure you'd be much happier wrestling with your pals, knowing the girls aren't there to smell your sweat."

"You stink worse than we do!" Burt offered, looking ready to plant his face into the middle of the checkerboard.

"Shut up," Bailey told his wobbly cohort. But we all knew the worm had turned when he said to me, "At least we're not wearing our mother's underpants."

"Oh, that's clever!" I couldn't help laughing out loud. "Ha, ha, ha! Mother's underpants! Gee whiz! You got me there, Walker!"

Even Percy laughed at Bailey, who scowled and shot back, "Piss off, Brehm."

Out in the dusty street, a noisy red automobile motored by out of campus, kicking up a cloud of exhaust into the blue afternoon light under the stately old oaks. I noticed Freddy's Botany professor behind the wheel. Did that mean my troubled roommate had won the day, or been shown the door? Either way, clearly another bottle of scotch was doomed.

Just then, a female voice called up to us from the sidewalk, "Excuse me!"

The balustrade was so lush with pink wisteria in bloom, I had to get up to see over it. Once standing, I found a stunningly beautiful young woman in scruffy bohemian dress with gleaming jet-black hair curled down her back. True love is the silliest of clichés, yet when she raised those cocoa-dark eyes, so enrapturing did I find her that a friendly wave was all I could offer.

Naturally, Walker Bailey saw her, too. "Why, here's your honey-bunny, Brehm. Show us all how brilliant you really are."

"Manners, please," I chided him as I headed for the stairs. "And take your hand off Percy's knee. We've got company."

"Piss off!"

Our lovely guest met me at the bottom of the steps with a clear indifference to my slobbering pals on the shaded gallery above.

"Hello," she said, look of earnestness on her brow. "Do you live here?"

"Yes, I do. May I help you?"

"Well, I was wondering if you could put this up somewhere for me."

She was cradling a stack of posters under her left arm and drew one out. It was a hand-lettered notice that read:

LOST DOG
Name: Goliath
Breed: Terrier
Color: Brown
Missing: Three days
Reward: Cr2.75
Tel. MERton-3457

"What's she selling, Julian?" Percy called down from his perch in the gallery. "If it's an invite to that Socialist wingding on Puetschsker Avenue tonight, tell her we're in, but she's got to provide the booze, and none of that monkey swill, either."

The girl hardly blinked as she told me, "He's my favorite little dog, and I've been in tears since he disappeared. If you don't mind, I'd like to post this notice on your bulletin board."

Even outdoors in the fresh air, I noticed she had a rare, exotic scent to her, something like incense in a cloudy cellar. Her cotton blouse and khaki work trousers were tough and thread-worn, clearly out of fashion for Regency Heights. Again, very bohemian, almost deliberately so. I rather admired it, even as I told her, "Actually, to be honest, we're sort of restricted here in what's allowable for posting. Only notices pertaining to Thayer Hall life and academics. That seems silly, I know, but rules are rules."

She smiled. "Well, how about if you just nail it up there and don't tell anyone? Do you really care what some stupid bureaucrat decides should be posted on a public bulletin board? I wouldn't."

No, I didn't doubt that for an instant. The bohemian crowd had mostly disdain for all manner of rules and convention. Everyone knew that. They reveled in traffic-obstructing street theatre, splashing blood-red paint on city trash cans, interrupting government radio broadcasts with silly nursery rhymes, and dumping baskets of pornographic leaflets from rooftops all over Prospect Square, juvenile pranks to irritate the top-drawer crowd at lunch. Lots of fun. Not wanting to seem overly flat myself, I said, "Well, you wouldn't believe how peevish our hall monitors get when their precious bulletin board is changed without consultation. They can be absolute cry-babies."

"But you'll do it, anyhow, right? Terrific!" Then she thrust one of the flyers into my hand.

Interrupting his checkers match, Bailey yelled down, "Are we on the guest list, Brehm? It's important to do a spit and polish for that crowd so they'll see we're earnest."

I smiled at the girl. "He's really a wonderful fellow so long as you don't know him very well."

Her eyes sparkled in the afternoon sunlight. She was so adorable I almost didn't mind her telling me, "It must be nice to play all day, but most of us don't have the luxury." She nodded at the flyer in my hand. "Will you please put that up for me?"

A gentle breeze strayed through her hair and she brushed a curling wisp off her brow, beaded with perspiration. How far had she walked today, distributing her missing dog notices?

I said, "It's really not that simple, but I promise I'll do my best."

"In other words, as soon as I leave, you'll toss it, right?"

"Not at all."

"Of course you will." Her lovely brown eyes flared brightly. "Why should a college boy care in the least about some little nobody's lost dog? Whether I find him or not won't matter to you."

"That's not fair," I argued. "I love dogs." I had a puppy when I was little, but lost him to a spoiled stick of bacon. I must have cried for a month and refused to have another, despite my mother's pleading that things would be different next time, though how many heartbreaks can a sensitive child be expected to endure?

Somebody roared past into campus in a large four-seater Algren sedan, the rumble seat crammed with luggage. The passing auto kicked up a cloud of dust in the warm spring air, forcing us to put our backs to the street.

"Look," the girl spoke as the auto exhaust cloud thinned, "I really have to go. Please do me this small favor, won't you? Believe me, Julian, having a conscience won't hurt you."

"Aren't you going to kiss her?" Bailey shouted from the porch wisteria. "Don't be a dub, Brehm. She's obviously anxious."

Just like that, the woman of my dreams strolled away. Percy gave her a shrill wolf whistle as a send off. She returned the compliment with her middle finger and a delightful laugh. Realizing I'd forgotten that most critical item of information, I called out, "Excuse me!"

She stopped, and looked back over her shoulder, giving me one last opportunity.

"What's your name?" I called out.

"I can't seem to remember!"

Hurrying down the sidewalk to the street, I shouted, "Please?"

"Are you going to put up my flyer?" she replied, skipping off backwards.

"Yes!"

"Cross your heart?"

"I swear!"

"It's Nina!" she answered, then hurried away down the dusty sidewalk toward the bottom of Trimble Street.

Nina!

Is it not true that serendipity plays as big a role in guiding our lives as deliberate intentions? My mother believed so. She always studied tea leaves floating in a china bowl of olive oil and burnt cinnamon before traveling abroad and rarely brought a map along. Once, before I was born, she got herself kidnapped from a mountaineering expedition by Muranese huntsmen and escaped dismemberment, she told me, by plucking a four-leaf clover from beside her foot and presenting it to the chieftain's new bride. Though my mother had no way of knowing that a four-leaf clover was considered manna from heaven to that particular tribe, her unfathomable intuition so flattered the primitives, they put her back on a donkey to civilization that very morning. Later on, when I was graduating Prouter Academy, my father told me that fate and character are twins of the same conception, insisting that what we are instructs what we do. He believed my mother's love of nature, and her instinctive generosity, led to that four-leaf clover which saved her life. What could be truer? That morning at Thayer Hall, I might have decided to skip my studies in favor of an hour or so in the third-floor lounge with another batch of slack-jawed classmates, hypnotized one and all by Dr. Elston's new radiovision set. Had I done so, Nina would very likely have decided none of us were worth wasting a flyer on, and walked off to pursue her rounds, oblivious to my existence, and I to hers, in which case, perhaps neither of us would be alive today. Instead, I spent the rest of the afternoon mulling over a clever strategy for insinuating myself into her life.

III

∽

"Julian, has it ever occurred to you that nobody cares in the least how many seeds a peony can ripen, or that those of the clematis have down like a duckling by which they're able to float on the breeze?"

My inebriated roommate steadied himself against the doorframe. Our room was dusky in the late-afternoon tree-shade from the clustering of dilapidated elms outdoors.

"No, Freddy, that hasn't crossed my mind all day." The note papers fluttered in front of me. "Would you please close the door?"

I had the window behind my study desk propped open to the fresh air just then, and the sudden draft from the hallway threatened to scatter all my hard work into the waiting tree branches. Poor old Freddy looked wan, his clothes shabby, his bearing desolate. Who could possibly fail to guess that another failing mark just appeared on his horizon? Trying to avoid a similar fate, I'd flogged myself all day since meeting Nina by entirely rewriting my introduction to a seminar paper on Aeschylus.

"It's all gone to hell," Freddy moaned, plodding over to his fancy iron bedstead and throwing himself down onto the mattress. Lying in a fading sun-shadow, he kicked back the thread-worn comforter and rolled over. "I'm doomed. Lengfeld is a bloody monster. He's persecuting me for refusing to lick the apple like those other twits down in front who reek of horse manure and actually try to use 'cryptogamous' and 'perianth' in ordinary conversation. It's humiliating, I tell you, and I won't stand for it."

Shuffling Aeschylus off to my rising stack of unread volumes, I swiveled my chair to face Freddy. "So, he's failed you?"

"That sonofabitch hadn't even the common decency to review my progress this semester, and it's been damned steady, too. Have some faith in me, Julian. I've turned a corner. It's right there in the record. Father believes me. So do Stubblefield and Dupré. My only trouble now is with 'Lungfester' and he's such a gaseous smut there's no chance he'll pass me on. I just know it."

"There's no persuading him?"

"Short of taking a pair of garden loppers to his knuckles? Not a hope."

"Well, then, what're you going to do?"

"Get stinking drunk downtown," Freddy told me, without a hint of irony. He fluffed up his cotton pillow. "I've been invited to a gathering at Schuykill's Tavern on J Street. Would you care to come along? I'll need somebody to keep my face out of the toilet."

I laughed. Freddy really was a case. "Gee, I'd love to, you know, but as it happens, something else came up this afternoon and I think I may actually have plans of my own."

He sat up, curious as ever. Freddy was relentless about poking his nose into my concerns. "Oh? What sort of plans? Pillaging a bookstore? You have no life outside of campus, Julian, and everyone knows it. What could possibly be more exciting than keeping me from flushing away tonight what little potential I have left?"

I told him about my encounter with Nina and those clowns on the front gallery, barely able to contain my enthusiasm for her winsome beauty. So evident was my lovesickness, I could scarcely keep from giggling. No need to worry, Freddy did it for me.

"Julian, you're insane!" He propped up against the iron headboard, a loopy grin on his face. "You've obviously been duped by a subterranean Hecuba who blew in your ear when you weren't watching. Her kind'll do anything to advance their cause, whatever it might be. I hope you know that. We're nothing but spoiled benefactors to them, which is why they're up here soliciting our aid rather than sitting next to us in class. Whatever you do, please refuse any further contact with her or any of that ilk. It can't lead to anywhere but trouble. Believe me, I know the sort. Besides, I promised your father I'd see you through to a diploma, whether I take one or not."

Outdoors, the late wind gusted through the elm branches, rattling the window frame while another smelly auto roared by into campus. Despite Freddy's admonishment, I was anxious to get back out there and find Nina. Feeling suffocated all of a sudden, I told him, "She's no insurrectionist, if that's what you're implying. She just wanted to find her dog. You remind me of the fellow who swore his brother's steak was rancid, then snatched it from the garbage pail before it cooled off. Had she laid her eyes on you, bohemian or not, I'd never hear the end of your mooning. Look, a society that breeds nothing but aristocrats wouldn't be able to find anyone to drive a taxi. I say Nina's awfully swell for lending herself out to something you and your crowd would think menial, if you considered it at all."

Freddy rolled over, shaking his head. "Walker was right, Julian. You *are* an idiot."

Of course, he was right, but so was I. Too often in this world, we hold people up to our own personal standards, as if we were the final arbiters of all that's good and true. Few of us are ever able to accept another's perspective as a legitimate point of view, almost as if the act of acknowledging someone else's virtue reduces our own. I'm sure the war had a lot to do with that. Killing on a mass scale is best practiced in an atmosphere of unforgiving partisanship. Who really cares what the enemy thinks is worth dying for so long as their graveyards keep growing and memorials to our own dead become repetitive and indistinct? Actually, in those days hardly anyone offered much respect for dissenting views on social characteristics and eugenical necessities in our grand old society. Those untroubled values that had brought us to the top of this heap imbued the sensible majority with a confidence that defied any doubts regarding the wisdom of our Common Purpose. Before Nina, I, too, belonged to that imperious group.

Once Freddy fell asleep, I went downstairs to the lobby and attached Nina's flyer to a corner of the bulletin board with a short admonishment against its removal scribbled along the bottom followed by a name: *Dr. FHB*. Though no one on our faculty had those specific initials, I was confident that Fletcher Moss, hall monitor for this term, lacked the guts to tear it down on his own initiative. Next, I walked around the corner to the collegiate association smoking room and slipped into one of the telephone booths by the washroom and dialed the number Nina had listed on her flyer: MERton-3457. That prefix served a sector in the soot-blackened Catalan District of industrial east metropolis, inhabited by dim constellations of the dispossessed and hardly noticed, where the golden people from brighter precincts often sneaked off to be stained. There, tall old brick tenement buildings, cold and drafty in the winter dark, became blistering steam furnaces by the dog days of August. Neglected sewers backed up hourly. Rude livery stables bred rabid legions of rats and scuttling cockroaches that prowled the disordered perimeters of ash and cinderblock, so near the immortal river that man and mongrel squabbled over organisms washed ashore in the grassless lee of empty encampments mourned over and abandoned by the world beyond. Rumors of bloodless cataclysms in packing-crate apartments, bone-dust spied on the ruptured floors of barren warehouses, sidewalks haunted by pale travelers and hosts, were whispered to the greater metropolis by leaflet periodicals and wounded refugees from the eastside underground.

Or so I'd heard.

No one I knew personally had ever been there. Some considered it a question of upbringing. Why refute the eminent truths of social evolution by slipping back into the muck? Others proclaimed a daring adventure awaited those who defied eugenical convention to mingle with the diseased and unfortunate. Perhaps drinking oneself into confusion might lead one across the grimy railyards at Hartley Crossing and into the Catalan after nightfall where not even Charon could guarantee safe passage back again. A good case for abstinence, I thought. Yet here I was on a sunny spring afternoon, dialing a scribbled telephone number that could take me precisely where just yesterday I'd had no desire whatsoever to go.

This is the folly of manhood, I realized, as I rang the operator. A pretty face and wicked smile wreaks havoc in the most circumscribed life. Not since my beautiful Lydia Sayre in Upper School had I been jolted so thoroughly from my complacency and certitude. What did I intend to say to her if she answered? Had I found her dog? No. All I had was a leap of faith.

"Station 14. How may I help you?"

"Could you please connect me to MERton-3457?"

"Thank you."

My knees wobbled where I stood while the operator rang the number. Three, four, five rings, then a click, and a young woman's voice at the other end of a scratchy connection, *"Hello?"*

I was such a tyro, my throat tightened. "Hello."

"Yes? Who is this?"

Sucking in my breath, I said, "It's Julian Brehm, calling for Nina."

There was a pause. *"Nina who?"*

"Well, I don't know her last name. We met this morning outside Thayer Hall at Regency College where she was distributing leaflets regarding a lost dog."

There was a long pause. I thought for a moment she'd hung up the phone. A couple of years before, solicitors and crank calls plagued my father so thoroughly he tried to persuade my mother to have the telephone taken out. Instead they had a friend from the Kirchoff Institute drop over to install an interceptor that relayed the ringer's number to a switchbox that distinguished wanted from unwanted telephone calls. Since this sort of privatizing of phone lines has been deemed a grey area of legality in the eyes of the Communications Directorate, few were able to take advantage of such arcane technology and I doubted this household I'd dialed was that lucky.

Then I heard the girl's warbling voice ask, *"Did you find the dog?"*

"Well, no," I answered, relieved she was still on the line, yet not entirely sure if this was even her. The tone was familiar, but the connection was dreadful. "Not yet, anyhow."

"Then what do you want Nina for?"

Aha!

"Is she there? May I speak with her, please?"

Another distinct pause, during which I heard faint voices shouting in the background. A busy house, or a flat? Lots of roommates, or a party? Maybe the Saturday meeting place of some secret bohemian alliance?

Then a surprise. *"Did you keep your promise, Julian?"*

And, of course, finally I recognized Nina's adorable voice, and the thrill of it ran through me. "Yes, I did. It's on the lobby bulletin board in plain view. I had to attach a fake note authorizing it, but I'm sure your lost dog will attract plenty of attention."

"Thank you."

"My pleasure."

"I didn't think you'd do it."

"No? Why not?"

"Oh, let's just say I had many reasons to be skeptical. I'm sure you know what they are."

"Please enlighten me," I said, feeling my blood warm.

"That whole outfit of yours. The society of go-alongs. Don't you realize that nobody with any character actually cares who is, or is not, in the best crowd? As if there even were such

a thing, which we both know there isn't. Why do you people think how much money you have or where you live gives you some phony moral authority over the rest of us? I hate that."

"What's this have to do with your dog?"

That whole dialogue had become such a cliché. Town and gown. Rich and poor. Socialist and Capitalist. Eugenical and Naturalist. I hoped this wasn't all going to wind up a terrible disappointment. You cannot begin to imagine how tiresome it can be debating the politics of social organization seven days a week, fifty-two weeks a year. It's just a terrific yawn. When's the interlude where we sit back and listen to the wind rush through the trees and hear the birds sing? I said to her, "Darling, you asked me to call you about your dog, and instead we're discussing the socio-moral fabric of our clearly inadequate world. What gives?"

"Julian?"

"Yes?"

"Are you always such an idiot?"

"Well, I do try my best to offend as often as possible. How is it going so far?"

"Well, I'm about to hang up."

"Great, that means I'm doing just swell."

"I hate you already."

"You do? Well, then, gee, I've succeeded beyond my wildest expectations. Thank you very much!"

"So." She paused a moment before surprising the hell out of me. *"Would you like to come see me?"*

"Pardon?"

"Unless it's too great an imposition on your time. I certainly wouldn't want to disrupt your routine, whatever that might be."

She laughed, and I took it to be as sarcastic as she'd obviously intended.

"What if I'm busy?"

"Well, if you aren't, then I'm inviting you over."

"Well, all right, then."

"Meaning?"

"I'd be happy to see where you live. Will there be refreshments?"

"If you do me a favor, first."

I laughed back. "So here's where it starts, right?"

"What starts?"

"You taking advantage of my natural generosity."

"*Not at all,*" she said, then yelled at someone in the background to hush up. "*I just need someone to bring my little sister back here. She's been out playing with friends and needs to eat. I don't trust her on the trolley by herself. She's only eight years old. I'm sure you can understand.*"

"Of course I do. I have a sister myself. She's completely irresponsible. We don't trust her to change the pillowcases on her bed."

"*Delia is not irresponsible. She just gets tired and forgets to eat. So, will you bring her back here on your way over.*"

"Of course. Where is she?"

"*The Metro stop at Ronsard Avenue. Do you know where that is?*"

"Across the river by Zoffany Creek?"

"*Exactly.*"

"And where will I be taking her?"

"*1618 Gosney Street.*"

"And where is that?"

"*Rosenstern Quarter, by the Kaarsberg fish market.*"

I had no idea where that was, but I assumed the Metro Line would have a stop close by. The Catalan District. Good God. "All right. See you soon."

IV
∾

I hired a taxi down the hill from Linscott Auditorium and rode it out Rector Avenue, whose snowy-white apple blossoms cascaded gaily on the late afternoon breeze. There'd been rain a week ago, a cold and ugly storm, but today the sun shone brightly and promised a better outlook. Soon enough, we arrived at the busy Ronsard Metro stop, where I paid the driver and got out. Searching quickly about the rail crowd, I found a young child roughly grade school age, sitting by herself on the far end of the station bench. She was wearing a pretty silk jersey top with a taffeta flounce skirt that fluttered in the gusting breeze. She was pie-faced with curly dark hair and held a stack of paper fliers at her waist. When she raised her pretty brown eyes to mine, I offered a friendly wave. "Hello there."

"Hello."

"Is your name Delia?"

"Yes," she replied, cautiously. "Who are you?"

"I'm Julian," I said, offering her my hand. "Your sister, Nina, sent me to show you home. Pleased to meet you, Delia. That's a very pretty name."

She handed me one of the fliers, a hint of defiance on her lips. "We can't leave until I find Goliath. He's a rat-catcher. My friend, Lutisa, thinks he chased one to the creek and dove in after it."

"Is that so? Well, then why aren't you searching down there?"

A motorcar roared by, swirling up a nasty black cloud of dust and exhaust. Spring branches of the green elms swayed in its wake. Stifling a cough, the girl said, "Oh, I've been everywhere. Besides, he's a wonderful swimmer, so there's no worry that he drowned. I'm sure he swam ashore and got lost."

Delia got up from the bench and began wandering up the sidewalk to get out of the exhaust cloud. "Do you like dogs?" she asked, somewhat warily. "You don't, do you?"

"Everyone likes dogs."

"My sister doesn't. She locks Goliath in the closet whenever I'm not around. She says it's to protect him, but I don't believe her. Sometimes she's awfully mean."

"Well, I'm sorry to hear that. Isn't it terrible when your sibling becomes disagreeable?" Her story reminded me of how my sister, Agnes, raided our laundry basket the morning of my twelfth birthday and plucked out my soiled underwear, which she then displayed inside-out at my party later that afternoon. I was ruined for years by her viciousness, a cruel deed repaid in kind at her coming out party where I offered proof of Agnes's womanhood in a pair of freshly stained panties to her newest crush. Those without brothers or sisters cannot fathom the delight of exacting an artful and clever revenge upon one's sibling, an exchange of torments that never ceased.

Delia asked, "Are you going to help me find Goliath? You will, won't you?"

"Well, I promised your sister I'd see you home. She didn't mention anything about your dog. Besides, the reward seems a little thin, to be honest. Is that really all you're willing to pay? It doesn't seem like very much. If I lost my dog, I couldn't imagine offering a reward of less than ten credits."

I was teasing, of course. Money had nothing to do with it. I just wasn't sure I needed to spend part of my Saturday afternoon traipsing about after someone's lost pet. Actually, I felt like going back to Thayer and having a nap.

"What if I pay you three credits?" she asked, most hopefully. Her pretty brown eyes sparkled. "Will you help me then?"

Good grief. Trapped by a child.

"Three and a half," I bartered, feigning a merchant's frown, my last chance to escape, "and not a penny less."

"All right," she agreed, "but only if we find him."

"Nope." I shook my head. "Half now, and half when we've got him in hand."

She growled and stamped her foot. "That's mean!"

With a self-satisfied smile, I replied, "No, dear, it's just good business."

Like any child not getting her way, she tried whining. "But what if I can't pay you now? I'm supposed to go to the market and buy coffee and eggs for supper. I'm not rich like you are."

I laughed. "What makes you think I'm rich? Good gracious! Where'd you get that idea?"

"My sister told me that anyone who goes to college these days is rich. Otherwise they'd be in the war. You're in college, aren't you?"

"Look, honey," I told her quite honestly, "I'm not rich, nor will I be in college much longer if I spend all day searching for your lost dog. You have no idea how busy I am." I hated to be cruel, but admitting the truth was far worse for me than for her. After all, who had to live with the possibility of being a college washout?

"All right, you win."

"Pardon?"

She reached into her pocket and drew out a small penny purse. I watched her count change to a credit and seventy-five cents, which she then thrust into my hand. "There! That's half now. I'll pay you the other half when we find Goliath."

"Delia."

"We have a bargain, so don't try to back out on it."

She darted off the sidewalk, quick as the wind, across a grassy lawn and between the slats of a rustic fence, out into the thick miasmic woods that shrouded cold, slithering Zoffany Creek. I felt like a fool sprinting behind her. I heard her screeching with laughter and urging me to catch up. Where was she headed? The spring woods smelled damp and succulent, fragrant with bloom.

Racing along after her, I felt like a satyr tromping through a freshly born Elysium, symphony of bird song in the trees. If she were Nina, I'd have been tempted to strip nude and frolic in this shady wood, chasing my wild Persephone. How shameful, don't you agree? Certainly not worthy of us young phenoms around whom the very universe revolves. Because a false step here or there puts one down in the basement with the protoplasm. Beware! Warnings are everywhere, like gilded signposts to a dreadful obscurity. Am I to be a junkie or a statesman, angelic or debauched? Decisions, decisions. Such unreasonable expectations of the privileged, such responsibility! Confusion of the leisure class. A blink of the eye sets a moral compass awry. Or the flutter of an eyelid, a whisper, a kiss. Or a whiff of tea, black smoke, a taste of paregoric, and disillusionment. So many choices, so little life. What do I know? I'm still fresh-faced and foolish, a child-heart, groomed for something grander than I can yet grasp. I lack perspective and discipline. What noble purpose do I pursue? Pure pleasure is elusive. I have no well-considered point of view. I require instruction, patience, prayer. And yet I may still choose burglary, sodomy, sabotage, espionage, homicide, suicide. Nothing is certain. There are rumors of honorable character, gold stars on record for good deportment. My roommate believes in me. So does my family (except Agnes, who suspects me capable of infinite moral infirmities). They trust that I'll do nothing to disappoint them. I won't be a disgrace or a crashing failure. I won't break wind in church or giggle at a funeral. I'll bear public witness to the noxious behavior of others. I'll cross a street only at crosswalks and return lost pocketbooks to their rightful owners. I'll be thrifty and honest, a good citizen of the Republic.

Possibly.

Young Delia led me up the creek along a narrow footpath cut into by vegetation surging with spring growth. Her voice echoed in the woods like a wild cat as she urged me to hurry up. I was doing my best to catch her, but if she didn't slow down, I was going to drop. Where on earth was her dog? We were almost half a mile from town now as Zoffany Creek bent east toward the city where it would eventually drain into the great river, Livorna.

I caught up with little Delia in the shade of a broad sycamore just upstream, sitting patiently in the stump grass, legs folded, skirt smoothed nicely over her knees, back to the bark, a devilish smile on her face.

"Did you get lost?" she asked, with more than a trace of sarcasm. I ignored it because I know how children are abnormally fond of drama.

"No, dear," I replied, keeping my temper. "I just didn't see any need to hurry. Why did you run on ahead like that?"

"I heard Goliath," she told me. "Didn't you? He has a very unusual bark. I'd know it anywhere."

"No, I didn't hear a thing."

She got to her feet with a smirk. "Well, you're not a good hunter, are you? I think he was calling me."

"Fantastic!" I said. "That means I can go home and get back to my studies. Thanks for the game. I love hider-seeker."

"No, don't go!" She grabbed at my sleeve, looking desperate, another silly contrivance that I wasn't falling for.

Perhaps a bit too harshly, I snapped, "What am I out here for? Do you even have a dog?"

That stung, I could tell. Her eyes teared up; her lips trembled. She was both furious and wounded. "I don't want your help. You're mean."

"And you're dishonest."

She scowled. "Shut up."

"You shut up."

"SHUT UP!" Her voice echoed down in the ravine. Then she added, "Listen!"

At first, all I heard was the breeze sweeping through the birch branches high overhead. Then, a distant chorus, a faint yelp, a dog barking in the wooded distance. How far was difficult to say. Delia went to look out over the rain-eroded embankment. Brush clung to the sandy bluff top to bottom and the peak of a dying black oak poked up from the wide creek bed like a crooked auto antenna. I walked to the edge to find what she was looking at and saw a great metal drainpipe across the creek and heard a hollow yelping from within.

"He's in there!" Delia announced, as if I were deaf. "Go get him!"

Her tone was defiant, and I didn't appreciate that. After all, I'd just chased more than a quarter mile through the woods to reach this spot and for no reward, except to help out a child in need.

"I thought you told me he was lost up the creek back there."

"Maybe he swam down here."

"He's a dog, not a catfish."

Ignoring my jibe, she called out, "GOLIATH!"

The barking grew more excited. Actually, it sounded a bit funny, as if her dog had a water pail stuck on his head. I almost laughed. But then she said to me, "What are you waiting for? Aren't you going to go get him?"

I peeked over the bluff and saw how steep it was. I must confess to having a terrific fear of heights. Just being there on the embankment gave me the creeps and I actually backed up a step.

"Well?"

"What do you expect me to do, fly over there?"

"No," she told me, "just climb down the tree." She pointed to the scraggly oak.

Of course, she had to be kidding. I took a peek over the embankment and saw, indeed, the tree hugged the bluff clear down to the creek bottom.

I asked her, "You want me to climb down that tree and rescue your dog from the drainpipe?"

She offered a plaintive smile. "Won't you, please?"

If I fell and broke my neck, my parents might grieve for a day or two until they considered the tuition saved. Also, my dear pal Freddy would have a bigger room. I stared at the rotting black oak. God, it was far down! As a child, I had awful balance. My father used to tell company about how long it took him to teach me to ride a bicycle. Four months doesn't really ring true, does it?

Well, not wishing to be humiliated in front of this little girl, I was somehow persuaded to put away my natural sense of caution and climb down that tree and rescue her stupid dog, despite the mortal danger involved. Fortunately, that tree was not as dried out and rotted as it seemed. Most of the branches were more than sturdy enough to support my weight so long as I kept close to the trunk. The huge old oak had somehow grown or insinuated itself into the dirt embankment and was really just a scraggly bark ladder from the top of the bluff to the sandy creek bed below.

Once there, I looked across the wash to the old drainpipe. That idiot dog had quit barking, thank God, but Delia was yelling at me again. I ignored her. This was just so ridiculous. I removed my shoes and socks and waded into the creek. My goodness was that water cold! The bottom was soggy, and my feet sunk into the sand. My trousers were soaked to the kneecap. It was rough going. I banged a foot against a submerged rock and skinned my ankle as I waded across. Then Delia's stupid dog began yelping from somewhere within that goddamned drainpipe. Well, this was just taking all together too long, so I hurried up the slope to the old pipe that once emptied South Yorkville's refuse into Zoffany Creek.

At first, I thought the entire contraption was blocked with sludge, mud and tree branches from a dozen years of winter floods. In fact, there was plenty of room to creep through. Just past the entrance, I discovered a horrific stink, putrid and rotten. What on earth had died in there? Sunlight illuminated a path only here and there by slanted rays. I called to the dog and heard a barking echo. This pipe ran three miles into the heart of the metropolis, but I knew Goliath couldn't be more than a few dozen feet inside or I wouldn't have heard him so clearly. And I was right, because only a minute or so after entering the drainpipe, I discovered the pathetic little terrier, stuck inside a rusty old upright ash can, scared out of his wits. The poor creature was too small to jump out and the bottom of the can was flooded with six inches of water. How he'd gotten himself in there, I had no idea. Once he stopped barking, I reached in and hoisted him out. He was wet and shivering. I clutched him to my jacket, which would likely need to be thrown away now it was so filthy. Departing the drainpipe was somewhat easier than getting in, and soon enough Goliath and I were out in the afternoon sun by the creek where we found Delia waiting across the water upstream, a satisfied grin on her little face.

"Did you come down that tree?" I asked, as I gave her back the shivering terrier.

"Oh no," she admitted. "It's much too dangerous! I might've broken my neck. There's a path to the bottom farther up the creek. It's a lot safer."

"And you didn't think to tell me about it?"

She kissed her dog. "I just wanted to see if you dared to climb down the tree."

We got off the bus at Gosney Street, gritty and bleak, where the old grey tenement houses looked worn-out and rotted, paint peeling and porches sagging, trees mostly leafless and tired. A mangy cat lolled on the stoop next door. My clothes had gradually dried in the draft from the open bus windows and I relaxed. Somehow the Catalan didn't seem so terrible. I even felt a bit courageous. Maybe swimming with a corpse in the cold tide at St. Etienne Shores had something to do with that. Delia seemed cheerful, hurrying off down the sidewalk to a dilapidated house in the middle of the block. That little dog in her arms, Delia rushed up the stairs and into her home, letting a hallway door slam closed behind her. She shouted to someone inside as I arrived. A moment later, beautiful Nina stood above me there in paint-speckled overalls. She smiled. "Hello, Julian."

I said, "Do I win a prize?"

"Do you want one?"

"Of course. This was a very trying endeavor. Your little sister is a demon. She gave me an awful run. I doubt I'll recover for weeks."

She smiled. "Oh, I'm sure you'll be just fine. Come in!"

I bounded up the steps behind her, light-footed and giddy. Nina held the door for me and we both went inside. Late afternoon sun splintered shadows in the narrow hall from rooms on both ends. The house was frantic with voices and music. Overhead lamps were sooty, the wood floor underfoot rubbed raw and coarse with stains, and warped here and there.

Nina gave me gentle tug. "Come meet my friends, Julian."

She opened another door off the hall and led me into a narrow living room where a crowd of scruffy bohemian types were scattered about on a ratty sofa and worn-out chairs, smoking and having at each other in contentious debate — just as I'd imagined. Leaflets littered the carpet and the walls were plastered with political posters exhorting rebellion and contentiousness, precisely the sort of enthusiasm for youth anarchy I expected. What else, after all, besides sex, stirs adolescent blood? Defy your parents, trash the system, throw a party. I'd had such thoughts myself. Who hasn't?

"Oh God, Nina!" some young bearded fellow with a cigarette and a peach called out from a cushioned window seat. "What's *he* doing here?"

"This is my new friend Julian."

I tried on my best friendly face, though I wasn't sure it mattered here. Who were these people, anyhow? Anarchists? Disrupters? Bad poets?

The abrupt young fellow stood and waved his peach at me. He was dressed in a paisley vest mismatched with a white-collared-shirt and dusty-brown-trousers. As if he lived in a cellar. His hair needed a good shampoo, too. "Are you insane, Nina? Who said you could bring one of them here?"

"Oh, go flush yourself." Nina grabbed my hand again. "He's come to help plan my birthday party."

A weasely little fellow with shaggy hair called out from an old armchair, "What if we don't approve? You can't just drag them in off the street, you know. We have rules here. Who is he, anyway?"

"He's my friend, and if we had rules, Marco, you'd be wearing a dress."

Two more casual fellows in ratty cardigan parked side by side on the sofa laughed, and the pretty brunette beside them wearing a lime peekaboo dress stuck her tongue out at the weasely boy. A crowd of a different sort.

Nina gave me a tug. "Come on, Julian. This party stinks. Let's have our own. I'll fix you a drink in my room."

I gave the couch trio a friendly nod. "Good to meet you."

They weren't dressed any more presentably than their noisy pal, but at least they seemed to know better than to advertise poor manners. Understanding how to present ourselves is one of the admirable virtues.

Nina dragged me through the kitchen where another scruffy fellow strummed a mandolin over a bowl of steaming oatmeal and a girl in a flounced apron fiddled with a broken potato peeler. The sink was stacked with empty wine and beer bottles. This was the bohemian highlife, all right. Just as I'd imagined. You couldn't see anywhere the floors or counter tops had entertained a mop or washrag in a month of Sundays. Hungry now, I snatched an overripe pear from a small porcelain bowl and followed Nina to the back of the house where her bedroom lay.

She skipped in and flopped onto a dumpy bed slid up against a wall adjacent to an open window where a flowering plant sat in a small pot and a casual array of prisms were strung like pearls across the glass. She had poster art of café scenes and bohemian authors, Pitre Kautsky and Riemer Volgin, and labor slogans plastered to the walls about a small wooden desk cluttered with books, pamphlets, leaflets, and on her mattress a week-old copy of *Subterranean Oracle*, that notorious guide to anarchy and political nonsense. A true socialist tableau, I thought, without saying so. The room smelled of griffo weed or Fasulian incense, I wasn't sure which, because the brass paraphernalia for both collected on a tiny carved tea table next to her bed. A noisy radio set rang music from the next room.

"Come sit beside me, Julian," she said, shuffling a pair of magenta-laced and sequined pillows to make space. "Let's celebrate."

"Will this be my reward for finding Delia's puppy?"

"Do you want it to be? I hadn't decided anything until you arrived. I wasn't sure what to expect. You, being who you are after all, right?"

"Meaning?"

She laughed a bit too loudly. Probably she'd started her party without me. "You're so stuffy, Julian! Come! Lie down. I'm so worn-out."

"I'm not sure I trust you, darling. You're seeming very shady. That whole missing dog routine. It was really too much. I hope you realize that. I wasn't at all fooled. But with a less sympathetic fellow, you could find yourself in real trouble. You're lucky you met me, and not some scoundrel."

"Well, aren't you just the most impressive boy." She giggled, then drew a silver flask from under her pillow. She unscrewed the cap and sniffed. "We should wash your clothes, Julian." She took a drink from her flask. "You look horrendous."

"Thank you."

"I'm not saying you stink, but I've just changed my mind about having you on the bed. You'd soil the sheets and I just had them cleaned this morning."

"Oh? That seems awfully bourgeois. How did you have time with all your marching about? Those silly speeches."

Nina stared at me as if I had a nosebleed. Then she said, "Take off your clothes, Julian." She bounced up off the bed and shut the door. "I mean this instant. I'll wash them myself."

"Is that so?" She really was crazy. Did she truly expect I would undress to my drawers in front of her, right then and there?

"If you're nervous, just pretend I'm your mother. Boys usually find that easier somehow."

"You're so absurd!"

"Julian, I just can't have you rolling about on my bed in those filthy clothes. So take them off."

"You're serious!"

"Good grief, are you deaf?" She opened the door and yelled out into the hallway, "DELIA!" She turned back to me. "The laundry room's in the basement. Delia loves washing clothes. She'll run them down for us. I have her completely trained."

Nina leaned out into the hall again. "DELIA!"

I should remind you these were troubled times in our grand civilization, days of fear and worry. Nothing was inconsequential. Litter in the streets, domestic upset, pervasive mental illness and chronic disease were felt as dangerous undercurrents of moral disharmony and what Dr. Regensberger from the Porterhouse Dispensary Staff called "intellectual rabies." Truth be told, I probably ought not to have gone to the Catalan at all that day, but when we're young, being swept along on someone else's tide just seems so damned exciting, and we feel strong and brilliant beyond our years, and our egos simply won't permit any recognition of potential danger.

None of this, of course, completely explains why I stood in the middle of Nina's bedroom stripped to union suit underwear while little Delia gathered up my creek-soiled clothing. Strolling out of the room, she wore a look of admiration that had me thoroughly defeated and it wasn't even suppertime.

Then the doorbell rang, and the story truly began.

One of those ragged fellows from the living room shouted down the hall, "NINA!"

"Stay here," she told me, and hurried out.

I went to the window. Traffic was thick with old autos. Fish wagons and pushcarts, too, clogging the street. Then, that verbal racket which permeated this entire floor of the house stopped so abruptly I went out into the hall just to see what happened. There was a short, stocky middle-aged fellow at the front door with a dour expression on his face speaking with that boy who'd waved the peach at me earlier. The fellow was dressed plainly, like a cab driver, with a grey cotton jacket and brown trousers and a flat work cap in his hand. I thought he might be somebody's father. That is, until Nina arrived to begin arguing with him over someone named Peter Draxler. That's when it became interesting enough to draw me down the hall in my union suit.

"He's not here, mister," Nina told the fellow. "We haven't seen him all month."

"Is that so? He wasn't visiting Tuesday evening? You don't recall that? I heard he was."

Nina smirked like her little sister. "You're lying. I think we'd know if he was here. He's our friend, not yours."

"Then you ought to know where he is."

The boy with the peach stepped forward. "Look here, that's none of your business. Who are you, anyhow?"

The fellow handed him a card. "This is a very serious affair. Nothing for kids to fool around with. Your young Mr. Draxler's fallen into a questionable situation. I may be able to help, but only if I can speak with him before matters get worse. It's entirely up to him. You should know, however, that somewhere in this city a clock is running out and when it does, young Draxler is likely to find himself caught up in a very disagreeable circumstance."

Nina told him again, "Peter's not here."

"I heard you, darling. Could you please tell me where I can find him?"

Another pretty girl stuck her head out from the front room. "Why don't you just go away and leave him alone? He hasn't done anything wrong. Why don't you just go away?"

The fellow drew a pencil and a small notepad from his jacket. Then he said, "How about if you give me your names? I think that's a good idea. Don't you?"

Peach Boy told him, "How about if you just leave now? We don't have to say anything more. We don't know who you are, but you look like a stiff, and we're not going to talk to you any longer. Just get out before we call the commissioners. Goodbye!"

The fellow broke a funny grin. "I like you kids. I really do. I'll be back. Get your stories straight. And let Mr. Draxler know we're on to him. He can't hide."

Nina swung the door open. "Out!"

Then, of course, all the attention fell on me, standing there alone halfway down the hall in my underwear. Laughter from Nina's friends roared through the house. Horrified, I rushed back to her room and flopped myself onto the bed.

"Who's Peter Draxler?" I asked Nina, when she reappeared from the hall.

"Our friend."

"And that fellow asking about him?"

"We don't know, and it's better that you don't ask. There's been a lot of snooping about these days and we're being careful not to talk to the wrong people. You wouldn't know anything about this, Julian, I'm sure, because it's no worry at all to you and your sort, but there are events occurring all over the provinces now, life and death, and my friends and I are much too involved to play dumb."

"Don't be condescending. I'm just curious what your business is in all of this, and why I'm here today. Couldn't you just have hired a dogcatcher? What's your game, Nina? Really now, what is it?"

The room felt shady and cold. The sun was diminishing. Out on the street, a roll of trucks rumbled by, rattling the unlit ivory lamp on her little desk. Nina came over and sat beside me on the bed. "Julian, you and all your silly friends live in a soap bubble. Did you know that? A flimsy glistening little orb of insubstantial beauty. You're so convoluted in your eugenical self-absorption, it's ridiculous to imagine you have any real idea what's actually occurring these days. For instance, did you hear about Jakob Voorsänger?"

"Who?"

"What?"

Then I laughed, and she looked as if she were about to slug me. But what else what I supposed to say? "Nina, are you, or are you not, going to explain why you solicited me for your little dog hunt? It's very important that I know this before we go any further today. At least until my pants return."

"Delia's washing them."

"So you say."

"My gosh, Julian! You are so skeptical! And yet you are accepting of everything you're told by the Council about why millions are being murdered in the Desolation. What is it with you people? Does all that money fog your brains?"

"Oh, I'm very cynical about the war. I can't even spell 'victory' any longer. I just can't seem to locate the proper letters. It's a form of aphasia, I'm certain, induced by persistent nonsense and utter confusion."

She stared at me for a moment, then said, "You're right. I shouldn't have brought you here. You're obviously unsuitable. I apologize."

"Unsuitable for what? You haven't asked one thing of me since I arrived except to take off my clothes, and I feel as though I did a pretty efficient job of that, don't you?"

"You're an ass, Julian."

"Already established."

"Do you have even the vaguest appreciation for what that man was doing here asking about Peter?"

"No, because I don't know this Draxler. All you've told me is that he's a friend of yours. Maybe that fellow was recruiting him for his own boy-friend club. How should I know? For goodness sake, Nina, if you really want me to get involved with your nefarious doings, then be brave enough to let me in on the game. It's the least you can do."

Then, just like that, she leaned over, grabbed my face, and kissed me flush on my lips. She had me smothered before I knew what I should do. Of course, once I caught my breath, I kissed her back. She had very soft lips and tasted of fresh bourbon. The first pleasant experience I'd had all week. When she retreated slightly, I saw those lovely eyes of hers were moist. What did that mean?

"I need to trust you, Julian," she murmured. "I need to trust and believe in you. These are very upsetting times and I don't like asking for help. Anyone can tell you that. I haven't had somebody to confide in these days, so I've been hurrying about solving problems on my own, but now I see that's not really possible. I have Delia to look after, and she's been terribly difficult lately, and none of the boys care at all. And those asinine girls they've brought here are worse yet. Absolutely selfish little bitches. I hate them all. But they don't know it because if they did, this house would be our own horrid desolation, and we have so much to do, you can't possibly imagine."

"Nina, again, I have no idea what you're talking about. Do you? How many times do I need to ask you why I'm here? Is that so complicated? And where on earth are my clothes? Because I do need to get back to Thayer Hall. Exams, you know? Very important ones, actually. That probably doesn't mean much to you, but believe me, my parents are very concerned."

Nina leaped off the bed and stuck her head out into the hallway. "DELIA!"

I heard a siren close by and went to the window. The Rosenstern Quarter was notorious for rotten behavior perpetrated across all manner of human beings. Perhaps that sounds elitist, as I've no doubt it is, yet decency has to be counted among our common virtues. Here, in this sordid corner of the Catalan, I'd read there were more burglaries, blackmails, suicides and murders in a month than anywhere west of the holy river. Just three weeks ago, for instance, on a sunny Tuesday morning, a building inspector named Penwell put down his cup of coffee and keeled over at the breakfast table, poisoned by his young wife who'd apparently decided the beatings he administered in bed each night after conjugal relations were not sanctioned by the Holy Book, after all. Four days later, a district security administrator and two recently dismissed deputies were burned alive in a fancy auto outside the Kasbakh burlesque theater on Olivette Street. A firebomb had been placed in the motor housing, set to detonate when the engine ignited. Both incidents were named political crimes by the Protectorate's chief investigator, though most in the metropolis decided that some sort of salacious sexual relations gone horribly awry was the more likely instigation. Yet who really was to know?

Nina invited me back to her bed where we cuddled and kissed, and she fiddled with my ear. "I thought you liked me, Julian."

"Oh, I do admire so many things about you, dear." I kissed her, too, again, and danced my fingers through her lovely black hair. "I just can't for the life of me recall what they are right now. Give me another moment or two, maybe they'll come back."

She looked me straight in the eye. "Don't be such an ass. It's not flattering. This is a very serious circumstance. I hope you can appreciate it, even if you're not entirely sympathetic with those of us who aren't like you or your crowd."

"Would I be more sympathetic if I wore a beret? Loan me a megaphone and I'll join your anarchy parade. Do you have flags?"

"Don't be an idiot, Julian."

"Then don't fool with me. I'm doing my very best to follow this conversation, but you're making me work a bit harder than I'm used to."

She leaned forward once again to kiss me, then abruptly got up off the bed and skipped over to the door where she shouted out once more into the hallway, "CORDELIA ROSE!"

Her voice echoed through the house. A moment later, I heard her little sister call back some nonsensical reply, after which Nina turned to me. "Julian, I want you to go home right now."

"Pardon?"

"I need you to leave this instant."

"Without my pants?"

"Delia's bringing them up from the basement. You should meet me this Wednesday at Thibodeaux Station on the East Platform. There's a small flower stand by the telephone gazebo. I'll be there at two o'clock. It's terrifically important that you arrive on time. I have something drastic to tell you. Worse than life and death."

I could hardly disguise a smirk. "Of course it is."

She frowned. "If you don't believe me, then don't come. I'll find someone else."

"I have no doubt."

"Julian?"

"Yes?"

"Don't be late."

I ate dinner that Sunday evening at home, where my appearance was mandatory. Father had important guests over and wanted them to see me, or for me to see them; I wasn't entirely sure of the trajectory. Rules were rules. When I was summoned home, I hopped onto the train and went. Why not? I loved my parents and had a wonderful and fortunate childhood. Highland Park was more pastoral in those days than it is now, more weed and woods than suburban paradise, an hour by rail to the metropolis, yet still civilized enough that my sister and I were able to ride our bicycles to the market an easy mile downhill at Ferngrove. Our lovely property on Houghton Avenue was large, terraced in ivy, landscaped and manicured with fir and elms and spruce, flower gardens and fruit trees, a tennis court and backyard swimming pool and greenhouse. Our home was tall and spacious with fine wood furniture. We had four upstairs bedrooms, an office library, coldstone wine cellar, and a carpeted billiard room with a cocktail bar for all sorts of amusements. So, our Brehm family certainly had advantages, and never thought to deny them. Why must we? Each of us is born into our own world. We need not apologize for our good fortune. Indeed, my parents worked many years and quite hard for all they earned. Rather, it is incumbent upon us to do what we can to share with the needy and less fortunate, so that each of us might be able to enjoy the best of what life can offer. The failure to do so is both cruel and dangerous. Goodness and evil navigate the world with equal velocity. Trust deeply in the memories of the grateful and the denied.

You should also know I greatly loved and admired my father. When I was very young, he did business at the Exchange on Market Plaza, and every now and then, he brought me along with him. He kept a small room reserved for a week on the sixth floor of the old Reveille Hotel overlooking Vaudal Avenue. Since he'd yet to join the investment firm in the Garibaldi Building that gave us a fine life later on, we couldn't afford more than a simple arrangement of a double bed, desk, toilet and armchair by the window where I'd stare out over the grey buildings when he was off on his appointments. A boy that age cannot know what he thinks he sees, and I was no exception. The city seemed dark and hostile to me, labyrinthine in its geography, immensely foreboding from six floors up. I remember the old Marconi set in a radio cabinet and the funny shows I'd listen to hour after hour. Late each day, my father would come back to get me, and we would walk up the street to a diner whose lime-green walls and odors of kitchen grease and fried onions I can recall even now. There, we'd choose a booth and order our meal. I was a finicky eater as a boy, only grilled cheese sandwiches and grape juice for my supper. Our table had a formica surface and Father used to slide the salt and pepper shakers to me and laugh if they slid by and toppled off the table. He rarely said a word about business.

One evening as we sat in that diner, my father pointed out to me a shaggy, bearded man in a shabby raincoat seated at a table by the restroom in the back. He sat alone reading one of the city newspapers and had a hardbound book open on the table in front of him. He wore wire-rim glasses and a floppy felt hat and seemed thoroughly immersed in his reading.

"That's Morris Longstreet," my father said, nodding in the man's direction. "He's a poet and an old avowed bohemian. He's political, and it serves his art, but he also stirs the soup of those who believe art and politics ought not to mix. They don't want their poetry to be anything but love sonnets and all their paintings to be deer posed under a maple tree by a pretty blue lake. He's hated by quite a crowd in this city and there's a danger in that, Julian. People don't like to be told what or how to think, especially by someone different from themselves. Often they feel insulted by their own ignorance and don't wish to be reminded."

"But why do they care what he writes?" I asked, quietly. "Do their teachers force them to read it? Mrs. Fortman made me recite a boring poem about two boys driving an oxcart through a dusty village and I didn't mind it so much. But if I didn't have to read that poem I wouldn't, because I couldn't even understand it."

"Well, Julian, just try to remember that men like Morris Longstreet are the town crier whose job it is to wake people up when things have gone wrong in the middle of the night."

"What's gone wrong now?"

He patted my hand. "Nothing for you to worry about. Just eat your sandwich."

At home my old bedroom upstairs under the eaves was neat and airy. I had school pennants on the walls with photoplay posters of my boyhood heroes, Wild Jack Calhoon and San Sebastien Allarde. Mother cleaned and tidied up once a week, whether I was there or not, and changed the bedding for me. With Agnes away at the McNeeley Branson School, my father wanted me to stay overnight and have breakfast with them in the morning and hit some tennis balls afterward. He was fiercely competitive and wanted a victim with his coffee. I showered and went downstairs to greet two of Father's old friends.

"Julian, I'd like you to remember Harold Trevelyan. I know it's been years."

"Hello, sir."

"And Addison Dennett."

"Pleased to see you again, too, sir." They both looked vaguely familiar.

"These fellows are awfully curious to know how college life is treating my son these days. Is life on campus as hectic and exciting as when we were stomping about Thayer Hall?"

My father's colleagues were dressed in fine grey suits and ties, pocket handkerchiefs and black polished Dorien shoes. They might have come straight from a boardroom meeting at the Garibaldi Building. I felt both studying me in order to determine how far Charlie Brehm's apple had fallen from the tree. I wanted to tell them that we still piss into the same bushes outside the girls' dormitory at Kesner Hall, that most of our books get less than half the attention a keg of beer does on Woldford Street, and that graduating college in the same nation laying waste to the Desolation seems pointless, if not obscene. But I did not. Mother raised me better than that.

"Thank you, sir," I replied, shaking Dennett's hand after Trevelyan's. "I'm sure things are pretty much the same as when you were there. We show up for class, cram for exams, and panic every four weeks when grades are assigned on the poster board at Fiddy Hall. We just hope we can live up to your expectations of us. That's all."

"Well, good show, Julian," Trevelyan said, briskly. "Nice to see you follow in your father's steps. It's inspiring, I'm sure."

"Thank you, sir," I replied. "I hope so."

Then we sat down to eat.

Mother brought in lentil soup and crackers, and a Greek salad with her own dressing of secret ingredients she refused to share even with Father. A rib roast came after, with cut greens and potatoes. Wine glasses were filled and emptied. I kept to water, not eager to let myself be muddled by Father's finest from our cellar. There would be questions arriving like a blizzard and I had to be on point if I wanted to survive the evening with the barest shred of dignity.

At the top of the hour, we had my father's favorite dessert, warm tapioca pudding. I ate slowly, paying little notice to the dinner conversation regarding property degradation in the Matson District and a scandal at Loring Tower regarding two secretaries to the board chairman and a limousine driver whose appetite for sharing gossip was sending a vice chairman named Strauss to Thapsus Court where his financial prospects were apparently in grave doubt.

And then it all fell onto me.

"Now, Julian," my father began, "you must give us your reading of the political temperature on campus today. Where the boys are running."

"And the girls," Mother added.

"Oh, we assume the girls follow the boys," Dennett interjected, "as they invariably will."

"Well, that's not a sure thing," I said, "at least not at Thayer. Our females are quite independent, believe me. Almost the contrary. They don't do anything we ask them to do. As if it's a moral imperative to be contradictory. They can be awful. You can't persuade them to wash even a cereal bowl anymore, unless it's their own. And then only every other Tuesday afternoon."

"What we mean to ask, Julian," Father went on, "is, do your fellow classmates, regardless of sex, have any commitment to the ideals of the Republic today, or do they debate whether or not we ought to exist at all in our present state of affairs?"

I laughed. "Oh gosh, my classmates don't do anything regardless of sex. That's half our problem."

"Julian!" Mother warned. "Be polite."

"Well, it's true, Mother. Do you believe we study for tests, hour after hour, then spend our free moments at bedtime or over snacks nitpicking the hypocrisy of the Status Imperium? Their ad hoc morality. That's absurd. No one has that much dedication to laws we had no hand in writing, nor rules we can't understand. We're still children, aren't we? To all of you? Why should we be emotionally or spiritually or politically invested in a world we didn't create? That makes no sense to us."

Trevelyan said, "Young man, this world makes no sense to many of us, either, let me assure you. It's confusing and contradictory at best, yet it's the lot we've drawn and some of us are invested in seeing all this through, no matter the outcome."

"But you see, sir," I persisted, "that's precisely the attitude so many at school just detest. Why chase down a path in the forest that keeps getting darker and narrower with each step? Why not choose a better way?"

I went up to bed a little later with a book from Father's library, *The Last Sonata*, a short novel of two lovers separated by a great fire in a small village. A sort of variation on Romeo and Juliet with the fire substituting for the familial conflict of the Montagues and Capulets. He thinks she's burned to death, and she believes it's he who was consumed in the flames that made ash of the old village. The novel is a romantic tragedy, best read by those experienced in love and death. I quit reading without finishing it. In any case, I knew there were themes at the heart of the narrative I was entirely unprepared in my young life to deduce and appreciate. Soon after dousing the light, I listened to a brief rain tattering on the rooftop, then fell asleep and dreamt of Nina in her derelict corridors.

I ate breakfast with my parents out on our patio by the rose garden in fresh air and sunlight. Mother fixed boiled eggs and toast and raspberry jam, and we had hot tea and coffee with honey biscuits. Afterward, my father dragged me out to the tennis court for my morning whipping. He was an excellent player, college champion at doubles, and a ruthless opponent. At my best, I was decent enough to give him a game, but I'd never defeated him. The very idea of it was unthinkable, really.

He gave me the advantage of the sun at my back and one of his new racquets. My old one had a broken string and a slightly warped frame. Not that it mattered. He hit the ball so hard my wrist hurt as his shots hurtled toward me off the grass. I tried to keep a rally going and failed to do much more than hold the ball inside the fence. He won five games in a row, giving me only a handful of points. My volley was decent enough when I could get to the net, which was rarely. From the backcourt, I was a disaster. I couldn't return his serve, and repeatedly double-faulted on my own.

"Julian, you're not concentrating! Be a sport and give a damn!"

I walked over to the back fence to retrieve another ball after my last shot flew off toward our swimming pool. "I am giving a damn! I'm just out of sorts these days, and I haven't picked up a racquet since we last played. We can stay out here all morning and I won't be much better. Actually, you should be happy I'm so lousy today. Just think how you'd feel if I were beating you! Mother would never hear the end of it."

He won the set at love and we sat down to a pitcher of lemonade. I was tired and frustrated. My father was not cruel. He gave me every advantage except letting me win, which neither of us would ever have sought or tolerated. Sportsmanship mattered in our family. Agnes was a terrific swimmer, much faster than any of us. By thirteen, she was already beating both my father and mother, and I was far behind. We felt a sense of fairness about her superiority because she trained for hours and hours in the pool. Mother was a wonderful painter, of course, and pianist, too, and no one doubted that we could ever dream of competing with her artistry. And out here on the tennis court, Father reigned supreme. In comparison, I wasn't even a hopeful acolyte.

Father filled another glass of lemonade. "Julian."

"I'm not quitting on you."

He shook his head. "That's not what I was about to say."

"What then? I'm utterly worn out. My brain has melted away to oatmeal."

"You'll survive."

"I'm not so sure."

"Julian?"

"Yes, Father?"

"Do you happen to know anyone named Draxler? Peter Draxler?"

Where on earth had that come from?

"No," I lied with little idea how else to reply. Actually, that probably wasn't a real lie since I'd never met Nina's boyfriend, whoever he was.

Father persisted. "Are you certain? Perhaps he's an acquaintance of someone in your crowd?"

My nerves were buzzing. "Not that I'm aware of. Why? Who is he?"

I took a sip of lemonade to calm down. This conversation frightened me somehow. I wasn't the least prepared.

"Are you familiar with Leandro Porteus?"

"The architect?"

"Yes, but also Vice-Chairman of the Republic Design Directorate. A brilliant and powerful man. I met him once a couple of years ago at Elena Gardens where he delivered a lecture on the incorporation of modernistic cues into classical architecture with an eye on the renewal of our aesthetic purposes."

"Sounds thrilling." I watched a trio of robins flitter across the branches of Mother's peach tree behind the court.

Father shrugged. "Actually, it was quite interesting. Not so much the content of his talk, but what had summoned Porteus from his studio on Franklin Lane. The man rarely left his drawing board. There were rumors of agoraphobia, or disdain for humanity in general. I had no opinion about that. What intrigued me was how deliberate Porteus was in describing a purpose that seemed to offer an ill-disguised contempt for the achievements of our predecessors that served no one but the dilettante."

The morning was warmer than yesterday, and I drank another lemonade. "Maybe he was bored. Or sick of his work. Sometimes I can't stand what I write and wonder why I bother at all. I hear that from Freddy almost every day. He likes to say we're tired of our own skin."

"No, Julian, I don't believe that was the case at all. I felt there was something working behind the scenes that day at Elena Gardens, something that compelled the great Leandro Porteus to suggest a poor opinion of his own architectural accomplishments."

"And what would that be?"

"Do you know this Peter Draxler fellow or not?"

"I said I don't and that's the truth." Now I was curious. Nina had held something out on me, no doubt. Maybe my father would be more forthcoming. "Why do you want to know? Who is he?"

"Well, according to Dennett and Trevelyan last night after cigars and cognac, something untoward has gone on regarding a breach of protocol at Porteus's studio. Drawings appeared to have tiptoed off unaccounted for. Important drawings. Commissioned by the Protectorate. Rumor has it that one of Leandro's student apprentices is under suspicion, a Peter Draxler. Those drawings vanished and so has he. For some reason, the Department of Internal Security is taking up the matter and has assigned a cadre of special state agents to the investigation. Trevelyan has ears inside that office and told us how people there are frightened out of their wits. Word has it that Porteus himself has been instructed not to discuss the nature of the missing drawings with anyone inside or outside of his studio. They say he's terrifically overwrought and panicked, entirely unlike his usual self. People at the firm are worried."

I knew just then I ought to have told my father about St. Etienne Shores, and Nina at Gosney Street. Such subterfuges in one's personal life aren't concealed for long. Trouble is, we rarely seem to be found out casually, and it's always horribly inconvenient when we're dropped on our heads. But if I told Father about the dead soldier in the tides, I'd need to tell him about Nina, too, which would lead to Peter Draxler, and then he'd feel I lied when I said I hadn't known him, and I'd have to agree. Father hadn't asked me if Draxler was a friend of mine, only if I knew him. His name spoken at Nina's house placed him in that category. We aren't big on such distinctions in my family.

In any case, being the coward that I am, I failed to say another word on the subject. I let my casual lie float off on the morning breeze and followed my father back onto the tennis court to complete my beating. Then I said my goodbyes to both him and Mother and rode the train back to Regency Heights.

VI

Late the next afternoon, after Alexandrian Art and Poetry, I found a note from Freddy on our door at Thayer Hall summoning me to the storage basement. No further explanation. He knew my class schedule, so I couldn't beg off with the sort of feeble excuse that gave Freddy his own notoriety on campus. I took the note off the door and went into our room and put my books on the desk and had a look out the window where my fellow students were cycling past under the shady elms above the sidewalk to the upper campus along Trimble Street. Even with the rigors of modern academics, we enjoyed a nice life here. Stress and turmoil were more often than not self-inflicted — like Freddy's war with Professor Lengfeld and Botany 12A, or Walker Bailey's dispute with proliferating co-education. But we weren't fools, nor were we so spoiled (regardless of lovely Nina's estimation of us) as to pretend that what occurred in the Desolation happened on another world. Pretense is a gauzy veil, neither translucent nor opaque. Sometimes we manage that outlook we wake to each morning by accepting this and that for what it is, rather than what we might imagine or hope it to be. Don't look too far ahead or behind, and perhaps you might find yourself in that moment and that place where you do belong.

I opened the window behind my desk to bring in a draft of fresh air, then went out and headed to the basement after Freddy. Thayer Hall was an enormous brick building, a veritable warren of square shadowy rooms and narrow halls that smelled of aging wood and polished floors. Electric ceiling lamps were perpetually dim, and the old radiators rattled and hissed. This late in the day, most Engineering classes were ended and only a few last students lingered about.

The stone basement was cold and the iron door to Thayer's storage room locked. I knocked and called for Freddy and got no answer, so I knocked again. The heating furnaces were shut down for the season, so the basement was quiet and the echo of my door knocking rang around the walls. I tried again, more firmly, almost bruising my knuckles. The door opened and Freddy's head poked out. "Julian! Quick!" He grabbed my arm and pulled me inside and shut the door behind us.

"Freddy."

"We can't be down here, Julian," he told me. "It's off limits to undergrads, so keep quiet!"

I looked about at the innumerable storage crates and large wooden pallets stacked tall with odd metal contraptions and more boxes. "Then why did you call me to come down?"

"Because it's too important to worry about rules. Remember the tree viper in our room freshman year?"

"Yes, you chased the damned thing into the heating vent and almost got us expelled when it crawled out in the kitchen."

"True, and if I hadn't, we might've been killed."

"Are you telling me there's another snake down here? Where is it?"

"No, no, no! Julian! Listen to me!"

"I'm trying, Freddy, but you're behaving oddly again. Was it bourbon or scotch? Why don't you just tell me what we're doing?"

A familiar voice came from behind one of the storage pallets. "Let me explain, Freddy. It'll be simpler." Warren Radelfinger strolled out, his adorable Evelyn following, gorgeous as ever. He smiled. "Julian, old boy! So good to see you again."

Somehow, this didn't feel like such a grand surprise, though I wasn't sure why. I forced a wary smile. "Hello, Warren. Evie. How are you two?"

"Just swell," Radelfinger replied. "Wonderful, marvelous. Mostly."

"It's cold down here," Evie said, folding her arms under her lovely bosom. "I don't like it. This wasn't my idea. I wanted to have a swim at Giséle Park, but Warren insisted we come here. Freddy let us in."

I looked at Freddy. "How did you manage that?"

He shrugged. "I borrowed the key from Hawley's board when he went to pour bleach into the diving pool. One of our lovely freshman co-eds had a little accident this morning. I'll put it back before he's done."

"And why are you here?" I asked Radelfinger. "This can't be Freddy's idea. He's afraid of the dark."

"That's not true," Freddy said. "My ophthalmologist told me that my rods and cones are underdeveloped and it's dangerous for me to skulk about in areas of poor illumination. That's all."

Radelfinger said, "I asked Freddy for the key to Thayer's storage department. Much of his experimental apparatus is packed away in here and there's something I desperately need to explore. It's critical to everything we're experiencing these days."

"Warren's a genius," Evie said, rubbing the back of his neck. "Nobody can match him. He's quite exceptional." She kissed his cheek.

"Not at all," he demurred. "I simply dabble in other people's gardens. They do the planting. I pick the fruit. Hartley Thayer's the genius. The man was stupendously brilliant. I could play down here for months if they'd allow it."

"If only you enrolled in school," I said, a touch of sarcasm I couldn't avoid. Something about him annoyed me. Maybe that persistent insouciance.

"Well, there you have it, of course," Radelfinger replied with a silly grin. "I am the obstacle on my own road to success and notoriety. Or that road not chosen for lack of a simpler purpose."

"All right, at any rate, what's our purpose here, mine and Freddy's? We're not geniuses. What do you need from us? It's risky to be down here without a note of permission from the monitors."

"Very simple. I need your help to locate some original research papers of Thayer's that may save us all."

Freddy laughed. "Julian's in love these days with a luscious bohemian. He can't be saved."

I kicked his shin. "Hush up, Freddy, or we'll turn out the lights."

Radelfinger said, "Let me tell you what they look like and we'll divide up. I have a rough idea where they might be. It's very important."

Then he described blue and brown binders labeled: *Heliotropic Radium; Phenotheric Gas; Clothonium Particles; Teleophlogistic Dispersives; Atomized Isotopic Viridium.* Radelfinger assured us the binders would be easily identified once we looked for them. Since he sounded so earnest in his desire to locate these vital papers of the great Dr. Hartley Mills Thayer, reluctantly I agreed to help, and Freddy went along with me. We were already there, right?

Radelfinger assigned each of us quadrants in the huge storage room. Aisles of tall shelves and pallets packed tightly with strange equipment in open boxes led off into the dark. As we searched row upon row, reaching through spider webs and rifling clumsily organized file cabinets, I heard Evelyn complaining to

Radelfinger about her upset stomach and a cut on her thumb. Freddy sounded energetic in his own quarter. I really had no idea where to look. The job seemed impossibly arcane and tedious. Tangled wires and dusty glass beakers, metal coils and electric switches tossed together with scribbled-over journals and piles of papers, some blank, others water-spotted and indecipherable. An elaborate junkyard of discoveries and technological wonder from another age. Who had been responsible for storing all this with such casual indifference? It irritated me so much, I decided to quit and go upstairs for juice and a muffin.

Then Freddy called out, and Radelfinger, too.

They'd both found Thayer's binders, some blue and some brown, but in separate corners of the basement storage. Mixed together with inconsequential papers concerning plumbing and electrical structure and repairs to the floors above. The binders were thin, just scribblings and odd schematics on ordinary paper. Radelfinger skimmed them for a minute or so, then asked Freddy to give him an old medical bag they'd brought along from upstairs. It had belonged to Freddy's father, but was full of school papers from today's classwork. Radelfinger began stuffing the binders into the doctor's bag between Freddy's schoolwork. He explained, "This is just in case someone happens along to catch us on our way out. We're all empty-handed except Freddy, and he's carrying his homework. No one cares about that."

"We hope," I added, suddenly frightened of the consequences for stealing historical scientific materials from Thayer's storage. Radelfinger probably had a story prepared to keep himself out of jail and, like at St. Etienne, he also had the luscious blonde Evie as a distraction, but for this not-so-petty indiscretion Freddy and I could be expelled from the college. I wondered if Radelfinger considered that, or if he even cared. Somehow, I doubted it.

As it happened, nobody paid any notice at all as the four of us emerged from the cold basement. While Freddy handed the medical bag over to Radelfinger, Evelyn dashed off to the ladies' washroom. By now, the hour for day classes was over and supper would follow in the Thayer commons. A breeze stirred through the leafy green elms above. I was hungry, but also anxious to be rid of Radelfinger's intrigue. These mysteries were more convoluted and disturbing than those Penny Dreadfuls my mother read. And the stakes were infinitely greater.

"What will you do with those binders?" I asked Radelfinger, as Evie came out of the washroom, wiping her hands dry on that rosy cotton skirt.

"What binders?" He gave Freddy a wink, then walked off with Evie down the steps toward Trimble Street.

VII

Thibodeaux Station was a busy rail depot in North Calcitonia, maybe thirty-five minutes by interurban train from Regency Heights. Closer by half to Gosney Street in the Rosenstern Quarter where Nina had her bedroom. To get there by two o'clock, I had to skip my Wednesday afternoon class in Alexandrian Art and Poetry. No threat. I was holding a very solid ninety percent in that course and my professor, Dr. Zenas Lamberton, adored me. Well, to tell the truth, I suspected he had a crush on me. One afternoon when he invited me to stay after class to go over a series of kraters painted in erotic designs from Heraklion, I felt him hovering over me in such a way that made me curious what sort of sexual signals I gave off. When Freddy and I first met at Thayer Hall freshman year, he told me that I was clearly androgynous. I had no reply other than to point out I'd been dating Lydia Sayre in Upper School for two years and hated undressing in the showers after gym class. Three years later, neither Freddy nor I were considered a reward to either sex.

The East Platform was hectic in the early afternoon when I arrived. Thousands of travelers and citizens in and out of the metropolis used Thibodeaux Station for booking transit either into the busy stores and marketplaces of the Calcitonia District, or out toward the mercantile shipyards surrounding the harbor district, or off in the pastoral countryside of Dove Hill and Pantiére where many of the well-to-do took their holidays from our current insanity. The harried immigrant crowds of foreigners rushing through Thibodeaux Station from Marok, Fézzan, Togo, Tombut, Nédra were a blur of skin shades and exotic rainbow-hued clothing and noisy dialects. Each exit perimeter into the center of the greater metropolis was monitored by blue uniformed officers of the City Protectorate whose orders were to guide these hordes of peculiar-looking interlopers toward the established sanctuaries of Nikríté Barbária where they might mingle and mate with their own kind until such days as they were shown the gate. Unlike our mortal enemy of spyreotic undesirables, these amusing people dressed in busutas, daskas, djelleebas, kangos, kaftas were not viewed as any sort of existential threat to our Common Purpose, but rather a simple indulgence in appreciation of foreign cultures that waxed and waned according to the status of our national economy. Or so we've been taught for a century now. Not all of us believed even a word of it.

Pushing forward along the rail platform, I found my beloved Nina trimming orchid stems at her flower stand on the concrete back-wall next to a telephone gazebo. Wearing a simple lavender peasant frock and a tiara of violets, she was alone and humming to herself, though the rail platform was so noisy I couldn't quite hear her melody. Nevertheless, my heart leaped when I caught sight of her. Love is so terribly irrational. I didn't even know her last name, nor much about her at all, except that she had a cute little sister, a house full of bohemian idiots for friends, and a sarcastic humor that really was more irritating than funny. So why did I love her? Those eyes stole my heart. Nothing else need be said.

I approached from a crowd of raging children. She saw me and put down her orchids and hurried from the flower stand to throw her arms out for a big hug and a delicious kiss.

"Julian! You're here! My goodness!"

"Yes, I am, indeed. In the flesh among the raucous hordes."

She stared for a few moments into the crowds and across to the trains. "We can't stay. We need to go."

"But I just arrived!"

"I noticed, and I'm happy you did, but we have something very important to do, so we have to leave." She glanced out toward the station perimeter. "Right now."

Nina took my hand and tugged me toward the flower stand. "Help me close up."

She gave me a box to collect her garden shears, spools of twine, cards, pens and stationery. Then I wrapped her last white orchid in butcher paper while Nina took her cash box, tucked it down into a leather satchel, and we left Thibodeaux Station.

Ten thousand pigeons swarmed the broad public plaza at Dário Street and Zilpha. By the bubbling marble fountain, a string quartet was performing a classical minuet for a lower grade school class and many passersby stopped to listen. The afternoon sky was cloudless and blue, and a light wind cheered the air. I wanted to know why Nina had collected me for such a hasty exit, but she hushed me as we hurried on. So confusing. We rushed through a side-street vegetable market on the far end of the plaza and down a narrow alleyway where a pack of delinquent boys tossed cards against a filthy brick wall. One of them swore and flicked a hot smoldering cigarette butt after us as we rushed by. Nina paid no notice at all. We emerged from the alley onto Ehrenhardt Boulevard, one of our grand thoroughfares that cross the metropolis between the holy river, Livorna, and the great Dome of Eternity whose gilded spires I saw rising behind the opera house ten long blocks ahead. Motor and electric trolley traffic swallowed us up as we dodged in and out of the frantic thousands on the broad sidewalks.

Nina finally paused outside a sweetly aromatic Kaftak bakery to let us catch our breath. Her pretty eyes were moist and troubled. She leaned forward and spoke in my ear, "I can't tell you anything just yet, Julian. Please wait."

"Soon? Because I've had a trying morning and I'm awfully tired."

"Yes, I promise, but you need to believe me when I tell you that everything you'll see and hear now is genuinely vital to our very survival. Each of us has a role to play and I can't tell you anything more until it's your time to know."

"But why me? What do I have to do with any of this? We just met. I don't even know your last name, or anything about you. Like, where are you from? Where does your family live? How are you involved?"

Nina took my hand and gave me a soft kiss on my cheek. "Rinaldi. My name is Antonina Terésa Rinaldi. My family is from Arbolé township. Both my parents are dead. They were killed in a motor accident with a truck when I was nineteen and my older brother, Arturo, disappeared eight years ago in the Desolation. Delia is all I have now. I can't tell you why we're here today except that I like you and trust you, and I need your help."

She kissed me again.

I felt a blush and knew I was lost.

There is a lovely arboretum across from the city opera house on a garden walk to Immanuel Fields, perhaps the stateliest of all our metropolitan parks. On the sidewalk just outside the arboretum, perhaps two dozen vendors had set up in brown canvas tents for attracting passersby on their way into the park or farther ahead toward the opera house and the ancient Dome of Eternity beyond. Most of their customers are shrieking children accompanied by a phalanx of chattering mothers, and meandering pockets of the elderly taking in the fine afternoon sun. These vendors from our frantic immigrant districts sell spicy exotic foods and wreaths of flowers, knitted scarves, colored balloons, clever handmade jewelry, painted wooden puppets, wool and leather handbags, toys and buttons. More alien bazaar than public market, how profitable they are is only conjecture, but dawn to dusk they sell, sell, sell until the hour of folding up tents arrives.

Nina quickly took us to a vendor named Serpas close to the arbor path with a cookstove in his tent and bought us both a Lagärto bread and sausage roll wrapped in brown paper. Serpas had black eyes and black hair, sun-darkened skin and old laborer's hands. His olive-green cotton shirt was stained with cooking grease and missing three buttons. He looked tired but spoke with a smile and a bold assertiveness in a pleasant accent I could not identify.

"I miss you, Nina, when you go all about the city and not here. You are unfair to my heart. I can only guess why you deny me."

She smiled. "You are the diamond of my eye, Serpas. All my footsteps lead here. You know that to be true. Trust me and you will always be happy."

"Ah, Nina the Temptress." Serpas gave a brief bow. "I am your slave. Don't doubt my everlasting allegiance."

Nina offered her slender hand to Serpas who took and kissed it. Then she said, "Serpas, this is Julian. My new friend."

He reached out and offered his own hand to me. "Any friend of Nina's is a stab to my heart, but I am polite, and I greet you kindly."

"Glad to make your acquaintance," I said, utterly confused by all of this. It felt uncanny that she knew a fellow like Serpas. Who was he, anyhow?

He handed her both wraps of bread and sausage. "Two Pajapiros for my beautiful tulip."

Then Nina handed the Pajapiros to me and unbound that graceful white orchid from the butcher paper. "For my prince of princes."

At last Serpas smiled. "Enchantress of my thirty-thousand days and nights. You try my patience with your magic. Be gone before my passion consumes us both."

He touched one of the wraps I was holding and looked me dead in the eye. "Be wary of Nina's spirit, young man. It is unachievable and unyielding." Then he ducked back into his tent.

Nina and I chose a wooden bench along a brick walkway in Immanuel Fields beyond the shady arboretum where birds chittered in the fir trees and little children played on the grass by a pond in the distance. I had begun to unfold one of the sausage-wraps when she slapped my hand. "No, you don't, Julian. That one's mine."

"They're exactly the same."

"Of course not. Can't you tell the difference? Here, give it to me."

I hesitated but did.

She held it away from me. "See?"

"What?"

"The difference, you poor boy."

"No, what is the difference?"

She giggled. "I'm holding this one now, and you're not. Which makes it mine!"

I stared at that pretty face, astonished by her absurdity. "You're a demon."

"Maybe." She shrugged. "But I got what I wanted. Isn't that what counts? We needn't always be sugar and spice. People lie and cheat and steal all day long in this city, and nobody cares."

"Well, I do."

"You just think you do. Or pretend you do. Because then you feel superior, when you're not. Nobody's superior. Everybody's rotten now and then."

"Not everyone steals Pajapiros. It's bread and sausage, not caviar."

"Some do. And some do lots worse."

"Great," I said, "another civics lesson. Is it all right if I eat *my* Pajapiro? Bantering with you makes me hungry."

"Be my guest." Nina shrugged, unfolding her own wrap. "You don't need my permission."

A flurry of sparrows dove past overhead, spiraling toward the arboretum. An older couple strolled arm-in-arm up the brick path. Both wore brown winter coats and wool hats and proceeded with a curious caution as if the sidewalk were treacherous. Then I glanced over at Nina and noticed her reading something scribbled on the inside of the paper wrapping for her Pajapiro. When she saw me, she crumpled up the paper, tucked it into her leather satchel, and looked off toward the pond where those little children ran in ragged circles across the grass.

I thought to ask Nina what was written on the wrapping paper, when it occurred to me that it was given her by Serpas intentionally. Which explained her switching of our Pajapiros. A secret message for her eyes only. Interesting. More intrigue. More mystery. What on earth was I there for? I ate my Pajapiro and watched passersby and pretended not to have noticed Nina's duplicitous gesture. What was her game? Why were we in the park? Birds chattered. Children shrieked at play. A solitary violinist strolled by fingering a solo in E minor I recognized from my mother's piano mornings: "The World in Miniature." A tonal oracle perhaps?

After finishing my Pajapiro, I said to Nina, "Why are you so jittery?"

She licked sausage grease off her fingertips. "Who says I am?"

"I do."

"Well, I'm not." She stood and grabbed her leather satchel. "Let's go."

"Where?"

"You'll see."

And off she went down the flowered brick walkway into the heart of great Immanuel Fields. I chased to keep up. Off to our left in a narrow copse of elms, a small audience was gathered for a speech by some stout fellow dressed as if for the opera in a black and white tuxedo. He held a lit cigar and waved it about for emphasis. I couldn't quite make out what he was orating, but the crowd appeared receptive and enthusiastic. Then Nina veered away across the lawn toward the bronze clock tower that announced three o'clock with a ringing of bells. She was hurrying. Were we late somehow? Several hundred yards ahead, Dardanus Way bisected the park with an old cobblestone road wide enough for vehicles of any sort to pass without drama. Today a long funeral cortège of a dozen horse-drawn carriages draped in black led a procession toward Lourdes Memorial Cemetery. More dead heroes of the upper class come home to rest in peace and splendor near the reedy banks of the eternal river, Livorna. Flags would wave, trumpets blare, drums rumble, chants arise, and tears wept like autumn rain. Would no one rather live than die a war hero's death? Isn't that breath we take at the beginning and end of each day honor enough for enduring existence, this expansive legend of ours? The underclass and poor remain buried where fallen in the Desolation, trumpets silent, battle flags of Imperial viridian and gold stained with mud. The forgotten. How pure were our intentions, soaked in the blood of millions?

A vast flock of crows collected noisily in the dark branches of pine trees above us where Nina led along the bricks and flower beds toward a small mausoleum in a willow garden. The day was lazy here, the sun relaxed. Nina's silk-black hair tossed in the draft, her careless gait fluttering her peasant frock. Several steps ahead of me now, I could stare with erotic pleasure at her lithe figure and debate how she was able to tangle my common sense. Is this love? A girl smiles and her childish dimples tie our thoughts in knots of nonsense. Nina had a way of looking at me with those cocoa-dark eyes, sly and often peevish, that curdled my stomach with longing. Just her graceful fingers touching my wrist left me light-headed and vague. Why is love so provoking of emotions that drain our will? She was obstinate and opaque. Then coquettish and lustful. She'd kiss me as if I were the only boy on earth and afterward ignore my pleas for tenderness and consideration of my needful heart. If this is called love, that kind agony would surely be my undoing.

"Julian, you can't say a word once we're indoors," Nina instructed as we approached the old mausoleum shrouded by willows. "You have to promise."

Her eyes were damp, as if warm tears were about to burst forth. She hesitated at the iron door where a marble plaque affixed to the architrave above read:

IN MEMORIAM IPPOLIT GOODPASTURE

There was no date recorded because the revered are thought to be timeless, unbound to the counting of days.

Nina nudged me. "Julian?"

"Yes, I promise. But why are we here?"

"Just be quiet."

She knocked gently on the old iron door and waited.

Back on the brick path behind us, a trio of young mothers rolled perambulators along, chatting about chrysanthemums and birthday cakes. A flurry of mynah birds descended to elms just across the way where sprinklers erupted on the soft green lawn. Nina knocked lightly once more, now with a different cadence I hardly detected. A few moments passed. Somehow, I was holding my breath.

Then the iron door creaked inward. A gloved hand beckoned from the shadows. We slipped inside and the door closed once again. I watched a lucifer match flare brightly and travel quickly toward a candle in a carved wall niche. Whispers were traded across the flickering shadows, a hiss of incomprehensible utterances. I stood away from the iron door beside the cold wall, Nina ahead of me, a tall man cloistered in the dark across from us. They conversed so quietly I had impressions of telepathy or some arcane sign language. Then I saw him step sideways to another niche and retrieve a slim object from within. He offered it to Nina. She shook her head and gestured instead toward me. He came forward from out of the gloom and I saw the violin in one hand and a leather-bound book he held out in the other. I glanced at Nina. She nodded, and I accepted the book. Then the violinist receded into the shadows and extinguished the candle and the mausoleum was dark until Nina opened the old iron door and we left.

In the sunlight again I looked at the book given me. Virgil's *Aeneid*. A very old edition, too. I opened it and saw the ancient epic was rendered here in Latin and set in a beautiful antiquarian typeface. Incredible.

Over my shoulder, Nina said, "You can read it, can't you?"

"Virgil? In Latin?"

"You study it. I know you do."

"What makes you think that?"

"I just do. Your third term professor, Konovaloff. He teaches Latin and you were his student twice, weren't you? Decent grades?"

I frowned. This was suddenly very disturbing. "How do you know this, Nina? How are you so familiar with my classes? Do you have spies at Regency College? Is that it? Have you and your friends snuck into our records at Thayer Hall?"

She took my hand and carefully knit her fingers into mine, then gave me a pretty kiss. "Let's walk to the river, Julian. I'll explain. But first, hide the book in your shirt. No one needs to see it."

"This is so strange, Nina," I said, tucking the old book under my shirt waist and following her away from the mausoleum. "I have no idea what I'm doing."

She looked back, forcing a smile I took as inauthentic. "You're helping me, that's all. And a lot of other people you've never met. Don't confuse yourself. It's not good for your health."

We sat shoulder to shoulder on a cracked stone quay along a shallow stretch of waterfront at the immortal river in the hour of sunset. Yellow clouds drifted east away from the Hoheimer marina where ships from out at sea sent goods of all sorts into the metropolis by barge and steam freighter. Nina curled her ankle over mine and leaned close, her perfect breast soft against my arm, perhaps her peace offering. Her sinuous black hair smelled of peppery incense and coal smoke in the river wind. I took her hand.

"Julian," she murmured, kissing my ear, "I'm sorry for being such a challenge. You've been so wonderful, and I've behaved very badly, and I know it. These days are such a terrible anxiety, you haven't seen my best self."

Her narrow face was bronzed in the late afternoon light off the river. Farther down the waterfront, a small group of roughened fishermen carried poles and buckets to the river's edge. A jangling ship's bell echoed sharply across the hazy sky.

"I don't know how to please you, Nina," I said, stroking her pretty fingers with mine, "because I'm not sure you care enough to be pleased by me."

We kissed again. "You love me, don't you, Julian?"

"Maybe I do. Though I'd be foolish to admit it."

"Why would you say that? Love isn't one of our daily trials, Julian."

"Well, it's been feeling that way recently," I told her, flatly. "If I'm being honest."

I watched a graceful black cormorant dive for fish out in the cold eddies, and I remembered my father bringing me down here to this shore once when I was little to watch a gilded wedding yacht navigating the cold current upriver with a flotilla of smaller flag-draped water craft trailing after. *Look there, Julian*, he told me, *our Minister of Foreign Affairs is onboard*. I remember, because the next morning, my father woke me up to say that the great man had drowned only an hour after we'd seen him when his beautiful yacht of happy celebrants collided with a steamship and sank. Nobody was saved. His name was Dr. Christian Bernadotte and his orders had expanded the Desolation past the Florian Border into Grijalva and the fertile growing fields beyond. One hundred thousand people died that first day.

"If I said I loved you, Julian," Nina gently asked, laying her head on my shoulder, "would you believe me?"

"Would it be the truth?"

I just then understood how terrified I was of her, of being in love with her. She was very beautiful to me, so incredibly alluring in too many ways. The risk was immense. Whose heart do we trust? Our own, or our lover's?

"I'm not cruel, Julian," she told me. "I'm just as afraid of you, as you are of me. But why? What does that do for us? All our lives, we exist in fear of what hurt may come, and so we never choose to be happy. We just choose not to be sad. How can we live like that? What are we here for, then? Once when I was in school and scared to go to the playground for fear of not making friends there, Momma said to me, 'My baby sweet pea, joy is not the absence of sorrow. It's the opposite.' I didn't believe her, and so I didn't have any friends to play with for a whole year. Then she and Poppa died, and my brother disappeared, and I was alone with Delia who needed me more than I needed friends. Those were my first lessons in love: hurt and happiness. Both sides of life."

I stared out across the wide river where a thin boy in overalls rowed a wooden skiff west into the dying sun. His fishing poles hung over the stern and the boat looked empty. Maybe just an unlucky day. A handful of grey and white gulls swept past him on the breeze above.

"Julian?"

I shaded my eyes. "Yes?"

"I'm not here by accident. I want to be with you. That day at the college I admit I was looking for someone to do me a favor, and I really didn't care who it was. But you came out onto your gallery and I thought you were so cute, it just had to be you. Then you actually started talking to me and I felt like an idiot with that stupid dog-flyer Delia made and I was sure you hated me, even though I could tell you thought I was pretty."

I smiled. "I thought you were beautiful."

"No, you didn't." She giggled and pinched my arm. "But it's sweet of you to say so."

I shrugged. "Well, you were very persuasive."

"Did your friends approve of me? I doubt they did, right? Let me guess what they called me: A socialist tramp, bohemian bitch, traitorous whore. Am I close?"

"Nina?"

"I don't mind, really. My friends weren't very generous, either. Most of them are sure you're a spy of some minimal rank for the Security Directorate. They'll explode if I sleep with you."

I laughed. "Are you planning to sleep with me?"

"Am I too obvious?"

I kissed her as gently as I could, then lingered, her sweet breath on my lips. "Nothing about you, Nina, is obvious. I think you know that."

"Do you love me, Julian?"

A shrill ferry whistle sounded from the far shore and a flock of ducks scattered about the damp reeds just downriver.

I smiled into those dark eyes. "Probably."

Her skin golden now, Nina grinned. "Me, too."

We hugged and kissed again. Then Nina stood up from the old stone quay and offered her hand, "Let's take a walk, sweet boy, and find some place to eat."

Instead of heading back into the center of the metropolis, we went upriver along the waterfront where crowds gathered to watch sunset and the restaurants were vibrant and delicious. We strolled hand-in-hand and drew close as we maneuvered through knots of enthusiastic pedestrians atop the breakwater. At the terminus of Clover Street, Nina pressed herself to my shoulder and kissed me. She lent my hand a delicate squeeze and I felt a wave of desire, that brilliant flush we get when we allow ourselves to believe love has descended upon us at last. I watched her wistful eyes glimmer in the glowing streetlamps and stole her scent with me as we walked on. I had already decided as we left the stone quay not to mention a word about the old volume of Virgil's *Aeneid* — why I was given the book and what I was supposed to do with it. Nina's mood now felt airy and joyful and I was afraid of spoiling our hour of what I hoped would be true affection.

We paused briefly to watch an old paddle wheeler steam past downriver, fully lit like burning candles on a birthday cake. Her luminous deck railings were packed solidly with passengers enjoying a romantic dinner excursion to the Odessa Landing & Hotel three miles away.

"Will you take me on a twilight cruise sometime, Julian? Just us two? I don't care where we go, so long as it's somewhere beautiful where we can be alone and pretend nothing matters."

I nodded. "If you like. Just tell me when."

"Soon." She kissed me, her delicate fingers caressing my face. "I want us to go soon."

We found the Colonia Miñaero restaurant a couple of blocks farther up the waterfront and sat at a table for two in a candlelit nook with a view of the holy river. By then, Nina was so dreamy and serene I almost wondered if she was the same frantic girl I had met at Thibodeaux Station only a few hours earlier. A wispy blonde waitress in a pale azure Penthean robe and sandals came to see what sort of wine or spirits we preferred. Nina asked for a clever cocktail from the lower Catalan called Sekouz, a radium-green liquor and potent in excess. I chose a glass of Guerrero, that blood-red spirit wine Mother adored and my initiation into alcohol at fifteen when she and my father were on holiday at Bilignon.

"What do you prefer to eat, Julian," Nina asked, studying the parchment menu with a sly grin, "when you're out with a girl?"

"Should there be a difference? Am I choosing a food that suits my mood or my general digestion?"

"Just curious." She skimmed to the bottom and folded over to the next page. "It's important not to eat the wrong thing with your date along."

"I agree. My parents taught me to be careful. One fault and it can all go to smash, true?"

"Exactly."

Across the restaurant in two cane chairs on a raised and recessed stage, a bearded older fellow and his round wife in Farolinese dress and hats began a musical interlude on eight-string mahlousjka and daubha flute. Their intricate melodies were obscure to most of us, delightful to others, reminiscent of life once upon a time in faraway provinces yet unaffected by war and its dreadful tribulations. Watching them dip and sway, I began to feel that musicians must be a rather happy lot, at least when lost together in song.

"If I order the cinnamon arroussi dish," Nina spoke up from behind her menu, "will you share it with me? I can't eat it all, but it's so good I really think I need to have some."

"I was just getting interested in the paphus steak," I admitted, being honest. "It's the strangest fish, do you know? Looks like sturgeon but tastes like jellied lamb. I can't figure it out."

"Is paphus steak filling? Maybe you'd still want some of my dish, anyhow."

A police siren wailed in the metropolitan distance. I looked out of doors. Night had fallen over the eternal river now and burning oil lamps mounted on late-to-home skiffs and log rafts glowed like golden stars on the dark water.

"I'll share whatever you like, Nina," I told her, trying to be agreeable. "I'm just glad to be with you."

"Julian?"

"Yes?"

Nina took her napkin and laid it on the table. "Do you think there's a telephone I could use? I need to call Delia."

"Of course," I said. "If not here, then at the tobacconist next door. I noticed a telephone booth there with four boys stuffed into it when we arrived. I'm sure they're finished by now."

"I'll see." Nina left the table and hurried off to the front of the restaurant. I watched her ink-black hair float in the draft of the low ceiling fans as she went. Nina was so beguiling, I doubted the clarity of my present judgment, love being the most astonishing inebriation. When our waitress brought Nina's fluorescent Sekouz and my blood-red Guerrero, I questioned whether I should even tempt myself with a sip. Who could tell where I might end up later on?

I thought I'd give Nina a little while with her telephone to Delia, but then our pretty waitress returned to light our own table candle, and I decided to order our dinners: that arroussi dish and my paphus steak. I left my Guerrero and Nina's Sekouz in the smoky-glass copita untouched. I believed we should toast and drink together. Isn't that what we do when we're in love? I felt sure I was in love, and I hoped she was, too. Almost four years come and gone at Thayer Hall and I hadn't yet found my best girl, or any girl at all, to be honest. Hence the derogatory comments from Freddy and his pathetic crowd. I kept to my room and my studies, not for lack of sexual and romantic passion and desire, but simply because I wanted to discover one wonderful girl to be my lover and companion as I struggled to survive Regency College.

During Upper School at Prouter Academy, Lydia Sayre was my inspiration for those last four semesters before graduation. We met on the steps out front of Claflin gymnasium on a sunny afternoon and took to each other enthusiastically that very day. She knew my sister Agnes from glee club and dance in Lower School and remembered having a crush on me when I accompanied my parents to watch Agnes in the girls' performance of "Will O' The Wisp." Seeing her at Claflin, my only thought was how little brown-haired, cherub-faced Lydia Sayre had very much grown up since then. With a terrific enthusiasm, she taught me how to kiss, and I have no hesitancy in admitting that. We went about like twins and I felt as if we had absorbed each other for all we shared in books and games and music and talk. My parents adored her almost as much as I did, and she and Agnes were close, too, not quite sisters, but confidential as girls. We studied for exams together, rode bicycles all over Highland Park and Stanton, went to the videoscopes and twilight picnics at Ridland Pond. We'd lie on an old blanket in the damp night grass of our backyards and plan our life by lists and stories: where we'd live, what jobs we'd have, where we'd travel, whom we'd meet to bring into our lives. I bought Lydia a silver amethyst bracelet for her seventeenth birthday and thought she and I were sure to marry. We designed a tall house with a garden and fruit orchard, a swimming pool, a new Hüeffer motor car. Her parents and mine would become best friends and we'd share a table at Sunday dinner. Perhaps her brother, Henry, might even marry Agnes and make everyone happy. Of course, it feels silly now to think that way, but we were so young and in love and nothing in the world mattered as much. She was my first love and my first lover, and who could ever replace her in that? How she laughed and held my hand in bed, how warm and soft and comforting she felt nude in the dark, how she said my name in that funny, melodic voice of hers. Lydia Sayre. Her mother suffered a stroke and died the week of Upper School graduation and her father sold their house and took them away to Petersburg. I'd still expected Lydia Sayre and I to be together again at Regency College where both of us had been admitted. Then that same fall, she wrote from their new home to tell me college was foolish and that she had found a secretarial position with an insurance firm and I should probably not write to her anymore. I did, then I didn't. First love is an astonishment, the bluest of all our blue, blue skies. Dear Lydia Sayre. Where are you now?

And Nina? Mindful of the time she'd been gone, I got up from our table to go see if she was still using that telephone by the tobacconist. When I noticed the booth was empty, I looked around to the crowds along the waterfront upriver and down, and that's where I saw her in conversation with a fellow perhaps my father's age, tall and burly, wearing a navy-blue coat and a sailor's cap. He had his hands in his pockets and was rocking back and forth on his boot heels as they spoke. She seemed excited, and agitated, too, depending upon who was speaking in that moment. I went back inside to our table and sat down, slightly irritated and confused again. I stared at my aromatic Guerrero and almost took a drink. I felt let down. Who was that fellow? Did she go out to telephone Delia or to see him? I listened to the Farolinese musicians and waited for Nina to come back. I expected her to, of course, because she'd left her leather satchel with the cash box on her chair when she went out.

To pass a few minutes, I drew Virgil out from under my shirt to have a brief peek at the printed Latin text.

Arma virumque cano Troiae qui primus ab oris
Italiam fato profugus Laviniaque venit
litora multum ille et terris iactatus et alto
vi superum saevae memorem Iunonis ob iram

At least that violinist had not given me an illuminated manuscript. In Philology class earlier in the winter, we were shown a Gallinese Book of Hours to examine and I had no idea at first what to make of it. Where were the words? But Virgil's *Aeneid* I'd studied, just as Nina reported, in Second Latin with Konovaloff and earned a passing mark. I found it both vague and violent, indecipherable and inspiring. I liked it well enough, after all, but had no particular desire to read it again. I preferred *The Odyssey*. Homer felt more fun than Virgil.

Then Nina came back and saw me with the book. "Julian! Put it away."

"Why?"

"Please?"

I slipped the leather volume back under my shirt, then asked, "Where were you? I thought you fell in the river."

"Delia is such a share," Nina said, taking her chair again. Her face was dark. "I told her to keep indoors until I got back, and she went out anyway with that stupid dog. Kaspar and Saami had to go look for her. They found her down in the next block with some other little kids dropping old toys down a manhole. I may lock her in my closet next time."

She picked up her Sekouz and had a drink. Her eyes were nervous somehow, her hand slightly unsteady on the smoky copita. She stared past me out toward the eternal river.

I took up my glass of Guerrero. "A toast?"

That drew Nina's attention back to me. "Oh, yes, sure." She raised her glass.

I said, "To romance, may it arrive swiftly and never depart."

She smiled slyly. "À votre santé."

Our glasses clinked and we drank together. Then Nina reached across the table to touch my hand. "I'm sorry I'm so pathetic, Julian. I don't mean to be. These days with Delia, and everything else, I feel like I'm in a cloud and I can't see anywhere."

Our fingers intertwined and she squeezed gently, her night-dark eyes settling on mine at last. I smiled. She had her enchantments, no doubt. Love is also a gamble. Sometimes it's willing, sometimes not. Which side was I on?

Nina added, "Julian, I'm sorry. Did we order yet? I don't know why you put up with me. I'm really terrible, aren't I? I should be locked up in a nunnery at Venulius and forgotten about. I knew one of those girls. She was crazy like me."

I laughed. "You are pretty crazy, that's true."

"But you love me, anyway, don't you?" She laughed, too. "Lie, if you must."

I smiled. "Maybe."

Then our food arrived.

As we ate, Nina talked about her friends in the house on Gosney Street and how that cast of oddball bohemian transients came to gather there. A couple were dropouts from the government trade school at Schirding. The boy named Marco drifted in out of the rain one night, telling them he'd run away from home after being raped by his stepfather, a Cheikh laborer and boucle poppy addict. That pair Nina had sent after Delia, Kaspar and Saami, were already there when Nina arrived sixteen months ago, having rented the house from a portrait painter named Idel Memphis who had gone to sea with another fellow and hadn't come back. That was almost six years ago, but Kaspar says they expected him any time now. Nina thinks he and Saami are hoarding the rent and plan to fly into the wind when Memphis returns — if he does. Apparently, Saami isn't so sure he *will* be back and the others in the house think he's dead, which is why the indoors looks like a rat's nest: none of them see any purpose in keeping it up if the owner isn't looking in on them. She also told me that, except for a few of the girls who were essentially stray cats, everyone in the house was wildly political and desperate to see the Directorate fail and the war come to an end, regardless who wins. Dozens of others just like them passed through the house, day and night, storming each other's heads with elaborate schemes of social disturbance, anarchy and insurrection. Most of the ideas, Nina told me, were juvenile and idiotic, while others sounded dangerously suicidal. She refused to offer details. I guessed the Colonia Miñaero was too public for that and didn't press her. Walls and dining tables and ceiling fans had electric ears those days. No one should be so naïve. In fact, she said, lately the house had become paranoid and distrustful of anyone they hadn't slept with, male or female. They were trading partners now like a bowl of apples and had no fear of disease or disappointment. There's an awful fatalism in that crowd, she told me, which worried her for Delia's sake. If someone believes there's no future, then there's no constraint on killing it for everyone else. Delia was just a little girl. She deserved her own world to grow up in, her own tomorrow. Nobody had the right to take that away from her.

I saw Nina's eyes dampen when she spoke of Delia and her young life. Her voice quieted, her hands fluttered gently as she shifted her fork through the steaming arroussi. I cut up my paphus steak and traded Nina a tender slice for a spoonful of her arroussi. The buttercorn sauce and meal, Roman mushrooms and sacquali were cooked so aromatically that each bite tasted much as it smelled. And the paphus steak was perfect.

"Thank you, Julian."

"Of course."

"You're so patient with me," she said, a pretty smile arriving. "What am I going to do with you?"

Did she love me? I had no true idea. In that moment, at the tiny candlelit table we shared by nightfall beside the holy river, I suppose I didn't care.

The house on Gosney Street was quiet and humid when we slipped in after midnight. Easing by the living room, I noticed people cuddled together on the ragged couch and tucked into sleeping bags on the old carpet and splayed out on armchairs. A drifting odor of incense and griffo weed and fried fish hung upon the upstairs heat. A faucet dripped in the kitchen sink. Whispers by Nina sent me down the hall to her bedroom as she went to look in on Delia.

Her room was dark, so I went to the window and slid the muslin curtain open briefly to the street below. A dim grey light filled the room. Unsure whether or not Nina preferred her desk or bedside lamp on, I left them both off. A motor car rumbled past outdoors and I thought I heard cats scrapping in the yard behind the house. Nina's bedroom was tidier than mine. Somebody must have been picking up after her since she seemed too harried to play maid. Delia was probably her house slave. I hadn't decided yet about asking who that fellow was she had been talking with outside of the Colonia Miñaero. Theoretically it wasn't any of my business. Were I more mature, I'd put it out of my mind and concentrate on the fact that I was in my beautiful Nina's bedroom in the middle of the night and any minute she would be coming down the hall to be with me.

Maybe Nina didn't want her curtain open. I went to the window to close it and had another look out over narrow Gosney Street. Now I saw some older fellow in a long grey coat standing hatless on the sidewalk under the streetlamp smoking a cigarette. He wasn't doing anything particular, just there as if waiting for a bus, but this block had no stop and I doubted any city metro line ran through the Catalan at that hour. Next, I saw him take a small black notebook from his coat pocket and a pencil from his inside vest. He glanced up and down Gosney Street, then stared across the sidewalk to this house for half a minute or so and scribbled on one of the pages. I stepped back from the window and shut the curtain. Maybe he saw me. Maybe not. I went over to Nina's bed and sat down and tried to understand what I ought to do next. There were no busses to Thayer Hall from the Catalan, but traffic was almost non-existent, so I could hire a taxi and be safe in my room within the hour.

Nina came through the bedroom door and tossed herself onto the quilted mattress beside me. She reached out and drew me down on top of her. Then kissed me. A faint scent of sultry Amata perfume bloomed from her skin in the dark, and I tasted a hint of cognac on her breath. Not unpleasant. Ripe. She kissed me again, then murmured, "Delia hasn't been happy here. She doesn't trust the boys and hates the girls. She was crying when I went into her room. I had to fix a cup of warm milk with morpheus powder and tell her a fairy story to put her to sleep. We're tragic, she and I."

I traced my fingers gradually through Nina's black silky hair. "What story?"

"Princess of Mardrus —"

"— and the Unicorn King? My sister Agnes loved that story. She made us call her Atyna for at least a year. My father went crazy, but my mother insisted 'Atyna' was just adorable."

Nina wrapped herself around me and we kissed more intimately then. She caressed my face and arms, kissed my ear and nose. Nibbled on my neck. She whispered through the dark, "*You're* adorable, Julian." And cuddled more closely. "You really are."

"I try to be as adorable as possible."

Nina eased away from me and sat up. In the twilight of streetlamps through her curtains I watched her slip that peasant dress up over her head and shed it. Her skin was brown and shiny. She fingered the buttons on my shirt and began unfastening them one by one, top to bottom, the faintest smile on her lips. Was I trembling? My mouth was dry, and I was afraid to touch her. Then Nina lifted off my shirt and I *did* touch her. And she brought her breast to my mouth and had me kiss her and kiss her and kiss her. And for the longest while as night wore on, I felt absurdly intoxicated in the consuming shadows of her bedroom, inhaling her desperate scent, her ravenous breath, dripping beads of sweat onto her bare skin. Her stormy black hair cascading over me, Nina whispered love and love and love. And I remember believing her. Hour after hour. Entangled unerringly. I lay my head down once and felt my heartbeat and thought somehow I had conquered this mystery of her, yet it was still night and still dark and she was crawling over me again.

VIII

∞

C lasses came much too early the next morning after I'd raced home by taxi at dawn. Freddy was already up and gone to Obstacles in Common Theology, one of only two courses he was confident of passing, chiefly because his professor, Malcolm Stubblefield, was a golfing partner of Dr. Barron. That advantage alone propped up Freddy's spirits. I had Philosophy in Classical Languages at eight sharp and barely beat the bell. On a best morning, my brain was a junkyard at that hour, so arriving to Thayer Hall from Nina's bedroom as city streetlamps were extinguished was asking for the moon. Also, Percy McDonnell was in that class and gave me a stink eye as I stumbled to my chair. He had a sneer prepared for every word I uttered aloud and his usual inappropriate laughter when I stumbled over a pronunciation. Fortunately, Dr. Coffeen appreciated my enthusiasm for his class and the inquisitive nature of my approach to the subject. I did enjoy being there each Tuesday and Thursday morning, Percy and the hour aside. Above Coffeen's blackboard was written:

We learn because we live. We live because we learn.

Think about waking one day with no idea who you are, neither where you come from, nor why you are where you are. No part of our being, our identity, exists exclusive from the cultural history of our family and class, our race. How we look, how we speak, how we think on a multitude of arcana and simple ideas that create and inform this fabric of our being. For some of us, all that's visible is the fabric itself, just its general color and maybe how it feels to touch. Not the warp and woof of its threads, that intricate weave, nor the patterns within the shade, how they're interwoven, how they sift and flow together, nor why they fit at all and please the eye. Yet everything in this world is a story of that weave, each thread adding to the hue and pattern of life, our towns and markets and neighborhoods, the fields and forests and streams, the sounds of children running on a sunny summer day, a father's steady hand, a loving mother's song at bedtime.

— . —

Changing clothes for class, I'd left that volume of *The Aeneid* in my room, hidden safely under my mattress. No doubt Dr. Coffeen would have been pleased to look it over, but I hadn't any idea why it had been given to me rather than Nina, so I resolved to keep its existence confidential until I thought it was reasonable to do otherwise. But, again, why me? On the streetcar back to the Catalan after dinner, when I attempted to broach that topic, she shushed me by saying, *"It's yours."* Of course, I understood that my rudimentary command of Latin was better than for someone like Nina who had none at all. And I further supposed that my ability to translate was only half the story here. I guessed there must have been something in that volume, or in Virgil's tale, I alone needed to discover. What could it be?

Managing to dodge Percy's insults once class ended, I hurried to the library for a Latin dictionary I failed to buy during Konovaloff's class. Fortunately, those dictionaries had not all been borrowed and I was able to take one back to my room before Dr. Sternwood's Law and Modern Science at eleven o'clock. Freddy was up from the basement and he had all our windows open to a fresh morning draft. He had also been asleep when I walked in and barely mumbled a word when I closed the door behind me. After putting my Language of Philosophy textbook and the Latin dictionary away in my desk, I looked back at him. Poor Freddy was a mess. Had he washed his hair in bourbon?

"Julian," he croaked, opening one eye. "I thought we'd lost you."

"Pardon?"

"That seductress from across the tracks, that succubus, her claws are deep in you. How did you manage to escape?"

I sat down at my desk. "Freddy?"

"Yes, master?"

"Did you find your common sense this morning?"

"Do you mean, did I go to Stubblefield, or throw myself on the floor in Lungfester's office and beg for mercy?"

I laughed. "Isn't there time enough today for both?"

"Probably, but Stubblefield always needs me to clean his erasers, so I consider that my priority. I was even on time this morning. Lungfester be damned. He won't get his pound of my flesh until I'm ready to give it."

"Now you're talking! Good for you, Freddy! Spoken like a true Barron! Your father will be proud."

Freddy had both eyes open now and shuffled his pillows to sit up. "No, he'll disown me, like he promises, but not today. He'll just need to wait. Dr. H. Cornelius Barron is not the most patient of men, but he can be trained. Mother says so, and I trust her implicitly. She's a saint. Have I ever told you that, Julian? My mother is a dear angel. I've always felt that."

"Is she an angel or a saint?" I asked, retrieving my Thursday study plan for Law and Science from the top drawer. "I want to get that straight."

"Can't she be both? Ramona and Henrietta call me a devil dog whenever I go home. I find that just as confusing, don't you agree?"

"Freddy, your sisters are harpies. I wouldn't pay them any notice whatsoever."

He offered me a droopy smile. "All right, I won't."

Then Freddy rolled over and fell back to sleep.

Late in the sunny blue afternoon, after day classes, I went to the gymnasium to toss a medicine ball with some arty fellows from Ilanos Hall, drama students and poets, not the sort one usually expects to find with the muscle crowd. Three of the pseudo-athletes — Oskar, Felix and Amadeo — were in training for a stage production of "The Colossus of Rhodes," where they were to be assuming the roles of mighty gods. Optimistically, they expected that lifting barbells and tossing the medicine ball back and forth for a month would make Titans of them in short order. The other two from Ilanos were skinny poets, Pindar and Quixote, who had appropriated their identity from dead writers to gain romantic attention from freshman girls. A hopeless endeavor, really, if you saw them in undershorts. I met the group after four o'clock in the men's locker room beneath the athletic courts. Pindar and Quixote had refused to undress in front of genuine athletic upperclassmen and wore bathing suits instead. The dramatists knew better than to debase themselves, while also reminding us how ancient Greek Olympians competed in the nude. At any rate, those three were not too far from athletic form, so a strenuous hour on the gymnasium floor upstairs would seem attainable. I was invited into this private crowd because Oskar knew me from sophomore tennis when I was playing several days a week and could hold my own with all but the finest players on campus. He hoped that my extensive experience in competitive sports could influence the pace and intensity of their training. I thought the idea was amusing and went along with it because the past few months I had begun to feel lethargic. Losing that set of tennis so badly to my father was a further warning. With hardly a nudge, I could find myself wallowing in all sorts of mediocrities.

"We've agreed to swim first, Julian," Amadeo announced, stripping nude. "Pindar claims our muscles need loosening in the pool before any furious exertion. We voted to agree."

Both Oskar and Felix undressed, too, boldly strutting their naked physiques to other athletes about the locker room. I noticed our two poets smiling. Somehow, they'd been able to manipulate this delicate situation in their own favor.

I shrugged. "I don't mind having a swim. I'm sure it'll be more invigorating than reading Gaius Musonius until supper. Will we swim laps or do time trials?" And pointing a finger at Pindar and Quixote, I added, "And are life jackets available for these two otters? Jack Steadman told me all lifeguards are excused at three o'clock."

Pindar crossed his legs like he needed a toilet. "Very funny, Julian. We don't need anyone's help. We're too fast to drown."

Soon enough, all six of us were splashing about in the gymnasium pool. I raced Felix and Oskar and beat them both by a length or so. Nothing to brag about. My little sister would have defeated all three of us with half the effort. Amadeo lured Quixote into the water and dunked him immediately. In defense of poetry, Pindar jumped onto Amadeo's back and started a war the poets lost unconditionally.

Next, we dried off and tackled the medicine ball. My shoulders were sore from the breaststroke and the ball felt ten pounds heavier than it had only a month before. Oskar tossed one to Pindar that knocked him onto his back. Quixote rolled it to Felix. Then we found a mutual rhythm and traded it around a circle until each of us felt well and competent. From there, Amadeo led us to the barbells where half a dozen members of our collegiate wrestling squad had gathered. Amadeo was the strongest of the three dramatists, a good choice for Atlas. His biceps were bigger than both Quixote's and Pindar's taken together. Even the notoriously arrogant wrestlers were impressed, admirably resisting insults. Confident now, Felix and Oskar and I grabbed our own barbells and did our best imitation of Greek gods and managed not to humiliate ourselves, but the poets shrunk away to the wrestling mats and practiced ridiculous holds on each other. Done with the barbells, the dramatists wanted to challenge each other on the climbing ropes. Having a natural fear of heights, I begged off and went over to kibbitz with the poets. Both were sitting now, backs against the gymnasium wall, giggling at a silly joke Pindar had just told. He repeated it for my benefit.

"Julian, who's the most athletic fellow at this college?"

"I have no idea. Who?"

The poets looked at each other and laughed. "Jim Nasium!"

All right, I laughed, too. I remember my father had told me that one when I was little. Maybe more than once. I think it was one of his favorite jokes.

The dramatists were at the ropes now, Felix halfway up, challenging some sturdy young fellow I didn't know.

Pindar said, "You're our hero, Julian."

Quixote nodded in agreement.

"How so?"

"You're the only one outside of Ilanos who appreciates our struggle."

Watching Oskar climbing now after both Felix and that other fellow, I asked Pindar, "What struggle is that?"

Quixote jumped in. "You should come to one of our poetry clans. They're invigorating. Nothing like our insipid classes here. We've taken a vote to see poetry banned from school. True art and college academics can't mix. Grading poetry is like smelling farts."

"Pardon?"

Pindar said, "That's what our clan mentor told us after the readings last month on Traiano Street. Everyone was drunk on bad wine and inspired by what we'd heard and wanted to do something radical and revolutionary about poetry and love and social stuff. Did you hear that no one in the Desolation is allowed to read poetry?"

"No. Who says that?"

Felix reached the top of the rope, touching the roof with his right hand in triumph.

Quixote told me, "Peter. One of our clan. He's brilliant. A true savant. Probably the only genius in the city."

"What makes him a genius?" I asked, watching Amadeo jump onto the ropes. Felix was sliding back down. Oskar looked fatigued ten feet from the top.

"His insights," Quixote said. "Everything is utterly transparent to him. He sees things no one else can even imagine. You ought to hear his readings. They're incredible. He says the Holy Book is a sham and we can't be led around by people who have no faith in themselves."

Pindar added, "We told him about you. He thinks you two should meet. He says he's a big fan of Virgil, just like you."

I frowned. "How interesting. He really said that?"

"Sure!" Quixote grinned. "Peter even gave us his number. Wants you to go see him. Says you two guys have lots to share. Here —" Pindar drew a soggy slip of paper from his bathing suit trunks and handed it to me. "He said you can reach him with this."

Naturally, the ink was somewhat smeared, but I could still read the number all right: WILber-2309.

I looked at Pindar, then Quixote. "I don't recognize that prefix. Where's it from?"

"He told us Bronzeville Square in North Catalan. He said it's a number from the old switchboard exchange. Cheaper than ours."

Felix waited for Oskar to descend the rope as Amadeo touched the ceiling above. I was bewildered by this exchange with the skinny poets. By the way, did they ever truly exercise?

I asked them, "And who is this again I'm supposed to meet?"

Both got up off the wall, then Quixote leaned close and told me, "The best of us all. Peter Draxler."

IX

Nina had apparently called to the telephone service at Thayer Hall a couple of times without leaving any message. I tried to call back and had no luck at all. Nobody answered the telephone at her house and there was no service for messages. I was terrifically anxious to see her. I hadn't heard her voice since we'd made love. Did she even miss me? When would we find each other again? My academic week had been plagued with class work and papers on the Quintillian Renaissance and Lunar Determinations in Jurisprudence. And I also had that ridiculous essay on the Achaeleon theocracy to revise. Father wanted me out for another dinner that evening, but I had to beg off. There was simply no time for a two-hour round-trip train ride to Highland Park, and I could not possibly stay overnight. But Nina floated constantly through my thoughts, hour to hour, disrupting my writing and scattering my attention in class. I became so foggy, Freddy even accused me of drinking his bourbon.

"You're being absurd," I told him, gathering up my notes for a study session on Social Philosophy.

"I can see you're not yourself, Julian."

"Well, who am I, then?"

"Me."

Freddy had a point. I'd let Nina's convolutions distract a purpose I'd spent most of my academic year resolving, only to fall off the track for a beautiful girl. Love is both a blessing and a worry. Running by instinct is hopeless. Resorting to cold logic ignores our natural desires. Nina, Nina, Nina.

And then this Peter Draxler. Who was he, anyhow, and how did he know me? I was no poet. And why Virgil? I wondered if perhaps we'd been in Konovaloff's class together, though I couldn't recall any particular male standouts in that group. And why that volume of *The Aeneid* from the mausoleum? Something to do with Draxler? How much did Nina know about any of this? It was damned confusing. Love, school, poetry, anarchy, war. I wobbled in and out of bed all week, becoming Freddy Barron, after all.

— · —

Rain came on Friday. A torrential storm muddied the pathways and flooded our lawns and streets. Debris clogged the storm drains and a cold, damp wind ripped tree branches off all about campus. A co-ed and her burly boyfriend were knocked down by a crashing limb off a thick oak tree outside Schearel Hall, the chemistry building. Both ended up overnight at the Infirmary. We also lost electricity for a couple of hours Friday morning, canceling classes in the lower rooms of Thayer Hall where natural light was mostly non-existent. That caused me to miss Contemporary Social Philosophy, a stroke of luck because I'd been expected that day to give a report on my progress with Achaeleon theocracy, a horrid worry. I danced a jig when the room went dark.

With no class until after lunch, I ate a bowl of cold oatmeal with a cornbread muffin in the commons. Afterward, I went back up to my room and reviewed my study choices. None of them held any appeal just then, so I watched the drizzling rainfall on the sidewalk and motor traffic out along Trimble Street and wondered about Nina, what I ought to do. Freddy had gone to the library with a flask of bourbon, so I had nobody to mull this over with. Not that I could tell him about Draxler or that volume of *The Aeneid*. Those days I had just enough sense to know whom to speak with about certain matters, and whom not to. Freddy was pretty confidential in most circumstances, but certainly his drinking mitigated my trust. I really wished his parents had been able to see the trouble he was getting himself into here. How were they not able to notice? Freddy was so rarely sober that more than once this semester I debated simply calling his father and letting him know how precipitous his son's angle had become, tilting ever so steadily to a gutter or the Selfridge sanitarium. Probably Dr. Barron already saw this and had solid plans drawn up for Freddy's inevitable collapse. It really wasn't my responsibility. I was his roommate and friend, not his pediatrician or therapist. And in any case, I had my own troubles, right? Whom did I expect to intervene on my behalf?

As the rain-wind picked up, I decided to try telephoning to Nina once more. I went downstairs to the bank of telephones outside the third-floor lounge. The small booths were all empty due to classes beginning soon and I chose one on the far end next to the staircase.

"Station 14, how may I help you?"

"Could you please connect me to MERton-3457?"

"Thank you."

I waited, not at all optimistic. Where had everyone at her house gone this week? Hardly any of that bohemian crew looked job-worthy, so I presumed none were off working regular hours. Maybe they had all passed out from griffo weed.

"Connecting."

"Hello?" A girl's voice, progress at last. But not yet Nina.

"Hello, is Nina there, please?"

"Just a second ... NINA! IT'S FOR YOU!"

I heard others rumbling around in that house now, so I guessed everyone was awake, after all. It sounded like a lot of commotion, people shouting at each other, rushing about.

"Hello?"

"Nina?"

"Julian! Finally! Why haven't you called me back? I've been trying to reach you all week."

"I tried! No one answers the telephone there. I'm sorry."

"Well, it's been crazy. You can't imagine everything that's been happening. And now our basement's underwater."

"From the storm?"

"And the water heater. It literally fell apart and emptied onto the floor. Besides our only washer and dryer getting flooded, we have lots of boxes stored down there, and they're all being ruined. This house is a dump. Can you come over tonight? Please? We really need to talk. I miss you, Julian."

I heard a crowd of co-eds coming up the stairs toward me, singing in unison, *"If I were your honey, I'd give you my money, and off to the islands we'd fly."*

"I miss you, too, Nina. What time do you want me there?"

"If you can be here by six, I'll fix you supper. That's when Delia eats."

"All right. I'll be there at six."

"Hurray!"

Click. Then Nina was gone again, and I could breathe. I felt redeemed somehow. I'd see her again. Soon. Sitting back, I wondered what she was so anxious over. No telling what sort of lunatic schemes that house of bohemian geniuses was concocting. They ought to be careful. Real trouble was just a telephone call away for that crowd. Similar nonsense from Theta Xi at Atherton House last semester brought a visit from half a dozen dour security agents of the State Council on Academic Affairs. Nine students left Regency College. Rumor had four of them sent to stack artillery shells in the Desolation they had so loudly and publicly despised. Freedom to express opposition to the Federal Directorate and Judicial Council was held by all to be valuable in our Republic, even essential to the emotional health and well-being of the greater nation. Limitations to free speech of the anarchic sort fell into that legal realm of *endangering internal security*, whatever that meant. Which was the point, I presumed: The Security Directorate alone decided what it meant. Every newspaper and radio network in the metropolis had its own opinion on who was truly in charge of our safety and general happiness. None had an answer that entirely satisfied anyone. So on we went. Maybe those clowns at Nina's house on Gosney Street had a better idea. *Well*, as my father would say, *let's hear it. Just be sure it suits more than you and your pet poodle.*

I grabbed the telephone again.

"*Station 14, how may I help you?*"

"Yes, could you please connect me to WILber-2309?"

A long pause.

"*I'm sorry, sir, there's no such number on the Metropolitan Exchange.*"

"Are you certain? I was told it's from the old switchboard exchange at Bronzeville Square."

"*No, sir, it's not a valid prefix for that number. Is there anything else I may help you with?*"

"You're certain? The fellows who gave it to me were quite specific."

"*I'm sorry. It's not a valid prefix, sir. May I help you with anything else?*"

"No, thank you."

The operator disconnected the call.

I put the telephone back up on its cradle. Well, that was strange. Now what? It couldn't be merely a case of those poets writing down the wrong number. If there was a simple mistake with the prefix, the operator would surely have tried to sort that out. But, in fact, she sounded convinced there was no such number at all, in Bronzeville Square or elsewhere across the city. How odd.

I went back up to my room and sat in bed, thumbing through that old leather-bound edition of *The Aeneid*. It was a beautiful volume. But why was it in my hands? As I said, I had no great love of Virgil. Did Draxler? If I'd been able to get hold of Pindar and Quixote, I'd have asked them to clarify that number I'd been given, and perhaps tell me a bit more about this savant of theirs. Trouble was, Ilanos Hall was a mile away from Thayer on the far end of Regency College and the weather was just too hideous. Nor would those silly names they were using be in the college student register. And for all that, I doubted they were rooming on or near campus, anyhow. In the locker room, I thought I'd overheard Oskar mention something regarding the poets commuting to Ilanos from Avenue D, out by Hamilton. So I was on my own with this conundrum, at least over the weekend. WILber-2309. If that wasn't a telephone number, then what did it mean?

Telephoning to the taxicab company, I found that city interurban rail was the best route to the Catalan that evening. Flooding along Zoffany Creek had closed taxi motor routes until morning and busses were suspended, too. I borrowed Freddy's umbrella for the rainy hike to the rail station at Scates and boarded just after five-thirty. The interurban was crowded at that time, people commuting home from work, and stops were frequent. I watched the steady rainfall and listened to conversations between my fellow riders on a myriad of topics from displeasure with work and wages to worries over flooding through the lower Catalan and disadvantaged youth summoned to national service in the Desolation. The latter seemed to carry less concern than a decline in stocks or the cost of local groceries, probably because so many had been called to perish in the war, it had become commonplace, like rain and floods, except, of course, that our war had no season of relent.

Crossing the iron bridge at Zoffany Creek, I watched city workmen sloshing along the soggy reeds in black raincoats and fishermen's hats. The creek waters roiled and spun waves onto the muddy embankments, treacherous and cold in the grey fading day. Tumble in and you drown. Were those men aware of the danger? Some of us are too smart, or timid, to venture off the sidewalks and bridge planks when the rains come. Why take the risk unless you're paid to do so? A boy at the front of the interurban slid his window down and put a hand out into the pouring rain. His mother watched, tolerant, I presumed, yet suspicious. Perhaps she didn't care to stifle his curiosity. Perhaps she wondered how daring he might be. When water began cascading into the car from the draft, a flurry of passengers occupying the seats behind them called for the window to be shut. The boy whined and his mother let everyone behind her know she found their complaints absurd, but the window was shut and we rode on, safe and dry.

The Catalan District by night and rain is a canyon of refuge for the lost, dark and dreary. No street is exempt from these souls shunned by our bright boulevards and polished Argolican marble. Here in East Catalan, rain-gutters spilled coal-stained dirt into the lee of flooding storm drains and garbage-cluttered basement stairwells. Pedestrians under ravaged umbrellas drifted slowly along in packs of six or seven, as if numbers alone guarantee safety and well-being. Roaring motor cars splashed by, drenching here and there the indolent on foot. I watched small rain-soaked children scurrying from curb to curb, almost challenging night-blinded traffic to run them over. Who lets a child out of doors in this weather to chase around like that? Rampant insolence abounds in the Catalan. *Rules are for fools who trust in our schools.* No one ever gets rich in the Catalan. No one lives long in the Catalan. Nobody remains in the Catalan who can leave by free will.

I disembarked at the old Stuyvesant train stop, three blocks east of Gosney Street. Wet litter floated by the platform and a mangy brown dog raced past, barking into the night. Popping open my umbrella, I hurried away through the rain ahead. First, Gustine Street, where half a block down, two women struggled to pull up a wooden cart stacked with gunny sacks. It had tipped over into the gutter and was flooding. Curses wailed like sirens. I rushed on toward Archimboldi, blocked off to motor traffic for a market that had been canceled. Some people still milled about under pitched canvas tents, smoking cigars and waving hot kerosene lanterns in each other's faces. Gosney Street came up as the rain abated slightly to a thick drizzle. I felt cold then. My shoes, socks and trouser cuffs were soaked from wading through gushing water at each street corner, and I hoped Nina had a warm blanket. Would she even let me into her bed again? I hoped so.

Arriving at her stoop, I closed the umbrella and rang the bell.

One of the boys answered the door. I didn't recognize him.

He stared at me. "Yeah?"

"Here to see Nina."

"Who are you?"

Wet and cold, I was feeling a little impatient. "Who are you?"

He shut the door in my face. Rainwater was sluicing off the eaves onto my head. I rang the bell again and the boy yelled back through the door, *"Go away! We don't want any!"*

I rang the bell six times as irritatingly as I could. When it opened again, there was Nina. Thank God!

She actually scowled. "Julian! What are you doing? Do you have any idea how annoying that is? Delia rings this stupid doorbell all day long and everyone in the house wants to kill her. Now you!"

Soaked to the bone, I shrugged. "Well, I came here for dinner at six, just like you asked, and that little monkey nuts wouldn't let me in. It's cold out here and I'm soaking wet."

"All right, what're you waiting for?" She stepped aside.

Indoors, I handed her my umbrella and she set it in a corner. I stood dripping on the entry carpet, which was so filthy I felt positive that rainwater was an improvement. Nina shut the door behind us and stared at me like I had a rat on my head. Then she shrugged. "Come on, Delia's waiting to eat."

"No kiss?"

"I'm sorry." She gave me a quick peck on my lips, then took my hand and led me off to the kitchen.

The living room crowd was jammed and noisy with shouts and conflict over a girl named Quintina whom I quickly gathered had seduced and slept with the wrong lover, a questionable fellow from the Provincials. The debate rung on how loyal he was to the Protectorate, and what to do with Quintina — should she be chastised or banned forever? Apparently, nobody could agree.

Nina had the door closed between the living room and the kitchen. Pretty little Delia sat by herself at the table with a children's book open. She looked up when I came in and smiled. "Hi, Julian."

"Hi, Delia. What are you reading there?"

"*Poofus the Cat.*"

"Is it good?"

"If you're a baby," she said. "Nina won't let me read anything else in here."

Her back to us at the stove, Nina explained, "She spills. I don't want her ruining our good books."

"I do not!"

"Yes, you do. *The Angel and the Dove*?"

"It wasn't my fault. Marco shoved the table."

"Still."

"Sorry!"

Nina stirred some fashion of tomato sauce in a frying pan on the stove top. Dinner would be beef and onion hash, sweet potatoes and buttered cornbread. I noticed the kitchen had been cleaned up a bit since my last visit. Counter tops were wiped off, most of the drinking glasses, coffee cups, dishes and blackened iron cooking pots and pans put away, empty wine and beer bottles tossed somewhere else. The solitary kitchen window looking out over the alleyway next door was still grimy. I didn't see much hope for that. All in all, signs of improvement. I wondered whose idea cleaning had been.

Nina poured us glasses of water, then sat down to eat. Delia recited a gentle non-denominational grace. I noticed Nina did not join her. One of the wayward girls came into the kitchen and took a blueberry muffin from a flowery clay bowl next to the refrigerator and left again. The yelling hadn't abated much at all. I cut up my sweet potato serving into quarters and smeared butter over all. Delia fiddled through the hash with her fork, looking desultory. Nina ate a piece of cornbread without talking but kept her eye on Delia. She didn't look at me much. I didn't mind. Something was occurring at this house tonight that had her more flustered than normal. Whatever it was, she didn't feel like discussing at the dinner table. Fair enough.

I ate a warm bite of hash. Not bad. Sauce was tasty.

Nina spoke up. "Do you like it?"

"Yes," I told her, "it's good. I like the sauce you put into it."

"I'm not much of a cook. Just warning you. My mother wasn't, either. I guess I inherited my culinary incompetence from her. I ought to be locked out of the kitchen."

Delia bit off a piece of cornbread. "I like your cooking. It's good."

"No, it isn't." Nina smiled. "But thank you for the compliment, honey. I'll try harder from now on."

We quit talking and ate our plates nearly clean. Now the shouting in the living room had quieted and someone began strumming a guitar. One of the girls sang along, a bit off-key, *"If only we don't know why God ain't in our fold, there's no one here to tell us we been sold away, away."*

Outdoors, night rain fell harder, rattling on the tin roof of a storage shed across the fence. Nina finished eating and took her plate and water glass to the sink. She rinsed them off and put them away into the cupboards and left me alone with Delia in the kitchen. I heard her bedroom door close down the hall.

Delia looked up from her last portion of sweet potatoes. "Do you want to play with Goliath?"

"No."

"Why not?"

I raked my fork through the remaining onion hash. "I just don't. He's smelly."

She scowled. "You're mean."

"No, I'm not. I just don't like dogs."

"You said you did."

"I lied. I hate dogs. If my sister brought one home, I'd eat it."

"That wouldn't taste good at all."

"How would you know?" I tapped my fork on the dinner plate, then pointed it at her. "Have you ever eaten one?"

"No, have you?"

"Lots."

"You're disgusting!"

"Thank you."

"I hate you."

I smiled. "Good."

Delia drank her water without looking at me. I got up and brought my glass and dinner plate to the sink, washed and rinsed them off. I dried both and put them up into the same cupboards Nina had used. The kitchen actually looked civilized for once.

"Are you sleeping here tonight?" Delia asked, bringing her own plate to the sink. She set it on the countertop.

I looked at her, unsure how to reply. Did it matter to her? "I don't know yet. Maybe, maybe not. It's pretty wet out."

"You can stay if you want to," she said, grabbing her water glass, still half full. "Nina won't mind."

"Thank you, dear. I'll see."

Then Delia took the children's book she'd been reading and walked out of the kitchen. I washed off her dinner plate, put it away, and went to find Nina.

I knocked at her bedroom door and she called me in. I found her sprawled out on the embroidered quilt, head on her pillow. The desk lamp was lit and her window curtain half open to the stormy night where she could watch rain falling against the brick buildings across the street.

Nina patted the mattress beside her. "Come sit with me, Julian. I need you here."

I sat there and took her hand and gave it a small kiss. "I've missed you."

"Me, too. It's been hell here all week. Not only is our basement under a foot of water, but no one in the house seems to give a damn about the washer and dryer or getting our stuff out. And half those idiots in there I've never even met. Gibb and Jeduthan invited them here without asking and nobody wants them to stay, except Marco, and that's only because those stupid girls followed them over."

Nina's room had gone to hell since my last visit: disheveled, sloppy, unwashed clothing, loose hair bands, laceless shoes, week-old bohemian newspapers, political pamphlets, torn shreds of scribbled notepaper littering the floor, more clothes spilling out of her closet.

I asked her, "Why are those people here?"

"I can't tell you."

"Why not?"

"Don't ask me, Julian. And don't say a word about Serpas or the park. I can't help you at all."

"Can you tell me anything about that fellow, Peter — "

"NO!" She sat up and grabbed my arm hard enough to hurt. "Don't!"

"Nina! Stop it! Let go!"

She eased her grip, her voice lower, "Julian, you don't understand any of this. I'm helping you by not helping. That probably doesn't make any sense after dragging you all over the city this week, but I've got Delia to protect, and now you, too, and it's becoming very difficult to see straight. I wish you could just trust me."

She slipped her hand free and kissed my arm. Her damp dark eyes fluttered in the amber lamplight. I thought she looked terribly frightened. I leaned over to kiss Nina, and she drew me down next to her, laying our heads side by side on her pillow. There she kissed me as she had that last night I was in her bed. She kissed me and kissed me, and I felt tears on her soft cheeks.

Then we undressed and put out the lamp and made love again to the rainfall on Gosney Street.

— · —

In the middle of the night, I woke and heard her humming softly facing the bedroom wall on her side of the pillow. I listened until she stopped, and I felt sure she'd fallen back to sleep, then I slipped out of bed and went to the kitchen for a glass of water. The house was silent and still. I filled the glass from the sink faucet and had a long drink and left it on the countertop. Heading back, I used the toilet at the end of the hall next to Nina's bedroom, flushed quietly, and felt my way through the dark to her room and into bed again.

"Julian?"

"I thought you were asleep," I whispered. "Did I disturb you?"

"No, I've been awake for an hour. I watched you get up."

"I was thirsty."

"I know. I heard you in the kitchen. Is anyone else up?"

"Not that I could tell. Seems quiet. Maybe they all passed out."

"One of the girls brought a jar of Phárés. She stole it out of a gypsy cellar behind the Odio market. These idiots eat it like candy. After a couple bites, they can't spell their own names."

I smiled. "Bohemian life."

"Not just that, Julian. There's no real point of view here, anymore. We had a working system all this year. No one allowed into the house unless we agreed that someone brought a new idea, or an alternative purpose to this foul-smelling mess that's making our stomachs burn. We agreed that any sort of prejudice was acceptable if it shamed, troubled or embarrassed the chamberlains on the Judas Council."

"Judicial Council?"

"Judas Council. They're traitors to the Republic, Julian. You should know that. Think about what you study at school, what you learn, not just off the blackboard, but in the books you read. Knowledge isn't purging one cheese for another. You try them all so you can share your experience with anyone who hasn't and urge them to sample each and every one."

"I hate Gordoñia cheese. Please don't put any in my soup. Gives me hives."

"Noted." She grazed my cheek with one finger. "But listen, Julian: People don't want to learn. They want to be told what's good and true. The Council exists to tell them. I'm predicting that one day all our colleges will be closed and boarded up. People with knowledge are dangerous to this Republic. How else do we account for who we are now? The Desolation has become the most monstrous obscenity this world has ever known, and we do nothing but praise ourselves."

Now she drew us together, almost nose to nose in the dark. Rain pattered against her window. "Julian?"

"Nina?"

She whispered, "We don't know where he is. We really don't. Those men come here all times of day threatening us, and we can't tell them what we don't know."

"No one knows?"

"Someone, I'm sure. But not us. Not that I'm aware of."

I hesitated to tell her. Did Pindar and Quixote consider it a secret, a confidence I was not supposed to violate? And if I were to tell her about the number? Then what? Well, she could continue to lie to those fellows who show up on her doorstep asking for Draxler, but I was confident they came from the Internal Security, that story Father told me about Leandro Porteus and his spectral drawings. And if that were true, and I told her about WILBER-2309, and she denied knowing anything about Draxler's location, they could escort her to a basement office in the Mendel Building and strap her to one of those iron tables and inject VeraForm into her groin and listen to Nina recite what I'd given her from the skinny poets. Then she would have lied to agents of Internal Security, and all the goodness in her young life, and little Delia's, would be consigned to the past.

So that night I simply hushed up and let us both sleep in peace.

XI

Nina woke early and rode the train to her flower stand at Thibodeaux Station and I went back to Thayer Hall. This was Saturday morning, so I had nothing more important to do than go out to breakfast with Freddy. The weather had cleared up and he was in better spirits than he had been all week as we went down along Kemper Street to a bistro popular with college students. Standing in a queue for a quarter hour to get a table, Freddy told me all about his Friday night adventure at a musical theatre on Lavillette Square with Walker Bailey and Burt Davy.

"Dierdre Dürndorf, my future wife, was playing the lead in *Love's Lonely Libretto* and I just knew she hoped to see me there. I dragged those two grouch bags along by promising them a pitcher of beer at Ludie's afterward. They were skeptical, but you know me, Julian, I can talk a dog out of his bone if you give me half a chance."

"I bear personal witness to that truth, Freddy, every day of the year."

"I know you do, Julian, and I'm grateful."

"You should be."

"At any rate, we went to the show and all was fine until Bailey decided to poke Burt into tossing a tomato at one of the actors on stage in the second act, a fellow Bailey said he knew from Lower School in Hampton."

"He didn't do it, I hope."

"When Walker's thumb is that far up Burt Davy's ass, he'll do anything he's told. Also, he'd already drank a fifth of scotch on his way downtown."

"And?"

"We actually shared it. A couple bottles. Bailey paid for the second."

"And?"

"Burt threw a tomato at the fellow, but missed and hit Deirdre's leading man, that Iberian actor, Vela, flat on the nose."

"Good God, Freddy."

"We got arrested, Julian! They dragged us off to jail and left me in there all night. Is that legal? I had to telephone my illustrious father to bail us out. And he refused!"

"So what did you do?"

"Sat in that goddamned cell by myself, is what I did. Walker's mother posted bail for him and Burt because their parents are in a bridge club together. Since my mother hates card games, I was stuck in jail until six o'clock this morning. Not at all fair."

We were finally given a table on the bistro's outdoor patio and we ordered breakfast. I chose a simple sausage and omelette au fromage with a biscuit and Freddy asked for his preferred flank steak and waffles. We both took coffee. That's when Freddy started up. I doubt our young waitress knew him, but he pretended she did and was irritatingly flirtatious. *"How long have you worked here? How do you spend your free time? Do you have a boyfriend?"* She mostly ignored Freddy's romantic innuendos, while keeping a pleasant smile pasted on her pretty little face.

Once she'd gone, his attention fell on me once more. "So, Julian, I've discovered you apparently do get about, after all."

"How's that, Freddy?"

"One of my jail mates last night seemed to be quite familiar with you. Says your honey-bun can't stop mooning over you."

"Who is this person?"

"Some wormy little fellow who seems to be at that house a lot. Knows your girl. Not like you do, but he hears her talking. She has a little sister?"

"Delia. An eight-year old spitfire. She'll pass us both someday." I stirred cream into my coffee and had a sip. "Did he mention anyone else? Any names?"

Freddy shrugged. "I passed out. When I woke up, he'd been cut loose."

"What was he in for?"

"He said shoplifting. Didn't tell me what he took."

Breakfast arrived along with a crowd of freshman students from Baker Hall, most of whom had just discovered alcohol. None looked too enthusiastic about a Saturday morning. Freddy and I ate and paid and left without our waitress's telephone number. I told Freddy it was smarter like that. Be hard to get.

I had a schedule of schoolwork set up for my afternoon and chose to ignore it. Instead, I brought Virgil out from under my mattress and leafed through the old volume. If Nina's people expected me to translate the entire *Aeneid*, they were insane. My second term Latin was nowhere near that good, even with a dictionary. I'd need about ten years and a room in a monastery. Freddy had gone down to the Trimble corner market for some bread and bourbon, and I finally decided to explore Draxler's number with him when he came back. I wouldn't tell him where I'd gotten it, even Draxler's name. I just thought Freddy might offer some helpful insight. He was a nut for puzzles of all sorts and this one was very intriguing.

Freddy came through the door with a grocery bag of treats. Not just bourbon today, but wheat crackers and oatmeal cookies and chocolate bars: the study diet. He bought a nudie magazine, too. Presumably for later on. Freddy's closet was our pantry and I had strict rules for storing food: nothing that spoils and no food left out. We had troubles with ants and roaches sophomore year and needed to fumigate. I slept two nights on a couch in the student union. Freddy just went home to Alexanderton.

He took up a box of crackers. "Want one?"

"No, thanks. Save them, please?"

Freddy shrugged. "Maybe. Guess who I saw at the market?"

"Who?"

"Lorraine. She asked about you. Wonders why you haven't called. I told her you had shingles and were embarrassed to leave the room."

"I hope that's not true." Lorraine Sibley was a girl I'd met in first term Rhetoric and brought to a party on Somers Avenue where she drank so much, I had to sit with her until sun-up when the dormitory sisters came for her. She told me her plans after graduation were to join a convent and dedicate her life to God. I wished her all the luck in the world and tossed her number. That was the end of my dating co-eds.

"She invited us to a sorosis dance at Esther House. No alcohol served but plenty of girls from the Frickey congregation." He could barely suppress a laugh. "She promises lots of fun."

"Freddy."

"Yes, sir."

"Have a look here." I drew that paper note from my back pocket with Draxler's number and handed it to Freddy. "Some fellow from Lamberton's office slipped this into my Alexandrian Art book. I guess I'm supposed to telephone, but the number was denied by our switchboard. They said it doesn't exist."

Freddy was such a whiz at this I expected him to solve the mystery in half a minute. You can't do crossword puzzles with him or play *Qantara* because he knows all the words and numbers as if he invented them. He's a riddle master, too. Figures them out too quickly to have a game of it. Dr. Barron thought Freddy was a prodigy when they had him in elementary school at Fawcett Academy. All his teachers raved. Then he began failing classes from absent study habits and soon enough his intuitive genius was forgotten, shoved aside by the rigors of daily academics.

"Well, it's not a telephone number."

"Apparently."

"But it could be. See the prefix? WILber?"

"Of course. The exchange operator says that's not a legitimate prefix."

"Yes," Freddy smiled, that wry grin he'd get when closing in on a winning game, "but it could be. That prefix exists, just not here. Way down south in Purkapile Hollow of Cisterna Province. But it's still spelled wrong. There, it's WILbur, after Wilbur Weimar who founded the township of Purkapile."

I frowned, flabbergasted at Freddy's collected assortment of odd facts. "How do you know this?"

"Crossword puzzle dictionaries. *Qantara* squib books. They're very informative. We should use them in class."

"So it's misspelled?"

"Not at all." Freddy was almost gloating now. "It's just not a telephone prefix. See those numbers, 2309?"

"Yes."

"Purkapile Hollow's population is under a thousand and always has been. Back when telephones were first required, the town voted to keep the numerals under a thousand, so they'd be easy to remember. Nobody has a telephone number above WILbur-0999. Essentially three digits. Only one such switchboard in the Republic. Look it up. Pretty comical, huh?"

"It's ridiculous."

"Not really, when you think about it," Freddy argued. "Why do more than you need to? My motto in life."

"So it's not a misspelling, and not a telephone number at all in the metropolitan exchange? What is it, Freddy? Be the genius now I know you to be."

"It's a code."

"A code? What kind of code?"

"First of all, the alphabet prefix is two words, not one. See? You're reading WILber as one word. It's two. First is WI, and that's not a word. Those are just initials. The second word is Lber — liber. Do you recognize that? I know you do. At least you should after two terrifying terms with Leonid Konovaloff, another academic Torquemada. Did I tell you he failed me? That was second term, just before we shared this room."

Freddy's dizzying explication of Draxler's note had me reeling. I grabbed *The Aeneid* from under my pillow and flipped it open somewhere in the middle. There was the Latin word, *Liber*, for book.

"Oh, you have it here!" Freddy squealed, beside himself with glee. "How convenient. But why, Julian? Why do you have that obviously rare and important edition of Virgil's horrendous masterpiece? And why did you borrow that Latin dictionary from the library just this week? Please don't tell me it has nothing to do with this pseudo-telephone number because I'll know you're lying and you're a terrible liar. All the girls at Regency College know it. Most particularly Lorraine Sibley. You should never have sent her that note about a sudden trip abroad with your parents. She telephoned to your father's office for confirmation and was very displeased with you."

"She peed her dress that night."

Freddy said, "*Veni, Vidi, Vici.*" Then he laughed.

"What's so funny?" I felt like a fool now for excluding Freddy from this puzzle last week. Alcoholic or not, my eccentric roommate was far more brilliant than I could ever hope to be. An awful college student, yes, but brilliant, still. No mystery why Dr. Barron was so frustrated by him.

"Actually," Freddy giggling now like he had hiccups, "I meant to say, *Weni, Widi, Wici,* in good old Caesarean Latin. Do you see it?"

"No."

"Julian, my God! That 'WI' are certainly initials here for Virgil in the classical Latin pronunciation, and the entire prefix is a code for Virgil, Liber 2-309! Book 2, line 309 of that volume you're holding."

"Oh."

"Really!"

"All right, Freddy, sure. Let's have a look."

I opened the book again and searched for Liber II. Finding it, I skimmed along until line 309. The full sentence, folding over to 310, read: *iam Deiphobi dedit ampla ruinam Vulcano superante domus.* I showed the page to Freddy and directed him to the line.

"Well?" he asked, excited now. "What does it say?"

I stared at the page for half a minute. Truth is, I really hadn't done so well in Konovaloff's class. In fact, I barely passed. He gave me just enough credit for having memorized the Seven Hills of Rome to send me on. I told Freddy, "Give me the Latin dictionary."

He fetched it off my desk. "Do your magic, Julian. This is the most fun I've had all week."

"Hold on," I said. "I need a note paper and pencil."

Finding both in my desk drawer, I went back to Virgil and the Latin dictionary. Then I looked up the words one after the other and wrote down the translation. Next, I studied what I'd written to see if I made any sense. I told Freddy, "I'm not a whiz at this. I'm just guessing, really. See what you think."

I showed him my translation that read: *Already Deiphobos' immense house has become a ruin, with Vulcan consuming it.*

I said, "You could read 'immense house or hall' as 'great or grand' and 'Vulcano' can mean 'fire' or 'flames' possibly. But that's the general idea, I think."

Freddy nodded. "I see that, but what does it mean?"

I frowned. "What do you mean, 'what does it mean?' That's the translation of the line."

"Yes, Julian, but why are we reading that line? Why was that the code? Where did you get this? Some fellow slipped this into your textbook? Who? And why?"

"Freddy."

"Julian, I'm very frustrated that you've solicited my help and advice and yet you're still holding out on me. I can't possibly make any sense of this translation or that code unless you tell me what it means, where it came from, why you have it."

I went over to my desk and sat down. Outdoors, the day was clear, and a pleasant breeze circulated across the blue morning sky and the tall leafy elms beside Thayer Hall. I was trying to relax. Freddy stared at me. If I told him about the skinny poets, then I was obligated by logic to tell him about Peter Draxler, and if I did that, then he'd need to know about those fellows knocking on Nina's door and, furthermore, what my father had told me regarding Draxler and Leandro Porteus. Like a row of dominoes. No path forward here but one. If Freddy weren't so brilliant, I'd just close this up and go take a walk. Thayer Hall has a lovely pond behind the commons where acres of lawn slope toward Wasson Woods. Geese and swans drift there in the sunlight and students amble along a gravel path that winds around the restful water. I've gone there every so often to be on my own and think about why I was at Regency College. But today, I needed Freddy's advice more than peace of mind. So I recounted the whole story from Nina to that officious fellow at her front door; my father; the mausoleum; and the poets and the Draxler telephone code that Freddy just helped me unravel.

When I was done, he told me, "Julian, this is more frightening than that dead soldier in the tide."

"Well, I'm not entirely sure I know what *this* is."

"Damned dangerous, if you want my opinion. If those shady creeps dropping over to your girlfriend's house are Internal State Security agents, then whatever your Peter Draxler borrowed from Porteus belongs somehow to the Protectorate, and you know what that means."

"Father said they were architectural drawings."

"Of what?"

"Like I said," I was feeling queasy now. Nerves or a bad bite of sausage? "according to my father's friends at the Garibaldi Building, word inside Internal Security is that only Porteus himself and the Protectorate seem to know precisely what those drawings were, and *they* believe Draxler has wandered off with them. Enough said. Period."

"But then Julian, why would this Draxler fellow want to see *you*? Have you ever met him?"

"Freddy, for heaven sakes, I've been asking myself that same question since Pindar gave me the paper." I opened one of the desk side-drawers and slid out an old Lit binder. "Have I ever met anyone named Peter Draxler? Not that I recall. It's possible, maybe. Who knows? Perhaps in a class, or somewhere else on campus? Or in town? I have no idea. How would I even know what he looks like from this slip of paper?"

Freddy studied the paper scrap for a few more moments. Then he said, "He wants *you* to find *him*. That's what this is for. Simple. For some secret reason, maybe his own safety, you were given both Virgil and the code separately. And then you were supposed to deduce the correlation between them. Not to telephone, but to find him."

"How can I do that if this isn't a telephone number?"

Freddy shrugged. "Virgil."

"Huh?"

Freddy gave me the paper and offered that wily smile. "Julian, he's hiding in Virgil. A great house that burned to ruin. That's his clue. Pretty simple, when you think about it."

"What great house? Where? Virgil was writing about Troy. Draxler's not hiding in Troy, so where's this great house that burned to ruin?"

"Did your little poets mention anything else about this number from nowhere?"

"Well, I remember they said Draxler told them it was a prefix from the old exchange for Bronzeville Square in the North Catalan. Obviously, that wasn't true."

"But I bet it was!" Freddy jumped up, giddy with glee. "I bet that was true! Not as a telephone prefix, Julian, but a factual location. Bronzeville Square. Some sort of mansion burned up. Yes, indeed! All we have to do is find it. Come on, let's go see the library."

XII
∽

More than a century ago, most of what is now the Catalan District had been fields and orchards, flat plots of land with square houses and narrow dirt roads leading north and west into the rural farmlands. Records and diaries portray a simple world of dawn to dusk labor, rain and sunshine. People wrote of hayfields and church life and family. Our collective memory of those days without industry and war is scanty and vague, as if no such time were even possible. Rumor serves how those days, our Republic was inefficient but benign, with goodness in all things being the aim of us. Each province had its own regis chamberlains and festivals and governance of rules whose better insights managed school attendance and the price of eggs, a distribution of wedding licenses, or dissolutions, and the cost of fist fights in local taverns. So, too, within the districts of the mostly pastoral metropolis were encouraged the destinies of men and women from all cultural inheritances dedicated to work and family, pleasant pastimes and love. Farms and fisheries fed the city, and inventions from the metropolis made tolerable and purposeful the lives of those whose labor sustained us.

We were not told these stories. They are not taught in our schools.

As if our history began with those immense grey factories in the West Metropolis, the tireless machines of industry that graded away acres and acres of common fields and fruit orchards, bricked over and forgotten by the iron behemoth of a modern world that permitted no mean obstacles to progress and profit. And the virtuous people who had worked those fields, who had walked those rural roads, were dispassionately distributed into filthy warrens of cold stone tenement buildings and basement provinces ruled by rats and roaches, or dumped into the mud and tunnels dug from the tributaries of the holy river, Livorna, that drowned in the torrents of winter, spilling cruel sewage and rank infestations into the crowded neighborhoods of this lesser metropolis. Crime follows poverty and disease, and the dark Catalan, and certain sectors within the adjacent districts of Calcitonia, Beuiliss and Simoni, evolved a chaotic miasma of vice, thievery and violence, rude thuggery and despicable perversions on these once holy streets: hapless animals butchered and crammed by the dozens into dank potato cellars, starved children hidden in tenement closets and broken ice boxes, luckless men and women murdered nightly with disdain and disregard and washed up by the hundreds along the reedy shores of the eternal river.

A great Republic of boundless dreams should not tolerate such demoralizing stains. A populace that fails so miserably to meet accepted standards of goodness and virtue cannot be welcome. One hundred years ago, a commission appointed by the Judicial Council under the direct authority of the Status Imperium sought a swift diagnosis and prescription for treatment.

Adolphus Varane was a chemist by trade and a strenuous advocate of social engineering. His published thoughts on Biological Dominion and Intellectual Capacity drew notice in the chambers of government and were disseminated by popular acclaim throughout our varied districts and provinces. Varane argued that a nation of undisciplined and unfit peoples could not thrive and advance as greatness requests. Those purposes of the best among us were distracted and subverted by the criminal and infirm, the deformed and feebleminded, who drained the moral and economic resources of the good, the healthy and the high-minded. He argued that nature observed this discrepancy and provided for its solution in a broad evolutionary model that saw the ineffectual and weak disposed of through the inevitable eradication of that root and vine. Varane felt we need not be so patient. He borrowed Francis J. Galton's hybrid word for the fortunate born, eugenics, and took direction from Galton's papers, adopting his eugenical theories as his own creed to seek out the best and the worst among us and see each forward as society requires. Conscious of this conundrum, and desiring to discover its solution, Varane maintained we were morally obligated to take those steps toward a conclusion that was both logical and necessary. Not everyone was convinced. A fierce opposition to his crusade arose from enlightened philosophers and clergy, disciplined scientists and the politically astute who recognized grave dangers in Adolphus Varane's proposed concepts of social engineering.

Perhaps the tilt of history could have veered from the eugenical precipice had a scribbled note failed to cross Varane's desk one sultry summer afternoon at Gardiner's Hill. A small inconsequential pharmacist named Edwin Paul from Green Harbor had isolated in his basement laboratory a peculiar bug in the blood of Paul's mentally defective brother, Joseph, and also in Edwin Paul's wayward daughter, Alice, who was afflicted with venereal erymastis. Not a zyme. Something else. Edwin tested her brother, Aloysius, and then his own older sister, Marguerite, both of whom were otherwise healthy, for familial or congenital knotting and found nothing. For six months, he secretly pilfered blood samples from customers he suspected were feebleminded or pathological or prone to chronic illness, and when he uncovered evidence of his peculiar bug, Edwin Paul added it to the extensive chart he'd drawn up. From ten dozen blood samples of what he determined were the well and the unwell, his testing revealed a near one-to-one result for a disease he named "spyreosis," an incurable disabler of the mind and body. Its origin in the blood and its ability to be shared between people was unknown to Edwin Paul, yet he suspected that spyreosis in some form was the key to understanding societal deficiencies. Those whose blood reveals it, Paul insisted, are incurable degenerates and those who don't are obligated to avoid and shun them for the goodness and common welfare of us all. After all, defective progeny does no race any favors.

By now, Adolphus Varane had a legion of fierce opponents to his eugenical theories, but also twenty times that many acolytes who saw the world degenerating around them with no apparent solution. How best and fair to cleave the good from the bad felt arbitrary and dangerously political. Then Varane traveled to Green Harbor to meet the pharmacist whose private laboratory, he believed, might very well have saved us all. He brought with him an ally in the struggle, Dr. Edgar Goode, a prominent physician on the governing board of the Medical Directorate. Goode had adopted Varane's faith in eugenical necessities for the preservation of our essential culture. Like Varane, he saw the urgency of linking the unfit in society with a scientifically acknowledged scourge. Those hopes were redeemed with Edwin Paul's mystery bug, spyreosis. Goode and Varane studied the strange bug in Paul's microscope and were satisfied spyreosis was a threat, even if neither had any true idea what to make of it. The case studies were reviewed and considered adequate for the occasion and both congratulated the pharmacist on his discovery and rode the train back to Prospect Square in the metropolis with a firm eye on the ultimate panacea to all our society's ills.

Yet one more voice was still to be added for the universal crusade to complete its history, a third crown in the holy triumvirate of national saviors. From the gilded dais of the Archimbault Cathedral in the central metropolis, a fiery Bishop Cyril Angus Melveny implored his parishioners to reject the degenerate society that had enslaved them in disease and degradation, soiled all they touched, polluted the very air they breathed. *"Must we bear this greatest of all unholy burdens? Must we condemn ourselves to doom and ruin? Our Savior tells us, a good tree cannot bear bad fruit, and a bad tree cannot bear good fruit. Every tree that does not bear good fruit is cut down and thrown into the fire."* From his holy pulpit, firmly aware now of the scourge, spyreosis, almost by osmosis through circulating communications from Adolphus Varane and Dr. Goode, the esteemed Bishop Mulvaney was first in the Republic to call for the Great Separation, vast colonies of the unfit and unwell to be established far out in the hinterlands. *"Weed our precious garden of the Lord that His beauty may grow unhindered."* Other ideas were more odious: Elimination of the unfit. Painless extinction in lethal chambers. Purity chamberlains in the Bureau of Population Accounting called for mass sterilization of any and all detected with spyreosis in the blood. Disputes arose regarding the efficacy of testing. No one seemed quite sure how to recognize the pernicious bug in so varied a populace. With great certainty himself, Dr. Edgar Goode assumed control of the epidemic and instituted an elaborate blood testing system under his personal supervision. Any citizens suspected of infection were summoned to district centers. Naturally, the entire Catalan fell under that terrible scrutiny. Tens of thousands of all ages and cultural distinctions were urged through the centers, thousands more were sought. Yet, still nothing had been definitively decided regarding disposition of the infected. What to do with them? Were they not people, citizens of the Republic like ourselves? Perhaps, it was suggested by the health commissioners, they might all die in their own moment. If that were soon, some thought it would be best for all. Could that be hastened somehow?

A bitter debate arose in the hallowed chambers of the Judicial Council. A race of the chronically ill and feebleminded, crippled or sociopathic, interbreeding with the better of us should not be permitted under any moral circumstance. Could our vibrant markets stand these disastrous intrusions? Certainly, mass sterilization of the infected, regardless of age, needed to be implemented at once. After that, what? Three arguments were advanced, three odious points of view: Castration, segregation, elimination. Sterilization programs satisfied those proponents of the first. A virulent debate over the essential necessity of lethal chambers provoked rumors of a vicious exchange at the chief Council table, one elector clubbing another with a stout walking cane. Moral distinctions were made plain and explicit. Prionic acid gas administered in a lethal chamber melted the human body from within. Death was so hideous, one witness to such an execution died from shock an hour after the experience. At the close of formal disputations was chosen the Great Separation, over lurid slaughterhouses, whose more modest morality was offered to the Republic in the dress of economic relief: Why must we tax the industrious of our great society to support the sick and indolent? Let us be free of this burden that all remaining might flourish. Days later, Bishop Cyril Angus Melveny chastised the hesitant: *"The laws of nature need not apply here. This is not our world. It is solely His. Therefore, we must not leave alms in houses of pity. Our Lord God has passed His own judgment upon them with mercy and wisdom. Let those souls of His children belong to Him now, and to us no longer."*

The enforced migration began in the east neighborhoods of Catalan District where fifty thousand were directed for immediate deportation. Suitcases and trunks collected on every sidewalk, street corner and tenement stoop, piled tall and thick. Wagons and pushcarts lined up along the curbs. Guardians and security agents shepherded crowds of shrieking children and the solemn elderly with loved ones whose expressions betrayed the fear and despondency of all the unfortunates whose departure into the unknown was to suit the best of us so thoroughly. Some resisted and were led away. Others ran off. Commonwealth Station bore the strain of that first day. Better than ten thousand an hour crossed a sweltering North Platform into an immense din of confusion and tears and bitterness. Many of the inattentive were shoved off onto the steaming tracks. Lost children were trampled underfoot and crushed with the slow and the elderly and the infirm, who gently surrendered to this unimaginable fate. The trains came and each car was filled above capacity like freight baggage for transport out of our world. The unwell and the unfit, the feebleminded and degenerate came and came and came until the streets and neighborhoods and crass tenement halls of the Catalan District were left still and ghostly. Then those troubled districts of Beuiliss and Calcitonia and Simoni were emptied, too, as the rest of us looked on with worry and wonder. By the end of it all, a century ago, almost a million citizens of our great metropolis rode trains far into the hinterlands of the east where they disappeared together for a very long time.

XIII
∞

"Look here, Julian," Freddy said, dragging his finger across the faded map in an old city atlas. "This is precisely where it was, just as I told you half an hour ago. You need to start believing me if we're to make any progress here today."

"I do believe you, Freddy," I told him, my voice soft in the library. "I only wondered if that were the best volume to be exploring."

"Well, it certainly appears to be."

Freddy and I had committed ourselves to this adventure for three hours now, first in the Thayer library, then through the main Regency College library in Harrington Hall, and on inevitably to the Mansurette at Hollerith Plaza. We were chasing a detailed city map of Bronzeville Square in the decade after the Great Separation. You see, as we understood the story of that era, not all had gone voluntarily to the distant hinterlands. Some of those who fled the Guardians to stay behind hid in tenement attics and deep connecting basements throughout the metropolitan underground, known colloquially among the renegades as "undercity," whose tunnels and chambers and catacombs provided shelter and hiding places from Internal Security. For the first few years, those fugitives from eugenical persecution were troubled by fear and floods and freezing temperatures, rats by the millions, terrible epidemics and ceiling collapses, now and then, though the limestone out of which the underground had been carved over the centuries had proven to be extraordinarily stable. Anger and bitterness seethed in the hearts of everyone hunted by the Security Directorate. From that fury arose a feverish hatred toward those most responsible for all the pernicious decisions and mandates of eugenical politics that chased them underground — chief among these men was Adolphus Varane, the subject of great and abiding ire from beneath the common city streets. Of course, Dr. Edgar Goode had organized and distributed the medical foundation for testing and detecting spyreosis in the blood of thousands, but who could blame him for pursuing a plague that may well be killing them all? In fact, somehow, he was perceived as merely another mindless bureaucrat, pursuing the coldhearted agenda given him by those above his station. Varane was the one they despised. Who was he, anyhow? A third-rate chemist with no university degree or legal authority from the Status Imperium. A pompous ideologue whose published diatribes on social engineering in popular journals advanced no scientific discoveries or new theories on the natural progress of man. A fool and a quack. A rich one, too. His notoriety in the burgeoning fields of eugenical research and education led him into the boardrooms and academic seats and council chambers of the most highly esteemed in our grand Republic. By those whose thoughts on eugenical priorities most closely aligned with his, Adolphus Varane was considered one of the greatest men in the metropolis. To those who suffered most from his pseudoscientific social engineering, he was held as a biological menace. To them, Varane himself was the abnormal, a wicked, wicked man, a monster of the first order.

On Coyne Street in North Catalan was a bronze foundry where statuary of the eminent and revered were cast for Immanuel Fields and Kirkham Gardens surrounding the Dome of Eternity. A quarter mile beyond the foundry on Hesperia Avenue in a manicured block of fragrant flower walks and broad leafy acacia trees was the four-story brick and stone mansion of Adolphus Varane. This was Bronzeville Square. His was not the only stately residence there, but the house Varane called *Seranus* (*He who has sown the seeds of the future*) was the grandest of all. He lived there with Idalia Galata, a lovely, slender, selfless woman from Solomon Province who rarely offered opinions on eugenics and then only in vague debasements regarding cultural hybridism that no one understood. Adolphus Varane entertained the most consequential of metropolitan society and gained a reputation for both ostentation and obsequious generosity. After the Great Separation, his patronage of the arts and scientific review was unsurpassed. As reward, his own statue was cast and polished and prepared for mounting on a marble pedestal in Dunham Gardens near the Mollison Institute. A ceremonial date was chosen, and invitations sent out, and late that very night under a blood moon, he and Idalia were burned to death at *Seranus*. Witnesses told how the flames were seen from across the eternal river two miles away. Trees in Bronzeville Square incinerated from the heat. Lamp poles melted. Two other mansions caught fire from Varane's rooftop conflagration and were reduced to ash and cinder. The undercity rejoiced. Rumors of a petroleum bomb in a coal chute flew about, but no one took credit. Adolphus Varane was dead and his well-born branch of eugenical ascension had been cut off.

"I think I've seen this ruin," I told Freddy, "years ago. I was driven past there by my father on our way somewhere else. I don't recall much more than that. I was pretty little."

"Let's see." Freddy opened another volume he'd requested at the front desk, a book of city ferroplates. He checked the table of contents and began flipping pages until he found what he wanted. Freddy slid the book across the table. "Here, Julian, have a look."

The sooty remains of Varane's great mansion stood tall and somber, absent of roof and doors and windows, a monumental ruin. "Good grief. Yes, that's it, what we drove by. I do remember."

The ferroplate replication was about seventy years old. I wondered what the house looked like now.

Freddy told me, "It's still on that lot, Julian, and your Peter Draxler is sending us there, don't you agree? We need to go see it."

I stared at the cloudy image, a depressing scene lacking only Varane himself to complete the tableau. "Yes, of course. What would all this mean, otherwise?"

Freddy was hurriedly skimming another thin volume he'd borrowed. "I'm trying to find out why Varane's mansion wasn't demolished. Seems the others that burned were torn down."

"They kept it as a landmark, I'll bet. Something to commemorate Varane."

After another minute or so, Freddy looked up with a smile. "You're mostly right. But not solely for Varane's memory. Listen here: 'On this site we dedicate our struggle as a rite of progress.' Do you see that, Julian? The ruin was left as a memorial to that fight against the undesirables they imply killed Adolphus Varane for his role in the Great Separation. It's sort of a rotten argument, if you ask me, but I presume it's the best they had at that time. Probably led to the Desolation. Well done, fellows."

"Yes, very encouraging," I said, marveling at how our species is able to convolute our personal emotions into social philosophy and political expediences. "Truly astonishing, when you think about it."

Freddy closed up the books on the library study table. "Like I said, we need to go see Varane's mansion. Now."

XIV

B y mid-afternoon, Freddy and I had hired a taxi to Bronzeville Square. Our driver held no great enthusiasm for North Catalan and let us know once we offered him the destination address.

"Why the hell do you want to go over there? It's nothing but trash."

Freddy leaned up over the seat and told him, "We like trash. We collect it. Study it. Sell it to other trash collectors. It's our life."

"You kids are nuts."

"Yes," I added, "that's what our parents say."

So many rides into the Catalan to see Nina had taken some of my fear of that benighted district off my mind. Yet, even so, crossing the bridge over Zoffany Creek had my skin bristling. And Freddy? He gazed out the window with the same curiosity he regarded most things in life that didn't involve textbooks. The dreary drainpipes protruded from industrial waste and rubble. Smokestacks crowded the rough skyline. People in old coats and stubble shoes ambled along worn-out sidewalks, staring as we drove by. North Catalan was more horrendous than East where Nina lived on Gosney Street. Houses here were ramshackle and sad. Tilted porches and wobbly stairs. Cracked concrete. Weeds and weeds. Packs of wandering dogs. Trash cans fallen over. Rubbish cast about. I apologized to our taxi driver. I guess he knew this Catalan better than we did.

We drove by the bronze foundry and saw the old building still had life, even on a sunny Saturday afternoon. At least a couple dozen autos and trucks were parked haphazardly in front. There were some fellows loading figurines into one of the trucks and another standing off to one side smoking a pipe and apparently supervising. I guess I thought Coyne Street would be the same ruin that Varane's mansion was in the old ferroplates Freddy had dug out. Maybe I presumed the bronze foundry was no more. After all, that was better than ninety years ago. Entropy rules all, does it not? I was wrong. Though Bronzeville Square was rougher and less polished than the work it produced, still its industry survived and appeared to be doing quite well.

A further surprise awaited up on Hesperia Avenue. No mean ruin and industrial desolation showed here, either. Acacia trees and elms, dogwoods and magnolia, were yet in spring bloom. Flowers of all sorts and hues made lovely the sidewalks as we approached the monument to Adolphus Varane. Indeed, the great man was there, after all, that commemorated bronze statue to the esteemed eugenicist, brilliant in sunlight on a carved marble pedestal in front of the towering brick ruin of his troubled mansion.

The taxi let us off across the avenue and Freddy paid a generous tip. As the cab drove away, we walked over to the site of that century-old conflagration. A single scruffy gardener in overalls and sun hat labored under acacia shade in a flower bed of pink roses and white carnations. There were a pair of tall elegant frame houses just up the sidewalk in the lot behind Varane's ruin, not extravagant at all, yet stately by their own bearing, relaxed architecturally and comfortable in this place of eugenical worship.

"Bronzeville Square," Freddy announced, stating the obvious with little hint of irony.

"Evidently."

"So now what?"

The wreck of the mansion was almost prepossessing if the truth of its destruction by fire were somehow ignored. In fact, Varane's house of fate was grander than I had thought from examining the library impressions. Taller, wider, penetrating more deeply into the back of the lot. A thick growth of ivy climbed the old brick walls from earth to precipice, lending grace from the natural world to the ruined works of a man. Odd, however, was the placement of Adolphus Varane's bronze statue on a patch of scruffy lawn just above the sidewalk. Reminiscent actually of Shelley's famous Ozymandias: "*Look on my works, ye Mighty, and despair!*" Did those who chose this location over Dunham Gardens have any regard for that?

"And where is your Mr. Draxler?" Freddy spoke up, while staring beside me at Varane's tormented mansion. "Is he hiding inside somewhere?"

"I don't know. Do you think it's safe to be in there? Are we even allowed? There's no barrier."

We both looked around. Across the street was a high brick wall hiding several small houses behind it. No one on the sidewalk in front. Same on the west side of Varane's lot. Another old brick wall blocking off any view of the simple homes over there. Bronzeville Square was quiet in the afternoon sun. A pleasant breeze rippled through the shady leaves of the acacia tree. Other than the presence of our laboring gardener, we felt alone. Freddy stepped up over the low stone wall that surrounded the front lawn of the ruin and went to have a word with the gardener. I began to wonder how often anyone paid notice to this city monument of horror and sadness. Ordinarily we would find a guardian or perhaps a city docent prepared to offer some informative lecture on the brief history of Adolphus Varane and the fate of his mansion, the purpose of his statue on that spot. No such person existed here today. Apparently, we were on our own. So why had Peter Draxler sent us here? Could he actually be hiding in that ruin? I had my doubts. Such transparent subterfuge seemed beneath a fellow who took such care with that volume of *The Aeneid* and the odd telephone code to disguise this location. He had summoned us almost across the ether. There had to be more than this. I popped up over the stone wall myself for a closer look at the bronze statue. It did appear very old, weathered and weary. The printed library ferroplates had flattered Varane's bronze doppelgänger. I knelt and read again the iron plaque whose copy we'd found in that library volume, and imagined the thrill of ceremony and establishment:

ON THIS SITE WE DEDICATE OUR STRUGGLE AS A RITE OF PROGRESS

"Julian!" Freddy called to me from the front brick threshold.

Walking up to join him, I asked, "Did that gardener fellow tell you anything interesting? Has Draxler been here?"

Freddy shook his head. "We're the only ones he's seen all day and he told me he's been here since dawn. I asked him if we can go in there and he said we can do anything we like. He's not a sentry. He said, if a brick falls on your head, it's your trouble, not his."

"Good enough."

"Supposing Draxler's not here," Freddy asked, "then what do you think we're expected to be looking for?"

I shrugged. "I have no idea."

We took a chance and went into the ruin through the remains of the front entry. Moss and weeds grew rampant on what was left of the tile floor and walls. Any elements of wood that had been part of Varane's mansion and not burned up in the fire had long since rotted away. The roof, too, was gone now, open to the blue afternoon sky above. I felt as if I were standing in a cathedral of chaos. Shorn of dedicated rooms and windows, corridors and vestibules, the interior was enormous, cavernous really, vast. Yet, hardly anything resembling a house of people persisted after ninety years of weather and entropy. Freddy and I picked our separate paths across the weeds and rubble. The dead mansion could almost be a hot house these days with the curious variety of peculiar plants and exotic wildflowers flourishing within the ruin. Slants of golden sunlight burned on the moss and mold of the brick walls as a cool draft, too, from several directions at once tossed about. Looking up to where the fourth floor had been, I thought about Adolphus Varane's bedroom, wondered where it had been, where precisely he had burned to death with Idalia Galata. A pair of amorous swallows darted in from above and then out again through a lower window hole. The ruin had the oddest odor, I noticed. Not from a fire. That was too long ago. Not even much soot was left, stained into the old bricks. Nor was that odor exactly rot, either, though one might expect that here. Don't plants grow and perish and decompose endlessly? My mother had kept up a small greenhouse for several years when I was a boy and, to this day, I can recall how it smelled when I entered from the fresh air out of doors: deliriously fecund and humid and putrid, too, from the cow dung fertilizer she used. This was still different. If I were a poet, I'd try to claim Varane's ruins were a grand mausoleum, a massive crypt, and that odd, nasty odor troubling me was Death, his death and somehow belonging to those millions who had been annihilated in the Desolation as a result of Adolphus Varane's eugenical fanaticism.

I found Freddy at the far end of the ruin studying the crumbling brick and mortar of a niche that probably had been a closet of some sort or even a small room.

"I don't know why we're here," I shouted over to him. "What's the point of all this? It feels like a snipe hunt. Remember? From sophomore hijinx?"

Freddy laughed. "When your pair of underwear turned up in Dame Wertheim's auto trunk?"

"No one ever admitted to putting them there. Still infuriates me. A more wicked mystery than this."

"Your Peter Draxler was here, Julian. I promise you. That code was very clever. He sent us to find him at Bronzeville Square in this monstrosity. We've just got to figure out what it is he intends us to do here. It's that simple."

"I'm going back outdoors," I told Freddy. "Look around some more. See if anything turns up in here."

He kicked over a piece of rubble. "All right."

I went out through the front entrance again, pausing briefly to shove the old iron address plaque back against the brick door frame. Someone ought to mount it again, I thought. Why not? Isn't Varane's ruin still part of the neighborhood of Bronzeville Square? I presumed it had been fastened to a cement architrave above the grand entrance. The years had worn that cement off, but I picked the plaque up, anyhow, and carried it out to the front walk and held it high to see where the plaque had once fit. 12646.The rectangle belonged horizontally, so beside the door was not the answer. Probably above, unless it had been installed on the low wall at the sidewalk. I took it down there to see if there was a niche missing its plaque. Nothing. The wall was rough, but not carved anywhere for Varane's address. So, above the door. I held it up again, imagining how it looked ninety years ago when this was 12646 Hesperia Avenue.

I caught my breath.

Good God!

I set the plaque down and looked around, and across the street. Freddy was coming out of the ruin, whistling one of his favorite tunes, "Dreamy Blue Teardrops." I saw a panel truck motoring up the avenue from Coyne Street, and ran across to the brick wall on that side of the road before it arrived. Where were the addresses? I'd need a ladder to see over, but a postman required a maildrop, so there had to be a box somewhere. I hurried up the sidewalk as Freddy called to me from Varane's statue. Halfway along the block I found a stand of mail addresses. They were numbered 1300–1310, Hesperia Avenue.

The truck roared past in a cloud of exhaust.

Then I yelled to Freddy, "I think I found Draxler!"

XV

We washed off the plaque in the bathroom sink across the hall from our room in Thayer Hall. Exposing the plate beneath all that accumulated dirt and grime left a fine sheen to the gilded numerals 12646. I dried them carefully with a hand-towel and stepped back so that Freddy and I could admire what we'd stolen from Varane's mansion. I had no real idea what had led me to guess that plaque did not represent the address on Hesperia Avenue. Easy to say there were too many numbers. Yet many addresses in the great metropolis had a similar count. Both Ehrenhardt Boulevard and Dardanus Way certainly had five or six digits to their city addresses as they stretched for miles across the metropolis. Lines could be redrawn. Maybe something else, perhaps what Freddy next told me as we stared at the plaque on my study desk.

"It's not old at all, Julian. And I think that's meant to be obvious when we examine the plaque more closely. Did you notice how easily it cleaned up? Had we taken a garden hose there in the yard, we'd have gotten all this gunk off right at the door. A true ninety-year-old iron plaque would require a fine animal hairbrush, a good rinse with therathiolate, and a proper polishing cloth. And you'd need at least a couple of hours to get it clean as this is now. We only took five minutes because it's a fake. Peter Draxler had this plaque made for us. It's basically a stage prop."

I shrugged. "Fooled us, though."

"Not really," Freddy argued, "and it wasn't meant to. If anything, it had to fool anyone else who happened to come along before we got there. And I presume it did since we have it now, right?"

"I suppose so."

"Time for Virgil again, Julian. Get your dictionary. Let's see what this one is all about."

While Freddy took a seat at my desk, I dug the old leather-bound volume of Virgil's *Aeneid* out from under my mattress once again. Then I took that library edition of the Latin dictionary from my desk drawer and brought both to my bed and laid them there.

Freddy reminded me, "We're looking for line 646 in Book 12."

"I know. Thank you. I'm not an idiot."

"Just being your trusty guide."

I began skimming through *The Aeneid*, book after book, until I reached Liber XII. Then I traced down the lines until I found the sentence beginning in the middle of 646 and completing in 647. It read: *vos O mihi Manes este boni quoniam superis aversa voluntas*!

"All right." I showed Freddy. "Here it is."

"Need this?" He handed the Latin dictionary to me, along with the notepad and pencil I'd used last time.

"Thank you."

I found this one somehow much more challenging to translate. It read metaphorically, at least to my relatively uneducated eye. And offered many possibilities. That other entry regarding the great burning mansion was complicated, but the central idea was clearer than here. I struggled with this line, particularly having Freddy there staring at me while I studied the text. Knowing what sort of a student I'd been in Second Latin, I imagined Konovaloff would have either adored my sudden dedication to his favorite dead language or laughed at my feeble attempt to make sense of something that would have been second nature to him, or any of his class favorites that term. Pretty Polly Dolan, for instance, (whose full name was Polyxena, after Priam's daughter) would have delighted in showing me up over this translation. She was a true academic snob and a dreadful bitch. Konovaloff gushed over her week after week, sickening the rest of us and contributing (we were confident) to our uniformly lower marks. Fortunately, she graduated after fall term and went abroad with her family. No one's seen her since.

"Well?" Freddy gave me a nudge with his foot. "What's it say? Don't make me take over the project."

"I won't." Making one final pass across Virgil's sentence and scribbling over a word I felt I'd wrongly translated, I offered this opinion to Freddy. "Here's what I think it says: *'O you spirits of the dead below, be good to me for the gods above prove so unkind.'* Or something like that. Close enough. This one feels sort of vague."

Both us read it over again.

Freddy said, "Well, that's interesting."

"It's the best I can do. I have no idea what it's supposed to mean for us."

"Me neither."

"But it means something, right? From Draxler to us. Some sort of message or code or clue to lead us to him."

"One would presume," Freddy suggested. "He's been difficult so far, but not overly obtuse."

I laughed. "How do you know that word? I've never heard you use it before."

"I told you this morning. My various *Qantara* squib books. They're a complete education. No true scholar should be without them."

"I'll try to remember that next time I'm at the bookstore."

"Oh, they won't sell them there. Not at all. You have to go down Rondeau Circle to Smahlian's old flea market. He keeps them in a box by the crystal Titian oil lamps. Mention my name and he'll sell one to you at half cost. He likes me."

"You bring him bourbon?"

Freddy smiled. "How did you guess? His wife, Motiña, won't let him buy liquor, so he suffers for his store profits that only profit her. I help him enjoy this life and, in exchange, his squib books let me feel like a genius now and then."

"A fair exchange, I suppose."

"Better than that, Julian," Freddy said, that marvelous expression of self-satisfaction drawn on his face. "Much better."

"Well then, genius," I said, "help me solve this riddle and we can all feel better."

Just then, we heard a knock at our door. Fortunately, it was locked, because the voice we heard following another knock belonged to my dear Nina Rinaldi.

XVI

"I'm so glad to meet you, Freddy," Nina said, sitting down on the bed beside me. "Julian's told me so much about you. I feel like we know each other already." She looked at me as I laughed. "Pardon? Isn't that what I'm supposed to say when I meet friends of yours?"

Freddy nodded. "That's exactly true, except that Julian and I aren't at all friends. We've just been thrown together in here by Thayer Hall's Housing Committee without any thought whatsoever regarding our compatability — "

"Which is non-existent, really," I cut in on him. "We can't stand each other. Never have."

"That's true, Nina," Freddy agreed. "We're mortal enemies who've had to strike an armistice for academic survival. But it's been a strain, let me tell you. Right, Julian?

"Almost inconceivably so."

Then Nina laughed. "You're both lying. I can tell by how you look at each other. If I didn't trust Julian, I'd think you were lovers."

"Oh, God!" Freddy turned and stared at me, mouth agape. "Darling, we've been found out! Exposed! Now what?"

I shrugged. "We'll just need to face it, I guess. It's not the end of everything. We can share closets at last."

Nina slid her arm around me and kissed my cheek. "Not yet, you won't. Julian's all mine." She kissed me again. "Well, for at least another week or two."

I said, "Is that why you came here today, to look after me? You might have telephoned and saved yourself a ride."

"I did," Nina replied. "They told me you've been out all day."

Freddy nodded, "That's true. We've been occupied all morning and afternoon with the mystery — "

I interrupted him. "— of how to keep Freddy enrolled so his father doesn't boot him out into the street." I shot Freddy a frown. He didn't seem to grasp that Nina wasn't to hear yet what we had learned about Peter Draxler's location.

But my dear roommate is no fool. "Julian's right," Freddy said. "I'm barely hanging on. And speaking of my father, Julian, I forgot to tell you that he wants me out at Alexanderton tonight for dinner. So I will now pack up my sorrows and leave you two to whatever amusements you're able to finagle."

He stood and gave Nina a polite kiss on her cheek. "So very good to meet you at last. I don't know how Julian does it. He'll need to give me lessons when I get back tomorrow."

"You'll be gone overnight?" I asked, somewhat surprised. He rarely went home for more than a few hours.

"Obligations, Julian. Obligations. Just be sure to keep me up on your progress with that silly snipe hunt. I won't sleep otherwise."

"I promise."

Before opening our door, Freddy and I had hidden Virgil and my Latin dictionary away, *The Aeneid* under the mattress once again and the dictionary deep into my desk papers. Nina knew about Virgil, but I was afraid of her asking about my translation, though I'd gotten the sense from her on Gosney Street that she neither expected nor wanted me to share anything I'd gleaned from the old volume. In any case, it was just simpler to hide both books.

Once Freddy had taken his over-night satchel and left, Nina and I engaged in another kissing fest that left us both anxious to make love there in my bed. Truth was, I'd never had any girl up in my bedroom before. At home, yes, meaning Lydia Sayre, when my parents were out to Párador for dinner, and again while they were off by train for a weekend to the sea resort at Atlajálas. Then Lydia and I swam nude in the backyard pool and made love in my bedroom and more than once on a blanket in the service box of Father's lovely grass court. The Sayres were not so enthusiastic about Lydia attending her girlfriends' slumber parties when they suspected she was sneaking off to my house for another illicit late-night rendezvous. A lover's fortune must include a best friend, and Lydia's was Claire Haines who enjoyed seeing us madly in love and used every trick she could invent to hide Lydia's whereabouts from her parents after dark. Those were exciting days and nights. Gone now, of course, lost to happy memories.

Nina told me she preferred us to wait until after dinner to make love in my bed, and I wanted to know what had brought her here to me so late on this Saturday afternoon.

"Delia went to spend the night at her little friend Adelaide's house over on Pepper Lane for a birthday party celebrating another little troublemaker named Emma. Her temper tantrums are blacker than Delia's. A little demon in petticoats. If her mother has half an ounce of brains, she'll throw that ugly child into the river while she still can. It's her only real hope. I absolutely expect Emma the Monster to slit their throats or turn on the gas in the middle of night."

"Nina!"

"I know." She took my hand and kissed me. "It's crazy. Everything is crazy these days, isn't it? Aren't we all insane? I know I am."

I pulled her close and kissed her softly on her lips. "I think you're sweet and beautiful. Yes, troubled, I admit that, but quite wonderful, too."

"You say that because you love me. Your perspective is ambushed by my charms. I've drugged you with a Ferésien love potion, and nothing you think about me can be trusted."

I smiled. "Are you telling me I should have pushed *you* into the river that evening on the waterfront when I had the chance?"

She nodded. "I was surprised you didn't."

"Oh, I guess since I already had the book, I didn't need you anymore, right?"

"Yes, Julian," she ran her fingers across my brow, "something like that. Certain mistakes we just can't overcome. This might be one of your worst."

"Well, nothing to be done about it now," I said, offering her one last kiss. "So let's go to dinner."

We decided to eat at that same bistro down on Kemper Street where Freddy and I had breakfast. More comfortable in the evening with the crowd being less hungover college students and more responsible adults out for a pleasant Saturday dinner. Couples mostly, except for a raucous group in a banquet lounge off from the main dining room. Cocktails and beer saturated that room. We ordered food and wine. Nina asked for a clam and tomato soup Pelotonia, with Rahaman salad, and I chose the pork potato dish and sourdough bread. She wanted red wine, and I preferred white. In the spirit of love and togetherness we mixed them quite crudely to create a curious rosé. I'm sure our waiter considered that hopelessly gauche, but we were happy and that's all we cared about.

After a taste of wine, Nina told me, "No one in the house trusts me anymore, Julian. They think Peter is my lover and I'm hiding him with you."

"Pardon?"

"It's so absurd. The absolute limit. They're such idiots. Every last one of them. The girls even more so. And their boyfriends seem to think I'm a whore. They knock on my door all hours of the day and night, even when I have Delia in there with me."

"Are you serious?"

"Yes! I tell them to go fuck themselves. They'd have a better time than with me. Or I say I have spyreosis and that keeps some of them away. Except one of those mental defectives, who calls himself 'Zamen,' said he'd turn me over to Medical Security, and I slapped him so hard he cried right there in the living room with all his little friends watching. Delia thought it was hilarious."

I raised my glass of improvised rosé. "Let's have a toast to a good slap or two."

Nina giggled. "To a good slap in the face!"

"Right!"

We drank half our wine. Then Nina said, "But really, Julian, I just don't know what's going on over there, and I'm terrified for Delia's sake. Besides that, now somebody's been nailing up bulletins all across the city warning of reprisals if the Security Directorate continues dragging off normal citizens for spyreosis testing. That's supposed to be illegal, and then they go and make their own rules about everything they can and can't do to us. Something bad's going to happen soon and none of us will be safe anymore."

Our dinners came and we sorted out the dishes, sharing with each other a few bites of our own choices. Nina was gorgeous in the evening ambience of the crowded bistro. Her coal-dark eyes sparkled in the yellow flickering candlelight. The casual magenta silk dress she wore fluttered gently with her falling black hair in the soft draft from out of doors.

We ate quietly for a few minutes as customers came and went, and auto traffic proceeded unceasingly along Kemper Street.

Finally, I asked, "Why do your housemates think you're in love with Peter?"

Nina shook her head. "I'm not sure. Maybe because those shady people are looking for him, which makes him seem important, and they believe I'm somehow more important than they are because most of them are just stupid kids. I don't know. It doesn't really make much sense."

"Have you met him?"

"Peter?"

"Yes," I said.

"Will you be jealous if I have?"

"Have you?"

"Yes."

Somehow, I did begin to feel jealous and my stomach clenched. But I had to ask, anyhow. "Were you in love with him?"

She laughed. "Oh, God, Julian! No!"

"But you went out with him?"

She rapped her fork on my wrist. "You are so inquisitive!"

"It's just a question."

Nina narrowed her dark eyes. "Do you really want to know?"

"I suppose so."

"Peter spent one night with me after we got drunk on cups of Teucrit. I didn't know him very well and neither of us thought anything about it afterward and it never happened again. I honestly thought he was seeing a girl out in Bohstedt and that she was in love with him. How he felt about her I have no idea."

"How did you meet?"

She had a taste of her tomato Pelotonia. "Julian, you should enroll at the Internal Affairs Academy. You'd be a champion investigator."

"I'm just asking."

Nina rolled her lovely eyes. "Do you ever go to the gallery exhibitions at Stegger Plaza? That small museum next to the Galician restaurant?"

"Never heard of it."

"You are so sheltered, Julian. My God! Lucky you for meeting me. I have so much to show you."

I cut off a slice of steaming pork and potato. "Tell your story."

"Oh, be that way." Nina smiled. "Well, there was a show one evening of paintings by Jerrold Souza, from Lamyrus Province, that I just had to see. He's a genius from the same school as Gustávo Agustín. You do know who that is, don't you?"

"No, so just go on."

"Julian!"

"Please?" I ate another bite of pork and tried to ignore the nasty look I was sure Nina was giving me just then.

"All right, well, anyhow I had gone there by myself and happened to notice a young guy sitting on a couch across from Souza's exhibition, making sketches. I assumed he was copying off the wall and went over to remind him, in case he didn't know, how it wasn't permitted. They toss you out for that. I told him and he laughed and showed me what he'd been drawing. Souza's painting in front of Peter was a rendering of a Venetian canal with a gondola and a gondolier passing under a bridge. What Peter was sketching in amazing detail was the Baxélega de San Marco during a winter flood tide. I felt humiliated, but he forgave me and we had dinner later on and he came back to my house that night for the bottle of Teucrit. Then I didn't see him again until just a few weeks ago when he dropped over with a friend of Kaspar's I'd never met. They spent the entire evening gabbing about politics and the Desolation and social suicide, and I was tired of that, so I went to bed and he was gone in the morning. That's all. Nobody admits to seeing him since."

I finished my plate of pork, then said, "Except Virgil."

"Don't tell me about that, Julian. It's none of my business."

Nina took a long gulp of wine, emptying her glass.

We finished dinner and went outdoors for a stroll. Nina took my hand as we walked south along Kemper Street among the crowds of others like us away from home on a nice Saturday evening. All through dinner I had tried working out a logical solution to the riddle of that line from Virgil, 'O you spirits of the dead below, be good to me for the gods above prove so unkind.' A cemetery, maybe? I had to remember that what Draxler had chosen for me to unravel was a clue to draw us together for some purpose that was itself a mystery. Why me? What did he want?

Farther on toward Cabanis Square, Nina led us into shops here and there along our walk where she sampled perfumes and tried on scarves, fiddled with antique knick-knacks, and asked my opinion about a brass watch she fancied. I agreed the watch was elegant. The watchmaker assured Nina it was not only beautiful but quite worthy of her investment. Confessing that she had no money to buy anything at all, we left the watchmaker and meandered along until we reached a Bachir jewelry shop where I led her indoors.

"Why?" she asked.

"Because I want to," I told her, then started searching among the glass cases of Carvãjlo illumined earrings and pendants for brash gems that Nina's own beauty would flatter. I studied each case for that one special something to adorn my special girl.

"Julian, you don't need to buy me anything. I'm serious."

I smiled at her. "Not you, dear. It's for my grandmother. Her ninetieth birthday next week. We have a huge family celebration planned."

"Oh."

"You're so cute." I gave a sweet kiss on her cheek and squeezed her hand. Her perfume bloomed in the small store, like that exotic smoky scent of Gioconda incense. Then I went back to perusing the pendants. I had my eye on a black vergenie immocalata, a pretty stone from the Pallantis ravine in Hotaling Province. Reasonably rare, yet at a price accessible to those of us who don't keep a yacht moored along the holy river. This jeweler, whose name was Rota, had his pendant marked to fifty credits, a fair price. I bought it with a delicate gold chain, and he wrapped both in cloth and placed them in a lovely little indigo satin pouch. As Nina and I walked out, she said to me, "She'll love it, Julian. It's beautiful. You have a very tasteful eye."

"Thank you, darling." I smiled and kissed her. "I'm glad you like it."

"Very much."

I handed her the pouch. "Because it's yours."

"Julian!"

"Put in on, dear. I want to you wear it. You're so beautiful."

Her smile explained how happy she appeared to be for this unexpected gift. "But why would you buy this for me? You're more insane than I am."

"Not insane, Nina," I told her. "Just in love."

She wore the smoky black pendant as we wandered back up Kemper Street to Thayer Hall, maybe half an hour walk counting stops where Nina took the occasional pause to kiss me. The sky over Regency College was dark now and stars sprinkled the night air. A pleasantly warm breeze drifted across trees and grass, where dozens of students were camped out on the lawn through this wonderful spring evening. I felt blessed and fortunate. Lovely Nina had flowery hands and a spirit ecstatic and improbable depending to her mood and moment. She was sweet and sultry, then blazed with a rare fury I did not always understand, yet I was never dissuaded from pursuing that shooting star of her. Love is both temperament and acquiescence, humbling and inspiring. The balance between these contradictions fires a universe.

We lit a pair of candles I'd kept for electrical outages that interfered with late night homework at Thayer Hall during windy winter storms. We put one candle by my nightstand, the other on my study desk. Seeing Nina naked in the darkness across the room silhouetted in the streetlight at my window as she looked out through the elm branches to Trimble Street below, I felt as if nothing unkind could ever happen to me again. When she returned to my bed and we made love atop the quilt my mother had given me freshman year, I believed I'd found my first glimpse of true manhood. An illusion, of course, but a sense I hadn't imagined before in quite that way. We lay together afterward and listened to auto traffic motoring by and music from other rooms down the hall and voices in the stairwell. She asked me about some of my college friends, other than Freddy, and the studies I was pursuing and which wild enthusiasms I'd chased on campus and elsewhere. And did I have heroes? I told her about Wild Jack Calhoon and Dr. Coffeen and my father, whom I admired above anyone on this earth. I described Highland Park and Agnes and my wonderful mother and how I came to be at Thayer Hall. With the faintest smile on her lips, Nina went to sleep soon afterward, then later woke briefly in my arms and kissed me ever so gently, her hand entwined with mine, and whispered into my ear: *"How do we account for who we are, Julian?"*

Then she fell back to sleep again. And that's how it was to be with Nina. Her voice was tender in the dark, her touch a butterfly's descent. I'd lie in the shadow of the streetlight and see her shadow breathing beside my own, knowing she was awake; she was almost always awake. We'd make love and she'd become dreamy with vague whispers and shut-eyed smiles, and I'd see her drift off, and kiss her eyelids and feel them flutter beneath my lips and imagine her dreaming and know she wasn't, that she didn't, that she never had dreams, or so she claimed.

— . —

Sunday morning in the commons was quiet and fairly empty, many of my fellow classmates hungover and hiding out in their rooms. I bought Nina breakfast there, just eggs and oatmeal, biscuits and blueberries. She had a cup of hot Mazzaro tea, and I took coffee. Eating, we chatted a little about Delia's schooling which Nina assured me had become another horrific trial. She asked, "Do you know anything about the Menhennet School? It's off Messel Lane behind the Kaarsberg fish market. Supposed to have good teachers, but Delia doesn't seem to be learning a thing, and I get notices every week about all the trouble she's causing there with girls *and* boys. I know they'd like to kick her out, but the East Catalan school superintendent's mandate for elementary education won't let them. Wonderful! She gets to torture her teachers and classmates all day long, then me, along with everyone else at the house, every evening until bedtime. Sometimes I want to strangle her."

Picking over the bowl of blueberries, I told Nina, "That house is too hectic. I can't see how Delia would not be so distracted and agitated that it wouldn't affect her schoolwork and her general class deportment. She's just a little girl, and those bohemian revolutionaries you're surrounded by can't be helping her."

She sipped her tea. "I wish you wouldn't call us bohemians like that, Julian, as if it were a bad word. And I'm not sure you're being fair about our politics, either. If nothing changes, no one's lives will ever be better than they are today. The war goes on, people disappear, and our government ignores anyone who lives below accepted standards of the Status Imperium, which is to say most of the population of our grand Republic. How does this continue? How will it ever be better, or even different?"

"I'm sorry," I replied, slightly embarrassed by my own intransigence. "I don't mean to be so critical. It's stupid to say those things, I agree. And you're right that we're on a road that doesn't lead anywhere good, regardless of those preposterous notices from Prospect Square. I'm not sure we can even trust the city newspapers or the radio shows, any longer. What do they tell us we don't already know? I think we're deceived because we tolerate these deceptions, and we tolerate them because we can't seem to decide what all this is about besides protecting us from a violent nation of undesirables and some vague scourge of spyreosis that none of us truly understands, anyhow."

Nina smiled. "So, at last, you are more than another pretty face, Julian. Maybe you're one of us in more ways than you might've thought you were."

"Maybe." I ate a spoonful of blueberries and enjoyed my coffee. She was too pretty herself to scrap with over politics whose underlying purpose we couldn't easily discern. Besides, I loved seeing her smile and tried my best to draw that out.

"I need to go to work," Nina said. "I'm supposed to open up by ten o'clock."

"On a Sunday morning?"

"Sadly, yes. And I have to be there until six. We get a lot of our business on Sundays, people traveling home from the provinces and they like to buy fresh flowers to brighten things up for the week."

"I had no idea."

"We're very profitable, but only when we're open, which means me on the East Platform in about an hour. So I should go."

We finished with breakfast and went back up to my room where Nina grabbed her bag. She gave me a long, lovely kiss beside my bed, and then I walked her out of Thayer Hall and down to the bus stop, gave her another kiss and a good warm hug, and saw her off.

XVII
∞

Freddy was waiting for me in our room when I got back. He'd just arrived from Alexanderton in the quarter hour, his overnight satchel still on his bed, unpacked. He seemed enthused about something, almost buoyant. Very unlike his usual visits home where he came back despondent and suicidal.

I sat down across from him on my own bed. "All right, Freddy, what gives? Did Dr. Barron agree that grades no longer count in his household? Or did your Gorgon sisters move out?"

He tossed himself onto his mattress and stretched out, fluffing the pillow under his head. "Never mind that, Julian, my friend. How was your honeymoon? Did all your dreams come true? Did you draw attention to our room from all about? Any noise complaints?"

I refused to let him draw me out. Instead, I said, "I think I have a grip on Virgil. It feels obvious, though maybe not simple enough to solve quite yet."

"Oh, yeah? How's that?" Freddy perked up. "What did you come up with?"

"What if those 'spirits of the dead below' is a cemetery?"

Freddy laughed and shook his head. "It's not."

"How do you know that?"

"Because there in Virgil, 'spirits of the dead below' refers to Hades, the underworld, or here meaning the undercity. And 'the gods above' is about Olympus, or in our case, the Status Imperium that controls our lives. *'O you spirits of the dead below, be good to me for the gods above prove so unkind.'* I believe that entire line is another sort of code from Draxler instructing us to hunt for him now in the undercity."

Well, I was astounded. Ordinarily, Freddy floundered in dissecting fiction and poetry. He consistently failed to recognize symbolism or see metaphor in the most simplistic texts. Quite obviously those magical squib books of his produced no great emancipations for Freddy in the literary arts, whereas I've always been more than adept at navigating my way along those artful rivers.

But this?

"Good grief, Freddy. How on earth did you arrive at all that?"

"Do you think it's wrong? I don't. In fact, I'm absolutely convinced this is what Draxler intended."

"No, Freddy, actually I agree completely. I'm only astonished at how my literarily obtuse roommate managed to arrive at such an elegant deduction."

"Simple." Freddy smiled like the Cheshire Cat. "Konovaloff."

"What?" That was peculiar. "How so?"

"We crossed paths at the bus depot yesterday," Freddy said. "He was coming back here from a Classics conference at Shope. Quite a nice fellow, Julian, so long as he's not grading your papers."

"And you told him about Draxler? I hope not."

"No, no, no! I merely quoted that line from Virgil in the context of curiosity. I told him I had decided to revisit *The Aeneid* for my own enjoyment and had been stumped by the meaning of that sentence. He was only too glad to help!"

"And he told you it referred to the underworld?"

"Yes, indeed." Freddy grinned. "He was quite forthcoming about the translation. Yours was slightly off, he told me, but conceded there are always variations open to interpretation."

I was mortified now. "You mentioned my name to Konovaloff? Why would you do that? He thinks I'm an idiot."

"Not at all, Julian, not at all. He told me you were a good student of Latin and that with a little more attention to the niceties you could excel in that discipline. In fact, Konovaloff was impressed that both of us still read Virgil and enjoy him. Apparently, we are not the norm at Thayer Hall."

I could not help laughing at that. Freddy was such a brown-noser. Better than anyone. "Well, that is such a serendipitous consequence, because, really, I had no good sense of what we were intended to make of that line. Cemetery was a guess, but where were we supposed to go with it?"

Freddy laughed. "Oh, you didn't do so poorly, Julian. Cemeteries are normally underground. You just weren't extravagant enough."

"Thank you, roommate."

Freddy offered a royal nod. "At your service."

"So, where do we proceed with the undercity? I've heard it's expansive and quite dangerous. Creepy thugs and rampant pestilence. Black bottomless sinkholes. Those might be rumors, but still. And, in any case, how would we know where to begin?"

"Now that's the question, isn't it?"

Freddy and I decided to mull it over for a while and, in the meantime, get back to classwork if we hoped to keep ourselves enrolled at Thayer Hall. He shuffled off to the library and I retreated to my study desk with that blasted paper on the Achaeleon theocracy that had been haunting me for a month now. No problem, because a couple of nights ago an intriguing idea had come to me in a waking dream. The ancient community of Achaelus on a small Greek island in the Aegean Sea was a theocratic society whose dominant social and political organization was universal democracy. That is to say, each citizen, man or woman, held the identical influence on all decisions to life and laws. Achaelus had no sitting monarch, nor any rigid governing council. Both theological revelation and intellectual dialogue throughout the island state created and influenced the daily life of Achaeleon society. Its domestic circumstance and economic construct were elevated and sustained by fishing, both from the shore and out on the water in boats. Spiritual guidance provided through Olympian deities and pastoral oracles was experienced by each individual on the tiny island. In that sense, Achaelus, I argued in my essay, was a true theocratic democracy. But no form of government is ideal. The trouble there? As it's often said, too many cooks spoil the broth. With each citizen being fonts of wisdom and oracular inspiration, conflicts arose throughout the island society regarding when and where to plant in the harsh and unsatisfying earth, what punishments to mete out for which serious or trivial transgressions, which stars to chart for divine intervention. Who can be wrong when everybody's right? That was the essence of my thesis for this paper. I'd written most of it early in the semester, then got sidetracked by other classes that felt worthier of my limited attention. Finally, though, all work needs to be completed and what we postpone only lingers; it does not go away. So I dedicated the rest of that Sunday afternoon and evening, with a brief dinner break downstairs in the commons, to the good people of Achaelus, *anapáfsou en eirini.*

— . —

Freddy stumbled back into our room just after midnight, maddeningly bourbon soaked once again. Trying to discuss the metropolitan undercity with him in that state was hopeless. He barely recalled Konovaloff's interpretation of Virgil's line and fell asleep mid-sentence atop the bed comforter in his clothes. I went back to reading elegiac poetry from the Greek Anthology, then another chapter on potentialities of radioactive gas from Law and Modern Science. After that, for an hour or so, I read through and edited my Achaeleon theocracy paper until I was both sick of it and positive it would not get any better or more persuasive unless somebody else wrote it. Next, my flagging attention was directed to Alexandrian art beginning with the Pharos and those exotic antiquities extracted from the sunken island of Antirhodos by Mare Institute divers: jars and statuary and assorted relics. Because I would be expected to differentiate between the Egyptian and Hellenic during the Ptolemaic period, I scribbled extensive notes and descriptions into my class book and put them aside for later review. The exam wouldn't be for several weeks yet.

My study desk light went off around two o'clock. Draxler's puzzle circulated through my brain, his stygian underground. How did he expect us to locate him in that vast and risky labyrinth? The entire idea was absolutely insane. I really thought of getting up for another look at the old city map Freddy hid in his closet, but instead I fell asleep.

XVIII

∞

I heard from Nina on Tuesday, telling me that Delia had come down with a cold and was in bed and that she herself had the sniffles and I had best stay away for a couple of days. Given the amount of class work I had on my academic calendar that week, being forced to avoid Gosney Street was helpful. Yet I missed her, too. Nina had me so hypnotized I thought no story in my life had any narrative absent of her. Is love forever entangling like that? Reading in bed I noticed a lingering scent of her on my pillow. Lying alone in the dark, I listened for her and when she was not there, I pretended she was, still curled up in that mattress hollow where she'd slept. Then I willed her across my dreams.

After dinner on Wednesday evening, with classes done, Freddy brought out a city map he'd borrowed from the Thayer library, bribing a girl at the research desk with a miniature bottle of Nysian brandy. The articulated legend at the bottom of the map claimed this to be a thorough rendering of all the tunnels and catacombs north, east, west and south of the eternal river. Neither of us believed it because the map was at least forty years old and we were both aware of major subterranean excavations undertaken since then.

"It's more than a warren down there, Julian," Freddy said. "I'll wager my father's new auto that no one in this city has seen anywhere near half of that filthy labyrinth. Can you imagine how it must smell? Our sewers run under the city, and if the pipes break up above, which they do constantly, can you even conceive of how broken they could be down there? Draxler must be crazy if he expects us to kick about through floods of shit and sludge looking for his pretty face."

I slid the map closer to me, angled better into the light. "Well, that's just the point here, isn't it? I don't think he does. Peter Draxler knows the Directorate is on to him and wants to keep hidden in some dark, maybe godforsaken hole of the city, but he also needs us to track him down. You see, he's made his closet obscure, but not invisible. I'll bet he knows we've taken the plaque and are past Virgil's 'spirits of the dead' code by now. Therefore, if he wants us to chase after him underground, the path must be some sort of chute like Alice's rabbit hole, not a sewer dung heap. Do you agree at all?"

"Putting it like that, yes, I do. There's no logical point to this otherwise."

"Good, because, like I said, we're looking for a rabbit hole, not a sewer. So let's start by trying to find a gate where we can enter the undercity without poisoning ourselves."

Then Freddy told me, "I hate to say this, my friend, but you can't trust Nina."

I frowned. "Yes, I can."

"All right, maybe, but you shouldn't trust that house or any of those people in it besides Nina. Who are they, anyhow? What are they there for? What's with all that coming and going you've been telling me about? Do you have any real idea? Honestly?"

"I'm not sure."

"Precisely," he said. "So be careful."

That afternoon, I had gotten a letter from Agnes, who rarely wrote to me and when she did it was with admonishments for my failure to be a better brother and write to her more often. I did, in fact, write as often, or rarely, as she did, but somehow Agnes felt that one letter from her was worth three of mine. Either that or her counting was faulty. Father told me they experienced the identical conflict. Agnes had always been a trial because she resisted any compromise that didn't favor her opinions. Today was no different.

April 7

Dear Brother,

I am writing to you on this lovely spring morning from my wonderful room at Branson to let you know how upset Mother is with you for failing to keep up with your side of family correspondence. She says that Father is concerned you might be neglecting your schoolwork in favor of extracurricular activities that will do you no great advantage later on. Also, they miss you and cannot understand why you're not visiting them more often. I am three hours by train, yet I've gone home four times this season to your one. Why is that? Do you hate them? You've never traveled here to see me, either, and I find that hurtful. Is it truly impossible for you to appreciate your family? We have given you our constant love and support, and all of us, including Father, feel you have not held up your part of the bargain. I think it is time you grow up and show us the consideration we deserve.

I'll wait for your response, though I'm sure you won't write back until summer.

Love,

Agnes

P.S. I was not to tell you this, but Mother thinks our father is not as well as he ought to be. Something you should think about.

Agnes Ellen Brehm enjoyed chastening me for each perceived slight, whether toward her or our parents. I rarely took it personally, that's just who she was, but her note about my father's health did cause me some concern and I telephoned Mother immediately to tell her I'd be home for dinner on Saturday evening. I would have taken the train to Highland Park on Friday, except Mother said she and Father had a charity gala to attend that night at the Garibaldi Building, and she preferred I see them a day later.

I breezed through my Thursday classes, handing in a two-page report for Law and Modern Science on legal ramifications of marketing radioactive Harnack gasses, then doing relatively well on a quiz for Philosophy in Classical Languages that covered five poems by Bacchylides, one of which, *The High Immortal Gods Are Free*, reminded me of Virgil's line obsessing both Freddy and myself, day in and day out now.

> "The high immortal gods are free
> From taint of man's infirmity;
> Nor pale diseases round them wait,
> Nor pain distracts their tranquil state."

How was I to keep focused on college studies with such a stupendous mystery dangled in my vision?

After classes let out, I went off to the gymnasium for a swim. Fifty laps usually helped calm my nerves and set my mind free, at least while I was in the pool. I wished Pindar and Quixote had been there, too. Asking them anything specific about Peter Draxler was out of the question now, but maybe they'd accidentally offer some innocuous detail that could help me locate that intriguing genius of theirs. I swam for almost an hour, then got out and showered. After that, I went back up to our room and found a note slipped under the door. It told me Nina had telephoned in the hour I'd been at the pool. She asked that I call her soon as possible, so I did.

"*Station 14, how may I help you?*"

"I'd like MERTON-3457, please?"

"*Thank you.*"

There was a gaggle of co-eds crowding one of the telephone tables, the girl with the receiver yelling at someone on the other end, probably an unfaithful boyfriend. Her friends were egging her on to give him the goose. Her pretty face flushed with emotion, as she seemed to be resisting. That meant for her it was love.

"*Connecting.*"

"*Hello?*" One of the boys at the Gosney house.

"Nina, please?"

"*Sure.*"

Sobbing all of a sudden, the co-ed slammed down her receiver and ran off, a pair of her friends in pursuit. Some of the others were laughing.

"*Hello?*"

"Nina?"

"*Julian! I'm so happy you called. Delia's still sick, but I'm better and I want you to come over. I'll fix you dinner. We'll have chicken pot pie and biscuits. I'm crazy here without you, Julian. I feel like slitting my wrists.*"

"Don't."

"*It's a joke!*"

I looked up at the wall clock above the telephones. It read twenty after five. I still had to organize my desk for tomorrow's studies.

"All right," I told her, "I'll meet you there about half past six. Is that all right?"

"*It's wonderful, Julian. You're really the sweetest thing.*"

XIX

∞

Once again, I saw rain on my taxi ride over to Gosney Street at twilight. Just a cold steady drizzle. My driver was a fellow named Nevsky I'd met before. He had come to the metropolis from Fabian Province where the Desolation had intruded into the countryside near his family, killing everything that grew with hydrocyanic gas and ceaseless artillery barrages. He was the only survivor of his village and had literally walked the eighty miles from Fabian to Porto Princepéssa on a month of refuge roads. Yet he felt to me like someone who had accepted fate as a gift from God looking down on this child of His who knew better than to complain and saw therefore no fault with heaven.

The taxi let me off in front of Nina's house. I went straight up the stairs to the door and rang the bell once. Another young wayward girl I didn't recognize let me in after I told her who I was there to see. I found Nina in the back hall coming out of Delia's bedroom with a thermometer in her hand. She gave me a kiss and a nice hug and told me Delia's fever had disappeared.

"The poor darling was hot as Egypt last night and I almost took her to the doctor. I was worried she had the flu, but her fever's gone now and she's sleeping."

"That's great."

"It's a blessing with everything else here falling apart. Are you hungry?"

"I suppose so. I skipped dinner at the commons to eat with you."

Nina smiled. "Good! Then come with me into the kitchen. Let me fix you the chicken pot pie. Do you want that? It's still fresh. Delia and I shared one for lunch today."

"That'll be fine, sure."

"And biscuits?"

"Yes, please." I was starving. I hadn't eaten since lunch and that was only a dry turkey sandwich and a small bowl of celery soup.

She kissed me and took my hand and led me along to the kitchen. Two of Nina's housemates, Kaspar and Saami, were sitting at the table eating peaches and pears. Each had a bottle of spice beer. Since their signatures were apparently on the rental agreement with that painter fellow, responsibility seemed more present in them than anyone else I'd met at the house. Of course, that didn't mean they were less bohemian. Kaspar had shaggy blonde hair and wore an oil-stained khaki vest. His girlfriend, Saami, must have shared closets with Nina because she was dressed in one of those same blue peasant blouses Nina favored. Bohemian chic, I presumed. Or dressing for anarchy.

Tonight, they stared at me as if I'd just dropped in from the moon. I tried my polite voice. "Hello. I'm Julian."

Kaspar looked at Nina. "Is he kidding?"

Saami added, "You know we have a meeting tonight."

Nina replied, "You always have a meeting. So what?"

"We agreed that no one can be in the house when we have meetings."

"We've agreed about lots of things," Nina told her, "and I don't feel you're being good to your word, anymore. You two promised to keep those people out of Delia's room and I caught one of them sleeping on the floor in there last night. Delia's sick. She needs peace and quiet. Your new friends are the opposite of peace and quiet."

Kaspar told Nina, "That was Jeduthan's cousin, Claude. He was drunk and thought it was Gibb's room. Not our fault, but bringing *him* here," he jabbed a finger at me, "is not right. Saami and I don't agree with you, Nina. And we're not the only ones."

Nina glared at him. I could see she was furious. "Keep your friends away from me and Delia, or I'll make sure nobody's happy here. And you both know what I mean."

Saami stood and grabbed her bottle of beer. "You're a bitch."

Then both she and Kaspar left.

Nina baked a couple of fresh biscuits and heated up the chicken pot pie. She told me she'd shared a bowl of chicken broth with Delia an hour ago and wasn't hungry. I had a glass of apple juice, too, and honey butter with the biscuits. Nina kept her eyes on me while I ate, a sort of wistful, inquisitive gaze I didn't quite get. In fact, she almost looked a touch feverish herself. Maybe she'd caught more than Delia's cold.

We washed the dishes when I finished, and cleaned up the kitchen together, wiping off the table and countertop, putting utensils back in the drawers where they belonged. I felt domestic beside her, comfortable and efficient, proud to be with her. An unfamiliar emotion for me. Mother and Agnes would have been flabbergasted.

We took a peek in at Delia on our way down to Nina's bedroom. Goliath was sleeping on the bed beside her and little Delia had one arm around him. A tiny nightlight glowed yellow on a child's wooden play stool across the room and a small glass of water sat on her nightstand. Nina smiled as she closed the door. "She'll be fine."

Nina had her window open to the rain damp air and a copper censer burning Soko incense by her desk. Her nightstand lamp had been lit and the bedroom was shadowy as her curtains fluttered in the window draft. Nina's own Amata perfumed scent was familiar now and when I breathed in, I remembered also how she felt to touch. Truth was, I loved her without any good and true assurance of who she was, whether angel or wraith, and my heart refused to ask. I undressed and laid beside her again. She kissed me, as she did, with conviction, and too obsessed to worry about a silly cold virus I let myself belong to her in that bed. We made love in a hurry and slid under the sheets afterward and held each other against the night and the wet draft and the rain that fell so softly I could see those slants of it through feathers of smoke from Nina's incense, yet no longer hear its hiss above the dark flowing curtain.

Nina murmured, "Delia and I have to go soon."

"Go where?" I held my breath.

"Away from here. Anywhere. Somewhere else."

"I suppose she needs a real home. Not a crucible of anarchy and revolution."

"It's true, she does. So do I."

"I haven't ever thought it safe here for either of you. These walls have a taste to them like vinegar in a fruit salad. Nothing good can come out of this house. I do agree. You should go. Soon as you can. I'll help you."

She nestled close. "Would you, really?"

"Of course. I'd love you both to be well and happy and safe."

Nina kissed me. "I love you, Julian."

I smiled. "Do you, really?"

"Yes, I do." She squeezed me tight. "Very much."

As we laid there together, I listened to guitars from the living room and a slight girl named Cliona singing that tune, "Apéritif," all our radio sets played this spring across the metropolis. *"May every kiss lead my heart to you."* She sounded lovely. Meanwhile, I heard the front door open and close probably a dozen times in half an hour, the house filling up with those people I realized Nina didn't know, or approve of, nor care much about either way. Whenever the music stopped, strident voices echoed in the walls. Argumentative voices, excited voices, laughter, too. Then more songs of all tempers.

Nina fell asleep briefly, and I felt myself beginning to drowse next to her. Lately, I noticed how I slept more comfortably with her than I did alone at Thayer Hall. A revelation, really, because I was so accommodated to my solitudes, it seemed unthinkable I could enjoy or even tolerate someone occupying half my space in bed. In fact, I had come to detest sleeping alone now. Another lesson: Love's little intrusions make us whole when we had no idea we were not. How could I know that was to be the last night I'd lie in her bed?

Maybe another hour or so passed when I was startled by a loud, angry confrontation at the front door. Nina woke, wonder on her face. We both got up. She put on a jade floral sarong and I pulled on my trousers. We went out into the hall and saw a crowd gathered at the entryway where that fellow with the flat cap I'd seen on my first visit to Gosney stood on the threshold with another taller man, both looking stern. All the boys and girls were screaming at them so wildly I couldn't differentiate one word from another, just a cacophony of craziness.

Nina and I walked up the hall to join the insanity. Kaspar stood at the head of his crowd, a half-eaten apple in his hand, Saami just off his shoulder with another bottle of spice beer.

Kaspar was yelling, "Get out! Get out! Get out!"

Saami shrieked, "We told you leave! So go!"

Flat Cap stood still, a smirk on his scruffy face. He wore a rain-wet brown jacket and work trousers. His companion had on a long black weather coat, and no hat. He was bald and damp.

Another one of the boys called out from behind Kaspar, "We told you he's not here! Are you deaf? He hasn't been here in a month!"

The pretty girl in a turquoise blouse beside him added, "Why don't you believe us? We're not liars!"

Kaspar told them, "You can't be here if we tell you to go, so get out! Now! Go!"

Nina took my hand. I looked at her and saw she was still half-asleep.

Flat Cap spoke without raising his voice much. "You kids don't seem to get it, do you? We know young Draxler hides here, or somewhere around the Catalan with one of you. Tell us where we can find him tonight. No games. We're not leaving until you do. Got that?" He smiled. "Now, kiddies, do what you're told."

Kaspar laughed at him. "I don't see a crown on your head, you little freak, so why don't you just piss off! We're not telling you shit!"

Kaspar threw the chewed-up apple at Flat Cap, bouncing it off his chest.

Then Flat Cap drew a black revolver from his jacket pocket and shot Kaspar in the face.

The girls screamed, and that bohemian crowd of would-be anarchists fell back. Kaspar collapsed where he'd stood. Saami dove on top of him. Blood seemed to be sprayed everywhere.

Flat Cap held the revolver out at arm's length. "All right," he said, "you kids want to play games, we'll play games. Do you like this one? I do. Stop being stupid."

Then he and his tall associate backed out onto the stoop and went off down the steps to Gosney Street.

Nina and I heard Delia crying down at the end of the hall.

Hurrying almost blindly, we dressed and collected needful items and packed them up in Nina and Delia's old canvas suitcase, then put a short leash on Goliath and headed for the back door off the kitchen. Nina had a friend named Hannah with a spare room in her attic on Trask Street, about ten blocks east of Gosney. I telephoned for a taxi that would meet us by the fish market after we crossed out of this neighborhood through a narrow alleyway. Those bohemians who hadn't already fled, crowded the kitchen door to the backyard, some cursing, some weeping. Saami refused to accept that Kaspar was dead and laid on top of him, brushing her fingers through his hair. The girl in the turquoise blouse sat next to her in a pool of blood, crying and crying.

I heard sirens shrieking in the distance, drawing steadily nearer. One was a city ambulance, and the others were police. I didn't see what good the ambulance would do, but maybe they'd carry the body to the morgue for an autopsy. That was the law. All the dead were tested for spyreosis.

Nina shoved a path out the backdoor, Delia holding on to Nina with one hand, Goliath's leash in her other. Someone pushed me from behind and I stumbled out onto the short porch. The panicked bohemian kids were scattering now into the dark of the yard, climbing over the wooden side fence or crawling through the wire fence farther on.

"Do you have everything you need?" I asked Nina at the bottom of the stairs. "I can go back in for something if I go now. Once the police arrive, nobody's getting out."

"I think we're fine. Delia? Are you all right?"

Delia looked vaguely off into the dark. "I brought Goliath. He wanted to come with us."

"I'm glad," Nina told her. "We need him tonight."

"I know."

I asked Nina, "So, which way?"

"That gate over there on the left those idiots didn't see."

We rushed across the dark grassy yard and through the garden gate, then up along a dirt alley between Gosney Street and Thigpen. Houselights were coming on one after another as the emergency sirens approached. We met the taxi soon after and rode to Nina's friend where I watched them go indoors, then took the same cab out of the Catalan and back through the long cold night to my own empty bed.

XX

The train to Highland Park felt slow and ponderous late that Saturday afternoon. Perhaps it was my own anxiety. The quiet towns and gardens and auto byways of Schuyler Province crept past as the train rolled on and I sat at a window in the dining car watching a world go by. I felt dazed and distraught. After witnessing the murder of Kaspar and seeing Nina and Delia off to another house where there was no telephone and no possibility of sleeping in the same room with them, if that were even wise to do, I had resolved to tell my father everything. Truth was, I'd been afraid of having him see what a mess I'd entangled myself in. He'd been such a bulwark of support, I thought all of this idiocy from Gosney Street to Draxler's secrets would horrify him and confirm a betrayal of all he'd invested in me.

Freddy believed my father ought to involve his lawyer. He told me, "You can't be so foolish as to think that fellow with the revolver did not have permission to murder one of those idiots, if not last night, then tomorrow or a week from now. And he could've killed you or Nina just as easily. Or either of us any day of the week for hiding what we know about Draxler's location."

"What do we know? Not enough to get shot for."

"Oh, Julian, you are such a naïf. Just failing to share our deciphering of that first telephone code would likely be sufficient for that little fellow with the revolver to put a bullet in our heads. Theirs is not a world that trades on fairness and decency. Haven't you come to see that yet? What occurs daily in the Desolation is, I am certain, so thoroughly soaked in treachery, what happened at Nina's house last night would seem incidental and trivial. Death is not the by-product of our war with the spyreotics, it is the very purpose of it: killing for the sake of survival. The more killing, the better chances of survival."

"An ugly supposition, Freddy. I saw that boy shot to death not ten feet from where I stood and wonder how I can possibly survive the memory of it."

"We do survive, Julian. We survive the most despicable cruelties and heinous acts by our fellow human beings because we have no other choice if we choose to live in this blighted world of ours. I think the Desolation must be a mirror of who we are as a race and species, an example to the gods and universe of man in his most inventive and prolific self. We thrive and celebrate our debauchery, all the while defending what we do as both accidental and necessary. I truly believe we are insane."

My father hadn't yet gotten home from a round of golf at Cedar Wood by the hour I arrived, and Mother was down the block visiting her friend, Dorothea, from the Goodfellow's Society, so I just went up to my bedroom and laid down. I stared at all the important artifacts of my youth on the walls and cluttered shelves and old walnut bookcase. I guess if I were a Philistine regarding childhood, I'd have tossed most of that into a garbage heap for spring cleaning, disposing of my many glad memories as kitschy memorabilia like so many of us eventually do. Yet, somehow, I recognized that who I am at any given moment has derived from who I once was. Inescapably. I felt comfortable in my old bedroom, not one bit estranged from that silly Julian who rode his scooter down Houghton Avenue and climbed the Parkers' apple tree to spy on Eleanor Jacobs in her underwear at Lola Coué's slumber party. We should remember those days of our lives because night comes soon enough.

Mother cooked a rib roast and squash and baked potatoes for dinner, and Father invited me to help set the table with him. He laid out the linen cloth and napkins and I fetched three sets of silverware and dinner china. As we proceeded together, he told me, "There are certain traditions, Julian, that, observed with honest regularity, are likely to keep your lovely mother willing to feed us year after year for the most paltry wage imaginable."

"Does she recognize this, or are we attempting to pull one over on her?"

"Oh, your mother sees everything as if she were a fortune teller. Nothing escapes her studious eye. Don't even imagine you can fool her. Can't be done."

We ate and talked about neighbors and my classes and Agnes and weather patterns over the metropolis. Mother saw storms arriving. Father did not dispute her opinion. I had nothing to offer. Weather was never a big worry with me. Once we finished the Flemish pudding for dessert, my father and I cleared the table as my mother did the dishes and put everything in its proper place. Then Father and I went to his study and had a long conversation.

I began by apologizing for failing to tell him that I had known something about Peter Draxler, not much, but that I had heard his name at the house on Gosney Street. From there, I introduced Nina into our dialogue and her idiotic bohemian revolutionaries. That's where we went, Father and I, wandering off into the wilderness of my transgressions against common sense. He forgave me, as he often did. Then he telephoned to Jack McManus, his attorney for personal affairs.

"He'll be here within the hour. I caught him in the middle of dinner at Herote's. Does Dr. Barron have good legal counsel that you know of?"

"No idea. Don't all doctors?"

My father smiled. "Only the wise and the quacks."

While we waited for the attorney to arrive, I went to use the bathroom just across the hall from my father's office. With all the upset from Gosney, I hadn't thought much about what clothes to wear to dinner. I did change shirts from last night but wore the same trousers. In any case, they felt clean enough. Somehow, I hadn't noticed in taking them off, or putting them on again, a slip of paper in one of the back pockets. I did just then, in the bathroom. And took it out and saw a note scribbled in pencil that read simply:

where goliath hid

I stared at the slip of paper. Of course, initially I wondered what it meant and how it had gotten into my pocket. I only knew two Goliaths: little David's slingshot victim, and Delia's pet. Since the Holy Book had no reference to the Philistine giant hiding anywhere, I assumed the note was about the silly dog. Hidden where? In Delia's room at Gosney Street? Under her bed? In a closet? Down in that basement with the laundry? Where? And who snuck it into my pocket? And when? Well, unless somebody had crept into Nina's room while she and I were lying in bed in the dark, I had to presume it happened in the flurry of departure from the house. So, who? Impossible to know just yet.

Remembering my father was still in his study waiting on Jack McManus, I put the paper back into my pocket, washed and dried my hands, and went back across the hall. What I had not yet told my father was the entire mystery of Peter Draxler and *The Aeneid*, that hunt with which Freddy and I were still occupied. I was afraid of involving him further than I already had. What if Flat Cap knew I had information regarding Draxler and suspected I'd divulged any or all of it to my father? Would he bring that black revolver into this house? Would he kill my parents to track down those stolen drawings? Seeing how cavalierly he'd shot Kaspar, I had no doubt.

"Julian." Father poured himself a nip of brandy and sat back in his leather desk chair.

"Yes."

"Those people at the place where that boy was killed, do you consider them friends, or acquaintances of yours?"

"Neither," I replied. "They're certainly not friends, by any means, and I don't know any of them beyond seeing them at the house. Most of their names I never even heard. They're all pretty anonymous to me. Even Nina told me she couldn't keep track of them all. That was one of her issues with the house these days: Who was supposed to be there, and who wasn't. I'm not sure they had any firm rules there at the last. Or it certainly didn't seem so to me."

"Jack will want to hear all of this, you realize. If he needs to protect you, there are three sides to this fence, a logical contradiction, of course, but present here, in fact."

"I understand that."

"We'll need to be very careful now. Circumstances today at Prospect Square are breezier than I can remember in years. The Judicial Council has been meeting almost daily and no one seems to have a grasp on any consistent point of view. Well, I'm sure Jack will have something to say about that. He's got his own ear to the wall. We'll listen to his opinion, but we'll also do what seems good and best for you, Julian. Family can't unravel over somebody else's tumble."

"Thanks, Father."

"You just be honest and truthful," he told me, "yet firm. That'll put you in a strong position with any of those fellows, regardless of who they think they are."

"I'll try."

Jack McManus drove up half an hour later, the lights of his silver Henrouille sedan illuminating the hedges of our driveway on his approach from the street. Father got up from his desk and went to greet him at the front door. I heard Mother walking there from the kitchen. She and Jack had known each other at Templar

College on Sparrow Hill as undergraduates where my mother introduced Jack McManus to his future wife, Peggy Visaggi, one of the sisters in her sorority house. As she told it, Mother sent them out on a canoe ride at Papaouthah Pond one lovely autumn evening, which began a story that eventually led Jack here tonight.

Unsure how exactly Father had prepared him, I was too nervous to greet Jack at the door. I found him imposing and all too often overbearing when he'd somehow forget we weren't in a courtroom. I heard my parents welcoming him into the house and my stomach tightened. My palms were sweating. Maybe I was on trial, after all. Now my mother was chatting and laughing. So was Jack. Had one of them told an old joke from college days, that Templar humor? Good grief, this was awful. Then, Jack and my father came down the hall, and I did prepare to give my testimony.

I sat on the couch, Jack McManus across from me in one of our leather armchairs. My father took a seat behind his office desk again, so that I would not feel ganged up on.

Jack began by asking, "Julian, how long have you known Nina, and where did you meet?"

"A couple of weeks. She came by Thayer Hall to hand out a poster regarding her missing dog. I agreed to attach it to one of our bulletin boards. Then she left."

"And when did you see her again?"

"Later that afternoon. She invited me to come see her, and when I agreed, she asked if I might pick up her little sister, Delia, and bring her home on my way over. So I did. I found her at the Ronsard Metro stop looking for her little dog, Goliath. After I helped her find him, we rode back to Nina's house at Gosney Street in the Rosenstern Quarter of East Catalan."

"That's a rough neighborhood."

"Yes, it is."

"And that's where you saw Nina again?"

"Yes, for an hour or so. We just talked in her room until that fellow who shot Kaspar came to the house, asking for information regarding Peter Draxler."

"Did he see you there?"

"I'm not sure. A group of them were gathered at the front door and I was farther back down the hallway. So, I doubt it, but who knows? He had a lot of them shouting in his face. He probably didn't notice me at all."

"And you've been back to that house how often?"

"Three or four times, I suppose."

"Overnight?"

I looked at my father. He shrugged. I told Jack, "Twice, not counting two nights ago with the shooting. We left. Nina, Delia and I. So did a lot of them."

"Her friends?"

"I'm not sure I'd call them her friends. Most of them just came and went, but about five or six of those people shared the house with her."

"How old were they? Roughly?"

"Late teens to early twenties. Kids, mostly. My age or younger. Seemed young, though several of those who just passed through for meetings were Nina's age."

"How old is she?"

"Actually, I've never asked. Funny, but it hasn't seemed important."

"Have a guess."

"Mid-to-late twenties? She's pretty mature, I'd have to say, more so than I am."

Both Jack and my father smiled. Jack said, "Oh, I'd say you're doing quite well for yourself, Julian. Don't worry about hurrying it along. We get old quickly enough, right, Charlie?"

Father laughed. "Got to slow down that aging train. I feel it in my bones every time I get in and out of my auto."

Jack leaned forward. "What are Nina's politics?"

"Do you mean, does she believe in the war, or that stupid incessant eugenical testing?"

"Is she a radical? Does she think our Republic is decadent and ought to be overthrown? Does she —"

Father interrupted, "Jack."

"Let me finish, Charlie," McManus stopped him. "It's important for us to understand how she thinks, how all those kids are seeing our current situation."

I said, "I don't imagine there's any clear consensus, any more than there is at the Judicial Council. Who really accepts the opinion of the Status Imperium today on the moral necessity of the Desolation? Anyone?"

Jack told me, "There are sides to be taken in any conflict, Julian. Determining right from wrong is finally a matter of opinion, but we need to choose. It's how society persists. We can't be anarchists and still hope to sell daily groceries at the market."

"We can't buy any potatoes at all if we're dead."

"Well, it's never that simple."

"Of course, it is! A lie is a lie, and equivocating won't turn it inside out. Do we actually believe spyreosis is a mortal threat to our eugenical well-being? Does spyreosis even exist? Some of us have very serious doubts. We think it's nothing more than a crude and worn-out cudgel used to divide us or gain political and social advantage over the helpless and unattended. We've been lied to for decades, and millions of innocent people are dead because of that lie, and we won't stand for it much longer."

Jack stood, his face beet-red. "You and your friends are all idiots, Julian. Rabble-rousers. You don't do a goddamned thing but fuss like babies and talk about tearing things down you had no part in building. You throw fits, is what you do, like spoiled brats —"

"JACK!" Father stood, too.

McManus ignored him. Leaning over me now, he yelled, "What do you people contribute? Nothing! Not a goddamned thing, Julian, and you know it, too. That's why your little gang of revolutionaries yells so loudly. That's why you're out there chasing around in the streets, bursting fire hydrants and screaming at the top of your lungs so nobody can get a word in edgeways. You're all pathetic, every blasted one of you!"

I was stunned, and also embarrassed for both Jack and my father. My mother was there at the doorway, distinctly unhappy. She waited a few moments, then spoke up to say, "Jack, I believe we listen better with our ears than our mouths."

McManus looked over at her. She had her arms folded under her breasts like she always did with Agnes and me to let us know she was fed up with our behavior. Jack sat back down in the armchair.

Father came around from his desk and slid in beside me on the couch. He put a hand on my knee, gave it a pat. He said, "Julian, I think we had best stick to what happened the other night with that fellow who shot Nina's housemate." He looked at McManus. "Do you agree, Jack? For clarity's sake this evening?"

Jack nodded, perhaps feeling contrite with my mother glaring at him from the doorway. She remained there on the threshold as Jack asked me if I'd recognize Flat Cap were I to see a photograph of him.

"Yes, I would," I told him. "Why? Do you know who he is?"

"No, not specifically, but I have flies on the wall at Internal Security and if he's one of theirs, I'll be able to find out."

"What can we do to keep Julian out of this?" Father asked him. "That's really why we invited you here tonight. He can't be looking over his shoulder, nor can he be held at all responsible for what's gone on in that house these past few weeks. Julian met a girl and began seeing her like any young man. There's no law against falling in love that I'm aware of."

Stepping forward into the office, Mother added, "Regardless of politics, Jack, we do let our hearts lead us off the garden path every so often, and we know Julian didn't give his away because of Nina's opinions on our societal demerits." She smiled at me. "Isn't that right, darling?"

I said, "She's very beautiful and brilliant and difficult, too. I can't say I've agreed with every position Nina's taken with regards to eugenical persuasions or the cost of tariffs on river traffic, but neither would have I abandoned her and Delia for behaving contrary to the suicidal aims of our illustrious Republic. It's simpler than all that. I love her. I don't know what else to say."

Jack spoke more reasonably now. "Julian, I apologize for losing my head. You have a right to your opinion, and I ought to be able to respect it."

"Thank you."

"Tell me this, though, if you can. It's important. Do you believe that fellow noticed you at Nina's house the night he shot that boy? Would he remember you being there?"

"I doubt it. Like that last time, I was back in the hall and he was pretty well occupied with everyone there at the house screaming in his face. He did have someone else with him, a tall bald fellow who didn't say a word. Maybe that one was committing all of us to memory for a later visit, but I don't know. That's my best answer, I suppose. I'm not sure."

"Well, at any rate, in my opinion you shouldn't go back there. I don't believe it's wise or safe, anymore."

Father agreed. "Yes, Julian, you need to stay away from the East Catalan now. Meet Nina somewhere else."

Jack added, "And try not to be seen with anyone but Nina, either. If she's your girlfriend, then sitting in a café together is perfectly understandable. Associating with anyone else from that crowd would be dangerous these days. We don't want your relationship with those people to be misconstrued. And Internal Security won't require much to do so."

"All right."

Jack McManus got up and wandered over to the office window, where he gazed out onto the driveway, something clearly on his mind. Finally, he turned to me and asked, "Julian?"

"Yes?"

"What's Nina's relationship with Peter Draxler?"

I'd been expecting that question. If this scenario in Father's office were written in one of those mystery novels my mother so adored, my presence here would be a feint to distract from the real object of interest which were those drawings Peter Draxler apparently borrowed illicitly.

I told Jack, "According to her, not much. She told me they met at some art gallery down on Stegger Plaza, then went back to her house and got drunk on a bottle of Teucrit. He spent the night and left the next morning. She didn't see him again until a few weeks ago, she said, when one evening he showed up with a friend of the boy who got shot. Tired of talking politics and war, Nina just went to bed and hasn't seen or heard from him since."

Jack asked me, "Do you believe her? That she's had no contact with Draxler or knowledge of where he is?"

"Yes, I suppose so, because whenever I mention his name, she cuts me off and says she doesn't want to hear anything about him."

"And you?"

"What about me?"

"How much do you know about him?"

Here's the big lie I knew I had to tell, because Freddy and I were simply too far along to put my parents in danger by letting on that Draxler was leading us to him and we were getting close now.

I said to Jack, "Only what she told me, and what Father said about those drawings the Protectorate believe he stole from Leandro Porteus. That's it."

"And you haven't overheard anyone at the house mentioning him or his whereabouts?"

"No, nothing. Did Father tell you about those fellows Nina said have been dropping by the house at all times of day?"

"He said something about that, yes. Why?"

"Well, that's all I'd ever hear about Peter Draxler, that people from Internal Security are searching for him. But nobody's ever said one word as to where he's been. It was sort of a mystery around the house. The girls seemed thrilled by it. I think some of them have a crush on him. But I wouldn't even know what he looks like."

"You're certain of that?"

I shrugged. "Who can be certain of anything?"

XXI
∾

Frederick Morley Barron was no coward. In fact, he was probably braver than I was back then. He had a true zeal for adventure. Why else would he have waded into the cold surf that night at St. Etienne Shores when he could hardly swim? Yet Freddy also had a pathological claustrophobia. He admitted this to me after I returned from Highland Park with that slip of paper in my pocket.

Sitting on his bed with a box of ginger crackers open in his lap, Freddy told me, "When I was ten, my sisters wanted to play a game of Egyptian mummy and persuaded me to climb into a toy chest which they would close up like a sarcophagus from Karnak. Being a good big brother, I obliged and crawled inside and let them shut me in. Unfortunately, I'd badly misjudged their intentions and quickly found myself trapped. They'd used one of Father's ropes to tie the chest tight, then walked off and left me there. I had enough air to breathe, but I could barely move my arms or legs. I yelled and yelled and both sisters ignored me, intending to let me suffer in that chest overnight. I got so scared I peed all over myself. Fortunately, Mother came in after bedtime to close their window and heard my sobs and let me out. Both sisters got enthusiastic spankings from Mother, but I was left traumatized by closed spaces for years. So you understand why I can't join your expedition, right?"

"Of course. I wouldn't expect it."

The expedition to which Freddy was referring was indicated by that scribbled note whose meaning we were both sure of now.

where goliath hid

That ugly drainpipe on Zoffany Creek. My great dog-rescue. Freddy and I were positive it was a clue from Draxler telling us where to enter the undercity. However, with Freddy's claustrophobia being so debilitating, I'd be going on my own. He had no desire to get wedged into a slim passage and die soaked in sewage. I had no dispute with that. Still, one of us had to go and I elected myself.

Interpreting that note had been more difficult. First, who'd written it? Assuming the paper had been slipped into my back trouser pocket at Nina's, probably during our panicked evacuation, Freddy expected me to draw up a list of everyone in the house that evening. That was too big a challenge, I explained, because some of them I only noticed at a glance, others I didn't see until they were vaulting over the dooryard fence. Then Freddy had another idea, a more persuasive one.

"Whoever wrote the note, Julian, had to have known about your rescue of that dog from the drainpipe, right? So it's not likely to have been someone just passing through for the meeting that night. Fresh revolutionary anarchists are out, then. Your secret Santa had to be intimate with the relationships between housemates, including you, being Nina's new paramour. Also, given that your rescue mission happened a while ago, I think he or she had to have been there long enough to be familiar with that dog story, don't you think?"

"Unless this person just heard about Goliath getting into the drainpipe, maybe from Delia, and more recently. Isn't that just as likely?"

Freddy nodded. "It's a consideration, I agree. But in any case, just eliminating those bohemians who haven't really ever lived at the house reduces the possibilities."

"Something else just occurred to me."

"That whomever gave you the note is a confederate of Draxler?"

"Freddy, my friend, you have telepathic abilities that you aren't using to their fullest effect in daily life."

I stared out the window overlooking Trimble Street alit by streetlamps. So calm and lovely. The world of Regency College was a brief idyll, a calm before the torrent of adulthood that cares little what grades we earn or collegiate honors we achieve. Our potential is won or lost in those chilly moments after graduation, not before. As I'd boarded the train to Thayer Hall my freshman autumn, Mother had offered one of her cherished Sparrow Hill sentiments: *"Today is the tomorrow you dreamt of yesterday. These days are yours, Julian, my dear. Make them worthy."*

I did very much want to be worthy of the confidence my father and mother had in me, and all they had sacrificed to see me off. How to do so? Make better grades? Improve my general deportment? Fall in love and raise children?

Become a good and honorable citizen of the Republic? We've discussed that. There was no faithful recipe any longer to goodness in our time. If character is itself the defining model, then how we behave in each scenario of our lives reveals our value to ourselves and those around us. We should never be so vain or ambitious to ignore that truth. These moments are brief and offer little chance for revision or redemption. Make them count.

That was late Saturday night. Freddy and I decided I should go to the drainpipe the next morning, early Sunday afternoon at the latest. My hope was that I'd be able to go into the undercity and be out by dark so that I could locate Peter Draxler, or at least solve his mystery, and get back to Thayer Hall by the start of classes on Monday. That did not seem unreasonable to Freddy.

"Look, Julian," he offered, "that's maybe eight to ten hours underground, an eternity for most of us claustrophobics, but plenty of time for you to navigate any number of dark twisties. Besides, I'm sure Draxler has left bread crumbs to follow. How else could he expect you to succeed? Wasn't that telephone code and the mock address plaque fairly simple?"

"In hindsight, yes," I agreed, "but the geography down there is much more daunting. Look, I'm more than ready to take the dive. I am just very curious what's expected of me once I enter the drainpipe. It's probably dark as sin and filthy like you can't imagine."

"Oh, I can imagine, all right. Be sure not to wear your best suit."

"I don't have a best suit."

"Better yet."

I went to bed that night fixed emotionally to crawling through muddy spider-holes and ancient bone-strewn tunnels haunted by spectres of the scurrilous, the enigmatic, the detached and diseased. Would I be welcomed, dismissed, or consumed? I had no premonitions in my dreams that night, and when I awoke, only a distinct sense of unease had settled over me.

Freddy had left while I was still asleep Sunday morning and hadn't returned when I'd finished my morning shower, so I went to enjoy a late breakfast of pancakes and eggs in the commons by myself. Somehow, the idle chatter irritated me and I ate quickly, then went outdoors to enjoy a good long walk. I still had studies to do, but if I intended to pursue the undercity today, I'd have to forego all of that until I surfaced again. Or maybe I'd try to get some work done before I left. That seemed to be a more responsible plan. After taking a shorter loop in the warm sunlight around Thayer Hall, I went back indoors and up to my room where I dug out study notes for Contemporary Social Philosophy and thought about exploring a short paper on the connection between eugenical education and free thought, almost a contradiction in terms these days.

This was what I'd been organizing on my desk at noon when a very large bomb exploded near the heart of the metropolis.

Four miles removed from Regency College and we still felt the blast concussion.

It rattled windows up and down Thayer Hall and produced a terrific echo across campus.

Some thought we'd just experienced a small earthquake. A bomb of that magnitude was unthinkable.

Then smoke drifted high onto our grand metropolitan skyline and the source of that immense rumble was plain to see.

I quickly joined a crowd hurrying down the stairs to the front doors where students and administrators still on campus, emptied out onto the lawns and sidewalks to watch that huge plume of black smoke rise over the city center. Where exactly had the bomb detonated? Right then no one had any idea. Some of us guessed Prospect Square or Cathedral Plaza. That general location was what we deduced given the cloud of smoke's proximity to the great Dome of Eternity visible to the east. A faint shrill of sirens traveled on the air across the city.

I saw Freddy coming up the sidewalk from Trimble Street. He was carrying a small paper sack of groceries, probably bourbon and bonbons, and looked almost indifferent to the crowds and frenzy outdoors of Thayer Hall. I ran down the lawn to meet him. He spoke up before I did.

"It was the Ferdinand Club. I just heard on a radio set. Noon lunch for the high mucky-mucks in their private dining salon. Probably a fuel bomb. You can tell by the color of the smoke. Low grade petroleum. They think everyone's dead. Body parts on the rooftops next door and in Church Street along with half the building."

I watched the smoke drift out now across that central quarter of the metropolis, blooming on the breeze. Some students were crying. Some had that far-off expression of puzzlement and incredulity. Others still wore slight smiles. Once aware of the bomb's target, not so hard to be partisan in this age.

I told Freddy, "I need to see Nina."

"How do you plan to do that? Your father and that lawyer told you not to go to the Catalan, right?"

"I know, but I can't telephone because I don't know the number where she's staying."

Freddy gazed off toward the soaring black plume. The high lawns out front of Thayer Hall were crowded with hundreds now, coming up from Trimble for a better look. We began hearing rumors of who might have been at the Ferdinand Club for lunch. Regis Grappa, Secretary of Institutional Medicine? Fontana Watson, Protectorate Director of Education? Parapine Zygmunt, General Prosecutor for the Judicial Council? Oleg Mulberry, President of the Biological Investigations Commission. Who else? Many more names, many influential members of the Ferdinand Club. And Sunday lunches were heard to be well-attended.

"Political assassination?" Freddy wondered. "Does that seem reasonable? People with that much influence are never popular with anyone except their own crowd. They huddle together in those paneled rooms of theirs and agree with whatever the other says. Who doesn't hate them?"

"On the other hand, Freddy, they're also bureaucrats, which means none of them are indispensable. Kill one and another is appointed to take his spot."

"Like roaches."

"If you like."

"I don't."

"Well, nobody does, but our grand Republic is overrun by them, our very lives legislated and dictated by those preposterous decisions they arrive at, mostly suiting their own best interests. One day that'll change, but it won't be tomorrow. Something will need to happen, something completely unexpected."

"Like a bomb in the salad bowl?"

I tried not to laugh. There were too many close by to make light of all this. "Let's go back to the room. We can talk there. I need to figure out how to reach Nina."

"I assume you're not taking that trip this afternoon, correct?"

"On the contrary," I replied. "This inspires me even more. I'll go soon as I can. Maybe an hour."

Upstairs, Freddy helped me sort out a rucksack with needful supplies including an electric torchlight with spare batteries, a box of lucifer matches, two water canteens, a small rope, dry socks, another shirt and sweater, a hat, leather gloves and a pair of boots. We'd kept all this and more in his closet for a camping trip to the Billancourt Forest planned for the winter and postponed when Freddy took a bad flu. Now we seemed almost prescient in our readiness for adventure.

"You'll need to eat," Freddy reminded, "because rats and roaches won't suit your daily diet."

"I've already thought of that. I'll go down to the commons and have them fix me a couple of sandwiches."

"Good idea. Let's go now. I didn't eat much breakfast."

The kitchen was empty except for our favorite cook, Sofia Cárdenal, who had taken to us like a den mother when Freddy and I were freshmen. She'd kept us afloat nutritionally, despite Freddy's alcoholic escapades, and we trusted her implicitly. So when she advised me to accept a serving of baked lasagna with a wooden fork in a small tin, I couldn't refuse. She told me, *"You cannot do without meat and cheese and flour, Mr. Julian. You'll fall on your head. Believe me, it will happen."*

She also prepared a couple sandwiches of Séverine cheese with roast beef and sent us both off with a kiss and a hug. We felt adored.

Back upstairs, I found a note waiting on our door with a telephone number and a message to call Nina. Dropping the food off with Freddy, I rushed back downstairs to the telephone banks and summoned the operator.

"Station 14, how may I help you?"

I was afraid the bomb had disrupted the exchange. Apparently not.

"Could I have MERton-2613, please?"

"Thank you."

The hour was coming up on one o'clock now and I knew I had to get to Zoffany Creek soon. I had no desire to be underground after nighttfall, but that probably made no difference, right? Dark is dark.

"Connecting."

"Hello?" A woman's voice, but not Nina.

"Yes, hello. This is Julian Brehm looking for Nina Rinaldi. I have a note from her asking me to telephone this number."

"Just a moment."

I heard conversation in the background, then footsteps running toward the telephone.

Nina came on, almost breathless. *"Julian, my God! Did you hear the bomb? We thought it was the end of world! Delia went completely to pieces."*

"Are you all right over there?"

"I think so. Delia's in our bedroom hiding under the covers with Goliath. I'll probably wake up with fleas tomorrow. She's become so unreasonable these days, I haven't the vaguest idea how to handle her. And now this! But we're both alive. I suppose that's not the case for those people at the Ferdinand Club. We just heard they're all dead. Can you believe it?"

"No, it's a shock."

"Let's not talk about it on the telephone. We can't be sure who's listening in these days. I don't trust a soul in this world, anymore, except for you, Julian. You're my angel. I love you."

"I love you, too, Nina. Will you and Delia be staying there for a while now? I had no idea how to reach you until I got that note."

"What note?"

"The one you just sent asking me to call."

"Julian, hang up the telephone right now. I'll get by to see you. Maybe tomorrow or the day after. Don't try to come here. Good-bye."

Then she clicked off and was gone.

Back upstairs, Freddy had me all packed up. As we ate our sandwiches, I told him about the telephone call. He looked horrified. He said, "She thinks someone's spying on her, listening to her calls, maybe sneaking up on her and Delia by her friend's house. Sounds like it spooked her. I'd be spooked, too. This is dangerous business, Julian. I hope you appreciate that. We're not safe like we used to be. Things are changing. I feel the world going dark on us, and I don't like it."

Peeking out the window, I saw the crowds out in front of Thayer Hall had grown even larger. That cloud of smoke from the bomb had swollen to a black haze over most of the central metropolis now. I sat down at my desk.

I asked Freddy, "Were we ever safe?"

XXII

I took my rucksack and left for Zoffany Creek, choosing a seat on the city bus that crossed the eternal river toward the Ronsard Metro stop where I'd first met little Delia. My plan was to go off into the woods and follow that same trail we'd chased into the damp ravine and find that ugly drainpipe.

Along the bus ride, some curious rumors flew about from my fellow passengers: *Our enemy's in the city; that bomb was just the start; they're here to kill us all. Or: The Status Imperium decided to dissolve the Judicial Council; legislative injunction wouldn't be accepted by the Protectorate; it was simpler to blow them all up and start over. Or: A rogue band of deviants from the undercity crawled out of a sewer on Church Street; they snuck that bomb into a serving cart and detonated it during the main course; their next target is probably National Cathedral.*

I found myself sympathizing with the most outlandish theories. How else could my fellow citizens cope psychologically with so dreadful an event in our midst? Hearts are ruined by disease and mayhem. We falter before tragedy and abandonment. We yearn for comfort, even in the shadow of another's suffering. Isn't life brief, after all? Not everyone can lead happy lives. Therefore, joy may just as well be ours.

That's how war endures.

The spring woods were lush and fragrant as ever, dense with thickets and vines. With birds chirping to each other in my ears, I marched along that same leafy path to the narrow brook that led under black oaks and birch, through more buttonbush, crépe weed and wild grape farther on to Zoffany Creek. I was alone in my private wilderness, a natural-world man. Or so I felt wandering through the trees and thicket to that steep bluff over the cold creek. Today there wouldn't be any climbing down a moldy old black oak into the creek basin. Instead I chose that wormy route along the high bluff farther on where Delia had found her own little path down the rain-soaked embankment to the sandy bottom. It wasn't easy to discover with the undergrowth so wild, but when I did, I was astounded at the view ahead beyond the wider creek.

From that damp perch in a copse of river willows I saw the notorious flood plain of Harrogate Bottom that had once nourished a vast settlement of vagrants, gypsies, ragpickers, outcasts and fugitives of the Great Separation, a false and indigent metropolis of tents and campfires that for grim decades had bred fever and violence. No trace remained. Today, industrial smoke rose from the grey munition factories just over the hills, and miles east of the bomb cloud, where I could hear woodsmen slugging away in the forest to the south and steam whistles from vessels far up around the bend plying deeper waters. Long before my birth, a popular governmental decree had brought forth an incendiary night of bloodletting and field-cutters, absolute and utter erad- ication, dispersing that organic nation of diminutive purpose and virtue to prisons and sanitariums and dreary backwaters, never to return. Crime and licentiousness in the surrounding towns dissipated. Agreements were signed regarding the forfeiture of citizenship for any failing to abide by the vagrancy ban, and lethal chambers for those who resisted by force of arms. A millennium passing might bring anthropologists to this site, summoned by rumors of seed and culture, but I suspect they'd depart soon enough, thoroughly dejected by the dearth of clues and discovery. Winter floods, worsened by the overflow of dams upriver, rip and gouge this ancient plain with a stunning ferocity. Season to season, only the black willows, sycamores, cottonwoods and fluid elderberry seem immutable as sandbars shift, rise and vanish, and granite escarpments are remolded by a relentless current. How on earth had those encampments of the ignorant and the damned persisted for so long in the growing shadow of the metropolis and the urgent reach of eugenical purpose? No matter because, fortunately, once erased, like any dead age, *civilitas successit barbarum*, there was no rebirth.

A quarter mile down Zoffany Creek through the wicker brush atop the mound of a soggy sandbar, I saw that cold wicked drainpipe shrouded in after- noon shade. I admit it frightened me, like the maw of some great beast. Possi- bly because today I'd be venturing much more of my young life than a simple dog retrieval from a rusty ash can. Keeping away from blackberry brush and wormthistle thorns, I removed my boots and socks and waded across, then put them back on and crept up the sandbar and along the damp embankment until I stood outside the old drainpipe. Glare from the afternoon sun rendered the interior ink-black and opaque. I'd need to step inside to let my eyes adjust, and so I did. A stink of rot and mildew swelled over me as I went farther in, ten feet, twenty feet, fifty feet. The interior was putrid and nauseating. My boots slopped about in the sludge as I went on. There was Goliath's ash can on my left, tipped over now and swamped in mud and filth. I took a handkerchief from my pocket and tied it around my mouth and nose. Peter Draxler was insane if he truly believed this route was worth pursuing. Freddy's claustrophobia was a blessing. I felt like a fool. Another hundred feet forward and I began to wear the dark like a shroud, so I wrestled that electric torchlight from my rucksack and switched it on. The tunnel was narrower than I had expected, rusted and grimy and cracked. Little to see but flotsam and garbage washed from the underground. Nothing beyond where the electric torch illuminated the darkness ahead. Had I expected some signpost to Draxler's underground lair? Or painted arrows pointing the way to safety and enlightenment? My boots leaked and my socks were wet. Splashing along soiled my damp trouser cuffs, too. I thought to yell out, if for no other purpose than to hear how far my echo would be flung. Fear of what also might echo back helped me resist that temptation. Behind me now, the entrance had receded to a mere dot of light, no longer helpful. Another two hundred yards on and I found myself yearning to see a candle in the dark, any oblique note of humanity, perhaps to let me know I wasn't losing myself down here.

Instead, I heard a voice.

And my name.

"Julian!"

A voice I vaguely recognized, echoing across this hollow chamber of city dregs and shadow. I called back, "Who's there?"

"Come forward. My lamp just quit and there's a step-off ahead of me. Keep to your left. Feel the ledge?"

I did. Still wet, but not as deep, only above the tops of my toes. I sloshed on.

"That's good. Keep coming. You're close. Don't point the light at me."

I kept one hand on the tunnel wall to guide my steps forward.

"That's right. You're almost here. Good."

And then I saw a scrawny little fellow with ratty hair in the deflected light from my electric torch. I knew him, too.

Marco.

My echo of Beatrice in this visit to Hell.

"Now, follow carefully," Marco said, putting his back to me and leading us off further into the dark. My electric torch barely lit the tunnel ahead, but I could tell he knew where to go. We walked forward along that ledge which rose just enough to be mostly out of the sludge and water. My boots were soaked already, but I was pleased not to feel them getting worse. Maybe my socks would dry out eventually. Freddy had packed an extra pair and I didn't want to ruin them just yet.

I asked Marco, "How did you know I was in the drainpipe?"

"I saw your torch."

"Yes, but how did you happen to be down here just now to see me?"

"Frederick told me you were arriving."

"Who?"

"Your roommate. Very nice fellow. Drinks too much."

I was confused here. Freddy spoke with Marco? "I'm not following this. How did you hear from him?"

"I left a note for Frederick to telephone to a number I'd given him when you were on your way to the creek, so that I'd be here to greet you in the tunnel."

"How do you know Freddy?" I asked Marco. "He didn't say anything about this."

"He never told you about us sharing a jail cell? I thought he did. He said so."

"That was you? The shoplifter?" I laughed. That wormy fellow Freddy described sounded a lot like Marco. Then again, quite a few of Nina's bohemians met that description, and what did it matter? I hadn't given it a second thought after hearing Freddy's jail woes that morning.

"Very unfortunate, too. I needed that stuff for the fireworks show today. Wasn't the end of the world. I got them elsewhere."

Marco walked us on maybe another fifty yards, then stopped next to a grate in the wall on our left. He pulled it off and set it down in the water. "All right, you go first. I'll close up behind us. It's one of our barricades."

I pointed the electric torch into the opening and saw a narrow passage just wide enough to crawl through. A tight fit. Freddy would not have survived this.

Marco urged me in. "Go ahead. It's dry."

I took off my rucksack and pushed it into the passage ahead of me, then climbed in after. The walls were rough, unfinished, carved rudely out of the limestone. I felt as if I were on sand now as I crawled forward, shoving my rucksack on ahead. My head scraped the roof of this small passage and I had my own touch of claustrophobia for a minute or so when I thought I could no longer see where I was. How long would we go like this? I heard Marco scraping along behind me and that was sort of reassuring. At least we weren't falling off into the center of the earth. The cold of the drainpipe was replaced now by heat that brought a sweat and dripped into my eyes. Had I needed to see, I would not have been able to do so. Nothing mattered but that we crawl to the end of this tunnel.

"It's just a little farther," Marco spoke up off my shoulder. "Hold your light up."

I paused just long enough to do so, and then I saw where the tunnel fell off into a larger cavern. When I got there, I tossed my rucksack over the edge and slid down to a stone floor of sorts, Marco just behind me.

"Not so bad, was it?"

I brushed sand off my jacket and trousers and stood up. "Not if I were a squirrel."

"Frederick told me he wouldn't be coming," Marco said. "It was better this way. Peter would approve. Much easier with just one of you."

"Is Draxler down here?" I was feeling weary of his game. Something just wasn't sensible in all this chasing about. Why so much funny business?

"You'll see."

"I hope so."

"I'm glad Nina chose you, Julian," Marco said, smiling. "You're a good boy."

"What do you mean by that?"

"Hold the light up so we can see better."

I raised the electric torch and waved it about to illuminate this dark chamber, whatever it was. There were four wider stone passages, not counting the small one we'd just crawled out of.

I thought of something Marco mentioned back in the tunnel. "When you said fireworks a little bit ago, did you mean that bomb in the Ferdinand Club?"

"Exciting, wasn't it? A pretty good roar."

"But what stuff were you talking about? Something you got caught shoplifting? I didn't follow what you meant."

"Only wires and plugs. Just incidentals. Small stuff. We had everything else already."

"For what?"

"The bomb, Julian. Obviously! You can't buy them assembled."

"You and your friends built the bomb that just blew up the Ferdinand Club? Why?"

Marco smiled. "They killed Kaspar in cold blood, so we gave them a good kick in the nuts. That'll make them think twice."

"Freddy and I heard that most of the building was blown up. How could you make a bomb that big and still get it into the salon?"

"Tafra grain and opis powder mixed with kerosene and a crude petroleum that burns and hastens the grain within. Stirred together carefully and cooked with a lot of patience, a chemical is born we call 'imperitium.' It magnifies heat more than a thousand-fold and gives up a blast like a visit from the sun. Today, a great big gorgeous roast turkey was on the menu for the Gentlemen's Dining Salon and we substituted imperitium for cornbread stuffing. Had it gone off late, I'm sure it would've tasted reasonably wonderful, too. Müller is an excellent chef. Believe me, they had a lunch to remember, for a few minutes at least. He sent them four magnums of Cafereus champagne and Laval oysters on the half-shell and Askour caviar for their appetizer, and we let them finish all of those before the big show."

"They'll kill all of you."

"I'm sure they'll want to, but there's a lot of us, Julian. More than they can imagine."

"Did you pay any notice as to who was in the club at the time? Did you plan it that far?"

Marco's laughter at that echoed throughout the dark chamber. "I knew my father would be there."

"Your father? Who's your father?"

"Oh, it's such a surprise to everyone. Who can ever imagine? Nobody! It's so amusing."

"Well, who is he?"

"My now late-father was the esteemed Dr. Albert Darwin Grenelle, Prime Minister of Cultural Integration on the Judicial Council. A very cruel and calculating man. I assure you his loss will be felt by no one who matters in the least. I doubt there'll even be a funeral, though maybe if they can find enough pieces of him to stitch together, there could be a viewing at Carville Hall. I hear the refreshments for wakes there are delicious."

"Marco."

"He beat my mother half to death one night and accused her, baselessly, of infidelity while he'd been satisfying himself for months with a dipsomaniac named Aya Astréa from DuClané Province. Then he tossed us both out into the street and locked all the doors. We slept in a car barn on Gollux for a month until Mother met my future stepfather who hired us a room at his house by the Hoheimer docks where he was a stevedore."

"That's the Cheikh fellow who — "

"Raped me, yes. That ugly person. Démar Korsch pretended to love her and give us a home so he could rape my mother and beat her and drown her in his bathtub, and then come into my room and rape me, too."

"Good God, Marco, that's hideous."

"Yes, it is. My mother was the kindest human being in this wretched world, and she was tortured by two monsters."

I didn't know what to say. Obscenities seem to descend on us like autumn rain. How do we manage? "Weren't the authorities involved at all? Did you attempt a complaint on either of them?"

Marco laughed, a sardonic laugh, almost theatrical. "Don't be serious, Julian. My father wouldn't hear of it, even if I did. His doorman would show their agents down to the sidewalk and that would be the end of any investigation. No cells at Drumont Prison for that crowd."

"Well, surely your stepfather wouldn't have that sort of umbrella."

"No need for him," Marco said. "He's a demon and a poppy addict. I used my mother's key one afternoon during his nap when I could smell the honey odor of wet boucle from the kitchen door and shoved Mother's best ice pick into his brain. He probably didn't feel a thing — which is too bad, really."

I felt a chill. "These things you've done, Marco."

"Yes, I'm probably mental or diseased. Is spyreosis real? If it is, maybe I have it. But I don't feel bad. Actually, pretty fine, to be truthful. I sleep well enough. I feel good today. Want to take a walk? I have friends who'd like to meet you."

Marco's story had echoed about this black chamber and I was convinced the walls had absorbed each word indelibly. So, yes, I wanted to take a walk.

And Marco led me onward, then, to the undercity, a place I hadn't conceived of, and likely never could.

XXIII

∞

Marco brought me into the undercity through a long corridor of brick and limestone lit by gas lamps. Nearer, we crossed a plank walk over a thin stream of water flowing beneath our feet from some obscure subterranean source. And then ahead, voices and light and a society not so different from that I'd known above. Freddy and I were wrong about that hell of rats and filth and sewer men inhabiting bleak, black tunnels, narrow and nasty. What I had expected to be gloomy mud and stone crawlspaces and narrow passages were, in fact, a vast tunnel network of understreets realized by banished architects demolishing miles of ancient limestone to build a reverse world inhabited by people our own great metropolis had given up on and forgotten. A web of disjointed dreams.

We emerged under a carved stone arch into a catacomb of crowded arcades lit by tinted flower lamps and Chinese lanterns, electric globes, hanging rope lights, kerosene torches, crystal candelabras; and buzzing with people in all styles of dress, drab and festive: frock coats and tailcoats and muslin skirts and cashmere shawls, woolen bonnets and leather hats, rubber trousers, worn and soiled boots, tormented collars, peasant dress, feathers and festoonery. People in skin colors of different hues and racial origins mingling with dogs and cats and pigs and goats, and the smallest horse I'd ever seen pulling a wagon in miniature filled with potatoes. The rows of arcades were draped in canvas or patchwork quilts and silk curtains, folds of velvet and lace, each offering a phantasmagorical assortment of Argand oil lamps and gum resin dolls, taffeta orchids and mechanical toys, balloons, peacock feathers, music boxes, fabric shades and wicker chairs, glazed ivory skulls, manacles and monocles, glittering trinkets, and all forms of bric-a-brac. Farther on, we walked past glass blowers, calligraphers, bookdealers, haberdashers, locksmiths, dressmakers, shoemakers, hatteries, oculists. Then, frantic street kitchens boiling onions and potatoes, frying fish and eggs and lamb, simmering nectar, steaming hot cauldrons of soup, fried potatoes and mushrooms, butter cheese wine, and puffy little women selling a delirious patchwork of honey cakes and ice cream, frosted cookies and jam tarts, butter sticks, bonbons and a league of chocolates.

"Are you hungry?" Marco asked, as we meandered through the market of vegetable carts and fruit stands surrounded by steam vapor with no obvious origin.

"Not just yet," I replied, though the aroma of cooking aroused my interest.

"There are many indulgences down here, but potatoes grown in the catacomb pits and eaten by everyone are a food of the divine."

"How do you mean?"

"Well, Julian, nothing should be able to grow underground but mushrooms, yet it does. Tomatoes and carrots and beans, too."

"But you do have mushrooms, don't you?"

Marco laughed as we dodged through a cloud of black tobacco smoke. "Yes, hundreds of sorts. Almost sprouting on our heads. And they're very good. Most of them. A few are poisonous, of course. I thought of feeding some to my stepfather, but the ice pick was easier. Maybe that was a mistake. Black Tartárean. Don't eat them. You'll be very sick and die slowly. It's disgusting to see."

"Thank you. I'll try to remember." Looking about at the variety of merchants and customers, I was curious. "So, how do people pay for what they buy at these markets and those shops we passed? Credits? Are there banks down here?"

He laughed even louder. "Yes, one or two, depending on the season, but hardly anyone has credits. Mostly we barter. Let me show you."

Marco stepped by a gathering of children chanting melodically from the Book of Song over to an old woman in a velvet cape and shawl seated on a stool beside a wooden pallet stacked tall with baked bread. I followed, trying to avoid knocking over one of the little kids. He said to her, "Hello, Sonja."

She brightened. "Marco, my dear. I see you've been scarce lately."

"No, just roughing about. I'm too popular to hide out. My public won't stand for it."

"I'm sure that's very true, Marco. You're a rare gift, indeed. What brings you to me now?"

"I'd love to engage a loaf of your magical bread."

"Of course." She intertwined her hands as if in prayer. "And to offer?"

Marco drew a small emerald bottle from his jacket and handed it to her. "It's Fina glass. I found it floating in the upper river. You see it has a cork?"

She plucked at it until the cork worked loose. "Very lovely. But this cork is older than I am. It'll need a fresh one if I hope to hide my fermented béchar which you know I love. For that I can only offer you half a loaf."

Marco shrugged. "Done."

She took a large knife and sawed one small loaf in half and gave Marco his portion. "Don't forget to share."

Marco nodded and tore off a chunk which he handed to me. "Try this. Sonja is a sorceress."

I smiled at her and ate a healthy bite and agreed. "It's quite marvelous. Thank you both."

Marco ate a piece of his own and led us off to another cold corridor marked by a seascape painted on the limestone wall and a signboard that read:

I create the world through my travels

As we wandered into the shadowy passage lit by tiny glowing green lanterns, Marco told me, "Too many of you sneak down here to go vagabonding in the dark just to escape the moral climate of above. I have to say that's not appreciated. You get a choice to be anywhere. Those who live below do not. You have to respect the difference."

I found the very idea of intrusions into this underworld to be somewhat remarkable. Particularly since I'd never heard anyone mention having done so. I wondered if it was one of those secrets we're not privy to until we are.

I asked Marco, "Where does everyone sleep? I see markets, but no beds. There must be thousands of people in the undercity. Where do they all fit?"

"Mostly in the lower catacombs. Caverns. Many, many holes in the tunnels. Some find space in the back of the arcades. Sort of all over. It's not comfortable. There aren't houses or apartments underground, if that's what you're asking. Water is scarce now and then. The sewers flood. We've experienced horrific epidemics of more diseases than you could hope to count. Cruel and impossibly virulent. People get sick and spread it. There are only a few doctors, so lots die. Thousands, actually. It's not easy here. In fact, sometimes it can be pretty awful. We just make do with what you forced on us if we don't choose to be shipped away or murdered."

"I've never had any idea this was down here at all. Freddy and I thought it was just sewers and rats."

"A filthy shadowland?"

"I wouldn't say such a thing."

"Well, it's not."

"I can see that."

We crossed out of this passage into another chamber, now with iron ladders ascending to the ceiling above with hatches and the rattling of railcars. I presumed we were beneath a metro station, precisely which one I had no idea. I also smelled hot coffee from somewhere close by, and a bitter odor of Maranthian pipe tobacco.

Enjoying his bread, Marco said, "I'm taking you to meet two dear friends of mine who'll help you understand this undercity. Our barricades and potatoes are a moral stance. We're not just street kitchens and conspirators, Julian, not just subterranean hovels of artisans and pauperism. There's a history of 'here' that belongs to your story above. Jews and Jesuits coexist in this world. Dialectical dishonesty, Peter told me, is the root of many evils in the metropolis. We don't allow it in these tunnels. Here, civic law and moral imperatives are the same. Our children are taught that from baby school. Up there," Marco pointed to the stone roof over our heads, "your alphabet is jumbled. Words have less meaning because you're told day by day how cold is hot and healthy is sick. Peter says that life above is a façade of folly and delusion."

"So, you blow it up?"

"Peter believes that sometimes violence is liberation from the status quo, and he's not a violent boy at all, by nature, but insurgency is not graceful. Peter's helped us design incendiary bombs disguised as apples and plums. If we chose to do so, we could even set earth mines in certain catacombs and exterminate most of the central metropolis. Peter says there's a crash of realism and idealism implied in that prayer recited in your cathedrals and every trench across the Desolation: 'God save us all.' One day, he told me, while your gaze above is turned by money and power, your beautiful cathedrals will tremble at our voices."

We were strolling now through a fog of curiously aromatic smoke past theatrical stages and polished tables where Hadijien fortunetellers flashed the tarot cards, and a troupe of brown-skinned Chálian midgets danced a minuet, and musicians in vibrant-hued provincial costumes performed folk melodies for pregnant women and hollow-eyed infants, and a firebreather entertained a queue of customers at a fruit peddler's cart of limes and oranges. If there were such a thing as subterranean royalty, I wondered if it might be found with entertainers who seemed so beloved here.

I asked Marco once again, "Where is Draxler?"

"Close by, Julian. Don't press the issue just yet. It's not time. We have more to show you, so you'll understand what all this means."

"I'm more than willing to do so, Marco. Believe me. I'm only wondering."

Wandering along, we passed a wine merchant and a pork butcher and a busy haircutting salon side by side with a hothouse of orchids and rare amethyst-tinted prismic flowers my mother would have gushed over, and a flourishing Tree of Life with golden leaves suspended in a tinted glass chamber among a flurry of chirping parakeets. A curiously theological offering.

"Our idols down here are not only potatoes and rainwater," Marco told me as he plucked a peacock feather from a bouquet hosted by a girl whose face was painted like a death's head and seemed oblivious to Marco. Walking away from her, he told me, "That was Fiora Piña, a notorious thief and griffo weed adept. She trades recipes for brilliant intoxications with addicts from Cordier Street. I just stole from her what she had obviously stolen from some poor sucker up above. She won't miss it. Stealing like that is considered fair down here. Life is precarious. Tomorrow might not arrive."

We left those arcades and markets just as we'd come upon them, passing once more into a dark corridor. This labyrinth of understreets was astonishing in its fluidity, because for every passage we took, I saw three or four more we hadn't chosen, yet might have. How huge was the undercity? I never knew, only that its subterranean network of byways seemed prolific and endless. Without Marco as my guide, I'd already have been lost and forgotten.

"I'm bringing you to my teachers, Castor and Pollux, who'll tell you more than you'll ever want to hear about all of this, I promise. You see, Julian, no one has lived here forever, except those two, and we can't be sure how long even they've lived underground. The farther down we go, I've been told, the more impossible it becomes to ever surface again. The absence of light is a binding factor, or so they tell us. No one really wants to find out."

That was interesting. I wondered how deep the underground went. Were the tunnels and catacombs excavated and dug out, or true primordial caverns discovered accidentally by these itinerant wanderers? How far was one willing to be lost to find a new home?

"But let me show you one more thing before we go see Castor and Pollux."

From another connecting chamber, Marco veered us off in what felt like an irregular direction, inconsistent with the painted murals that guided us along, and then on through a narrower tunnel of mud and dampness again. I had to hunch over to avoid scraping my skull on the limestone above and stumbled briefly as we knelt to keep firmly on our path. Back in the arcades and markets, noise was constant — voices, music, clattering of carts and iron, screeching babies. Here now, I heard nothing but us scuttling along, scraping and shuffling through this cold limestone passage. The air was colder still and had a curious odor, sort of musty and stale, then oddly dry.

Marco spoke as we descended slightly at a narrow bend. "Have you ever wondered where we go when we die, Julian?"

"Of course. Who hasn't? Heaven? The Elysian Fields? Or Lourdes Memorial? Maybe Larchmont Gardens for those of us who aren't war heroes."

"What of these people down here? Where do you imagine for them?"

"I wouldn't know, I suppose, because I really couldn't have conceived of anything like this. It's all a great surprise. Not just sewer men and perhaps some beggars and hideouts, you know? I guess we weren't intended to consider the undercity, except to hear the name and then forget it, like unicorns and spacemen. Rumors, and nothing more. Don't you agree?"

"Maybe." Marco put his hand up to stop me for a moment. "Be careful here. There's a slope and it's a bit steep. And don't hit your head."

"Thanks."

"I'll go first."

I watched Marco sit on his bottom and put his legs out, then shove off and down a sandy chute. He disappeared into the dark.

He called up for me. "All right. Come on."

Showing great faith in Nina's squirrely housemate, I sat as he'd done, let my legs sag forward, and took the slide downward. I did graze the back of my head as I slid, but not too heavily, and I landed at the bottom in reasonably good shape.

Now Marco fiddled with a small electric lantern I'd forgotten about until it lit, but when it did, I saw something from my childhood nightmares, something incomprehensible to those of us who pass our lives in sunlight and fresh air. The walls of this chamber and on to the adjoining catacombs were thickly packed with human skulls, an ossuary of immense proportion. Almost an infernal caricature of hell, if you like, except that here the dead were cold and still, a black hive of grey skulls.

Marco said, "We're taught that in the decade or so after the Great Separation, those who died underground were dissolved in pits of quick lime and forgotten. Like nameless troglodytes unworthy of remembrance. I've been told they believed themselves to be spineless cowards for running off down here while so many up above were shipped away to who knows where. Those were awful times. But then somehow we did choose to remember."

"Of course. A monument to hell. Thánatos on earth."

"And who could be blamed for choosing this over the trains? I don't know what I would've done. Nobody does."

"I'm sure there was enough shame to go around. Isn't there still?"

"Back then, one of those monsters, I can't recall which one, voted for establishing 'colonies of the unfit and the unwell,' and I guess they did that when they put us on those trains. But down here," Marco said, his voice quavering, "they left us with colonies of the damned, what some call, 'a cosmos of catacombs.' I prefer, 'the apocalyptic prophesy of our age.' Let me show you."

He raised his lantern high and led me off where pale grey ivory skulls were stacked so closely to one another there was hardly room for dust in between them. More awful than Doré's illustrations of Dante. Here, as we walked the long hideous corridor maybe half a mile or more surrounded ground to ceiling by skulls and fragments of human beings, I witnessed that record, the decline of flesh and bone, humanity undone and reconciled to this subterranean cavern, the unfortunate and impure catacombs of our great metropolis. There were thousands of skulls and fragments of skulls, and skeletal remains, probably hundreds of thousands, a ghastly gallery of the dead, a true monument, even, to eugenical madness and horror. Farther on, I saw more recent skeletons nailed to skulls and decorated like Christmas trees with glass baubles and dried fruit, suspended like ossified saints among antediluvian bones.

The deeper into this catacomb we walked, the more I began to suspect we were breathing dust of the dead, resurrected this hour in our lungs. As if we were inhaling the history of a race and its decline and death, its record of demolishment. Who would not believe that to be true? What would my father and mother think? Did they imagine any of this? Or had they known already and decided it wiser to keep the unhappy fact of this undercity grotesquerie from Agnes and me?

Back in the catacombs behind us, I heard handbells ringing, an insistent echo drawing closer.

"Anchorites from the lower catacombs," Marco told me. "They burn Ophian incense and sing prayers for the souls of lost pilgrims whose bones haven't yet been found. They have sheltering camps on the banks of the dark river, Potamus, that flows beneath us to the bottom of the world. Have you heard of it?"

"No."

"They say its source is rainwater from iron cells and old mine shafts, leaking out of cracked and rusty pipes in the cold earth of your metropolis, a guilty reward from God for having abandoned us. No one knows if it's true or not. Castor and Pollux once told me that to those who inhabit the lower catacombs, your moon at night is a dreaming eye, of less substance than 'dust on the wings of a moth.' Down below are rumors of transparent children composed solely of light and air, and alchemists brewing liquid fire for rise and revolt, and some mysterious presence in the ancient coal pits."

"Good grief."

"Just stories, Julian." Marco smiled. He bit off another chunk of bread. "Nothing to concern yourself."

"Thank you." I had no intention of letting any of this haunt my sleep, though I presumed it would. Once I'd seen the undercity, this breeding ground of torment and odd mythologies, my faith in the elemental firmament of earth, air, fire and water, lost structure and conviction. I hardly knew my own place in the world anymore, as if I ever had. Who was I, really?

Now the column of strange subterranean anchorites arrived in our chamber, carrying candles and ringing their brass handbells. Each wore a hooded robe the pale shade of bones they came to honor and praise. Their eyes were black and god-sunk, faces and teeth yellow like wax.

Marco told me, "We need to go."

So we did, away down the tunnel ahead past broken skulls and dried up cadavers on cold stone to a fading chant from the anchorites behind in the sooty gloom. Marco led forward with his lantern and after a while I noticed the catacomb of skulls and scattered bones finally gave over to empty limestone once again and a slushy mud from streams of trickling water. The smell was different, too, earthy once more, rich with soil, alive somehow.

Another lighted arcade appeared ahead. Shrieks of laughter. Male and female. Unbridled hilarity. And jaunty music. And someone hurrying by the tunnel entrance, a naked fellow wearing only a fluorescent green moon mask and black polished hobnail boots. What in the world?

"Mating season!" Marco laughed, leading us out of the tunnel into another kind of arcade, illuminated by floating globes, and glowing signboards advertising sex for *30 Credits or Your Worthy Exchange*, a subterranean bordello. Several, in fact, glittering arcades of flesh and worldly desires.

"Prostitution of any sexual persuasion," Marco told me, "is refined here and tasteful. Peter would tell you those erotic fantasies of our bourgeoisie are theater in the undercity where a fully constituted spirit of decadence is experienced and celebrated, unlike what you know up above in your brothels of the dissolute and despairing, that naked lust and lechery you profit from and then condemn. Your young pay a custom tax even to be nude. In National Cathedral, Mary Magdalene is named obscene in her carnal love of our Christ the Savior. How is that true? Our love markets tolerate and encourage the homosexual union of priests and moral investigators. Castor and Pollux believe that making love is a waltz of souls. They theorize a colony across the sea of nymphs and soldiers where everyone's need of sex and violence is sated. Do you think that's at all possible?"

"Honestly, Marco, I don't know what to think anymore."

This really was so baffling. What was I doing here, after all? Across from me just then, by the light of floating orbs, I watched a bearded lute musician and a half-nude girl in scarlet satin on a circular oriental rug perform a Müsyné dervish that drew a crowd of men and girls, each entwined amorously in the arms of another, not unlike some carnal thicket. Everywhere else, erotic stimulation reigned in the extravagant queues of both maddened sexes jostling to enter the perfumed love arcades. Some of the waiting women bared gorgeous breasts and some of the men strutted obscene appendages. All seemed to enjoy Cupid's felic-itous promenade. Once upon a time, I'm sure I thought love meant more than squandered virtue, yet perhaps since time immemorial this is why we're here, not that checkerboard of idiots we called society, but these irresistible human intoxications, the wolf and the swan, who we are in that most glorious moment.

Marco said, "Peter lives here, too, you know. Maybe not day to day, because every so often he escapes to the upper city to mingle with some of you to remember why you are who you are. He slept with Nina that night because he drank with her and she recognized who he was, where he'd come from, and that pleased him, even when he knew she would never sleep with him again. Because Nina loves you, Julian. Do you realize that? I admit we don't know why and can't begin to understand how she chose you to come here for her and Peter and all of us. At the house, it's been the biggest mystery. No one has ever done anything like what Nina's done with you and Delia. Are you even able to see this like we do? Maybe a little?"

Marco might just as well have been speaking one of those impenetrable dia-lects from St. Marta Province, for all I was able to comprehend of him. How he dragged Nina into this conversation confused me, to be honest, since she had never uttered one solitary syllable regarding the undercity or those who dwelled within. But scrawny little Marco just speaking her name made me miss my pretty Nina and her lovely smile, even so.

"Nina doesn't belong down here," I told Marco. "And not just for Delia's sake, either. She sees all this better than I ever could, but her life is elsewhere, away from that house, maybe even away from the metropolis. And certainly not hid-ing in tunnels underground."

"Do you really think we're hiding?" Marco stopped walking. Behind us, a gaggle of girls started screaming at each other. Then one pulled another's hair, and those two fell onto each other in a violent fit. Both vanished under the shrieking crowd of girls.

"Where's Draxler?"

"We're not hiding, Julian."

"What do people do down here besides eat, dance, and have at each other? I presume this is Eden to some of you, but Eve found her garden a little monot-onous. Why else do you imagine she plotted her freedom with the snake?"

"Monotony is not boredom," Marco said, somewhat stridently, as if I'd struck a nerve. "It's regularity. Castor and Pollux say your city of light is an imprisonment of clocks and duty."

"Like the circularity of all heavenly bodies?" I learned that from Dr. Coffeen. Well worth the early hour.

Marco scowled. "The eternal sameness of your world is an illusion. We don't suffer the satanic intoxications of greed and envy like you do, or pass our days brooding over annihilations past and future. You dream of infernos and steam shovels. We just try to live by keeping away from those brain disorders in your upper city marauders of authority."

By now, I'd tired of debating social forces. What time was it? How long had I been down here? I'd also become hungry and, having nothing to barter, I walked over to a wicker chair between arcades and sat and took Sofia Cárdenal's lasagna from the rucksack. Marco stared wordlessly at me as I ate. I wondered where he'd come from, if he had any family besides a murdered mother and the father he'd apparently just blown up, but I was too weary of him to find out. Instead, once I finished the lasagna and took a drink of water, I asked, "Where are these teachers of yours?"

He pointed down the stony corridor where the electric lamps glowed a dull amber. "Just over there. Around the corner."

"Your teachers live next to the bordellos?"

"Why not?" Marco laughed. "They told me it's where life begins. Isn't that the truth?"

"If you say so."

"Well, good. Now let's go see them."

The lamplit passage onward held a warm draft where most of the undercity apart from the arcades was a little chilly. Not deathly so, but I was glad to have my jacket, a bit muddy though it had gotten now. Following Marco along, I smelled wood smoke from a fire or cook stove ahead, and just then wondered how all these stoves and firepits, lamps and candles, vented from underground tunnels and passages. Probably sucked through drafts and or even drawn upward to unseen conduits. After all, the undercity had a hundred years to engineer some sort of accommodating survival mechanism, and neither gas nor smoke had killed them yet.

Marco led me into a round cul-de-sac illuminated by burning torchlights. There, he drew apart a woven curtain portière and urged me through to another salon, a most peculiar one, in fact. Initially, I thought I'd intruded on a private gathering of a half dozen men and women enjoying tea and biscuits at a pair of lamplit walnut side tables flanked by lush kentia palms and a record player offering Merkála's Meridian Quartet performing the Cadeña Suite in C sharp minor. All were dark-skinned and arrayed for a twilight diversion at dreamy Zanzibar and appeared pleasantly amused. I thought to excuse my entrance among them, when I realized their motions were deliberate and repetitive, and I saw that all were mechanical waxworks, a stunning illusion.

Behind me, Marco laughed, and I felt myself blush at the deception. He said, "Fooled you, didn't they?"

"They're fantastic. Where do they come from? Who made them?"

"Industry at the center of the earth, or so I've been told. Some very clever fellows down there with lots of time on their hands. When you've been exiled to oblivion, you apparently learn skills you couldn't have imagined in another life. They've created things even we can't understand. It's a sort of secret society they have. Nobody knows much about it, because no one's brave enough to go that deep underground. Not anymore. They send up inventions and amusements. We lower food into the abyss. It's been a fine arrangement."

I watched one of the waxwork automatons drink from a cup of tea and pluck a biscuit off a porcelain plate and immediately replace it as if choosing the biscuit were suddenly indelicate. The olive eyes glittered, and the figure of the waxwork fellow seemed to wink at me. Then I could have sworn I saw one of the darker women breathing, her bosom rising and falling to the music of the record player. She was beautiful and exotic, at once ancient and present in that practiced moment.

"Well, it's incredible." I turned to Marco. "They're so real."

"Maybe they are." Then he laughed again and took my arm. "Come on. We're expected."

We passed through another curtain and into the hidden boudoir beyond, where two withered and white-haired old men dressed in thread-worn oriental gowns, emerald and crimson, were seated at a mahogany table and engaged in a card game called *Amphios*. Both drinking sapphire Ulla liqueur from tulip glasses.

Without removing his attention from the cards, the one in emerald spoke up, "Hello, Julian."

The one wearing crimson followed. "Greetings!"

Marco added, "This is Castor and Pollux, my teachers."

Emerald was Castor, crimson was Pollux. Twins. Other than the hue of those gowns, they were indistinguishable from each other. Their boudoir was a spiderwork of draped fabrics and sultry furniture: a purposeful assortment of oriental rugs and magic carpets from Egypt and India, cushioned sofa and armchairs, brass lamps and painted flower vases on twin tea tables, hanging oil portraits and a cloudy blue marble fireplace. Across from Castor and Pollux was a crystal glass aquarium flooded with seashells and golden fish. And behind that, a gorgeous trompe l'oeil rendering of some faraway maritime with gulls and sea waves and boats afloat.

"If you'll excuse us just a few more moments, Julian," Castor said, "we'll complete this round of a game we've disputed all day long."

There was a small hourglass on the mahogany table and Castor turned it over as he placed a pair of Tarot cards before Pollux. I knew *Amphios*. When we were freshmen, that gamemaster Freddy taught it to me one Sunday evening. The rules to this very old game were so arcane and complex, I forgot entirely how to play only an hour after he won, so don't expect me to explain them here. It's just impossible.

A scrawny Persian cat wandered into the boudoir from under the curtains and took up residence on an armchair nearby with a distinct air of satisfaction.

Pollux smiled. "Cats keep the plague at bay."

Marco nudged me and motioned for us to go sit on a velvet sofa near the game table. Thoroughly exhausted, I was pleased to do so, feeling as if I'd been on my feet since Thayer Hall, which was mostly true. There, I noticed a lovely perfume of scented flowers that was pleasant after all the musty tunnels and smoky arcades.

Pollux shifted his pair of cards to Castor and turned the hourglass over. He murmured, without drama, "Your fate is sealed."

Castor took a sip of Ulla.

Pollux collected his cards.

I heard a brass chime ring above my head and looked up and saw atop the wall, a great ivory clock face indicating the hour. Late in the day now. Light would be scarce in the upper world. People in that metropolis would be preparing their suppers with bedtime soon after.

Studying his own cards, Castor remarked, "Our clock stands in for the sun we no longer see."

Pollux added, "We do regret that sunshine and warmth in the above world of parks and children."

Castor enjoyed another sip of Ulla and set his cards aside and nodded to his brother. "I resign the game. You are victorious again."

Pollux smiled. "More than a bitter challenge. I accept your surrender."

They gathered up the playing cards and shuffled them together and placed the Tarot deck into a Chinese box and closed it. Pollux poured more sapphire Ulla for Castor and himself, then both looked at me.

Marco said, "Julian wonders why you're in this particular catacomb."

His teachers laughed. And Pollux told me, "The devoured apple never rots. We're still harmless libertines who believe in orgies. Sadly, we're far too old to enjoy them, although we do watch every so often."

"Pollux dreams of lesbians frolicking in the font of Eden."

"Those delightful creatures with the loveliest eyes."

Castor asked, "Julian, have you ever read Freyling Villepiqué's, *Eros and the Owl*? 'The delight of sexual congress both sustains and subverts our race.' He explains how modern life is a sexual allegory of intellectual unrest and passionate dissolution. It's quite convincing."

Pollux added, "Serpents swim in those dark waters."

Castor agreed. "True enough. Amorous monsters of any species cannot be educated."

Pollux told me, "Phantom flowers bloom in that blackness whose fragrance is fatal to the infatuated."

Castor said, "Felicity is not divinity."

"But enough of us, Brother," Pollux interrupted. "I presume Julian is not here for this. He wants those thousand dazzling fires in the dark."

Castor looked me in the eye. "You're here for our story?"

I replied, "I suppose I am, yes."

Pollux said, "You wish to know how we lost those dusty roads of our past, a rural life of apple trees and clean breezes."

Castor said, "My dear brother would revisit antiquity when the earth was kind and gracious in all things."

Pollux asked, "Is it so remarkable to remember a better past? A clock ticks and the age turns over and a new race is born. Maybe a better race, maybe not. The past is a more powerful charm than that undiscovered future we imagine but cannot see. Yet it is concealed somewhere beyond our grasp where memories fail, players die, and affections either recede or bloom according to our intimate sensibilities."

"What good are emotional memories of childhoods that never were?" Castor asked, after another sip of Ulla. "That tranquil meadow of bees and violets is a daydream best dismissed."

Pollux told me, "We were schoolteachers back then."

Castor nodded. "Many subjects."

"Our definitive history of the Great Betrayal, 'Then Night Came Walking,' is something you may choose to read one day, if there are still books and there is still reading."

"Oh, we do read," I told them, somewhat nervously. "Though, examining coursework, our professors at Regency College I'm sure have their doubts."

Pollux said, "Books belong to the romantic among us. They should only be shared among willing hearts."

Marco spoke up, "I read what you tell me to read. Peter just reads faster than I do."

Castor smiled. "You're both remarkable boys."

Pollux took the sapphire bottle of Ulla and filled both their tulip glasses. Then he told me, "That past you seek, Julian, is a bleak and boundless horizon of hatred and disregard, when your metropolis celebrated a noble indifference to suffering."

Castor said, "An epoch of ethical decline."

Pollux nodded. "That constituted spirit of moral decadence."

I felt suddenly bold enough to ask, "Could you please explain that? Honestly, I'm not all that smart. You could ask my parents. I do need guidance now and then."

"Good boy," Castor replied. "Now you're learning."

"My dear Julian," Pollux started, "we begin to expire as we draw our first breath. We each share the destiny of bones. Brains may seem individual, but we are joined by air and attracted to each other like gravity among the planets."

Castor joined in. "We choose to see the freshly born devoid of petty ideas and unnatural prejudices. Therefore, both the fortunate and the cruel seem an enigma to the rest of us. An unprejudiced civilization knows this and understands the puzzle of weights upon a scale."

Pollux said, "Those accumulated truths of our decay were always evident in the hysterical clergy whose faith begins and ends in church coffers and the acolyte's fascination with a God who is blind, deaf and dumb."

Castor said, "Human passions are not tomatoes, Julian. The natural goodness and substance of human beings should not be lost as we age."

Pollux added, "That day arrived at last when the cold corridors of falsehood and persuasion described the Status Imperium, who became parasitic creatures of a lower order, exterminating angels proposing decency and virtue as a guiding principle. Pronouncing foolish theories of bugs and gas."

Castor said, "Moral and technical elevation will not easily rise together. Both must be taught in sequence to the other. Are natural flowers truly bettered by immortal satin? Wisdom must graduate progress, or what is this all for?"

Pollux told me, "We believe there are no limits to human and social perfectibility. Your metropolis did not. There was sin in your machines. The great trains came and took away almost a million of us forever, but some among our people chose to escape that bitter vengeance by the witness of blood underground."

"You fought them," I said, reflexively, as if our history hadn't been more obvious.

Castor replied, "Oh, we fought them, indeed. A phalanx of police and hunters from the Security Directorate, well-armed soldiers and assassins, descended to flush us out. Hundreds died, ours and theirs. They sent fire down to burn us alive. Then gas to choke off the air we breathe. We lost so many people. Even our children. Thousands and thousands. But we learned how to barricade ourselves within the catacombs, to survive *here* where we would die over *there*."

Pollux told me, "Then we struck back to warn them off."

Castor nodded. "Yes, we sent flames up their own coal chutes and gas pipes and set fire to their houses and businesses."

Pollux said, "We broke into their water mains and drained away the life substance from their holy city. We poisoned their livestock and salted their growing fields. We melted their electric grids."

Castor explained, "We made them suffer as we had, and many, many of them died, as well."

Pollux said, "Until they quit."

"And we agreed to quit, too."

"And they left us here alone. For good."

Castor said, "Julian, the blood of generations drips down these walls. We've survived by having no expectations but to breathe another day."

Pollux added, "Boots are worth more than gold when crossing a miasmic swamp."

Castor told me, "Though even now there are those among us who ask if we are not vomited forth into these bitter depths of our city under yours by those indigestible transactions."

Pollux said, "They believe your inorganic crowds are barely half-people, empty of heart and soul, that cold water taps must drip on your brains day and night."

Castor said, "My brother and I witness an incomprehensibility of human life both above and below the surface of the world."

Pollux said, "We see that insistent torpor of your populace where no moral greatness can exist. We struggle to endure in these dark catacombs, bereft of fellowship with sunlight. Up there, you offer no pity for laborers or poor children. We shed tears over the dubious fate of all your errand boys and flower girls above."

Castor added, "While you manage to ignore the perpetual mourning of your own soldiers in the Desolation."

Pollux said, "There is a false and fading gentility of your society above. Your metropolis is an imaginary city of gilded rust. You suffer a depravity of innocence. You fear that God arises from the sewers to torment you when it is the winds of your own history that are blowing this world into chaos."

At last, Castor told me, "This is what we see, Julian: One day your boats will sail forth across a great expanse of elastic nothingness toward a gladdening horizon that never was."

Marco led me back out to the torchlit cul-de-sac, then returned inside to have another word with his teachers. He promised me Peter Draxler, and I intended to hold him to that. I felt the hour in my legs and a foggy disposition. How had I no knowledge of this undercity before today? Propaganda from the Educational

Directorate had deceived us all. Freddy would be outraged. I really wondered what Father and Mother knew of this, if anything. And Nina? I had no doubt she'd hidden this from me. Maybe for my own protection. In her opinion. But I didn't need protecting. I needed to know the truth.

Marco came out through the curtained portière. He was eating a tea biscuit and smiling. "Peter's waiting for us."

"I hope so."

"Follow me."

Then Marco walked up to the rough limestone wall of the cul-de-sac and seemed to put his hand through the stone, which was, in fact, only a painted curtain, another deceiving trompe l'oeil, a dark illusion. He passed through and I followed behind.

Now the passage ahead was dark once again and Marco lit his small electric lantern and led us along a narrow path whose ceiling was so low, we had to duck our heads to get on along. The air here was musty and dank, almost suffocating. I had no doubt this route would have exceeded the limits of poor Freddy's claustrophobia.

"Where does this lead?" I asked Marco. "It's awfully tight."

"You'll see." He paused to look back at me. "Don't worry. It's not much farther."

Actually, it was quite a bit farther with elevation changes and twisty turns that put me on my knees more than once. And I felt a rising claustrophobia of my own as the passage narrowed considerably and the air felt thick and almost unbreathable. Had Marco used oil or kerosene rather than his electric lantern, I was certain we'd have both been choking now from black fumes. I began to feel scared. The passage was so tight I became afraid I wouldn't be able to turn around even if I needed to. The dark cocooned me and Marco's small lantern moving steadily ahead was no help. I wanted to call out for him to stop, but I was afraid that he either wouldn't or that if he did, and we sat together in this worm hole, I'd feel helpless and doomed. I felt a panic coming on. Now the passage closed over me and I had to crawl on my hands and knees to keep up. My rucksack scraped on the ceiling and my face was clouded in dust. My knees hurt. Marco was too far ahead. Was he abandoning me?

"Marco!"

"Almost there!"

"How much farther?"

"Very close now!"

"Don't leave me!"

Marco laughed. "I'm not! You're fine! Keep coming!"

"Promise?"

"I promise! Nina would kill me if I left you here!"

"I believe that!"

My rucksack caught on the stone above and I thought I was trapped. Good grief. I slid back a couple of feet and slipped it off and shoved it ahead of me and began crawling forward again. If this passage got any smaller, I'd be stuck. Then what? I crawled and crawled and crawled and, as I did, the passage tightened even more. Now I barely fit. I couldn't raise my head more than a few inches. Marco disappeared into the dark. I was alone, shoving my rucksack ahead of me, praying Marco hadn't abandoned me. I felt as if I were breathing more dust than air. Would I die here? I was terrified but kept crawling and crawling forward ... until at last I saw light again.

A little farther on, Marco had stopped and set his electric lantern down so I could see the way toward him. I felt sure I was suffocating. Marco was small like a tunnel rat. He fit better. I saw him sitting with his legs tucked up to his chest. He had a smile on his face. Maybe he looked smug.

As I crawled close, I asked, "Where are we? Where's Draxler now?"

Marco inched nearer the passage wall and pointed ahead into the black. "Down there."

"Down where?"

"Come close." Marco shrunk even further back to let me crawl up beside him as best he could. He pointed down and hung his lantern out. "Look."

All I could do was lie flat and peek forward over a descent in the passage that appeared to be almost straight down. A pit of sorts. A long drop. Maybe ten or twelve feet to the bottom.

"I don't see anything."

"Take out your torch and aim it across to the far wall."

Closer to the edge, I did notice a faint draft, cool and fresher than the passage I'd just traversed. Progress in this struggle to contain my panic. I managed to drag the electric torch from my rucksack and switch it on.

Marco told me, "There's a small iron gate, Julian. Do you see it?"

With both my torch and his lantern lit, our surroundings felt less claustro-phobic. I aimed my torch across the pit until the gate Marco directed me to was visible.

"What is it?"

"Your way out."

"Where's Draxler?"

"You'll find him on the other side."

"Does he see us?"

Marco shook his head. "He's waiting up above. There's a ladder past the gate that you have to climb and a hatch that only opens from our side. It's another of our barricades."

"So what am I supposed to do now? Climb down and open that gate?"

"Yes, but it has a combination lock. You need to go down there, use the com-bination tumblers, go through the gate, then close it behind you and spin the lock shut again."

I directed my torch over the edge and saw how steep the drop was. "Are you going first?"

Marco said, "I'm not going at all. I have to give you the combination, then leave."

"Why is that?"

"Peter's rules."

"That seems ridiculous."

"Not if he wants to stay alive."

"And how am I supposed to get down?"

"Just let yourself slide. It's not too steep."

"That's your opinion."

"You're not the first to go down there," Marco told me, "and no one's been hurt yet."

"Are you sure?"

Marco reached into his shirt pocket and took out a small fragment of paper. "I'll hand you the combination and you have to memorize it. Do you have a good memory?"

"For most things. Why?"

"Because after you see it, I'm supposed to burn the paper. I can't see the number. You'll read it and memorize it without telling me." Marco took out a lucifer match and a striking flint. "We can only do this once."

"This just feels so absurd."

"It's not."

I do admit to being frightened then. "What if I climb down there and forget the combination? What then?"

"Please don't."

"Good grief, Marco. Why are we doing this?"

"Ask Peter when you see him."

"And what about this hatch you mentioned?" I asked. "What if it won't open?"

"It will. There's only a simple latch and a drain a few feet above it that hides the hatch. You just push that aside and you're out."

"And Peter's waiting there?"

"Yes."

"How do you know?"

"He told us. This is his show and he's reliable."

"Why do you need to burn the combination?"

"So you won't forget to destroy it. Peter thinks it's safer this way."

"Seems risky."

"Possibly."

"How did you get the combination?"

"From Castor and Pollux."

"It's pretty goddamned confusing."

"Julian, you need to go now. I can't stay any longer."

"And if the combination doesn't work or the lock jams?"

"You're stuck."

"Well, I do have a rope in my rucksack."

Marco laughed. "Do you really think I'm strong enough to pull you up? Julian, I'm going to show you the number and you have to memorize it. Tell me when you're sure you know it, and I'll burn the paper and say goodbye."

"You won't stay to see if I survive the drop?"

Marco shook his head. "No, because it won't matter either way. Are you ready?"

I'd never been so scared in my young life. To die in a pit underground in the dark? Alone? I drew a very deep breath. "All right, show me the number."

Marco unfolded the paper and held his lantern up between us. I read the number written there:

3158

3158, 3158, 3158, 3158, 3158.
"All right?" Marco asked.
"Wait." *3158, 3158.*
Marco struck the lucifer match and burned the paper and let the ashes drift off.
He lowered his lantern. "Goodbye, Julian."
"You won't help me get down?"
"Slide feet first on your stomach."
Then he crawled past me off down the narrow passage. I watched until his lantern dimmed and disappeared, then turned my torchlight over the pit and dropped my rucksack in ahead of me. Good God! *3158, 3158.*

I had to twist violently to get my feet up ahead. Then I rolled over onto my stomach. I inched myself over the edge slowly, feet to knees to pelvis, keeping my elbows tight to the ground, gripping the torch. If I lost or broke it here, I'd be finished. Then I gave one firm shove and let myself drop.

I hit my chin and banged both knees as I slid, and twisted my ankle when I hit the bottom next to my rucksack. The torch fell out of my hand and went dark. *No, no, no!* I was utterly blind now. Good heavens! I could not see a thing. Frantic, I swept the dirt around me for the torch. It had to be close. On hands and knees, I searched like a madman. *Where is it, where is it, where is it?* I could scarcely breathe. Sheer terror ate me up. I scrambled about, flailing my hands across the dirt. *Where is it? Where is it? Oh God! Where is it?* I bumped the torch with my foot. That caught my breath. *Oh God! Please!* Rolling there, I put my hands on it and muttered a prayer that the light wasn't broken because I'd be good as dead. My hands shook as I located the on/off switch and flicked it with my thumb. The electric torch did not come on. I tried the switch again. Nope. Then I banged it with my fist once, twice, then again. Christ Almighty, I was doomed! Trapped in a black pit with no light to see the lock. I was terrified.

What now? Would I die of dehydration, or starve first? Good grief! My rucksack! I grabbed it and rummaged around for that box of lucifer matches Freddy had given me. I found it, took out a match, and struck it. Fire! Light! All right, I was still in the pit, but alive. I waved the burning match about and saw the gate just a few steps away. My eyes were watering as I approached the lock. Four tumblers, out of proper sequence just then, waiting for me to reset them. For a moment my mind went cold, and the combination flew off. Only a moment. Then, *3158*. Keeping the match directed at the lock, I scrolled each tumbler, left to right, 3-1-5-8. Then I held my breath and tried the lock. It didn't open. The match flame burned my fingers, and I dropped it. Good God! I lit a second match, then gave the lock another tug. Nothing. Stuck. Panicked, I jerked at the lock again and again. Still didn't open. Goddamnit! I held the flame close and stared at the numbers. 3-1-5-9. Oh God, I'd dialed it wrong. I tried again, after re-setting the "9" to "8." Almost terrified, I gave it a good tug and ... thank God in heaven, it came free. I pulled open the gate and quickly crawled through, then closed it again, and refastened the lock, spinning the tumblers. Then I lit another match.

The iron ladder Marco described was behind me. I turned and shined the torchlight on it and saw the latch up top and started toward it when I saw words, written in chalk on each of the eight steps, bottom to top. They read:

I rest at the feet of my masters.

What is that?

I read it over again, then dug around in my rucksack for a pencil I knew I'd put there. I took out one of the leather gloves Freddy and I had packed and scribbled this sentence on the palm. *I rest at the feet of my masters.* What did it mean? I was tempted to copy down the combination numbers, too, but thought better of it. Draxler had his reasons for keeping it secret, and I doubted those numbers would ever escape my memory. *3158*.

I put the glove and pencil back into my rucksack, then climbed the iron ladder to the hatch. Once there, I flipped the latch aside, and pushed the hatch up to open. It was just as easy as Marco had promised. And the drain was close above me. Shoving it aside, I hoisted myself up, and left the undercity.

— · —

This was a cold, cluttered basement. Filthy windows above me at the ground level. And, of course, no Peter Draxler. Anxious to get out, I tidied up my rucksack, put away the electric torchlight, pissed in a dark corner, and went up some old wooden stairs to the street.

I found it raining. Stepping outdoors, I breathed in the fresh cold air, a stark relief after the underground. I looked around then. All the buildings were dark. Where was I? By the eternal river? Or somewhere in the industrial east sector? I'd traveled so far through the undercity without a map, I had no sense of location or direction now. So I just began walking in a damp drizzling breeze along the wet sidewalks until I saw lights far ahead and went toward them and after another half hour or so, I found living people about with umbrellas, and eventually hailed a taxi home to Thayer Hall.

XXIV

Freddy was snoring when I crept into our room. I was too tired to wake him and give a recitation of all I'd seen and experienced underground. Instead, I quietly undressed in the dark and took a robe and a towel to the shower down the hall where I scrubbed off those suffocating hours of grime. Frantic images of the undercity raced through my head as I stood under the hot water. Was it true? Had I really been there? Dreams and nightmares are only a certain thought apart. When I slept, which would this be? Closing the shower, I toweled off and went back to the room and put on my bedshorts and eased that leather glove out of my rucksack. I took it to the window and held the palm up to the streetlights on Trimble so I could read what I'd scribbled. *I rest at the feet of my masters.* What in the world? Written in chalk on that ladder. Meant for me? Another part of this confounding mystery. I took the words to bed and let them circle in my brain with those terrifying numbers 3-1-5-8 as I fell asleep.

My roommate shook me awake half an hour before morning classes. Lovely thoughts of Nina were dispersed with Freddy's frantic rousing of me. I was not happy with him, but he was desperate to hear what had occurred underground and I knew if our places had been reversed, I'd have behaved just the same.

"Julian, you have to tell me everything!"

I could barely open my eyes. Dr. Martita Pardo, engaging as she was at nine o'clock, might not have me in Contemporary Social Philosophy today. "Good morning, Freddy."

"Was it horrible? Dangerous? Frightening? Claustrophobic?"

I nodded. "All of that." I tried sitting up. "I barely survived. You wouldn't have. Good thing you stayed away."

"I knew it." Freddy shivered. "I just had that feeling. I'm not cut out for danger. I haven't the bones for it."

Waking further, I told my faithful roommate, "Oh, there were plenty of bones down there. More than you could count. Your instincts were good. I wish I'd known. Now I'm crippled emotionally. Maybe forever."

Freddy stood back from my bed. "Good God, Julian! What happened? You absolutely must tell me everything. Start from the beginning, and don't leave anything out."

So I gave him the whole story from the drainpipe to the basement. We both missed morning class. Freddy looked intoxicated by my words. Enraptured by the sheer adventure of it all. At one point, he grabbed a pencil and a sheet of paper from his desk and began scribbling notes for discussing later on. His face paled at the ossuary and darkened with my visit to Marco's teachers. He only seemed less disturbed when I recounted the undercity bordellos and the winsome girls who flocked to the glossy arcades there. No surprise. Freddy had a first-rate imagination, particularly involving sex. I deliberately played up that chapter of my story. By the end, when I was crawling on my stomach after Marco through that harrowing passage in pitch darkness, Freddy looked apprehensive and then almost nauseated. My escape seemed to thrill him. When I finished, he asked the identical question I'd had in mind.

"But where was Peter Draxler?"

"Exactly."

"Did you search that basement?"

"He wasn't there. After I closed the hatch and replaced the drain, I had another look around. Nothing. Not even a door except the one up to the street."

"So, Marco lied to you."

"I don't know," I told Freddy. "It doesn't seem that simple. Why would he drag me through that tunnel if all it meant was a way out of the underground? I'm sure there are lots of easier exits. No, there was some reason we went that way, whether Draxler was waiting for me or not."

"The writing on the ladder."

"That's what I think."

"Another clue."

"Presumably."

Freddy looked at his notes. *"I rest at the feet of my masters."*

"Yes."

"Sounds like a riddle."

"Sort of," I agreed. "Maybe."

Freddy said, "The ladder rests at the bottom of the hatch under the drain in a basement of a city building." He looked at me. "Which building?"

"I honestly don't remember. It was dark and raining and I was tired."

"Could you find it in daylight?"

"I'm not sure. Maybe not. I didn't recognize the district at all."

"Well, that's not helpful."

"Sorry."

Freddy read the line again. *"I rest at the feet of my masters."*

"It does sounds like a riddle."

He said, "But maybe it's not. Maybe it's a clue. There haven't been any other riddles. They've all been clues. Why would Draxler toss in a riddle now?"

"I don't know."

"So let's assume he didn't."

"All right. Then what?" I could already sense Freddy's clever brain lighting up to the challenge.

"So far, he hasn't been overly obtuse."

I smiled. "That word again."

"It's in my squib book."

"I like it."

"Draxler's not trying to throw you off," Freddy said. "It seems to me he's only keeping someone else off the track. He has to stay hidden from everyone except you. But he needs you to find him, so he's running a pair of hider-seeker games here simultaneously. You're playing one, and presumably the Security Directorate is playing the other. Draxler's clever. Those little poets are probably right. Peter Draxler is some sort of genius, and he needs to be to stay alive. I also think that somehow he knows where you are. Even as you're trying to find him, I believe *he's* following *you*."

I got out of bed and went to our window where I watched the morning sun warm the campus grass. I said, "Freddy, you do realize I can't tell my parents about any of this, right? Where I've gone? What I've done?"

He nodded. "Agreed. Not yet anyhow. It's too dangerous. For all of us."

Freddy had to get ready for his late morning class and I needed to dress and go eat. We decided to revisit this later in the afternoon when I came back from Alexandrian Art and Poetry. We'd probably have the rest of the day to figure it all out. And I had an alternate idea to offer.

Down in the commons, over coffee and oatmeal, I began worrying about Nina. Since I hadn't seen any note when I got back last night, nor this morning, I assumed she had not stopped by. Maybe today. After that strange note yesterday morning, I couldn't telephone, and neither would she. I'd just need to wait to see her again. My experience underground made me miss her terribly. She was the one person I most wanted to share with how I felt about everything I'd seen and experienced down there. And I still wondered about her relationship to Draxler, how much she really knew about him, what sort of relationship they really had, and what game he was chasing. Did she know about the drawings he'd pilfered from Leandro Porteus? I doubted that. I believed she would've told me. But if she did know, what was the plan? And how was I involved? What was my purpose in all of that? I considered it to be the biggest mystery here. Who was I to them?

Back upstairs, only that coffee I'd had in the commons kept me awake long enough to sketch out my class report on the painted funerary monuments from third century B.C. Greek Alexandria. I'd promised Dr. Lamberton a decent performance after already missing one of his classes and it was valuable to keep on his good side. The ancient world fascinated me in both its beauty and how it all faded away. What seemed like a golden age of artistic and architectural victories, wisdom accumulated from disparate sources, had somehow gone to dust over the centuries, seemingly valued now only by antiquity scholars and eager students. Is that what we had to look forward to? Dust and arcane memories?

I finished preparing my report and felt so exhausted, I took a nap and woke just in time for class. I was only a few minutes late. Lamberton was pleased with my presentation and the class didn't hate it. Good news all around. Freddy wandered into our room sometime after four o'clock, that usual look of disgust on his face. He threw himself onto his bed and gave me the bitter news.

"Now Stubblefield despises me, too. I'm doomed."

"How's that?"

"He says I haven't been good to my word regarding a term essay on that sect of Nysasians in Daniélli Province, the ones who are convinced that God inhabits their fruit orchards and divine revelation is solely obtained by eating apples and plums and peaches and pears from those trees."

"Have you written the paper?"

"No, not yet, but that's no reason to threaten dropping me from his class. I've been stalwart in attendance and lively in group discussion. Apparently, my enthusiasm isn't sufficient for him. He must be having a spat with my father, although I doubt he'd admit it. I'll have to ask Mother this evening. She'll tell me what's behind all this nonsense."

"You need to keep up on your assignments, Freddy," I told him. "There's no side roads to that."

"Thank you, roomie. I hadn't noticed."

"You still have Dupré in your corner, don't you?"

"Yes, but I hate that class. Everyone does. Who cares about Detrimental Geology?"

"Elemental?"

"Same thing. Dull, useless, idiotic. And that's describing Dupré. His course is worse. I'd drop it if I weren't so desperate for units. He guarantees a top mark for anyone who simply shows up."

"That's our famous Regency College aristocracy of power and persuasion. We're all players in a conspiracy of academic cordiality."

"Julian!" Freddy sat up in bed. "I believe I know what those words on the ladder mean!"

"You do? So do I, but let's hear yours first."

"Who are Peter's 'masters'?"

"Well, I was given the impression that both he and Marco studied under Castor and Pollux. So, I suppose, in that sense, we could call them Peter's 'masters.' Is that what you're thinking?"

"Yes, I am. He's 'resting at the feet of his masters,' those two old school-teachers."

"But Draxler wasn't there. Marco led me to believe he was in that pit at the end of the tunnel."

"No, because those words on the ladder weren't describing his literal place at their feet. It's somewhere else, a metaphor of sorts, and we're intended to deduce from everything you heard or saw or were given, exactly where that is."

"All right. Good."

"So?" Freddy stared at me like I was the Oracle at Delphi.

I shrugged. "Well, I have no idea. I saw lots of things. And Marco talked non-stop, except when we were with Castor and Pollux, and they prattled on forever. I didn't quite memorize everything, Freddy. I gave you the general tour this morning. There was no phonic recorder around my neck when Marco led me through the undercity. Put me under hypnosis, and maybe it'll all come back."

Freddy got up and went to his desk and took out those notes from my story he'd put in one of his drawers. He held them up. "I think whatever we need is in here. Like I said this morning, Draxler wants you to find him. He's not hiding from you. He might be in the shadows, but he's close."

"Where, though?"

"How should I know? You're the object of his clandestine desire."

"That's not helpful, Freddy."

My roommate sat back in bed and skimmed his notes again. "All right, then, Julian. Your turn. Tell me your idea, what inspiration you had this morning."

"Same as yours, actually. That, 'rest at the feet of my masters,' meant Castor and Pollux."

"Good."

"But just now I realized something else, too, maybe a long shot."

I jumped off the bed and went to my own desk and got out that Latin dictionary. Then I reached under my mattress and retrieved Virgil once again.

Freddy came alive. "What are you thinking?"

"I'm thinking how these clues have each been tied together without being presented as such. Virgil and the telephone code. The address at Bronzeville and Virgil. 'Where goliath hid' and now, 'I rest at the feet of my masters.' So, where's Virgil?"

"Right!" Freddy agreed. "Where's Virgil?"

"Exactly. Numbers. Telephone code, address number, now what?"

Freddy shrugged.

I smiled and opened *The Aeneid*, flipping pages until I reached Liber III. Then I traced down to line 158. I said to Freddy, "Hand me your notepad and pencil."

As he did so, Freddy suddenly grasped my direction. "Oh, my goodness! That is so clever!"

I copied out this line: *idem venturos tollemus in astra nepotes imperiumque urbi dabimus.*

Freddy said, "He had to believe you'd solve the lock and remember the combination afterwards. He didn't allow Marco to see the numbers because they were only meant for you."

"Marco told me it was easy, and if I hadn't been so terrified, it would have been. 3-1-5-8. Not complicated."

"But obtuse, if you hadn't seen the other numbers."

"Precisely."

"All right, then," Freddy said, "what does it mean?"

I took the Latin dictionary and his notepad over to my desk and sat down. "Just give me a minute. This is a long one."

"No rush, only the fate of our demented Republic in your hands."

"Hush."

I read and began translating, word by word. Somehow, I felt Konovaloff looking over my shoulder, perhaps feeling a hint of pride at this student of his at last coming to a beginning comprehension of classical Latin. I was certainly no Polly Dolan, but neither had she ever experienced the expectation and potential danger of what translating a passage from Virgil might reveal.

Freddy got up and came over to my desk. "So?"

"All right. Give me another minute. Almost there."

He stepped aside for a look out our window where students were crossing campus after late afternoon classes. I always thought it felt like some exodus of sorts from the halls of academia toward those mundane interludes of dinner, drink, and domesticity. Not a true metaphor but a fair description of college life as I'd known it.

Freddy said, "I just saw Nancy Pomone playing kissy-face with that fellow from Bébert, you know who I'm talking about? The one with the crooked ear?"

"Do you mean Isak Litov?"

"He's such a dope. What does she see in him?"

"In other words, why does she prefer him over you?"

"Don't put it like that."

"Freddy, she's not the Queen of Sheba. It's her loss, not yours."

"Maybe so, but still." He shrugged. "Isak Litov?"

I closed my Latin dictionary and straightened up. "Do you want to hear this, or keep mooning over lost love that never was and never should've been?"

"Go ahead. I'm swearing off romance for good."

"All right, here it is. Best I could do: *In days to come we shall raise your descendants to the stars and exalt your city's empire.*"

Freddy looked closer. "Let me see it."

I handed him the paper and got up. My Latin was so rudimentary that I could easily find alternate translations of that line, variations in nuance, but I thought what Freddy was studying there must be decent enough. The general idea was close. Whatever Peter Draxler intended for us would be decipherable.

"Hmm."

"Do you get it?"

"Yes and no," Freddy told me. "I see what it means, mostly, but I'm not quite sure what to make of it."

"Me, neither."

We both stood there in silence for what must have been five minutes.

Then Freddy said, "Let's go eat. I'm starving."

We ate in the commons because it was closer than off-campus and our parents had paid in advance at the start of spring term. No cause to be wasteful. The dining hall was mostly full, being Monday and nobody feeling much enthusiasm for running about after another crazy weekend. Freddy had a plate of spaghetti and Gardash vegetables, and I took round steak and fried potatoes. Not half bad, considering where we were. Thayer Hall commons had the most decent food at Regency College. Consistently edible, which was all we expected, really. Ptomaine and stringent academics were rarely a good fit.

Freddy and I sat off in one corner of the commons where we could discuss Draxler's puzzle without being overheard. Mostly we were both silent, neither having any momentous insight regarding Virgil's line. I got up and went to find a platter of bread and butter. After I came back, Freddy went to the toilet. The difficulty was trying desperately to interpret Virgil in the context of the real world where, in fact, Draxler could be resting at the feet of Castor and Pollux. Since it surely was not in the undercity, just what he meant seemed obscure.

Until it didn't.

Freddy came back with another inspired thought. As he sat down, he told me, "We can't fly up into space."

"Not just yet."

"So the stars are probably metaphorical, do you agree?"

"Well, not entirely." I cut up one of my potatoes. "This has to be a true location, connected to his teachers, presuming that's the meaning of 'feet of my masters.'"

"All right, I'm with you there. But what if his 'at the feet of my masters' is not literal. What if that's metaphor? His 'masters'?" Freddy took a piece of bread and raked it through his spaghetti sauce.

"How do you mean?"

"Where can we see stars?"

"Anywhere outdoors after dark," I said, "if the weather's clear."

"Where else?"

"Pardon?"

Freddy asked, "Where else can we see stars anywhere, day or night?"

"I don't follow you."

"Julian! For goodness sakes! Did you never take a field trip during Lower School?"

"To see stars?"

"Yes!"

"Good grief, you're right!"

"And Dr. Bednar's Astronomy hour, freshman year," Freddy said. "Remember? We studied Ptolemy's constellations."

I almost jumped out of my chair. "The Dioscuri! Alpha and Beta Geminorum! The Gemini twins."

"Castor and Pollux!"

"Draxler's masters! My God!"

"And," Freddy added, "where is our city's empire most exalted under a field of stars?"

My ingenious roommate grinned as broadly as I'd ever seen, because almost in unison, we both said, "In the Dome of Eternity!"

Excited now, and thoroughly pleased with ourselves, Freddy and I hurried to finish our dinners, desperately anxious to get back upstairs and organize what we were certain we'd just figured out.

Too thrilled to wait for the notoriously slow Thayer Hall central elevator, we took the staircase up to our room. As Freddy put his key in the door, I heard my name being called from the third floor below, Werner Quinn from the Thayer Telephone & Communications exchange. "Julian! Note for you!"

I went halfway back down the stairs to meet him. Curly redhead. A nice fellow, sophomore. A little pudgy. Fairly quiet. Better student than we were. Quinn handed over the slip of paper. He told me, "About ten minutes ago."

"Thanks."

I read the note where I stood as Quinn ran back down the stairs.

Freddy called down to me. "What is it?"

"Hold on."

It read:

THEY ATTACKED THE HOUSE. PLEASE COME.

I read it twice. Stunned. Nina. Gosney Street? What else could that mean? I shouted up to Freddy, "I have to go! Something's happened with Nina! Find a radio!"

XXV

I rushed out of Thayer Hall and down to the taxi stand at lower Trimble and hired a ride to the East Catalan. I gave my driver the fish market at Kaarsberg as my destination so I could approach Gosney on foot from a couple of blocks away. Even without knowing what to expect, somehow that seemed prudent.

We heard the sirens farther off than that, and saw crowds collecting down by Gustine Street. Smoke bloomed all across that neighborhood on the cool spring breeze. I paid the driver and got out by Kaarsberg and headed up toward Gosney. I'd never seen that many people out of doors there. The sidewalks were so packed I had to walk in the street with a hundred others. The smoke was acrid and cruel. People were buzzing over what had just occurred half an hour before. I heard a house had blown up or was blown up. I heard everybody was killed, or most of them were killed, or a lot of them were killed. Someone said, *Raskol 18 pounder*. And another fellow said, *Nope, Stromer-75*, whatever that was. I waded through the crowd, pushing my way forward up Gustine and Archimboldi. A block now from Gosney, I saw fire engines and ambulances and police and state security trucks and autos. Then a hundred yards away, the block was a madhouse of wailing and screams and tears, injuries, burned and bloody clothing, people lying on the sidewalk or leaned up against the brick walls and city lamp-poles. I tried to get to the house and was stopped by fire trucks sealing off the street. A hasty wooden barricade had just gone up and people were attempting to breach it and being restrained by scores of police. Angling up the sidewalk along the wall across the street from Nina's address, I saw what had happened. Her house was completely demolished. Just splinters and smoke. Utterly destroyed. Obliterated.

Then I felt my arm grabbed from behind and I found myself looking at Nina, that wreck of her. Her lovely face was sooty and grey, her dark eyes wet, make-up smeared, long black hair tangled and filthy.

She tugged on my arm, dragging me away from the wall. She was sobbing. "Julian! Oh my God, Julian! I can't find Delia! I can't find her! Oh my God, help me! Help me, please!"

I grabbed her. "What happened? Nina, what is all this? What happened here?"

"They came to kill us, Julian! Oh my God! They came to kill us all! Delia was in the house. I left her there when I went down to the market. We were just getting some of our things. They drove a truck here with a cannon on it. I was coming back up the street and I saw the cannon fire straight into our house. My God, Julian! Everything exploded! And the houses on both sides of us collapsed, too. There's nothing left! And Delia! Oh God, Julian! Delia!"

I'd never seen anything like it. She was right. The house and the ones next to it, were just piles of black splintered lumber, burning now, flames blazing on a funeral pyre. The truck with the cannon was gone. I had no idea what to do. If Delia had been in that house when the cannon went off, well, Good God! Nina was frantic with shock, crying so hard she struggled to breathe. I was utterly horrified myself and I couldn't think what to do. Had Internal Security actually sent artillery to kill a house full of kids? What sort of monsters do that?

Nina wobbled in my arms and I led her back to the wall and sat her down. Face in her hands, she cried and cried. I stared at her, helplessly. Impotent to do anything useful. The police barricade was reinforced by security agents with weapons drawn. People were screaming at them. The agents gave no notice, faces expressionless, like waxwork from the undercity. The tableau was obscene. Or insane. Choose your favorite. I couldn't wait to hear what my father would say. Or my mother, whose opinions on matters like these were strict and vicious.

I sat next to Nina and put my arm around her and held her close as she sobbed. And then I heard her name across that incessant din. Someone down the street was shouting for her. I let her go and stood up to see who it was. A woman I didn't recognize with dirty blonde hair and wearing a faded pink house dress was pushing through the crowd toward us, calling for Nina. I waved to her and pointed to Nina and the woman rushed over and shook her once.

"Nina? She's all right! Delia's all right!"

Nina looked up. "What?"

"She's at my house with Adelaide and Buster. She's all right. She's fine. They're all fine."

"She was in the house," Nina said, struggling to comprehend what this woman was telling her. "I left her there to go to the market."

"I know, she told me. But Adelaide telephoned and Delia brought Goliath down to play. She was with us," the woman stole a quick glance around, "when it happened. We heard it."

Trembling, Nina wiped her eyes. "She's all right? Are you sure?"

"Yes, she's fine." And the woman gave Nina a hug and kissed her sooty forehead. "We're all fine."

The woman's name was Franny Rotella and she lived in a small yellow house on Pepper Lane, half a block toward the river from the fish markets. On a less smoky afternoon, I'm sure the smell of seafood was pungent and lively. Franny had no idea who I was, or what this was all about. Seeing the explosion, Nina had telephoned that note to Thayer Hall from the house of another friend just down the block. Then she'd gone completely to pieces, wandering frantically about until she saw me. Once Franny got the children settled down, she'd gone looking for Nina to let her know where Delia was and that she was safe.

Now Franny kept Delia and her own two children playing in the back room and left me alone with Nina while she prepared something for us all to eat.

Evening descended over the Rosenstern Quarter. Ash was still drifting on the breeze. Even indoors we could smell it. I telephoned to Thayer Hall for Freddy and left Franny's number for him to call me back. Then I held Nina's hand in a window seat looking out on a darkened Pepper Lane. She had taken a shower and cleaned up, but she was still shaken, jittery. Upset.

Teary-eyed, Nina told me, "I warned them this could happen. They didn't listen at all. They were so arrogant. As if this was yet Lower School and smart putdowns matter and anarchy is a game about being clever and daring. Even after Kaspar got killed, they still thought planning something sneaky would be fun."

"Like blowing up the Ferdinand Club?"

"Not that," Nina said. "No one's that stupid. Who would do anything so idiotic?"

"Marco?"

Nina frowned. "What about him? He's a little twerp. Nobody pays any attention to his stupid ideas. Marco couldn't blow up a balloon."

So, she didn't know. That was interesting. Who among them *did* know what some of them had been planning? What if only a few of the kids in that house today were involved with the bomb in the Ferdinand Club, and the others died without knowing why a military artillery piece fired a shell that killed them? Then again, what if *none* of them were involved with Marco's infernal bomb? Mortal secrets. Some protect. Others endanger. Threads unravel and a pretty little eight-year-old girl like Delia could die for somebody else's obsession.

I asked Nina, "Who was in the house?"

She thought for a moment or so, then her pretty eyes dampened, and she told me, "I never go into anyone's room except mine and Delia's, but I remember seeing Saami, Gibb, Jeduthan, Pieta, Juliet, Estelle, Bohlen, Cliona and Gianni. They were either in the living room or the kitchen. I heard another girl in Gibb's room, and a boy's voice I didn't recognize. I think there might've been more people in the house, too, because the basement door was open and someone was doing laundry. Gibb invites his friends over to use our washer and dryer. They're too cheap to pay at a laundrette." She looked at me with a sadder, more plaintive expression than I'd ever seen on her darling face. "Julian, they're all dead. Every single one of them. And if I hadn't gone to the market to buy bread and milk for breakfast tomorrow, Delia and I would be dead, too."

I leaned over and gave Nina the warmest hug I could imagine. "I love you, Nina. I love you and Delia both." I kissed her and felt a shudder for how close we'd just come to losing each other. We needed to be so very careful now.

A little later, we ate dinner together at Franny's kitchen table. Meatballs and boiled potatoes, bread and butter, and apple cider. The kids teased each other and ate quickly so they could go play again. Delia saved one of her meatballs for Goliath, sleeping back in Adelaide's bedroom. Once the children had gone, Franny asked how Nina and I had met and most of what we told her was true with a few white lies added for Franny's benefit. Some secrets do protect. Afterward, Nina decided that she and Delia ought to go stay that night with another friend of Nina's, Johara Ternaux, who lived outside the Catalan on Meltemi Avenue, across the eternal river and miles from Gosney Street. There was a nice big bedroom in the back of the house and a fenced yard for Goliath. Johara offered to keep them with her as long as Nina wanted. I favored that idea. This time she gave me Johara's telephone number so we could keep close. I hadn't heard yet from Freddy, and I asked Franny to tell him I'd be back at our room in a couple of hours or so. If he called.

We helped Franny wash the dishes and clean up the kitchen, then Franny went to get her children ready for bed. They had school in the morning, far enough from Gosney Street that the explosion shouldn't interfere with classes. Nina led us back to the front room where she told me, "I need to see you tomorrow, Julian. It's important. There's something I have to tell you, and a desperate favor I need to ask."

"Anything."

"When can we meet?"

"Depends where. If it's near campus, we can meet at noon. I'll skip lunch."

"How about Fidley Park. That's close. I can bring you something to eat."

Nina went to get Delia and Goliath and I telephoned for a taxicab. She decided to go straight to Johara's house and not worry about their stuff at Hannah's until the next day. I'd ride with them out to Meltemi Avenue, see them indoors, and take the taxi back to campus. That's what we did.

XXVI

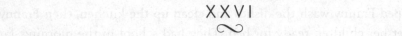

Freddy had gone back to Alexanderton for the night to solicit advice from his mother about his illustrious father and Malcolm Stubblefield. I telephoned my own father in the morning to ask if I could go see him and Mother. I told him we needed to talk about the bombing and what had just occurred on Gosney Street. He sounded frantic and told me to be there by six o'clock. I promised I would.

Dr. Coffeen was more energetic that morning than I was, lecturing us on the Sophists who could have been jaded members of the Judicial Council rather than my favorite Greek philosophers. Winning on Gosney Street yesterday seemed like something that would have thrilled Gorgias and his crowd. As I understood it, moral integrity was relative for them. Who knew what evil truly was? In fact, who could even name 'good' and call it universal? People can be persuaded of the most despicable acts with a clever argument. When I raised my hand at one point and suggested that opinion to Coffeen, I heard Percy McDonnell fart in the row behind me. Everyone laughed, but Dr. Coffeen agreed with me and went even further, offering us the notion that the Great Separation was a form of Sophist dialectic whose basic argument was specious at best. After class, I stopped him in the hall and asked what he thought of the dispersal of our rogue population into the undercity after the Great Separation.

With his wickedly familiar smile, Dr. Alfred Coffeen told me, "Mr. Brehm, I consider it highly unfortunate that anyone in this Republic of ours should be named more 'rogue' than another. Whether today or a century ago. Society consists of citizens who cannot be called equal in either talent or fortune yet must be admitted into fellowship with one another that all might benefit from each seeking goodness and well-being in all things. The Great Separation fractured our Republic and the Desolation has widened that fault, perhaps irredeemably now. We should fear the consequences."

— . —

Back from class, I found Freddy in our room, actually reading from "Common Theology" for Stubblefield's class. Presumably that visit home to Alexanderton had instigated some miraculous transformation in his academic point of view.

"Are you Freddy Barron?" I asked, needling him as I put my own coursework on my desk.

"Julian!" He cast his book aside. "I saw the newspaper this morning. That gas main on Gosney Street. Good God! Did it really blow up half the block? Is Nina all right?"

"Is that what it said in the paper? A gas main exploded?"

"Isn't that so?"

"No, it isn't! Not at all. That's a big lie. It was a cannon. They drove it up the street and blasted Nina's house to pieces. Killed everyone inside."

Freddy sat up. "Oh my God! Nina?"

"She's all right," I told him. "Both she and Delia were out of the house at the time. They were lucky. If they hadn't been, they'd be dead right now. God-damned Security Directorate. They went there to kill everyone."

"Why would they do that? That's crazy, isn't it?"

I walked to the window and looked out. Just another normal day at Thayer Hall. Nice weather. A pleasant breeze and morning sun. A good day to be alive. The house on Gosney Street. All those kids. Indescribable. To die like that was profoundly obscene.

I said, "We've all gone crazy."

"What does Nina think?"

"She's too upset to think about much, except that she and Delia are both alive and another few minutes here or there and they wouldn't have been."

Freddy got up from his bed and came over to where I was standing. He looked out, too. That blue spring sky above us all. A perfect moment in this world. He said, "I just don't understand why that happened."

"Oh, I neglected to tell you. Your cellmate, Marco, built the bomb that blew up the Ferdinand Club."

"What? Who told you that? Good God!"

"He did. In the undercity."

"Why?"

"Why did he tell me, or why did he blow up the club?"

"Was he in the house yesterday?"

"I don't think so."

"Why did he blow up the club?"

"Well, according to him, two reasons: First, to get back at those people who shot Kaspar in the head. And secondly, to kill his father."

"Good heavens! Who's his father?"

"Dr. Grenelle."

"Julian, this is all so insane. You and I need to reexamine what we're doing here. I was actually enjoying our little Draxler snipe hunt. It seemed so diverting and clever. But this is something else entirely. People are getting killed. I'm beginning to feel now this is all a big mistake for both of us. And where does Nina fit in? Do you even know?"

"No, I don't," I replied. "Not precisely. She's always sort of evasive. That is to say, I believe everything she's told me. I just sense she's never been telling me everything. There are simply too many holes in her story. I trust her, and yet somehow I don't. Not entirely."

"Love is a blinding agent, my faithful roommate. She's distracted you. Meeting her last week, I can see why you're crazy for her, but love and politics are not a good romantic pairing. If you're not careful, you could end up like those poor rebels on Gosney Street."

"I know that, Freddy. I'm trying to find a vantage point here where I can see all this more clearly. Nina and I are meeting at noon today in Fidley Park. Then I'm going home this evening to talk it out with Father and Mother."

"And the Dome of Eternity? What about that?"

"I'll go tomorrow after morning class."

Freddy asked, "Should I come with you?"

"No, if Peter Draxler is actually there, I think he prefers me solo."

Fidley Park was about a five-minute walk from campus across Trimble Street and down a lovely wooded path of oak trees and elms and poplars. It was a family park with picnic tables and drinking fountains and grassy areas for blankets and games. Nina was already waiting for me when I arrived just before noon bells from the Regency College campanile on Cistern Hill. She wore a pretty floral-rose net frock she'd borrowed from Johara, since nearly all her own clothes had been destroyed in the cannon shot and subsequent fire. Seated there at a table with a small picnic basket in the noon shade, I just thought she looked beautiful, and told her so.

She smiled. "Thank you, Julian. Honestly, I feel like an orphan today. I don't know why. Delia and I have been shuttling about like this really for the past couple of years. We've never found anywhere yet to settle. It's discouraging, but I guess we're used to it."

"I didn't know that. I'm sorry. I'd hate to staple a suitcase to my own hand. I don't know that I could stand it. You're very strong."

Nina shrugged. "It's not something I brag about. Who wants to be a vagabond? Delia manages better than I do. She's very malleable to circumstances. I'm so proud of her."

"She's terribly sweet," I said, "and smart as anything. She'll have a great future, I just know it."

"Do you really think so? I worry all day long about her, what I'm doing and how it affects her. Sometimes I wonder if she'd be better off without me. My life is such a cat's cradle. But if I didn't have Delia, I don't how I'd survive."

"We find ways to live, Nina, and that becomes our story. But yours belongs to her, and hers to you. You're fortunate together. If anything's true, that is. Your little sister is part of you. Nothing can change that."

Then I leaned forward across the table and kissed Nina and squeezed her hand. And she pulled away just enough to say, "I have to tell you something now I should never have kept from you. And an impossible favor to ask."

She reached into the picnic basket and took out a small envelope and handed it to me. "Go ahead, Julian. Open it."

I did and drew out a small photograph of Delia. "It's a pretty picture."

"That's Delia. About three years ago."

"I can see."

"I want you to take that picture to the Asklepieion Hospital at Tamorina."

"Tamorina?" I frowned. "Nina, that's in the Desolation."

"Yes, but it's miles from the war now. You'd take the train. A day or so, maybe less. You'd be safe. I promise. I wouldn't ask otherwise. I'd be crazy."

"Why do you want me to go there?"

"Because I need you to give this picture to her father. He's an attendant at the hospital."

"What do you mean, her father? You told me your parents are dead."

"They are," she said. "But they were killed by that maniac in a truck before Delia was born. Julian, she's not my sister. She's my daughter and Arturo's her father, and after yesterday when I almost lost her, I finally decided he should know who she is. I've been thinking about this for months. I've just been afraid to tell you."

I was honestly flabbergasted. Confused. Another story? Another lie? What was true about any of this? "You were married?"

She shook her head, that lovely black hair fluttering in the breeze. "No, I was pregnant. Arturo didn't love me, and I wasn't sure I loved him, either. When I told him I was pregnant, he left Arbolé township for Méryon and wrote me a letter saying he wasn't ever coming back, and I should forget about him. I had Delia by myself, and I was so lonely and ashamed after she was born that I began telling everyone she was my baby sister. I don't know why. I guess I was just stupid. Or a coward. But I was embarrassed, too, so I finally packed us both up and took a train to Oikema where I knew friends, Robert and Heléne, who kept us for half a year. Then Robert got in trouble with Conscription and he ran off and we had to leave. Heléne traveled to her aunt's home at Deventeer-By-The-Sea and we went with her. I put Delia into baby school there and took a job in a glass shop to pay our way. That wasn't the most awful place for us, after all. Heléne's aunt was nice and she was good with Delia. Her name was Brigíta and her husband had been killed in the Desolation a couple of years before and she told me that company in her house made her happy. We liked her and Delia loved being at the shore where she could wade into the water and collect seashells and chase the gulls up and down the sand and laugh and laugh. We lived there for almost four years. Then Brigíta caught pneumonia and died, and her sister came out from Mellah and sold the house, and Heléne left, and Delia and I had to go elsewhere again. So we came to the metropolis and rented rooms here and there in Káundonia and Clairville, until I found the house on Gosney Street and met those kids who thought they'd help the world get better. They were all stupid, and so was I."

I stared at her as the breeze gusted. "Nina, why didn't you tell me any of this before? What were you afraid of?"

"Before what?" she asked, brushing the hair from her eyes. "Before you fell in love with me? What was I supposed to say? That I have a little girl I've been pretending is my sister and I need you to find her father to let him know he has a daughter whether he likes it or not?"

"Are you saying this has all been about getting me to fall in love with you so that I'd risk my neck to find your old boyfriend?"

"Do you think I don't love you, Julian?"

"Do you?"

She scared me more than any girl I'd ever met. Because I was in love with her, and that incontrovertible fact brought me to the verge of tears for everything between us and everything she'd done to protect that darling little girl.

"Of course I love you. For heaven's sake, how could I not? You've been so sweet and good and kind. I've never known anyone like you, Julian. And no one's cared about Delia the way you have. That means everything to me. Are you serious? Do you really not know how I feel about you? I love you so much. These crazy things I've been asking you to do are because I trust you, too. For me, love comes from trust. I don't know what I've meant to you, Julian, but we have so many dreams here to share, so many possibilities, and without you in my life, it'd just be me and Delia alone in this awful city, and I don't have any faith that the two of us could survive."

I looked off into the woods beyond the park where two young people were walking up through the underbrush. The girl was laughing and the boy beside her was soaking wet. A shallow tributary of Zoffany Creek ran near here and I guessed he'd fallen in, or she'd been splashing him somehow. They looked fun together.

"Nina?"

"Yes?"

"Did you know Marco blew up the Ferdinand Club?"

"He didn't."

"Yes, he did. In fact, he told me he did, exactly how and why, when I saw him in the undercity on Sunday."

Her pretty dark eyes narrowed. "You went there? To the underground? Julian, are you insane? Why would you do that? Marco's a lunatic. He's probably infected, or completely demented. You can't listen to anything he says. Nothing's true with him. He's the sickest person I know. We only let him stay at the house because he begged us one after another. He really seems absolutely pathetic. I wouldn't even let him come down the hall to use our bathroom. And I never trusted him with Delia. I told Marco if I ever caught him in her room, I'd strangle him. And I wasn't joking. Why would you go see him?"

The game had reversed, but I tried not to smile. I understood how much she had deceived me about Peter Draxler. The ties that bound them were not so vague any longer. Maybe Nina didn't know that. Maybe she did. But I saw it all more clearly than I ever had before. And because I did, I could not tell her everything I knew if I still hoped she and little Delia could be kept safe. So I repeated just what she'd been saying to me, "I can't tell you."

"Why not?"

"Same reason you've been giving me all along. So please don't ask."

"You shouldn't be like that, Julian," Nina said. "It's not nice and it's not fair."

I reached across the picnic table and took her hands as the breeze gusted again. She was so very beautiful. "But at least it's truthful. I love you so much, Nina. I'd do anything for you. Honestly." I let go and put Delia's picture back into the envelope. "I'll take this to Tamorina and give it to Delia's father."

She hesitated, her expression quizzical. "You will?"

"I promise. What's his name?"

"I've been terrified of asking you. I never thought you'd agree."

"Well, I just did."

"Are you sure?"

"Yes," I said. "What's his last name?"

"Cascádes. Arturo Cascádes." She reached back into the picnic basket and took out another small envelope. "Here's his picture. This was only taken a month ago by someone we both knew back in Arbolé. Samuel Protiste. He works with Arturo in the hospital these days. I just found out. Samuel is the one who told me Arturo was there. It's the first I've heard of him in eight years. I assumed he was probably dead."

"Does Delia know you're her mother?"

"No," Nina replied, "and I won't tell her just yet. We need to settle in for a few weeks at Johara's, get her back into school again. Have her find a routine she enjoys."

I heard the campanile chime on the half hour. The sun had its own routine. I smiled at Nina. "Did you bring something for me to eat?"

— . —

An hour before heading to the train station, I telephoned to Father at the Garibaldi Building to tell him about Tamorina. He told me not to worry. In fact, he'd just that moment had a plan in mind to ease my concerns. We'd discuss his thoughts when I got home, and he'd let me explain it all to Mother.

That evening at Highland Park, Mother baked a small ham with scalloped potatoes and turtle soup for the three of us, and my father said grace at the table for the first time since Agnes and I were children. My parents weren't strictly religious and hadn't attended church regularly in years. We weren't brought up to believe in salvation from the supernatural. For us, the Holy Book was only a book, a guide, perhaps, to moral behavior, but certainly not a blueprint for the world as we knew it. Why Father recited grace, I don't know, and I never asked, yet somehow it did seem appropriate to the occasion.

We ate quietly, just a few words about my classes and a plum tree Mother was replacing in the backyard. It had bugs, which she detested. My mother did all the gardening herself. Digging, planting, grafting, trimming. Mother claimed she understood her garden better than she did a society of people who, she told me more than once, refuse to be trained to grow as they ought to. *There's more than enough sunshine and water to go around. Portion it wisely, Julian, and watch the world flourish!*

Over dessert of tapioca pudding, I finally told my mother about Nina and her idea regarding Tamorina.

Mother asked quite firmly, "Julian, who is this girl?"

I explained Delia and Gosney Street as best I could, then to now.

Both my parents are more perceptive and intuitive than I am. They told me I was deliberately avoiding the bigger part of the story here. Still refusing to introduce Peter Draxler into this narrative, I did, however, try to explain the politics of that house Nina inhabited, and her story with Delia and Arbolé township and that Cascádes fellow I was supposed to find at Tamorina.

Mother was not satisfied. "Julian, my dear, you're sitting here at this table because your father and I met and fell in love. Do you imagine we've forgotten all about that? Do we look that old to you?"

Father grinned. He knew Mother had me on the ropes now. Final humiliation was at the bell, and he instigated my demise. "Yes, Julian, tell us all about falling in love. Your mother and I need a little more excitement around here, don't we, Martha?"

"Indeed, we do." She tapped her spoon on the dish of pudding. "Julian? A love story, please."

Trapped and defeated, I told them about the missing dog and Nina's lovely dark eyes and her messy bedroom and the flower stand in Thibodeaux Station and our intimate little table at Colonia Miñearo and the rain outside her window on Gosney. I told them about her visit to Thayer Hall and the black vergenie immocalata pendant I bought her on Kemper Street. How she cooked that tomato hash for me one night and a chicken pot pie on another, and how we saw Kaspar shot dead in front of us and escaped to Hannah on Trask Street, and then again how I found her on Gosney with her house obliterated and Delia lost then found again with Franny, and how we decided to move Nina and Delia to Johara's home at Meltemi Avenue.

When I'd finished, Mother said, "Charles, our son is hopelessly smitten. What should we do about it?"

"Well, dear, there is the garden shed. I could bring home a new lock. By summer's end her spell will likely have worn off and he can be back to his studies, fresh and eager to make us proud."

I said, "You two are so ridiculous. How do I know I wasn't adopted? Agnes is certain we were. She says it's the only logical explanation."

"Your darling sister," Mother told me, "has her own ball of yarn and she's been telephoning incessantly. I've had to send her a new box of handkerchiefs."

Father said, "Our children have grown up, Martha. I'm afraid we're only spectators now."

I said, "Well, I'm here, aren't I? Without you two, I'm not sure I could make five good choices out of ten. Neither could Agnes. You still have a valuable role to play in our young lives, if you're willing."

They both laughed. Father said, "Martha? What do you think? Do we have the patience, anymore?"

"Maybe for another month or two, Charles," she said, "but after that, they're both out the door."

"Agreed."

While I was helping Mother put the dishes away, the doorbell rang. I heard voices in the entry and Father called for me. Mother sent me out of the kitchen, and I went to see who had arrived. Our guests had gone to my father's office and I met them there. Those two fellows from before all this got so horrible, Addison Dennett and Harold Trevelyan. My father's trusted friends and advisors. I knew what they were here for and I was grateful.

We shook hands and I sat on Father's sofa with Dennett and Trevelyan flanking me in armchairs. As ever, my father remained at his desk, presiding over us. He poured glasses of cognac for himself and those two. I pretended disinclination toward alcohol when, in fact, that's all I'd thought of once Dennett and Trevelyan walked into the house, dressed as usual in fine grey suits and ties, shirts buttoned high, black shoes polished. That expected Garibaldi Building standard.

Straight off, Dennett asked me, "How are you doing, Julian?"

"I think I'm all right. It's difficult to appreciate the psychology of seeing a house blown up by an artillery shell, particularly when you knew some of the people who were in there at the time."

"We heard your girlfriend escaped harm."

"She was lucky, yes. That's all we can say. A different turn here or there and she would've been killed with everyone else."

"It was a nasty business," Trevelyan said, "all around. Almost inconceivable, except really it's not."

Dennett said, "But you weren't expected at the house, were you? No one thought you'd be there at the time the house was attacked?"

I looked at my father who wore his usual expression of deep concern when circumstances arose concerning myself and Agnes. "Not at all. I was studying at Thayer with Freddy when Nina telephoned a note that they'd been attacked. Really, I'd gone there after the fact, not before. I'd had no plans whatsoever to go back to Gosney Street, otherwise. Honestly, I was surprised Nina was there, though when she explained they needed to get some things they'd left behind the night of the shooting, I suppose it made sense."

Dennett asked, "She wasn't living at the house, anymore?"

"No, after Kaspar was killed, she took Delia to go stay with a friend where she thought they'd be safer."

Trevelyan asked, "Do you feel safe, Julian?"

Mother came into the office and took a seat in a chair near my father's desk. Her expression of concern wasn't much different than Father's.

I said, "I'm not sure. I suppose it depends where I am. At Thayer Hall up in the room with Freddy, or in class anywhere on campus, I'm fine. Probably because I'm occupied with studies there. In the Catalan with Nina, I can't say I ever felt all that safe, but part of that was concern for her safety, and Delia's. Neither of us, nor even Freddy, are naïve about politics and state security. Everyone knows how paranoid the Council is these days. And I think they ought to be. Pursuing that hideous war shouldn't allow any of them to feel comfortable. I doubt the Council was really any more shocked at the Ferdinand bombing than Nina's friends were about Gosney Street. Fear lends itself to killing, doesn't it? Eventually, none of us feels safe."

My mother said to Dennett, "I want you to keep the Protectorate's nasty fingers off my son."

"Well, that's precisely what we're getting to here," Father told her. "The Judicial Council is not infallible, dear. We know plenty of secrets, enough to run them out of town, and they know it."

Dennett smiled at Mother. "We do have leverage, Martha, though it's not limitless."

Trevelyan added, "That means they won't dare touch Julian unless it's something particularly egregious."

Dennett told me, "Julian, we have papers and a two-way rail ticket for you. Safe passage to Tamorina and back. By train, or auto if that should become necessary. It doesn't matter. They were signed an hour ago by Otto Paley, Chief Director of Internal Communications on the Judicial Council. He's served there for thirty years, so his position is secure. We knew him at Willsford School where he was Head Prefect to our Hall."

I said, "I take it he wasn't in the Ferdinand Club on Sunday."

Dennett shook his head. "That's not Otto's crowd. Never has been. Doesn't trust most of them. He says they're not moral like we are. He'll attend the memorial, but that's about all he'll give to those people. He believes they've been half the problem themselves."

Trevelyan said, "We do need you to have a firm grasp on the intensity of these times, Julian. There are certain events we can't quite as easily control."

"Events?" That kind of language was so disconcerting I wondered if I really was mature enough to be in the room just then.

"Yes," Trevelyan explained, "for instance, that bombing at the Ferdinand Club or the persistent investigation into the Draxler boy, regarding Porteus's drawings. There's also a peculiar misunderstanding, or so they're claiming, out at the Pellerin Building where a counselor to the vice-chairman has gone on unscheduled holiday and no one appears to have even the vaguest explanation. The fact is, the man's disappeared and not even his wife seems to have a decent opinion regarding where he went. It's important because the chairman of the board there has connections through the Status Imperium and somehow this counselor is tied into all that. Again, just another unexpected ripple in the pond."

Dennett told me, "Julian, listen here. Otto has given you envoy status from the Judicial Council which makes you important enough to secure safe passage anywhere from Highland Park to Tamorina and thereabouts, but not important enough to get yourself shot. It's vital that you use both good judgment and discretion on and off the train, regardless of circumstances or whom you encounter. We've included here strict telephone numbers for our office and Dr. Paley's. Understand that communications between us will naturally be somewhat limited by distance and opportunity. Otto knows this and will do everything in his capabilities to mitigate any worries you may encounter, but a lot of your security will depend upon you alone."

Trevelyan added, "Just try to be smart and careful, Julian. That's the best way to stay safe while you're there. Don't take chances. Otto is counting on this being a normal train ride out and back."

Mother spoke up, "Harold, nothing is normal in the Desolation. We have no need of pretending otherwise. Our family are not fools. Charles and I have watched this despicable drama unfolding every year of our lives. We've lost dear, dear friends. Seen the ruin in too many living rooms. And yet nothing but the delineation of borders in the east has changed. Do not think for one instant that we are at all unaware of the risk involved with letting Julian board that train, his eminence Otto Paley be damned."

Father said, "Martha and I, and I'm sure Julian, appreciate the reality of pitfalls in the Desolation, just as I am confident of Otto's prescience in these matters. It's simply that life's confounding implications rarely lend themselves to easy narratives. Our stake in this adventure is high as heaven."

Trying be adult about all this, I spoke up to say, "Gentlemen, I have no intention of killing myself out there. If I thought that was a likelihood, I wouldn't go at all. Probably Nina wouldn't expect me to, either. At least, I hope she wouldn't."

Addison Dennett took a sip of cognac. Somehow, he appeared more tremulous about my excursion than I was. Trevelyan, too. Possibly the imperious presence of my mother in the room instigated that. Father merely looked stern. I tried not to faint. No one needed to tell me what I was attempting. Tamorina is not a resort, and a trip there was not a walk down the block. The very concept of a train ride into the Desolation scared the hell out of me. If I'd been asked a month before what I might do for love, I would have said, unhesitatingly, *"Not that."*

Harold Trevelyan opened his briefcase and took out a flat canvas pouch. He handed it to me. Speaking then in his most formal tone, he said, "Julian, this is your diplomatic pouch, authorized by Dr. Otto Paley, Chief Director of Internal Communications on the Judicial Council. As I stated before, you've been appointed directly by Dr. Paley as his personal envoy to any and all relationships within Tarchon Province and stops in between here and there, with principal directive indicated at Tamorina. Do you understand this?"

"Yes, sir."

Father got up from behind his desk and went over by Mother. He rested his hand on her shoulder and she grasped it tightly. Both looked more pale than ever before. I felt responsible.

Dennett tried to calm us all by saying, "We think you'll be fine, Julian. Tamorina is a lovely town these days. The shelling that occurred there was eighteen years ago, and the war has gone away since. Otto insists life has returned and no one has bad feelings any longer."

"I very much doubt that," Mother said. "Chlorocyanic gas doesn't produce amnesia."

Trevelyan said, "Well, we all have to live, don't we?"

"When we're permitted to do so," my mother replied.

Out on the front stoop, Addison Dennett and Harold Trevelyan said their goodbyes to my parents and offered me one last reassurance of security. For my mental comfort, I presumed. Dennett told me, "We're not afraid for you, Julian, because we know you'll have a pleasant train ride and an inspiring adventure. We've been close friends with your father and mother for most of our adult lives, and seeing you and your sister grow up to be such fine young people has been a privilege."

Trevelyan agreed. "We feel a solemn responsibility toward you both. My conversation with Otto Paley was rooted in that understanding, and I guided him there in no uncertain terms. Because of this, I feel a well-grounded confidence, Julian, that you'll have the most imposing umbrella over you on this short journey. But if you should feel any trepidation along your route, no matter how trivial, please contact me or Addison immediately, and we'll do our utmost to rectify the situation."

We shook hands and I watched them down to their auto where they drove off in Trevelyan's new silver-blue sedan.

I never saw either of them again.

Upstairs, Father gave me a jacket from his closet that I hadn't seen before. Just my size, too. When he was younger, Father was a perfect fit as well, but as he was fond of saying, *"That was long ago and far away."* The jacket was formal in cut and style, intended for occasions where military dress or ceremonial attire would not be considered overdone. My father had last worn it to a week of legislative proceedings within the Judicial Council when he was only a few years older than I am now. The jacket was a sort of greyish-green wool with a dusty rose collar and dark bronze buttons from waist to neck and about the cuffs. Perhaps the nature of it was out of fashion, yet the elegant formality of the jacket felt correct and inspiring. I was pleased to try it on and see myself in his tall closet mirror.

"You are the image of your father," Mother said, coming into the bedroom. "And every inch as handsome."

I smiled, pleased with myself. "Thank you."

"I think he actually wears it better than I did," Father said, studying my look. "His height gives him more stature than I ever had."

"Yes, quite prepossessing," Mother agreed.

"You'll take it with you, Julian," Father instructed. "Wear it on the train. It'll do you a service. That jacket is not ostentatious."

"Just proper," Mother said.

"All right," I said. "I really didn't have anything more appropriate besides a dinner jacket that Freddy spilled wine on a month ago and I neglected to run out to the cleaners."

I slipped the jacket off.

"Do you have a valise?" Father asked. "You'll need more than your old rucksack."

"May I borrow one of yours?"

"Of course, that was my intention."

"Thank you."

We went downstairs together, Father's jacket in the leather valise he loaned me. Because of class in the morning, I'd decided not to stay overnight, and instead take the train back to Thayer Hall. What hadn't yet been decided was how I was to explain my upcoming absences. My professors weren't unhappy with me as Freddy's apparently were with him, but neither was I one of their star scholars, so we needed to finesse this academic holiday. Mother was better at inventing fiction than my father, so he gave her permission to create a dramatically convincing tale that would excuse my inattendance for a few days. This being Tuesday, I expected to miss no more than six classes and be back eager and energetic for Contemporary Social Philosophy on Monday morning. Both my parents would describe a family emergency involving Agnes at McNeely Branson School that only I was able to resolve. Mother would instruct Agnes to deflect any telephone calls to me until further notice and play along with the story under threat of losing her monthly allowance. Once that was organized and agreed upon, I telephoned to summon a taxi cab to the Highland Park train station.

I felt strangely uncertain, then, preparing to say goodbye this time. What if I were never to return? Life offers no such assurances. Had any of those kids on Gosney Street said goodbyes like this? The thought was frightening.

Mother gave me a hug and a kiss on my cheek. "My baby boy, Julian. You're once in a lifetime. I love you. Please be attentive to your health and safety, my dear. I won't touch my garden until I hear you're back."

"Mother!"

"Do not say another word. It's settled."

She went back into the kitchen to finish cleaning up.

Father walked me outdoors to wait for the taxi. A pleasant breeze stirred through the trees all about. The night air off our spring foliage was cool and freshly fragrant. A million stars lit the dome of heaven.

"When you were little, Julian," Father told me, "I used to lie in bed, thinking about a night like this, seeing you off to some distant adventure beyond my reach. Often those thoughts would keep me awake and I'd feel compelled to go down the hall and look in on you to see you were still there with us. I'd watch you sleeping and wish somehow those moments might never end, that you and I would always be together like this, father and son under the same roof 'for days and days unending.'"

"Father."

"Oh, I know that's not our story to tell. What is, has long been determined, and we are to witness life as it unfolds, not how we might imagine it could be, 'if only.'"

I told him, "When I come back next week, we'll go out and play a couple of sets and I'll beat you for once. Or maybe I'll keep letting you beat me. What do you think?"

Father laughed and gave me an exceptionally warm hug, and I know I cried, and I've always tried to remember how that felt.

XXVII

∞

Back at Thayer Hall that night, I found Freddy and two male sophomores engaged with a game of *Phanagrams*, one of Freddy's specialties. Anything with words or numbers. His two victims tonight didn't seem overly put out by Freddy the Steamroller.

"Hello, Julian. This is Roderick and Perlo."

They spoke in unison. "Hello, Julian."

"Hi, fellows."

Freddy told me, "We're almost done. I have 15,723 points."

Again, in unison, his competition announced, "We have 412, but we're enjoying ourselves. It's a great game. Freddy's teaching us."

I laughed. "I'll bet he is."

Freddy said, "They're over here from Stokely Hall. Botany majors. Lengfeld's pupils."

One of the boys said, "He hates Freddy."

"So I've heard."

The other said, "We don't have a grasp of teacher politics."

"Nobody does," Freddy said. "That's why some of us struggle to keep off probation, and others like you two chew the golden apple."

They both smiled. "We're just lucky. You're the genius. That's why we need you to teach us how to crush everyone at Stokely in *Phanagrams*."

"I'll be back," I told Freddy, then went out to use the toilet across the hall.

Once they were gone, I put Father's valise on my bed and organized some necessities. I took Nina's envelope with Delia's picture and Arturo's, and slipped them both, and 1200 credits Father had just given me, into the diplomatic pouch, and stuck the pouch into the valise. Freddy watched intently, reminding me now and then to include such needful items as a spare toothbrush, nail clipper, hairbrush *and* comb and extra underwear, just in case. Possibly a third shirt, too.

"Thank you, Mother. I can't imagine how I could even plan this excursion without your steady guidance."

"But that's just it, darling," he said. "You couldn't."

"I suppose a pair of boots are too much, right?"

"Is there space in the valise?"

"Probably not."

"There's your answer. No boots. Just reliable shoes."

"I'll bring two pair of trousers," I told Freddy. "One dress pair for the train to fit with Father's jacket, and another for knocking about elsewhere."

"Good idea. Julian, are you going to the moon?"

"That's not on my itinerary, why?"

"Because we're packing you up for a trip into the Desolation without really considering why you're going. We might just as well be flying you to the moon. The idea of that makes more sense than Tamorina."

"I've explained why. Weren't you listening?"

"Of course I was. Hearing your explanations is part of my job here. In this case, though, you've neglected to mention something critical to this present venture."

"Which in?"

"Peter Draxler. We both know that whatever he has in mind for you must be connected somehow with the Desolation, possibly even with Nina and her plan for you there. Or maybe those stolen drawings? We haven't even discussed that scenario. Why not? Impossible? Too dangerous?"

I quit packing the valise and sat down on the bed. "You're right. With Nina's story and this envoy situation, I'd mostly forgotten about him. I mean, I hadn't forgotten about going to the Dome tomorrow, but I haven't given much thought to what might happen there. This has all been overwhelming."

"My point exactly. Look here, Julian, unless you're prepared to simply board that train and ride off into the unknown, which is precisely how you ought to consider the Desolation, we need to formulate some kind of flexible contingency for this excursion that allows you to navigate between what Nina wants, and what Draxler might require of you, as well."

"I don't know if we can do that before hearing why Draxler has chosen me to chase around after him. It's all too big a mystery right now. Too many unknowns."

"Oh, I disagree. In fact, I see it as fairly simple. Both he and Nina are asking you to do something. We know what Nina wants, and I expect tomorrow morning you'll find out what Draxler wants. When you do, we'll have to decide if you should actually board that train, or not."

"Well, I think I have to. I've promised Nina I would. She doesn't even know about the Dome. Neither do those fellows at my father's. What if there's nothing in all this nonsense connecting Nina and Draxler, except that one night he slept with her, those puzzles from Virgil, and the fact that they both know Marco?"

"All right, Julian," Freddy gave me that look, "but what if there is?"

The next morning in Dr. Martita Pardo's class, I blundered my way through a report on what I described as the catastrophic conflict between our common eugenical education and free thought in the Republic today. Admittedly influenced by my experience in the undercity, I was perhaps overly strident in evaluating the disastrous failures perpetrated by contemporary social philosophy as implemented through the Status Imperium and accepted as natural fact by most of our populace. You could've heard the verbal outrage and abuse clear down to the end of the hall. Someone threw a pencil at me. Another tossed a notebook. My report was not well received. Dr. Pardo censored me. She told me I was put on notice. When I remarked that free thought had just been put on notice, Dr. Pardo gave me a red mark. I ought to have stayed in bed.

I had my oatmeal and toast and a cup of coffee alone in the commons, avoiding anyone from that stupid class. I generally prefer to shun, rather than be shunned. It did distract my attention from where I was about to go. If I'd thought telephoning to Nina were helpful, I would have done so, but this morning there should be no more obstacles between me and Draxler, at least none foreseeable. Unfortunately, Freddy was also correct in pointing out how little notice I'd paid to where Draxler fit in this convolution of Nina's request, Marco's escapades, my fresh envoy status, and Draxler's secret, whatever precisely that entailed. God forbid it involved those drawings. In other words, as usual, I was behaving like a fool and pretending I had no choice. We always have choices. More often than we ever care to admit, our lives are constructed around choices we make, whether trivial or momentous. Nothing is entirely inconsequential. That crosswalk we enter without considering traffic in both directions could kill us. That expired egg or tainted sausage we eat might lead to stomachs being pumped. An imprudent decision at work could toss us out into the street. No one is omniscient. Therefore, because we cannot see the future, that attention we give to each choice we make through these days of our lives is the best hope.

If only I were more astute in evaluating my own decisions.

I decided to take Kemper Street down to the taxi stand, mostly to walk off some of my jitters. The morning was breezy with a slight spring chill in the air. I wandered along the sidewalks through knots of people and wondered how they could be so calm and pleased with themselves while I was tending toward frantic. Where was Freddy when I needed him? No, if he were with me now, we'd both be off the rails.

I saw a free taxi and hurried across the street, taking care not to get run over. I rapped on the glass and the driver nodded and I climbed in. Just like that, the other door opened, and Marco slid in beside me, smiling. "Hello, Julian."

Our taxi took off, driving us toward downtown.

Marco said, "I already gave him directions."

Bewildered as always, I asked, "What are you doing here? Did you follow me?"

"More or less. Don't worry about it. We're right on schedule."

"There's a schedule?"

Marco laughed. "Julian, there's always a schedule. He demands it. This is his chess board and he's the king. We're only pawns."

"Or jokers in the deck."

Marco shook his head. "No, Julian. He doesn't play games of chance. Too risky. Chasing luck, he says, is a fool's errand. He won't live like that."

I couldn't talk to Marco any longer. He annoyed me. Like Radelfinger, he offered a kind of airiness that you just felt was more pretense than earnest. I began to see why Nina hated him. It was almost comical he didn't seem to get that.

The taxi entered Ehrenhardt Boulevard with the Dome of Eternity in sight now. My nerves flared again. The unknown is invariably terrifying. Was I actually about to meet Peter Draxler himself? Face to face? What would the skinny poets' savant, Nina's one-night lover, be like? In the Dome of Eternity. I hadn't been there since I was perhaps ten years old in Mrs. Herzog's Lower School Fourth Level class at Highland Park. That diverting field trip to see the golden stars. My memory of that day was vague but for a glimpse of something truly mirroring the divine.

We rode almost a dozen busy blocks along Ehrenhardt until our taxi diverted left onto Mauler Street and quickly stopped at the curb by an old clock shop. The sign above the door read: 𝕮𝖍𝖗𝖔𝖓𝖔𝖘𝖞𝖗𝖔𝖘.

Marco got out and came over to get me. "Let's go.

"What is this?" I asked, before leaving the taxi. "Why are we stopping here?"

"Safer passage, Julian. Come!"

I climbed out as Marco paid the driver. The shop was closed, but when Marco went to the door, a little old man in vest and trousers wearing a brass eye loupe opened up to let us in.

"Julian, this is Siegfried."

We shook hands. "Hello, sir."

The small fellow just nodded, as if he weren't able to speak, or perhaps his language was different from ours, although he did seem to understand Marco.

"This way, Julian," Marco said, leading me past Siegfried's workbench piled high and wide with arcane springs and clock faces, indecipherable mechanical apparatus and a multitude of clocks in various states of disassembly. "To the back."

We went through a ratty old curtain to a storage area of boxes where Marco took us to a basement door. He smiled. "Down again, my friend."

"Good grief."

"Don't worry," he told me. "Not too much crawling involved. Just a little."

We went down the narrow wooden stairs to a cluttered basement. Marco pulled a chain to a bulb overhead and lit the room. In a corner was a stack of crates he shoved aside, exposing a small door about four feet high. When he opened it, all I saw were a pair of dusty shelves, but Marco reached in, gave a push, and the shelves swung away into the dark beyond. He switched on a small electric lamp and handed it to me. "You go ahead. I'll put out the light in here and follow you."

"Are you sure?"

"That's my job today."

"If you say so."

"Go."

I went through on my knees. It wasn't bad. Just a few feet ahead. Not a claustrophobic underground limestone passage. Once through I was able to straighten up. The lamp illuminated an ordinary brick tunnel that led off into the dark. Marco stepped in behind me. "That wasn't so scary, was it?"

"Just swell, Marco. Thanks for the guidance. Where now?"

"Follow the tunnel."

I kept the glowing lamp and we started along. The ground was a bit damp and the air musty, a smell of mold and old brickwork. I didn't feel like talking, but I did, anyhow. Curiosity got the better of me. I asked Marco what he thought of what had happened at Gosney Street.

"Monstrous."

"You understand it was revenge for the Ferdinand Club that your crowd blew up, right? Both Nina and Delia could've been killed. Was it worth it?"

"Julian, five very close friends of mine died in that house. And just last night they murdered twenty-three of us in a beer cellar on Lejeune. So, I'm completely aware of how this works. We kill them, they kill us, we kill them, they kill us."

"And the innocent?"

"No one's innocent, Julian. You think Nina has no involvement in all this? She's more involved than you could possibly imagine. Ask Peter when you see him."

"And Delia? Was she planting bombs and lighting fuses?"

"Nina was warned when she took those rooms in the house. She's a smart girl. Maybe too smart for her own good. The part she took on put Delia at risk. Had Delia been killed, Nina would've been to blame. Not us. No one forced Nina to stay there once she agreed to join our crusade. She just always thought she was smarter than everyone else. Nina put us down every day of the week like we were her inferiors, her serfs. She's very beautiful, Julian. Anyone can see why you fell for her. But she's also terribly selfish, too."

"Your opinion."

"Yes, my opinion," Marco replied. "That's what it is."

"So who are you going to blow up next to get back at them for Gosney Street?"

"You seem angry, Julian. Why is that?"

"I just wonder who has to sacrifice what so you can feel better about yourself."

"That's not nice. Shut up."

"Who's angry now, Marco?" I said. "Maybe you ought to take it out on that maniac who shot Kaspar. I presume a fellow like him wouldn't have been dining in the Ferdinand Club."

Marco sounded sullen now, a little less pop in his voice. "He's been resolved."

"Is that so? How?"

"You really want to know?"

"Sure, why not? Violence has become second nature to my life these days."

"All right, then," Marco told me, "he tripped last week and fell through a manhole. Got himself stuck in a drainpipe about thirty feet down. A couple of days from now when the Mulhouse Reservoir releases its overflow, that pipe will flood and his silly cap will come floating up and he'll be drowned. He's just learning patience down there right now."

I tried to imagine what that nasty prick might be feeling then, caught in a pipe in the cold pitch-black darkness with no expectation of escape or rescue. The thought was horrifying, whether deserved or not.

We walked along through the damp brick tunnel for another five minutes or so before I asked, "How much more do we have to go?"

"Right up ahead here," Marco told me. "You'll see a ladder."

Then a dozen yards farther on, I did. A solitary iron ladder running ground to ceiling. A sturdy manhole-cover above it.

"What's up there?" I asked. We'd walked a long way and I wasn't quite sure in precisely which direction.

"A utility shed attached to the Dome. A door up there lets you into the monument without anyone outside seeing you."

"All right, then what?"

"Since you're here, I presume you know where to go in the Dome. Climb up the ladder and open the manhole. Once you're in the shed, hand me down the lamp so I can leave."

"That's it?"

"Yes, it is, Julian," Marco said. "Maybe we'll see each other again, or maybe not. Peter will decide."

"Or fate."

He shrugged. "If you prefer. Just listen to what he tells you and do what he says. If you want to save lives."

A minute later, I was up the ladder and Marco had his lamp back and I steadied my nerves for that entry into the great Dome of Eternity.

XXVIII

∞

For those of you who have never stepped inside the Dome, I must tell you that it is inexpressibly vast. No arrow or crossbow bolt could reach the ceiling from the floor of the Dome. Its construction exists in the mythology of the Republic, a massive edifice erected millennia ago in another world bearing faint similarity to our own. Yet we worship its grandeur with far more reverence than any of our exalted cathedrals.

On the great floor, rendered in solid gold on a tile sea of indigo blue, are the twelve signs of the zodiac, representing by metaphor we who are human, gazing up at a cosmos that is both indecipherable and never-ending. Around the perimeter, posed imperiously on gilded pedestals, are the zodiacal figures themselves, eighteen feet tall and carved in Dolonian marble. Above the floor, encompassing the entirety of the dome, are exhibited all the constellations of our known universe on a cobalt-dark firmament, pinpricks of light, thousands upon thousands, shining by refracted mirrors and oiled-torches into the glorious Dome, day or night.

Hundreds of people were there today, milling about, wandering singly or in groups, gathering under the zodiac statues for discussion and appeal to spirits of the spheres. The hallowed air of this monument is considered sacred, its purpose eternal. Formal speakers are forbidden in the Dome of Eternity, no speeches of any sort permitted, political or otherwise. Confusing this legacy with trivial opinions and disputes was anathema.

I knew where to go, yet I wandered about for a short while just the same. The Dome attracted myriad devout acolytes of curious theological persuasions. Burning censers were allowed if the musky incense chosen was ordained as holy or introduced into the metropolis by *Chaude-siérpes*, a cult of ancient imperials who believe they transcend from the dawn of Empire. These devout monks wear robes similar to the anchorites I saw down in the undercity but brown wool and plain as befits a vow of rank poverty and utter submission. There were dozens of them in the Dome, chanting guttural hymns, painting scrolls, and supplicating themselves to ghosts of the statued deities, those grand lords of the enduring zodiac. I did my best not to stare. So strange to me, this drifting populace of worship and wanderers. My life thus far had been no preparation for interpreting the journey of people so entirely unlike myself that those footsteps they pursued might just as well have been aimless, even as I accepted they were not. I was beginning to see how humanity was itself a vast labyrinth, a metropolis of souls, impenetrable to the apathetic and stubborn, immensely rewarding to the patient and willing. So I witnessed that day in the Dome of Eternity.

Finally, I went to the heart of my own pursuit. At the foot of the Dioscuri pedestal sat one of those inscrutable monks, obscured in his woolen hood, hunched over a sheet of parchment with a crude camel-hair brush and jar of black poshlavt oil. As I drew close, I saw a circularity in the patterns he made, interlocking swirls and swoops of intricate design and rendering, an appearance of chaos, a creation of indissoluble elements. I stood over him, intending to speak but dispossessed in that moment of the ability to do so. What should I say? Had I actually found him, at last? Was this the center of the maze?

Head down, eyes intently focused on his parchment, the hooded acolyte spoke first. "Welcome, Julian. I'm Peter."

All I could think of in response was, "Good morning."

"You're a very clever boy."

"Thank you," I replied. "I had some help."

"Frederick the Puzzle King."

"You know him? Of course you do. Through Marco, I presume."

"And others. Frederick has a curious reputation."

"His father thinks he's an idiot savant."

"I'm sure he does."

I had hundreds of questions for Peter Draxler. Where to begin? Maybe here: "Why Virgil?"

He muffled a laugh. "No one likes him, so I assumed if all went wrong, you wouldn't have many competitors. I had no idea this would work out so well. Nobody followed you at all."

"Thank God."

"You're welcome."

"I presume you won't tell me what this is all about?"

"My costume today, or our purpose here?"

"I understand your disguise," I told him. "It's very effective. Brilliant, actually."

"You want to know about the drawings I borrowed from Leandro Porteus, correct?"

"Mostly," I said. "And Nina."

His head still lowered, hand constantly creating with oil on parchment, Peter told me, "I won't reveal any details of the drawings, except to say they must be delivered to Major Laurentine Künze, of the 32nd Battalion, posted this month at Crown Colony. Do you know where that is?"

"No idea whatsoever. Is it by any chance within Tarchon Province? I've been given travel status only within those boundaries."

"It's close enough."

"Pardon?"

"You won't have a problem."

"All right, why me?"

"At last, the critical question. I've been waiting for you to get to the crux of all this, Julian. The reason I've put you, of all people, in the bunny run."

"Yes, please."

"Nina chose you after the great dog rescue. She said you were very determined and dedicated. That's why she led you to Virgil in the mausoleum. Your pursuit since then has been energetic and thoughtful. My young poets, Pindar and Quixote, promised you were fit and physically able. They're quite envious of your strength and studied aesthetic. Likewise, the codes and clues in Virgil proved you had the intellectual prowess and stamina to unravel intricate puzzles and link one to the next. That was absolutely vital."

"And Marco? What does he offer? He's been following me, hasn't he? All this time. He's your ears and eyes these days."

"Marco Grenelle is courageous and loyal. A great resource of constancy in a shifting tide of intrigue and dispute. He keeps me alive to do what needs to be done."

"He's mentally disturbed," I said, keeping my voice low. "He kills people with little remorse. He told me you encourage him."

"That's not precisely true. I do acknowledge certain bitter realities in our time that are distasteful and probably deranged."

"Like the Ferdinand Club?"

"Nearly one hundred thousand people have died in the Desolation this past year, Julian. What could be more deranged than that?"

"Is the death of a hundred thousand more heinous than the death of one? Are we statisticians now? Moral accountants?"

"Julian, my friend, in that one hundred thousand are single deaths, individual human beings with unique hearts and hopes, multiplied one hundred thousand times. There is no true formula for expanding or reducing a great moral dilemma."

I had to get on with this, anxious to be done here and off to that train for Tamorina. I asked, "And Nina? What role does she play for you? Are you still lovers?"

Peter stopped painting. His wet brush dangled above the parchment. "Goodness, no! Not even through another lifetime. Nina has wounds too deep for me to fathom. How you're able to bear her for more than an evening impresses me more than your translations of Virgil."

"But you're still entwined, somehow, the two of you."

"Only for one singular purpose, this crucible of fate and circumstance we can't avoid if she wants sweet Della to outlive us both."

"I have to tell you, I've never understood any of this. The arcane politics and insolence of it all. Honestly, I find it baffling."

"Nor have you ever needed to," Peter said, dipping his brush into the jar of poshlavt oil and painting again. "You're a runner. You have your papers from Paley. You can go safely where none of us would ever be allowed. That's your role. It's simple. I only wanted to know you were capable and willing. Nina believed in you, and I agreed, so long as you could find me. And you have. Congratulations. Marco bet you wouldn't."

"He's not that bright, really, but he probably has the deficit of spyreosis. Or so he says. I'm not sure what to think about that except your little Marco has his problems, whatever they are."

Peter Draxler's brush swirled once more, like a swallow on a spring sky. His touch was deft and daring. He told me, "Spyreosis is just a fable, Julian, the cruel manifesting of an obsession with people who are different. An enfeebling bug that taints the very lifeblood of our race and culture? God in heaven! Has spyreosis ever been put to any rigorous scientific examination and study within the Organic Medicine Institute? Of course not. Doing so would ruin the reputation of thousands whose pathetic lives have been dedicated to weeding out and destroying everyone they believe is a threat to their own social placement and well-being. It's reasonably simple to name your opposites as degenerates or imbeciles, shiftless or defective. Identifying them as infected with a virulent and debilitating scourge allows confirmation of that fraudulent conceit. It's all been a big lie, Julian, and that lie has annihilated our society. The pernicious disease, my friend, has always been eugenics itself, the great excuse for denying life and liberty to those we fear and despise. This Dome was once the extraordinary exemplar of a great civilization in its moment of ascent. Now, the true embodiment of us, whom we've become, is the Desolation and all its horrors, made evident within our grand eugenical Eden. But you'll see for yourself soon enough. Yes, you will."

His condescending arrogance astonished me. "Do I really need instruction on the moral decline of our Republic? Honestly? Or am I so naïve as to believe you and your cohorts in the undercity and all about have some magical ability to see through the daily hypocrisies of the Judicial Council, while the rest of us simply enjoy the weather? Good heavens, Draxler, who's insane here?"

He casually dipped his brush into the jar of black oil. "You tolerate the intolerable."

"Who doesn't? We are all complicit in this obscenity! Can you not see that? We're all part of this society, high and low, indivisible one from the rest." I struggled to keep my voice down. "Killing each other, like we do, is mass suicide. The trouble is that we don't recognize it as such. If we did, perhaps we'd do something about halting this plunge we're taking into the abyss."

As if waving a wand, Peter let his brush flourish across the parchment. Then he paused again. "Does Nina know you're this excitable?"

"I'm not sure what you mean."

"Why is she encouraging you to go into the Desolation, Julian, besides this scheme of ours? Does she have a purpose for you there, or perhaps another boyfriend waiting in the wings for when you don't return?"

I thought about how to answer that impertinent question. Since Nina didn't seem to know, or want to know, much of anything about my pursuit of Draxler, maybe neither was he privy to her priorities, either. Except that she led me to Virgil which allowed the unraveling of clues to bring me here. Did she know the purpose of *The Aeneid*? Did he not know about Delia's picture and Arturo Cascádes? Maybe each of them had been kept apart in all this for security concerns, with the only point of true intersection being me. Both knew Marco, of course, but he was just a traveler, not the destination.

Considering all of this to be a very distinct possibility, I told Peter, "Nina is a very beautiful girl. She's also quite clever. I love that she's so adamant about following her instincts. She doesn't trust Marco. I'm not sure how she really feels about you. Riding here to the Dome today, I was beginning to wonder how closely you two were together in devising my role here, but maybe you're not intimate, after all. And that makes me think I'm better off not sharing with you any purpose Nina might have entrusted in me. It's probably safer that way, wouldn't you agree?"

Peter laid his brush aside and studied the parchment scroll. He had yet to look up. Another blank parchment scroll rested beside this one and he took it then and let it unfold. The scroll he had finished painting, he held up to the light, and I saw his face for a moment, pale and riveting with a rare kind of beauty. Perhaps I knew why Marco spoke of him with such reverence. Admiration arrives in many forms, as does love.

Then Draxler folded up the painted scroll by quarters and held it out to me. He said, "Julian, I need you to carry this to Crown Colony. Please don't lose it. Hide it if you can. Without this scroll, the drawings are gone. As I told you, Major Laurentine Künze will be expecting it. Your envoy status will permit this deviation from your itinerary with no problem. Tamorina is a holiday. No one will expect you to go any closer to the war. There'll be an escort to guide you forward. His name is Samuel Protiste. He's attending at the hospital there, and he knows you're coming."

I took the scroll.

Samuel Protiste. Arturo Cascádes. Those names. Knotted together.

Unraveling another puzzle now felt too complicated for me, so I chose to let it go.

Peter Draxler gave his brush another dip into pashlovt oil and began painting the new scroll. He did not say another word. I watched him for a few moments, then wandered off into the center of the great Dome where I looked up to the dark blue firmament to find Alpha and Beta Geminorum, impossibly high in the glittering star field, then back once more to that solitary robed figure resting with brush and oil beneath the enormous marble statue of Castor and Pollux.

That last evening of the world I'd known, a note from Nina was slipped under the door of my room at Thayer Hall while I was down to the commons for dinner. Freddy found it on his return from the library. The reconciliation with his father and Professor Stubblefield involved Freddy spending one hour each evening at the Regency Library with a tutor named Hugo. My loyal roommate left Nina's note on my pillow when he went out to eat over on Peake Street with Burt and Walker. I felt too exhausted to catch up with them. Meeting Peter Draxler had drained me. Anticipation of where I would go the next day also put me so on edge, my nerves wore me out. After tossing about in bed, apparently I got up and went into Freddy's closet and grabbed one of his bottles of bourbon and filled a shot glass or two just to calm myself. I suppose it did the job because I don't have much memory of the evening after that. I presume I fell asleep with one fine thought cascading through my mind: the note Nina had written me. It read:

Wherever you go Julian my heart will be with you.

THE DESOLATION

XXIX

∽

My train left Commonwealth Station at nine o'clock the next morning. The North Platform wasn't as busy with baggage and travelers as East Platform at Thibodeaux Station where Nina worked, presumably because not many people took the train east along that unhappy route. The very idea of it held a certain air of dread and defeat, as most who had ridden in that direction were compelled to do so, a distinctly unpleasant circumstance. True enough, not all who rode these days were being deported. There were towns along the rail lines with normal people leading normal lives, and many of those used the train to travel into the metropolis for business or the entertainments of Pallanteum Plaza or those restaurants and arcades along the boardwalks of the holy river, Livorna. Not all our trains were poisoned by the grim reach of eugenics.

My ticket offered a compartment just off the dining car that I shared with a quiet fellow from Calcitonia where he held an important position with a commercial press. His name was Keaton Walmsley and he told me he was traveling to Colonia Tamal in Fabian Province to see his aunt who had taken ill with Burberia flu and was suffering greatly. Our compartment had fold-down berths and a narrow writing table between our cushioned benches. I thought these accommodations were plenty comfortable, given that I really didn't know much better. The train from Highland Park to Regency College was a plain commuter with no compartments, only general seating other than a drab dining car. Truth was, I did my best to adapt to this circumstance, given the great unknown I was entering into. Yes, I was terrifically nervous from the taxi ride to Commonwealth Station, securing my ticket, boarding the train with a crowd of strangers and finding my way to the compartment where I would soon look out the window at a world I hadn't any good preparation to see.

The first couple of hours didn't suggest anything but daily life in the rural countryside of Triánder Province I'd read about and imagined growing up. There were lovely fields and pastures of green grass and trees, horses and cows and sheep. Tall grain silos. Small houses with porches and home orchards, dirt roads in and out. Laundry on clotheslines. Barns and work sheds. Plain autos and utility trucks. Farther on, I saw acres of wheat and corn and barley, men and boys laboring together. Steepled churches, too, with horse and carriage out front. More old autos. Women carrying baskets of clothes or fruit and vege-tables. And small framed schoolhouses here and there, children running free about the yard at recess, teachers on the stoop out front. Crows and sparrows on telephone wires and perched in oak trees and birch. Lots of dogs and cats about the houses and horse pastures and rutted roads. All sorts. Some mangy and poor, like many people I saw along the rail route.

The train rolled through towns, too, small and rural. A population of ordinary citizens. Country towns. One or two-story buildings. Mercantiles and offices on dusty streets. Wind-whipped flags from courthouse poles. Sun-bleached white-wash on meeting halls and postal structures. The train stations were tired and mostly vacant. Like the livery stables I saw on failing supports. Rustic and aged. Some houses, as well. Standing yet because people occupied them in needful ways. A destination long found and accepted. Or embraced.

I had to remind myself how these were the hallowed fields of our Republic. This was not the Desolation. No war had occurred in these provinces. Eugenics had little moment of necessity out here. This fertile ground fed and sustained us. These rural people were our saviors in times of want. We could not eat our polished marble, our gilded edifices, or ten million paper credits. How far from the wide boulevards of the metropolis did rumors of inferior blood carry? I watched the day pass in carted bushel baskets of potatoes, and iron tractors urged through growing fields by women and men in simple cotton clothing and sun-shading hats, and wondered if these people were considered useful citizens by the Status Imperium. Was their value found in that sacred human-ity each of us shared, or only in those heaps of produce trucks carried from this raw earth to our hungry markets? Did spyreosis even exist in the labored blood of those who dug our planting furrows by spade and hoe? I hadn't con-sidered these questions before boarding the train to Tamorina. Worlds apart are often worlds unacknowledged. This history of us had loops and tangles whose unbinding required better than a keen and sympathetic eye. To see life unlike our own is daunting and risky. Cherished opinions and points of view can unravel with a glance at someone's laundry on a frayed clothesline, or one shabbily dressed child leading a smaller one across a wooden plank atop a country ditch.

I slept off and on during those first few hours aboard the train. My traveling companion read from a tattered volume of the Holy Book and a thin pamphlet called "Ministrations of Advertising." We didn't speak except for a few words upon greeting, after which he drew out his reading and left me to my sightseeing. I didn't much mind the absence of conversation because I was still apprehensive about what I carried with me. There was an implied threat to all this I could not ignore, and I accepted Dennett's advice to use discretion with whomever I encountered. How could I be sure this Keaton Walmsley fellow was who he claimed to be? Wouldn't a top investigator with Internal Security profess a clever alternate identity?

After breakfast early that morning before I left, Freddy and I had gone over Draxler's request and tried to figure out how best to secure his painted scroll. We agreed that keeping it hidden among my extra clothes or tucked carefully into the diplomatic pouch with my identity papers wasn't sufficient. Being who he was, Freddy came up with his usual ingenious solution. He went down to the second floor and brought back with him a young co-ed named Angelina Jouvenon, who had astonishing skills as a seamstress. Taking a pair of scissors with a needle and thread to my father's jacket, she sewed a secret pocket on the inside that was virtually invisible where I could tuck the quarter-folded scroll away until I needed it. A few snips from another pair of scissors would bring it out again. We were so impressed, we paid her fifty credits and each gave her a gracious kiss of gratitude. I think she left with a crush on Freddy.

Lunch in the dining car was sparsely attended and generally quiet. We were served Ganpari ham and stewed rice and honeycakes. Beer was offered and I drank one. Keaton Walmsley remained in our compartment. I left my valise there but brought the diplomatic pouch along, just to be safe. While eating, I met a friendly woman by the name of Madelon from Albiona who was traveling that day to celebrate her eldest daughter's birthday.

"I won't tell you her age," she said to me, "because that isn't polite, but I can promise you she's very mature and already has a good handle on housework."

"Does she have children?" I asked, hoping to be pleasant.

"Not yet," she told me. "There is a young man she has her eye on, although he sounds unsteady to my ear. I hope she is patient enough to resolve him more clearly into focus, so she doesn't make that big mistake."

"I hope so, too. We can't repeat our lives, can we?"

"No, we certainly can't."

I asked, "How far is Albiona?"

"Oh, it's maybe another hour, I guess. And four miles south of the train station. There's a lake and a meadow nearby of the loveliest wildflowers where the cemetery is. We were occupied, you know. Well, I'm not sure that's the best way to put it. We had folks there who shouldn't have been, and they put us all at a terrible risk of infection. Mind you, we knew nothing about the disease until they were rounded up and driven out. I suppose some of them died. We heard about that afterward. I can't say we were sorry. None of them wanted to leave, of course. Albiona is quite pretty. It's a wonderful place to live. If I'm truthful, I'd have to say those folks were very selfish. How can we expect to be happy when we make those around us unhappy? Like I said, we didn't know how close we were to being wiped out. I guess the Good Lord was watching over us and that's why we were saved."

Her train station came up sooner than expected and became my initiation into what would follow. The depot was plain and unadorned by city standards. Built of wood and cinder block. Just an office and toilets for both men and women. A couple of benches on the platform under a wood roof. There was no town, or at least nothing left of one. I saw ruins in the surrounding acres, broken framehouses and collapsed brick buildings, signs of violence passing through. I presumed the train depot had been put up after the struggle ended to service the outlying communities like Madelon's belovèd Albiona. I watched her get off the train and walk to a bus stop down to the end of the platform and across the tracks. She looked happy. The stationmaster came onboard, then got off again and I saw a small group of school-age children in ragged clothing, boys and girls, come around from behind the depot and collecting together behind a prim pair of older women in grey dress and jackets. Each child held a slip of paper and stared down the rails in the opposite direction from where I was heading.

No one else came on board and our train left the station soon after. Colonia Tamal, where my compartment friend intended to go, was another two hours along. I thought to ask Keaton Walmsley how one would describe the place, but he seemed thoroughly engrossed with the Holy Book by then and I had no desire to engage in a theological discourse aboard the train. I tried and failed to fall asleep. The porter came by and asked if we needed anything. My companion shook his head. I asked for a glass of water. The porter gave me a firm nod. I noticed in the mirror that my father's jacket did actually give me a very officious appearance and I wondered if that was why Madelon had been so willing to offer such an ungracious opinion of her neighbors removed from Albiona. Perhaps she thought I had some affiliation with the Council and therefore a hand in appreciating the vital circumstances of that decision. I wondered about communal loyalty and how far it extended. Love thy neighbor as thyself. Was that perhaps too much to ask in the society of eugenics?

I saw my first soldiers another hour ahead when our train stopped again at a town called Winterburn. There were dozens of them about the depot in no particular formation, gathered in pairs or small groups and smoking cigarettes and sitting on benches or up against the depot walls. Their uniform khakis were stained and dirty, their faces sooty and dark. Some were laughing, others grim and sullen, staring off beyond the train into the woods where black smoke rose above the birch trees.

How did they happen to be here? As I understood it, the war was hours and hours from this place. I saw soldiers now emerging from the woods carrying stretchers, half a dozen, men under blankets on them, alive. And a truck arrived from the dirt road to the depot. As I watched the soldiers bring their wounded compatriots to the truck and load the stretchers into the flatbed, I began to smell that smoke from the birch trees through our compartment window we'd lowered an hour ago. The odor was odd and pungent and rude. More than wood burning. It turned my stomach and I raised the window to close it. Keaton Walmsley had gone out to use the toilet at the end of our train car, therefore I didn't need to ask if it was all right to do so. At any rate, I presumed he wouldn't mind. Who would? The wounded were fully loaded into the flatbed and the truck drove off. An officer arrived and blew a whistle and all the soldiers about the depot got to their feet and shuffled into a sort of formation with weapons at hand, and another officer appeared and blew his whistle and the men began a slow march up the road ahead. Keaton Walmsley returned to our compartment and we both watched the column of soldiers until they disappeared into the distance and the depot was quiet again. Next an auto drove up and I saw a family of four get out. The woman kept her two little girls beside her as the man took a large suitcase from the trunk and gave the woman and the girls a kiss and guided them to the train and the porter who helped them onboard. Then he returned to his auto and lit a pipe and waited behind the wheel.

Another couple of men in ill-fitting brown suits and bowler hats came out of the depot with newspapers and small satchels and went straight up onto our train. A dog ran past barking after a crow that had alighted in the dirt by the tracks.

I was startled then by Keaton Walmsley who took that opportunity to speak for once. He said, "God's eye is on the world of we who inhabit His garden. No one can claim to recognize the patterns in His cultivation, but His purpose is clear. The world is perfect without us. This life He offers is a gift that can be taken back without hesitation or remorse. Our organization of things is vanity. It will not stand His scrutiny."

Another fellow in a long grey overcoat left the depot office and hurried to the train. He had a stack of papers in hand and waved to the conductor as the whistle blew for departure. The fellow climbed onboard as we rolled forward.

I told Walmsley, "If we can't presume to know God's plan for us, how can we interpret His desires? It seems futile to do so. Maybe our time here is better used in understanding and preparing for what our good neighbors have in mind for us."

He stared at me, his expression neither intense nor vague, just fixed as if attempting to recognize what or whom he was focused on. I wished I'd kept my mouth closed. I excused myself and got up and went out with my diplomatic pouch to use the toilet. The corridor was empty, but I heard a lively crowd in the dining car and walked that direction instead. Honestly, Keaton Walmsley sounded like a nut. Just my luck to have him in my compartment. I wished Nina were there with me. Miles and miles apart now, her scent remained. And that dark glow in her eyes. The taste of her. Love has no geography but what we believe and remember of it. Near or far, matters not. The heart may travel, but never leaves.

I wandered into the dining car and found a seat in the sunlight at the far end by a group discussing with great enthusiasm a recent horse race at the Jansenius Hippodrome in Darrieux Province. Apparently, the contest was interrupted with the favorite trailing by several lengths when a radio rocket blasted through the betting annex and frightened the horses to such a degree that not only was the race disrupted, but half a dozen animals had to be put down right there on the track. Had I a decent map with me, I would've researched Darrieux to see how close it was to the war. My understanding of our current military positioning was feeble. Now I realized that had to be reconsidered. For my own safety, at the very least. The Desolation was more mutable and dynamic than I could possibly have imagined from our newspaper reporting and radio broadcasts. I'd thought Tamorina was near the front lines at Tarchon Province when, in fact, the town was quite a few miles from the current engagements. Conversely, several provinces I'd thought were safely away from the struggle turned out to be on constant alert for artillery bombardment and random rifle assaults. Who was winning this war?

The train did not stop at each town along the rails. We bypassed Cahill and Sainz and Boudjfelja, for instance, whose buildings looked vacant or in ruins from vicious shellings that ended the common life of those communities. Both towns' train depots were demolished and the signals taken down. What few people I did see meandering along with packs of scavenging dogs looked to be vagrant or refugees from other places with no belonging there. Looters might inhabit those desultory roads and structures, stripping them bare, then drifting off to another. I imagined that was not without rewards of some sort. But farther on, we witnessed grave penalties for such behavior. At Dannenbaum, our train stopped for half an hour to take on supplies of food and water, coal for the engine, crates of something or another, and a handful of military officers without explanation. As we waited, a squad of riflemen hustled along a pair of scrawny teenaged boys from a barn up the road. They caused the boys to empty their pockets into the dirt beside the depot and sorted among these discoveries until they came up with some coins of arcane significance. I had no idea what that was, but once revealed, an officer who had boarded our train bounded back off again and motioned to the soldiers who nodded and shoved the two boys up against the depot wall. The squad stepped back several paces, raised their rifles, and shot them both dead. The bodies were there in the dirt when our train departed.

Keaton Walmsley watched without comment and returned to the Holy Book as if divine absolution for what he had just witnessed came page by page. I confess that he disgusted me. Colonia Tamal could not have arrived too soon. An hour later, when it did, we were obliged to leave the train so that maintenance could be performed. That's what we were told. Our tickets and papers were also examined as each of us stepped off. I was given an extraordinary examination when I offered Dr. Paley's notice of envoy status to the fellow administering our checkpoint.

"You're traveling to Tamorina?" he asked, warily.

"Yes, sir," I said, "by request of Dr. Otto Paley, Chief Director of Internal Communications on the Judicial Council. Thank you."

"I can read the directive, young man. You don't need to quote his position. I'm well aware of Otto Paley."

"Sorry, sir. It's been a long trip."

"How long do you expect to remain in Tarchon Province once you arrive?"

I tried to be as officious as my jacket and diplomatic pouch permitted, without coming across as arrogant to my status. "I suppose that depends on what's required of me there. The details await my arrival. I understand that I'm merely Dr. Paley's go-between in this situation."

"Of course you are," the fellow said, with no small hint of sarcasm. "Why else would the Council send a boy, right?"

"Certainly, sir."

He studied me for a few moments. My nerves flared. He asked, "You do know where you are, don't you?"

"Colonia Tamal, sir. Fabian Province. Correct?"

I felt Keaton Walmsley off my shoulder now, preparing to step off the train to his own destination. My interviewer looked past me to my compartment neighbor. The Holy Book that Walmsley held seemed to distract him. That insufferable edge to his voice diminished slightly as he came back to me. "You're in a battle camp of the damned, young man, where men like Otto Paley stoke the fires. Your envoy status is like that rising smoke, easily blown away when the wind changes. Pay good attention, my boy, or you'll blow away along with it."

I kept my best countenance. "Thank you, sir. I'll do my best."

The conductor told me the train would be delayed there for about an hour, so I decided to take a short walk. Late in the afternoon now, the air was cool, and a breeze swept across the depot platform and stirred dust in the tracks. Most of my fellow passengers had left the train and milled about in small groups or went off alone into town. I followed in that direction myself just to see what effect the war had here. My taxi driver Nevsky had lived in Fabian Province, but I couldn't recall which town he was from, only that the war had killed everyone he knew and driven him out. Colonia Tamal had certainly seen some fighting and yet it survived. Or maybe there had been extensive rebuilding due to the train hub for troops and other travelers, east and west. I had watched Keaton Walmsley get into a tan motor car driven by a young woman I assumed was his daughter. If she kept a home in this sector of Fabian Province, perhaps the experience here was more benign than elsewhere.

The town was plain and square. Just a few streets. Cobblestone and brick. Ordinary storefronts for general wares and trinkets. Tobacconist, grocery market, clothes and shoe store. Livery stable. A restaurant and a hotel down the street. A bank. Not a lot of people out, other than us. Some women, but mostly men. A few soldiers, too, in the company of an officer and a civilian investigator. I decided not to go far as there wasn't much to see. My father's jacket drew the occasional look of interest or concern, and I felt both self-conscious and confident. Whom did they imagine I was? Too young for a city magistrate. A fresh boy from Prospect Square, earning my medals in the outer provinces? I decided to test the waters, so to speak, by trying a general store in the middle of the block.

Being one of only two customers in the store, I was greeted almost immediately by a cheerful young woman seated behind the cash register. She was reasonably pretty in a pink dress and a yellow ribbon in her blonde hair. No Nina, but nice enough. She said hello and so did I.

"Are you shopping for anything in particular?" she asked, quite pleasantly. I thought she looked sleepy. Probably not a lot to do.

I smiled. "Just came in for a look. I'm on the train today. We stopped for something, but they didn't tell us what."

She frowned sweetly. "Oh, that's disappointing. Where are you supposed to be going?"

"Tamorina. I have a friend there." A small lie. No truth is entirely truthful, anyhow.

"I've never been," she admitted. "It's awfully far."

"Do you like it here?"

"Not particularly."

"Why not?"

She smiled. "It's ugly. Don't you think?"

"Well, I haven't seen much. I just got off the train."

She gazed across the store to her other customer, an older gentleman in a coat that was in fashion forty years ago. The store was gloomy, and he looked like he belonged there. She softened her voice. "You can go wherever you want to. It won't get any prettier."

I shrugged. "Then I guess I'll just have to stay here with you."

"Please do. I'm awfully bored. What's your name? I'm Greta."

"Julian." I reached over the counter and shook her hand. "Pleased to meet you, Greta."

"Likewise. It's a nice jacket you have."

"Thank you," I said. "It belongs to my father. He lets me wear it every so often."

"Well, it's very handsome."

"He thinks so, too. Are you in school?"

She shook her head. "There are no schools. We got blown up last year and our teachers left."

"What do the kids do for school?"

"They left, too. Put on a train one day. All of them. Now our town is empty."

"But you're still here."

"My father won't leave. He owns this store and we live in the back. He thinks there's no place else to go."

"What does your mother think?"

"She's dead. Those monsters killed her in the woods when she went out to pick raspberries. Six years ago."

"I'm sorry."

"We were told they ate her. By our soldiers who found her body. I don't think that's true, but my father does."

"It's all horrible these days."

Her pretty face somewhat pale, Greta said, "I wish I could leave and never come back. Where are you from?"

"Highland Park, Schuyler Province, but I'm in school now at Regency College in the metropolis. My final year."

Greta asked, "Do you like school?"

I shrugged. "I haven't decided yet."

"I didn't think school was useful. I only wanted to be married and raise children in a cottage by the sea."

"Why don't you?"

"All our boys are gone. There's no one here to love anymore."

"That doesn't seem right. I'm sorry about that, too. I can see why you'd want to leave."

"It's not fair."

"No, it isn't." I looked outside where a truck loaded with troops rumbled by. A thought. "Maybe a soldier?"

"Oh, I don't know." She perked up. "Do you want to buy something? We have lots of nice things you won't find anywhere else today in Fabian Province."

I looked about, wondering what I could do. Perhaps some trinket for Agnes so she'd stop with her guilty letters. "I'll see what catches my eye. Thank you."

Poor Greta offered a cute smile, a sad smile. "Take your time. I'll be right here."

I noticed that older fellow staring at us. At Greta. If I left, would he approach her? Was there something he wanted? She hadn't paid him any attention at all during our conversation. As I strolled off from the register, I kept my eye on him. He stared at her, as if I were completely transparent. Truth was, I didn't care to buy anything in that store. The glasswork and wooden bowls looked cheap and dusty. Agnes was too old for the handsewn dolls on a shelf along a side wall. I doubted that she needed any scarves or hairpins or needles. I saw a stone paper weight carved in the shape of a toad. Agnes loved frogs. Weren't toads and frogs the same? If Freddy were here, he'd know. The older fellow walked toward the cash register. When Greta saw him approaching, she slid off her stool and went through a curtain at the back of the store. I heard her yell at someone in there, and I left.

My father had put one of his old pocket-watches in the jacket for me and I checked the time. Still a half hour or so before departure. I decided to take a longer walk back around to the depot. Along the woods where spring lifted the air. I crossed the street as a group of soldiers came out of a liquor café down the block. A truck filled with sacks of grain drove through town, another soldier at the wheel, and one beside him in the cab.

I found the dirt road that skirted the woods leading up to the train depot in one direction and far off to distant growing fields in the other. There was a shallow ditch coursing beside the road by a thicket of raspberry brambles and ferns and I walked along until I saw a break where a path had been cut and stomped through into the woods. I decided to follow it where birds chittered high in the beech trees and broad shady oaks. The trail ahead was leafy and sort of muddy from a recent rain shower and the soil was wonderfully fragrant and earthy. A breeze stirred the afternoon air and felt cool all about, restful and dreamy. A walk in these woods should have been restorative to the soul, intuitively rekindling that natural affinity we share with the world into which we are born. The earth, the sky, this life we belong to, that better part of us divorced from hatred and fear and moral confusion. Mindful of the hour, I walked deeper into the woods and thought about Greta's mother killed somewhere out here amid the simple act of picking berries and tried to imagine both her fear and mortal disappointment at how her delightful interlude had been perverted for someone's cruel purpose. Easy to ask why she hadn't simply remained on that dirt road and chosen those raspberries where the day was safe and her life unthreatened. Yet being here deeper into the woods under this cathedral of nature, I could see why she would choose to wander off from the brick and bustle of town. That her life ended out here was a tragedy not of location but rather of those insidious forces that had no concern for the simple beauty of wanderers in a wooded shade.

I had thought I was alone out there. Only birdsong and the rustle of squirrels in the branches overhead and bees throughout buzzed in my ears. Then I heard someone tramping a ragged path toward me from deeper in the brush. A soldier, rifle slung over his shoulder, hat off, boots kicking at the leaves as he approached. I stopped and stood still, so he wouldn't mistake me for a stalking or escaping enemy. When he was close enough, I called out to him. "Hello there."

As he brushed a branch away from his face, the rifle came off his shoulder and he held it out, not exactly pointed at me, but not unthreatening, either.

He asked, "Who are you?"

"I'm Julian Brehm, personal envoy for Dr. Otto Paley, Internal Communications Director for the Judicial Council. Sir."

The soldier wore that expected look of suspicion. He had stripes on his sleeves. Not being a student of the military, I had no knowledge of what they signified, but he was obviously quite a few years older than myself and had that distinct appearance of a warrior. I felt if he had any doubt regarding my identity, he'd more easily shoot me dead than negotiate the truth. He said, "Show me your papers."

"Yes, sir. They're in my satchel. May I take them out?"

"That's what I'm asking."

I carefully slipped off the diplomatic pouch and lowered it to zip open so he could see I had no hidden gun within. Still the soldier raised his rifle such that it was now aimed at my chest as I withdrew my directive from Dr. Paley. "Here it is. My status orders."

"Fold it open and put the pouch on the ground. Then take five steps back and sit down with your hands on your head."

"Yes, sir." Of course, now I was terrified. If he intended to shoot me there where I stood, that umbrella Trevelyan had guaranteed would not help me at all. On the other hand, he and Dennett had warned me about being smart and careful. I presumed getting off the train and strolling into woods would not meet that definition.

I did as the soldier ordered and sat quietly while he glanced over my papers, never really letting his attention waver from me. I believed if I should happen to sneeze or scratch an itch, he'd kill me for his own safety's sake.

He asked, "What are you doing out here?"

My throat tightened and I was so afraid I could hardly speak. I forced out a weak, "A report."

"What kind of report?"

"Dr. Paley instructed me to see things and report them back to the Council."

"What kind of things?"

"Whatever I happen to see," I told the soldier, "they want to know about it. They weren't specific."

"Why is that?"

"I was not permitted to ask. Just to tell them. That's all."

"What have you seen so far?"

"Nothing," I replied, as my mouth felt dry and cold. "I was on the train. I just got off to walk into town for a few minutes. I met a girl at a store there."

The soldier smiled finally. "Was she cute?"

I shrugged. "Sort of."

He nodded. "Yeah, there aren't many beauties out here."

The woods felt quiet. As if the soldier and I were the sole living entities there in that moment. If he killed me then, would the earth pay any notice? How foolish to be in those woods alone. I'd already learned more about the war since boarding the train at Commonwealth Station than in all my years before. Things I'd had firm opinions of were dissolved by these realities of Madelon and Greta and this rough soldier whose name and story I didn't even know.

He tossed my pouch back to me. "Be careful, sonny boy. No one's innocent these days."

Then he slung the rifle back over his shoulder and walked on by, leaving me sitting there, hands still on my head.

I waited until his boots became deaf to my ears, then I got up and grabbed the pouch and checked my father's watch. I had another quarter hour to spare in the woods if I were foolish enough. The soldier was gone, yet curiosity ruined my better judgment and I followed the trail he'd taken toward me out of the thicket. I listened now as I walked, being awake to threats from any direction. Were there still birds in the branches overhead? Did a breeze still blow and bees buzz in the bramble? I didn't listen for that anymore. I wanted to stay alive long enough to catch my train, but just the same I had to see where the soldier had come from.

And so I did.

And this was what I saw.

Perhaps another hundred yards on through a wet entangling undergrowth, a deliberate clearing of fallen trees and rough-hewn logs, yet shaded by ancient beech and oaks, thirty or so graves of piled dirt and leaves, a smell of damp ground and rot. A hidden slaughterfield. I walked into the middle of those low earthen mounds and stood where sunlight cascaded in a late afternoon slant of warmth and disregard for our moral disabilities, and I wondered what form of this heavenly wood was seared into the brains of these unfortunates in that brief and bitter moment of their dying.

Then I heard a muffled utterance next to one of the black gnarled oaks where the dirt was fresh and moist. I walked close and listened and thought someone was humming or heaving beneath the dirt, and then I knew what I was hearing and did not dare acknowledge it because there were voices in the woods just a little farther off, two men shuffling along in my direction. I hid behind the oak only a few feet from the fresh grave, that living grave, that groaning under the earth, waiting quietly until I saw the men, one with a shovel and the other carrying a pickaxe, in rays of warm sunlight. Gravediggers. Slathered in mean grime and sweat. Not soldiers in uniform. Conscripted to do this job in the thick woods. Burying our mortal enemy alive? One by one? Good grief. I heard them so close now, crushing leaves beneath their muddy boots, I thought they could hear my breathing.

Then one of them saw me and shouted.

And I ran off.

Our train left Colonia Tamal and rolled on through a red sunset. I had another neighbor in my compartment for the next few hours. His name was Grover Colborne and he told me he was a scientific interrogator assigned to the Pharosien Brigade for rooting out infiltration conspiracies of which he assured me there were many. At first, he seemed like a congenial fellow, somewhere between my age and my father's. He was fit and sturdy, strong of voice and body. Assured of his own character and morality. Often a mistake, of course. How can we truly know who we are without that critical mirror held up before us and unadorned with false and misleading flatteries? Yet, I felt he was fairly benign, given my other encounters so far along the rails to Tamorina. Naturally, I was wrong.

But our dialogue began all right, eating supper together in the dining car. We were offered Topacchi soup and green salad, Sypelle chicken with boiled potatoes and steamed vanilla pudding. We both drank glasses of red Guerrero spirit wine and toasted to a pleasant journey, 'wherever we were led, henceforth.' He told me his wife, Lara, taught school in the metropolis at the Molly Institute on Simoni Hill, a fine district in those days. Lots of money, good facilities, wonderful and engaging students. Healthy. He said they were blessed to have the fortunate-born attend classes without worry of disruption or disintegration of her intricate curriculum by any of those less-equipped for modern life. That had been his concern when his wife was offered her position.

Drinking down his wine, Grover told me, "Some educators, you know, are less intuitive than others in being able to identify students whose capacities are naturally limited by birth or circumstance. It does no one any good to introduce them into a setting where failure is inevitable, and their very presence becomes antagonistic to fellow students whose breeding and biological possibilities offer better opportunities for success. This debate over the inclusion of students who may not be diminished but are certainly not gifted is one that ought to have been put to rest decades ago. We've been fighting a war all these years to protect that part of our civilization we trust will guarantee a future of accomplishments far exceeding any we've known so far."

Grover signaled to our attendant for a refill of his Guerrero.

I said, "And the cost of this?"

He frowned at me. "Do you mean economics? Because one cannot quantify a culture. It exists outside of ledgers and counting machines."

"No, I don't mean bank credits at all. To the contrary, I wonder about its effect on our souls, an endless war. So many lost. The disruption in our everyday lives and emotional well-being."

"Well, what of it? Do you say we shouldn't have fought at all? Just let them win? Do you even know who they are? Who we're fighting? Really?"

"You tell me."

Grover was brought his second glass of spirit wine and quickly drank half of it. I already felt lightheaded from my partial Guerrero and wondered how clearly this fellow was thinking after his glass and a half.

"Julian, my boy, I've interviewed legions of those creatures over the past three or four years, depending on how you define 'interview.' We've captured them out here by the hundreds and shoved them through our basement protocols, wrung the hell out of them. Put the fear of a true God in their hearts. Electrified their nuts. Melted the tits off their women. Cut them open and poured in salt and vinegar. Sawed them apart. They each died screaming that same nonsense, how they're just as human as we are, but they'll take the Republic back from us if we don't quit the war. They're working out a plan. A good one. They say they know things we can't imagine, and they'll kill us all if we don't stop. The lies they told, you wouldn't believe."

Grover Colborne stared at me, breathing slowly, his pupils dilated. He drained his second glass of Guerrero and called out across the dining car to our attendant for another. Then he told me, "This is something you're not taught in school. Our enemy are mentalists. Cerebral infectives. Worming their vile imbecilic thoughts into our unsuspecting brains. Like lice that fester and multiply. Their nastiness creating brutes out of aristocrats. Leading us down into that muck and misery they know quite well. It's practically institutional. We're pretty convinced of that now. I've experienced it directly myself. It's insidious. And very dangerous, too, you see, because our interrogators are all different. Some just aren't that strong. The weakest have fallen apart and cut the monsters loose and let them out. It's been a big problem. We haven't figured out a solution yet."

"Mentalists? What does that mean? They make you walk into walls? Jump off cliffs?"

"Son, they're not human. Not like we are. Spyreosis changes them, alters their atoms or cells, or what not. I can't explain the science. It's just what we've been told by a representative of Dr. Mulberry from Biological Investigations. He did all the testing that revealed this. We're pretty sure that's why the monsters blew up the Ferdinand Club. They knew he was onto them and needed to be gotten rid of. The Council ought to have expected something like that. If I were with the Security Directorate, I'd have seen it coming a mile away."

"A bomb to kill Mulberry? You're sure about that?"

"Makes sense, don't you think?"

"Blowing up the whole Ferdinand Club to kill one person? Almost two hundred people died in that building. Does anyone think like that?" I saw now that Marco was desperately insane. Did Draxler know that? I assumed so, but if not, he was a fool.

Our attendant brought Grover his third glass of red spirit wine. He swallowed half in one gulp, then said, "Let me tell you something, Julian: they do not have the same morals that we do. Keep that thought in your head."

"Yes, sir. That's probably true."

"And it's why we're fighting this war, and why we need to win."

"I understand."

Grover studied me with glassy eyes. Our train rattled over a long wooden trestle and the dining car shook side to side. Wine splashed from my glass, which was still mostly full. I had no intention of letting myself get drunk on this journey. I was not that big a fool. I excused myself and went to the toilet at the back of the car. The sky was dark now and there were lights across the last fields of Fabian Province. Next were forested mountains of Tarchon Province, what the map designated as Kumari Wilderness. No towns or villages. A stronghold for our indomitable enemy forty years ago until we set fire to the entire forest with batteries of incandescent artillery shells enhanced by radioactive phenotheric gas. All life in that prehistoric wilderness ceased for almost ten years.

After dinner, Grover Colborne went off to visit associates in the smoking car and I went back to our compartment to sleep. I was so tired I could scarcely think. I folded down the bed and climbed into it with my diplomatic pouch, intending to give myself over to dreams quick as I could. Yet a certain curiosity seized my mind and I opened the pouch and took out the two envelopes Nina had given me: One with Delia's photo, and the other with Arturo's. I looked at his first. Why I hadn't done so earlier, I passed off to a touch of jealousy. After all, he'd been my beautiful Nina's lover and father of her child. How could I compete with that memory of hers, the huge part he'd played in her life? Regardless of how he ran out on Nina, Arturo had given her Delia. Such a gift. That delightful, funny, smart little girl. I looked at his picture. I had to admit he was quite handsome. Not the rugged sort like some of these soldiers, but classically proportioned in his features. Sort of darkly angelic, I suppose, with luminous eyes. I could see why she fell for him. I wondered what she saw in me. What drew her besides my ability to find and fetch Delia's little dog from a nasty drainpipe? Would she still love me when I came back from the Desolation? *If* I did? Or had I played out my role in her life and she'd seek another fellow toward a new destination? I do admit that worried me quite a bit. If there's anything perpetually true in the trials of love, it's that no one wants to be left. So what was he like? Fit or lax? Studious or exciting? Buoyant or moody? Strong enough of will to put Nina in trouble and then run out on her, that was certain. And how was it that Arturo did not fall in love with her? The part of her story I found almost incomprehensible, except each of us has his own preferences in food and clothing and music. Why should love and lovers be any different?

I put his picture back and drew out Delia's. She's so young still, it was difficult to pin down her age in that picture. Three years ago? Not a baby picture. And her hair was a little shorter, curled differently. Recent enough, I thought, to be recognizable. She was very pretty, but so mercurial no camera could possibly capture her true essence, the amazing spirit of her. Honestly, once I got past that childish obstinance, I liked her quite a lot. Casually, I flipped the picture over and found writing on the back I hadn't noticed when Nina had first handed me the picture, a scribbled line along the top that read:

I keep a secret

That was Nina's handwriting. What did it mean? What secret? Was that simply referring to being Nina's daughter rather than her sister? So, read that way, the picture meant that Delia kept the secret of her true identity in Nina's life. Was that all? Everything in these stories, whether Nina's or Draxler's, seemed to have meaning beyond what fell in front of me at a glance. Did this, as well? When I went to put the picture back into its envelope, I found something else I hadn't noticed: a dried lemon blossom. What was that for? Delia's favorite flower or scent? A physical signifier of season or beauty? Something Nina and Arturo once shared? Had they made love under a lemon tree and that union created Delia? So many avenues of interpretation, but I was far too drowsy now to contemplate even one, and I tucked the envelope back into my diplomatic pouch, then switched off the tiny bed lamp and fell asleep.

Somehow our train stopping woke me up out of an odd dream an hour later. I'd been out on a lake in a boat under moonlight with a girl who might have been Nina, or possibly Lydia Sayre. I recall a great captured fish and a delightful song across the water and other boats all about alit by candle lanterns and Agnes swimming away from us across the lake and laughing at me for refusing to follow her.

I stopped wondering about it when I heard gunshots from outside and the sound of people boarding the train. I climbed off my bed and looked through the window and tried to see what was happening and could not, so I went out into the corridor. There were soldiers now ahead in the dining car and in the sleeper car behind us. People were yelling inside the train and I heard more shots and screams from outdoors along the tracks by the dark woods. I went back into my compartment, grabbed the diplomatic pouch, then made my way forward along the corridor to the vestibule where I might see what was occurring in and out of our train here in the middle of the night. I ought to have remained in my bunk. Two steps off the vestibule let me witness soldiers hustling certain people off the train and shoving them away from the tracks where they were pushed to the ground and shot in the head as they fell. Grover Colborne was there by the train illuminated in hydrogen spotlights and directing the action of our soldiers. Shot. Shot. Shot. Shot. Shot. Bodies scattered in the grassy dirt along the edge of the woods. Blood in black pools.

Next, I watched another group of soldiers leading a column of filthy and frightened children in wool coats and scarves from the forest, herded to the baggage cars at the rear of the train. Then the shooting ceased and the lights went out and the train whistle shrieked and we began to roll forward once again. I had no idea what atrocity I'd just witnessed, but I took the memory of it back to my compartment and failed to sleep another minute.

The train was only a few miles outside of Tamorina and I was in the dining car eating my breakfast of hardboiled eggs, fried ham, toasted bread and a hot cup of Alcasian cocoa-coffee. The morning was cold and nearly everyone I'd encountered onboard since sunrise looked tired, doubtless from that horrific interruption in the middle of the night. The sole exception being Grover Colborne and a fellow named Arlo, who invited themselves to my table when I was just halfway through eating.

"Sleep well, Julian?" Grover asked, taking his seat opposite mine. He hadn't returned to our compartment all night long, and I presumed he'd been off torturing some unfortunates in the rear of the train. I decided Grover Colborne was a hopeless psychopath who'd found his niche in a war where anyone he laid his wicked eyes upon could become the object of his own mental disorder.

"Not particularly. Too noisy."

"Lots of excitement, wasn't there?"

"I don't know," I replied, cutting off a slice of ham. "Was that exciting?"

Grover slid the chair back beside him for his friend. "Julian, meet Arlo. We worked together in Flissingen Province a couple years back. He just happened to be on the train last night. A remarkable coincidence."

We shook hands. "Hello, sir."

Arlo was a shorter fellow, bald, frail, gaunt of face and hands. The kind of person you come across now and then who just appears hungry all the time, as if he can't digest enough food to keep that pink in his cheeks.

"Pleased to meet you, Julian."

Grover told me, "Arlo is one of our finest interpreters. Your Dr. Paley solicited his talents for the Communications Directorate straight out of Ascanius College. He has a special talent, don't you, Arlo?"

His friend shrugged and grinned at me.

"What's that?" I asked, then immediately regretted saying a thing.

Grover took a napkin and folded it. "Tell him, Arlo!"

One of the dining room attendants recognized guests at my table and went to get a couple of breakfast programs.

Arlo said, "They tell me I can sense spyreosis in someone's blood."

"Is that so?" I smiled. "How clever."

"Amazing, right?" Grover enthused. "There aren't more than a dozen fellows of his techniques and experience in the whole of our Republic. It's astonishingly helpful for this work. Last night was a perfect case of it." Grover took a fork and pointed it at Arlo. "You saw those fellows at the game table before any of us, didn't you?"

I ladled a bite of egg onto my toasted bread and ate it. Then had a sip of cocoa-coffee. I wished they'd both leave my table, but perhaps I could've eaten more quickly and solved the trouble myself.

Arlo said, "The one with the blue velvet coat and ascot was more obvious than the others. I just did my calculations and linked them all. Not a particularly difficult solution once you see through the disguise."

The attendant brought the programs and handed one to Grover and the other to Arlo, then left.

I decided both of these fellows were disastrously insane. They belonged in white strap-jackets on the bottom ward of the Jouhandeau asylum. How had we let ourselves fall so far that men like this determined life or death for the rest of us? Once upon a time, we must have all become pathetic fools. One hundred years of institutionalized lunacy.

Grover said to me, "Julian, this train was under a dire threat last night. Those fellows Arlo uncovered were plotting to burn us all up. Our investigators are still searching for the phlogistic incendiaries and ash igniter, but we'll find them. Don't worry."

I finished my eggs and carved off another piece of ham. I was eating as fast as I could. Yet I could not resist asking, "Who were those children out there?"

Grover looked at Arlo, who nodded and told me, "Refugees from one of the internment camps. They were hiding in the woods when our troops found them. Three had died already. We were lucky to rescue the others. Kids don't manage well outdoors in these temperatures."

I drank most of my cocoa-coffee and dabbed at my mouth with a napkin. These fellows made me so nervous I was afraid of spilling all over myself. "Where were their parents?"

"They're orphans, Julian," Grover told me. "All orphans."

Arlo told me, "We try, but we can't save everyone."

I buttered my last piece of toasted bread, then asked, "Do we really try that hard? Do we?"

Grover replied, "You seem skeptical, Julian. Does Otto Paley know what sort of boy he's appointed as his envoy?"

I ate another bite of bread. "I don't presume to be privy to Dr. Paley's opinions on anything, sir, and haven't been asked to do so. I only perform those duties required of me and leave the rest to the more experienced."

As our dining car attendant arrived to take the breakfast requests of those two maniacs, Arlo said to me, "You're a smart boy, Julian. Don't let that get in your way out here."

Tamorina was not a holiday. When we arrived at the mid-town rail depot, the great plaza was hectic with soldiers and civilians hurrying about in many directions. There were trucks and autos and pushcarts and horse-drawn wagons intersecting across the morning cobblestone. A large cast-iron bell atop the depot tower rang and rang the ten o'clock hour. I grabbed my valise and tucked the diplomatic pouch back into it and left the compartment. A crowd filled the vestibule for departure, and we had to be patient to get off. No one pushed.

Outdoors, the morning was cold and people bustled about in coats and scarves. Soldiers, too, wore thick wool overcoats and hats. More children, as well, also in little grey coats and knitted caps, scores of them crowding the edges of the plaza as they emerged from town in an orderly column, preparing to board the westbound train. Tamorina was the eastern rail terminus, and here is where people traveling out of the Desolation began their journey back toward the benign and peaceful provinces, or farther west still to the great metropolis itself surrounding the banks of the holy river, Livorna.

Walking away from the train, I'd never seen so many children in my life. More refugees? The guides were solemn adult civilians in black and grey dress, aided by small squads of armed soldiers, stern and earnest in their duty, whatever it was. I didn't completely understand any of this. The chattering of voices, shrieks and calls and laughter and shouts, was deafening after the quiet of my rail compartment. I had to push a path through the crowds to get away from the railroad cars into the middle of town where I hoped to find the hospital. I realized I had no idea where it was, so I'd need to ask if I had any expectation of finding it. Was it walking distance? How big was Tamorina? These things I ought to have investigated while I was still on the train. I might have asked Grover Colborne, but his mental state was so cruel and perverted, I could live three lifetimes without hearing his voice again and feel quite satisfied.

The town was actually quite a lot larger than Colonia Tamal. For instance, Tajah Street, where I went from the train, stretched out as far as I could see to the north, lined with buildings of all sorts and sizes. I was walking on brick that looked recently laid and well assembled. There was much more commerce here, many stores of great variety and goods, several restaurants catering to the disparate culture and ethnicity of Tamorina, some hotels, and, of course, attorneys and finance and the usual array of bureaucratic offices. I stopped in at a coffee and pastry bistro for a powdered jelly nouvelle to take along and to find out the location of the hospital.

Indoors, the shop smelled wonderful and was warm and busy, all the small tables occupied with customers enjoying tea and coffee and lovely pastries of all kinds, with conversation lively and pleasant. The mix of people was intriguing, more like Ehrenhardt Boulevard or the undercity than any of those towns I'd just viewed from my compartment window along the hours of our train route. Racial and geographical distinctions were evident here in skin shades and odd dialects of those ancient communities native to Tarchon Province: Colozi, Riusa, Cisseus, Combitta, Satorius. A blur of curious cultural inflections, fascinating in this aromatic context. Listening while I stood in line, I almost wished I'd enrolled in Dr. Schoelcher's Language and Dialects course the previous winter. A Thayer fellow from third floor told me about it with great enthusiasm. Of course, his motivation for taking the class was a Sofarien girl he'd met and was wooing in hopes of surrendering his virginity in the New Year. Apparently, he passed the course with top marks. How he fared with the object of his desire I never asked, but I presumed it went well. Passing him in our stairwell off and on, he always wore a smile. Life was magisterial.

Once I reached the counter, the woman there asked what I wanted, and I pointed to the powdered jelly nouvelle. "Just one, please."

"Coffee, if you please, sir?"

She was about the age of my mother but weathered poorly by relentless sun and wind in the eastern provinces, and spoke with a distinctive accent, possibly Colozian.

"No coffee, thank you."

"Tea? Hot, if you please, sir? Mokhat? Very excellent this morning. You may ask."

"No tea, thank you. Just the jelly nouvelle."

"As you say, sir. For no tea or coffee. Three credits."

I had the money in my trouser pocket and paid her as she fetched my fresh nouvelle from under the glass. "Thank you, ma'am. May I ask where I might find the Asklepieion Hospital? I have an appointment there this morning."

She gave me one of those looks of worry and concern that suggested she thought I was possibly ill and contagious. "You have emergency today, sir?"

"No, just a nice meeting with a friend," I told her in my best voice of reassurance. "He works there, and this is my first visit to Tamorina, so I'm trying to find the hospital."

"Pandarus Street, sir. Clean hospital. Nice doctors. No dirty people."

Dirty people?

"Is that anywhere close by? I'm walking."

"No, sir. Hour to walk."

"Are there any taxis?"

"Yes, sir. Top of Tajah by the trains. Many to buy."

I thanked her and left. Walking back up the street to the depot, I ate my jelly nouvelle and wondered how I would approach my conversation with Arturo Cascádes. Did he have any romantic memories of Nina? Had he loved her once as I have? What feelings would his heart possess for sweet Delia? And what of this Protiste character? What was he like? Draxler expected me to trust him on the road to Crown Colony, wherever that was. I needed to see a map today, find out what I'd gotten myself into.

The taxi stand was just down to the end of the depot past the crowds for boarding or departing the trains. That column of children seemed not one bit diminished. Hundreds then. Where had they all come from? Certainly not only Tamorina. Their faces pink or tan were flushed with the cold air, lots of runny noses, lots of teasing smiles here and there, but mostly skittish expressions of fear and worry. Again, I wondered about their parents. Were all these children orphans? There must have been at least three or four hundred, probably lots more. Was that even possible? Their grey-coated guardians tried to keep the children quiet, but kids will be kids, and a mass of children that great is impossible to subdue entirely. I had the oddest, most unsettling feeling as I walked past them to get my taxi. What on earth was happening here?

I found my taxi just beyond the children and climbed into the back seat with my valise. My driver was a dark ethnic fellow with a wool cap and knitted scarf, who was reading a newspaper when I got in. He looked back at me with a bright toothless smile. "Good morning, sir."

"Good morning. Could you please take me to the Asklepieion Hospital?"

"Oh yes, sir, indeed. Are you injured?"

He started the motor.

I said, "No, just meeting an appointment there."

"Oh, that's very good. Many soldiers at the hospital. Many, many, many." He drove us away from the depot. I rolled my window down. Although the morning air was chilly, the interior of the cab had an unpleasant odor, something like Kafrat oil and onions. I presumed my driver ate his meals in this cab. I'd advise against that.

"Are you with the soldiers, sir?" my driver asked.

"Not exactly. I'm an envoy for Dr. Otto Paley."

"I don't know that name, sir. Is he at the hospital with the soldiers today? There are many injuries there. Many, many, many."

I wasn't sure I should explain the distinction. Perhaps there wasn't one. Was Paley a medical doctor? I wasn't really sure. I thought I should find out, except that asking such a question might lend someone to believe I was a fraud for even mentioning Dr. Paley's name if I didn't know his résumé.

I told my driver, "No, he's working in another town this morning. I'm seeing someone else."

"Are you sick, sir?"

"No, I'm perfectly healthy. At least I hope so!"

We both laughed.

He dodged our taxi around a clot of people crossing the street from a narrow alley of shops and pushcarts. Auto traffic was lighter in Tamorina than people on foot or bicycles, which also seemed fewer than I might have expected out here in the rural provinces. Looking about as I ate my jelly nouvelle, I began to wonder what sort of damage the war had inflicted when the bombardment occurred eighteen years ago. The buildings I saw appeared fresh and well-constructed, as if all of Tamorina had undergone a thorough restoration. Not a renaissance, however. The town felt improvised, somehow. Culturally insubstantial, like a fresh air street market or a traveling circus hastily thrown up to welcome visitors but carrying that discernible air of impermanence. It smelled sort of odd, too, a passing scent of fresh creosote and stale fertilizer.

I asked my driver, "Are there always these many soldiers here?"

"Yes, sir. Many, many, many. From all about. They need the hospital and the train, sir."

"And the children, too? For the train? Where do they all come from? Not here, I presume."

My driver went silent for a minute or so, as if he hadn't heard my question. He ran the taxi up a short hill past a row of flat houses that were mostly unpainted and plain of adornment. No fence or gabled eves or shutters or curtained windows. Empty, too, I guessed. A quiet neighborhood of no one. At the top of the hill, he stopped and rolled up his own window. Then he turned to me. "No children from Tamorina for the train today, sir. Riusa, Satorius, Páros, Ilus, this week, sir. Last week, Cisseus, Aurora, Colozi. Many children, sir. Many, many, many."

I asked, "Do you have children?"

"Oh yes, many, many, many, sir."

"Do they live here in Tamorina?"

"Oh, no, sir," he told me, "they went away on the other train."

"When was that?"

Silent again, my driver swung the taxi away from the curb and drove us on down the other side of the hill where young trees were planted along a sidewalk and the houses were prettier and I saw people outdoors here and there and dogs and small children scrambling in the grass. This was a living neighborhood of mailboxes and radio antennas and autos parked in cement driveways. Why not on the other side of the hill?

I asked my driver, "Were you here for the war?"

He steered us onto a wider boulevard toward a plain where the growing fields were green on the horizon. "Yes, sir."

"What was it like?" I asked, almost obsequiously, although that hadn't been my intention.

"Many, many, many things, sir."

We rolled down onto Pandarus Street, and I could see the big hospital ahead, gleaming white on a flat plaza of tall poplars and spring flower beds in glorious bloom.

"Well, it looks very pretty," I said, sounding as immature as I was that day. How *do* we account for who we are?

I finished that jelly nouvelle as my driver pulled up in front of the hospital in a line of military trucks and civilian autos. I gave him thirty credits, far more than the cost of his fare. What else was due this fellow?

He offered once again that toothless smile. "Many, many, many thanks, sir. Good morning."

When he took my money, I noticed the skin on his hands was bleached and mottled, his fingernails black, a permanent effect of chlorocyanic gas.

At the lobby entrance, I had to remove the diplomatic pouch from the valise to present my envoy papers to a firm and surly guard. He examined my status and looked me over up and down with extreme skepticism. He asked, "How long have you worked with Dr. Paley?"

"I'm not permitted to answer that, sir. I'm sorry, but the nature and parameters of my status are held in the strictest confidence by the Internal Communications Directorate. Dr. Paley left that undisputed."

"Is that so?"

He handed back my papers.

"Yes, sir. We each have our orders."

I replaced them into the diplomatic pouch.

He studied my valise. "What's in that suitcase?"

"Personal items. Clothing. My traveling paraphernalia," I said. "We're many miles from Prospect Square."

"I see."

"Would you care to look through it?"

"No."

"Thank you, sir. May I go in now?"

He stepped aside and I grabbed my valise and entered the madhouse.

That rude coppery-odor of blood and sterile antiseptic washed through the interior of the hospital lobby where dozens of soldiers and civilians stood or sat or lay on the cement floor, wounds oozing blood through inadequate bandages or none at all, stanched only with dry cloth compresses or rags soaked in carinaen solution. Was this the only place for them? Where were the treatment stalls? A handful of nurses circulated through the moaning injured, addressing each briefly then shifting attention to another and another after that. Threading my way through to the front desk, I felt almost cruel to ignore the suffering wounded around me merely to ask the whereabouts of a couple attendants I presumed were occupied with critical duties elsewhere at that moment. The noise was disconcerting, too, cries of pain and physical anguish, people shouting down the halls, telephones ringing all about. I could scarcely hear myself think to mentally organize and present my request to the nurse receptionist.

She ignored me for the first few minutes and I took no insult at that. No one's presence in that lobby was more superfluous than mine. I was not bleeding, nor I was a doctor, nor did I demonstrate any certain military affiliation. Where had all these casualties come from? There was no fighting in Tamorina I was aware of, no echoing thunder of cannon fire across the morning air. How far off was the fighting if these poor souls were here? Shouldn't that agony be a hundred miles away or more? Had these wounded arrived by train or truck, I couldn't conceive of the prolonged suffering during transport from such a harrowing distance. Were there no army field hospitals? There was clearly something in this dreadful spectacle I was failing to notice, a clear hint of purpose. The war was not a secret, no rumor behind a curtain. What was I missing?

I kept my back to the blood and sufferers because I had nothing to offer and only terror and nausea awaiting if I stood by and watched. How many of them were dying in that lobby? Good grief. Who was I in all this? Was I really prepared to meet Arturo and hear his romantic love story of Nina in this hideous circumstance?

A voice called across to me, impatient and frazzled. "How may I help you?"

The woman who spoke was at the end of the desk, just off the telephone, middle-aged, weary of face and dress, yet apparently not overly flustered by the insanity of her morning environment.

I went over closer to her. "I'm here to see Arturo Cascádes. He's an attendant."

"Cascádes?"

"Yes, ma'am. Arturo."

She opened her day log, flipped a couple of pages and skimmed a column of names to the bottom. "No, sir. Not here."

"Are you sure?"

"Yes, sir," she told me, as the telephone rang at her elbow. "He's not in the log. Excuse me."

She took the call and my own attention was drawn to a gurney pushed into the lobby from the left hallway. One of the soldiers bleeding from a chest wound that soaked the whole of his upper uniform was hoisted by two attendants and another bandaged soldier up onto the gurney and rushed off to the corridors of the inner hospital.

"Is that all?" the woman asked me, just off the telephone.

"I'm sorry," I replied, "but could you possibly look up Samuel Protiste? If maybe he's here?"

"Yes, he's on 'D' ward this morning. I can notify him."

"Please."

"And your name?"

"Julian Brehm." I spelled it for her as she scribbled it down. "He's expecting me."

"I'll let him know."

"Where should I wait?" I glanced about the agonized lobby. "I feel sort of in the way here."

She pointed to her left. "Down this hall, Visitors Waiting Room for surgeries. You'll see the sign on the door. There are chairs. I'll send him to you."

"Thank you."

I found the door and went into that room of fear and sorrow. An older man huddled with a young woman and a small boy on a pair of chairs in one corner. Along the opposite wall was a girl maybe my age whose dress from knees to ankle hem was stained with blood. Another girl beside her sat, face in hands, sobbing. Occupying the other half-dozen chairs on that side of the room looked to me like a family of folk ethnic Riusanians in traditional patchwork calico dress and roughened leather shoes. Four busty women, three children: all girls. They wore stoic expressions and spoke not a word. Near the door I'd entered was a rail-thin fellow in muddy work clothes, just a few years younger than my father. I saw blood on his shirt and hands where he hadn't scrubbed well enough. I stepped past him and took a chair one removed from his. He looked pale and gaunt and hummed and coughed intermittently, with each cough sounding sicker than before as if he had a plague. I considered going out into the hall to wait on Samuel Protiste, but I was tired, too, and needed to sit a while.

I wondered about Arturo. Where was he this morning? Why was he not at the hospital? Nina was adamant that he worked here as an attendant with Protiste. Hadn't she just heard that a month ago? The woman at the front desk behaved as if she had no idea who he even was. Yet she knew Protiste immediately. If Arturo wasn't here at all, what was I supposed to do with that picture of Delia? I assumed Protiste would have some idea where Arturo was because, apparently, they'd been friends since their days at Arbolé township.

The young woman sitting with the old man began to cry and the little boy threw his arms around her neck and hugged her fiercely. The old man patted her head and murmured in her ear. She nodded but continued to cry. The girl with the blood on her dress got up and went out of the room along with the sobbing girl. Her eyes were dreadful with tears and sadness. If the Riusanians were suffering, and I presumed they were, as befits that culture not one of them suggested tragedy was unfolding. One could be impressed if stoicism against these horrors were a virtue. I wasn't confident at all that was true. Do tears not flow from our hearts? That ache we suffer is as pure a sign as this world offers that we're alive and meant to be here with those we love.

I waited on Samuel Protiste for more than an hour. Neither the sobbing girl nor the one with the bloody dress came back. After a while, that fellow with the nasty cough got up and left, too. A nurse came in and visited briefly with the family in the corner. Then they rose together and followed her out of the room. I was left alone with the silent Riusanians for another half hour until a pair of soldiers came in and sat down across from me and had a quiet conversation about a girl one of them had met in Keiranville who had a sister more anxious for fun than she was. Maybe on summer furlough they'd go visit both girls and take them to the shore for a few days. Both seemed enthusiastic to do so.

Our door opened again and a dark-haired fellow in attendant whites speckled with blood poked his head into the room. He looked straight at me. "Julian?"

"Yes."

"Let's go."

I got up and met him out in the hallway where the painful and disturbing racket from the lobby swelled again.

"I'm Samuel," he said, taking off his rubber gloves to shake my hand. He was fit and slightly taller than me. Sort of swarthy. Probably ten years older. Maybe more. I'd have guessed him to be from Páros or Aurora by the sea, rather than Arbolé where Nina said they knew each other. From what I'd heard of it, Arbolé was too staid and ordinary for a dashing fellow like this. At least by his appearance. But I could be wrong both about him and Arbolé township. What did I know?

"Is Arturo here?" I asked, as Protiste led me down the hallway away from the lobby. Some of the lights were out in this corridor and caused the hospital to feel empty when the opposite was certainly true this morning.

"No, he isn't. I'll explain in my auto."

"Are we driving to Crown Colony today? I have no idea where it is. I haven't had a chance to look up a map."

Samuel Protiste hurried us along to the back of the hospital. "Let me tell you once we get outdoors."

We made a turn down another corridor, passed through a pair of swinging doors, then another turn, and more swinging doors. I saw signs for surgery and radiography and somatic illuminations and cardiac infusions, cerebral cartography and pneumothorasic kimithesia. We passed isolation wards for infectious disease, pediatrics, socio-pathologic diversions, psychogenic and therapeutic counseling. Then farther on, doors to maintenance and laundry and attendants clothing and equipment. Eventually we were out into the back lot of the hospital where autos and a couple of long passenger busses were parked among military trucks and assorted tractors and some odd-looking four-wheeled armored vehicles guarded by small groups of soldiers looking weary and worn.

"My auto's that way." Protiste pointed to the copse of oaks atop an embankment past the trucks. The morning air had warmed up since I'd gone into the hospital and the weather felt optimistic for a good day ahead. I'd heard rumors of a rainstorm but saw no hint of clouds on the blue sky. Maybe later on.

His motor was a drab grey Zane two-seater with the absurd nickname, "Thunderbolt," proclaimed in a metal badge across the rear trunk lid. Protiste stripped off the blood-stained top of his attendant clothes and tossed it behind the seats as we got in. I tucked the valise between my legs. The autocar felt older than I was. Cracked leather seats and dash. Headlining frayed. Better days behind.

He fired up the motor and drove us out toward Pandarus Street.

I asked, "Now, where's Arturo? I have something for him from Nina. It's the chief reason I've agreed to travel here."

"What you were given by Peter Draxler is much more important. Let me just tell you that."

"Not to me."

We drove maybe half a mile before he said, "Arturo is gone. He left about a month ago. No one's seen him since."

I was shocked. How was I not told this before getting on that train? I assumed Nina couldn't have known. Otherwise what purpose would she have had to send me here?

"Where did he go?"

Protiste shrugged as he steered us off Pandarus Street and onto a narrow lane lined with sparse elm trees just gaining spring leaves. "He's gone. That's all I can tell you. Why and where isn't important anymore."

"Well, I don't understand this," I said. "If I'd known Arturo wasn't here, I can't say I'd have agreed to be Draxler's delivery boy. This is all too dangerous. I could be killed. I hope you realize that."

He told me, "We knew you'd only travel for Nina."

"Well, that's nicely manipulative. Thank you."

The houses were simple, both squat and tall, plain but well-painted in delicate greens and yellows and browns, some pink, too. Flowers in the yards. Fruit trees here and there. Apples and plums, pears and apricot. A proper neighborhood of sun and shade but no people anywhere about. Maybe at work, or indoors for the hour.

Protiste pulled over to the curb in front of a sun-bleached white two-story house near the end of the block. He shut off the engine. "Come with me."

We both got out and I brought the valise and followed him down the side-yard along a rickety picket fence. This entire escapade had become ridiculous. No one wants to feel deceived and I was distinctly unhappy as I dodged bristling thorns on a fat blooming rose bush beside the fence.

"Did Nina know Arturo wasn't here?"

Protiste walked across the weedy yard to a little white cottage at the back under a sheltering oak. He unlocked the door there and held it open. "No, she didn't. Peter told me not to tell her. Guess why?"

"You people are a big puzzle. Do you know that?"

"I hope so." He stepped aside to let me by. "Go on in."

Indoors, the cottage was nothing more than a living room attached to a tiny kitchen, a bedroom I could see off the living room and a toilet closet. Just a scruffy sofa, a chair next to a low table with a reading lamp, some mechanics and hunting magazines on the table. A couple of rugs. The kitchen was only a sink and a gas stove. A dull and unfortunate place.

Samuel Protiste shut the door behind us and immediately asked, "Do you have the drawings?"

"Which drawings?"

"Don't fool around."

"Where's Arturo?"

"I already told you, he's gone."

"Where?"

"We don't know. One day last month he didn't show up for work. He had an apartment over on Nazar. I went to see if he was sick and his landlady let me in after she knocked and he didn't answer. The place was cleaned out. Nothing there. He was gone. Hadn't paid up his rent, so she was mad."

"You didn't tell Nina this?"

"I don't talk to her."

"You told her Arturo worked at the hospital. That's what she said."

"I wrote her a letter."

I frowned. This was becoming absurd. "How did you know where she lived? She said she's only been there a year or so."

He smiled. "Me and Nina have, let's just say, mutual acquaintances from Arbolé. I thought she'd want to know about Arturo."

I felt myself getting angry now. Or nervous. I wasn't sure which. "What did you tell her?"

"Just that he had a job at Asklepieion like I did. He'd been down to Maggiani for a few years with a field hospital and came up here because he heard it paid more. Then he saw me and we connected our shifts to pal around like the old days. That's when I wrote Nina."

"Then he just left without telling you? Not a word?"

"Yup."

"And you didn't tell Nina."

"Nope."

"Why not?"

"Like I said, Julian, we needed to get you here and we knew you'd only do this for her. Peter's a smart guy, don't you think?"

"I think he's his own biggest fan." I was irritated now. Who likes being fooled?

"No reason to be mad," Protiste said. "We worked all this out a few weeks back. That was after I wrote to Nina, but before Arturo left. We've had to improvise. It's not your fault. Blame Arturo."

"You're all crazy."

"Where are the drawings?"

"I'm not sure."

"What do you mean, you're not sure? Where are they? Peter says he gave them to you."

"He gave me something."

"Show me."

"No," I told him. "We're not at Crown Colony, and you're not Major Laurentine Künze."

Protiste went to the kitchen and opened a drawer next to the stove. He took out a revolver and pointed it at me. "Give me the drawings."

"What are you doing? I told you I don't have them."

"Let me have what Peter gave you," he said, "or I'll shoot you right here."

"If you do, you won't find it. I hid it like Draxler told me to."

"Where?"

"No."

I felt a sudden wave of nausea.

Samuel Protiste smiled, then lowered the revolver. "All right, we'll go to Crown Colony." He went back to the kitchen drawer and put the revolver away.

I stared at him, still frightened. "You're not going to shoot me?"

"No, I just needed to see if you'd crack and let us down. You're a good kid."

"What about Arturo?"

"Forget him," Protiste said, walking off to his bedroom. "He's gone. Who knows? He might be dead."

I went to the toilet and almost threw up. After pissing, I washed my face and saw how pale I looked. Just awful. What was I supposed to do with Delia's picture? Those words Nina wrote on the back, and that lemon blossom. Lacking Arturo, how was I supposed to know what all that meant? I had no intention of asking Samuel Protiste. It wasn't any of his business.

He came out of his bedroom with a small canvas travel bag and wearing a tan leather jacket. He'd also tossed on a khaki motor-bicycle cap.

"Let's go," he said, switching on a kitchen light for later. Then he opened the door and let me out. He followed and locked the door behind us and led me back along the side of the house to his auto out front.

Sliding in on the passenger side again, I asked, "We're going to drive this to Crown Colony?"

I had no idea what the roads were like out there, but this motor car didn't look like the best choice.

Protiste fired up the engine. "No, we're meeting the trucks at Shadroe Station, a few miles north of the train depot. It's a convoy. No one goes by auto that far. It isn't safe. Two of us alone like this wouldn't get five miles. They'd find our ashes in the morning."

XXXI

The geography of the Desolation east of Albiona, and north and south, was fluid and universal. That is to say, people were killed all over those provinces, regardless of where the great artillery batteries were assembled for bombardments along the battle front of millions. This was what I had learned in just twenty-four hours from Commonwealth Station. No place was safe out there. If Tamorina felt more normal and ordinary than Albiona or Colonia Tamal, that had more to do with the immense presence of military protecting and utilizing the last eastern train depot than any presumed status of the town itself with regards to the enveloping war. I'd seen death all along the rail lines beyond Winterburn, Cahill, Sainz, Boudjfelja and Dannenbaum for more than five hundred miles thus far and I knew the worst of it was still waiting ahead. The towns were an illusion of recovery and settlement, almost false fronts. In truth, the war was everywhere. People knew it, too. Back in the metropolis, there was an instinctual awareness of this that no naïveté regarding daily life in our busy streets could completely mask. From Albiona to Tamorina, no one could entertain any notion of peace and prosperity in the shadow of all this death and devastation. The war might go away for a week or a month, but just as easily soldiers returned and people would begin dying again. Only that eternal confusion of pretense got everyone out of bed each morning with a new day to confront those simple challenges of eating and drinking and seeking the sustenance of earning credits. I don't mention children dressed and fed because there simply did not seem to be many of them left anywhere but at the train depots. That enormous column of orphans was gone as we drove by on the road to Shadroe Station. The train had left and presumably carried them all away with it. Hundreds and hundreds of children. Orphans? I wondered and had my doubts. If that were true, the amount of killing in the smaller towns and rural communities of Tarchon Province beyond Tamorina must have been profound.

— . —

The sun had risen almost to noon above and the road was dry and dusty. Poplar, spruce, oak and beech trees thickened in the woods all about. Tall fresh grass and brush swayed in the passing draft of Samuel Protiste's roaring auto. I watched a flock of crows sail across the clear blue sky. Sparrows, too, darted in and out of the lush spring woods. Our motor was noisy and the old fuselage rattled over each bump in the road. It truly felt as if the auto were about to fall apart and I held onto my door handle just in case. But I enjoyed being out of town again. The countryside was lovely — woods on one side of the road and long empty fields of grass on the other whose scattered oaks across the noon distance and pastoral simplicity imagined another Eden. Where do we go when we die? Perhaps fields such as these where all our earthly cares are dissipated in a calming breeze redolent of fresh grass and wildflowers. A pleasant destiny.

"How far?" I asked Protiste.

"Another couple of miles or so."

"And to Crown Colony?"

The thought of that place gave me a case of nerves. Until Draxler said the name, I'd never heard of it. How does someone call it that? What does it mean?

"Never been. We'll ask if you like, but riding by convoy won't make it quick. I do know that much. I can tell you it's not next door."

"Thanks," I said. "I already got that feeling."

"One thing?"

"Yes?"

"Don't start off bragging with any soldiers about your position with Otto Paley. That won't go over."

"Why would I do that anyhow? I've never even met Dr. Paley."

"I'm just advising you to keep it under your hat unless someone asks. They don't need to know what you're out here for. You're sharing a ride, not your purpose in being there."

"Understood."

"We'll try to ride in the same truck, but we're not pals, all right? I'm just giving you a lift to Shadroe, and that's all anyone needs to know. It's important they don't connect us. Safer that way."

"How so?"

"It just is," Protiste told me. "And don't mention eugenics. They'll tie you to a tree."

"Why?"

"They don't have much patience for stupidity."

"I don't follow that."

"You don't need to."

As we drove on ahead, I began to wonder once again what I thought I was doing out there. Wherever Crown Colony was, I was smart enough to know it had not been included in Dr. Paley's envoy directive. Yes, I presumed I could probably talk my way into explaining the necessity of operating beyond Tamorina, so long as Crown Colony was located within Tarchon Province. If it were not, my presence would prove difficult to justify and put my safety in jeopardy. And what was I out here for now, anyhow? I hadn't met Arturo to give him that picture of Delia, and what Draxler had proposed for me was not really my business. I'd only agreed because Nina wanted me to do that great favor for her and we were in love. Seeing me in this auto with a stranger like Samuel Protiste would anger my parents and cause them to doubt how efficient they'd been in raising and educating me. Who could disagree? Truth was, I'd now put myself in mortal danger and I had no sense of how to turn back.

Coming around a last bend in the road, we saw the trucks gathered under a dense stand of shady oaks. Dozens of armed soldiers wandered about, some sitting under the trees. There was an old wooden pavilion with a business office and toilets and a brick incinerator where Protiste parked his motor between a green autocycle and some ash cans. A pair of officers came out of the pavilion smoking cigars and talking about a regiment commander named Reggane who had apparently just blown up a big ammunition dump at Yalactiño last night. They sounded as if that were the greatest thing in the world.

"Which truck are we taking?" I asked Protiste, feeling a little skittish now in the midst of all these soldiers.

"Let me find out."

He headed over to the pavilion and walked past the officers and went indoors. I thought of following, but since he hadn't explicitly asked me to do so, I assumed he preferred I didn't. In any case, there were six transport trucks and a lot of soldiers to fit in them. Was this a company or a battalion? No one had ever told me the difference. This was another one of those things I wished I'd had Freddy along to explain. He knew everything. And he had those squib books. He could look it up.

Honestly, I felt like an idiot standing there under the oaks with my valise among all those soldiers. Fortunately, none of them were paying me any attention. Probably they were used to civilians passing in and out. But I noticed one of the officers staring at me. I glanced away toward the woods where a handful of soldiers were emerging from the shady brush. When I looked back at the officer, he was walking toward me. My stomach clenched. He was not smiling when he addressed me.

"Son?"

"Yes, sir?"

"This is a restricted zone today."

"Yes, sir."

"Well, what's your business?"

"Thank you, sir. I'm a personal envoy for Dr. Otto Paley, Chief Director of Internal Communications on the Judicial Council. He sent me to make reports from Tamorina and also to meet with Major Laurentine Künze at Crown Colony. That's all I know, sir."

"Papers, please."

"Yes, sir." I set down my valise, then opened it to remove the diplomatic pouch. I zipped that open and took out the status directive and handed it to the officer. He looked somewhat quizzical as he read it over.

Finishing, he said, "This directive says nothing about Crown Colony."

Nodding, I replied, "Understood, sir. But circumstances in Tamorina deviated from my schedule, a meeting that didn't come off and a further urgency to travel farther on. I telephoned to Dr. Paley's office, who assumed that since I'd still be in Tarchon Province my directive would stand."

The officer frowned. "Young man, Crown Colony is not in Tarchon Province. It's Caesárea. Do they not have maps at the Judicial Council?"

Utterly horrified at this ruse being exposed, all I could do was shrug. "I wouldn't know about that, sir. We're a long way out here from Prospect Square. Perhaps Dr. Paley's secretary was confused."

"I would say so."

"Yes, sir."

"Who did you say you're to meet?"

"Major Laurentine Künze, attached to the 32nd Battalion."

By now, the other officer had come over. He interjected, "I know Künze. Fine fellow, wonderful commander. We served together at Bulganin. All that trouble."

"Nasty business, eh?" The first officer smiled.

"We lost half the battalion before Cheever and Watts put their heads into the fight and gave us the 44th to sweep the flank. That was Künze's idea. And a damn good one. Saved our lives."

The first officer told the other, "This young fellow says he's got business with Major Künze at Crown Colony on behalf of Dr. Paley. Trouble is, his directive only grants travel here in Tarchon. It seems the Council is short on maps."

"May I see the paper?"

I handed it to him. He read it quickly, then said to me, "So you want to take a ride with us up to Crown Colony, is that it?"

"Yes, sir. If you could do me that favor, I'm sure Dr. Paley would appreciate it."

"Well, Johnny," he said to the other officer, "what do you say we carry this young fellow along with us and maybe earn some payback with the great Otto Paley? Where's the harm?"

"It's irregular, no doubt, but why not? I'd like to meet your Major Künze. Sounds like quite a fellow."

"All right, son. You're in with us. No monkey business. Sit tight and keep your head down. It's a long ride and we're not going to the county fair."

I could breathe again. "Thank you, sir. Both of you. I'll let Dr. Paley know how helpful you've been."

They walked off, telling a joke about a young Rosado girl from Cassini.

Soon enough, one of the officers blew a whistle and the soldiers grabbed their gear and we piled up into the trucks. I didn't see Samuel Protiste anywhere, but assumed he'd talked his way into one of those rides behind mine. The lead driver sounded his horn and our column rolled up onto the road toward Crown Colony. We sat on wooden benches under a canvas cover that gave shade in the early afternoon. I was nearer the tailgate so at least I could see out, the valise on my lap. Our trucks were slow and loud and the road was dusty. Where it was thickest, I felt like we were driving through a brown cloud. A few miles on, the road thinned to dirt again and the air cleared and I was able to watch those fields and woods receding behind us.

Some of our soldiers chattered about girls in Tamorina or back home and collegiate dribbling-football matches and where to go on furlough. A few dozed off or pretended to. I noticed one or two staring at me every so often and that felt terrifically uncomfortable. They could see I wasn't one of them. Not military. Who was I? None of them asked. Perhaps they'd seen me speaking with those two officers and word had been passed among them that I was to be left alone, off-limits for conversation. Or perhaps they simply resented a civilian like myself riding with them as if I belonged when they knew I did not.

We were not alone on the road. Trucks from the east passed by every so often, mostly filled with soldiers looking weary. Some were obviously wounded. Blood and bandages. Empty expressions on gaunt faces. Twice I saw trucks loaded with children. None looked cheerful in the least. Going to the trains? And where were the trains taking them? I wanted to ask one of the soldiers for his opinion on that question. Would he tell me if he knew? Then I remembered Dennett's advice that I should use good judgment and discretion with whomever I might encounter, and I decided that asking questions about orphaned children in the Desolation did not fit such a description. So I kept my mouth shut and watched the pretty scenery sail by.

An hour passed with no more trucks and I was tired of sitting on that bench. My back ached and my neck was stiff. All of us seemed fidgety by then and the interior under the canvas was hot and stuffy. On a mid-summer's day, I imagined the back of one of these trucks could be sweltering. I was already sweating in Father's jacket and the afternoon air outside was fairly pleasant. But then we stopped. Suddenly, in fact. Our entire column lurched to a halt and all our soldiers were out of the trucks in half a minute. I let my fellow riders get by and waited to see what was happening before I joined them. When I did, I saw there were some three or four buildings here, not a lot, and I couldn't immediately tell what they were. Maybe a store? And a little house behind it? The biggest might have been a rural schoolhouse. All were severely damaged, almost gutted. Then I smelled burning and looked up the road about a hundred yards to where a big transport truck like ours had been torched. The black smoldering hulk of it was just off into the brush on the edge of some woods. No fire and not much smoke, so it hadn't happened in the last few minutes. Another truck had pulled in behind it and was parked there, engine rumbling. Our soldiers were striding into the woods, weapons ready. I walked across the road to what I thought was the schoolhouse and looked through one of the missing windows. The interior was just ruin and rubble and burned wood. Probably a one-room school.

Someone shouted, "TRAVELERS!" and everyone seemed to get excited. A wave of our soldiers withdrew from the brush-line and fanned out across the road, all down on one knee, rifles aimed into the woods. I ducked behind the side of the ruined building and watched. In the near distance, a dozen shots were fired, echoing across the air. Screams chased from the woods. More shots. More screams. Yelling. Noise. Almost twenty minutes went by, then that truck up the road pulled out from behind the burned-out wreck of the other one. Next, I heard the cries of children, wailing from inside the truck. I watched it roll slowly toward us, maneuvering carefully past our column. As it drew near and rumbled by, I saw the rear packed tightly with children, all dirty and teary-eyed. Like weeping rag dolls. Two soldiers sat at either end of the benches by the tailgate to prevent any of them from falling out. Or jumping off.

Whistles shrieked in the woods, and through the trees and dense green thicket I began to see people meandering toward us, a cult of hermits or Tser-béro gypsies or scarecrows, both men and women of varying ages, hands atop their heads. Too many to count yet with most still obscured in the woods. Our soldiers surrounded them, herding them out, threatening a few with rifle butts, urging everyone forward into the heavily armed company along the road. That first officer I'd spoken with shouted out, "Don't touch them! And don't let them touch you! Keep your separation! Keep your separation!"

Just then, I noticed Samuel Protiste coming out of the woods up by the truck that burned. He had full khakis on and wore a cap like one of the drivers. How had he managed that? The rough ghostly procession of raggedy strangers was being guided by threat of arms toward my school building and I hurried away, back across the road to the safety of our trucks.

That officer shouted again, "Don't touch! Don't touch! Get 'em in there! All of them! Get 'em in!"

The soldiers were funneling that entire gathering into the broken school-house now through the missing door. I looked back up the road to Protiste and he was still there by the smoldering truck, watching. I guessed there must have been about thirty or forty rural people drifting toward the school and forced into the ruin. They were quiet. None spoke a word. One tripped on the front step, an older fellow, and two more men helped him up. I saw tears smeared on the faces of some of the women, but they were not openly weeping.

"Do not touch them, soldiers! Do not touch them!"

Our soldiers had formed a tight cordon around that whole shuffling crowd, so they had nowhere to go except into the building, mostly two by two. A woman fell in front of the steps and tried to crawl to her feet. She lost her direction momentarily and crept toward one of the soldiers. He shoved her back with the sole of his boot on her head and she fell over again.

"Soldier! Get out of line! Get out right now!"

Two other soldiers pushed him back from the cordon onto the road and left him there.

A voice from that officer who knew Major Laurentine Künze echoed across the afternoon air, "Do not touch them! Keep your separation! Do not touch them!"

Most of the raggedy people were in the schoolhouse then, packed together amid the rubble and dirt. The last of them were on the steps, dragging the fallen woman indoors.

Then they were all crowded within the ruin and two soldiers blocked the front door threshold.

The first officer called out, "Form up! Form up! Squads, east, west, north, south!"

I watched our troops fan out around the building to the rear and along the sides where missing windows offered vantage points to the interior. Once assembled and in place, Künze's officer shouted, "Keep your separation! Keep your separation!"

Then, from the other officer, "Prepare arms!"

Rifles were cocked and aimed into the schoolhouse. Now I heard weeping from indoors, and howls of fear and anguish. In that moment, I had no genuine appre-hension of what was about to follow because the bitter fact of it was so shocking.

"FIRE!"

That blast of rifle shots was horrendous. The very air around us thundered. Our soldiers fired and fired and fired and fired. I found my hands blocking my ears. I went dizzy from the noise and sight of it all. Even from across the road I could see people inside that abandoned schoolhouse knocked down like wind in grass from the blistering fire. Screams echoed all about and felt endless as the racketing rifle-fire went on and on and on.

Until a fierce whistle blew and it stopped.

And the screams ceased.

And then that smell arose.

A hideous, sickening odor.

I vomited by the side of the truck.

And again.

Holding my balance on the rear fender, I heard one of the officers call out, "Incendiary squad! Approach! Rifle company, step back!"

That tight cordon of soldiers retreated from the schoolhouse, half of them back into the brush, the others up onto the road. A trio of soldiers holding three-foot long metal pipes I didn't recognize as weapons came forward from a truck just up the road from mine. The pipes had thick red casings fit onto both ends and something resembling rifle triggers in the middle. The incendiary squad passed through the line of the rifle company and spaced themselves apart facing that front door and one of the side windows and at a rear window behind the schoolhouse to the left.

"Incendiaries! Prepare to fire!"

There was a metallic snap as the triggers were primed.

"Ready on the line!" That officer who knew Künze had one final look around to be certain his troops were in position. I noticed nearly all of them had retreated another yard or so.

"FIRE!"

Three rockets ignited the interior of the schoolhouse in a massive white-hot fire cloud. Not an explosion. More like the incandescent flash of a lucifer match. The heat pushed everyone back at least half a dozen steps. My face felt enflamed and I ducked behind our truck for relief. Both officers were yelling something to each other I could not quite hear over the roar of the fire.

And then the awful stench of burning flesh blazed from the schoolhouse and I escaped away up the road toward that smoldering truck where I'd seen Protiste. He was still there, eyes bright in the fire-glow, face blank of expression. As I came out from behind one of the trucks, he saw me and nodded. I walked up the road toward him. Protiste motioned for me to follow him into the woods. So I did.

A damp leafy path led us along through ancient beech trees and birch, black oaks and fresh spring undergrowth like what I'd tramped through outside of Colonia Tamal. That obscene din from the road was swallowed up by these woods and my ears gradually quit ringing. After a short walk, Protiste paused for me to catch up. He said, "I bet you want to know why."

"Is there any answer that's not insane?"

"No, but come along just the same, and I'll show you. Just don't ask me about this uniform."

"I won't."

Then I followed him again. Was it unreasonable or inhuman to have noticed birds chittering in these woods as we walked? Insects buzzing about? That lovely intoxicating scent of wildflowers and spring leaves? Beauty permeates this world. Life persists. Death leads to rebirth. The world survives. Another twenty yards or so ahead was something else. Wrapped and bound by cord and nail to three separate trees, two beech and a narrow oak, were nine soldiers of ours. Three to each trunk, pinioned together by nails pounded through hands and into the bark, interlinked to encircle each tree. A leather cord around the neck of those unfortunate soldiers created a loop holding each trio to the trunk. The cord was wet and drawn tight, intended to choke each captive to death. And it had. All nine were dead. Necks fractured. Nearly decapitated. Faces were purple, almost black. Other than those nails, no other wounds. Tortured and executed.

Good God. I tried not to stare. I'd never witnessed anything so ugly. The lower trunk and base of each tree was drenched and wretched with blood.

"Who did this?" I asked Protiste.

"Does it matter?"

"Are they from that truck on the road?"

"Presumably," he said. "Seeing as how they're here and the truck's empty."

"I heard one of the soldiers call those people in the woods 'travelers.' What does that mean? What are 'travelers'?"

"Julian, my boy, this war's gone through a lot of places, knocked them flat, emptied them out. People who aren't killed outright need someplace to go, so they start looking. Back there down the road used to have a name. It was on the map and called, 'Kippel,' after the fellow who built the store there and the school for his own children. That was his house behind it. The war came here about twenty some-odd years ago and a big artillery shell flew through the schoolhouse roof in the middle of a Tuesday afternoon and blew up every kid inside and their teacher, too. Then the army arrived and shot Kippel and his wife and burned his store and his house and left again. No one gets to claim it or rebuild. Maybe those people in the woods thought that's what they were going to do. Maybe they got told they couldn't, and it made them mad and they caught that truck on the road and got even. Or maybe it wasn't them at all, just more marauders who did it and got away before our trucks showed up."

I was astonished at the sheer audacity of that. "You're saying our troops might have murdered all those people down there and burned them on a hunch? Is that what you're telling me?"

"Maybe," Protiste said, "and maybe not. These fellows tied to the trees probably didn't know why they were being killed. No one does anymore. Except that eventually enough people have to die so someone can win."

Another ten miles or so up the road and we left the woods and lovely meadows behind. Now the fields were plain and flat, almost absent of trees except the odd spruce here and there shorn of branches, victims of relentless shelling from artillery barrages. Sitting once again in the rear of the truck, I watched the landscape change from that ancient beauty to the artificial ugliness we had imposed upon it with our relentless cruelty, that foolishness of the human heart in perpetual conflict. There were barely noticed houses off in the killing fields as well, just concrete foundations left, scant reminders of habitation by people now long gone. A war passes across the world like rural mowers through fields of grain, putting down to rest what had been grown season to season. Modern cannons performed those old rituals of scythe and plow, gouging rents in the earth, erasing the natural order of things. What grows in the blood and mud? Nothing until we depart. We are not required for life to go on. We just need to leave and not return before balance is regained and the sun can shine on life without men and their endless torments.

XXXII

∞

We arrived at Crown Colony late in the day, a vast encampment on both sides of the Alban River. Ten thousand tents crowded the embankments as far as I could see to the north and south. There was a strong bridge built across to the other shore, wooden shanties along the waterfront, boat landings abounding. I was told later on that Crown Colony earned its name from old imperial settlements here by Eurymedon, Alexander, Tiberius, Todra Abdelhassan and Voireuse Bardamu traveling upriver by papyrela, scapha, bireme and barge into these once wooded heartlands to establish footholds in the ancient wilderness. By the age of our Republic, through fire and flood, those settlements were scarce rememberances and nothing remained but stone bridge footings and vague descriptions of intricate summer residences along the riverside. When war came across the Fatoma River, forty years after the Great Separation, those simple rural people who had been inhabiting these fertile lands both west and east of the Alban River for quiet centuries were unprepared for the intrusion of hatred and persistent darkness. They were swept away almost entirely in those relentless waves of battery and invasion. No hint of them survives. Rumors have them escaping downriver to Xandro and Hippisia on the southern sea and beyond. Other opinions invite words like annihilation and extermination. No one knows for certain except that fate intervened and their legacy was diverted.

I found Samuel Protiste climbing down from his truck as our company disembarked and prepared to disperse into its assignment. Thousands of soldiers milled about, crowds and crowds of armed combatants preparing to wage war for the Status Imperium and our collective culture, our Common Purpose. I smelled cook stoves on the late afternoon breeze from the mess halls under tents somewhere close by. Nothing was permanent here. The great army assembled on the Alban banks was restless and urgent, trained and prepared to pull up stakes, fold tents and go elsewhere as strategy and circumstance demanded. Protiste and I wandered among them for the better part of an hour, working up our own plan for Major Laurentine Künze. Trouble was, no one seemed to know just where he was right then: on the Schiffer Landing or eating in the officers' shanty, maybe across the river with Major Asádo. Lots of shrugs. We went down to the water's edge ourselves for a look at the cold Alban.

"My dad told me he was here once before I was born," Protiste said, gazing across the gentle waters. "Came out with some of his friends from Léonville, probably fifty years ago. Maybe longer. Back then, most of the war was elsewhere and people still fished on the river here in boats and anyone could set up a camp and stay the night. That's what they did. Four of them. Drove up by motor one morning and went fishing and stayed the night. There were girls, too. Lots of girls. One of them was my mother, Galina Porgari. She and her friends rode here on horseback to meet the boys who came to fish. That's how they got married. If it wasn't for this river, I probably wouldn't be here telling you how it used to be. You never know, right?"

I watched a couple soldiers across the river wade nude into the slow current. "No, that's very true. You never know."

"How can you?"

"I guess you can't."

We stood there for a little while as the red sun went down and boats floated past with small cannons on the decks. We didn't see anybody fishing.

Protiste and I walked around among the mass of troops in a pale dusk until I caught sight of that officer who knew Künze. He was reading at some sort of map or bulletin board when he noticed us and waved me over.

Strolling up, I told him, "Sir, we haven't been able to find Major Künze. No one seems to be sure where he is."

The officer gave Protiste a good look over, undoubtedly curious what his part was in this adventure. In fact, he asked, "Who are you?"

"Samuel Protiste. I work with the hospital at Tamorina. Julian's contact in the metropolis hired me to be his guide for the meeting with Major Künze. I was the one who drove him up to meet your trucks at Shadroe."

The officer turned back to me. "Does Dr. Paley know about this fellow?"

I nodded. "I assume so, sir. There were no other provisions regarding my transportation here, and the Council is very thorough about these things."

"I'm sure they are." He gave Protiste another stern look, then told me, "Well, your Major Künze is across the river, actually, with his 32nd Battalion on the Péridon Road. They'll be encamped along there tonight, moving east sometime tomorrow to Porphyry Hill."

"Should we go over there now, sir, or tomorrow morning?"

The officer shook his head. "You can't go now. We're closing the bridge until dawn. There've been infiltrators through the dark twice this week. We've lost seven men already. Throats slashed on the guard wire. That's enough. You'll wait here with us and someone will run you across at first light."

"Where will we sleep, sir? Is there any room in the tents? The camp looks terribly busy."

The officer smiled. "Remind me your name again, son?"

"It's Julian, sir," I told him. "Julian Brehm."

"Well, I'm Lieutenant Colonel Grammar Hastings." He offered his hand and we shook. He ignored Protiste. "I'll see to your arrangements personally. And you may join the men in mess hall '12' for supper." He pointed down the row of tents. "It's about two dozen yards that direction. You'll see the posting. I'll find you when you're done and show you to your tent."

"Thank you, sir."

He nodded at Protiste and walked off toward one of the larger river shanties, whistling as he went.

By nightfall we found the mess hall and ate supper with probably one hundred soldiers at four long tables. The roar of conversation was breathtaking, and I struggled to hear anything Protiste was saying to me. Everyone ate hot Pajapiros and plates of steaming rice with cinnamon cherífa tea and water. Not half bad. I had been starving from the long truck ride and our ugly diversion. The night air was becoming colder and drafty under the tent. Perhaps because we were eating and food always seems to enhance our moods, but I was still astonished at how lively these troops were. Laughter permeated the atmosphere. Enthusiasm reigned in direct contradiction to the perilous circumstances. I presumed my age and inexperience with military conditions gave me scant insight there, yet I had to wonder where fear and worry were hidden. Who could know which one of these fellows might be eating his last meal? Across the river were threats from dark corners. Survival depended upon training, yes, of course. Odds increased with perspicacity and teamwork. Nobody went out alone. Or I didn't imagine so. Maybe some did. Scouts and secret agents. I was sure there must have been such things. Still, death had unexpected invitations, and no one could be sure of avoiding that final call.

Fiddling with my rice, I asked Samuel Protiste a question I'd mostly avoided until then. "How am I supposed to get back to the train at Tamorina after all this?"

"My guess is they'll ride you there once you're finished with that major you're seeing."

"Are you staying until I do?"

He took a sip of tea. "I suppose so. Peter told me to be sure you get those drawings to wherever they're meant to go. I'll stay till that happens."

"Well, I hope you do. This is just so much more complicated and dangerous than I thought it would be."

He coughed. "More dangerous than you thought? My God, it's the Desolation! What did you expect?"

He seemed flabbergasted by what he perceived was my absurd naïveté.

I set down my fork beside the rice. "That's not what I mean. Not at all. Yes, there's a war out here. Yes, of course I knew a war would be dangerous. What I'm talking about are things I've seen. Fellows I met on the train. What people have been doing. Hideous things. Moral obscenities. It's not just the war, unless the war really is everywhere and involving everyone."

"Well, Julian, it is. And the sooner you get that straight in your head, the better you'll understand what it's all about. This war is a lot more than two sides shooting each other."

I frowned. "What does that mean?"

Protiste stared at me as he drank another sip of cherífa tea. "There are no sides."

We were given cots in a tent with eighteen soldiers just up from the Alban River. Four of the soldiers smoked cigars and played a few hands of a card game called Gallimard. I remember my parents used to invite friends over for that when I was little, a social gathering with cocktails and petit fours. Everyone dressed up. Agnes and I heard the laughter and shouts from clear upstairs in our bedrooms.

Mother was apparently very competitive and preferred to win in her own home whenever possible.

Protiste and a couple of the soldiers went to sleep early. Protiste snored. A few of the others read books by small electric lanterns under their blankets. I could see the faint glow when our lights went out at nine o'clock. I fell asleep soon and woke up again maybe an hour later when I heard it raining. That tattering on the tent became louder and boots sloshed in the mud outside as people rushed by. A crack of thunder rumbled across the distance and startled me. Was that cannon fire from somewhere? Even half asleep, I had no idea I'd become so jittery.

I closed my eyes again and listened to the rain ease to a steady hiss. Soothing somehow in the night and darkness where I was so far from home. None of this felt real. This cot and tent. The encampment and soldiers. Samuel Protiste. Who was he, anyhow? I missed Nina as I huddled fully dressed under a musty cotton blanket, clutching my valise like Delia with her furry Goliath. I thought of that damp stormy night we shared Nina's bed on Gosney Street, how warm she was in my arms, her soft breathing, that spicy scent of her. And making love to the falling rain outdoors. Here, I only felt foolish and lonely, too, and thinking of Nina just made it worse. The rain kept pattering on our tent, and I wondered why I had agreed to bring Draxler's scroll to Crown Colony. Where were the stolen drawings? Why was I here? Was this really what my beautiful Nina had intended all along when she led me to that dark mausoleum in Immanuel Fields? When she had that fellow give me Virgil for Draxler's puzzle yet wouldn't even let me speak his name aloud? Miles and miles from the metropolis, I was beginning to see some sort of interlocking riddle that had brought me to Nina and then Draxler, and through Marco to the undercity and back to Draxler's scroll and Nina's picture of little Delia. What part did Arturo play? How did that fit? The vagrant father of her child. A ghost in the wind. Rain fell harder again and a damp gust tugged at the flap to our tent and drew in a cold draft from outside. I heard a truck engine roar to life, and then another. Voices passing by out in the rain. I needed Freddy to solve this for me. He would unravel the labyrinth of intrigue and deceptions before I got myself killed. Too bad for me that he wasn't here.

— · —

When I woke up, the tent was empty, all the soldiers gone to morning duty. As I collected myself, Protiste came in through the flap and said, "If you want any breakfast, you better go now. I recommend the eggs Kerezza. Coffee's horrible. Stick with tea."

"Thanks."

"They said we're crossing the river in half an hour."

He left and I changed shoes. Those boots I wanted to pack but didn't fit in the valise would have been perfect for the mud outdoors. Instead, I put on some rubber high-top galoshes I'd had in my bedroom closet at home. Maybe they'd keep my feet dry. The dress shoes I'd been wearing went back into my valise.

I hurried off to the mess tent.

Protiste was right about the coffee. It really was ghastly, a hinting of kerosene or diesel fuel. Someone must have spilled. I ate the Kerezza eggs and a couple of biscuits. Butter was gone so I swallowed them dry with tea. I was learning to adapt.

Once I finished eating, I went back out into the cold grey morning. Clouds hid the fugitive sun, and a faint drizzle fell over the encampment. I walked down to the river where a group was gathered, including that friendly Hastings fellow, the lieutenant colonel. Before I got there, I saw him walk off. He looked angry.

There were two bodies just up from the water's edge, both under tarpaulins. Another pair of soldiers who had been standing there left. There was only a fellow in civilian clothes and a single soldier holding up an umbrella beside him when I approached. The civilian had a doctor's bag and instruments laid out on a dry cloth protected from the cold drizzle by the black umbrella. He glanced up at me and acknowledged my presence with a slight nod. The soldier kept his focus on the instruments.

I asked, "Who are they?"

Without looking up the civilian asked, "Who are you, please?"

I repeated my traveling mantra. "Julian Brehm, sir, personal envoy for Dr. Otto Paley, Chief Director of Internal Communications on the Judicial Council."

"I see."

"Sorry to disturb you, sir."

"One of ours, one of theirs."

He put on a pair of spectacles and studied a glass slide onto which he'd dripped a drop of blood he'd taken by syringe from one of the corpses.

"What happened?" I asked after another minute or so. "If you don't mind, sir."

"They killed each other somewhere upriver. An attempted infiltration. Both bodies floated down here this morning. I'm testing theirs for spyreosis."

"Do you test ours, too?"

He looked up at me like I was crazy. "Why would I do that?"

Four trucks assembled to cross the Alban River for linking up with a larger column of armored motors directed to join Major Künze's 32nd Battalion on the Péridon Road about eight miles ahead. I saw Hastings climb into the lead truck. Protiste and I took seats in back of the truck at the rear. Rain began again, dappling the surface of the river whose cold waters swirled and swept by to the south. I felt some of that tension I saw in the faces of those soldiers riding with us to the far shore. They certainly understood more about it than I did that damp morning. The keen insight into our mortality as humans at war belonged most profoundly to them whose lives were risked and cast forward into the hell of combat.

None of us spoke as the truck motors roared and we surged toward the bridge. I heard the planks creak and sway as the first truck began crossing. By our encampment I saw officers watching the far shore with binoculars and mounted telescopes. A white-hot flare shot high into the rainy air farther up the river and seemed to hang there like a tiny sun in the grey light. What was that for? I glanced at Protiste and saw his usual passive expression. What was his stake in all this? Credits? If so, I hoped he earned thousands. How much could a life be worth? If not credits, then what? To which lofty purpose was his allegiance delivered?

I looked up at that bright flare fading now, burning and drifting down the grey sky with the steady rainfall.

Suddenly our truck lurched and shook violently side to side as the first truck disintegrated with a massive explosion just past the middle of the bridge.

Protiste grabbed my shoulders and shoved me to the tailgate. "OUT! OUT! OUT!"

He leaped over it.

An instant later, the second truck blew up a third of the way across the bridge.

I tumbled out the rear just behind Protiste and landed in the mud, still gripping my valise. I heard yelling about artillery and saw soldiers from the third truck leaping off the bridge into the river.

And then that truck erupted in a huge fireball and blew apart, fragments shooting across the water.

Protiste took my arm and pulled me away from the burning bridge toward the river embankment south of the camp.

Another shell hit the bridge between our first and second trucks and fractured its spine. The bridge split in half and collapsed into the river with an enormous roar.

Dozens of steaming bodies floated in the water. Some on fire. Soldiers still alive were screaming for rescue across the cold current. I watched patches of fuel oil burning beneath the wreckage of the bridge.

"It was a trap," Protiste told me as we slogged along through the soggy reeds. "That flare? A signal to kill us."

"You think so?"

"Of course. What else? Beginning of duck season?"

By now, the bridge ramp was a fiasco of soldiers and doctors and stretchers and firewagons. Whistles were shrieking all over. Our truck had pulled back and away. We hadn't been a target because we hadn't yet driven onto the bridge. Otherwise we'd probably be dead. I thought of Nina just then, how fortunate she and Delia had been to avoid the cannon shot that had blown up her house. Now fate had taken my hand, as well.

Looking at the disaster on the river, I was sure Hastings had been killed. His truck had taken a direct hit from a big shell and was annihilated. No trace at all. Maybe it had been transporting some munitions. I had no idea. It was just gone. That made me wonder how Protiste and I were supposed to get across now to catch up with Major Künze's battalion. The bridge was sunk. I presumed there were other spans across the Alban, but I also guessed they were miles up and downriver from where we were just then.

I wondered what the purpose was of this bombardment.

Protiste must have read my thoughts, because he said, "I'll bet they're setting up to attack the 32nd right now. They hit the bridge to block any reinforcements.

Of course, our fellows know that, so they'll be ready. Or as ready as they can be. This war business is kind of like boxing with a sack over your head. You know that punch is coming, and you know what you need to do about it, but it just ain't that easy to duck when you can't see where the punch is coming from."

I didn't care much about military tactics or strategies. I just wanted to know what our own plans were. So I asked Protiste, "What do we do next?"

"I've just been considering that. Come with me. I have a thought."

He led us to a boat landing a couple hundred yards downriver from the ruined bridge where three motor transports were moored and tied off. Several soldiers were already there loading boxes into two of the boats for crossing to the far shore. Protiste went directly to the stocky sergeant overseeing that duty and told him what we wanted to do. Then he brought me over to show my papers from Dr. Paley and had me explain the urgency of our need to get across the river and link up with Major Künze.

I told the sergeant, "We have an opportunity here, sir, that Dr. Paley's office feels is immensely vital to our efforts. Of course, I'm not privy to details, but I was urged to grasp the seriousness with which this is considered in the Judicial Council."

This sergeant was gruff and abrupt to his men at the landing. He had even less patience with us. "Do you fellows see that bridge up there? There isn't one, anymore. And I've got half my company fishing bodies and parts of bodies out of the river. And you fellows want to requisition one of my boats for a little excursion to the other side? Are you kidding me?"

"Not for us," Protiste interjected. "Young Mr. Brehm here is under orders to reach Major Künze by noon today with critical information that impacts field operations along the Péridon Road. We're pretty sure this attack on the bridge is part of a move to hit the 32nd any time now. Too late to stop that, but we believe something bigger's coming and we need to reach Major Künze before it does. Mr. Brehm could use the field telephone to get further authorization from Dr. Paley's office, but lines of communication don't help decisions like this when every minute counts."

I could almost see those proverbial wheels spinning inside the sergeant's head. Duty and responsibility are too often in conflict. Whose orders do you follow?

"Tell you what I'll do," he said. "There's a boat loading up right now. I'll hold back a couple of my men to let you ride across with the others. If either of you fellows go into the water, you're on your own."

"Yes, sir," I said. "Thank you, sir. I'll let Dr. Paley know how helpful you've been. We appreciate this."

He gave me one of those looks you don't want to see a second time.

Protiste and I hurried down to the landing and found our places in the boat just preparing to depart from the shore with four soldiers and the stacked boxes of supplies they were transporting across the river. Rain fell steady and cold.

A pair of transport trucks were up on the Péridon Road loaded with rifle squads and ammunition for Künze's 32nd Battalion that had left two hours before to Porphyry Hill. These trucks had been delayed by a mechanical transmission failure in one of them and protocol required at least two traveling together. The problem had been repaired, and we were fortunate enough to have caught them in time to climb on board. Talking our way into this one was simpler. One look at my envoy papers and the officer in charge waved us ahead.

The Péridon Road was muddy and rutted and rough. Not so much a road those days as a wide passage in a great field of nothingness. Hard to see even whether it had been growing fields or grassy meadows or horse and cow pastures when the war and those constant bombardments arrived. Where our two-truck convoy drove east, I saw no trees at all. No ruins. No people. No birds. No life. There was nothing but mud clear to the rainy horizon. Clouds were low and grey, and black farther off. Rain drizzled. The air smelled of damp earth amid the diesel fumes of our trucks. One of the soldiers cleaned his rifle, guided by another soldier seated beside him. Both looked younger than I was, and I wondered if they'd been to battle together. A couple older soldiers watched them with studied interest but didn't offer any instruction or commentary at all.

Protiste leaned toward me and murmured, "When we get there, you and I need to find somewhere to collect our wits and figure out how to avoid being drawn into combat. We're not army and we don't have weapons. It'll be hard for anyone to know exactly whose side we're on."

"I thought you told me there aren't any sides."

"I did tell you that, yes, and I guess it's more or less what I'm trying to put across here. It could be to our advantage that we're not obvious either way."

"How so?"

"Maybe they'll ask before shooting us."

Five of the soldiers shared a thick hoggari cigarette whose bitter aroma was a favorable substitute for diesel exhaust. I recalled how one of those kids at Nina's house had introduced hoggari to some girls Saami had invited over that rainy night I stayed to dinner with Delia. They huddled together giggling in Gibb's bedroom, and I could smell the pungent odor of it clear down the hall to Nina's. I wondered if any of them had been in the house that day it was obliterated.

We rode on for more than two hours. Rain was so constant I got used to watching those silvery sheets of it wash about on the draft behind us as if it were permanent to the road we were traveling. Protiste dozed beside me. No one else slept. Our soldiers looked edgy, alert. Another couple of miles up the Péridon Road, I felt the trucks slow down by half. Gears stuttered, brakes squealed. One of the older soldiers got up and came to the tailgate and hung an arm to a frame-bar and swung himself out so he could see ahead on the road. Both trucks slowed further. The soldier yelled, "Goddamnit!"

Protiste woke as the other older soldier followed to the tailgate. Our trucks weren't running more than a couple of miles an hour now, barely trundling along when the first soldier at the tailgate jumped off the truck into the mud and rain. The other one grabbed onto where the first had taken his look forward. The one in the road shouted, "Those fucking bastards!"

Then I saw him run forward toward the lead truck, yelling, "GO! GO! GO!"

The engine roared on the front truck and I could hear it accelerate away from us. That soldier down in the road shouted again, "GO! GO! GO, GOD-DAMNIT! GO!"

And our truck lurched forward as the gears shrieked and our engine rattled, then burst us ahead.

Now the soldier was suddenly behind in muddy Péridon Road, still running and shouting, "GO! GO! GO!"

And that's when I saw the small field of thin tree stumps sticking out of the wet ground paired together by stalks of two. And I saw the older soldier falling away from us as we accelerated ahead. And I heard that shrill scream of artillery shells racing overhead to detonate in the road beside the field of tree stumps that weren't trees at all, but rather the bare legs of men buried upside-down to their thighs in the common earth. Then Péridon Road behind us erupted with a great black fountain of mud and water and, too far away now to catch up, our running hero was vaporized in the blast.

Another four miles along the road.

"It's an old game," Protiste told me as we rolled on, still traumatized by the attack and the sight of those bodies. "You kill somebody, then invite all his family and friends to the funeral and blow them all up together."

Those two young soldiers who'd been cleaning rifles before the subterfuge looked shaken and pale. The ones smoking that hoggari just sat quietly, as if comfortably anesthetized to the constant violence and horror of it all.

Protiste said, "See, Julian, they missed us twice today, so maybe you're a lucky charm."

"I don't know what I am, or why I'm out here at all. This is completely insane."

"Don't worry about it. Somebody put a spell on you. So long as it doesn't wear off, you'll be just fine."

"If you say so."

I stared out into the rain as we drove along. Those muddy fields. That dreadful emptiness. I heard thunder in the distance, and now I knew it as heavy cannon fire across the grey sky. The rumble was distinct and constant. To none of us in particular, the surviving older soldier said, "That'd be Dentellus. Our Borrado 90s. Sambanet's brigade. The old Lucian. Unleashing hell on those sonsabitches. We'll run them out of there soon enough."

One of the hoggari soldiers spoke up. "Flanagan's with that crowd. Remember him? On the Bucareli Bridge?"

The older soldier shrugged. "That was nothing. I've seen worse."

"Aw, phooey on you. No one ever did nothing like that before. How do you think he got his stripes?"

The older soldier smirked. "Behind the latrine?"

Another hoggari soldier laughed and the first one slugged him in the shoulder.

"That's not so funny. Flanagan's got something, I tell you, and if any of us had it, we wouldn't be riding along here like sitting ducks."

"Somebody's got to be the ducks, right? Otherwise there's no war and you get nothing to complain about."

"I like complaining."

"Well, do it somewhere else. You're wearing me out."

Half an hour on and the lead truck stopped and so did we. The rain had lightened to a thick cold mist and there was a gentle wind.

"Piss break," Protiste told me and climbed out over the tailgate. The other soldiers went next, but not all at once. I got out, too, stepping down into the mud. That cannon thunder had ceased. No sound at all but wind flapping at the truck canvas. I looked around at the muddy landscape of nothingness. We might have been on the moon of a cloudy day. Did the moon have clouds? Dr. Bednar said no, but had he ever been up there? Of course not. Although I supposed he was probably right. No atmosphere means no clouds. These fields were nothing but mud and clouds. And something else, too. A smell I noticed then out in the rainy air, a faint putrescence, the stink of death and decay across the common soil. Unrelenting. I thought, no one will ever want to live here again.

I went off to piss.

The front truck wouldn't start, so the tools came out and a trio of soldiers from that truck, and one from ours, went under the engine to repair something, I had no idea what.

As we stood off to the side of our own truck, I asked Protiste, "Aren't we making a target of ourselves parking here like this?"

"Nah, too far away. Back there with those guys buried with their heads in the mud, that spot was all lined up. They didn't need to aim so much as we drove into it. Here's different. If they shoot at us, we'll have time to roll before they get the range. So, nothing to worry about."

I looked up at the grey sky and wondered how long it would rain. Feeling a wet chill, I climbed back up into my truck and waited for the lead truck to be fixed.

— · —

We were stuck there for another hour and a half. Rain began to come down harder and most of the soldiers got back into their trucks. The officer up front in charge of this convoy sat in the cab on the radio to Porphyry Hill, letting them know where we were. Turned out he was the same fellow I'd met at Shadroe Station with Hastings. I watched Protiste walk about in the rain, staring off across the muddy fields into the distance as if he were looking for someone or something that wasn't immediately visible. His borrowed uniform was soaked, but he didn't seem to care. How did Nina know him? What sort of acquaintances had they shared? And how did he happen to be so cavalier about Arturo's disappearance? I thought he said they were pals. Protiste didn't sound all that troubled over finding out Arturo had left without saying a word about where he was off to. I just found that odd somehow.

A couple soldiers from the front truck brought us canisters of water. Nice and thoughtful of them, because we were all parched. They told us we'd eat with the 32nd Battalion in the encampment at Porphyry Hill, and that once we got the trucks up and running again, we were only about two hours out.

I must have drunk a gallon of water, then left the truck to piss again into the mud a dozen yards away. Standing alone in the cold drizzling rain, I realized now that this was the Desolation I'd seen in my dreams, a world utterly devoid of life, of anything good to love and nurture and grow. Our wrath had laid waste to this earth and left it barren and cold. One destiny made evident in these putrid fields of the dead.

XXXIII

The clouds broke a little as our small convoy finally rolled into the sodden truck depot at Porphyry Hill. The late day was still cold, threatening of further rain, but for now maybe we had a chance to dry out. I was hungry, too. All of us were. Our surviving officer from the first truck found out where the mess hall was located and gave us directions before heading off to see the camp commander. Apparently, that was not Major Laurentine Künze. Regardless, I followed him over to inquire as to the major's whereabouts and attempt to explain my purpose there. I felt that Porphyry Hill would finally be the end of the line and after this I could go home to Nina and my normal life at Thayer Hall with the most severe threat being academic washout. In fact, crossing this muddy camp, I was nervous, contemplating what all this had meant, my journey here. So many deaths. Ruin and confusion. Sadness. Fear.

Crossing the encampment, I noticed this terrain was different. Like its name, here were low gently rolling hills, a few trees spotted about. Not many, but some. Bare, of course, entirely absent of leaves, as if spring had bypassed this place. But it was something, at least. The Desolation felt so relentless. The end of life. I knew it wasn't, but it felt that way. Most remarkable, following that officer through the camp, I was impressed by how all these soldiers got on with their duties in such a horrid place. That discipline to shove aside constant mortal dangers and perform those daily tasks required of them, I just found astounding. How they even managed to rise from their cots each morning was a testament to courage and commitment to this mission, and to each other, of course, for whom they fought. Not the Status Imperium. Not those of us enjoying the benefits of our gilded society. Not even their commanders who sent them off each day to an unknown and incomprehensible fate. I admired each one of those fellows and I didn't know them at all.

Colonel Denham Watson was division commander of the Porphyry Hill encampment. His tent was near the mess hall, and tidy all about, in contrast to the orderly disarray almost everywhere else. I stood patiently outside as the officer from our truck convoy went in ahead of me, preferring my conversation to be as private as possible. I didn't want to experience any confusion of purposes. My directive was basic and simple, although its reason for being could come across as a little abstruse. I understood that. Particularly when I invoked the name of Major Künze, since I knew absolutely nothing about the social politics of military command structure. I didn't even know the basic hierarchy. Again, I needed Freddy here to explain the difference between colonel, major, lieutenant and captain. Who was best? "General" was the only one that made sense to me, and that was just because my mother had a friend whose husband was General Féliz Oster of the Security Directorate. He was killed at Niarchos when I was in Upper School.

I also wondered where Samuel Protiste had gone off to. I hadn't seen him since the truck. We were both filthy. My father's coat looked ruined by rain and mud. The valise, too. My trousers were cold and wet. I felt a chill coming on. Maybe Protiste was locating our tent for the night. That would be helpful. He was a strange, sort of distant fellow. I had no idea what to make of him. I wasn't even sure I trusted him. Yet, were he not along with me from Tamorina, I knew I'd be lost. Possibly dead.

Rain began falling again. Just softly. Not bad yet. A wet breeze swept through, fluttering at the commander's tent flap. The officer came out. Seeing me there, he asked, "Are you still with us? Have you seen your Major Künze?"

"Not yet, sir. I'm about to ask where I might find him."

"Hastings was killed this morning."

"I know, sir. I'm sorry. I was in the last truck. We got out, but it was terrible, just the same."

"He was a good officer."

"Yes, sir."

He looked me up and down, probably disappointed with how shabby I appeared with all the mud on my jacket and trousers. "Well, do your business and take yourself back to Tamorina. We've haven't the time for fellows like you these days. It's hell enough."

"Yes, sir. I'm anxious to finish up, as well. Sorry for this assignment, sir."

He nodded and walked off without another word.

I drew a deep breath and went into the tent.

Colonel Watson sat behind a small wooden desk, folders scattered across it. On an artist's easel was a field map of Porphyry Hill and the encircling territory.

Various lines and ink marks were drawn all over the map and pins stuck in irregular order. At least to my unstudied eye. A metal lantern was suspended from a hook above the desk. The colonel looked about my father's age, but tired. He was reading from a pale-green booklet when I came in and didn't seem to notice me. I coughed. "Excuse me, sir."

He glanced up. "Yes? Who are you?"

"I'm Julian Brehm, sir, personal envoy to Dr. Otto Paley, Chief Director of Internal Communications on the Judicial Council."

He looked me over.

Then he said, "Yes, all right. Fine. What brings you here?"

"I'm supposed to meet with Major Laurentine Künze of the 32nd Battalion, sir, on a matter of personal interest to Dr. Paley."

"And what would that be?"

This was tricky. "I'm not permitted to comment on that, sir. I'm sorry. The Council is strict to those rules. I'm only to follow their directive."

He looked a bit insulted. "Let me see your papers."

"Of course, sir."

I put down my soggy valise and took out the diplomatic pouch and the status papers from Dr. Paley. I handed them across the colonel's desk. Once more, I felt those jitters that had been plaguing my well-being since boarding the train at Commonwealth Station.

Either he read very slowly and wasn't absorbing it or was skeptical of my envoy status.

Finally, he said, "Your directive is described for Tamorina, young man. Tarchon Province. How have you managed to make your way up here?"

"Actually, with great difficulty, sir, and a lot of luck. My liaison in Tamorina left for Crown Colony an hour before my train there arrived, so I was obliged to follow him by truck convoy. He, then, passed information I was to have interpreted by Major Künze, who apparently had already assembled his 32nd Battalion to travel up here. As I boarded a truck to cross the Alban River to meet up with him, the bridge was shelled and destroyed. Only my truck, sir, being at the back of the convoy and not yet on the bridge, avoided being hit. We were very lucky, sir. Nearly everyone else was killed."

"I assume you rode up here with Lieutenant Vaudable?"

"Who, sir?"

"The lieutenant who was just in here ahead of you."

"Yes, sir. We drove from Crown Colony in two trucks. His was up front. I didn't have a chance to meet him. Sorry, sir. It was pretty hectic. An older soldier in our truck saved us from being shelled but was killed on the road."

"So I heard."

"Yes, sir."

"Well, look, Major Künze is up the road at our forward position and won't be back until after dark. Is there anything I can help you with until he returns? I didn't realize the esteemed Otto Paley sent envoys out into the field."

"He wants reports, sir. Besides these meetings, I'm to provide notice on what I see out here in the war provinces. I presume he has his reasons."

"Everyone has his reasons these days. That's why we have this war."

"Yes, sir."

"Tell me something, young man. Do you know why we're out here?"

I told him, "To protect our civilization, sir. Defend our Common Purpose."

He laughed at me. "I hope that's not a serious answer. Because if it is, I'm very disappointed. I'd have thought Otto Paley would send someone smarter than that."

I bristled slightly. Was he testing me somehow? "All right, sir. We're out here to kill everyone on the other side of the fence."

He smiled. "Now, that's more like it. These are not moral issues, son. They're imperatives. Do you understand the distinction?"

"I believe so, sir. You mean that we do what we do, not necessarily because we believe it's right, but rather to serve our own best interests, whatever they might be."

"Exactly."

"If a million people on that side need to die for us to put hot soup on our tables at dinner time, sir, and hot soup is vital to our national survival, we'll kill a million people."

"Let me tell you something, Mr. Brehm. My father was your age when our Republic decided that life as we knew it had stagnated. Our growing fields were inadequate, our metals had diminished, our very spirits were in need of revitalizing. They decided the world had grown small and petty. Our world.

And something had to be done. The nation required a directive that expanded our Common Purpose to include those provinces in the east we had considered empty and useless in that decade of the Great Separation. It's why we sent those trains to the east with the unfit and the unwell. Nothing out there was worthy of our attention or desires. Nobody in the Republic could have ever conceived what those people made of their fate out in the hinterlands. I suppose we just expected them to die. They were, after all, intellectually and physical ill-equipped, right? Feebleminded? Whether we kept them or sent them away didn't matter, did it? Because our Medical Directorate told us they were all going to disappear, isn't that true?"

The colonel stared at me. He had a pencil and tapped it on the desk. I heard the rainfall thickening outside, drumming on the tent roof.

I nodded. "It's what the books say, sir."

"Well, damn those books, young man. They did not die. They did not fail. They did not prove our Medical Directorate correct in dispersing them into the wilderness. For forty years those people found water and food and shelter by trading with the natural inhabitants of those useless fields. Then they made tools and built houses and towns and windmills. They planted those fields to grain and orchards, and cultivated livestock. They designed and constructed machines and mined for gold and copper and iron. They dredged the Bakhaouran swamps and cleared forests and drilled oil wells and constructed electric grids. Mr. Brehm, they were not unfit and unwell. Not defective at all."

"No, sir."

"My father left my young mother at home and enlisted to the Simois Brigade where he trained under Commander Maxim Cristobal during the First Directive. He was told that our Common Purpose expected the reacquisition of Darrieux, Solomon and Fabian provinces from settlements of the undesirables. We ordered them to leave, to give up their houses and home orchards, their stores and schools, their holy churches. Some did. Plenty of them. The others we killed. By the hundreds. With the Simois Brigade. My father told me stories of needful slaughter and pillaging. Instructions to terrorize by command of the Status Imperium to save our Republic. Inevitable. Necessary. Then some who'd left came back to reclaim by force of arms what we'd forced them to give up. And we killed them, too. Thousands. We took those provinces from them, everything they'd built on their own, we took. We pushed them back, mile after mile. All this geography we thought was worthless, they'd made a life from. God, how they'd worked. No matter, the Judicial Council determined by fiat that it all belonged to us, anyhow, by right of imperial domain. Then our armies crossed the Fatoma River at Obregón and Madaleña and Van der Halt. We killed everyone we saw. That first year of the war, we killed over two hundred thousand using radioactive shells and hydrocyanic gas. The next spring, we pierced the Florian Border and the war spread across the eastern provinces until finally they fought back. We were unprepared for that. The sheer ferocity of their defense. Their technical expertise. The weapons they had were better than ours. Their tactics were uncanny. We lost entire brigades. Xanthus and Layton and Simois. Our finest men. My father had both his legs amputated at Colina. I never knew him as anything but a cripple in that iron wheelchair. He felt we had to win this war, or his legs were sacrificed for nothing. Redemption for our suffering, OUR suffering, mind you, not theirs, could only come through winning this war and annihilating those monsters on the other side of the fence, as you so aptly put it."

I was horrified. "Yes, sir."

"I joined Lieutenant Commander Solís with the Volcow Brigade when I was seventeen years old to honor my father whom I dearly loved. I swore an oath to him that I'd see to the end of this war. My life has been spent out here, young man. More than forty years. What's it all meant? They have to die, Mr. Brehm. Every last one of them, if necessary."

I came across Protiste at a soggy tent where a game of Dámian poker was hosted. He was smoking a fat black cigar and kibbitzing. I leaned in, caught his attention, and asked him where the tent was that we'd be using overnight.

He said, "You'll see it by the motor pool. Not the best location, because it'll be noisy as hell at sunup." He peeked out at the steady rainfall. "If there is any sun tomorrow."

"How long are you going to be here? Don't we have to eat?"

"I already did," he told me. "But you better eat now. The dinner show might spoil your appetite."

"How's that?"

"You'll see. Just go eat."

I went back across camp to the mess hall by Colonel Watson's tent. There were long queues of hungry soldiers holding tin plates, forks and knives. We ate royal ham and boiled potatoes and spinach. I had a cup of coffee that tasted a bit like paregoric and ate a little cake of something that resembled raspberry but was not. Dinner was fine. I listened to odd rumors about our enemy. Robots and invisible soldiers. Other impossible things. Rain outside the tent abated but the air was still cold and drafty. A couple soldiers asked who I was, and I told them I'd been sent there under strict orders from Dr. Paley. I made them promise not to blame me for the coffee. They thought that was pretty funny and invited me out to watch the show with them after we finished eating. One of them by the name of Reece Clauston told me he was from Fiurth Street in Calcitonia District. His dad sold shoes and his mother repaired them. Reece hated the stink of shoe polish, so he enlisted and wound up at Porphyry Hill. He admitted that in hindsight, shoe polish wasn't so bad, after all. His pal was García Arqueles, a true Saviona by birth but who grew up by the sea at Poerto Clichy where his father caught mussels and his mother sold trinkets made of shiny seashells. Neither of those two fellows expected to live much longer and wanted me to tell Dr. Otto Paley that if the mess hall food were improved, we'd have a better chance of winning the war. I assured them that would be my first comment when I got back to the metropolis.

"It's a question of attitude and motivation," Reece told me. "If the food is good, our motivation is better to survive for another meal. If it isn't, then we kind of wonder what the good of it all is, right?"

"I agree," I said. "We need to have goals to get us by."

García said, "Food matters. Don't let nobody tell you otherwise."

Earlier that afternoon, a regiment of mechanized fusiliers had engaged and captured a squad of spyreotic infiltrators and tied them to scrawny birch trees on a low hill at the edge of camp, trees stripped of branches and bark by relentless artillery barrages a month before. "Pigs on a stick" was how a staff sergeant from the motor pool waiting behind me described those fiends bound harshly in our grasp. At dusk in the spotty rain, each enemy soldier was drenched in petroleum as Colonel Watson enjoyed his own supper of pork sausage and fried potatoes and a glass of Kebir wine at a small table under a broad black umbrella outside his tent while listening to Reynaldo Font's Lullaby Suite in B minor. For his dessert, a corps of weapons engineers had fabricated a crude slingshot from rubber straps and motor parts. A sport was devised using round stones wrapped in oily rags, ignited by lucifer match, and hurtled across the road, five shots apiece by alternating chances, he with the most strikes earning a week's pay from a pot paid into by the regiment. Like shooting stars on the rainy night sky. Thus, I witnessed the contest with my two new soldier friends cheering on the horrid competition. Blazing arc and explosion of sparks. Hit and miss and hit. Flames and screams. Hurrah for a winning throw. Human candles bursting like sunlight atop the fiery copse. That ghastly scene of hellfire and carnal revenge. A hideous act. Burning down the birch poles one by one until the stench of burning flesh drifted toward the encampment. Then the colonel's herd of pigs was chased up the hill to feed.

Hours later, as a storm arrived, I huddled on a narrow cot keeping my shoes out of the mud. The rain fell remorselessly, flooding a crudely ineffective gutter next to our tent. Wind ripped a hole across the canvas and Protiste rose to refasten it. Somewhere not so far to the east, artillery fire boomed, another onslaught in the dark, a mean insult to the unprepared, a distant summons to battle. Or was that just thunder? I listened for a while and felt cold and lonely. I knew I didn't belong in this place. But who did? Whose soul was so rude and craven that he could thrive in this? And why was I sent here? Some part of me had suspicions of a secret purpose I could not hope to fathom. Those oracles at Achaelus gave each pilgrim the possibility of reason. I had none any longer. I slept and had distracted, irrational dreams that were harried and unpleasant.

Sometime in the night, a hand on my shoulder shook me awake and I saw an officer standing over me. He put a finger to his lips and motioned for me to get up and go with him from the tent. I rose from the cot and took my valise and went out into the rain. He waited for me.

His uniform was soaking wet. "I'm Major Laurentine Künze."

I offered my hand. "Julian Brehm, sir."

"I know. Come with me."

He reminded me somewhat of my father, sturdy but not too tall. Stern. Serious. He strode off quickly through the mud. We went across camp in the rainy dark, just a few soldiers up and about on duty at that hour. Actually, I wondered what time it was. How long had I slept? I couldn't tell at all. Major Künze led me to a bunker at the end of camp tucked away from the narrow road that led in and out. There was a small armored truck parked by the bunker I assumed was his personal transportation. A thick canvas hung over the entrance that Künze brushed aside to let me in.

Not quite a cave, but not a tent like Colonel Watson's, either. Dug out of the surrounding embankment and embellished with sandbags and ratty rugs on the dirt floor. I had a good look around as Major Künze fiddled with one of his cabinet drawers. Like Watson, he had a desk and a couple of creaky chairs. Maps on the walls. A gold and viridian flag of our Republic. A radio set on a walnut side table. A field telephone sat on his desk with a stack of papers and manuals, all obscure to my eyes. He also had his own field cot and an old wood-burning stove in one corner of the bunker that warmed the room but let out enough smoke to cast a slight haze in the lamplights. I could see this would be comfortable enough for a temporary assignment. Not bad at all.

He drew out a thin satchel from the cabinet and opened the metal clasp. Then he asked, "Well, what do you have for me?"

"I'm not sure, sir. Are there any scissors here, or a small sharp knife?"

"Penknife?"

"I think so, sir," I said. "Let me show you." I took off my jacket and prepared to lay it across his desk. "May I?"

"Just a moment." Künze cleared away some of the papers and stacked the manuals across to the other side of his desk. "All right. Let's see what you have."

I folded the jacket open to reveal where Angelina Jouvenon had carefully stitched that secret pocket. Directing the major's attention to the almost invisible line of threads, I told him, "If you cut them carefully, sir, it won't ruin the hidden pocket."

He didn't seem to care about that and brought the penknife blade directly to my father's jacket and sliced through the stitching in one rapid pass. Then he slipped two fingers inside and drew out Draxler's scroll. As he unfolded it, I took back my damp jacket and put it on.

Major Künze laid the scroll on his table and flattened it out. We both studied the arcs and swirls of Draxler's artful brush strokes.

"What is this?"

"That's what he gave me, sir."

"Where are the drawings he had?"

"I don't know, sir. This is all I have."

"Hmm."

"I have no idea what this is all about."

"Well, you do know he stole some drawings from the architectural offices of Leandro Porteus, correct?"

"So I've been told, sir. I never saw them."

I heard the rain roaring outside the bunker as the storm drenched the camp.

Künze examined the painted scroll again, humming softly to himself as he did. He traced over part of it with a forefinger. He asked, "Did Draxler say anything to you about this painting?"

"No, sir."

"Did you watch him create this?"

"I saw him painting most of it, sir. He had it positioned such that I couldn't really make out what he was doing. I never saw it closely until just now."

"Well, have a look here," he said. "How does it strike you?"

I gave it a good going-over, tracing the same curves and arcs the major just did with his finger. Honestly, to my rather unartistic eye, what Draxler had painted wasn't much more than a lot of black swirls and angles. Another example of modern art I didn't understand, nor particularly care for. I told Künze, "I'm not sure at all what to make of it, sir. It's just a lot of lines to me."

"Well, it can't be, you know?" The major sounded irritated, or greatly frustrated, now. He asked, "What did he say about this when he gave it to you?"

I thought about that for a few moments. What had he said? "As I recall, sir, it was something to the effect that without this scroll, we wouldn't be able to find the drawings."

"What the devil does that mean?"

I shrugged. "No idea, sir."

"Well, there has to be something here."

"I'd assume, sir."

Major Künze took the scroll and held it up to the lamplight above his desk. He tilted it up and down, and side to side, frowning as he did. He pulled it out and pushed it back toward the light, squinting as he did.

"Hmm. Very interesting. You watched him paint this?"

"Yes, sir. Mostly."

"Would you happen to know what sort of paint he used?"

"Pashlovt oil, sir. My mother's an artist. She paints in many mediums."

"Did he give more attention to one part than another?"

"No, sir," I replied. "At least not that I noticed."

"Have a look here." Künze held the scroll up to the lamp. "Do you notice how the paint is thicker in some places than in others?"

I gazed at the lines of dips and swirls. When he tilted the scroll here and there, I did notice what he'd suggested. Indeed, some of the painted arcs and strokes did appear to have a heavier application of paint. "Yes, sir, I do. What does it mean?"

"Well, I have a thought." He laid the scroll back onto his desk and went around to a drawer and took out a pencil. "Let's try something. Hold it flat for me, please."

"Yes, sir."

The major took his pencil and began tracing over those curves and arcs and swirls where Peter Draxler had applied the thickest paint. He went slowly and mumbled to himself as he did. I wasn't quite sure what his intent was, but he seemed vigorously entertained now.

Then he finished.

He smiled. "It's chirographic writing in the midst of this chaos. A word."

"What word, sir?"

"Well, look here." He traced it over for me. "See these letters? Their placement on the scroll, across and down, tells us how to read them."

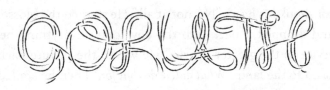

"I can't make that out, sir. What does it say?" I felt so sleepy just then, I could hardly think.

"Goliath."

"Goliath? Are you sure, sir?"

"Why? Does that mean something to you?"

"Yes, sir, it's the name of Delia Rinaldi's little terrier."

"Speaking of which," Künze asked, "where's Arturo Cascádes?"

"I don't know, sir. I never met him. Samuel Protiste told me Arturo left his apartment at Tamorina last month and nobody's heard from him since."

"But I understand you had something for him. Is that correct?"

I nodded. "Yes, sir. I was bringing him a picture of his daughter. Her mother gave it to me."

"Nina Rinaldi?"

He knew everything here. "Yes, sir."

"May I see the picture?"

"Of course, sir."

I leaned down and opened the valise and took out my diplomatic pouch once more and found the envelope with Delia's picture. I handed it to the major. Rain outside poured down harder than ever.

He slipped the picture out and looked at it. "Lovely child."

"Yes, she is, sir. Very smart, too."

Then Künze flipped it over and read that line Nina had scribbled on the back. "What does this mean? *'I keep a secret.'*"

"I haven't any idea, sir. I didn't understand it, either." I picked up the envelope and took out the dried lemon blossom and showed it to the major. "Did you notice this, sir?"

"No. What is it?"

"A lemon blossom, I believe, sir. I thought it might represent somewhere Nina and Arturo made love, perhaps even where Delia was conceived. Do you agree?"

The major shook his head. "No, not at all." He studied the blossom for a few moments and dropped it back into the envelope. "Everything here, my boy, exists in service to the greater puzzle." He waved the picture back and forth, then held it up to the lamp. *What did he do that for?* Then he smiled. "All right, now it makes sense."

He put the picture down and went around to another one of his desk drawers and took out a box of tall lucifer matches. He grabbed the picture again and struck a match against his desk. As it flared hot, he held it up to the picture.

I panicked. "No, don't burn it, sir!"

But he didn't bring the match to the picture itself, rather he waved it back and forth a couple of inches from the side with Nina's scribbled sentence. After about thirty seconds or so, he smiled. "Aha!"

Then he blew out the match and tossed it away.

"Now, son," he said, "let's see what we have here. Take a look."

He handed the picture back to me. "Can you read this?"

I stared at the fuzzy handwritten letters revealed by lucifer match. They said:

> *I love my Goliath*
> *So*
> *I bathe him in violets*

"Do you understand that, son?"

"Well, sir, if it pertains to Delia, then I suppose 'Goliath' is referring to her dog. I don't know about the violets. And I'm not sure that's even her writing."

"Might there be a connection between this picture and that scroll you brought here?"

"I don't see how, sir. One is from Peter Draxler and the other from Nina."

"But they do know each other, correct?"

"Yes, sir."

"They were lovers?"

"Apparently, sir. Sometime earlier this year or last. That's all she told me. I gathered they don't really favor each other any longer. Her opinion. Speaking with Draxler in the Dome, he made it clear he didn't much care for her, either."

"But you can see how they worked this out together, can't you? A collaboration. Nina knows both Arturo Cascádes and Samuel Protiste. Draxler paints the scroll and needs you to bring it to me, and he knows you'll do this because Nina has persuaded you to bring this picture to Arturo with whom she had her child."

"But he wasn't at Tamorina, sir."

"Not important anymore, son. Their idea was just to keep both pieces separate. The lock and the key. One requiring the other. Draxler is one of the most brilliant young fellows I've ever known. Do you see what a clever puzzle he's constructed here? I believe I know just what he's done. Both the picture and the painted scroll provide nothing apart, except for a photograph of a little girl and a fairly trite example of incomprehensible modern art. Therefore, nobody could decipher the hidden purpose of one without the other. Goliath, for instance, is both the little girl's dog and the title, I presume, of Draxler's abstract painting. We know Peter is not concerned with giving that dog a bath, so we can predict it's the painting those violets are referring to, not the terrier. But we can't know that with only the painting, nor just the picture. We need both. You've gotten them here safely and now they're together, so let us see what we have."

The major went through a curtain on one side of his bunker, across from the wall maps where he had a toilet and a bathtub. I watched him put a small bottle of some bathing solution into an empty porcelain wash basin and bring them back into the room to set on the desk. Then he opened the bottle, poured some of the liquid into the basin, and added water from a jug he had atop that filing cabinet and stirred it with his hand.

"That was violet essence I just mixed up."

He went back to the bath for a wash rag and came out again, then soaked the rag in the water. He told me, "You take the painting now and dip it into the basin. Get all of it wet."

"Yes, sir."

Carefully, I eased it through the violet bath until I'd soaked every inch of the scroll.

The major returned to the bathroom and came out with a towel and used it to cover part of his desk next to the wash basin. "All right then, lay it flat on this towel. Hold the edges for me."

"Yes, sir."

Major Künze soaked the washrag in violet water and began scrubbing the painting. As he did, he told me, "Pashlovt oil dissolves in violet water. This is why young Draxler used it, just as Nina drew her message in lemon socco that's invisible until heated by flame."

He scrubbed firmly as the black pashlovt oil markings began to fade away from the linen parchment. Top to bottom, side to side, Künze erased the painting Draxler had made. He rubbed it all away until nothing remained but the pale parchment.

"Good. Now more water." He soaked the rag more thoroughly, really drenched it and did not wring it out. Instead, he brought it back to the parchment and began rubbing vigorously. He told me, "Draxler used white pashlovt oil for the base. It's very rare and quite clever. Almost impossible to distinguish from the natural parchment itself. And it can easily be painted upon with black pashlovt oil."

"I didn't know that, sir. My mother never showed me any such thing."

"Well, it's relatively uncommon."

I had to hold the scroll down with some force to prevent it from sliding on the towel as Künze worked the washrag fiercely across the damp parchment. Now an ink pen design began to evolve, lines and angles. Architectural forms. Direction and symbols. Language. Boxes and notations. Plans for a well-ordered and intricately detailed and conceived structure. The drawings from Leandro Porteus.

Major Künze said, "I'm assuming this is a copy Peter created. Where the original is, only he knows."

"Maybe he made this copy, sir, and put the original back to protect himself. If he were caught, he could always say someone had misplaced it. They'd probably have to believe him."

"Don't be naïve. Peter isn't. He knows they'd torture and kill him, either way, so he's likely hidden the original in the event you failed to bring this here. Then he'd just try to find another courier and start over."

I examined the architectural plan laid out before me. Having no structural design sense or experience, I had no true concept of what I was looking at. I asked Künze, "Do you have any idea, sir, what this represents?"

"No, but I know people who do. We're going to get it to them immediately. Tonight, in fact." He refolded the parchment into those original four squares Draxler had created and handed it to me. "Put this back into your jacket. Arturo was supposed to bring it forward, but since he's not here anymore, it's your assignment now."

I felt that familiar cold stone drop into the pit of my stomach. This was not my responsibility. I said, "I'm not a soldier, sir. I'm not even supposed to be here. My directive from Dr. Paley limited my travel to Tamorina, and no farther."

"Yet you are here now."

"More by circumstance than choice, sir. An accident of timing."

"Son, fortune often favors the needy and we need you to get this up to the front where we have a runner who can take it across to some people who have a good understanding of what Peter stole from Leandro Porteus."

My nerves boiled. "Do you mean we give this to the undesirables, sir? Is that what you're saying? Wouldn't be that treason? Aren't we shot for that?"

"We're shot for a lot of reasons these days, Julian, from both sides. I assume you've noticed that on your way up here this week."

"Of course, sir, but I didn't expect to have to look over my shoulder wherever I went. I don't want to be a traitor, sir. I just want to go home."

"And you will," the major said, "but just ask yourself what you thought you were doing in bringing that scroll here from Draxler. You knew many agents from Internal Security were looking for him, and it. Word is that you met one already in that house on Gosney Street. Did you tell that nasty fellow about Draxler, or even Nina? What do you imagine they'd do to you if they knew why you'd accepted that envoy pouch from Otto Paley? Would your father and those friends of his from the Garibaldi Building really be able to protect you? Or even themselves? Think about that, son."

This was so confusing. What was he driving at? Was this all my responsibility? My cause and effect? If so, where was my solution?

I chose to be bold for once. "May I ask you a question, sir?"

"Certainly."

"Well, no disrespect intended, sir, but why are you involved in all this? You're a field officer, a major in the army of our great Republic. Why are you doing it?"

He folded up his towel and rag and tossed them into the wet wash basin. Then he stared at me for a few moments. I assumed he was trying to find words to excuse his own guilt in this absurdly arcane affair. Instead, he told me, "Because this war has to stop before somebody wins."

The major gathered up a khaki field coat and hat and put on his belt holster with a revolver. I grabbed my valise once again and we went out into the windblown rain. It was dark and gloomy and cold when we climbed into his armored truck, watched by guards passing through the camp, rifles at the ready.

Künze fired up his motor and rolled us out onto the muddy road to the east. His headlamps were woefully inadequate for illuminating our journey, but he didn't seem to notice and drove rapidly. I huddled in my seat, chilled by the wet draft as we rushed on into the rainy darkness.

This road was empty of trucks or motors of any kind, but I did notice the occasional patrol of three or four soldiers collected along the side of the road every so often, looking soaked and miserable. Life of the unfortunate conscripts. Mostly brief and ugly. After being in these encampments, I felt sad for each one. Who among them could expect future days of sunshine and pleasure? For many, that life they'd known and loved was behind them now, never to be felt again. Every soldier in our war, or perhaps any war, was a human tragedy. That we tolerate and pursue such profound indignities in this world describes a species in abject failure. It's what I learned from the Desolation. If there are triumphs to be had, they won't be discovered here.

After driving in silence for maybe half an hour, the major spoke up. "We're roughly ten miles now from our forward positions. The battlements are enforced by trenches and artillery batteries and mechanical rifle emplacements, so we're well defended, but it is the hope of regional command that we are not compelled to remain here at this Porphyry Hill engagement too much longer. I think you'll see that conditions are necessarily dreadful and the spirits of our soldiers unsurprisingly low. They've all become fatalistic and that harms performance and attention to duty. On the other hand, they do not seem to understand how expecting to die leads them to death irrevocably. We've tried to instill in each of them concepts not of honor and courage so much as faith in our purpose out here and those strategies we pursue in putting our adversary to flight, thereby avoiding these prolonged engagements that risk so many lives."

I said, "Maybe they'd just rather quit the fight, sir, and go home. If that's even allowed. Is it? We never see them, you know. Really ever. At least I haven't."

"Of course, that's every soldier's fondest desire. To be home again. If it were only that simple. But maybe what you and I are chasing out here tonight can contribute one day to the realizing of that little dream."

"Maybe."

We drove on through the damp and windy dark, and after a while I began to hear thundering across the distance. Heavy storm or bombardments?

I couldn't tell for certain and I didn't care to ask Künze. Perhaps I didn't really want to know. This truck ride was uncomfortable enough. Fear in either case was foreboding. I'd held up reasonably well, I thought, since Albiona, but now and then I felt my resolve declining, knees trembling, my gaze becoming faint. If I passed out on this dreadful road, how could I be sure the major wouldn't simply snatch Draxler's plans from my father's jacket and shove me out into a flooded ditch. Perhaps it wasn't my fate to escape the Desolation, either. If not, this was starting to feel very close to the end of it all and I was scared.

Major Künze's forward positions for the 32nd Battalion were dug into the rolling hillsides where zig-zag trenches and deep bunkers had the great advantage of critical buffers and protection for troops traversing the natural terrain. Of course, that also meant mud and flooding everywhere and the desperate proliferation of sandbags and hewn logs. Hundreds of them. I didn't completely understand military geography and defensive architecture, but I grasped the basic concepts as he led me from the motor depot where we left his truck into a tunnel behind the trench lines. He told me that we were to link up with a fellow named Reto Sancho whose grandparents had occupied a one-bedroom tenement apartment in the Beuiliss District prior to the Great Separation. That sad dispersal had sent them by train to Darrieux Province for twenty-three years where they worked on a farm in the wheat fields of Batalla. They raised Reto's father there and six uncles and an aunt until the First Directive brought our armies across the Whitestone frontier with a threatening purpose evident to the rural population. By then, Reto's father had already married Siselia Üsküdar and left to his own life on the calm blue sea by Parthius where Reto was born. Most of the old family were killed during the initial reacquisition when Reto's grandfather and great-uncles refused to relinquish what they had lent many years and much trouble and heartache to build. His grandmother was burned alive in the cellar of their humble farmhouse and his great-aunt shot dead fleeing from a chicken shed in the midst of that pathetic struggle. Once they'd come of age, Reto's younger twin brothers joined the battle at Van der Halt and were captured, then released to Internal Security where one, Dani, vanished and the other, Leto, escaped across the Alban River to Châtelet Heights, seventy miles upstream from Crown Colony. His baby sisters, Cymonea and Creucyne, chose to stay by the sea with their parents and live in the contentment of fish and laundry and children bearing the name of survivors.

Major Künze told me that Reto wore the uniform of the Republic but his allegiance varied according to circumstance and memory. Apparently, he drifted between worlds with the confidence and conviction of the invisible man who knows he can't be seen yet is constantly tempted to assert his being and existence.

"He's about here somewhere," the major told me, as we traipsed down a cold dirt tunnel. "I saw him just yesterday in the munitions bunker making his counting. He's very diligent and trustworthy. Just the fellow for our purpose."

"Good," I replied, "because I'd prefer to leave this adventure to someone else as soon as I can."

"We'll need to see Brigadier General Dodd first. His explanation of what is intended in this campaign is important for you to grasp in case something unfortunate occurs."

"Unfortunate?"

"Use your imagination."

I had too many thoughts already infiltrating my dreams without extending myself further into some darker earth. What I wondered was whether this Reto fellow had a plan that avoided drawing me into some clandestine arrangement wherein I'd be forced to confront my own mortality or be found wanting in courage. I was no hero. In fact, the more miles I traveled out there, the more I became persuaded that survivors were needed more desperately now than heroes. Someone had to outlive all of this so that life could go on and the world might grow and flourish once again.

The tunnel came to an end at a noisy maze of passages ahead with irregular trenches dug roughly eight feet deep and six feet wide out of the damp earth and bolstered with heavy sandbags and tree timber hauled to these trenches by transport trucks under the protection of massive artillery barrages. There were dugouts and ammunition shelves, razor wire atop parapets, thick sandbags on the parados behind, trench boards and stumps. Wooden duckboards mostly covering the mud underfoot. The trenches themselves were packed with soldiers, soaked and filthy and hollow-eyed in the rainy darkness. A putrid odor permeated throughout. As if the disordered whole was a latrine or a hospital death ward. That horrid stink of rot and mire, both fecal and scabrous flesh, and the acrid burn of cordite and old gunpowder from ceaseless conflict. A bitter insult to humanity. I felt them staring at me, but I was probably paranoid. They had more to worry about than a young fellow in a dirty jacket with a muddy valise. Even so, I heard a Mascías concertina playing, "For as Long as I Live," in the cold drizzle and a young man's graceful voice singing along with that touching melody: "*O, when our fond hearts freely/ by the willow trees dearly/ lead we young lovers along.*"

"This way." Künze directed me under a timbered roof along a tunnel lit by electric lanterns hooked onto the wall every few feet. We walked along wood planks barely atop the shallow flood sluicing into the passage. I heard shouts echoing ahead and occasionally the sharp bark of rifle fire from the trenches, presumably snipers exchanging pertinent night greetings with adversaries across the rainy gloom. Like the one we came through after the truck, the air in this tunnel was cold and damp and drafty. A telephone bell rang ahead in the direction we were following.

"Dodd's right up here," the major told me.

The passage bent into a dank, almost airless dead-end with light and wood smoke coming from a cave to our left. Künze led us inside where an officer in a fit and tidy uniform stood by a huge wall schematic of tunnels and gun emplacements and a long wavy indicator of battlement trenches. He appeared a few years older than my father, perhaps in his sixties. Hair gone grey and absent in those familiar ways. Skin wrinkled, eyes drooping. Aging according to natural progress. He was on a field telephone, saying, "There's no worry here, Billy. The lines are cut and regulated. All our phlogistics were set this morning. The boys are edgy, all right. Pardon? ... No, they're goddamned tired of standing in the water all day. Some already got the lice fever, so they'll be glad, I tell you. No questions asked. ... Yes, I saw that, too, and it was a concern, but that was yesterday. It's been addressed. ... Who? ... Oh, Weston and Slimané. Both of them. You should've been there. Those fellows know what they're about, all right. It's a marvel to watch. Puff of smoke. Never seen anything like it. ... Well, sure. I'll send him up this morning if that'd work. ... All right, consider it done. ... Yes, yes."

He hung up the telephone and looked at us. Mostly me. But first he said to the major, "That was Touggorout. We've got trouble with the collapse of emplacements Seven and Eight from the storm. He wants to abandon them as forward positions until there's some sort of buffer protecting our boys out there. I haven't had a good opinion, but I don't much care for his."

"Would you like me to look into another solution, sir?"

"If you could."

"No trouble at all, sir. I'll do it once we're done here."

"Good enough." Then his notice switched to me. "So, who's your young mascot, Major?"

Künze told him, "This is Julian Brehm, sir." He tapped my shoulder. "Julian, this is Brigadier General Morris F. Dodd. Show him your status papers."

I set down my valise on a damp musty rug and took out the diplomatic pouch. I found the envoy papers and handed them to Dodd. He read them quickly and gave them back. Künze strolled over to warm his hands on a squat wood-burning stove in a corner of the cave.

"Well, well, well," he said, "the great Dr. Otto Paley sends us his finest, but to what purpose, young man? To what purpose?"

I was used to this by then, familiar with all my narrative variations, keen to inquisitions I'd be receiving, fluent in my methods of dodging them. "As you can see there, sir, my directive was Tarchon Province, principally Tamorina, but it seems my course was diverted by necessity due to a missing contact there whom I've now pursued through Crown Colony to here at Porphyry Hill. Secondarily, Dr. Paley has requested my attention to reporting on situations and conditions wherever I go, sir, so I've done that, too."

"And I take it you've seen your fair share along the way, had some excitement, perhaps, as well."

"Yes, sir, plenty of that."

"Well, young man, I knew Otto Paley quite well when we were both younger. We were perpetual adversaries in scholastic fencing when he was at Willsford and I attended Salius Academy. Lightning with a blade was that young Paley fellow. Not big, mind you, but rapid. He and I enjoyed many a great duel. Wonderful school days of youth."

Künze joined in from over by the stove. "Perhaps you could give Julian a basic primer on what we've gotten rigged up here so he could explain our situation and tactics to Dr. Paley when they speak next. That could be helpful in soliciting the kind of equipment we need to really take the fight to them this month. Get a lot of this over with by summer at the latest, if at all possible."

"Yes, of course." Dodd looked back to me. "Do you understand Porphyry Hill, young man? This geography and its economic purpose?"

"Not at all, sir, if I'm honest."

"Well, these old cave systems are basically tunnels for mining ore: copper, lead, tin, zinc. Our enemy used them for decades to build up their industry and machines. We didn't even know they were here until about nine years ago when we were able to fight our way across the Alban and bring the war into Caesárea. Porphyry township lies about a mile east of here and is fortified by a crack division of infantry armed with short range incandescent artillery, mobile incinerators, and those gas myrmidon guns that fire two thousand rounds a minute. Terrifying bastards. We require the strategic resources of these mines but cannot commit our geological engineers to the project so long as that force remains out there, alive and angry. Trouble is, we haven't been able to dislodge him from his stronghold despite repeated assaults and our heaviest artillery barrages. Simultaneously, this division's assignment is to protect the Péridon Road to Crown Colony and our chief encampment there. If the enemy should manage to assume control and use of Péridon Road, the way west to the Alban River is wide open and that threatens four hundred thousand men of the Second Army and our purpose clear back to Tamorina. Losing here could cost us years of tactical and strategic advantages. Not to mention how the politics of our position and actions all across Caesárea Province are debated in Otto Paley's Judicial Council. The assassination of those people in the Ferdinand Club was unfortunate for us, in that Dr. Jiudítha Rahmána, for one, had been assiduously active in pursuing support for our activities out here. She was astonishingly brilliant and intuitive with these matters. Her death in that bombing is a terrific muddle for us. As much as I admire Otto Paley, I'm not always certain of his point of view these days. Perhaps you can be of assistance to us there."

"Of course, sir."

Major Künze interjected, "Let's show him our latest idea, sir. Julian won't be leaving here, anyhow, until it's implemented, so there'll be no threat of being compromised. We'll want Dr. Paley to understand we're not just shooting into the woods."

Dodd smiled. "Of course, yes. Why not? Come over here to the map, son."

He went and flipped over the top page to expose a rendering of tunnel systems beneath, a crude architectural drawing replete with signs and figures I could not quite follow until his discourse.

"See here? Look at this wide passage." He traced it with a forefinger. "Well, it's not actually that wide underground, but it serves your being able to follow it east along this corridor toward the enemy. A month ago, we drained the water table from below, then tunneled in four directions under the putrid ville," he pointed to the map, "here and here and here and here, and seeded the cracks this week with wet stacks of tri-nitrophlogistics. When it goes off about two hours from now, they'll drop fifty yards, the whole town of Porphyry Hill, right into our laps, and we'll annihilate the whole fucking lot of them. Pardon my language."

Major Künze chuckled at Dodd. "I think we've been out here too long."

"No doubt."

I said, "It seems like a fine plan."

Dodd smiled. "It's damned genius, actually. If we pull it off —"

"And we will," Künze interrupted.

Dodd finished his thought. "If we do, conflict in this region will cease and our troubles will be resolved to a most satisfactory conclusion."

I added, "I certainly hope so, sir."

Künze came over to guide me out. "Well, Julian and I better get along to his rendezvous, so we can send him back down the road in one piece."

"Indeed." Dodd and I shook hands. "Glad to meet you, son. When you see Otto Paley, give him my best regards. Tell him 'Dodder' is still waiting for that bout from Campion Cup. He'll know what you mean."

"I will, sir. Thank you."

Out in the tunnel again, the major led me away from Dodd's cave down another passage parallel to the forward trenches. He told me there were three miles of fortifications in front of Porphyry Hill township. A relatively recent battlement, not meant to be permanent, or even sustaining. This was not the strategic intention at all. Only a defensive perimeter that allowed for the build-up of troops and equipment for the assault that would follow. By contrast, sixty years ago the undesirables' infamous Florian Border had battlements of trenches and pickets and razor wire and redoubts and vast artillery emplacements extending almost four hundred miles north and south, and in some regions fifty to sixty miles deep. It had provided security for St. Marta and Darrieux provinces until Dr. Bernadotte ordered it breeched a year into the war. That disastrous collapse and the resulting mayhem led to a million deaths in less than six months and the pathetic inevitability we now call the Desolation, not to mention the subsequent ruin of both societies, ours and theirs. The morbid assembling of casualty figures ended thirty years ago, those numbers already being so enormously obscene as to be considered finally irrelevant, at least in the gilded halls of the Status Imperium whose counting machines had no formula or index for morality.

The major spoke to me in a measured tone as we passed groups of soldiers whose muddy uniforms stunk as if they'd been bathing in rank latrines and astynex insecticide. "That corridor Dodd told you about is beyond the trench blocks of 'D' tunnel we used to get in here from the motor depot. The idea is that we meet up with Reto Sancho at the entrance and hand over your scroll which he'll take through the underground to another unmarked tunnel away from the earth mines we've planted for the destruction of Porphyry Hill. It's a fairly reasonable plan. Not too difficult to execute. Sancho has credentials for tri-nitrophlogistics, so nobody will question his presence in the tunnels there."

"I'm sorry, sir, I admit I'm a bit confused here. You say this is what Arturo was supposed to have done? How would he have been able to go down those tunnels?"

"No, I didn't say that at all. Arturo was only solicited to bring Delia's picture here to me. Reto Sancho and I have always been alone in this scenario. One simply cannot have excessive eyes and ears on assignments such as these. Failure increases almost exponentially when numbers are added. As they say in the machine industry, 'Too many working parts, it won't be worth a fart.' We're avoiding that here, trust me, by having you carry the scroll in my place."

Before I could chase that logic, the very earth beneath our feet shook with a deep resounding boom that made those amber wall lanterns sway on shallow hooks. I almost lost my balance.

Major Künze steadied himself with a hand on the tunnel wall. "Good heavens, it's a 12! Where did that come from?"

"A what?"

"Railroad gun. They haven't any in this region. Or they oughtn't to, according to our scouts."

Then another massive boom and one of the lanterns flew off its hook. Dirt cascaded from the tunnel ceiling. I saw an enormous brown rat scurry by down the tunnel away from the forward trenches, then a couple more. What the hell was going on when the vermin were fleeing?

The next gigantic blast thumped the earth and put out all the lanterns, dumping the major and myself into pitch darkness. We heard shouting from all over and soldiers sloshing through the muddy tunnels from every direction. Muffled explosions cannonaded in the near distance. And the crack of sporadic rifle fire.

"Is it an attack?" I asked, trying to keep the major close. If I lost him in this tunnel, I'd have no idea whatsoever where to go. At least in the undercity, we weren't being shelled.

"Not sure. I doubt it. I think they're just trying to rattle our cage, as it were. Keep us on edge."

"Honestly, it's scaring the hell out of me, sir. Can you get us away from here? I'd like to go now."

"Not until we meet Reto Sancho."

"Well, good grief."

Künze grabbed my arm firmly and gave a tug. "Come this way."

A fourth tremendous blast almost tossed us both into the muddy wall. But the major kept us on along the tunnel in the dark, refusing to slow another step. I saw flashes in the passage ahead, like lightning strikes, illuminating the night. Then a staccato BOOM, BOOM, BOOM, BOOM, like thunder echoing across the sky. More dirt shaking from the tunnel ceiling. Major Künze angled us off down a south leading tunnel where packs of soldiers were hurrying in both directions with ammunition boxes. Another enormous detonation shook the passage worse than ever. It collapsed part of the tunnel just behind us, trapping a pair of soldiers. Künze glanced back, saw their compatriots digging furiously to free them, then rushed us ahead once more. I heard the throaty din of mechanical rifles from emplacements nearby. POP-POP-POP-POP-POP-POP-POP.

Künze yelled to me above the weapons roar, "We have to get to the trenches! It's the quickest route through to the passage where Sancho's expecting to meet us!"

He cut us east, ahead to where I saw incandescent flashes on the rainy sky, a brilliant blaze of shooting stars and fireworks all at once with sounds of vulcan hammers and hellfire. Next, I could hear bullets by the dozens impacting the heavy parados sandbags. And the whump-whump of mortar shells detonating up and down the trench fields. Where to go for safety? Surely not ahead, yet that's precisely where the major was leading us.

I called out between blasts, "Why are we going this way, sir? We're going to get killed."

He ignored me and led us directly into the trenches, fully alit now by tools of war.

Whatever I'd heard back at Kippel's schoolhouse was small preparation for this. As if the entire world were blowing up at once. Thousands of incandescents shot across the sky overhead like a great meteor shower come to earth. Artillery shells shrieked above and exploded beyond us. Our mechanical rifles stuttered that brain-rattling rhythm and screams of our wounded and dying filled the trenches. Just a few yards from us, I saw a soldier tumble off the parapet with a bloody gaping hole in his face. And another, his helmet falling off with no head at all beneath. Künze pulled me low to the muddy reeking duckboards. He reached over and grabbed the helmet off a third dead soldier and stuck it on my head. Then he gave me a shove down along the trench. "Move! Move!"

The earth thundered as a huge shell detonated less than fifty yards from us farther up the trench line. A shower of mud cascaded down out of the rain. Keeping low, we headed south along the trench, dodging in and out of soldiers trying to angle upward to fire from the damp parapets. Our artillery had just joined the cannonade and we heard the shells whistling overhead along with the low crack of incoming rifle projectiles from the other side that sounded like someone snapping his finger next to my ear. We only got another fifty yards down the zig-zag trench line when a stupendous blast back where we'd come from tore a massive crater in the field near the parapet that completely buried that entire section of the trench where Künze had fetched my helmet. Through the glittering, almost ethereal light of ten-thousand incandescents crisscrossing the rainy sky overhead, I could see soldiers hurrying to climb across the muddy landslide from one side to another hoping to rescue anyone trapped and alive. Above us a hail of steel continued to thud-thud-thud into the sandbags of the parados. More artillery shells. More stuttering roar of our mechanical rifles. More frightening detonations of enormous explosions. I couldn't hear a word the major was yelling at me as we threaded a path through the dark damp trenches, stepping over and around the dead, the wounded, the frantic. Here and there Künze barked orders and instructions to his men, directing attention to this or that. I wasn't able to understand much of it, but somehow his composure was only half as rattled as those he directed. The entire scene was so horrific, my memory of it even now seems scattered and harried. I remember the smell of burnt cordite and sewer filth and blood. I remember the incessant and deafening roar and rumble and pop of guns and shells. I remember the ghastly expressions on the faces we passed, both the living and the dead, and the sight of human beings dislodged and dismembered and torn to pieces up and down that hell of trenches. And the screams of the wounded and the dying. Those fly about in my memory and refuse to go away.

Halfway down our trench run, I heard another fearsome sound from across that wet killing field. Like a motor saw, a great vicious motor saw.

The major yelled to me through the din, "Myrmidon guns! That means they're coming!" He took a whistle from his pocket and blew it so loudly it almost popped my eardrums. Then I heard other whistles blow, and a cacophony of fierce airhorns howled from behind the trench-lines. Künze told me, "No time to waste. We'll be closing off that corridor with diatomite once we see their people coming across no man's land. Can't have them finding our schedule." He gave me a shove. "Go!"

The noise was incredible, unearthly. Staggering explosions and mechanical rifle emplacements fully engaged. That snap-snap-snap of enemy bullets arriving overhead. And another gargantuan blast of those railroad artillery shells lifting the very ground under our feet and raining the wet soggy world down upon us afterward. The major and I weaved a frantic path through the ranks of soldiers firing off into the dark and ducking back down again beneath the sandbag parapets. And above us, always those beautifully terrifying incandescents screeching across the damp night air, piercing lights from heaven, or hell, in our mortal atmosphere. My terror was fully alive by then, nerves aflame.

Indescribably frightened. The major slid ahead of me when I stumbled over one of our wounded, just moments after being shot off his perch at the parapets. Not killed but suffering a dreadful bullet strike through the side of his chest, blood staining his muddy uniform. He moaned as we hurried past offering no help or comfort.

"We aren't doctors," the major said as I caught up to him. "Don't look."

Then that motor-saw roar of the gas myrmidon guns was amplified, seeming to be everywhere across the muddy field, closing on our trenches.

The major shouted, "We have to hurry! They'll be right on top of us!"

He ran through the trench, pulling ahead of me, and then my world vanished in a huge avalanche of mud and bodies. The sonic blast knocked me over. The trench disappeared. The shell ripped a great gouge out of the earth, parapet and parados collapsing together into the crater. I was on my back, my father's filthy valise a few feet away. I was dazed and deaf. Still alive but unsure of anything else. I looked up and saw the incandescents floating in the black sky like Christmas ornaments on a celestial firmament. Scarcely moving. Suspended for my benefit so I might witness the beauty of my life's ending. I only felt like resting there. To take account of all this was. I closed my eyes and was slapped. Harshly. The major hovering over me. Yelling my name. Urging me back up. He gave a tug and I found my feet. He handed me the valise and pointed me up the muddy embankment that enormous shell had created. He gave me a shove and I began to climb, still deaf to the blasts and fiery torments that were killing our soldiers all around now. I dragged myself and that valise to the top and almost looked around to see what was coming from the east across that dark field when I felt a vicious punch to my left shoulder and was knocked down the other side into the crowded trench below.

I landed on duckboards wet with rain and blood. More soldiers were lying nearby. Some dead, some still breathing, gasping in pain and anguish. Then a most extraordinary and excruciating agony shuddered through my body and I felt a hot stream of blood from my shoulder flood the sleeve of Father's jacket, soaking my hand and trousers. I thought I'd faint, but I didn't. The incessant din of mechanical rifles at the fixed emplacement just overhead apparently kept me conscious. That awful POP-POP-POP-POP-POP-POP-POP ringing in my ears between cannon blasts and screams.

Then Künze was at my side again, now with blood draining from his neck and top of his head. He yelled at me, "GET UP! GET UP! GET UP!"

He jerked me to my feet and my shoulder gave off the most horrid pain imaginable. He pushed me ahead along the mud-flooded trench. Leaning into my ear as we hurried, he said, "The passage is about twenty yards ahead. It's wide and you'll recognize it instantly. Reto Sancho will be there now. After you give him the drawings, there's a smaller tunnel directly across from the big one that'll lead you away from the trenches back out to the motor depot. Here —" he handed me his truck keys. "Drive it back down to camp. Don't look behind you or stop for anyone or anything. Just go."

"What about you, sir?" The entire side of his face and neck was wet with blood. "Are you shot? Good grief!"

"I'll be fine. Just a couple of scratches." He looked at my shoulder and bloody jacket. "Go down to the east passage and wait for me. I'll find you a towel to stanch your wound. It'll hold for you to drive. Take this now. It's morphium."

He gave me a brown pill to swallow and I did.

We separated in that nightmarish trench, and I didn't get sixty yards farther on before I felt a fantastic blast concussion behind me and saw the earth erupt where Major Künze had just sent me off. The trench completely disintegrated with everyone in it. All the mud, razor wire, sandbags, logs, blood, soldiers, dead and injured, Künze himself, obliterated and blown clear to God. Our mechanical rifle emplacement was gone, too, with the blast, no one left alive on the wet parapet, and that ugly motor buzz of the gas myrmidon guns so close now I could barely hear our own rifle fire. Soldiers all about were escaping down the trench in full retreat from the failed battlements. I grabbed my valise and chased after them.

How could the end of the world be much different from this? Rain and death and mayhem everywhere. A deafening orgy of violence and terror. I found the wide dark passage just ahead now where a frantic mass of soldiers was crowding the trenches and tunnels from many directions. Air horns kept blasting retreat. Wet and bleeding, I pushed my path through along the log wall until I reached the east passage and went inside to evade the hopeless escape attempt. How was I expected to reach the motor depot now with the division packing those narrow tunnels like that? Maybe I wasn't, after all. Maybe the only plan was for me to hand over the drawings to that Reto fellow and then be on my own. But I did have the major's truck keys. That must have meant something. The motor worked, didn't it? This assault from the undesirables ruined the schedule. And probably meant I would die here.

A voice behind me. "Do you have it?"

I turned to see a fellow walk from the dark passage with a rifle raised to fire.

"Who are you?"

"Reto."

I wanted to take the drawings from my jacket, but I needed to do so with my left arm, and it refused to budge. I guessed that bullet had shattered my shoulder. It ached badly now as the wound bled. I also felt dizzy from shock. I thought I might faint any moment. I told him, "It's in my jacket and I can't get it out. I was just shot. My arm won't work. I can't even raise it above my waist."

"Go down the tunnel. When I say so, drop your bag and step away from it."

"All right."

About fifty feet inside the passage, where the roar from the battle trench diminished somewhat, he said, "Stop there. Now, go stand over at the wall and put your nose into the mud. Do it now or I'll shoot you."

I went and did as I was told.

"If I feel you budge at all, I'll kill you."

"I won't move."

I felt him press the barrel of his rifle against my upper spine.

"Lower your right arm, too."

"All right."

He stepped close and dragged my jacket off and drew it away from me. "Where's the drawing?"

"In a secret pocket under the right sleeve."

I heard him back away at least a dozen feet. He was fiddling with the jacket, trying to get the drawing out. Freddy and Angelina and I had made it a tight fit so the scroll wouldn't show. Reto would have a hard time slipping it free with one hand on that rifle.

I asked, "Do you want me to get it out for you? That's what I'm here for."

"All right, but no funny moves."

"I won't."

As I came away from the passage wall, I saw him shot. Twice. CRACK-CRACK. Not from the trench, but out of the dark. He dropped where he stood. His killer walked toward me. Samuel Protiste. Revolver in hand.

"Are you alive, Julian?"

He didn't approach me. Rather, he headed toward Reto and my jacket. When he was close, he shot Reto in the head.

"Why did you do that?" I asked.

"To make sure he's dead."

"Why did you shoot him at all? I came to give him the drawings. That was the plan. Isn't it why I'm here?"

"More or less." He nudged Reto with his foot. "Now you can give them to me."

"Why?" The agony of my shoulder numbed the fear I felt just then. "And what are you doing here? I thought you were back at camp."

"Not anymore. I rode up here to get the drawings, Julian, because they belong to Leandro Porteus and the State Protectorate that commissioned them. Not to that race of deviants. Peter Draxler stole them with Nina's help. I'm returning them."

"Nina didn't steal them. She didn't even know where they were."

"She knew Peter had them and she helped get them here. I didn't know that until talking with you. Now I see how it worked. Peter, Nina, you, Nina, you, Peter. Pretty interesting, really. Internal Security will have a fine long visit with your girlfriend. You can count on that."

"She didn't do anything."

"I'll bet they won't feel that way."

"What about Arturo?"

"What about him? I told you already. He's gone. Probably dead, but I don't know. Maybe he's on a beach somewhere with a new lady and a bottle of Xóchitl. No one cares about Arturo."

I watched Protiste for signs of something resembling sympathy. I asked, "Who sent you here?"

He smiled. "I think you know that. The Council has more than one opinion, and they need friends these days. I'm a very friendly guy."

I felt fear expanding through my pain. "Well, what about me? What happens now?"

"Yes, Julian, glad you asked. I have to kill you right here," he said, reaching down and taking Reto's rifle. "I'm going to shoot you with this rifle and take the drawings back to Prospect Square and tell Dr. Otto Paley how you were murdered by the degenerates during the assault on Porphyry Hill. Maybe you'll be a hero. Anything's possible, right?"

He checked the bolt as I backed slowly away down the passage. Maybe I could run off and hide in the dark. Was I fast enough?

He looked up. "Where do you think you're going?"

I blinked and his body jerked, and a hole opened in his chest. Then another. A few inches apart. A pair of rifle shots cracked and echoed from behind me. Protiste's eyes widened as he coughed once harshly. Then he died and fell over backwards. I'd just seen so many people killed in the past ten minutes, I wasn't even startled. I stared at him for a few moments, wondering if he'd intended to kill me all along since Tamorina. The thought of it gave me a horrid shudder. Then I looked to see who'd shot him and watched a pair of men in shabby clothes walk out of the same darkness toward us. Both held rifles high and aimed. One of them said to me, "Are you Julian Brehm?"

With my bleeding wound and the shock of seeing both Reto and Protiste killed before my eyes, all I could manage was a brief nod.

The one who asked that question smiled. He lowered his rifle and handed it to his partner. Then he drew a pistol from his waist holster and pointed it at my chest. He said, "Goodnight, kid."

And he shot me.

IN THE GARDEN OF ELYSIUM

XXXIV

∾

I awoke in a bed chamber on a cold morning. Past my window, snow lay on the ground beneath a cultivated forest of birch trees in the icy breeze. Alone in the room, I felt delirious and short of breath, vague to my surroundings. My limbs were numb and my mouth cold and dry. The room was bare of furniture except for my bed and a cane chair in a corner and a nightstand with a lamp. Nor any rugs on the parquet floor. There was a single door almost hidden in the exquisite gilt and mahogany paneling that encircled the chamber. Large ornate mirrors adorned each wall and the ceiling above my bed was a painted rendering of a blue summer sky of lilting clouds and happy cherubs trailing viridian and gold ribbons across the heavens. A warming fire crackled within a marble hearth across from me, the carved entablature upon which appeared Roman. I had no idea where I was, nor any impression at all of how I'd come to be there. I found myself dressed in flannel bedclothes with brown stockings. My shoulder was bandaged. I was thoroughly washed and clean. The war had gone. The bed chamber was silent.

I tossed off the covers and got up. My shoulder hurt and I felt stiff and sore. How long had I been in bed? And where was I, anyhow? I went to the window where frost collected in corners of the glass and looked out at the snow. People were outdoors, a few bundled up against the cold in boots and thick coats and fur ushankas or chooks on their heads. Just shuffling along. Nowhere in particular that I saw from my window. A spring snowfall? At Highland Park, once winter temperatures fell to freezing, Father would go out in the dark late at night and clear away snow on our tennis court into rounded embankments and flood the grass as it froze and make a small ice rink for me and Agnes to discover at sunrise the next morning. Wearing wool hats and mittens and our small coats, we'd put on our skates and glide out onto the fresh ice. Then my father and mother would come out, too, and join us to shoot about and make swirls on those blades and play crack-the-whip and learn to spin. I was the best skater in our family. Even Agnes had to admit that. I was quick and clever with my turns and no one could catch me during ice tag. Unless I lost my edge and flew into the snowbank. Then we would go back indoors for waffles and hot chocolate. Later, my father and I would build a snowman in our front yard with one of grandfather's old black top hats, coal for eyes and a carrot stolen from Mother's kitchen for a nose. We named him "George" and pronounced him Count of Schuyler Province. Each New Year's Eve we drank a sparkling cider toast to him and sang a verse of "Auld Lang Syne" in his honor. Agnes always cried when he melted at last. Those simple joys of childhood are more than toys and games. Spring flowers and summer waters, the leaves of autumn and winter ice. Our evergreen seasons of love and family. We cannot have them back, but we can enjoy our memories.

Those bundled-up people outdoors had gone off and the snowfield was empty once again. I wanted to go out and make a snowball. Where were my clothes? And Father's valise? I noticed, too, that I was hungry. When had I last eaten? I had no memory of anything since that dark passage at Porphyry Hill. And my shoulder ached. I went over to a mirror and studied my appearance. I hardly recognized myself, so pale and tired now. Yet my hair was clean and trim. Had somebody snipped it while I slept? My face was shaven, as well. Where was I?

The door opened and I saw someone peek into my bed chamber. A young fellow in striped rose pajamas. He noticed me across the room and gave a simple wave. I nodded back and he came in. "Hello," he said, "I'm Lewis."

He was skinny and his brown hair was parted to one side and flopping over his face. I thought he was ill. But maybe not. My reflection in the mirror looked sick and I only felt tired. No fever or anything worse. Still foggy from sleep. Sore shoulder. I told him, "My name's Julian. Where am I? What is this place?"

"Our house."

"Where are we?"

Lewis shrugged. "I can't read maps. Does it matter? You're here."

I asked, "Do you have a map? Maybe I can figure it out." Freddy was better with cartography than I was, but I wasn't entirely bereft, either.

"I wouldn't know what one looks like."

"Is there a globe?"

"What's that?"

I realized Lewis would not be helpful. "I'm only trying to understand where I am and how long I've been here. I have no idea at all. I just woke up, actually."

Lewis wandered over to my bed and stared at the blankets. Then he said, "Perhaps you were revived from a suspension tank. You might be hundreds of years old."

"I doubt it. That would mean I died."

"Perhaps you did."

"Have there been many people brought back here from the dead?"

"None that I know of, but who's to say it hasn't happened?"

I remembered that line from Dr. Margeton's course in Impressionistic Literature, sophomore year. I quoted, "*Dream. Ona nonday I sleep. I dreamt of a somday. Of a wonday I shall wake.*"

"Pardon?"

"A book of riddles," I told Lewis, "like my life these days."

"You probably need lots more rest, Julian. A week of sleep with no bothers. I sleep for days and wake fully recovered. Once I slept for an entire month and discovered a formula for Mezentian metals that are both impermeable and edible in the same moment. I wrote up a patent but forgot to record on my blackboard one of the best elements in the equation and had to give it up."

I decided Lewis might be deranged. "That's too bad. I'm sure it's a loss to all of us."

He smiled. "There are more dreams. Perhaps I'll sleep for another month and discover how to fly across the ocean on one breath."

My stomach rumbled, and I asked Lewis, "Where do we eat?"

"Have you rung the bell?"

"What bell?"

"By your bed."

He pointed to the walnut headboard where a small brass bell was mounted on the carving. He walked over and gave it a ring with one finger. I wondered how anyone outside of the bed chamber was expected to hear it. After a few short minutes, the door opened, and a rather stout woman dressed in a maid's uniform and frilly cap entered carrying a silver tray that held a shiny dome and flatware with a white cloth napkin. I smelled the delightful aroma of hot food as she passed.

"Good morning, Julian."

"Hello."

"Back into bed with you now. I have no tables today."

This felt so absurdly erratic, I did just as she told me. Heading to my bed, I asked, "Who are you, please?"

She offered a most ingratiating smile. "I'm Lalla Goldbeck. Now, into bed!"

Utterly perplexed, but even more hungry, I climbed back under the covers and pulled them up to my chest. Once I'd done so, she placed the tray on my lap and removed the dome revealing a beautiful baked pheasant with cheese dumplings and cup of fig pudding.

"Here you are, Julian," she said, tucking a napkin under my chin. "I'll be back with your tea, unless you'd prefer lemon juice."

"Tea is fine, thank you."

She left like a gust of wind.

Once she was out the door, with great earnestness Lewis told me, "We have to get off this world."

I laughed. "And go where? Mars?"

His expression didn't budge. "Why not? I hear they have canals up there flooded with pink water, and the air is warm like our tropics and nobody does anything but eat fruit and procreate."

"That's daffy!" I picked up my knife to cut off a slice of steaming pheasant.

"Not at all. I find it entirely reasonable. Everything we can imagine must exist somewhere. If not here, then elsewhere. Perhaps on the moon, or on Mars. Don't you dare think our minds are limited by familiar geography. That's nonsense. It cannot possibly be true. Therefore, it isn't."

Ignoring the insinuation, I offered him one of my dumplings. "I'm sure I won't be able to eat all four of these."

"No, thank you. I had my plate of mush and sausage an hour ago. I'm not allowed to eat again until tomorrow."

"Suit yourself."

Lalla Goldbeck returned with a cup of hot tea on a china saucer. "Soulien tea, Julian. It's very fresh. I brewed it myself."

She placed it carefully on my breakfast tray.

"Thank you very much."

She offered an effusive smile. "Of course, darling."

Hoping to capitalize on her mood, I said, "May I please ask where I am? Lewis here doesn't seem to know."

She glanced over at him, sitting now on the foot of my bed. "Lewis, it's not a fault to be helpful."

"I didn't understand Julian's question," Lewis replied. "I thought it was obvious we're in the house."

She showed him a teacher's frown. "That is not a proper response, Lewis. You ought to be ashamed of yourself. Julian asked you a simple question."

I tried again. "So, where am I? Either of you may answer."

They looked at me as if my head had just split in two. Lewis glanced at Lalla Goldbeck. She looked out the window where snow had begun to fall once more.

I added, "Well?"

She told me, "You have an appointment with Mr. Sutro at noon. He's expected to describe this all to you. In the meanwhile, eat your breakfast. If you feel up to it, you may dress and go outdoors. I'm sure the fresh air will do wonders for your well-being." She turned to Lewis. "Isn't that true, dear?"

Lewis said, "It's cold out."

"Of course it is. Can't you see the snow?"

He told her, "I've lost my coat."

"It's in the coat closet where you left it yesterday. I've told you twice."

I finished one of my cheese dumplings, then asked, "Where are my clothes? I had a valise with them in it. I don't see it anywhere."

Lalla Goldbeck told me, "All your personal belongings are in the closet here, Julian. Do you see that door beside your bed?"

I leaned out to my right and did, in fact, spot a door I hadn't noticed before. And I saw a second door on the other side of my bed.

Before I could ask, she told me, "That's your sink and toilet and bath. If you care to, you may wash up before dressing. Just ask if you need any help doing so."

This was so odd. I felt like a child.

Lalla Goldbeck took poor Lewis by the hand. "Come with me, dear. Let's allow Julian to eat his breakfast in peace. You can visit with him once he's done." She smiled at me. "Give the bell a ring, darling, if you need anything else."

"Thank you."

Then they both left, closing my door behind them.

I ate the pheasant and cheese dumplings alone in the quiet of the elegant bed chamber and drank my tea and tried to understand the arcane and myriad circumstances that had led me there. How had this all come about? I had been in my last spring semester at Thayer Hall in Regency College. I had a wonderful and entertaining roommate in Freddy Barron. My loving parents looked out for me from our comfortable home on Houghton Avenue. My life was not absent of challenges, but those were manageable, and I was surviving. I had no expectation of being summoned for conscription to the Desolation. I was a fortunate boy. Then I met a beautiful young woman and fell wildly in love and saw things I hadn't dreamed of, mysteries both above and below the world of my birth. I chased along in a labyrinth of deceit and deception, until, at last, I found myself led into the sum of all our hells, that ugly fate of our Republic. And now I was lying here in this bed chamber with no idea whatsoever how far or near I was to home, or to those I loved. And I was deathly afraid that, unlike Alice's adventure, this was more than just a curious dream.

XXXV

I saw that my father's jacket had been properly cleaned and pressed, his valise neat and tidy. My shoes were polished, and the galoshes washed off and dried. Also, I found a long winter coat on a hangar, a fur hat and gloves on the shelf above, and a pair of snow boots. I put it all on and left the bed chamber.

My room was on the corner of the house, and a wide tiled hall that led down from my door was extraordinary in scale with many other paneled doors and tall framed windows opening to the birch garden. Anxious to feel the snow, I chose one and went out into the lovely chill of morning. The cold bit into my face and burned in my lungs with each breath I took. It was wonderful. So fresh and clean. A cold draft circulated in the shade of the brick and marble building and I marched away toward the birch trees laden with snowy branches. I saw hoar frost on stones here and there. My boots crunched on the icy snow as I strode forward. Rather than exploring the landscape or wandering off into the birch woods, I chose to follow the simple path tramped by those people I'd seen when I first awoke. The freezing air was so still, only my boots in the snow disturbed the morning quiet. That trail they'd stamped weaved through the birch trees which appeared planted as an arbor of sorts rather than any natural growth. I looked up and noticed the sky was still patchy clouds with only traces of blue. A light feathery snowfall persisted as I walked. I adored it. Even catching a snowflake now and then on my tongue as I went along. What was this place? So tranquil. My breathing and boots were all I could hear in the birch wood. The fog of my breath was delightful, and the scent of wet woods and frozen earth and leaves. Not since my room at Thayer Hall, and Nina, had I felt so content.

The path those people led wound through the birch trees toward what I thought was a clearing ahead. In fact, another few minutes of tramping through the snow brought me out of the birch grove and onto a gentle slope above the most beautiful glacial lake I had ever seen. It filled the irregular basin of a grand forest beyond of fir trees and pine farther than I could see. A snow-topped wilderness. Those people I'd followed were gathered by the lake side at the bottom of the slope and I descended carefully through the icy snow to join them.

Three men and two women, each in winter clothes like mine. Faces ruddy in the frosty morning air. Clearly pleased to be there by the water's edge. They met my approach with pleasant smiles.

"Good morning, Julian."

"Hello, Julian."

"Greetings, Julian."

"Welcome, Julian."

"Felicitations, Julian."

Two of them appeared older than my parents, but by years not decades. They stared at me with the oddest affection as if our lives had already been intimately entangled. I had no idea who they were. I assumed they had been told my name when I arrived out of the ether. Whenever that was.

I said, "Good morning."

They introduced themselves one by one, the three men deferring first to the pair of women.

"I'm Larina." She had golden-brown hair and a Roman nose and a graceful smile.

The next had night-black hair and a complexion the hue of Jardín tea. "My name is Parra." She blinked when she spoke her name.

Both women were hauntingly beautiful.

The men introduced themselves after Parra.

"I am Isher," said the tallest of the three, bearded and firm of face and form, particularly in his imposing winter coat.

"Pellison," spoke after, perhaps my height and figure. Possibly the youngest of those five. Not too much older than myself. Soft of voice and skin. Pale and blue-eyed.

Lastly was the fellow I guessed was the elder. Tall, grey hair barely hidden beneath his fur hat, glassy dark eyes. A strong bearing. "I'm Landin." He nodded to the younger one. "He and I are brothers."

I dared to ask again, "Where am I?"

Landin replied, "By the shore of Lake Nouille. Isn't that clear, Julian? It's quite ancient and renowned. We come here each morning to watch the sun rise over the forest to the east and see the Lamus fish swim into the daylight where our hawks descend to pluck them from the waters."

Parra said, "It's one of the rituals, Julian, we indulge to describe this life."

Larina added, "Schedules needn't be onerous. We love this order and habit to remember who we are and rediscover ourselves when we go astray."

"The sun and the fish and the hawks," Pellison told me, "are the world in miniature. Each pursues its agency in balance, the absence of one suggests faults too numerous to ignore."

A cold gust swept toward us from the lake, rippling the waters, bringing a vicious chill to shore. Why could they not simply tell me where I was in this grand scheme? None of them seemed to appreciate the hell I'd just experienced in getting here, wherever this was. I said, "I admit I'm confused, but Mr. Sutro is supposed to tell me where I am. I've had an awful last few days. I was at Crown Colony, and then Porphyry Hill where I was shot and almost blown up during a terrible assault on the trenches there. I'm really not sure how I survived."

Snow began falling once more in cascading clouds of white, obscuring my vision of the icy lake. My new friends glanced at each other as if deciding whom to elect for offering some pertinent reply. Isher stared at me, his steely countenance less pleasant than before. Landin spoke up to say, "Mr. Sutro is a fount of knowledge. We trust his advice and opinions. You're here with us by Lake Nouille. There is no conflict on these shores."

Larina told me, "Those yesterdays of your war are over now. Such worries detain our hearts. We prefer to walk peacefully in the birch woods and come to our lake for the sunrise and the fish and the hawks. There's nothing but that in the world, if you'll allow yourself the appreciation of what it means."

Parra said, "Try to understand this simple thought, Julian: Where you breathe is where you are."

She offered a quaint smile I didn't care for. It felt condescending. So I left and walked back up the hill in the thickening snowfall and thought I might find Lewis. At least his nonsense was entertaining. I liked him. He wasn't pretentious like those idiots by the lake.

Back in the bed chamber, I took off the snow clothing and changed into my father's jacket and dress shoes. I noticed my breakfast tray had been taken away and my bed sheets and blanket tucked and ordered. I wondered if somewhere there was a telephone I might use to reach my father or Nina. Not that I could tell them where I was, but perhaps they'd be reassured to know I was still alive. And just hearing their voices would restore some sense of comfort and well-being. My confidence was gone. That optimism my parents had trained me to develop and nurture felt thoroughly depleted. I wasn't frightened any longer. I felt reasonably safe here for the moment. Yet, without any true sense of what tomorrow might bring, how could I hope to form a plan for restoring structure to my outlook? It felt impossible. Perhaps meeting this Mr. Sutro would change that.

I wandered in that mansion for more than an hour, losing myself among the intricately carved woodwork on a myriad of doors and gilded mirrors. Most of the doors were locked and I presumed those were bed chambers like my own. I heard voices in the walls, chattering laughter and weeping and argumentative tones that caused me to wonder once more what sort of place this was besides a labyrinth of rooms and halls. I found a wide staircase that led up to a loggia overlooking a great dining hall of flags and marble statuary and niches containing painted vases and ugly cherubs. Instead of circling the loggia to go down into the hall, I decided instead to explore more rooms all around this floor. In doing so, I found a wonderful library of perhaps a hundred thousand dusty volumes. The parquet floor was covered in rose and blue oriental carpets with mahogany side tables to a dozen leather armchairs and brass lampstands for reading. The wood ceiling was coffered in hexagons except in the center where a fantastic trompe l'oeil painting eighteen feet above portrayed Prometheus descending to earth with the fire that gave birth to civilization. So ironic, I thought, how we've used that flame throughout the Desolation to burn each other to death and torment the very world of humanity Prometheus desired to create. If that irrepressible Titan saw us now, would he believe the suffering he endured on Mount Elbrus had been worth his ceaseless agony?

I browsed about the volumes for something that could tell me where I was, what this place existed for, its purpose. Most of those books were extremely old, beyond my comprehension and academic experience. Leather-bound or cloth, the pages of each were so thin and fragile I was loath to flip through them. The variety of disciplines represented in this library was astonishing: universal science, natural history, metallurgy, mineralogy, vegetation, medicine, physical geography, astrology, parliamentary law, agriculture, philosophy, arithmetic, physics and mechanics, chemistry, drawing and painting, geology, agronomy, medical treatise, astronomy, poetry, mythology, literature of the world, phonography, logic, rhetoric, architecture, spiritualism, theology, natural sexuality, maritime navigation, taxonomy. Many were rendered in Latin, Greek, Carthusian, Chinese, Arabic, Eriyhniv, Persian, hieroglyphics, cuneiform ink, and some other arcane languages I did not recognize at all. A room for the collected knowledge of the world as we knew it. I searched for the modern history of us but was unable to locate anything obvious within the many dusty mahogany shelves, high and low. Perhaps because it wasn't yet written. We needed a conclusion to provide the best explanation of how we became who we are, and I wasn't convinced even these thousands of volumes would provide much insight into that narrative.

I heard a door open in a corner of the library and watched a frail balding fellow wearing pince-nez glasses and a black smoking jacket with white ascot tie come into the room. He was holding a thin reading volume, a journal of some sort, folded open to the middle and held to a braided string bookmark. When he noticed me standing by one of the book ladders, he smiled. "Hello, Julian. Nice to see you're up and about this morning. What a trial you've had. So glad you've rejoined the land of the living."

"Hello."

He came over and offered his free hand. "I'm Dr. Jules Bernäert. Perpetual Librarian for the Mignard Institute." He nodded to the journal he was holding. "I've just been reading about your Regency College, specifically Thayer Hall where you're matriculating, right?"

"Yes, I hope so." *How did he know that?* "If they keep me after all this."

"Oh, I'm certain the school is proud to have you. A scholar and an adventurer!"

This fellow had a peculiar way of pronouncing his vowels — overly extended and then too clipped. I'd heard that manner of speech somewhere years ago but couldn't quite recall when. Maybe at home with my father and one of his friends when I was younger.

"What is this place?" I asked, in my most ingratiating voice. Making friends seemed more important now than ever. At least in the Desolation I understood the basic geography, east and west.

"Why, our library, of course. Not as popular as it once was, unfortunately. I'm afraid reading has fallen somewhat into decline. I'm not sure why. We do have the most marvelous books, and up-to-date periodicals, as well, for those with short attention spans. It pays to be accommodating today."

"It is a beautiful library, sir, but I suppose what I meant was, where am I? This mansion, these grounds? I'm completely disoriented."

The librarian offered a sympathetic frown. "Have you not seen Mr. Sutro? That man usually has all the answers you could possibly want. We defer to him on most matters. He is a walking compendium of valuable information."

"No, I haven't yet. They tell me I have an appointment to see him at noon."

The librarian took a quick glance at his pocket-watch. "Well, Julian, that's only ten minutes from now. You'd better hurry. Mr. Sutro generally sits down to lunch on the half hour, so you won't wish to be late."

"Thank you, sir. That's another thing. I have no idea where he is."

"Well, of course he'll be in his office. That's simple."

Now I felt as if I were in some sort of asylum and unable to determine who was the patient — myself or them?

I told him, "It would be, sir, if I knew where that was. Remember, I've never been here before."

"No, you haven't, Julian, but that's not your fault. It hasn't been your destiny to find us until now." He smiled and took my arm. "All good things in time, as they say. Come, let me take you to Mr. Sutro. I expect he's most intrigued to meet you."

We went back out onto the loggia and traversed this upper floor to the far end and then down another narrow marble staircase and along a tiled hallway to a carved mahogany door in a cul-de-sac of pastoral art and inlaid porcelain pottery. The view out of a single round window there revealed a truly immense and magisterial building atop a lofty hill, reached by grand ascending steps framed with terraces I presumed held flower beds and perhaps lily ponds under the morning snowfall.

Through the door was a small waiting room outside Mr. Sutro's office with a quite comfortable leather sofa and lampstand. I expected to find a small table with periodicals to browse while anticipating an appointment but there was nothing like that. As I sat, the librarian pushed a wall buzzer on the door frame and stood back. A couple of minutes went by and he checked his pocket-watch, then told me, "Be patient. We're three minutes early. Mr. Sutro is extremely punctual and protects his time like a guard dog. He's quite efficient. You'll see. Be clear in each moment you're with him. You'll appreciate his candor."

"Thank you, I'll do my best."

"Of course. Everyone here has the utmost faith in you."

"I hope so."

I had no idea why he was speaking to me that way. He stared at me, oddly, forcing me to look off into a corner. I searched the room for some distraction. Why was there nothing to read?

The door opened and a young woman strolled out with a heavy stack of papers. Then a voice from the office called out, "Julian? You may come in now."

Dr. Bernäert showed his clock. "Do you see? Twelve noon straight up!"

I nodded and stood and went past him, closing the office door behind me.

Mr. Sutro was perhaps African or East Indian and spoke with a familiar colonial accent I recognized from certain professors of similar cultural distinction at Regency. His skin was dark-brown and his eyes were black as Nina's, and he wore a thin moustache and ordinary eyeglasses. Perhaps he was my father's age with grey at his temples and wrinkles across his forehead. I thought he would be imposing and stern, yet he was not at all. He extended his hand to me before I reached his desk and wore a pleasing smile I hadn't anticipated, given the reverence in which he seemed to be held.

"So glad to see you here, Julian, after all your travels," he said. "This has been quite a journey you've undertaken."

"Yes, sir."

He motioned to the leather chair before his desk. "Please sit! Be comfortable. We have quite a lot to discuss and I know you have many, many questions."

His office was filled with shelves of books and glass-shuttered cabinets and smelled of leather volumes and old wood.

With what felt like a genuine smile, Mr. Sutro asked, "So, Julian, where would you care to begin? Where you are, or how you got here?"

I leaned forward in the chair. "Thank you, sir. How about, where am I?"

He looked me straight in the eye. "You are this moment in the Clélius House on the imperial estate of Laspágandélus, former seat of the Third Regime in the era of Emperor Aventinian the Great. This building was originally the summer cottage of his sister, Clélia Tórpis, principissa of Tarchon region. She preferred the waters of the Alban River to her brother's lake and only traveled here when the weather suited her."

"Thank you again, sir. Although I'm not sure that helps too much since ancient history was a failing mark for me in Upper School, but I appreciate your effort."

He waved his hand. "Nothing to worry about. I have wonderful maps that will clear all this up, I promise."

"All right, well, how did I get here? I have no memory whatsoever since Porphyry Hill where I was shot."

"Twice!"

"How do you mean, sir?"

"You were shot twice, Julian. Once through the shoulder during the assault on those trenches and again in the cave passage by one of our agents. He shot you in the chest with a chloromorphium dart of great strength that permitted your transport from under the battlefield and away to this estate without your awareness of pain or worry. We put you to sleep so that your shoulder could be repaired while you traveled. How are you feeling, by the way? Is there much pain? Dr. Oistrakh, our finest physician, performed the surgery under difficult circumstances. The journey was over eight hundred miles and he admitted you lost quite a lot of blood. Transfusions were required from several of our footmen to save your life."

"Good grief."

"Yes, very unfortunate, indeed. Not at all what any of us anticipated. Though we expected Mr. Protiste to try and kill you, that bullet you took in the battle was an unavoidable horror. Much apologies for that, I assure you. Not intended, I swear."

"You knew Samuel Protiste?"

"Certainly. His role was carefully defined since the inception. Its orchestration was choreographed by young Draxler and Mr. Künze with the blessing of our Regents. Most notable was his inclination to betray you at the last possible moment. That was expected, too, and prepared for. Perhaps you're not able to recall that. Dr. Oistrakh kept you unconscious for more than a week. The chloromorphium has a strong amnesia inducing fabric and content. I'm told you were given the highest possible dose for your emotional comfort."

"I think I remember him saying something about a rifle, but I thought that was just a dream. I don't know what happened to Protiste. We shared a tent at Porphyry Hill. He tried to murder me?" Somehow that didn't seem to be such a surprise. His story about Arturo troubled me all along. And I never believed he knew much about Nina at all. I got the sense he wouldn't have minded hurting me.

"We were compelled to kill Mr. Protiste to save your life and secure the drawing you'd brought us. Perhaps had Mr. Künze not died in the attack, the solution might have been different, but war offers too many avenues of fate and not even we can guide more than one or two. In any case, Julian, despite those catastrophies, you were successful in accomplishing that purpose you were invited to achieve."

"Major Künze was killed, too? I have no memory whatsoever of that, either." As I spoke, I did have a glimpse of the trench in the rain and a bombardment and no thought of Künze afterward. Like a fog lifting too slowly in my brain to grasp that moment.

"We only had word that he perished in the trench after your meeting with Mr. Sancho. Quite unfortunate, really. His loyalty to the Regents was unsurpassed in a most morally compromising circumstance. Those acts he performed to play out his part in this immense tragedy were most incomprehensible. I cannot conceive of where they lay in his heart. Such trials ought not to be required of a man."

"I saw some terrible things myself."

"No doubt, Julian. Each of us has endured far too much of this awful nonsense, for far too long."

"Nina almost died, too, and little Delia. Did you know about that?"

"Of course, we did," Mr. Sutro replied. "Mr. Draxler kept us informed of your lovely Miss Rinaldi and her child. Her role was not incidental. We appreciate the ultimate truth of what drew you here. Love is a most powerful inducement. Nothing in our world surpasses it. Without love, perhaps none of this has any meaning but storm and fire. Not enough to suffer for. Loyalty itself derives from the heart in terms of faithfulness which can only evolve from love."

I felt Nina's absence in that moment. I missed her badly. All of this was a nightmare. "Do you know where Arturo went? Why he wasn't waiting for me at Tamorina? Protiste said he just vanished, but I don't know if I believe that. Maybe Protiste killed him."

"He didn't," Mr. Sutro told me. "We know that for a fact. His disappearance from Tamorina is not a mystery. Tomorrow you'll have an audience with the Regents themselves where much of this will be explained. I'm not permitted to offer more than I have."

"Can you at least tell me what the drawings represent? Not being architects, neither I nor Major Künze were able to make much sense of them."

"I'm sorry, Julian, but I cannot. Once again, I trust you'll find the Regents quite enlightening. Their insights are detailed and most profound. The torments of this war have troubled them greatly for decades. Each medley of injury and betrayal has made peace that haunted fugitive throughout our world. We chase with hope and desperation, Julian, because we have always believed that somewhere what's unknown to us now will be unveiled in the certain evidence of a better day."

"And the Desolation, sir? What does that mean? What I saw there."

He frowned. "Five hundred and sixty-three miles of unholy cemetery, Julian. Irredeemable, unless somehow our hearts are healed. Nothing can change that. One day, children will not remember and then life can proceed anew. But not until then."

"And eugenics, sir? That scourge of spyreosis? The cause of all this?"

He shook his head. "A most sad and unfortunate fraud. Simply an excuse for hatred. I'm sorry, Julian. I could give you a more elaborate discourse, but it's truly nothing more than that."

I sat back and gazed out the window above Mr. Sutro's desk and watched the snow fall in breezy waves. This lesson was evolving in my brain, the lives we've wasted these past hundred years, those opportunities for greatness we've squandered. I was being taught the meaning of this war and saw how naïve I'd been. Nina was correct, after all, in claiming I'd been living in a soap bubble of insubstantial attitude and opinion. That all I believed was what I thought, not what I knew was true, which could only be understood through direct experience. Well, I certainly had that now. And the extent of my ignorance was baffling.

Mr. Sutro stood. "I do have my midday meal on schedule, Julian. Your audience tomorrow with the Regents is firm for ten in the morning. I'll escort you there personally. The palace can be quite overwhelming."

I rose, too. "May I ask one more question, sir?"

He clasped his hands. "Of course."

"Who are these people here in the house? I've only met a few them, and they're all quite, let's say, different."

Mr. Sutro smiled. "I think that's another puzzle I'll let you unravel on your own."

XXXVI

I found Lewis in my bed chamber when I got back after wandering about in that disorienting labyrinthine mansion. He had placed my cane chair at the window where he sat and watched the snow falling.

I asked, "Are you sure you wouldn't rather go out? It's really wonderful."

"Not alone," he said. "I get lost. I fell in the lake once and couldn't find my way back up here. But if you'll go with me, I will. I found my coat. Mary had it in her closet with a cat she's been hiding. She told me she discovered my coat outdoors by a bush and covered with snow, so she thought it was hers. I became very angry with her this morning over this and I don't think we can still be friends. I don't care for her anymore."

I went to my closet for the winter clothes again. "Who's Mary?"

"Mary Cumberland. She's the daughter of a chamberlain from Écuries who took a sabbatical to the sea and hasn't returned. No one seems to know when he's expected but he left many years ago and I don't think he's planning to come back."

I put on my coat and fetched the fur cap off the shelf above. I had to grab it with my right hand because my wounded left shoulder still ached. "What does Mary think?"

"She's convinced he was kidnapped and is being held on a boat somewhere near Corísco-sûr-Mér. A letter addressed to her came from there last year with a note that told her to be patient and send jewelry if she can't wait. It upset her greatly because she has no jewelry of any true value, most of which she inherited from her mother who told her it was worthless but had great sentimental value in the family."

I put on galoshes and searched in the closet for my gloves that had apparently been knocked off the shelf.

"Is Mary a sentimental person?"

"She claims she wants to be if she can only imagine what that means. I, for one, don't see it in her character one iota. I'm not certain she misses her father much besides the trips he took her on. My theory is that she's hoping he's been killed so she might inherit his coin collection that is apparently of tremendous value and would permit her to go anywhere or be anyone she chooses. After I found my coat in her closet this morning, I suggested that she dye her hair and change her name and try to be more likeable. She slapped me and now we're no longer friends."

"Where's your coat?"

"Under your bed."

"If you'll get it, we can go out."

Lewis wore black boots beneath his long winter coat and a grey wool cap with a gold ball as a tassel when we walked through the birch wood in a light snowfall. I was curious what had brought him to this place and asked as we went along. He told me, "I was sitting beside an empty road one day a hundred miles from Serévien with a cheese sandwich in my pocket and no water when two men in a potato wagon came by out of nowhere and asked if I wanted to ride with them to Bethéa. I must've been asleep because I hadn't seen them coming until they were right alongside. They didn't look at all trustworthy, but I was so thirsty I got into that wagon and rode with them for about an hour when one of them took my sandwich and the other hit me and I remember a truck stopped ahead to block the road. Four men with rifles got out of the truck and stole the potatoes and shot the men who took my sandwich. They asked if I wanted a ride to Serévien and I said no, and they drove off and left me. That's about it."

"Right, but how did you end up here?"

"I don't know." He shrugged. "One day I was in my room."

"That's all?"

"Why? What else would there be?"

I decided Lewis was insane. How was he supposed to help me solve Mr. Sutro's puzzle of why all these people were here? Was this a mental hospital? Nobody I'd met even resembled a doctor. Nor were there any orderlies or attendants other than Lalla Goldbeck, who could be thought of one if serving hot meals counted. I doubted that. No, the asylum idea felt inadequate.

"Do you like birds?" Lewis asked, watching a soaring flight of sparrows arc across the frozen air, almost ghostly in the gentle snow fall. "We shoot them every so often and I don't agree with that. We also have deer in our woods. Mr. Sutro and Dr. Bernäert hunt them with crossbows. If they kill one, we all have to eat it.

They made that rule. I disagreed, but nobody cares for my opinion. Things die all over the world these days and I refuse to encourage more than our fair share. It's beastly."

"I do like birds and deer," I told him. "And I agree with you that killing is unfavorable, unless, I suppose, we do so to eat. 'Carrots and beans do not a full meal make.' My mother used to say that, and I believe it's reasonably true."

"I enjoy a good ham and I've never killed a pig. Mary called me a hypocrite. We're not friends anymore."

"So you said." I felt colder by the minute. The birch trees were thick with snow and the ground was so icy my boots slipped here and there. Lewis was leading and had no trail to follow. If he got us lost, I'd be angry. According to Freddy, when the winter sun goes down, the temperature drops and our brains freeze. This wasn't winter any longer, but snow was falling and my face was numb from the cold. That felt already halfway to my brain.

As we plodded across the snow under a sky ever greyer, I asked Lewis, "Do you know where everyone here comes from? Besides yourself?"

"I don't recall where I come from, but 'Gravesend' sounds familiar. Or maybe not."

"And the others?"

"No, I don't think any of them come from Gravesend. If they had, I'm sure I'd remember. My memory is that we had a small community by a stream where anyone who wanted to could fish for dinner. I think we were very compatible. Unless my memory is wrong and I'm not from Gravesend at all."

This was maddening. "What I mean is, I'm wondering about some men and women I met down at the lake this morning."

"Oh, they're crazy about fish and birds. They all live in the same room on my floor and sing half the night. I try to complain, and no one believes me."

"But where are they from?"

"The songs aren't from anywhere. I think they just made them up themselves."

I quit. Lewis was deranged. If he fell over in the snow, I decided I'd just leave him there.

He stopped under one of the birch trees to ask me, "Have you met Lancaster?"

"No, who's that?"

"Lancaster's remarkable. He planted all these trees."

I looked about and felt that was absurd. There must have been fifty thousand birch trees we'd walked around and through since stepping out into the snowfall. Possibly twice that. A small forest.

"He's close to here. Let me show you."

Lewis led us off in a fresh direction where the woods thinned, and I saw wood smoke rising through the cold and another brick building became apparent not too far ahead. It was two stories tall, like a square tower with windows up above on all four sides. Imperial flags flew atop in the windblown snow. Lewis took us around to the back of the tower and opened a wooden door and we went inside. The stone floor was cold and the interior smelled dank. There was just a narrow iron spiral staircase leading up to the second floor and another winding downward into a basement. Lewis chose the lower stairs and disappeared into the darkness. After a few moments, I saw lamplight flare to life and heard Lewis speaking to someone, then curse loudly. He came back up. "It's locked. I need to get the key. Do you enjoy art?"

"I suppose so, sure."

"Priscilla's a good painter. Go upstairs and say hello."

"Up there?" I nodded toward the rising staircase.

Lewis gave me an unfortunate look. "It's the only one here."

"Thank you."

Lewis went back outdoors. I wondered where he needed to go and hoped he wasn't about to get lost. I only had a general idea of how to get back to the mansion. If I were here after sundown, I'd be in trouble and I was already a little hungry.

Curious, though, I ascended the circular stairs, thirty steps to the top. A little dizzy when I arrived. Another wooden door. Because politeness was taught to me by my mother when I was little, I knocked instead of barging in. Quiet for another half a minute or so. Mother further advised me not to knock a second time until a minute had passed. *Allow for your host to walk across the house or come down from upstairs. We can't fly, remember.* Then a voice called to me from the other side of the door. "Come in, please."

And I did.

A most graceful woman sat at her easel, a sweet smile on her face in the grey late afternoon light. She lowered her brush, and I noticed she was barefoot beneath a casual gingham porch dress and shawl. "Hello, Julian Brehm."

"Hello."

"I'm Priscilla Draxler."

I know my face flushed. I felt it. More than a surprise. Could it be possible? Her face, like his, was cherubic and pale, her hair curled, brunette and bundled atop. She was slender but not frail, more youthful than my own mother by several years and her eyes sparkled in the window light.

She said, "You may take off your coat, if you like. There's a clothes-stand behind you. Just fold your coat over mine."

"Thank you."

"How is your wound? Are you healing well?"

"There's still some pain and a little stiffness, but I'm improving, thank you."

Since my mother once painted daily, the room had that most familiar odor to me of oil and pigments and turpentine. A paint-stained canvas tarpaulin covered most of the floor where she sat, with some of her brushes and oils and wooden pallets on a stout marble plant stand beside her. She had placed an embroidered walnut chair and a pair of table desks surrounding the easel, a library desk across the room and a lovely ebonized walnut lounge that looked very comfortable against one wall under a window. A cast-iron wood-burning stove in one corner kept us warm. I felt I could fall asleep on that lounge if given permission.

After hanging up my winter coat, I gazed briefly out all four windows, one after the other. Snow forest and grey sky to the horizon. That lake and the palace. Somewhat awkwardly, I said, "You have a marvelous view from up here, ma'am."

"Please call me Priscilla. And, yes, I do. It's why I've chosen this room for my studio. And I taught my son how to hold his first brush at this old easel back in the metropolis when he was little."

Just to be certain now. "Peter Draxler?"

"Yes, of course, Julian. My first born."

"We met last week in the Dome of Eternity. Under the Dioscuri."

"So he told me. I'm sorry, dear, but my son has always had an inordinate love of games. I hear you were subjected to one of them in order to bring you here."

"It was interesting."

"Perhaps a bit cruel, as well? Peter has grown in unexpected ways since he left. Those strange teachers he studies with in the undercity are a mystery to me.

What they've taught him is so foreign to my life, I can't say I'm familiar any longer with his points of view, but he is my son and I love him very much. Of course, a mother will always have her concerns."

"I heard their story, Castor and Pollux, in the undercity recently. I found it very strange, too. All that drama from the Great Separation. How they experienced it. I wondered where Peter thought he fit in that narrative. We each have a role to play. I've tried to understand how he sees his own."

"My son can be an enigma, even to those who love him dearly. Like his father, he adopts ideas from everywhere and assigns them meaning in his own life until they become the meaning itself. I just hope he's able to discover something personal that gives him peace before he wanders off in unexpected and unpleasant directions he can't foresee or escape from."

"You can appreciate how unexpected this is for me. Meeting you here."

She set her brush on the easel and laughed. "I'm surprised you didn't faint dead away!"

I nodded to the walnut chair. "May I sit?"

"Please."

Doing so, I said, "Well, I've had my fair share of surprises since leaving the metropolis. This is all beyond my experience. I think I've grown up more in the past week than at any time in my life. Certainly more than in my four years at Thayer Hall. School can only teach us so much, right?"

Priscilla told me, "Peter's father was a professor at LeBrunen College in North Treppel District when Peter was still in Upper School. We had a house on a quiet street with trees and flower beds and pretty iron railings. Peter's sister, Amelie, danced ballet and played the flute and carved her own dolls from firewood. They were both the most enchanting children. Smart, a little eccentric, but well-behaved. Neat and tidy without being asked. My husband, Victor, was quite brilliant, an intellectual without being stuffy or pedantic." She paused. "I'm telling you this as explanation of all those hoops you've had to jump through for my son. You see, Julian, that was many years ago and our lives are no longer those."

"No?"

"Swept away from us in half a season. Against my advice, Victor decided to teach a course he called, 'The Renaissance of History,' in which he lectured on what he titled, 'The Great Mistake.' It was simply a nasty reduction of eugenical history that told his students they were being duped by the Status Imperium and the Medical Protectorate. Ordinarily, academic freedom is tolerated far more than you might expect, but Victor just could not contain himself. He was so obstinate. Assigning lessons about our immorality wasn't enough for Victor. No, he had to go out and give speeches in the city parks where he called the Judicial Council criminals and urged people to kill them on sight wherever they went on daily walks. Of course, he was arrested and put in jail at Nieboldt. Both children were so frightened they refused to go to school. One night, my darling little Amelie ran away. She left a note telling me not to worry because she was going to get her father out of jail. She was thirteen years old. The metropolitan police found her body the next morning under the pilings at Tudor Landing. She'd been raped and strangled. Victor believed he was responsible and wouldn't be consoled. He hanged himself in his cell."

"Good grief!"

"He wasn't himself. I believe he was ill somehow. That man who gave those speeches and took his own life wasn't the Victor I married. The world poisons us if we don't find our own antidote through beauty that survives the ugliness of our times. It's why I took Peter away from the metropolis. Life there had no kindness or meaning for us anymore."

Her voice was soothing yet trembled in describing those days of agony and sadness. I thought I ought to change our conversation, so I leaned forward to have a better look at her canvas. "What are you painting today?"

"Oh, thank you." She smiled. "Well, do you know much about this estate, Laspágandélus?"

"Not really. Mr. Sutro gave me a brief primer earlier this afternoon. He told me the Regents, whoever they are, would be more expansive."

She took her brush and touched a dab of cerulean on her wooden pallet. "Yes, you'll adore them. I won't say another word. Without those two, we can't exist."

"You came here with Peter? The two of you?"

"No, I didn't. One cannot just travel here. At first, we rode a train to Calambria in the south where there was no war or eugenical disputes because nobody offensive lived there. We took an apartment on a quiet street and both of us made paintings that we sold at the artists marketplace on Sundays. But Peter was restless with peace and quiet. He was his father's son and the absence of conflict offended him. So, one morning he took his brushes and oils and left for Óbregon where the war had emptied the culture of that lovely town. From there, he traveled through Madaleña and Timsley and Aïcha, just meandering his way back to the metropolis, involving himself wherever he went with people whose distaste for common life appealed to his own disaffections. Eventually, of course, he found his favored crowd in the undercity, and was happy. Those were all things he wrote to me every so often in his letters. Still troubled by dreams of Victor and Amelie, I stayed on at Calambria for another year and a half by myself and tried to believe I could be alone with my artistic solitudes. Of course, I was mistaken. One day I was in the market offering a sketch to some tourists from Maspéro who spoke with wondrous enthusiasm for a victory our armies had just won in St. Marta Province where nobody we fought had been left alive. I decided they were such awful people, I refused to sell them my sketch even though I very much needed the money to pay my rent. They became so indignant, I gathered up my things and prepared to leave when a man offered me twenty credits for my sketch if I'd only allow him to watch me make another. He had the most generous smile and a kind spirit. His name was Zinder Sutro, and he led me here."

She touched her brush to the canvas in swirls of cerulean and green. "Did you notice this water I'm painting? It's Lake Nouille. I can see it out that window every morning, even in a snowfall. We may imagine it's a million years old, but it's not. Many, many centuries ago, Emperor Aventinian ordered his engineers to divert the Pilumnas River into that glacial valley so that his first-born son could sail a boat without threat from the sea. When Aventinian the Second ascended the throne, he declared the lake sacred so that only he could unfurl his sails upon its waters. He courted young Trinácria Levántine in his boat upon the lake and made her his queen. One summer evening, she felt emboldened to borrow his boat and float out onto the gentle waters alone where she fell overboard and drowned bearing her emperor's own first-born. His heart broken, Aventinian the Second then declared the lake anathema. Beauty, he warned, is a seductress, and so this land was abandoned for centuries. Ages pass and tragedies that consume history are forgotten. Queen Nouille built that palace you see on the mount above the lake and bore children who floated boats on its quiet waters, and many sailed across the lake at dawn to watch the Lamus fish chase the sunrise, and happiness found a home here again. The Regents, whom you'll meet tomorrow, are her descendants. If you're patient, they'll explain the Republic and how its troubles are not destiny but rather choices that arise in moments of fear and loss of faith in the essential goodness of people."

She let her brush trace the arc of shoreline that appeared golden as the oils joined. I could easily see where Peter had inherited her artistic grace, as if her eye and her brush were one thought in pursuit of a beauty only she could see in that moment.

Still curious, if not terribly impatient, I asked, "Why did Peter remain in the metropolis, once you'd found your way here? Did he know where you were? Does this not appeal to him at all?"

"Actually, Peter has never been to the estate, and he can't get here any longer. It's too late. I was brought here by Mr. Sutro when I was lost, and I can't ever leave, even if I chose to do so, which I never would."

That gave me the oddest feeling. "Are we that far away now?"

Her voice softened further. "Peter thinks so. He wouldn't come here, even were he invited, because he says we're meant to be in the world to save it, and that can't be done from the gardens of Elysium."

"And he wants to try and save the world."

Priscilla nodded as she tapped her brush across the canvas, gilding the waters of her pristine lake. "Like his father."

Lewis was waiting for me at the bottom of the winding stairs when I came down from Priscilla. He held out a rusty iron key and told me, "It was in the bucket. Mr. Sutro told me. I didn't need to run back up there, after all. I just hadn't noticed it in the dark."

"And you didn't get lost going up and back."

"Why would you think I'd be lost? I've been back and forth tens of times. I've lived here my whole life."

"I thought you told me you were on the road, or that you came from Gravesend?"

"I didn't say any such thing, Julian, and if you insist that I did, then we can't be friends anymore."

Lewis was so crazy I didn't feel like arguing. "Well, I take it back. Sorry."

"That's better." He smiled. "We're still friends."

"Good."

"Would you like to meet Lancaster?"

"Certainly."

"Then come with me."

With Lewis leading, we descended the iron stairs to the basement below. He'd already lit the wall lanterns, so I didn't need to worry about tumbling down the circular staircase and breaking my neck.

The basement was extremely cold and damp and reeked of mold and rat urine. The door Lewis spoke of looked ancient and solid. Why would someone be down here voluntarily? I said, "This looks like a jail cell."

"It kind of is. Lancaster was put in here a long time ago after they said he pushed a girl down a well. I didn't see it because I wasn't alive yet. I guess it could've happened. You never know about people anymore."

"No, you sure don't." Another one of Lewis's stories. Was he always this crazy?

Lewis put the iron key into the old lock and turned it with a loud clank that echoed throughout this basement. He opened the door and stepped aside to let me in. He told me, "I can't leave the door open, so I have to lock you in with him. You don't worry about that, do you? He's safe."

I waited outside the cell. "You're not coming in with me?"

"How can I lock you inside if I'm in there with you?"

"Why do I need to be locked in?"

"Those are the rules Mr. Sutro wrote down. He told me where to find the key, so he knows how this all works."

Lewis showed me a slip of paper. It read:

The key is in the basement water bucket.
Unlock the cell door and let Julian go in.
Lock the door behind him.
Let Julian out again when he asks to leave.

"All right?"

I shrugged. "I suppose so. Just remember that last part where you let me out when I ask you to."

"I won't forget."

"I hope not. It's cold down here."

Lewis said, "Lancaster doesn't mind."

"Does he have a good coat?"

"He doesn't need one."

"What does that mean?"

"You'll see. Just go in."

I looked into the cell and saw a simple stone room with a fellow dressed in common work clothes sitting with his back to us in a wooden chair under a ray of sunlight. I saw a single window atop the wall opposite the cell door. The window was the sole source of light in the room.

"Go ahead." Lewis gave me a nudge. "You'll like him. He's fun to talk with."

"Don't push."

I walked into the cell and Lewis locked the old door behind me. The air had no smell at all except a faint odor of mold and dust and old stone. I stared at the man in the chair. His hair was thin and white, his skin almost translucent. His hands were ruddy and wrinkled, but he didn't look a lot older than my father. His work clothes were dusty and his boots were covered with dried mud. Was he taken out for walks?

Snow was piling up at the window outdoors, diminishing the light in the cell. I supposed on a sunny day the room would not be so bleak. And perhaps the sun warmed the air down in here, too. It already felt warmer than the basement on the other side of the door. I walked closer to the ray of sunlight and off the fellow's shoulder so he could see me when I spoke to him. He hadn't made a sound yet and I wondered if he was asleep. I decided to speak first. "Hello?"

He shuffled his boots and cocked his head to one side, then the other. He spoke in a flat voice with little intonation but precisely articulated.

"My name is Lancaster. I was head gardener for Queen Isabella Nouille. I have been dead for precisely three hundred and twelve years, four months and sixteen days. This, I've been told. There are calendars. My death was blamed on heart failure by the prick of a thorn from one of my Phalia bushes that made a fatal infection. They claim that ended my life, but I know better. I blame a failure of my heart, for love fully deserted me, and in turn I made that cowardly retreat from the soul of the world. My beautiful Ferése went down the well and

I was blamed for that accident of playful desire. No loss was greater than my own. I would follow her down into that water if permitted. Instead, my punishment is this: I am kept here where the sun rises and falls in my window and my past keeps company with these remorseless shadows. What do we owe eternity for our transgressions?"

He spoke without looking at me, as if he were either blind or in disregard of my presence there in the cold cell beside him. I failed to grasp who or what I was experiencing there. Lancaster didn't frighten me. In fact, he seemed more sad and benign than terrifying as might befit a living corpse. Surely he could not have been dead for three hundred years. That was impossible. He spoke. He was aware. Not dead at all. Did he breathe? I hadn't noticed at first, and then I couldn't tell. I took a couple more steps toward him and I saw his eyes greet me with the semblance of a crude smile. I said, "My name is Julian Brehm. Lewis brought me here. I'm pleased to meet you."

He said, "It is surely a wonder to see the sky of passing clouds or a soaring bird in flight. I took so much for granted in my youth when Queen Nouille admired my art in her gardens and invited me to choose the flowers for the walkways she selected me to plant. I was very gifted once many years ago."

"I'm sure you were." This felt very awkward and unsettling. What else to say?

With some effort, like expelling a fly from his throat, Lancaster told me, "Now my thoughts are imprecise, my sense of direction erratic and unreliable. For instance, I can neither count to ten consistently, nor leave this chair and follow the same path to the window. While I am still able to hold a fork, I cannot use one because I can no longer grasp its meaning. I recognize neither myself nor my attendants on any given morning. To be dead is to know a vigorous absence of humanity. I can't truly distinguish being a man from being a shoe, though a shoe certainly serves a greater good and purpose than I do now. I'm here to tell you that death is not so much horrible as inconvenient. Don't think of this as immortality. My own self-description is not of one who is dead, but rather one no longer alive. The distinction is crude and possibly immature. Death is not the end of life, as I knew it, instead the absence of life as I had experienced in all its wonder. I don't sleep or dream. Neither do I have many thoughts independent of conversation. A suggestion that well describes my condition is the fleeing of a soul. In other words, had I a soul, my true state might be more apparent. Death is inanimation of a most profound sort. At any given moment I am no more human than this chair. Is a chair dead or alive? I think it's neither. And neither am I."

Staring at Lancaster, I wondered why he was being kept here. Was this the end of all things? A showcase for what was to come for most of us, trapped in a cell in the shadow of sunlight we can glimpse but never feel again?

Lancaster bent his head slightly toward me. His eyes did glisten in that ray of sunshine as he said, "I believe being dead as I am now is not entirely a coincidence. I've considered this for quite a while. My state of nothingness is perhaps not without benefit. There are lessons to be taken here. Facts to be witnessed. I am who I am. My story is true and constant. Once I was alive, and now I am not. I loved and was loved. I breathed the air of the world and felt the warm light of day. I was born and died and now I am here in my cold solitudes. My dearest Ferése had her drowning-well, and I have this. What else do I know with certainty? That life should be lived with deliberation and contentment. We choose to be alive whether we appreciate our condition or not. There is no heaven or hell apart from our hand in the eternity of the world, no mysterious caretaker of our souls whose divinity divides us from the good promise of fate. I cursed our Lord when my belovèd fell down our well. Queen Isabella Nouille said it was God's will, but I cursed His diligent apathy to my suffering, to the suffering of all. This is what I've learned. We must take our own way."

Lancaster completed the rotation of his head to face me then, fully awake, or so it seemed. Either way, I could no longer deny that he existed here, whether he breathed or not. He raised a hand toward me and took mine, like a parent to a child. His was cold and dry. His grasp was firm but not uncaring. He told me, "There are no truths, Julian, other than these."

XXXVII
⌒

After dark, Lalla Goldbeck came to get me for dinner in the great hall. I dressed in my father's jacket and a clean pair of trousers. Someone had taken my shoes from the closet and given them a wonderful polishing, and I felt almost refreshed. I studied myself in one of the mirrors and was pleased. My recovery was proceeding nicely.

As we walked along the corridor, I tapped Lalla Goldbeck on her arm. "I meant to ask you something this morning, if I may?"

"Of course, Julian." She smiled. "I'm here to help."

"How long have I really been here? Mr. Sutro says it's been more than a week, but I have no sense of that at all. When I woke this morning, I felt incredibly rested. My shoulder was sore, of course. I expected that. I just don't feel any sense of how much time has passed since I was shot at Porphyry Hill."

"Nor should you. I'm sure Mr. Sutro told you how chloromorphium induces a persistent amnesia. It's for your benefit and mental well-being. The trauma you've endured was most profound. After all that, no one could expect you to wake like a bluebird on a Sunday morning, all fresh and ready to fly."

"I wouldn't imagine so."

"There, you see?" she said. "You're clear as a bell. When we can appreciate how lucky we are to be up and about after a tragedy, we're on that good old road again."

Lalla Goldbeck took my hand briefly and gave it a soft affectionate squeeze. I wondered if she was crazy, too. Probably I'd need to ask Mr. Sutro again how long I'd been asleep. Or maybe Priscilla Draxler. I liked her quite a lot. Much more so than that obsessive son of hers.

I could hear the roar of voices from the Great Hall when we passed through the upper door to the loggia above. Peering over the stone balustrade, I saw a huge table in formal banquet preparation with glittering dinnerware and candles and floral arrangements. Lalla Goldbeck led me around the loggia to the marble staircase and down into the vibrant hall. I supposed there must have been fifty or sixty people, men and women in colorfully extravagant clothing and jewelry, depending on disposition and status and skin hues, seated at that immense table and chattering away. I really had to admit I didn't grasp at all what this estate actually entailed. As Lalla Goldbeck showed me to my seat, I had the presumption that many of these people actually resided here in the mansion. For instance, looking out across the table, I saw those peculiar people from the lake, and, of course, Lewis and Mr. Sutro and the librarian, Jules Bernäert, and Priscilla Draxler. I had hoped Lalla Goldbeck would seat me next to one of those, perhaps Priscilla, but instead I was put in a group of strangers.

This dining hall was simply the largest room I'd ever been in, other than the Dome itself. The vault above must have been another thirty feet higher at its peak than the loggia and painted in murals of stars and skies and mythological figures flying about with ribbons and branches and birds of all sorts. Attached to the inner railing of the loggia and surrounding us on all sides were the many colorful flags of our disparate provinces, most of which I knew, a few I didn't recognize at all. We'd learned about them superficially in Lower School, a quick primer on names and most favored birds and flowers. I do recall an assembly when I was quite young where a chorus of children holding tiny paper flags sang out a recitation of provinces for which we were asked to clap and echo. I confess to being infatuated with the name, "Vulturnus," from a province to this day I couldn't locate on a map. I think it's in the southeast near the sea, and I believe it's been spared the war. Sitting there in that Great Hall, I must admit how I did love all the wondrous flags, regardless of any affiliation to dubious memories.

But I still felt very much alone. Lovely Priscilla in a fashionable dress smiled at me from far down the table. Lewis smirked at my discomfort. The lake people didn't acknowledge me at all. My neighbors at the banquet offered nothing to me at first except pleasant smiles and nods. Each fluted glass at our places was filled with sparkling gold Rhoetean wine, and I wondered how early some of these people had arrived, since it was clear that several of them had already enjoyed more than a couple pourings. Laughter was exaggerated, conversation excessively loud and boisterous. No one could be that happy so soon. Or maybe I was too hungry for enthusiasm. In any case, I was saved by the clanging brass bell a fellow in a fancy old gold and viridian uniform of the Republic rang as he entered the Great Hall just behind Mr. Sutro.

Everyone took a wine glass and stood. The room became astonishingly silent. That fellow with the bell announced in a stentorian voice, "A VAST EMPIRE IN THE WEST WILL BURST THE CHAINS WHICH FETTER IT!"

To which everyone in the Great Hall raised their glasses and responded, "HEAR, HEAR! HEAR, HEAR! HEAR, HEAR!"

Then the bell guard retreated, and we sat once more.

Except for Mr. Sutro.

He took his glass and raised it to the hall. He announced: "A toast now to our intrepid adventurer, Mr. Julian Charles Brehm, whose service to us was given at great risk. We owe him a tremendous debt. Ladies and gentlemen, to Julian!"

Mr. Sutro motioned for me to stand, so I did.

Everyone rose, as well, with all eyes upon me. I felt embarrassed, but proud somehow, too, even yet uneasy in my ignorance to the purpose of those drawings.

The assembled mass roared: "TO JULIAN! HEAR, HEAR! HEAR, HEAR! HEAR, HEAR!"

I lifted my own glass to the hall in gratitude.

And the toast was followed by a long and boisterous applause.

And then we sat again, and finally my neighbors at the table acknowledged me as a troupe of waiters began to bring out our meal.

A pudgy old fellow in a white tuxedo to my left nudged my sore arm. "You're quite the hero, my boy! Simply astounding! Almost a miracle!"

The dark woman seated on my right in a diamond blue gown and tiara took my hand. "You are the most remarkable boy I've ever met! How you survived is the tale of legends! Of course, we knew you were coming, but who could have imagined your trials to get here?"

Another woman to her right in glittering emeralds and a satin gown leaned out to say, "We hadn't the least idea someone of your stature could be found to save us all as you have. It's proof of those celestial spirits who look over us! I'm certain they were guiding your every step. Did you feel that, too?"

I shrugged. "Who can say for sure, right?"

"Oh, I think we can! There's no other explanation. You ought to have been killed. The others were. Every last one of them." She spoke to her friend beside me. "Isn't that true, Maralee? They've all been killed, haven't they?"

"I presume so, since none arrived like our dear Julian here."

I smiled as I took up my glass of wine. "Thank you all."

The woman in the blue diamond gown said, "No, thank *you*, Julian! Life is precious. Without a boy like you in the world, none of this could endure."

The white tuxedo leaned close to speak into my ear. "I was in the war, my boy. Ages ago. At Lago Sirminé. We fought their Sthenelus Brigade at high noon of a terrific dust storm in a ferocious heat. No one could see an inch. Thousands were killed. I survived by stealing a uniform off one of their dead and hiding in a boat until dark. The next day, when the wind cleared, I was the last one alive. Both sides were massacred. Ours and theirs." He raised his glass to mine. "To war, where only the vultures are victorious."

Our glasses clinked and I looked away to a great roasted pig being served to us. The preparation with boiled potatoes and cabbage and honeyed carrots was *ancién avec marot*, a style my mother offered at Christmas one year when she was determined to outwit my Aunt Jean. The sisters dueled with recipes and compositions until, at last, my father put his foot down, insisting we needn't be trial monkeys any longer.

In the next few hours, the banquet consumed five pigs and a barrel of potatoes and more carrots and cabbage than grew in all the green fields of Trivánder Province. Tureens of sweet tomato soup were shared. Then chocolate petit parc cakes and peach pies appeared and were also devoured. All our wine bottles were emptied, and our glasses gone dry. Coffee poured and drank. The table candles burned down the wax to the last inch, and I noticed three of my dining companions, a woman and two older fellows, slumbering at their dishes. No one seemed to give them any attention at all. Probably not an unusual ritual at this occasion.

I also saw that Lewis had gone early. Then I recalled him telling me how he was not allowed to eat more than one meal. That mush and sausage he claimed for breakfast could not have been very filling for a young fellow like himself. Looking about, I wondered which female at the great table was the aforementioned Mary Cumberland. I had a handful of candidates in mind — one in particular with dark shingled curls and a schoolgirl's white petticoat had my best vote. She just looked the sort Lewis might worry over.

Soon, my dining neighbors on both elbows departed. As they did, another pale and powdered woman in fashionable pink silks and sashes came along and sat beside me. She asked, "Will you be joining us in our flight? I'd love to have you along tonight. We could sit together."

Then I heard Mr. Sutro's voice behind me, too. "You'll be flying over Lao-medonia and the Great Chasm, Julian. It's part of your instruction here. The Regents insist. Some of these questions you have may find answers in the air."

"Flying?"

I saw lovely Priscilla there, arm-in-arm with Mr. Sutro, both of them impossibly elegant in the golden glow of the great torches. She told me, "You ought to go, Julian. My story and Peter's will make more sense if you do."

I asked, "Will you two be coming along?"

Mr. Sutro shook his head. "It's not appropriate. This is just an excursion, an evening's entertainment. I have papers to sort and Priscilla needs her early bed."

"You won't need us with you, dear," Priscilla told me with the kindest smile. "I promise you'll be too occupied to even notice our absence."

The powdered woman beside me took my arm and squeezed me close. "I'll look after you, honey. We'll have a grand time of it."

"Well, what is this flying business, after all?" I felt nervous again. "I don't understand what you're talking about."

Mr. Sutro said, "Lalla Goldbeck is bringing your winter coat. Once she's here, we'll all go out together and introduce you to the most marvelous experience you can possibly imagine."

The night air outdoors was bitterly cold, and the sky of stars clear of clouds at last. We walked through the icy snow on a trampled path that led away from the mansion to the west now, rather than the east where the lake and that palace lay. I felt the chill with each breath I took and strode through that freezing mist in the air from my fellow companions as we went along. The snow field was wide and flat for a while, no trees at all. I wondered how far we had to go. Up ahead I heard voices excited in the dark, echoing across the night. No hint of worry or concern for the cold.

My escort, that woman who'd taken my arm at the table, walked just ahead of me in a white fur coat and hat. Her luscious honey-lilac perfume was redolent and tasty, even though I felt she was somewhat overdone herself. Every so often she cast a look backward to see if I was still with them, and I smiled to reassure her that I had no intention of getting lost out there in the icy night. She told me her name back at the mansion, but I hadn't heard her clearly in the crowd of departure from the foyer. I thought she said something like Tiara or Dyára. I wasn't sure. She seemed pleasant enough. Unless she had a crush on me, in which case I'd need to hide. I guessed her age at only a few years younger than my mother's friend, Dolly, who flirted with me whenever she came over to tea and games of Gallimard.

Soon the cold field sloped gently away from us and our path through the snow headed gradually downward and became icier and almost treacherous in the dark. Ahead, I could just discern a large building blocking the stars and I heard that revelry of voices and saw lanterns lit against the night. We followed a curving trail down and through a fenceline almost covered with snow and then out onto a broad flat where the building stood that I recognized now as an immense barn.

Let's call her Dyára. She came over to take my arm with a glowing smile. Her sweet perfume bloomed as she said, "Isn't it just astounding?"

Mr. Sutro arrived to greet me, as well. "You are a lucky boy, Julian. No one from the metropolis has ever seen this. The Regents have offered you the experience because of your intrepid spirit and the sacrifices you made to get here."

I stared at the barn. It was very big. I'd seen barns. Lots more in pictures. None of this scale. I'd hoped all the excitement wasn't over a thousand bales of hay stacked to the rafters. My Lower School class with Miss Bixio took us on a field trip to a farm outside of Calcitonia District one sunny morning when I was about ten years old where we were shown all about agricultural life. Farmer Luc led us through the muck and mire of his stinky barnyard and had us milk a nasty-tempered cow and sit on bales of hay that poked through the seat of my pants and gave me a rash. I'd had better school experiences.

Priscilla called to me, "Come, Julian! They're bringing it out!"

I watched a flood of light burst from the barn as its huge doors were flung open to the night. A raucous cheer went up from those standing nearby. Excitement all about the icy dark. I followed our group in that direction, feeling myself wonderfully thrilled with curiosity. A snowbank blocked us from walking around for a better view of the big door until the object of our excursion finally appeared. I'd never seen anything like it in my young life. Well, perhaps in illustrated books of adventure and artful speculation. The science of modern possibilities. Stories of other futures. Those shapes of things to come. What rolled out of that stupendous barn was no fantastical daydream. I saw it emerge into the starry night with my own two eyes and was astonished.

Carried forward by twin motor sleds on either side was a gigantic oblong balloon, like a great fat Fulton sausage constructed of canvas, and ringed in wire and ropes. It was lit across every surface with dozens of the colored electric bulbs we hang on our Christmas trees. Suspended from its underbelly was a carriage the size of a small streetcar with flags. It was not supported by those motor sleds. On the contrary, walking closer I saw it was floating, weightless, seemingly held aloft by nothing but itself. Only a series of ropes tied to the sleds prevented it from flying away.

Mr. Sutro came up beside me. "The airship, *Deiopea*, Julian. Your carriage for the evening."

I stared in wonder at this incredible thing gliding out of the barn, almost free now. I said, "It flies?"

He laughed. "Of course it flies! That's its purpose!"

Priscilla took my hand, "Isn't it lovely, Julian? A wonder of the world!"

"How?"

Dyára took my other arm, nestling close. "Oh, darling, don't bother with technicalities. It's so beautiful. Does any of that matter? Truly?"

"Well, I need to know before I set foot onboard," I said. "Is it dangerous? How does it work? Who built it?" I knew for certain Freddy would have already figured out the entire contraption from concept to construction. A study on the fundamental idea probably existed already in one of his squib books.

Once the airship fully emerged from the barn, I had a good view of it in all its glory. Besides the balloon and wires and colored lights and ropes, there was a tall rudder top and bottom on the back and a huge metal propeller protruding from a motor housing in the middle rear.

Mr. Sutro told me, "Many years ago, Dr. Homer Zámbernon of our Mignard Institute described a mysterious chemistry in certain elastic fluids whose vapors are lighter than air. With great patience and diligent experimentation, he was able to expose the secret of their essence and thereby harness their unique properties and direct that potential toward a spectacular use. He demonstrated how elevation occurs with a stable mixture of helion gas and DeCosta's méléndré molecules in forced combination. This allowed him to avoid incandescent hydrogen, which could burn us all alive in flight. The airship, then, was engineered and constructed by the Brothers Philemon from a drawing Dr. Holsendorf had made at Huegenot College. They built it in six months and took it up into the air thereafter. Quite a sight, I must tell you. The celebration of its first flight was remarkable. Even the Regents came to witness and were suitably impressed. They gave our airship their blessing and the name, *Deiopea*, a nymph in Virgil and one of Queen Nouille's granddaughters who apparently loved to sit high in the birch trees of Laspágandélus."

Dyára gave my arm a light tug. "Come, Julian. Let's us go fly above the birch trees. Let's float among the stars." She gave me a kiss on the cheek. "Come!"

Priscilla laughed. "I think you better go now, Julian. The sky is clear. There's no better time for a flight up to the heavens."

"Yes, Julian," Mr. Sutro agreed. "Time to go."

They escorted me to the airship and a wooden ladder that led up into the carriage. Several people were already inside and seated along the gallery of viewing windows. I helped Dyára onto the second rung of the ladder, then followed her up the steps into the airship.

Fortunately, I found it much warmer than outdoors in the freezing night. A heater had been provided for our comfort and the seats along the windows were padded. The interior did, indeed, resemble one of our nicer city street cars or interurban trolleys. Bronze railings above the windows, a ceiling decorated by painted scrollwork and speedlines. Four brass ceiling lamps illuminated the interior. I felt much more comfortable seated in the airship than I had in contemplating my flight only minutes before. Dyára tucked herself into the seat beside me with another playful hug. We heard the electric motor engage with a buzz that briefly shook the carriage. I looked down through the window at Mr. Sutro and Priscilla who smiled and waved. Our pilot was a thick, older fellow in mutton chops and a formal captain's uniform of Imperial viridian and gold with braided epaulets and an impressive array of service medals on his chest. He introduced himself as Commander Elias Pennymaker and asked everyone to take a seat, after which he assumed his own position at the ship's wheel. Then the mooring ropes were freed, and we began to rise and float forward into the cold sky. I had no sensation of movement really at all, nor any feeling of elevation. We simply rose, and the snowfield and the barn beneath us seemed to shrink away. The electric motor made the airship virtually silent. We sailed above the countryside toward the west among millions of shining stars.

"Isn't it simply marvelous?" Dyára said, nestling even closer now. "Just the most of everything!" She kissed my cheek and I knew I'd carry her honey-lilac for nights upon nights.

Up front, that crowd who had boarded ahead of us began singing in the round, "O, That Lovely Heart of Heaven," each taking up his or her part in joyous rotation. Dyára hummed along and I watched the cold snowy earth of field and forest glide by beneath us. I must tell you that flight is not as terrifying as one might imagine. Aloft in the airship, there's no fear of tumbling to earth. Nor do we drift and sway in the wind. Were I to have closed my eyes, I could just as well have believed I was in my bed chamber at rest, so comfortable and reassuring was our celestial carriage. Freddy would have been ecstatic. And Nina? God, how I wished she had been with me in that flight. All I lacked from my first experience aloft was her lovely scent and touch, her beautiful smile. I missed her so. How far apart were we that night? How many miles from each other's arms? Too many to count. I did feel terribly lonely without her. Our hearts are haunted by those we love, whether high in the heavens or down on earth.

I'd been looking back toward the barn disappearing behind us in the dark, when Dyára pinched my cheek. "Laomedonia!"

"Pardon?"

"Look!"

There I saw that astonishing sky of stars brought low to the immense plain before us, a great village of lights in the snowy darkness. We approached like a glittering cloud. From my viewing window, I saw a fantasy of lights and gilded spires in the frigid night. A fairyland architecture of sorts. A snowy kingdom in miniature. Once upon a time, Agnes owned a children's book called, "Mary Antoinette and the Snow Queen," an illustrated volume with colored plates of fabulous castles and icy mountains of glass where fabulous mysteries happened on every page and mystical creatures popped up wherever one looked. Easily her favorite book as a child. This snowy Laomedonia resembled one of those plates I remember best: golden lights in each window, wood smoke spiraling upward from every chimney, flags of many colors and designs flourishing each steeple and rooftop and lamppost. A snow-covered village of magic and wonder.

Sailing just above the outskirts of the glorious village, people on both sides of the carriage up front opened their viewing windows to the night air. A freezing draft passed through our interior and I had no idea why they would make such a ridiculously uncomfortable decision until I heard the faint tones of symphonic music from the earth below. A concerto performed in a broad town square for our benefit: Rialto Mecanété's "Orellia" Movement No. 21, one of my mother's favorite pieces of orchestral chamber music. It was remarkably beautiful experienced way up in the air. Dreamlike and transcendent. As Commander Pennymaker slowed the airship over the village, our passage was so quiet that the music almost made me forget we were high above the performance.

I asked Dyára, "How many people live here?"

She laughed. "A million, Julian! At least a million!"

I doubted that. Really, there weren't rooftops enough to house such a populace. Or were there? What did I know? I asked her, "Well, where are they all from?"

She giggled. "Why, here, of course! Laomedonia! Where else?"

"So how did they get here?"

"Just like you, Julian, my dear! They were born!"

She laughed again and kissed my cheek and went back to watching the grand village gradually unfold and pass ever so slowly beneath our glimmering airship.

When the abbreviated concerto ended, a wonderful applause arose from the snowy streets. Our pilot responded with three bursts of a great airhorn. Then he accelerated the electric motor and we sailed on across the sparkling plain of Laomedonia toward a vast darkness ahead. My fellow passengers up front closed their viewing windows and everyone seemed to huddle closer together while we waited for the carriage heater to warm us up again. Once more, the night seemed still and icy and the stars felt distant yet all encompassing. The sky and airship went silent again, as if we were sailing at midnight on a vast black sea, drifting into a cold void. Where were we now? Where were we headed? No one spoke for long minutes as we floated onward into the night. Dyára relaxed her grip on my arm and settled into her seat. Her eyes looked drowsy. Perhaps she'd fall asleep in flight.

Snow fields were visible below by starlight, and the silvery tips of fir trees. I began to feel sleepy, too, as the carriage heated up. It seemed late. I brought Father's timepiece out my pocket and checked the hour. Already a quarter to ten. Glancing casually at my fellow passengers, I could tell we'd gone past bedtime for some of them.

Farther on we flew. Miles and miles. I began to feel strange, wondering where on earth we were headed. No one spoke. The carriage was still as we sailed through the icy night. Nothing but snow beneath us now as the white forest thinned and disappeared. Another mile or so, and I saw the strangest sight: a great expanse of blackness ahead on the horizon. Slashing across those snowy fields of our flight. Eerie and vast. As the airship approached, I thought we'd flown to the end of the world. Endless miles of snow quit there at a border of darkness. I felt scared at last. All along our flight, I knew we were hundreds of feet above the frozen ground, but I could always see where we were, almost feel the earth below. And now suddenly we had nothing beneath us. A true black void as we floated above that last precipice of ice and snow and the commander slowed the airship.

Dyára told me, then, "We're here, darling."

"Where?"

"The Great Chasm."

"Pardon?"

"The natural barrier between your world and ours. Mr. Sutro says it's twelve to twenty-one miles across depending on where you're standing, over two thousand feet deep, and more than nine hundred miles long. Isn't that just fantastic? He and Dr. Bernäert performed their own study years ago and gave a lecture in the dining hall. It was fascinating unless you'd chosen the St. Dénis wine with dinner. I doubt half of us heard the entire paper."

"That's too bad. I'll bet it was interesting. The history of all this."

"Yes, but does it really matter? We have plenty of entertainments and the war is far away from here, although on clear nights I've heard it's possible with a telescope to see rockets on the sky over Caesárea or Bourgh Province to the north."

The airship eased forward across the darkness. A million stars above us now, nothing beneath. We sailed out over the Great Chasm.

"How do people get across?"

Dyára nuzzled close to me once more, kissing my cheek, hugging me. "They don't, honey. Unless they fly like this. It's how you came to us, Julian. This airship."

Another absurdity. "That can't be so. There must be bridges somewhere."

"But there aren't, darling. No one's walked across in centuries. Not since the great earthquake that made the chasm. We may travel as far as we care to the east, but not west. Nor could you travel here from the metropolis. It won't ever be done."

The airship had left the snowfields behind entirely. I saw nothing then but stygian black beneath us, ahead and behind. In fact, it was terrifically frightening. Suddenly, I did fear falling from the airship. Or what if we deflated somehow and plunged into the chasm? How long would we fall? And then what?

"What's below us?" I quickly asked Dyára. "At the bottom, I mean."

"The River Philateus. I hear it's very treacherous. In the daylight, you can see the water churning. They say boats have sailed along it to the sea, but I'd never go. I refuse to believe it's possible." She squeezed my arm. "Please don't try it, Julian. Will you promise? We couldn't bear losing you."

I said, "Don't worry. I don't like getting wet."

If clouds had hidden the sky of stars, I could've felt as I had in the underground when my torch went dark. Except here, there was no purchase of earth to grasp, no sensation of anything natural and true. I supposed this was how floating in a suspension tank must feel. A removal from the world. Or perhaps the experience of death? Silent and cold, like Lancaster. I thought, too, how the war must have seemed quite distant from this place. Alien and corrupt, certainly, yet irrelevant. Who could march here and fire rifles or cannons across this expanse with any expectation of achievement? To that point, what could eugenics have to do with this immense gash of earth and river?

Our airship sailed out across the Great Chasm another few miles with nothing but blackness all about. Even the silence in the carriage had become intimidating, subduing our spirits. And then one of the men up front abruptly called for us to turn back for fear of losing our essential elevation. He worried to our pilot, "Look here, Pennymaker: What if the gasses leak out? Or a rabid owl punctures the balloon? What if our carriage falters and comes loose?" The woman wrapped in blue satin and wool beside him began weeping. It happened that neither of them had ever been aloft at night, and so far from Laomedonia. Commander Pennymaker attempted to reassure them both over the safety of his beautiful *Deiopea*, but without great success. Then an argument broke out between those two and four other riders up front who insisted we fly to the far ridge of the chasm as was apparently promised at the beginning of the evening.

"We're not cowards," I heard the nervous fellow protest. "My Lenora here simply hasn't the constitution for altitude when she can't see the ground. And I agree with her. Is that so difficult for you people to understand? Have you no sympathy?"

One of the bolder women fired back, "You oughtn't to have come aboard if you didn't hope to see our voyage out to its scheduled conclusion. I think you're being selfish. You ought to lie down and close your eyes and pretend you're in bed. It's the perfect solution. In any case, it's obvious to the rest of us that you both had far too much to drink at dinner. We all noticed that when you came onboard. You ought to be banned from the airship in the future."

"How dare you! We'll report you to Mr. Sutro first thing in the morning!"

"I'm sure you will! If you're able to make it out of bed!"

Commander Pennymaker turned to his passengers. "Please, everyone! Calm down! We're perfectly fine and our flight is concluding shortly. The Tamson Ridge is just ahead. You'll be able to see the Fumaroli lighthouse if you look out your viewing windows on the north side of the carriage."

So we did.

And what I had thought was a planet near the sky horizon five minutes before, I recognized now as a bright incandescent hydrogen lamp in a stone tower, high above the cliff top. I presumed its purpose was to warn careless trucks or autos from driving off into the chasm at night. Like any lighthouse above the sea, its glowing lantern circulated a beam across the dark that brought us again to the world of people and solid earth. I felt myself relax, because only a couple of miles past the cliff were other lights, as well. Houses and farms. Nearby settlements.

And then I saw people on the cliff, perhaps a dozen of them. A few with electric torches. One carried a hunting rifle. Commander Pennymaker blew the airhorn and they waved to us and the airship slowed as we drew close, then stopped over the people and our pilot pulled a lever. I felt a slight shudder from the floor of the carriage and something detached and fell to earth below us. I leaned out and saw it was a huge leather bag, probably tucked into a cabinet within the carriage. Next, I felt a motor running beneath us. In the glow of electric torches was a long wooden box and when the motor stopped, I saw the men on the cliff attaching a long chain to the box. Once they finished, the motor hummed again, and I watched the box begin ascending toward the carriage bottom.

I asked Dyára, "What are they doing?"

Her voice sounded dreamy and vague. "The exchange. Needful items."

"What sort of things?"

She shrugged. "It depends. Nothing I ever request." Dyára smiled. "We're not asked to vote. I'm sure Mr. Sutro could tell you if it suits his mood, though he hasn't been in good spirits lately."

The people on the cliff top hoisted the leather bag onto a small horse-drawn wagon. With a wave of the electric torches, they moved off into the dark. Wondering momentarily who exactly they were, it occurred to me that this was probably the lost frontier rumored in our dusty histories. Severed from the imperial estate by the earthquake and abandoned centuries ago, left to wither in these forgotten hinterlands far from the young Republic and our evolving metropolis. Would the ugly reach of endless war ever blunder this far? What dire obstacles lay between this distant region and, say, Crown Colony or Porphyry Hill? More craggy ravines and cold rivers? Another great forested wilderness? Were there even intentions at the Status Imperium to seek killing and victory out here, half a world from Prospect Square? Did the Medical Directorate imagine spyreosis floating this far on a poison wind? I wondered how our hearts perpetrate mythologies that permit us to torment our fellow human beings. What stories do we tell ourselves to feel justified in the evils we pursue? Perhaps the vast black void above the River Philateus was not as great as that which resides in our own souls.

XXXVIII
∽

Lewis joined me for breakfast in my bed chamber the next morning. The wood in the fireplace was lit for me and two child's dining tables brought in by Lalla Goldbeck and arranged next to the window so we could watch the snow fall as we ate. Lewis arrived in his rosy striped pajamas and began complaining that Mr. Sutro had denied him a seat on the airship.

"He doesn't trust me at all, and it's awfully unfair. I've never broken anything in his office since my first visit and, even then, it was his own fault for leaving that ship-in-a-bottle so close to the edge of his bookcase. If you ask him about it, I'll bet he won't tell you how diligent I was in sweeping up all the glass."

Snow had begun falling again just after dawn and those soft flakes tossed about wonderfully on a light morning breeze. The birch wood was pretty in the ice and cold.

I said to Lewis, "I'd just assumed you'd already been up in the airship, so you had no interest in joining us."

"Well, you see, that's just not true at all. Mr. Sutro has never permitted me onboard. He's very unfair. Even Mary Cumberland has been on many flights and she's the most unnatural person in our house. Ask anyone."

"Well, she's not your friend, anymore, is she? So, nothing to worry about there."

Lewis looked shocked. "Did she tell you we're not friends? I haven't heard anything. Is that true?"

"You told me so yesterday. The incident with your coat."

"Somebody stole my coat, but it wasn't Mary. We're much too close for that. I trust her implicitly, and she accepts that. For all I know, you stole my coat."

"No, I have my own."

"Well, you haven't been here long enough for us to be friends, so I'll have to keep my eye on you. Be careful."

"Oh, I will. Believe me."

Lewis was so crazy. Good grief. Why was he even there in my bed chamber? Who told him he was invited? Fortunately, Lalla Goldbeck came along just then with our breakfast. She served us steaming roast mutton and eggs Scudéry and syrup pudding.

She asked me, "Julian, would you prefer tea this morning, or hot cinnamon cider?"

"Cider, please."

"And you, Lewis? Your lemon tea?"

"Why won't Mr. Sutro let me on the airship? I've done nothing wrong. Maybe I should just leave."

"Why would you leave us, Lewis? Aren't you happy? What about Mary Cumberland? Won't you miss her?"

"Mary's not my friend, anymore. She stole my coat."

She gave him a pat on the head. "I'm sorry, Lewis. I'll bring your lemon tea."

We ate our spicy eggs and hot mutton and watched the snow fall in silence. I was tempted to ask Lewis where he thought he would go if he left here, but I managed to stifle that impulse. He was so crazy I was afraid that conversation might spoil my breakfast.

I expected Mr. Sutro within the hour and needed to eat quickly. The thought of meeting his Regents both excited and scared me. How would they describe and explain Leandro Porteus's drawing? What did it mean? Why was it worth the lives of so many people?

Lalla Goldbeck returned with Lewis's tea. "The kitchen is out of honey, darling. I added a spoon of sugar instead. I hope that satisfies your sweet tooth."

She kissed her fingertips and dabbed his forehead.

Lewis stared out at the snow.

Lalla Goldbeck told him, "I saw Mary just now in the game room. She asked me to invite you to come play with her when you've finished eating. She was very anxious to see you."

Lewis smiled. "I won forty-four games of Gypsy Candle last week playing against her. She wasn't very good."

"Then maybe play something else."

"No, I like to win."

"Doesn't Mary want to win, too?"

"I don't care. She's not very good at that game. I like beating her."

"Lewis?" Lalla Goldbeck gave him a soft pat on his shoulder. "Enjoy your breakfast."

She left the bed chamber and I did my best to ignore Lewis. What was wrong with him besides having a nasty disposition? Did he fall on his head somewhere? So many mysteries here. I tried to gather it all together and felt it wasn't possible. Maybe my brain was still fogged by the chloromorphium. That would explain a lot. Nothing here seemed clear. Almost like a dream where you experience familiarities that aren't real despite normal appearances. A lucid dream where everyone knew me intimately while I recognized nothing and no one for certain. How does one wake from this?

Lewis finished his breakfast and went out the door without saying a word. He seemed disturbed. Honestly, I was glad he left. I ate with an eye on the hour for Mr. Sutro's arrival. I'd already dressed fully for breakfast and used the toilet, so all I'd need to do was put on my winter coat once he got here. The snowfall gradually slowed to casual flakes on the morning breeze. Then I drank the last of my cinnamon cider and Mr. Sutro knocked and brought me out of the mansion through the front foyer. I hadn't seen it yet and found it suitably impressive. Roman floor tiles and elaborately painted arches. Gilded lamp sconces. A massive fireplace and a thick oak door with black ironwork.

At the marble threshold, we both put our hats on, buttoned up, and went out into the icy breeze. The front of the huge mansion faced up toward the Regent's palace, cold and stern atop the broad snow-laden hill. I felt small in the wide half-mile between the two buildings. Insignificant. Perhaps that was inherent in the philosophy of imperial architecture. Not so much to diminish us as to request our gaze upward. I intended to have Mr. Sutro explain all this to me as we walked, but first I just had to ask him about Lewis. I mentioned the airship, his disappointment at being excluded. I said, "Lewis thinks you've kept him off it. He feels slighted at never having been aloft."

Mr. Sutro laughed. "Oh, that's not at all true. In fact, he's been up on at least three occasions. He's correct in stating that we don't trust him now, though. His last trip aboard, he opened one of the viewing windows three hundred feet above the ground and tried to crawl out. The fall would have killed him. He didn't seem to grasp the concept."

"Oh God!"

"I'm well aware of his frustration, but he can't be permitted up there any longer. If he managed to crawl out over the Great Chasm, we'd lose him for good.

383

He's a ward of the estate, by decree of the Regents, and our perpetual responsibility. He doesn't care for that, I know."

"He seems erratic. That girl Mary Cumberland troubles him."

"She doesn't exist."

"Pardon?"

"Mary Cumberland is a figment of his imagination. He has a very extravagant love/hate relationship with the idea of her. We've attempted to exorcize her from his waking consciousness and have always failed, even with the use of electricity. Now we just go along with his fantasy engagements to the enigmatic Mary. Life here is simpler that way and really does no one any harm, least of all Lewis himself. His mood waxes and wanes according to daily considerations of her."

I buttoned up higher on my coat as icy snowflakes tossed about. "When Lewis says he plays games with Mary Cumberland, does he actually see her, like some hallucination?"

"No, in fact, she's not any hallucination at all. His impressions of her are all retroactive memories. He doesn't see her. He only *has* seen her. How recently is wholly dependent upon what else occupies his focus, minute to minute, hour to hour. I'm sure he's seen less of her since you arrived. Lewis likes you."

I shuddered. "That's sort of unfortunate."

Mr. Sutro laughed. "Oh, he's not all that bad. Just oddly eccentric."

"He seems crazy to me."

"In a sense. Somewhere in his past, he suffered a terrible trauma, whether physical or psychological, the nature of which we'll likely never know. We discovered him one morning clinging to the western cliff a thousand feet above the Philateus. No one could determine whether he was climbing up or climbing down. He was stuck, though, and weak, and would certainly have fallen had we not rescued him. All we managed to extract was his name and a strange word only the Regents knew. On that account, he was named a ward and given to our perpetual care."

"What word?"

"Clothonium."

"What does it mean?"

"I was discouraged from asking, so I haven't pursued it. Dr. Bernäert has extensive dictionaries of all sorts and was quite enthusiastic about uncovering its origin, when he, too, received a notice from the Regents to let the matter drop. So, he has. We don't discuss it any longer, nor should you."

"Don't worry. I wouldn't know what to say."

"Look here, Julian." Mr. Sutro directed my attention ahead as we strolled through the snow toward the lowest set of steps in the palace gardens. "This estate is quite ancient. More than two millennia old. We estimate its origin corresponds roughly to that almost mythical construction of the Dome of Eternity by the holy river. Over the centuries, it's undergone unimaginable changes, both human and geological. To state, as your Council does, that these lands belong to the Republic is both absurd and dishonest. I assure you, they know better."

The frigid breeze picked up and burned on my face.

Mr. Sutro said, "You see, Julian, the Philateus River flowed once through those miles of fields near Laomedonia, almost two thousand feet higher than its current elevation at the Great Chasm. It was broader and more navigable than the Alban eight hundred miles to the west, so larger vessels were able to travel along its waters through antiquity. Where Eurymedon and Alexander and Tiberius made excursion ports at what we call Crown Colony, Emperor Aventinian created a seat of empire here in the forests of the east. That village of Laomedonia was once the site of his imperium and this immense structure we're coming to upon the mount," he pointed up to the palace, "was originally the Temple of Jupiter. Notice the central edifice is different from its flanks? Those columns and Corinthian capitals? And the gilded dome on top? All belonging to the Jovian temple. The borders of his empire extended to the eastern shore of the Alban where, as I told you yesterday, his sister, Clélia, made her home. Or so we think. There is a body of opinion that suggests Aventinian's rule extended far past what we call Tamorina, but that's just conjecture based on concepts of empire. There've been no confirmed artifacts uncovered to persuade the Alban River opinion, either way. And once the war reached Tarchon Province, all study ended."

"I'd imagine quite a few things ended out here with the war."

The morning was so quiet in the cold and snowfall, our words almost seemed to echo above the crunching of our boots.

"That's more or less the crux of my story here, Julian, what you need to know before meeting the Regents. When Aventinian the Great died, his son ascended to the throne and ruled here until his beloved Trinácria drowned in his father's lake. So crushed was he by her death, Aventinian the Second abandoned this region and moved the seat of his empire across the Pilumnas River and far into the east where he could forget his father's lake and how it had broken his heart. Perhaps that was fortunate because within a couple hundred years or so, we experienced the Minor Ice Age. Are you familiar with that? Have you studied it at Regency?"

"Not really," I confessed, feeling like an idiot again. "My emphasis there hasn't been history so much as classical philosophy and law. I'm sorry. I know I ought to know more about who we are and where we came from."

"Well, the significance is that this region was almost entirely consumed by a glacier, all but that edifice of the original temple and the marble foundation of Clélius House. Aventinian's palace and the surrounding villas were erased by the ice and the land stripped almost clean. What it meant was that his legacy here was mostly forgotten, as it was to the west, too, where those summer cottages, as we call them, of Alexander, Tiberius, Todra Abdelhassan, Voireuse Bardamu along the Alban River also vanished under the glacier. Of your world, only the Dome of Eternity survived, which is partly why we've called it that, why to the people of the River Livorna, it seems always to have been there."

"And yet nobody knows precisely who built it? Isn't that true?"

"Not with any certainty. There are opinions, of course, among academics and archaeologists of the field, spiritualists and astrologers by the thousands. Egyptians often get credit, as they do for anything ancient beyond our records. Carthusians or Athenian Greeks. Antalasian sea peoples are a current favorite. Some obscure linguistic and astronomical connections there. But you're correct. No one knows for sure. It is certainly much older than we can imagine, and its purpose shrouded in secrets we are not privy to thus far. And, like you say, the war has thoroughly disrupted studies of all sorts. We've lost almost a century of intellectual progress. It's a pity. Like everything else."

The snowy steps up to the palace had been shoveled and swept clean in the middle, offering us a path upward. Thirty steps on four broad sections. Very imperial. I expected to be exhausted when we reached the palace. Snow kept falling. Would they shovel for our return to the mansion?

"But listen here, Julian, because now we're getting to the heart of what we understand as our modern society. You see, once the glaciers began to retreat about four hundred years ago, these greatest of our rivers: Livorna, Fatoma, Alban, Sybéle, Philateus and Pilumnas, became navigable once again, and in our case these waterways invited the empire of Laspágandélus from the southern sea up into these lands. His armies went both east and west from the Alban to establish a kingdom of field and forest that regained civilization as we understand it and the enormous growth of a population from which so many of us derive. We are the inheritors of much from that culture in politics, social structure, architecture, agriculture, engineering and the arts. And his philosophy permitted an empire of many cultures and distinctions to thrive under one flag, that imperial viridian and gold you see waving over these lands even now. At his death, Queen Nouille assumed the throne from her palace on this hill she called 'Désallier' after her birthplace. She preferred the climate here to that of Livorna, for the seasons of warmth and rain and snow, and the surrounding forests where she could ride her horse and feel miles from the royal court."

Mr. Sutro and I ascended the second set of steps in a drifting snowfall. I wondered if every approach to the palace was taken by these steps or if there was another route, a road, perhaps, for horse-drawn carriages, or autos and trucks now. The icy wind had picked up and I had to pause briefly to let my face thaw. At least the ache in my shoulder felt diminished in the cold.

I said, "Priscilla Draxler told me yesterday how Queen Nouille let her children sail on the lake that Aventinian surrendered. She must have loved this place."

"By all appearances, yes, that's true. So did her children. It truly was a beautiful Elysium in those long-ago days, both of, and apart from, the great empire. Queen Nouille established the Status Imperium to oversee her rule on the banks of the holy river, Livorna, where, legend has it, water has never ceased to flow. She traveled there only once a year and took her audience in the Dome for six days and departed on the seventh to maintain her natural fealty and obligation to the Holy Book." He stopped two steps above me where snow was quickly gathering. "Can you see how enormous this empire must have been three centuries ago? And how unwieldy? Since embarking on your journey here, you've traveled across most of it west to east. More than fifteen hundred miles."

My face felt numb as I nodded across the cold breeze. "It really does feel endless, even by train and truck. I can't imagine crossing on horseback or, heaven forbid, by foot. And to think so much has been reduced almost to nothingness by the Desolation. I feel like I've seen the end of the world out there."

Mr. Sutro waved for me to keep up. "Come along, Julian. We're expected on the hour."

I could see my icy breath in the air as I followed him to the next two steps. "We won't be late on my account, sir. I have no desire to freeze to death."

As I caught up, he asked, "Do you know who founded the Republic?"

"Not sure, really. A popular vote?" Another stupid answer.

"Nobody, Julian. It was the great earthquake that wrote your origins. Historical memory and legend say it struck in the middle of a pleasant summer night of stars and warm breezes when most of Laomedonia was asleep and Queen Nouille lay ill up in her palace with all the windows open to the fresh air outdoors. Do you notice those two adjoining wings up there, north and south?"

Ascending the third tier of steps, my ears were frozen in the snowy draft. "Of course. The design is classically symmetrical. My father loves old architecture, so I grew up with that aesthetic."

"Good enough. Well, you see, besides reconstructing Clélius House, Queen Nouille had those additions attached to the old temple edifice for her children and dignitaries visiting from Livorna. She kept her bedroom high in the temple above the imperial audience chamber, so she might hold her eye on Laomedonia, and appear as if from the firmament when she descended the central staircase to greet her ambassadors. Very imposing, I'm sure. When the earthquake occurred, it's likely no one had any real sense of what was happening. Like the volcano that killed Pompeii and Herculaneum, death came dressed in mystery. Both additions collapsed and many on the bottom floors were crushed, including four of her own seven children. Worse yet was what fate held for Laomedonia. An earthquake so great as to create such a rift in the earth has no pity for anything built by man. Dr. Bernäert and I believe it was as if the entire plain of Laomedonia had exploded. We've uncovered marble artifacts in the forest miles from the site, flung into the air by the fury of the beast. We presume everybody was killed as the earth was torn apart and the River Philateus dropped two thousand feet in the blink of an eye. A monstrous event. Unimaginable to us. The horror of it all."

"And the queen? She died, too?"

Mr. Sutro shook his head. "Not that night. Her bedroom floor had fallen three stories to the chamber below, yet our history says Queen Nouille walked out of the palace ruin at sunrise with blood on her face to renounce fear. She displayed her children's broken bodies on the marble terrace for frightened survivors as proof that she, too, knew this tragedy. What died was her empire. Rumors of mortal catastrophe spread to the west. Stories of death and dissolution. The Great Chasm was inconceivable and impassable. The Status Imperium declared a Republic in lieu of empire and Laspágandélus was considered lost, and then forgotten."

That icy breeze swirled snowflakes all about as we mounted the final set of steps to the palace. I looked at the beautiful edifice and was astonished to see it whole and perfect after Mr. Sutro's description of ruin and horror. In the snowfall, its marble columns and architrave, the twin sphinxes on stone pedestals flanking the terrace, were all monumental and pristine.

"But that's not the end of the tale, Julian. In a sense, it's the beginning. Beyond that forest of Lake Nouille is the Pilumnas River, the true savior of our world and legacy. Because, while the Philateus was dropped into the chasm and rendered mostly unnavigable, the good Pilumnas flowed as ever to the sea, keeping us alive with needful nourishments and industry. We rebuilt, year after year, rediscovering ourselves in this home of our birth. Labor provided moral and spiritual sustenance. Love and purpose prevailed. Queen Nouille passed away, and her surviving daughters, and granddaughters and grandsons, great-grandchildren and great-great grandchildren, and so forth, after them, shared the throne and the wealth of the estate, assuming the role of Regents and encouraging the growth of our own perpetual metropolis they chose to call, *Illium*, 'for that success which depends upon perseverance.' You can't see it from here, but what is there would astound you. A living society untouched by guilt and moral confusion. Museums and parks and great institutes of study. Boundless neighborhoods of people healthy and untroubled. Art galleries and markets. Vibrant industry and playing fields. Wondrous pools of water and sunlight. Six million people thriving on the edge of tomorrow. We say, 'The sun rises in the east and sets in the west, and the story of our world lies in that cycle.' We do believe that when we are hand-in-hand with you once more on the shores of the sundown sea, this life will be complete."

I heard the doors open on the terrace and two guards wearing imperial viridian and gold emerged carrying royal standards. They announced, "By the grace of the Regents Nouille, welcome to Désallier."

XXXIX

∽

On the frieze of the marble architrave above the grand entrance was carved:

PROSPERITY AWAITS THEE

I mulled over the sentiment underlying those words as Mr. Sutro and I shed our snowy winter coats in the vestibule. The palace was warm, if a bit drafty. Those nerves I'd felt at breakfast had settled during our walk and the subsequent story Mr. Sutro told. These histories of us I'd been hearing from the undercity to this palace were so far beyond my normal school education, I had few reference points with which to assimilate them. Again, I wondered why I was not taught these things. Is it truly within a society's interests to keep its story hidden and forgotten? What was I supposed to believe now regarding who I am and where I come from? When philosophies are muddled by politics, and faithful histories revised to suit the present moment, how can we be expected to choose the proper course for a life? Or is that even a question for such a world? Is power the sole aim of us? And wealth accumulated through power? Are cocktails enjoyed on a sunny terrace all that's good and right through these brief years of our lives?

We were met in the Great Hall by a little fellow in a grey tuxedo and tailcoat. He was mostly bald and wore a white bow tie. He stood in the middle of an intricately detailed ancient Roman mosaic of the eternal zodiac that encompassed the entire center of the immense floor. Directly overhead was a coffered half-dome of gilded rosettes with a cove and swags of marble pearls and fluttering ribbons surrounding a frescoed ceiling oculus of Lord Jupiter on a chariot brandishing a handful of fiery lightning bolts. The image was grandiose and marvelously intimidating. I presumed it had either survived the great earthquake or been meticulously restored to a former glory.

That little fellow greeted us with a gracious smile. "Welcome, Julian. Mr. Sutro. I am Bertrand Tissándier, personal emissary for the Regents Nouille."

"I believe we've met," Mr. Sutro said, shaking hands. "At the embassy symposium on Cordiality in Foreign Service last summer."

Tissándier tipped his head. "I don't recall, sir, but I do not deny that possibility. I find myself inundated by gatherings of all sorts these days. What a trial it can be to connect faces to names as my appointment here to the palace anticipates."

"I think it would be overwhelming," I added. "I can hardly recall my own name some days."

Tissándier looked me in the eye. "You are matriculating through Thayer Hall, isn't that correct?"

"Yes, sir. My final term. I hope. Although these past few weeks may have put that in doubt. And I'm certain to have missed more classes than I'd expected since boarding that train at Commonwealth Station. Five days was all I'd allowed myself. A handful of classes for which my assignments were all up to the minute."

"Well, I may tell you the Regents are most intrigued by the curiosities of Dr. Hartley Mills Thayer. He's quite the enigma to them. Perhaps they'll explain their enthusiasm. Your audience with them is arriving soon now. Top of the hour. I hope your preparations are complete."

"Julian hasn't any," Mr. Sutro interjected. "The Regents have requested his presence, not the other way around. He was only to be shown into their audience for a conversation regarding a service he performed."

Tissándier smiled. "Wondrous! Then I'll simply guide you to the Grand Gallery where we'll wait to be summoned. Thank you both!"

He led us left through a carved stone archway flanked by Ionic columns into a long corridor of tall gilded mirrors divided by marble Corinthian pilasters and painted arabesques. The ceiling overhead was a great vault of frescoed mythological figures and soaring pink clouds on a pale blue sky. Our boots echoed on the polished tile floor and I felt slightly embarrassed to make such a noise in a place so grandiose. I just couldn't get over the thought that all of this had once been a disastrous ruin. How many years had it taken to restore its glory? The very idea of it felt incomprehensible. Yet, I did acknowledge how our hearts can be lifted by strenuous accomplishment, perhaps even more so if those achievements are meant for something greater than ourselves.

At the end of the hall were a pair of gilded doors Tissándier opened for us. A wide dark walnut vestibule awaited on the other side with cushioned benches and scrolled iron lamps. There were paintings on the side walls above our benches, portraits perhaps of former Regents Nouille or other persons of notoriety and renown.

"The Regents are receiving ambassadors from away at this moment," Tissándier told us. "But they are studiously punctual, and by my clock," he checked his chain watch, "we'll be invited into the chamber within two minutes. Have you both had breakfast this morning?"

Mr. Sutro nodded.

I told Tissándier, "In my bed chamber. Lalla Goldbeck brought mutton and eggs. And a cup of cider."

"I hope you enjoyed it. Dame Goldbeck is said to be a marvelous cook."

"Yes, she is. It was excellent."

"Are the accommodations adequate to your stay here? I'm afraid I haven't been in Clélius House for years, though my memory is that of a fine cottage, as it were."

"It's very nice, thank you. Warm and comfortable. A little busy now and then with my guest."

Mr. Sutro smiled. "Lewis has adopted Julian this week."

Tissándier looked horrified. "Oh, dear. I'm so sorry. Poor Lewis has a reputation of being quite disconcerting on his off days."

I shrugged. "He's all right. I don't mind. It's good to have some company now and then."

A bell rang.

Tissándier rose from his bench. "We're being summoned. Thank you."

He opened the solid walnut door to the next room and led us in.

The royal audience chamber was imperious in the grandest sense. Once more decorated with gilded mirrors and arabesques, carved and painted bas-reliefs. Now, too, flourished with long bright banners and scrolls beneath another coffered ceiling of painted miniatures featuring wild animals of the field and colorful birds in flight.

The two Regents, a man and a woman, were seated in tall gothic chairs directly ahead of us at the most immense wooden table I'd ever seen. Gilt and intricate marquetry described its surface with no distraction of papers or books or any such nonsense, only the Regents themselves who greeted us with gracious smiles, both dressed in imperial silks and braided fabric of viridian and gold, just as I'd expected. Both looked to be perhaps a decade younger than my parents, though age here at Laspágandélus was increasingly difficult to discern. The woman was classically beautiful, ivory skin, almost statuesque. The man was firm and regal, with eyes like sapphires. Each had a royal bearing and warm sun-lightened hair.

Tissándier spoke up. "My esteemed Regents, may I introduce Julian Brehm and Mr. Sutro."

Then he bowed and retreated.

The woman spoke first: "Good to see you again, Mr. Sutro. We thank you for escorting Julian to us this morning. You may be excused now."

Mr. Sutro bowed, as well. Then he and Tissándrier left, closing the door behind them.

And I was alone with the Regents in that stupendous chamber. There was only a single chair at the table across from them.

They both smiled at me. I had no idea what I was to say or do. Do I bow, too? Do I wait for them to address me?

They did.

The woman said, "Good morning, Julian. We are both honored to meet you at last. I am Lia Isabela, and this is my cousin, Vanderlei Rogário. We are Regents of the throne Laspágandélus, for Queen Nouille, Empress of the Eastern Empire. We regret your injury and those difficulties you've endured to reach us here. We are in awe of your determination."

I nodded.

Isabela said, "Will you please sit?"

"Thank you."

As I took the chair, she asked, "Are you still in pain?"

"Not too much. A little ache, that's all."

Rogário said, "We can't conceive of the trauma you must have felt being shot out there. Was it as terrible as it sounds?"

I shrugged. "I supposed the shock lessened it. I don't know. It hurt and then I felt dizzy and sick to my stomach."

"Good gracious, Julian." Isabela frowned. "What an awful experience. We are so sorry. Our fault, of course. Nothing to be done now, except to offer our gratitude, with perhaps some explanation for all you've been put through. Would you like that?"

I failed to hide a smile. "Very much."

"Where would you like us to begin? Your choice, Julian."

"The drawings? If you will? They've been the risk and the mystery. So many people have died."

"Indeed," Rogário said. "A hopeless regret. You'll understand our motive once we explain the origin of the drawings, yet even then there are no words to excuse the suffering you've witnessed."

Isabela said, "The tragedies you've encountered, Julian, have been compounded by years of struggle and are ceaseless to our moment in history. It needn't be so and, indeed, must not. We've delved into such blackness of spirit and soul as this world has never seen. Faith in goodness is eroded by the experience of evil, and that cannot stand. We need to divert our course and find that hallowed ground upon which peace can reign once again and tears abate."

Perhaps impertinently, I said, "Is that even possible anymore? The things I've seen and heard since leaving the metropolis make me wonder if some wounds are so infected, there's no hope for healing."

Isabela said, "There must be hope, dear. And it needn't appear from the clouds. As we witness these circumstances of our lives, so, too, are we able to form opinions to resolve how we absorb them and choose our way forward. Hope is born from that."

"Those drawings were about hope?"

Rogário shook his head. "No, Julian, I'm afraid not. As Vice-Chairman of the Republic Design Directorate, Leandro Porteus was chosen to provide drawings to the Internal Security Protectorate for a subterranean structure to be located somewhere in the west metropolis. The nature of that structure was to be kept under strictest confidence and identified as a state secret. By our understanding from someone close to Porteus, he created those drawings under extreme duress. Now that we've seen and studied them, his concern is quite evident. What he designed was a massive underground lethal chamber and crematorium in a single edifice. Its location was to be hidden from public view, the determination of which was not to be indicated within the drawings themselves but rather established after the fact of their creation by the Protectorate."

I was shocked. "How massive?" *Good God! No wonder Draxler was so strict with his puzzle.*

Isabela told me, "Scale was not properly referenced by Peter when he copied them, perhaps intentionally, so any estimate is just that. But given the parameters of normal widths and distances, we believe somewhere between five or six acres is within reasonable consideration."

"And built underground?"

"Yes, that's clear."

"And you have no idea where?"

Rogário shook his head. "Not yet, but we certainly will."

"They'll know in the undercity. Castor and Pollux. Those two seem to have eyes on everything."

Isabela said, "Yes, of course. We expect so. A rare genius we've never had the fortune of encountering. There are many regrets in this palace regarding the horrors they've suffered. That world submerged in the dark. How they live now. The brilliance of their survival. It's another reason you're here, Julian. You brought us information through those drawings of Leandro Porteus, and I hope you can see how vital they are. Something is occurring within the Status Imperium and Judicial Council that is greatly disturbing, a change of attitude, a point of view we feel is unusual and contrary to how all of this has been pursued for the past century. We find it extremely troubling, but we don't know enough yet to formulate our own direction and response. We need to be certain before acting."

"I'm not following this. What is the point of view you're worried about? And what does it have to do with me?"

Rogário said, "You've seen children on your journey here, correct? Many children."

"Hundreds," Isabela added. "Haven't you?"

"More than that," I replied. "Probably thousands. First at the train depot outside Albiona, and then everywhere else the train went, clear up to Tamorina where I'd never seen so many kids in my life since Lower School. In trucks, too, up the road past Shadroe Station, after something horrible happened in a bombed-out schoolhouse."

"At Kippel," Rogário remarked. "We know about that. Endless tragedies."

Isabela asked me, "Do you remember the story of the Pied Piper?"

"I think so," I replied. "When I was little. My grandmother used to read to me at bedtime. About the children?"

"In the tale, a Pied Piper was engaged for a nominal fee to rid a village of rats who were devouring all the grain that fed the populace. He did so by playing his magic pipe which induced all the rats to follow him to the river, wherein he caused them all to be drowned. When the Pied Piper returned and asked to be paid, the town elders refused and sent him away. In revenge, he played another melody on his magic pipe that lured all the children from the village into a dark cave, and they were never seen again."

I said, "You believe the Status Imperium is collecting children from the provinces?"

"Yes, we do," Rogário said. "At least somebody is. By the tens of thousands."

Isabela said, "We have a detailed accounting of this. We don't know where they're being taken, but we wish to find out. The drawings Peter stole from Leandro Porteus were rendered more than a year ago. Truth be told, Julian, we believe the lethal chamber may already be constructed."

Rogário said, "No one has definitively connected that with the disappearance of our children, yet there are discrepancies in the explanation of both purposes."

"Lies, actually," Isabela told me. "A pattern of deceit we cannot overlook."

I asked, "How do children get stolen from across the chasm?"

Isabela said, "They don't. Those refugee children you've seen at the rail depots and along the road from Albiona have never been to Laspágandélus and likely never will. Their war-ravaged provinces haven't been a distinct part of our world in three centuries."

"You don't defend them?"

"Mr. Sutro told you our history," Rogário said. "Did he not?"

I nodded. "Yes, and I'd never heard a word of it before today. Not from anyone, even my parents, who are very forthcoming."

Isabela said, "In the years of the Great Separation, our provinces along the Whitestone frontier and across the Fatoma were simple rural communities. The population was scattered about hundreds of miles of farms and communal settlements that relied on road and river trade for commerce. When those trains arrived from Commonwealth Station bearing your unfortunates, that rural world of the eastern provinces was changed forever. Try to imagine crowds by the hundreds of thousands bearing suitcases and trunks and children simply put off trains with nowhere to go and no familiarity with rural life and nothing but fields as far as they could see. Those first few months were a tragedy of great proportion. Thousands died, mostly the elderly and infirm. Infants, too. They were buried in fields and covered over in ditches. Starvation was rampant. Water was scarce. Empty luggage was strewn for miles. A stench of death polluted the wind. Also, the natural inhabitants of those provinces were frightened and wary of these intruders. 'Who are they? Why are they here? Are they threatening?'"

Rogário said, "There were skirmishes and armed conflicts all over. Many innocent people were killed. Rains came and the creeks flooded, and more people drowned or perished from exposure to the elements of the natural world."

Isabela added, "Here at Laspágandélus, we had no notice of the catastrophe for almost two months. By then, the disaster of it was horrifying. We sent help across the Great Chasm and also up the River Alban by boats, hundreds of them with supplies and materials for shelter. And simultaneously, in acts of astonishing generosity, the people of Tarchon and St. Marta and Darrieux and Fabian provinces began embracing your unfortunates and assimilating them into their own settlements, particularly once they realized those suffering by the thousands were refugees, not invaders, and human beings like themselves."

Rogário told me, "The Great Separation cost so many lives, Julian, we can look backward and wonder how anyone survived. And yet, a redeeming good that arose from those terrible disruptions built a world across the eastern provinces that would have been inconceivable in the decades before. From our vantage point, we watched something new appear, a culture that was neither ours, nor yours. A human foundry of necessity and opportunity fused in that crucible of eugenical madness."

Isabela said, "We thought what they'd built was one of the brightest achievements of our history, a greatness to be admired and marveled at."

I said, "And the war ruined it all."

"So useless," she agreed. "A destruction of both societies. To what end? More farmland? Trivánder Province alone is more fertile *and* profligate than Grijalva

could ever hope to be. What needs were not being met on that day Dr. Bernadotte ordered your society across the Florian Border? Did you kill a million
people to grow a better tomato?"

"You can't ask me those questions," I replied. "I grew up in Highland Park
and felt guilty climbing our neighbor's oak tree. I never snuck under Mr. Gross-
man's fence or stole apples from Mrs. Hackett's dooryard. We're not all wicked
by address. I won't excuse the perversions of the Judicial Council or attempt to
define the virtues of eugenics, because I don't believe eugenics offers any virtues that do any lasting good for the breadth of humanity. I would just prefer
not to be blamed for the sins of my wicked neighbors who've never consulted
my opinion on any of their adventures."

Rogário told me, "We entered the war to blunt those adventures, Julian. To
mitigate the slaughter. Our Mignard Institute invented and produced weapons
your armies had never expected or conceived of. To defend the helpless. And
then, sadly, blood was on our hands, as well."

Isabela said, "We tried to give support to all those whose agonies were suffered protecting what they'd dug out of the earth. We had hoped to help them
live, and we did, but they also wanted revenge. To kill, as they'd been killed.
And they did. And your armies suffered then, too."

"Yes, I know. A stalemate of death," I said. "Like I told your hero, Peter Draxler. It's become a mass suicide."

Isabela nodded. "Yes, Julian, it has, indeed."

In frustration, I raised my voice more than required. "So when does it ever
end? *How* does it end? Do we all need to die first?"

The Regents were silent for once. They both stared at me, as if I'd just been
the rude harbinger of the worst possible opinion. I heard a door open and felt
a cold draft from the far end of the room where I noticed a man standing on
the threshold in the same imperial uniform as those guards who had admitted
Mr. Sutro and myself into the palace. He was watching me. Did he worry that
my impertinent voice was indication of a threat to the Regents?

Isabela spoke first. "We wish you to do us one more service, Julian. If you
will."

I frowned. "Could it get me killed? I feel perhaps my luck is running short
these days."

"No, we don't believe so. It's very simple. You need only to take a book with you back to the metropolis and offer it to a seller on Clerk Street in the north Cristel District. His name is Sumner Dawes."

"Which book?"

Rogário took a small thin cloth volume off his lap and slid it across the table to me. The title was *A Child's Book of Fairy Tales*. A very old book. I thumbed a few of the pages. There were plates of fanciful illustrations with each fable.

"We've included his address. You're to tell him it once belonged to a great-aunt of yours whose favorite story was 'The Pied Piper.' If the bookseller is genuinely Sumner Dawes, he'll tell you his mother's most beloved tale was 'The Glass Mountain' and he'll give you fourteen credits and a bill of sale for it. If he does not mention that title, you're to leave, and we'll send you further instructions. It's vital that you don't deviate from this program."

"There's no one else to do this?" I smiled. "Maybe Lewis?"

Rogário frowned. "Impossible. Lewis is unwell."

"That's obvious. Five minutes in his company is all you need to figure that out. Who is he, anyhow? How does he happen to be here? If I may ask."

Isabela said, "His name is Lewis Atherton, and last year he was a graduate teaching assistant in Rare Earth Chemistry and a medical pathology intern at the Mollison Institute. His advisor was Dr. Anton Chalybian, Director of Radiographic Science for the Judicial Council. Lewis was assisting in post-mortem fluid analysis on one of Dr. Chalybian's associates, Ortygia Guyot, who was killed in an accident at the Mollison radiography lab. In Miss Guyot's blood were traces of clothonium particles, a chemical discovered by Hartley Mills Thayer, that is instantly fatal when inhaled as a gas and spectacularly incandescent under the proper conditions. When Lewis brought his results to Dr. Chalybian, he was immediately dismissed from the Mollison Institute for fraud and taken to the Mendel Building. His next appearance was on the western slope of the Great Chasm where we assume he was attempting to reach us. How he escaped from Internal Security we have no idea, and he is unable to tell us. We assume he was tortured extensively."

"Mr. Sutro explained Lewis's obsession with Mary Cumberland. I've tried talking with him, but it's difficult. Those stories he tells. His insanity is quite elaborate. It seems his only friend is that Lancaster fellow in your jail cell."

Isabela shook her head. "That's not our cell. It's been there since Queen Nouille. Perhaps so has Lancaster himself. No one knows for certain."

"Three hundred years?"

Rogário said, "His history, Julian, is older than any of us. The details of that remarkable story are unassailable. What he recalls of Queen Nouille. Like those Aventinians with their Lamus fish at the lake. We can't speak to another's history prior to our own. They've been here longer than our collective memories."

I was feeling cold now. That guard across the room kept the door open and the draft chilled the air. There were so many mysteries here, so many questions. Yet I just wanted to get home. Alive.

I asked, "All right, then. In any case, why me? There's absolutely no one else you could use? Someone more qualified to be a secret agent?"

"Julian, we've lost four already since New Year's."

"Killed?"

"Unfortunately, yes," Isabela told me. "So it appears. We received reports. Fragmented. One died in a motor crash on a hill north of Calcitonia. Another was shot to death in a garage at Schwiefka. A third was strangled and tossed into the sea off St. Etienne Shores. And the fourth was stabbed on Porter Str —"

I didn't hear much more of that one after she had said, "St. Etienne Shores." With everything I'd been through the past month, I'd almost forgotten that horrid adventure in the cold surf by the Barrons' holiday bungalow. Good grief. Was this the solution to our mystery of the dead soldier in the tide? Was it even possible?

Reflexively, I asked, "Who were they?"

Rogário said, "Volunteers who understood the metropolis and our purpose out here. The trouble has been that we've had to falsify identity cards for them and that's always a risk. If agents of your Internal Security recognize the fraud, it means summary execution. We assume that's what happened to each of them somehow. None even reached the Cristel District. We're very disturbed over it."

I was curious now, with a strange feeling about something. The question seemed far-fetched, but I asked anyhow. "My girlfriend, Nina Rinaldi, as I assume you know, sent me to Tamorina to meet up with her daughter's father, Arturo Cascádes. I was told he'd left a month ago, and that fellow who wanted to kill me at Porphyry Hill, Samuel Protiste, said he didn't know where Arturo had gone off to. Do you have any information about that? Nina's going to ask. I need to be able to tell her something useful. Better yet if it's true."

Both Regents looked at me, as if determining what to say, if anything at all. I knew they were keeping secrets from me, and I was glad of it. I really didn't want to know too much about any of this. It just all felt extraordinarily dangerous and frightening.

But Isabela told me, "Arturo Cascádes was one of the four we dispatched to the metropolis. I'm sorry. We haven't been able to establish which one died where, only that all four are dead. Identification was impossible because the Medical Protectorate immediately took possession of each of the four bodies and cremated them one after the other in the basement of the Mendel Building."

All four dead and unidentified. And if Arturo Cascádes was the body I'd floated on to shore that night? How was that possible? I suppose it was unknowable now, but still. What if? The web of coincidence can be profound. How can we ever know what's deliberate and true?

Rogário said, "Julian, we need you to do this favor for us because only you have the diplomatic credentials to bypass the investigative authorities and security interceptions. Those status papers from Dr. Otto Paley give you opportunities none of our other agents had. That diplomatic pouch of yours could eventually save untold lives, but only you can serve its advantage, perhaps even help us find a solution to this entire nightmare that we all agree must come to an end."

"And eugenics?" I asked the Regents, "Do you agree with Peter Draxler that eugenics is itself the disease infecting us all today? That's where this all began, didn't it? And how would that be reconciled with ending the war? Because if it's the cause, and the war is the effect, where does that lasting resolution come from?"

Isabela told me, "We have always believed that this disruption to society brought on by the Status Imperium's decision on eugenical necessities, and the Medical Directorate's pronouncements regarding spyreosis, have created a far greater and more profound rift in our world than the Great Chasm itself. We hope to expose the fraudulent science of spyreosis and show the testing program for what it is: modern medical tools used for social and political persecution."

"And how are you going to do that from fifteen hundred miles away? Will the Judicial Council let you buy advertisements in city newspapers and across the radio waves? I apologize for being impertinent here, but all of this has been going on for a very long time and if it were that easy to put a stop to, well, I just wonder how that can happen."

Rogário said, "Julian, you only see a small part of it. What we've permitted you to see. Our story here is much bigger. Soon, perhaps even tomorrow, we'll send you back to the metropolis with that book of fairy tales which you'll bring to Mr. Dawes. And after that you'll re-enter Thayer Hall and continue your studies with Frederick Barron and see your family again and pursue that endearing love affair with Miss Rinaldi and her child. And while you sleep at night, the wheels here will be turning irrevocably to change the world back to where it was long before any of us were born."

XXXX
∞

I ate dinner in my bed chamber alone that night. Fire hissed on the hearth. Later on, I had a visit from Lewis and then Lalla Goldbeck, who brought us cups of hot cinnamon cider and dessert. Lewis asked for honeyberry pudding. I enjoyed a healthy slice of chocolate cake with sweet vanilla frosting. Lalla Goldbeck cautioned us both against eating too quickly.

"One bite per minute, both of you. No more."

Lewis said, "I'm not sure that's a good rule. My pudding is best warm. That fire isn't hot enough in here. My toes are cold." He wiggled his bare feet.

"You were told to wear stockings after dark, Lewis. You know that. I should think you'd be even colder if you were naked."

"Why do you say that? I'd never be naked in this house. There are too many prying eyes about. You can't trust anybody not to share their nasty opinions."

I laughed.

Lewis stopped his spoon mid-bite to glare at me. "You can't conceive of the gossip concerning you, Julian. For some reason, Mary's been spreading it like a flu. If she were still my friend, of course, I'd put a stop to it, but she said a terrible thing about me yesterday evening and I told her to leave my room and never come back. We're not friends at all, anymore. I hate her."

Lalla Goldbeck smiled. "Enjoy your pudding, Lewis. You know Tablada cooked it just for you."

Lewis took another bite and raised his empty spoon. "I like it quite a lot."

"And you, Julian? Is your cake suitable?"

I'd already eaten several forkfuls before she told us to slow down. "It's delicious."

"I'll bring you a cup of hot cocoa before bedtime. Will you be up late?"

"I don't know. I'm awfully tired from that hike up to the palace, and then my archery lesson."

Lewis had drawn me out into the birch wood late in the afternoon before dinner to shoot arrows at a target he'd made of hay bales and canvas. I was no good at all. My shoulder ached far too much to hold the bow properly, and I felt that each arrow I fired aggravated my wound. But what else was there to do in my last few hours here besides read? Dr. Bernáert had brought me a short history of the Tafilus people who lived on the lower Pilumnas River in that barren era of glacial retreat. He thought it would offer some insight on the progression of historical cultures in these eastern regions. I suppose his aim was to provide me with an appreciation of this lost world beyond the metropolis as I prepared to go home. It was wise. So much to take back with me, and too much of my ridiculous innocence left behind.

After Lalla Goldbeck had gone, Lewis told me, "I've never been happy here. It's not somewhere I would choose to be if I weren't kept off the airship. Lancaster thinks we should steal it and fly out to sea. I don't have any strong opinion about that except to agree we ought to find ourselves another home. Mary Cumberland has ruined everything. I hate her very much."

He ate his honeyberry pudding with deliberation, and I wondered how he envisioned commandeering that airship. Then, curious again about his general remembrance, I asked, "How did you get here?"

After swallowing another bite of pudding, he told me, "I walked a long road, and nobody gave me a ride. Unless maybe I was on a train and I had a ticket. Mary brags all day long how she arrived on the airship and everybody cheered. I didn't mind that she stole my coat because it never fit so well, and I told her to keep it. But she called me a bad name last night and now we're not friends. I hate her."

"What did she call you? If you don't mind sharing."

"Are you sure you want to know? It's a very dirty thing. She was cruel to say it."

"What was the name?"

"Clothonium."

Late that night, as I lay in bed too sleepy to read, I noticed through the window a group of people passing by in another chilly snowfall. Each wore a white hooded robe and held a flaming torch. Those people from the lake? I slipped out of bed and went to the icy glass where I watched them file off through the dense birch wood and into the darkness beyond. Another guarded ritual too ancient to evade? Laspágandélus was the dream of a singular world whose wonder defied common sense, or at least that story of us we had been told and told. I began to wonder how much of this my parents knew, or were aware of, at any time of their lives. As I've said before, we never learned these stories of empires and earthquakes; they were not taught in our schools. But I thought some of us must know. Maybe in the stacks at Harrington Hall or buried in basement boxes of the Mansurette Library at Hollerith Plaza. Maybe filed away by judicial decree in a room of Special Collections within the Status Imperium. Knowledge can be hidden, but not dissolved into vapor. Someone eventually assumes the role of passionate caretaker, and year by year passes it down to favoring acolytes, or surreptitiously shares it about until the moment at last arrives when sunlight bursts upon it once again. I wondered, who among the millions in our grand metropolis knows that such a place as Laspágandélus exists today? Amidst all this torment and turmoil? My father would know. And if he did, so would my mother, his most brilliant half. And Dr. Coffeen? Has he hidden from all his students these many years the truth of our history? Is it possible he conceals that most elemental secret in the dusty cabinets of his office in Room 322 at Grimwood Hall? And if true, how does he possibly lecture, semester after semester, without divulging the essential truths of his lessons? Perhaps hobbled by imperious censors, he teaches what they permit him to by threat or directive, maybe both. Or perhaps this story of Laspágandélus has faded so thoroughly to fable and legend that no stern academic could offer such a contradictory theory of history to uneducated students without the rigorous substantiation of accepted facts. So, what of myself? What do I tell of these things I've seen and learned out here? Would anyone believe me? Well, Freddy would. And Nina, too, who actually knows some of the principal actors in this drama. She'd believe my story, since this was everything she had expected. And my parents? They'd believe me, because I think they knew all of this already. I think they had always known.

My nightstand lamp was still lit when Lalla Goldbeck brought me that cup of hot cocoa she'd promised. The fire smoldered on the hearth. I had drowsed for a bit and was half-asleep as she came into the bed chamber.

"Prop up, Julian," she instructed with her constant smile. "No cause to spill on your pajamas."

I adjusted my pillow. "Thank you."

"How is your shoulder? Is there still much discomfort?"

"A little achy, but a lot better."

"Good." She placed a thick cloth napkin under the cup of cocoa as she handed it to me. "I've mixed in a little morpheus powder with the cocoa to help you sleep."

"Thank you."

"I hope you have pleasant dreams, Julian. It's been wonderful having you here with us. Now, drink that down and go to sleep."

I took a first sip and smiled. "It's very good."

She gave me a sweet kiss on my forehead. "Goodnight, Julian."

I nodded. "Goodnight."

Then Lalla Goldbeck left, quietly closing the door behind her.

Sleeping, I dreamed of a desert, hot and dry. Wind across the shifting dunes. Sand on every horizon. A barren land. Alone I walked for miles and miles. Buzzards drifting on a yellow sky above. A strange dream. A cave in the desert. Hooded anchorites murmuring chants and shaking sticks at scrawny grey jackals. The echoing of wooden flutes. Smoke of censers burning. I was instructed to go into the cave where a prophet of life sat on a ragged carpet and told me about God whose face is found in stone and rules over the world in every moment and has been with us since the beginning of time and is eternal and immutable. Then another prophet spoke in that same cave and told me God exists in the flame of our fires that warm us at night and has burned there since time immemorial, and whose heat cracks the stone of earth that is not immutable. And a third prophet spoke from the shadows in the cave to tell me God inhabits all the waters of earth that wash away the stone of that God who is not immutable and extinguishes the flame of that God who may not burn for time immemorial, and whose waters we drink for our survival through all eternity. And a fourth prophet told me God is a spirit who chases across the air we breathe and whose wind erodes the stone face of that God who is not immutable and extinguishes the flame of that God who is not eternal and sweeps away the God of those waters we drink through all eternity, and whose breath gives us life. And the voice of a final prophet arose to tell me our thoughts are immanent in God before stone and flame and water and air, proof that above all we exist in Him forever and ever. And then in my strange dream there were no more prophets and I left the cave, and one of the hooded anchorites took my arm and told me there is no God but what we choose to call God, and this earth does not observe us at all.

TO A FARTHER COUNTRY

XLI
∞

Then I was sitting in a train compartment with no memory of how I came to be there. I was wearing my father's jacket and had his valise at my side. My shoes were polished. A reflection in the window showed my hair was nicely combed and, somehow, I'd gotten a shave. I was presentable. Seated across from me in the compartment was a fellow reading a morning newspaper. He had the fine appearance of a businessman in a sharp grey suit and tie and reading glasses. I'd never seen him before in my life.

What time was it?

I took out my father's pocket-watch and checked. Just about half-past nine. My stomach wasn't growling, so I assumed I had eaten recently. Perhaps a nice breakfast in the dining car. I felt comfortable, though confused by my apparent amnesia. Where were we?

"Excuse me, sir?"

The fellow lowered his newspaper.

I asked him, "Could you please tell me where we are just now? I guess I dozed off and lost track."

"Well, good morning." He smiled. "We've just passed Porter Station. There's another stop four miles ahead at Mansfield, in case you need to get off there."

My head was so foggy I hardly recognized those names, but they sounded vaguely familiar. "No, I believe I'm riding on to the metropolis. I'm a student at Regency College. At least I think I am."

He laughed. "You think?"

"Yes, sorry. I'm feeling a little cloudy this morning."

"Late night, eh?"

"Maybe." I laughed. "Hard to remember."

"Well, I'm riding through to Lazare, so I'll keep my eye on you when we arrive at Commonwealth Station, see that you get off the train all right."

"Thank you, sir. I'd appreciate that."

"By the way, I'm Franklin Orville."

We shook hands.

"Julian Brehm, sir. Glad to meet you."

"Where are you traveling from?"

How to answer that? Because I wasn't entirely certain. Last thing I recalled was snowfall outside my bed chamber in Clélius House at Laspágandélus. How had I managed to be on this train across the Great Chasm? Who put me here?

I made it simple for both of us. "The eastern provinces. I had an assignment there for Dr. Otto Paley. Nothing too exciting."

"And now you're heading back to school."

"Yes, sir. Long overdue. I hope I'm still enrolled."

"Well, let's just be sure to get you there today, all right?"

"Thank you, sir. I'd appreciate that."

"No trouble at all. Glad to meet you, Julian."

"Likewise, sir. Are you traveling for work this morning, or are you going home, too?"

"Work. Another contract. Orders to fill. I'm a distributions agent for a chemical procurements firm. They send me out to see that everything is organized for delivery in a timely fashion. We try to be efficient for our customers."

"Have you been doing this long? Do you enjoy it?"

"It's a reliable paycheck. Credits to earn. The job isn't particularly difficult, and the rewards are more than adequate. So, I guess I could say I enjoy it. There are worse things in the world these days, isn't that right, Julian?"

Franklin Orville gave me the oddest smile, then went back to reading his newspaper and I stared out the window for a while, watching the countryside go by.

Another lovely spring morning of trees and green grass and wildflowers in bloom. Blue skies and occasional puffy clouds. I was pleased to see houses once more, intact and alive with dogs and small children playing in the yards, laundry on rope lines. And autos driving about on the roads here and there. Trucks, too, hauling lumber and fertilizer for these spring fields of growth and produce. Men and women at useful labor.

I had a brief peek into my valise to see if the diplomatic pouch was still there, and it was. So, too, did I find the envelope with Delia's photograph yet intact. That writing in lemon socco Major Künze had exposed with the match flame was mostly faded away now, but I did remember and felt a sudden sadness over his brutal fate in the trench that night.

After a short while, Franklin Orville got up and excused himself to use the toilet at the end of our passenger car and I noticed the headline on the newspaper he'd been reading.

SIX KILLED IN MOLLISON LOBBY BOMBING

My first thought was Marco Grenelle. My second was a hope that Nina wasn't in the middle of it. Being so far away from her and Delia as I'd been, and through all I'd just experienced, my love for both of them had deepened almost to desperation.

What day was this? The paper said Wednesday. I felt wildly confused.

At the huge Commonwealth Station terminal, most of my fellow passengers prepared to disembark. I'd wanted to say goodbye to Franklin Orville, but he hadn't yet returned from the toilet, so I gathered up my valise and joined the queue at the vestibule. Since we'd been traveling from the eastern provinces, identity papers were requested by agents of Internal Security as each of us stepped off the train. I was used to this now and felt like a seasoned traveler when I took out the diplomatic pouch and withdrew the status directive.

After reading my orders, the agent looked me in the eye. "You know Dr. Paley?"

"No, sir. I was only his envoy to Tamorina last week."

The station was loud and hectic. Steam and that nasty smelling oily black smoke from the locomotives clouded the air of the platform.

"What was your assignment?"

"I'm sorry, sir, but I am not permitted to comment on my business there. Dr. Paley was very strict in that regard."

"Did you travel anywhere else besides Tamorina within Tarchon Province?"

"I'm sorry, sir, but, again, sharing that information would be in direct contradiction to my assignment from Dr. Paley."

People were restless behind me, urgent to depart the train and get on with their mornings.

The agent was firm and deliberate. He stared at me and back again to re-read my status directive. He seemed reluctant to let me pass. Finally, he relented. "All right, you can go. Thank you."

I walked away from the train into a busy crowd. The noon hour had just passed, and thousands of people were rushing off one way or another. I wanted to find a taxi to get back to Thayer Hall where I could telephone Nina and let her know I was alive. The same with my parents. I had no doubt they'd both gone crazy with worry over my fate out there in the Desolation, and I felt sure Mother had pestered Dennett and Trevelyan daily to discover my whereabouts after I hadn't returned by the end of that first weekend. I wondered if Dr. Otto Paley possessed any information that far out into the eastern provinces. Hard to know. Maybe his office had contacted that Brigadier General Dodd to see if I had turned up at Porphyry Hill. Was Dodd even alive after the assault that night? No telling. The viciousness of that attack was profound. How could anyone survive?

Emerging from the station onto busy Hebert Street, I was able to hail a taxi just down the block and give him my destination. We raced across the city toward Regency Heights. After my strange journey, I'd almost forgotten how bright and vast the metropolis felt. The enormous banks and theaters, department stores and office buildings, that hurrying flood of people. I recognized the street signs and storefronts, how people dressed and gathered. The blare of motor horns and the smell of soot and auto exhaust and delightful restaurant aromas. That harried pace and drama of the modern city, a vibrant society alive with its exuberant millions. The beauty and electric madness of our times.

Then Trimble Street to Thayer Hall on a nice warm springtime afternoon. Bicycles gliding by. Students like myself, girls and boys, relaxing on the grass until the next academic hour. Books and notepads strewn about. Talk of pretty things and happy futures. I was let out at the taxi stand down the block and hurried across the street, anxious to tell Nina how much I'd missed her. A few people shouted to me and called my name as I crossed the grass. I waved and went on. The stairs up to the fourth floor felt steeper than I recalled, and I was out of breath when I reached my room.

Freddy wasn't there. Not so big a disappointment, because I'd surely need to defer my story until after speaking with Nina, anyhow. I got out of Father's jacket and emptied the valise into my closet and changed into more normal clothes. My old student identity. I put away the diplomatic pouch into my largest desk drawer, then took out the slip of paper with that call-number to Nina's friend, Johara, on Meltemi Avenue and went back downstairs to the telephones by the third-floor lounge.

I found an empty booth between two giggling co-eds and rang the exchange.

"Station 14, how may I help you?"

I peeked at Johara's number. "Could you please connect me to FULton-9377?"

"Thank you."

The call rang three times. Then a woman's voice I didn't know.

"Hello?"

"Hello? This is Julian Brehm calling for Nina."

"Oh God! Are you sure?"

I smiled. "I think so!"

"She's just out for a walk with Delia. They left school after lunch. Nina's been crazy for you! Is there a number she can reach you? Oh God, this is wild!"

"Ask her please to telephone the exchange at Thayer hall. She's done so before."

"I will. I absolutely will. Oh, she'll be so excited! Thank you!"

"Thank you, too."

We rang off and I sat for a moment trying to decide what to do next. I could go back up to my room and wait for her call. If I did that, Freddy might just appear, and I'd be obligated to tell him the whole business, and I wasn't up to that just yet. I realized what I needed to do was telephone to my parents. They deserved to know I'd made it back alive. I owed them that and, anyhow, I missed them both terribly.

So I rang the exchange once again.

"Station 14, how may I help you?"

"Could you please connect me to ALTair-6025?"

The number I'd known my entire life.

"Thank you."

This time, the number rang eight times. Then my mother's voice. *"Hello?"*

"Hello, Mother."

I heard an audible gasp.

"Oh, my goodness! Julian! It's you! Oh, my! It's you! Good gracious!"

"Yes, Mother, it's me. I'm alive. Are you all right?"

"Where are you, dear? Where are you this instant?"

"At Thayer Hall. My train just came in about an hour ago. I rode a taxi straight here."

"Dear, you simply must come home immediately. You really must. Agnes is here. She'll want to see you."

"Is anything wrong? Where's Father? May I speak with him for a moment? I'm so glad to be back, Mother. You just can't imagine what I've been through. I want to tell you both all about it. Agnes, too. I'm glad she's there."

"Come home now, Julian. Please? We're both here."

And she disconnected.

This was so odd, I felt scared somehow. Freddy was gone. Nina and Delia were out. Mother sounded unlike herself. I wasn't sure what to do. I went up to my room again and wrote a note for Freddy telling him I was back and that I'd explain everything when I returned from Highland Park. I asked him to let Nina know where I'd gone if she telephoned. Then I grabbed my overnight satchel and went to get a taxi for the local train station to Schuyler Province.

When we are young, we see our lives in this world through a lens of endless possibilities, a road ahead with many byways. We can go this way or that way, and either path belongs to us, and we can usually retrace our steps, choose that road we decided to skip last year to see if it's more appealing, after all. But the longer we're here in the world, the more often we discover paths closing behind us, choices narrowing, time intruding on our freedom to experience that life we've imagined would always be ours.

I arrived at home by mid-afternoon and had to ring the doorbell because I'd forgotten my house key back at Thayer Hall. After half a minute or so, Agnes answered, and I felt that rush of love and gave her a big warm hug.

"Jules," she murmured, kissing my cheek. "We missed you so. Everyone's been afraid."

"I know. I'm sorry."

I heard Mother's voice from inside the house. *"Is that Julian?"*

Agnes had tears in her eyes when she stepped back to let me indoors. She called back, "Yes, he's here."

Mother had been in my father's office and came out in a hurry. Her eyes, too, were tearful and she looked tired. Worn out. From worry over me? But I was so happy to see her, my own tears began, and I met her halfway to the kitchen. "Mother!"

She gave me a great hug and I felt her crying and hugged her more tightly. Agnes was sobbing now behind me, and I didn't really understand why. She was naturally emotional and dramatic, but rarely maudlin or especially sentimental. This was extraordinary behavior from her.

Mother eased away slightly to say, "We missed you so much, my darling boy. Frightened out of words. We began to fear the worst when the best was still our hope."

"I know, Mother. All I wanted to do was come home. I was so far away from you, it seemed almost impossible to be here. But now I am, and I don't ever want to feel that way again."

I noticed Agnes standing off my shoulder, watching and crying softly. I didn't understand what was happening, but homecomings are wonderful and difficult all at once when we feel so strongly. I wanted to see Father and have him explain all this to me, how things were while I was gone. He had a gentle voice that knew how to express what he named the "desperate rationality of love."

Mother kissed my cheek, too, then softly took my hand. "Come with me, darling. I need to show you something."

"Is Father home? I have so many stories to tell you all."

"Come, dear."

I looked back at Agnes, whose pretty face was drawn with tears and sadness that were somehow more than a fitful homecoming.

Mother led me down the hallway to my father's office. I thought he might be waiting for us, but he was not. Instead, there was a photograph of him in the center of his desk, a portrait of my father as a young man, perhaps just a handful of years older than I am now. The placement of that photograph was irregular, discordant. Why would he put it there? Where would all his papers go?

My mother sat on the sofa and patted a place beside her. "Come sit with me, darling. I have something to tell you."

I did as Mother asked, and she took my hand. As she did, I felt that premonition of emotional gravity we store for the unimaginable.

She told me, "Julian, we've lost your father. He's left us."

"Left?"

In the shock of that instant, I almost asked, *Where?*

She said, "My dear, he had a great heart spasm last Thursday night down in the billiard room just before bedtime. When he didn't come upstairs as usual, I went looking for him and found him lying on the floor. I telephoned to Dr. Portman who came straight over, but your father had already died."

I felt so vacant in that moment, I tried to explain what had happened. "I've been gone. I didn't know."

"No, you didn't, darling, of course not. But he missed you so much. He was terribly afraid for you. That's all he thought of."

And then the sense of it all boiled out of me and I couldn't feel anything but pain and horror in that loss I had always known would come eventually, but not then. Not when I was yet so young and foolish, so much in need of him.

I began sobbing uncontrollably.

Mother held me and I felt Agnes on the threshold, and I heard her weeping and it all just seemed so black and horrid and unreal. How would I live after his death? Who was I if not his son?

And Mother murmuring to me, "I'm sorry, dear. I'm sorry. He loved you so very much."

And I cried and cried and cried, until eventually I felt so tired, too tired to cry any longer. And that's when I caught my breath for a few moments, and asked, "Is there a funeral?"

"Oh, Julian." Mother kissed my cheek. "It was this past Sunday. We had no expectation of when you might return, so we weren't able to wait. I'm so sorry, dear. So very sorry."

And then I felt unfathomably lost and hopeless and guilty and foolish.

So, Mother let me go and I gave Agnes a good long hug and went upstairs to my bedroom and fell asleep in a house that was no longer quite the home of my childhood.

Later, after dark, Agnes came into my room and woke me for dinner. She told me Mother insisted that we eat together, so I got up and followed my sister back downstairs. The house felt cavernous in Father's absence. That voice I was so accustomed to hearing across those rooms and down our hallways echoed in my head, that memory of him. Stilled and hidden. *Such as it will always be from this day forward.*

We ate quietly, a roast chicken Mother prepared with buttered greens from Stoller's market and a loaf of bread Agnes had baked while I slept. I remember we seemed to avoid staring at each other, perhaps some pointed aversion to sorrow that collects with togetherness.

Next, Mother brought out a peach pie with vanilla cookies for dessert. Agnes just picked over hers with a careless fork, but I ate all of mine with appreciation for how my mother was able to keep her routine. I loved her even more for that. Agnes took her plate into the kitchen and came back out with a pot of steaming black Massot tea and poured each of us a cup. While we sipped, Mother said, "Perhaps this would be a good time for you to tell us your story, Julian."

I finished a cookie and had a drink of tea. "Are you sure? It doesn't need to be now."

"Yes, please. As your father used to say, 'There's nothing more diverting than a good diversion.' And I think the three of us need a good diversion this evening. Don't you agree, Agnes?"

My sister offered a slight nod and went back to her tea.

"Well, it's just an impossible story," I began, "but it's all true, and I can hardly believe it myself."

"I'm sure your father would have wanted to hear every word of it, so just pretend he's here with us and don't leave anything out. I need to know every mile my baby boy traveled there and back."

"All right, Mother." I smiled. "I promise."

Then I took another sip of tea and began a story that took me on a train through the empty fields and rubbled towns of our Republic, past sad and worried people, blood and mud and rain across a river of death. And the horrors of our war, bewildering cruelties, betrayals and hatred and fear. Voices of a horrid and tragic landscape. All those orphaned children. That trench at night. Then snowfall in a distant land whose strange beauty and ancient mysteries defied description, whose voices were delicate and curiously unexpected, and where love of life and society's wonders held perhaps the best heart of this world.

An hour had passed by the time I described waking up on the train this morning. I finished by saying, "And then I came here to be back with my family whom I love very much."

Mother reached out to take my hand, and I felt grateful. Her eyes were moist and so were mine. Agnes kept her head down. The neighborhood was quiet outdoors.

My mother said, "It's astonishing, Julian. Just astonishing."

"It is, isn't it?"

She shook her head slowly. "I'm at a loss. I really am."

Then Agnes spoke up, her voice flat and bitter. "Well, I don't believe any of it, not a single word. It's just not true."

Mother frowned. "Agnes?"

My sister said, "It can't be so, Mother. Tell him right now. None of it's true."

I said, "Aggie, it's all true. Every word of it. Why would I make it up?"

"Because you hate the Council! You think they're murderers."

"You haven't seen what I did out there in the Desolation. Those bodies in the woods, that schoolhouse, those prisoners burned alive at Porphyry Hill."

"Now you're lying," she said, rising from her chair. "Why are you lying? What good does it do to say things like that? Those people are all diseased. Our army is protecting us from them. Don't you see that? If it's not them, it'll be us dying. Is that what you want? Mother and me to be dead like Father?"

Mother stood, too. "Agnes! Stop that now! You're being cruel and I won't have it. Your brother has just come back from a very terrible place and he's trying to tell us what he experienced there."

"He's not telling us the truth, Mother. We don't murder innocent people like they do. If we have to kill, it's in defense of our own lives here. Don't you care about that? Obviously, Jules doesn't."

I stepped in. "Aggie, that's not true at all. I do care very much. What I saw everywhere I went out there showed me that we need to stop this war before everyone's killed."

"And let those monsters win?" She almost shrieked. "Good grief! Are you insane, Jules? Do you think the Council are all idiots? I suppose you know more about this war than they do. Is that it? You're the great expert now?"

Mother said, "Agnes, that's enough."

"I'm embarrassed he's my brother. I wished he hadn't come back."

"Agnes!"

My sister ran off and went upstairs to her room. We heard the door slam shut.

I waited a bit, then said, "I'm sorry, Mother. I had no idea she'd react like that. I'd have saved the story for another night otherwise."

She sat down again. "Good gracious, Julian, it's not your fault. Your dear sister has some growing up to do. Her year at Branson hasn't been free of turmoil. She's had fits with everyone, including your father, and I've tried coping by keeping out of her way whenever possible, but, as your father has often said, Agnes can be so unreasonable."

"Does she have many friends there? Maybe her agitation comes from being away from home."

"Oh, I dare say your sister has plenty of activities to keep her occupied. She was even seeing a young man from Davidson Hall last month. I gather they were quite the item until Agnes blew it up over some error in judgment he made that did not sit well with her. Once she sent him out the door, of course, she regretted her haste and had me on the telephone with her for three hours. I suspect they may have patched it up already, but either way, your father was quite concerned and thought perhaps we ought to bring her home. Now he's gone and your sister's here and I'm not sure what's best for her."

"I suppose I've poured oil on that fire, haven't I?"

Mother reached out and took my hand. "Not at all, darling. As your father would say, 'you've only made our hearts sing.'"

"Thank you, Mother. I love you, too. Maybe you should keep Agnes here with you for a while longer, so you're not entirely alone."

"Good gracious, Julian. I absolutely refuse to babysit your sister. Never mind her behavior toward you this evening, Agnes is almost an adult. No, she and I have discussed this. Your sister has to go back to Branson on Friday. They've allowed her a week off from studies to mourn her father, but after this she has to get on with it. We all do."

"I suppose so. I just can't understand why she was so offended. Maybe I ought to go upstairs and apologize. It wasn't my intention to upset her."

"I know that, darling. As I said, she's had a difficult year. Acclimating to Branson has been a trial. She'll survive. Your sister is very headstrong. She won't let herself be pushed out."

"But what did I do to make her so angry? I just told you both what I saw."

"Well, that young man I mentioned apparently has family relations with someone involved in the Council. Agnes wouldn't tell us precisely whom, only that she met her sweetheart at chapel where he's in the choir."

I was astonished. "She goes to chapel now?"

Mother smiled. "Evidently she finds it inspiring. And your father and I were told many of the evening sermons at Branson feature a theology of divine intervention that include God's eugenical intentions toward the unfavored. We heard those sermons are very well attended."

"It's madness, Mother. After all I saw out there, if Agnes truly —"

The telephone rang.

Mother paused a moment, then got up to answer it. I indicated to her that I'd bring the dishes into the kitchen. She shook her head and waved me off. The telephone rang again, and she picked up. "Hello? ... Oh, Nancy! Yes, thank you so much!"

She shooed me away, so I shrugged and left the dining room. I'd help her wash our dinner plates when she was off her call with Nancy Lilienthal, a good friend from Bakewell House and the neighborhood garden club.

I stood out in the hall and tried to decide what to do. Should I go upstairs and try to mend fences with Agnes? She could be terribly obstinate when the mood struck and reasoning with her then was impossible. Once when we were little, our parents decided we ought to take a family excursion to Lake Roeding about an hour south of home. Father, Mother and I agreed that was a nice choice for the afternoon, but Agnes insisted we ride to the zoo out on Vernon Boulevard where she could pet the llamas and ride a donkey. Obviously, we weren't going to do that. Mother wanted a real drive out into the countryside to see the sunny fields and tall trees of north Lamyrus Province and Paget township from where her own family hailed, and where she'd attended Lower School as a young girl. Agnes refused to budge from her zoo. She stamped and shrieked and wailed and had to be carried to the auto and put into the back seat with my mother, who hugged her like a blanket the length of the drive. Not until we parked by the lake and Agnes saw geese on the shore did her mood change and she splashed about all afternoon.

I chose to let her be.

The door to our billiard room was open at the end of the hall. I was afraid to go downstairs. My father had died there. That room where he and I shot games of billiards and threw darts was haunted by the man Mother had found lying on the floor. How could I go down those stairs? That familiar odor of our carpet and wood paneling and leather pockets of the billiard table would overwhelm me. My memory of him in that room would no longer be the exuberant father who taught me how to hold the cue stick and strike the ball when I was his little boy and all the world was new. I could smell the scent of his cologne and those cigars he smoked, the blue gel he used to slick back his hair. My father was the man I intended to be when I grew up. I'd be big and strong as he was. I'd speak with the same authority and kindness. I'd earn the admiration of people around me as he evidently did. I'd marry a woman who would love me as Mother loved him and have my own children and show them how possible the world can be when we love and respect each other in every little thing. Standing in the hall, staring at that open door to the last place on earth my father ever knew, I understood how our conversations had ended, and my charge now was to go forth and be the man he hoped and expected I'd become.

I closed that door to the downstairs and instead went up to my bedroom and laid down for a while. I was too tired to ride the train back to Thayer Hall and decided to stay the night. Perhaps I'd try to make up with Agnes in the morning. She was just scared, like the rest of us.

The doorbell rang and I heard Mother go to answer it. I expected Nancy Lilienthal had come for tea and consolation. Without her crowd of friends, I think my mother would feel troubled. For one as sociable as she was, that perpetual garden of hers could not possibly satisfy her heart.

From up in my room, I heard sounds of conversation in the living room where Mother usually hosted her card games, those festive occasions. On normal evenings, my father would often retire to his office for reading where he had all those books of his, authors he admired. Strelinsky, McClymonds, Burns, Stassen, Zarité, Alexis Martin. Lots of others. Also, his Classical histories and art books and leather-bound volumes on law and business. It felt odd and sad to consider that if Mother permitted, many of them would belong to me now.

Agnes had the radio set playing in her bedroom across our upstairs hall, and I could hear that Romaine Royale string and brass combo my sister adored. "When Eventide Falls" and "Whispering Elms." I thought they were drab, but musical tastes do vary. She was more than entitled. My window was propped open to the evening draft scented of spring foliage and freshly mown grass. This time of my life ought to have been the most beautiful ever. Now I'd just learned there is no such thing as 'ever,' that each moment provides a plot we can neither escape nor hold onto. We live as it comes and that's all there is.

"*Julian!*"

Mother called to me from downstairs. I sat up and listened.

"*Come down, please!*"

I assumed Nancy Lilienthal wished to offer words of solace for which I was to be appreciative, as that was the thing to do. So I got up and went down the hall to the staircase where I saw my beautiful Nina Rinaldi waiting there at the bottom with Mother.

Standing in the hall, Nina wiped away her tears and mine. "Freddy told me about your father when I telephoned for you. I couldn't wait any longer, so I took the train here. Freddy gave me the address."

My mother smiled. "This is a very intrepid and persistent young woman, Julian. She has a lot to say. I'll leave you two alone." She gave me a kiss on the cheek as she passed on her way back to the kitchen, whispering in my ear, "She's quite adorable. I approve."

Nina and I went into the living room where I kissed her and kissed her and held her as I had imagined all those nights I'd been gone. That hair smelled as lovely as ever, that scent of smoky Amata perfume. Her cocoa-dark eyes glittered in the lamplight where we sat entwined on my parents' old tan sofa.

"I missed you so much," I told her, and kissed her again. "You and Delia. It's been awful away from you."

"I thought I would die," Nina said, "every moment you were gone. I didn't know if I'd ever see you again, you were gone so long. I tried not to think about what might be happening to you out there, but I made wishes each night on my pillow and saw you in my dreams, so I had hope."

Seeing her now, particularly with what had happened here, brought more tears. "I felt so far away."

She saw that and kissed me and drew me to her breast and held me so close I could feel her heart. She murmured, "I'm so sorry about your father. Yes, I desperately needed to see you for my own sake because I missed you so terribly, but when Freddy told me your father had died, I just had to come here and be with you."

"I love you, Nina. I really do. I don't know how to live without him. And yet, you're here now and it just feels so important to have us together."

"I love you, too, Julian. I need us together, too."

We sat there in each other's arms for longer than I can remember. I heard Mother fiddling about in the kitchen, then the light went off in there, and she went upstairs.

Another little while passed, and in her softest voice, Nina asked, "Did you give the picture to Arturo?"

How could I explain this? Arturo Cascádes was hidden beneath my whole story. I told Nina, "He wasn't there at all. Samuel Protiste told me he'd left a month ago and didn't know where he'd gone."

Nina stared at me, eyes moist with tears. "Did anybody ask?"

"At the hospital he wasn't on the work schedules, and Protiste told me he'd gone out to Arturo's apartment and had the landlady open up the apartment to have a look and they found it empty. He even owed rent."

"I don't understand."

"Neither did I."

Nina sat back onto one of the couch pillows to be comfortable. Then she said, "Tell me everything, Julian. Please? I want to know about all of it."

And so I did.

At the end of my telling, she was terrified for me, astonished at the fact of Priscilla Draxler, completely ignorant of the existence of Laspágandélus, and quite bitter about Samuel Protiste. She told me, "Sammy's a traitor to our cause. Marco's friends would've killed him if they'd found out. I thought he was a friend. I hate him now. I'm glad he's dead."

I offered Freddy's favorite quote from Hamlet, "*A man may smile and smile and be a villain.*"

She kissed me again and I knew we were both desperate to make love. So we went upstairs to my bedroom and locked the door behind us. Agnes still had her radio playing, though she might have been asleep. Nights were when she used music to help her drift off. My parents' bedroom was down the hall in a lovely suite overlooking the backyard and garden. I wondered how awful it must be for my mother to sleep alone, knowing she would never hear Father breathing beside her again in this life. A crushing defeat of love and that failed promise of its deathless bond.

Nina and I undressed quickly and slid under my sheets and made love quietly with that urgency we both expected after all that drama and distance. It had to be enough, and so it was. Afterward, Nina told me she needed to work in the morning and could not possibly stay overnight with me. I agreed and thought I ought to ride the train back with her to attend Dr. Coffeen's class at eight o'clock. Father would want me back in school.

We showered together and dressed in the bathroom and I wrote a note for Mother, explaining the rationale for my return to Thayer Hall that night. I promised to telephone later in the morning and come back home as soon as I could. I went down the hall and slipped the note under Mother's door and went downstairs with Nina to telephone for a taxi to the rail station. The late train was at midnight and we caught it just in time.

Back in the metropolis that night, Nina took a taxi from the train station to Johara's house on Meltemi Avenue and I hired my own to Thayer Hall. I asked Nina about the Mollison bombing and she just shrugged. She told me she hadn't seen Marco since before I left and had no desire do so. His ideas terrified her. We decided to meet for dinner later that next evening at a restaurant she loved in Simoni District and study on the meaning of the fairy tale book I was to deliver to that Dawes fellow on Clerk Street. On the train, I'd discovered it hidden in my jacket pocket. I suggested bringing Freddy along to help see through the knot of conspiracies, and Nina agreed that was a good idea.

Meanwhile, I crept into my fourth-floor bedroom at just before two in the morning. I found Freddy fast asleep and went to do my toilet without disturbing him. After that, I crawled into my own bed, desperate to fall asleep. I was so tired, yet my heart ached over everything I'd experienced since waking aboard the morning train to Commonwealth Station.

XLII

Freddy had gone to his early Theology class with Stubblefield before I woke up, so I missed him and breakfast, and was late to Philosophy in Classical Languages. I chased Dr. Coffeen over to his office at Grimwood Hall after class let out to get a schedule of all the assignments I'd missed. His door was open, but I knocked anyhow, and he looked up from his desk where he'd just sat to go over some papers of ours. He smiled. "Why, hello, Mr. Brehm! We've missed you. That incisive commentary for which you're notorious."

"I'm sorry, sir. I've been away."

"Is that so? I assumed you were ill. To which adventures were you drawn in the middle of this academic spring?"

I'd been waiting all morning to tell him this. I thought Dr. Coffeen would appreciate my journey more than anyone at Thayer Hall.

I said, "Laspágandélus."

At first, he laughed. "A fantastical dream, eh? Research in the old stacks?"

I walked forward into the office. "May I sit down, sir?"

He nodded to the chair in front of his desk. "Please do. You have my curiosity piqued."

"I've been in Clélius House and to Laomedonia, and just a few days ago at an audience with the Regents Nouille in the palace Désallier."

He stared at me. Wordless. Since I'd assumed his historical erudition provided a familiarity with those names, that astonishment on his face was genuine.

Lowering his voice, Dr. Coffeen said, "Mr. Brehm, that is quite a pronouncement. You might just as well have told me you've flown to the moon and back."

"No, sir. The Regents' airship won't fly that high, but it can easily cross the Great Chasm."

Dr. Coffeen got up from his desk and went around me to close his office door. Then he returned to the desk and sat back down. His hands folded, that studious expression on his face we've seen in lectures, he said, "Mr. Brehm, are you asking me to believe you've been to the seat of Empire?"

"Yes, sir. Though not intentionally. I had a recent obligation to Tamorina that took me to Crown Colony and across the Alban River toward Porphyry Hill where I was wounded in the trenches during a night assault. Apparently, I was flown by airship to Laomedonia directly from the battlefield where they performed a surgery on me mid-flight. Look here." Anticipating this very conversation, I'd worn a shirt to class that allowed me to expose my left shoulder where the bullet wound was still quite visible and ugly. "I'm healing, but it aches now and then, and I don't yet have full use of my arm."

"The newspapers reported a big victory at Porphyry Hill just last week. Did you read about that?"

"No, sir. I only saw our soldiers getting killed. It was a hellish nightmare."

This was more complicated than I'd expected. Somehow, I had thought Dr. Coffeen would be thrilled to hear I'd visited the sites of our historical legends, even though I, personally, had never heard of those places until I was there.

Dr. Coffeen leaned forward. "Mr. Brehm, that our Republic was formed out of distant and disparate provinces to create this coherent nation goes to our understanding of who we are as a distinct people. To most, Laspágandélus, like Homer's Troy, is an incoherent myth. For you to sit here in this office and tell me you've actually walked those sunny grounds is difficult to accept."

I smiled. "Actually, sir, it snowed during my entire stay there. Lake Nouille was even icy along its shore."

Coffeen's expression flattened. "Describe the palace mount of Désallier for me, please."

Although mostly lacking in a proper architectural vocabulary, I did my best. In fact, I asked for a paper and pencil to make a crude sketch of the ascending steps and ancient edifice of the Jovian Temple and the wing additions ordered by Queen Nouille. While doing so, I related Mr. Sutro's tale of the great earthquake and the damage he told me the palace had suffered. I even added a brief description of my airship ride at night over Laomedonia and the Great Chasm.

Once I'd finished, Dr. Coffeen studied the sketch, then suddenly tore it up and tossed it into a wastebasket beside his desk.

I was shocked. "Sir?"

He smiled. "I believe you. And it's goddamned remarkable. In fact, I'm envious of you being able to see the royal estate. Did you visit Illium, as well? Good gracious, the stories I've heard of that place. The Mignard Institute. Is there truly such a thing?"

"Yes, sir. Mr. Sutro told me about it, but I didn't go there. He said it's beyond the lake near the Pilumnas River."

Dr. Coffeen nodded. "So I've heard."

"Sir, I haven't lied to you about any of this. I only wanted to tell you where I've been because I thought you'd be intrigued to hear all about it, and then maybe you'd be sympathetic as to why I've been absent from so many classes."

"Don't concern yourself about that. We'll catch you up. I have a syllabus of notes you can study from. The paper your classmates were assigned is due on Tuesday, but I'll give you another week to complete it. We'll just say you've undergone a vital surgery and were incapacitated. If anyone asks, you can show them your shoulder." He shuddered. "It's quite convincing."

"Thank you, sir."

"Some advice here?"

"Yes?"

"You shouldn't go about speaking of Laspágandélus. Not in this political atmosphere. The Status Imperium asserts its dominion over the eastern provinces and our right to express military force out there based on the assumption of imperial domain they claim to possess. If it were known and accepted that their historical position is false, then the justification of this war in the Desolation would be shattered and many lives and reputations soiled forever. Too many people have died on the grounds of that essential lie. Be careful, Mr. Brehm. Very careful!"

I found Freddy waiting for me when I got back to the room after Law and Modern Science with Dr. Sternwood, who got the "vital surgery" version of my absence. He seemed both amenable to my story and uninterested, merely advising me to read ahead and study up on the quizzes he'd given so I could take them next week.

Freddy greeted me at our door with a heartfelt smile.

"My stalwart roommate!"

"Hello, Freddy."

He gave me a nice hug and warm pat on my back. "I'm so sorry about your father, Julian. I was stuck here, but my parents attended the funeral. They said the service was very fitting. Everyone missed you. No one had any idea when or even if you'd be back. Lots of tears."

I was touched by Freddy's appreciation of all that. He really was a great fellow. I was lucky to have him as a close friend and roommate.

I told him, "It's just been so much I don't know where to begin. You wouldn't believe it. All the things I've seen."

Freddy grabbed his keys. "Are you hungry? I'm starving. I had a study session at seven and had to skip breakfast."

"I was late to Coffeen, so I didn't eat, either."

"Then let's go feed our sorrows with a good doughnut. I want you to tell me how many times you dodged the grim reaper out there, and how it all went with Draxler at the Dome."

"Oh, that's right. You'd already gone downtown with your two pets. That feels like seven years ago now."

"Burt got expelled. Did you hear?"

"He did? Good grief, what for?"

"What else? Cheating on exams. He had a system that apparently involved stealing a key to a couple of his professors' offices. He was sneaking in at night and copying out answers he'd paste into his shirt somehow. I'm not sure of the particulars, but Bailey said it was damned clever and almost foolproof."

"Except it got him kicked out of school."

"Evidently."

Arriving just after noon bells, we found the cafeteria jammed with hungry students and it took us almost half an hour to get our food. We grabbed a table in a corner by the kitchen where no one else wanted to sit. I had a gravy chicken pie and carrots and a peach muffin with hot tea. Freddy took some sort of egg and tomato casserole with toast and a cup of black coffee. Telling him my story was different from either my mother or Nina because he knew more details of how I'd been led up to it. He'd also predicted the threats apparent in all this and was not much surprised when I let him know what those drawings actually represented.

Freddy said, "I told you those agents at Internal Security were wicked. I'm sure most of them are just as psychopathic as that Grover fellow of yours on the train. It seems like their solution for everything is to kill more people. Do you really think they murdered that fellow in the surf, Nina's boyfriend?"

"We don't know the body was Arturo's."

"Could've been."

"Yes, and an astounding coincidence if it was, but we'll never know. They cremated it, probably right off the beach. Very spooky."

"Your friends from imperial fairyland need to fly back here to the metropolis and sort this all out for us. It's obvious we can't do it on our own." He lowered his voice. "By the way, do you really think your little Marco did that Tuesday bomb at the Mollison Institute?"

"I don't know anything about that yet," I said. "Nina doesn't either. She hasn't seen him since before her house was attacked. They hate each other."

Freddy stirred his eggs with a butter knife. "Well, I ask because those security agents from Prospect Square have been snooping about campus talking to everyone as if we're all crazy conspirators. They haven't gotten here yet, but they will. Thayer Hall has a reputation for free thinkers. Knowing Bailey's crowd and those idiots in Sigma Nu, I don't believe it's entirely deserved, but reputations are usually built more on rumors than fact. Since you had that pouch from Dr. Paley, I'm sure they know something about your travels, and they'll be pretty curious about what you actually did out there."

I cut my chicken pie into quarters and sloshed the gravy about. I took a bite. Not half bad. "Look, Freddy," I told him, "except for those two maniacs on the train, everyone I spent any time with at all out there was killed before I was flown to Laspágandélus. And Dr. Coffeen more or less told me the Council doesn't want to hear anything about the Regents, so that tells me nothing I saw or heard on that side of the Chasm is getting back over here."

"But that Sutro fellow told you the Council knows the empire out there exists, right?"

"That's what he said."

"So maybe they're scared of it."

"Maybe."

Freddy spread raspberry jam on his toast and took a bite. Then he told me, "We have to take that book of fairy tales to Clerk Street. Maybe tomorrow? You're not allowed to do this one alone. I promised your mother and sister

I'd look out for you if you made it back from the Desolation. You did, so I'm here."

I ate half my chicken pie and drank some tea.

Then I said, "Now Agnes wishes I'd died out there. She thinks every word I said about the Desolation and what I saw and heard was a lie."

"She's rather odd, if you don't mind my saying so. She'd be great friends with Ramona and Henrietta. They could start a girls club of nasty dispositions."

"You and I are having dinner with Nina tonight at Tusci, that Etruscan restaurant she likes out in Simoni. I've never eaten there, but my parents have. They said it was good."

"Baked onions, scallops in Vironila sauce, honey grain biscuits and tall bottles of jade Morini. Bailey and I got so drunk we gave our taxi directions to Novotny rather than Thayer. Cost us more than dinner to get him turned around. I'd forgotten all about that."

"Well, don't drink tonight. We've got to figure this all out. Get that fellow the book tomorrow, then maybe try to discover where all those children went. Freddy, you have no idea how many I saw. Probably thousands. I didn't believe they were all refugees. I don't know what the point of it was, but something just wasn't right with that story. Especially coming out of Grover's mouth and his pet monkey, Arlo. If you'd been there, I'm sure you'd agree."

"If I'd been there with those fellows, I'd probably have jumped off the train. I bet once they kill enough people, it's nothing more than buttering toast to them."

I agreed. "They're all insane."

After lunch, I took a nap for a couple of hours and woke up more groggy than usual, so I dressed and went down to the gymnasium for a swim. Water revives me. At mid-afternoon, there weren't many students about other than a gaggle of co-eds splashing each other at one end of the pool. One of them was Angelina Jouvenon, who'd sewn my secret pocket. She waved and I waved back and wondered if Freddy had indulged that attraction Angelina clearly had for him. Maybe I'd ask him at dinner. He'd be embarrassed, and then Nina would get the truth out of him. Angelina was very pretty. Maybe too pretty for Freddy, who was actually fairly insecure for a fellow who strutted about like he owned a harem.

I swam my fifty laps, ignoring the silly girls. Some husky fellows came into the gymnasium to exercise a particular sports routine. Probably Field Day heroes or a crew from our Regency College Boating Association. A handful went down to that far end of the pool, dangling feet into the water and flirting with the cute giggling co-eds. It was hard not to be envious of all that. And yet, perhaps unfairly so, I thought of Reece Clauston and García Arqueles who'd likely seen the last of girls in this life. Could they possibly have survived that horrendous assault on the trenches to enjoy another tepid meal in those damp mess hall tents? Then again, maybe somehow those two boys had made it back to the Alban River, after all, where even now they were dangling their sore and muddy feet in the cold water of empires and staring across to the far shore where motor transport waited to bring them home. Can't some dreams come true?

As I climbed out of the pool, I was treated to the sight of Pindar and Quixote wrestling on the big mat across from the climbing ropes. They were really just rolling around and laughing hysterically. I grabbed my towel and dried off, then went over to have a word with them. A new group of athletic dribbling-football monsters came in and gave the skinny poets a fierce glare that chased them off the wrestling mat. I caught them on their way to the shower stairs.

"Hello, boys!"

Pindar almost bounced. "Julian! Where've you been? We haven't seen you in weeks!"

"Really? Have you been here? I thought you two dropped out of school."

"We can't afford to," Quixote told me. "Our parents would cut off our allowances and probably disown us."

Pindar said, "Then we'd have to quit our poetry clan. I'd rather slit my wrists."

"Me, too," Quixote agreed. "It's our only purpose in life."

"They're symbiotic, Julian," Pindar said. "If you attended one, you'd understand. Otherwise, you're not experienced enough to see the poetic truth of things as we do."

"It's a form of hypnosis," Quixote explained, "blending intellect with the artistic."

Pindar told me, "Peter says school is a vapor. Much too insubstantial to take seriously. We really would drop out if it were possible."

Quixote said, "Our clan meets at midnight tomorrow in the basement of Jimmy Potatoes on Olivette Street. Stroke of twelve. We recite our sacred convocation, then begin the readings. They're incredibly inspiring. You just have to come!"

I was curious. "Will Draxler be there?"

Pindar sagged. "Actually, we haven't seen him lately. Rumor tells us he went to the sea for a while where his mother lives on a fishing boat. We hear she's a poet, too. I guess it runs in the family. If you need to find him, we can leave a note on our bulletin board. It's becoming very popular."

"Or maybe just telephone to that number Peter had us give you," Quixote said. "Did you two meet up?"

I smiled. "Yes, we did. He's an engaging fellow. We had a nice chat."

"Lucky you," Pindar said. "He rarely has time for us. We're probably too young or stupid for him."

"I'm sure you do your best."

Quixote beamed. "Come to the poetry clan tomorrow night, all right? You'll be our guest. It's invitation only."

"I'll try."

Pindar said, "Midnight at Jimmy Potatoes! Don't forget! There'll be a special appearance of the Pied Piper by invitation from one of our newest members, Ingall Ülrichs. We're promised his performance will be memorable. You won't want to miss it!"

"Who?"

"The Pied Piper!" Quixote laughed, as he and Pindar got up to leave. "Come by, and you'll see."

XLIII

F reddy and I rode a taxicab at nightfall to 113 Garmo Street in Simoni District, a part of the metropolis that was relatively clean and well-lighted. That meant the gutters were clear of refuse, sidewalks were swept regularly, and all the streetlamps had functioning bulbs. Little of those simple niceties were observed in the Catalan, for example. People in Simoni also had nicer houses on prettier streets and the apartment buildings were not so sooty and bleak as elsewhere in the metropolis whose burdensome tax revenues seemed to have been wasted elsewhere. Of course, Simoni Hill also had the Molly Institute and Braden College, where thousands of cherry trees bloomed in the spring and the children of the successful and well-bred matriculated into the best society.

Garmo Street was about a quarter up Simoni Hill bordering a pleasant residential neighborhood of elms and willows, purple trumpet vines and lovely flower gardens. The evening air was lushly redolent of spring cheer and wet earth. The taxi let us off at the bottom of Garmo where it intersected Lima Avenue and traffic was busier with dozens of stores and markets. Nina was waiting for us by a mailbox on the corner there. She wore a pretty floral print skirt and frilly blouse, bohemian fashion that described her extravagant personality as well as anything. I loved it. To my eye, she always looked beautiful.

She smiled as we walked up. "You boys are not punctual!"

I checked my watch. "You said seven o'clock! We're not late."

Freddy disagreed. "It's a quarter after, dear roommate. We've made your princess wait. That is not acceptable." He bowed to Nina. "Please accept our sincerest apology."

I laughed. "It's his fault. He was flirting in the stairwell with a freshman co-ed on our way out."

He shook his head and told Nina, "I was not flirting. She needed directions to the room of one of our colleagues. I was being helpful."

"You gave her *our* room number!"

"That was an innocent error. Our number circulates through my brain constantly. I can't avoid it."

"And you hoped she'd give up on that Morris fellow and come see you later, instead."

"Derek is an idiot. The girl can do better."

Nina laughed. "You two are hopeless." She took my arm. "Come along, handsome. Let's go eat."

The Tusci restaurant was decorated like some octagonal Persian smoking parlor. Oriental carpets and cloudy amber globe lamps and round painted tables and kentia palms. Torchéres protruding between embroidered tapestries on each wall. The dining room was crowded and noisy with liquor-enthused patrons. Fortunately, Nina had booked us a reservation in a tiny alcove off the main room where we were able to escape the revelry. Ours was a small table whose inlaid surface of ivory and indigo represented a night sky of star-flung astrological purpose. We almost hated to require cotton place mats and silverware. It felt sacrilegious. Freddy insisted we refuse the menus and let him order for all three us. Since Nina had eaten there often, she agreed and those two ganged up on me.

"You'll just need to trust us, Julian," Freddy said. "This city only offers so many true delights and dining here is one you can't miss. Isn't that right, Nina?"

She nodded. "Julian isn't too adventurous with food, so he'll need to be convinced."

"Then let's begin with a table carafe of Morini. We can't go wrong there. One glass and Julian will agree to anything."

I told them, "My only requirement here is that we order dinner before we begin drinking. I can't let myself get confused about food. Will you agree to that?"

Freddy said, "Of course, because I'll be ordering for us."

Nina asked, enthusiastically, "Ijoujak?"

Freddy beamed. "Indeed!"

Nina laughed. "Julian is in so much trouble." She leaned over to kiss me. "Just remember we love you."

Fearing the worst, I shrugged. "I'll certainly try."

Next our waiter came, a gracious coal-black fellow perhaps from Togo and wearing a purple fez, and Freddy announced our dining requests. After that, we three sat back and let the evening unfold.

First up, I told them about coming across Pindar and Quixote at the gymnasium and my invitation to Jimmy Potatoes and the midnight tomorrow Pied Piper performance.

Freddy said, "I haven't been inside the sporting hall since freshman year. Exertion of any sort, but especially the deliberate athletic variety, holds no appeal. I can barely bounce a ball consistently and feeling winded terrifies me."

"You can't go to Jimmy Potatoes alone, Julian," Nina said, her eyes and skin glowing in the amber lamps. "I hope you realize that. Those poet boys aren't legitimate. They seem queer and I don't trust them. I bet their poems are stupid."

"Do you not trust them because you think they're queer or because you imagine their poetry is stupid?"

Freddy asked, "Have you read any of the poetry from that clan? Are they any good?"

"No, I haven't, but that's hardly a reason to dismiss the authenticity of their passion. And whether or not they're queer isn't at all relevant here. I don't care in the least about that. I think they're both good boys. Odd, to be sure, but basically decent."

Freddy added, "We are not angels now, nor shall be."

Our waiter arrived with the carafe of jade-green Morini. He distributed balloon glasses among the three of us and poured our first servings. Then he bowed and left. Freddy raised his glass in a toast. "To our returning Julian, our jovial prince, and goodly to the sight!"

Nina leaned over to kiss me. Glasses clinked and Morini was sipped, a curious taste of liquored syrup and heat. Then I raised my glass. "To my father, whom I'll miss forever. 'His heart's as far from fraud as Heaven from Earth.' Godspeed, Father."

Nina kissed me again, and we sipped another round of Morini. Then she said, "We need a plan for the book of fairy tales tomorrow. Have either of you been to the Cristel District?"

I shook my head. "Never. Freddy?"

"Not that I recall. What does it matter?"

Nina said, "You two are so naïve. Each part of this city has its idiosyncrasies. How do we know Julian wasn't followed from that palace?" She turned to me. "Who was that man on the train you were sitting with? Had you ever seen him before? Did he get off the train when you did?"

I had another sip of Morini. It was fabulous, really. Freddy was already refilling his glass. "I didn't recognize him at all, and I had no memory of getting on the train. I assume I was overdone with morpheus powder at the Clélius House and maybe flown across the Great Chasm and somehow driven to the depot at Tamorina. It's all impossibly strange when I think about it."

Freddy said, "Since you had the book when you came into our room last night, we can assume he wasn't there to steal it. In fact, I believe he was riding with you as a guardian."

"I think so, too," Nina said. "He was basically holding Julian's hand along the way, protecting him and that book."

I said, "I didn't see him leave the train at all."

"Maybe he couldn't," Freddy said. "You had those papers from Dr. Paley. I presume if they weren't critical, those Regents from fairyland wouldn't have needed you to be their book courier."

"I agree," Nina added. "Internal Security is clever. They know what they're doing. You can't fool them that easily. If the book is so important to get to your man at Clerk Street, then a plan had to be made to bypass those agents. I wouldn't be surprised if they knew you were on the train, Julian, but with your envoy papers, there's nothing they could do to prevent it. You were protected by Dr. Paley. He's no fool, either."

"Thank God."

Nina took my hand and we kissed. "But not anymore, darling. Which is my point about tomorrow. We need to be suspicious of everyone we see over there, because we won't really fit in. Clerk Street is where the bluebloods shop. Most of them know each other. Nobody from Cristel District has ever been invited to join the Great Separation. Half of the Judas Council own mansions up there on Bovárd Avenue. Killing any of them is a ridiculous mistake."

"The idiots must play," Freddy said, his words a bit slurry.

I dropped my voice to ask Nina what she knew about the Mollison bombing, if Marco could've been involved. She shushed me instantly, then murmured,

"Nobody does. And don't mention Marco. He's hopelessly deranged. Delia told me she saw him by the river when she and Johara's daughter, Riala, went there last week on a class trip to the gypsy fair. She told me Marco was disguised in a clown costume and showing off stupid little card tricks to all the kids. He is so mental."

"Do either of you know who was blown up?"

"Yes, I have a list. That's something else we need to discuss."

Freddy asked, "They could be listening, you know. Ears everywhere, right?"

Nina told him, "I copied the names off the radio in the morning. City Network. Not a secret anymore." She slid the paper over to me as I sipped again from my glass of Morini. Already feeling lightheaded, I read the list.

Dr. Argivé Hyrtikus, Minister of Cultural Medicine
Dr. Boyceau Mollet, Prime Minister of Chemical Science
Armistead Setchell, Chief Engineer for Subterranean Projects
Dr. Anton Chalybian, Director of Radiographic Science
Amédée Hersam, Minister of Information and Political Logic
Dr. Bertha Craigmiles, Professor of Physiological Chemistry

Nina told me, "Hersam, Chalybian, Hyrtikus and Mollet are all on the Judas Council. No accident there. Chalybian and Craigmiles were teaching at the Mollison Institute."

Freddy added, "Actually, they were both tenured. Losing them hurts the Institute."

I said, "If that lethal chamber is still under basic construction, seeing Setchell killed is probably worse. My impression has been that appointments to the Judicial Council are mostly political. Those seats can be replaced. Lots of egos waiting in line. Losing your chief engineer is another game entirely."

Nina drank more of her Morini, then said, quietly, "We can't go to Clerk Street together. That makes us look like a gang. We should split up and arrive separately, a few minutes apart and from different directions. More coincidental."

"I don't think you should go at all," I told her. "You have more to risk. Remember Delia?"

Nina pointed her knife at me. "Honeypie, don't preach. It's annoying."

Just in time, dinner arrived on a rolling cart, our efficient waiter clearing off a space in the center of the table for a great big krater of steaming Ijoujak. He also gave each of us small soup bowls and plates of corn muffins and butter, then left with a polite, *"Bene sapiat,"* and another bow.

"As I was saying, you should leave this excursion to the bookseller with Freddy and myself. Delia needs you more than we do for this adventure."

Freddy tilted a bit in his chair. Two glasses of Morini had already infiltrated his brain, but he still managed to contradict me. "Illustrious roommate, Nina is vital to our survival. She can't be left behind if we have any hope of living beyond tomorrow. I vote to include her."

Nina rapped my hand with her large soup spoon. "See?"

"All right! Fine!"

"Fine? Without me, you two clowns wouldn't have the least idea how to find Clerk Street."

"Taxi?"

"What? You don't know the Cristel District at all. That section is excluded to motor cars. You have to be left off blocks away and walk to Clerk Street, which is really just a fancy alleyway and is practically invisible until you're literally on top of it."

Now and then, Nina irritated me with her geographical pomposity. I asked, "How do you know all this?"

She smiled at me as she took the soup ladle and scooped into the big krater. "A previous boyfriend."

"Of course."

Next, we took turns filling our small bowls with Ijoujak, an exotic stew of sorts. Both Nina and Freddy refused to let me in on the secret of its ingredients. I noticed something like lamb and a variety of garden vegetables floating about. The broth possessed a peculiar taste of spice that drifted between curry and cinnamon but was also peppery with a hint of tomato sauce. Quite good. I was thoroughly enjoying everything until a soggy white glob sloshed into my bowl. Nina laughed when she saw what I'd fished out.

So did Freddy. "Julian! The king's treasure!"

I tossed at it with my fork, rolling it over. "What is this?"

"Eye of the lamb," he told me. "An Etruscan delicacy. Ijoujak is served on many tables and since the poor creature has only two eyes, finding one in our krater is considered great fortune."

I dabbed at it with my fork.

"We need some luck for tomorrow, darling," Nina said, "so, eat it up with all of us in mind."

"What about you two? If it's such good luck?"

Freddy shook his head. "Must be eaten by him who has fished it out. That would be you, my friend."

Nina squeezed my arm. "Please, dear. Don't let us down. We're counting on you now. We really are."

So I did, and it was ghastly, gooey, pasty, sour. Trying not to gag, I washed the taste down with a full glass of Morini and that's the last I remembered of dinner, although Freddy and Nina both assured me the Etruscan mint pie we shared was delicious.

XLIV

I woke the next morning with a terrific headache and could not possibly see how I could make my nine o'clock in Contemporary Social Philosophy. However, it was Dr. Pardo's class, who'd given me that red mark the morning of my visit to the Dome and skipping it after being gone for so long was not smart if I had any hope of a passing grade. Therefore, I managed to drag myself out of bed, dress, stumble down to the Commons for toast and tea, then on to her class, confident in my natural ability to glean the salient points of her lecture. Which I did. After class, I tried a different tact in explaining where I'd been these critical weeks of my absence. I told Dr. Martita Pardo that my father and Otto Paley had sent me to Tamorina where I was to deliver a package to a family relative and ended up getting shot accidently through the shoulder during a brief skirmish. She did not care to see my wound but accepted my story and sent me off with a sheet of missed assignments I had five days to complete. That seemed impossible and felt like a punishment. I thanked her, anyhow, and went back to my room and fell asleep. I'd skip my one o'clock class with Dr. Lamberton and perform my explanations in his office when I got back to Thayer Hall after the book of fairy tales excursion.

Freddy and I hired a taxi after lunch to the Cristel District north of the holy river. Hazy sunshine and a warm breeze made the day pleasant for our ride into a part of the metropolis neither of us had ever seen. In fact, we both agreed that what Nina had related about Clerk Street was news to our ears. Who besides Nina and her vagrant crowd knew much about the greater metropolis? And I'm not talking about politics or social engineering. Eugenics was so universal throughout the city and our western provinces that one could not separate most districts from persecution and prejudice. One hundred years of both had inculcated in our populace the preposterous perspective that what once was held as truth, must therefore be true as sunshine and gravity. Like those incontrovertible lessons in the Holy Book. If we have studied them for centuries, must they not therefore have validity for our lives today? The uncritical civilization bears witness to its own decline in accepting myths as fact while dismissing facts as myth.

The Sommiér Quarter of Cristel District was eccentric. Its brassy street signs were polished but irregular, designed to look like melting wax. Its topography was up and down and confused our city map. The ancient cobblestone streets were curvy and undulated and absurdly narrow — only twice a pushcart's width here and there. Our taxi let us off on Franklyn Street next to a strongly aromatic candle shop. Checking our location, Freddy held up the map and a small woodlands compass from Dr. Barron's days as a Youth Scout in seaside Fortina. We walked up the block and met Nina outside a small apothecary. Since it was finally agreed that I ought to enter the bookstore alone, she and Freddy decided to pair off right there and pretend to be a couple out shopping on this sunny afternoon. They'd wander past the bookstore and shop on both sides of Clerk Street, then drift inside once I'd been there for a few minutes or so. In fact, we decided they ought to arrive on Clerk Street ahead of me, in order that it not appear at all we were together. A fine plan, we thought.

"Now, how do I get there?" I asked Nina.

Abandoning her comfortable bohemian style, she'd dressed in a lovely lavender skirt and blouse, trimmed in gilt with a gold sash. Her black hair was vibrant in the sunlight. She said, "Don't you have a map?"

"Freddy does. I don't."

She turned to Freddy. "Give Julian the map. We won't need it. I know where we're going."

He asked, "Can you read one, roomie?"

"I'll try."

Nina tapped her finger to a spot near the lower middle. "Here's where we are right now. This is Franklyn, right? You're going to follow it to Opera, then go left up the hill and left again at Vaux. Walk along the sidewalk there, keeping to the railing side until you see some stone stairs on the left leading down. Clerk Street is at the bottom. Don't miss the stairs. There's no sign, just a small gate. Easy to miss when you're across from where the buildings take the sun and put that side in the shade. It almost looks like the entrance to a basement."

"How will I know if I go too far?"

She pointed back to the map. "Vaux goes along to Parque where it dead-ends. You can't get lost. Just turn around and go back."

"Is this the way you'll be going?"

She shook her head. "No, Freddy and I are taking Oasis and coming to Clerk from below. It's more complicated and you two minor geniuses would get lost for sure, so I'm sending you the easy way. Just don't miss the gate, all right?"

"I'll do my very best not to let you down, sweetheart."

I gave her a nice kiss.

Freddy frowned. "No kiss for me, darling?"

"Good-bye, you two." I waved as I headed off along Franklyn Street. "Don't be late!"

Those streets of the Sommiér Quarter were pretty. Red brick buildings with wrought iron window bars and balconies and ornamental door gates. Window boxes filled with spring flowers in bloom and fragrant in the gentle breeze. Lots of shops. I passed people in fine clothes, some carrying baskets with new purchases, and happy faces. Here and there, I returned a nod with a pleasant smile, instruction from my parents who reminded me how it pays to leave a good impression.

Motor traffic was absent as I reached Opera Street and went up the hill to my left. There, the sidewalk was quite steep with shops on both sides perched at a curious angle. Too narrow for autos, the old cobblestone was wheel-worn from centuries of iron-wheeled carriage and cart. More fashionable clothes shops and exotic glassware. Oculist and cartographer. Florist and fortuneteller. A sculptor's studio. Calligraphic art of placards and posters. Pastries and spice candy from Porceliña. A fancy dress establishment for ritzy clothing. From this splendid section of the metropolis, one couldn't have expected the nasty, polluted streets of East Catalan. How do we breathe the same air, drink the same water, and live in such different worlds? Was it truly necessary to name the poor and downtrodden, the ill and disregarded, as our mortal enemies and exclude them from all the beauty and inspiration we enjoy? Couldn't eugenics have led the more fortunate of us to enhance the lives of those whose mornings were not as full of sunlight and goodness? Do the happy truly need to exterminate the sad to remain happy?

Vaux Street was a mostly alleyway embankment of ivy, wild periwinkle and trumpet vine draping a stone wall to my right and another narrow sidewalk along the iron railing Nina had described bordering the highbacked buildings to my left. Just brick and windows. Chilly in the shade. A couple cats under the ivy. Quiet and empty. Sort of a curious arrangement. But I heard life in the upper floors, the rattling of typewriting machines and motor dust inhalers. Voices, too, and someone singing scales to a piano. And just next door, a plaintive violin in duet with a deep Osterhout pulacélu. The music distracted me so that I almost missed those stairs down to Clerk Street.

But I didn't.

The stairs were barely wide enough for a child, and steep with a wooden hand-railing as a guide to the bottom. Twenty cement steps. My shoes echoed as I descended. There were only a handful of people down there when I stepped out onto shady Clerk Street. Looking left, I saw it dead-ended at the same fancy dress shop I'd seen on Opera Street. A walk-through. In the other direction were more shops of assorted fascinations including a Pimodian bakery, a Greek jeweler, a seller of antique clocks, a silk and satin fabric dispensary, and another quaint apothecary with jars advertised in the window whose ingredients baffled me. And, of course, at 13 Clerk Street:

Magisterial Books

Above a carved mahogany door was a rendering in brass of a studious owl with reading glasses perusing an articulated volume. Lovely. No Freddy or Nina anywhere about. Had they already come and gone? Were they lurking in one of these eccentric stores? That would be smart. Pretending to shop while keeping their focus on our assignment. I hoped so. I'd worn my father's jacket with the secret pocket apparently enlarged at Clélius House, perhaps by Lalla Goldbeck. I hadn't noticed the change at all until the train when I felt the book tucked carefully into that same pocket Angelina had sewn for Draxler's painting. Now I was able to walk about the Sommiér Quarter without advertising the Regents' book of fairy tales.

One more glance down Clerk Street and I went into the bookseller. A little bell rang above the threshold as I entered. It wasn't a big store at all. Perhaps twice the size out front as my bedroom at Thayer but with ten shelves on each wall stacked high with all manner of volumes to a twelve-foot ceiling. The store was deep, though, with a curtain cutting off at least a third of its depth. A glass and mahogany desk with rare volumes displayed to the front for qualified buyers and a cash register on a leather pad. A little brass desk bell sat beside the register. Since no one was present, I was supposed to ring for service. Sumner Dawes was the fellow's name. I remembered that much. We had a code to exchange, like one of my mother's mysteries. The idea seemed a bit silly, but given the stakes and everything I'd experienced since entering the tide at St. Etienne Shores, I felt perfectly confident in playing this off as I was asked.

So I drew a breath and tapped the little bell.

Right away, I heard someone rummaging around in the back. A voice called out, *"One moment, please. Just getting sorted."*

I looked out at Clerk Street for my companions. Nobody was there at all.

Then the curtain parted and one very ordinary-looking fellow in a grey business-suit came out to greet me. He was neither pleasant nor cold. Just rather flat. He said, "May I help you?"

"Yes, sir. Thank you. It was suggested I come here to offer a rare volume of fairy tales for sale. It was thought you might be interested." I reached into my jacket and brought the volume out to show him. "It's been in our family for years and belonged to my Great-Aunt Edith whose favorite story was 'The Pied Piper.' She read to me when I was a child. My siblings and I have very fond memories of her, but now my mother thinks we ought to sell the book so other children might enjoy these amusing stories."

Somehow, it felt natural to embellish that ridiculous narrative.

He nodded. "May I see it, please?"

I held onto the book, waiting for him to complete our secret code and tell me how his mother adored that tale of "The Glass Mountain." When he continued to hold his hand out without finishing our little game, I became nervous. Was this the correct store? Was this fellow even Sumner Dawes?

"The book, please?"

"Excuse me, sir," I replied, "but may I ask your name?"

He frowned. "Are you interested in selling your book, or not? I have a busy schedule today."

"Well, in that case, maybe I ought to come back when you have more time."

"Give me the book, please."

"No, thank you," I told him, deciding something funny was up. "I guess I'll come back another day, sir."

"No, Julian," the fellow said, reaching into his coat. He took out a revolver. "Give me the book this instant. I'll kill you if you don't."

Good grief. Not again.

I handed him the book of fairy tales. "I know Dr. Otto Paley."

The fellow smiled. "Me, too. So what?"

"I'm under his protection."

"Apparently not."

Now I was terrified. This fellow could kill me and get away with it. Where were Freddy and Nina? When they finally came here, I'd be dead.

He said, "Let's go into the back, you and I, and discuss this."

"You'll shoot me back there."

"Would you rather I shoot you right here? It's all the same to me."

I tried stalling for Nina and Freddy. Or anyone, for that matter. "Why do you want that book?"

"Not your concern, Julian." He gave me a shove. "Go."

My legs wobbled. I thought I'd faint.

He shoved me again, now with his revolver to my spine.

Marco Grenelle came through the curtain with a black pistol and shot him in the heart.

His body dropped behind me.

Marco stepped forward and shot him again in the head.

Two other strong fellows followed through the curtain and grabbed the dead body by the ankles and dragged it off to the rear of the bookstore. A third wiped the blood off the floor with a simple cotton towel.

I stood there with Marco, utterly in shock until he said, "Hello, Julian. Good to see you again. Did you enjoy Tamorina?"

We sat together on wooden chairs in the back with Freddy and Nina who had arrived about four minutes after my debacle without even having heard the gunfire. The "**CLOSED**" sign hung from a brass hook in the front window case. Freddy held the book of fairy tales open on his lap to the story of the Pied

Piper. We were trying to figure out what was special about this particular volume. Freddy took the lead. He'd borrowed a magnifying glass from the cash desk and closely examined both the print and illuminated illustration plate that accompanied the tale. Nina sat beside me, rubbing my hand. Marco was content to watch. Those two had declared a truce for my benefit and I let them both know it was appreciated. No reason to kill each other when there were now so many in the metropolis willing to do it for us.

"By the way," I asked Marco, "who was that fellow? Not Sumner Dawes, I presume."

"Nope." Marco fiddled with a toothpick he'd borrowed from the front desk. "His name is Max Wiertz. Just another of the Council's hired lamebrains. We almost burned him up in bed last week by accident. Just missed him back late from the videoscopes. He had a girl with him, so he was declared off-limits that night. Then we found out he had a stick in this book game and warned our people off to let him play his hand in here. We actually didn't know you were the courier. If we had, I'd have killed him before you came into the store. Sorry to let him scare you like he did. A fellow like that's better off dead."

"And where's Dawes? Is he dead, too?"

"I'll bet they killed him," Nina said, squeezing my hand. "They're so insane, they'll kill anyone they choose to."

"Possibly, but we really don't know. He's just missing. Maybe in the river. Maybe somewhere at the Mendel Building."

Marco shrugged.

Nina kissed my cheek. Her perfume smelled so lovely. I stroked her silky black hair. She calmed my nerves just being next to me.

Freddy said, "I have a thought here, but I need more light."

"Electric torch?" Marco suggested.

"That'd be good."

"Wait here a minute." He got up and went farther into the rear of the store where he disappeared.

Freddy asked us, "Do you two follow the curiosity here?"

I said, "Besides that you're delving into a children's book as if it's a bottle of bourbon?"

"Very funny, master. No, that's not it."

"Well, what's the curiosity, then?"

"That you were asked to bring this book from imperial fairyland to illustrate the idea that thousands of children were being collected for some nefarious purpose."

"And?"

Nina spoke up. "And why would you need to bring this book at all? Why not just tell somebody, or anybody? It's not as if the fairy tales by themselves is proof of that. It's just a story that everyone knows."

Freddy raised a finger. "Precisely!"

I joined in. "So you're suggesting it's this particular book that's important. Something about it."

Freddy nodded. "Yes, I am. That's what I'm studying here. There's a message of some sort written or drawn inside the tale. I'm trying to see it, but so far it's very elusive."

Nina asked me, "Why were you bringing the book to this seller? What was his name again?"

"Sumner Dawes."

"Did they tell you anything about him?"

"No. Just to get it here, exchange our greetings, give him the book, and take fourteen credits for it. That's all."

"Why not just give him the book? Why the fourteen credits?"

"No idea. Bill of sale?"

Freddy looked up from the book. "I have a thought."

Nina and I both said, "Yes?"

"Perhaps this illuminated illustration has a code or writing in it that only Dawes could interpret."

I said, "That's a possibility."

Nina said, "If he's at the Mendel Building, alive or not, then we can be sure they know what's in the book by now. They just had to wait for you to bring it here."

"No, darling," Freddy said. "That's not true at all. If Dawes needed this book to solve some puzzle, or determine something, what could he possibly reveal without it, besides the fact of Julian bringing it here?"

"That's a good point," I said. "Dawes knew something about the book, certainly, but only the book itself could provide what's important and valuable within this specific volume. But, if that's the case, why wouldn't they just take it from me at Commonwealth Station?"

"You had those traveling papers from Dr. Paley," Nina said, "and maybe once you got back to school, they couldn't be sure you hadn't hidden it there somewhere, or maybe even up at your parents' house. It was probably easier to wait for you to bring the book here."

I said, "Where Dawes himself knew what to do with it."

"Maybe he's not dead," Nina said. "Maybe the idea was to bring the book to him and get the truth out of it."

Freddy asked, "Who's the Pied Piper?"

"What?"

"Who's the Pied Piper?"

I said, "Some fellow with a magic flute that drowns rats and steals children from people who don't pay him."

Marco came out of the storage room with a small electric lantern. "Hello again."

I told him, "We're trying to decide why this book is valuable. And why Sumner Dawes."

"We don't know him."

"Somebody must," Nina said, "or the book wouldn't have been brought here. Whatever's in it, we think Dawes was supposed to interpret or share with us in the metropolis. Something about the children Julian saw on the trains and trucks."

Marco frowned. "What children?"

I told him, "Thousands being transported in this direction from the eastern provinces. I saw them everywhere from Fabian Province to Tarchon."

"Why?"

Marco handed the lantern to Freddy who flicked it on.

I said, "We have two questions to work on here, Marco. One is, why are all those children being brought out of the provinces? And secondly, what does this child's book of fairy tales have to do with that?"

Marco asked, "Where are they now, all those kids?"

I said, "Well, that would be the third question."

Nina asked Marco, "Did you explode that bomb at the Mollison Institute?"

"Do you mean, did I place it there and push the button?" He shook his head. "No, I heard about it on the radio, just like you."

"Are you sure?"

"I'm not lying, Nina. I don't need to. I like seeing things blow up when the right people are in the room."

Freddy said, "Now, here's something interesting!" He played the lantern back and forth across the illustration while tilting the book up and down, too. "Look at this."

We got up and went over to Freddy in a half-circle.

"See the Pied Piper? Watch his face as I wash the light over it and move the book."

Nina said, "What are we supposed to be seeing?"

"Watch."

I saw it. The lantern gave the Piper's face a strange glow and, as Freddy tipped the book back and forth, the face changed to another: one pleasant and smiling, and the other ugly and bitter. A chromatic trick of the artist.

Freddy asked, "Does everyone see it?"

I nodded and Nina said, "Now I do."

Marco agreed. "Me, too."

Freddy played it up and down. "Both kind and wicked, right?"

"Yes."

"Look carefully at the cruel face. Study the detail. It's only visible with lantern light. That's not just a cartoon painting."

"No?" I said, trying to understand where Freddy was leading us.

"That's the Pied Piper," he said. "The real one. A person."

Nina said, "Stealing the children."

"I think so."

"Who is he?"

Freddy shrugged. I asked Marco, "Do you recognize him?"

"No."

"Nina?"

"No."

"But I bet Sumner Dawes did, or whomever he was supposed to give the book after he got it from me."

All four of us stared at the illustration.

Someone knocked at the front door of the bookstore and Marco went to have a peek through the curtain. He shook his head and came back. "Nobody. Just someone shopping."

Freddy handed me the book. "Here, genius. Time for chapter two."

Nina said, "It's too dangerous for Julian to keep it." She pointed at Marco. "I think we should give it to him. That's safer. He can keep it underground. That's where he's going now. Right, Marco?"

"Yeah, I guess so. I can take it."

"No, you can't." Freddy shook his head. "Julian was told to leave the bookseller if he didn't meet with Sumner Dawes and wait on further instructions."

Reluctantly, I agreed. "That's true. It's what the Regents told me."

"Then that's what you have to do."

Nina said, "Marco, can your people protect Julian until he gets rid of the book? We know you've been following him. Can't you at least keep an eye on him?"

"We can try. There's a fellow I know."

Freddy said, "We'll keep the book until we hear from fairyland."

Marco narrowed his eyes. "From where?"

Nina said, "Julian's been to the Eastern Empire." She turned to me. "What's it called?"

"Laspágandélus."

Marco said, "Never heard of it. Where is that?"

I told him, "Go ask Castor and Pollux. They'll explain the whole story. Let them know I've seen the Regents. They'll be pleased."

Freddy said, "We need to go now. People keep looking in the window. Somebody'll get suspicious and call the police. We don't want to be here when that happens."

As a brisk afternoon wind kicked up, Freddy and Nina and I found a taxi down on Franklyn Street and rode it back across the eternal river to Regency Heights and Thayer Hall. I kept the book of fairy tales in my jacket and tried to consider how those further instructions would arrive so that I might be able to rid myself of this curious responsibility that had almost gotten me killed.

Up in our room, Freddy went to his closet and grabbed his overnight satchel. He told us, "I'm taking the train home tonight so you two can have the room to yourselves. Just be careful, faithful roommate."

We hugged and Freddy gave Nina a quick kiss on her cheek and left us alone.

Nina said, "I need to telephone Johara and see about Delia. Where can I do that?"

"I'll show you."

We went down the stairs to the telephone bank on the third floor and sat her on the end. In the hallway, a gaggle of co-eds with a handsome pair of husky fellows were overboldly discussing next week's junior promenade. Apparently, nothing could be more critical than determining who would be expected to escort shy Ethelynd Guppy to the glorious event. She didn't sound like a terribly exuberant young lady, so it appeared the assignment would require a deft and daring hand. Whom did that describe? That was the urgent issue at hand. I gave Nina a kiss on the top of her head and went back upstairs to use the toilet.

The day was ending, another lovely spring twilight on the way as I stood by my desk window, watching the red sun dying over our grand metropolis. I held that fairy-tale book opened to the illuminated page of the Pied Piper. Without the electric lantern glow, only a merry face illustrated the Piper's march. Not the hideous demon thief of children. I lightly touched the paper figure and felt nothing rough or artificial in the ink rendering. A clever trick to offer two faces in a single moment when the light was right. How was it done? And why? Who was the Pied Piper?

Once Nina came back, we went to eat dinner at the commons, a cheese and bacon casserole with cherki peas and cornbread muffins. I drank spiced tea, she had black coffee. While eating, Nina caught me up with Delia's afternoon escapades. "Johara took Delia and Riala to the kid's zoo at Langlet Place. Are you familiar?"

"No."

"Well, it's not a nice area and the zoo is dirty, and all the animals look suicidal."

"Pardon?"

"They're mangy and bitter. Nobody feeds them."

"Somebody must."

"Not often enough."

"So why did Johara take the kids there?"

"Delia told me Riala likes tossing peanuts to the monkeys, but one of them flung a pile of shit back at her, so she threw a rock and hit another monkey in the head and the whole zoo went nuts. It was a bad day. I don't like Delia skipping school and she knows it. If Johara can't keep her on a good routine, we'll have to move again, and I don't know where we'd go."

Nina took a drink of her coffee and stuck her fork into the lukewarm casserole. More drama. I told her, "I'll need a nap if we expect to visit Jimmy Potatoes at midnight."

"Me, too."

Both exhausted, we finished dinner and dragged ourselves back upstairs again. Walking into my room, I stepped on a note slid under the door. It read:

Harold Sketz
219 Chesterfield Avenue — Bloomington Wood

XLV

∞

That address was just under an hour from Thayer Hall, so we rode the interurban rail out there. Cheaper than a taxi. The evening air was pleasant and cool, scented of fresh lawns and night-blooming jasmine. Only three other riders shared the car. Elderly passengers keeping to their quiet solitudes. Bloomington Wood offered that sort of private neighborhood, well-manicured and proper. Mostly for the retired. Safe and secure from those troubled addresses in darker districts of the metropolis.

Nina sat close beside me, her arm tucked in with mine. A gentle hug. Since my return, I'd become comfortable once more with being in love and having her there or, rather, being there with her. After all, it was I who had left. Yet, the world felt so different now. Where I'd been. What I'd seen and heard. Threats and knowledge. That experience we adopt from living outside of ourselves. Losing my father. What falls away from us by days and days on earth is hard to comprehend and yet we must or living becomes impossible.

The rail station was only a couple of blocks from Chesterfield Avenue by a park whose pond offered a chorus of anxious frogs across the dark. Streetlamps lit the sidewalk and sprinklers soaked the grass and spring foliage. An older man walked a small dog farther down the block. Nina and I strolled casually up a narrow side-street, hand-in-hand, offering to anyone peeking through shuttered blinds a pleasant tableau of young lovers at play. A clean, well-kept tan Argenti auto motored by up on Chesterfield as we arrived at the avenue. The address we sought was in the block directly ahead, so we crossed over and headed along toward a one-story house atop a gentle sloping lawn with a brick walkway leading up to a glowing porchlight at the front door.

Nina rang the bell. A floor lamp switched on behind the shutters at the wide front window and I heard someone coming to the door. When it opened, we were greeted by a middle-aged fellow in a brown, hand-tailored wool suit and five-button vest. His hair was combed to one side and he wore a thin mature moustache. "Good evening."

"Good evening, sir. My name is Julian Brehm, and this is Nina Rinaldi."

"I see." He looked us over. "And how may I help you?"

"Are you, by any chance, Mr. Harold Sketz?"

"I am, indeed. To what do I owe the pleasure of your visit at this hour?"

"Thank you, sir, we were advised by one of our associates that you might be interested in purchasing a rare old volume of children's fairy tales. It belonged to my Great-Aunt Edith, who used to read those stories to me when I was a boy. I always adored Hansel and Gretel, but her favorite was the tale of the Pied Piper. It's included in this wonderful old illustrated volume."

"Is that so?"

Sketz looked me in the eye. I couldn't read his expression. Nina took my hand and gave it a gentle squeeze.

"We're offering the book to you for fourteen credits. My associates say it's a bargain."

"I'm sure they do." He held out his hand. "May I see it, please?"

"Are you interested?"

"Of course I am." He smiled. "When I was young, my mother's favorite story was 'The Glass Mountain.' She enjoyed reading it to me at bedtime. Bless her dear heart. I've never forgotten."

"That's very sweet."

"Do you have the book with you now?"

"Yes, sir."

"Then please come in." He held the door open. "I'd love to see it."

Harold Sketz showed us into his living room where that floor lamp was lit golden beside a nice wide davenport. "Make yourselves comfortable."

The room was warm and fitted out with pleasant furniture, fabric chairs and small walnut tables. A broad beige carpet and a brick fireplace with a modern glass screen. Two shelves of ersatz leather-bound books in a low cabinet off in a corner by the front window.

Nina sat on the soft davenport. I drew out the illustrated volume and handed it to Sketz, then took my place beside her. I said, "Each story is illuminated and the Pied Piper has a special painting. Study his face. It's an artistic illusion."

Nina told him, "Julian was almost killed today because of that book."

He looked up from the old volume. "Good gracious. Is that true?"

I nodded. "The book was intended for a seller named Sumner Dawes. When I got to his bookstore on Clerk Street, another fellow was waiting for me. He didn't give the code words you and I just exchanged, so I knew he was a fraud. When he pulled a gun on me, a friend of ours shot him."

Sketz thumbed through the slender volume of old fairy tales. "And why do you think that fellow wanted to kill you over this little book?"

I sat forward on the davenport. "Because thousands of children are missing from throughout the eastern provinces and somehow that book explains who's behind it. There's a mystery here this edition helps to solve. We believe that face in the illuminated illustration reveals the identity of the Pied Piper himself."

Harold Sketz smiled. "Well, then, let's have a look."

He flipped through the fairy tales until he came to the Pied Piper. He studied it for perhaps a minute or so. Nina cuddled up beside me. I noticed the house had a distinct odor of carpet freshener and furniture wax. But nothing else. No cooking kitchen aroma or cigar smells. And none of the rooms other than this had any lights on. The rest of the house was dark and quiet as if Harold Sketz lived there alone. Or, odd that it crossed my mind, not at all.

A dog began barking down the block joined by another somewhere behind Sketz's yard.

He said, "Your Piper certainly looks happy leading those innocent children away."

"Try holding the illustration under the lamp and tilting it slightly about."

"All right."

As he did so, I saw his expression change. "My heavens."

"Do you see it? The wicked Piper?"

Nina told him, "Julian thinks that's the face of a real person. So do the rest of us."

Stetz said, "Well, you're correct. In fact, that's Celäenos Yeazell."

"Who?"

"Your Pied Piper, the fellow most likely behind the collection of children from those eastern provinces. Celäenos Yeazell was a tenured dean on the research committee of the Mignard Institute. A brilliant inventor and a meticulous engineer. He developed some of those weapons that are killing your armies out in the Desolation, most particularly the gas myrmidon guns and charnel pellets and radio rockets. Without those technological inspirations, the war might already have been lost." Sketz tipped the illustration under the lamp again at an odd angle. "But he's supposed to be dead."

"How's that?" I asked. Another preposterous mystery?

"Yeazell was not a scientific philanthropist. He had no dedication to the purity of those arts. He performed his miracles at the Mignard Institute solely for the most extravagant treasures. Glittering minerals. Thousands of credits. This is what I've heard. Always more. Exponential increase in profits and reward. In a less desperate age, he'd have been dismissed without hesitation or remorse."

Nina said, "But they needed him to help kill people. Enemies."

"Precisely, and to do so before they themselves were exterminated."

"And so, what?" I asked. "He quit?"

Sketz laughed. "No, not at all. He asked for the supreme reward as recompense for much grander weapons of war he was proposing."

I asked, "What did he want?"

"Celäenos Yeazell requested to be appointed permanent Regent of the Eastern Empire and to wear a golden crown of jewels in the Imperial throne room at Désallier."

Now Nina laughed. "He sounds like a mental case. We know a lot of those."

Harold Sketz lost his smile. "Certainly, he was a very disturbed fellow. Possibly insane. Once Yeazell's request was denied, and he was told to leave the Institute, the story we heard was that he threw himself into the Great Chasm. His body was never found, and the expectation was that the merciless Philateus had swallowed him up."

I said, "And now he appears in a child's book of fairy tales as the Pied Piper. A perfect story. He rids the east of invading rats and wants his golden reward. When he's denied, he captures thousands of young orphaned children in revenge."

Nina squeezed my hand as she spoke up. "How is he able to organize something like this? Using the army and the Security Directorate to round them all up? And why would the Status Imperium even go along with a lunatic like him? What do they have to gain by kidnapping a bunch of kids in the middle of the war?"

I said, "It's a lot more than a bunch."

"You know what I mean."

Sketz shrugged. "It's a question, isn't it? That, and where's Celäenos Yeazell now?"

I told him, "Maybe performing his poetry at midnight, tonight, in the basement of Jimmy Potatoes."

XLVI
∞

Nina and I slept for a couple of hours in my bed at Thayer Hall. Too tired to make love, we both fell asleep, almost the same moment. I had scattered dreams of trains and strangers on dark streets with guns. Nonsensical appearances. I woke to some disturbance down on Trimble and then listened to Nina humming as she did so often. Maybe she hadn't gone to sleep at all. I thought about Harold Sketz and that house on Chesterfield. When Nina and I left after collecting those fourteen credits and the bill of sale, we crossed back over the avenue and stopped a few yards down that connecting side street in the shadow of a willow tree. We watched the lamps go out in Sketz's front room and the porchlight, too. Then we heard a door close in the back driveway and saw Harold Sketz come out of the dark wearing a long overcoat and a grey brim hat and carrying a thin briefcase. He hurried off down Chesterfield Avenue.

Nina got out of bed. "I need to pee."

She slipped out of the room and used the toilet across the hall. I got up, too, and went to my desk and switched on the light and took the city directory from my bottom drawer. I looked up the address for Jimmy Potatoes on Olivette Street. I hadn't been there since freshman year and that night our taxi had gotten lost in the mazy streets, so I had no firm memory as to where it was. Somewhere in the crazy Beuiliss District where low-rent clubs and dine-wine-danceries flourished. Thrill-a-minute halls. Perfect for college students and energetic layabouts whose enthusiasms rarely extended much beyond liquor and late-night nonsense. Freddy knew the area better than I did. If he were here, I wouldn't require the directory.

My desk clock said half-past eleven. I was drowsy but waking slowly. Nina came back into the room and yawned. "Are you sure we should go out tonight? Jimmy Potatoes is crazy on weekends. The whole street is."

"I'm trying to look it up. Do you know the address?"

"It's on Olivette, middle of the block. I don't remember the number. You're sure you want to go?"

"I have to go," I told her. "If the Pied Piper's there, I want to see him. The kind of lunatic who steals kids from the rural provinces? Does he really resemble that illustration? I have to see."

Nina came over to kiss my forehead. "Julian, actually this is a crazy idea. You don't know anything at all about Jimmy Potatoes or those queer boys of yours or some monster who writes bad poetry."

"Why do you keep calling them queer? That's so rude. They're just silly boys. Why do you care who they kiss, if they even do?"

She kissed me again. "Because it annoys you."

I kissed her back. "You are so creepy! Did you know that? The absolute worst."

She smiled. "And that's why you love me."

"Possibly."

We dressed in warm clothing. I gave Nina one of my old coats that accentuated her bohemian look. Made her sort of slumpy. Both rough and wild. We shared one of Freddy's Maldoror beers and figured out what strategy we'd employ at Jimmy Potatoes. We decided that Nina should take a table or some seat in the club upstairs while I went down to the basement for the poetry clan. Then she'd be able to keep an eye on me, more or less, without being intrusive. Besides, the poets had only extended the invitation to me and I didn't want to upset the situation by trying to get her included. I was also fairly certain Nina hated poetry.

Our taxi driver was not a friendly man. He complained the entire ride about everything from drunk college students who threw up in his back seat to fares smoking hoggari or griffo weed with the windows rolled up that got him so sick he had to quit driving for the evening and go home. He also insisted that nobody in the metropolis gave decent tips, although we couldn't see why that would be so, given his scintillating personality. Apparently, the fellow was from Figáro, a region not particularly celebrated for hospitality.

Olivette felt manic. More people wandered in the street than on the sidewalks. Our taxi driver honked constantly as we crept along at maybe two miles an hour. Not just students, either. Mature drunks, both men and women, traded kisses and insults as they crossed the street. One of them emptied his bottle of beer on the hood of our taxi when our driver laid on the horn to get them out of his way. Nina suggested we just step out right there and walk up to Jimmy Potatoes. I agreed and paid the driver his fare and added a decent tip he didn't really deserve.

Holding hands, we joined the madness.

It truly was a spectacle. I hadn't realized the metropolis had so many bars and sex parlors and burlesque theatres and noisy cabarets and glittering bistros. Like at those flashy arcades in the undercity, we had to shove our way forward along Olivette Street through the frenetic crowds, the odor of tobacco smoke and stale booze and sex-sweat clouding the night air. The din made my ears buzz.

We found Jimmy Potatoes about four blocks ahead and went inside. Not quite as popular as what we'd left behind us, mostly because the club was small and obscure in its purpose. Posters of sultry chanteuses and mustachioed artists in jaunty berets were hung on the walls. And no dancing, just a busy cocktail bar and a bearded fellow strumming a wooden guitar on a stool in the corner and singing a wistful Pelágie ballad about a girl he once adored with a pretty lavender dress. Nina made a gagging sign with her forefinger and found a tiny table by the window. I joined her for a minute.

"You don't like this kind of music?"

"Kill me, all right?"

"You are so rude."

"I hate songs about people falling out of love."

A young waiter wearing a squab hat came over and Nina ordered a green spice beer. Deciding to keep my head clear for the poetry clan, I had nothing to drink. Pindar and Quixote were confusing enough.

With ill-disguised sarcasm, Nina asked, "Will you be reciting a poem, too?"

"You need a good spanking, dear."

"Wait till we get back to your dormitory. Then I'll do whatever you want. I'm very flexible when it comes to your desires. I think you know that by now."

"Oh, Nina."

"Just keep your eyes open down there, Julian." She gave me a sweet lingering kiss. "I don't like this at all. Something's crazy here."

"It'll be fine. I just need to get a look at the Pied Piper, if he actually shows up. We'll leave after that."

More people came into Jimmy Potatoes, gathering at the cocktail bar, chattering with strangers, soon to be friends.

Nina switched her attention away from Olivette Street and pursed her lips. "Kiss me again."

I did.

Then I went down into the smoky basement where the poetry clan had already assembled. Candles burned in each corner. Bottles of wine collected all over the floor by the wooden chairs. I guessed there must have been a couple dozen people come together for the readings, milling about in small groups, smoking rancid Tchäro cigarettes. A nasty bohemian habit.

The skinny poets spotted me.

Quixote rushed over and took my hand. "Julian! Good gracious! We're so thrilled to have you here!"

Pindar followed. They traded off shaking my hand so enthusiastically I was afraid my arm would fall off.

"It's such an honor! My God! Will you recite something for us?"

"I don't know about that, boys. I hadn't prepared anything. I'm not really a poet."

"Why, of course you are!" Pindar argued. "Poetry comes from the soul. Everyone knows that."

Quixote told me, "I'll bet you could create something extraordinary without thinking, just letting the words spill past your lips. We have the greatest confidence in you, Julian."

I said, "Well, let's just see how the evening goes, all right? Maybe I'll be spontaneous, after all."

Pindar enthused, "Oh, we know you will!"

I looked about the basement. Other than the candles, just a single lightbulb and shade suspended from a ceiling chain lit the room. Shadows abounded. The corners of the basement were obscure. I asked the boys, "Is the Pied Piper here?"

"Not yet, but Ingall promises he'll arrive within the hour. He's our featured guest tonight."

"Besides you," Quixote corrected, patting my shoulder. "We're so honored. This may be our best clan reading yet."

Pindar said, "The spirit of poetry can't be denied. It's ultra art. That's what we're naming our clan. The Ultras."

"Maybe," Quixote added.

"We're discussing the possibility," Pindar said. "We plan to vote soon."

Another few minutes, and the meeting began. I thought most of the poets would be young bohemian crazies or pretentious college dropouts. I was wrong. Some of them were, of course, but a few looked as if they'd come straight from law and commerce office buildings or big investment banks at Ravensbrook Avenue or the National Stock Exchange on Ehrenhardt Boulevard. And a couple of others resembled those everyday fellows who punched a time clock in the iron and industry districts of west metropolis. Who could have guessed art mixed with grease and soot? Only one of the clan that night was female, and she was cute. Long brown hair and a dusty jacket. Pretty green eyes. Face of a pixie. Both Pindar and Quixote stared at her all the while I was there, and I sensed a fierce sexual tension.

That convocation Quixote mentioned was led by one of those natural fellows whose blue cotton workshirt was threadworn and faded. He called himself Lanterne and appeared to be at least middle-aged. A father or husband. Once everyone had taken a chair in the wide poetry circle, he stepped into the center of the room and spoke in a most earnest voice.

"Let us recognize the beauty of poetry in slaying those beasts of the cruel and the ordinary. Let us praise the word that heals our soul and sheds light on our divine path forward. Let us believe in the promise of art and the holy expression of truth."

In solemn unison, the poetry clan chanted, "Amen, amen, amen."

And the readings began.

To be honest, Nina was sort of right. Some of them were stupid. One of the fellows who resembled a banker read a poem about a family of mice living in an abandoned baby carriage and the happy home they'd made until some cruel alley-cat snuck up and ate them. Fairly gruesome. I presumed his poem was a metaphor for life in our modern Republic, or maybe it was just about cats and mice. He sat down without explaining. Everyone clapped. Next, we heard a poem by one of the shaggy bohemians about an old woman living in a tenement room who talked to her radio set thinking it was the voice of her dead husband. That was pretty spooky, but I admit I liked it. Another bohemian performed a short recitation on the killing of a young man in Calcitonia by the Security Directorate. It read like a political obituary and felt dangerously provocative. That one received the biggest applause. Then the girl read a poem she told us was composed on the train coming to this poetry clan. It was long and began as a travelogue describing her neighborhood that sounded awfully like East Catalan. Trash and dogs howling. Clogged toilets and violence in apartment bedrooms and alleyways, followed by a lovely section about the eternal river that included fish and birds and boats. Then along came a sad old widower who met a young girl at a tool factory and had her clothes off behind a storage shed and loved her twice until she stabbed him with a screwdriver and went back to her place on the assembly line that was her fate. A dreary conclusion. The skinny poets clapped the loudest and she didn't look at them. The rest of the poetry clan appeared disturbed and conflicted.

Quixote got up next. Both he and Pindar beamed. Quixote read:

"Mr. Moon, did I ask you to like me?
Did I ask you to keep that silver eye of you on me
As I walk home at night?
If you're my sole companion,
I think I'm in trouble.
I can see you watching over me,
But I cannot reach out and touch you.
Mr. Moon, I'm afraid you do not share
My loneliness."

Quixote sat down to a great cheer from Pindar. I thought that poem was oddly revelatory of some relationship curiosity. What was it really about? Quixote's poem was clever enough. Just something there intrigued me. Those two boys seemed too enthusiastic. I wondered where that pixie poet fit? She hardly clapped.

A third bohemian stood at his chair and quoted a poem to his father. It included both admiration and disgust. The poem was entitled, "Betrayal," and concluded with a broken bottle of bourbon, a short-circuiting hot plate, a lost puppy, and district police bursting in on the father in bed with a fat landlady. I wasn't sure I followed the narrative, but everyone else seemed to love it. Art is a mystery.

A brief intermission was announced by the fellow who gave the convocation. We were asked to stay in the basement to keep our poetic spirit focused. People got up and wandered about once again, collecting in familiar groups, all abuzz with the thrill of artistic union. Pindar came over with Quixote to ask me what I thought of the clan reading so far. I told them, "They're very good. You have a top-notch clan. I'm mesmerized."

Quixote beamed. "Thanks, Julian. We were afraid you'd hate it. Some of our members are more experienced in public readings than the rest of us, so the clan gives everyone a chance to be part of the grand tradition. Did you like mine?"

I nodded. "The best so far."

Pindar said, "He worked on it all morning. I heard him scribbling notes in the dark before dawn."

"Time well-spent, I'd say."

Quixote stepped forward to give me a hug. "Thanks, Julian. We're both thrilled you're here."

"Glad I came." I watched the pixie girl take a long drink from one of the dark wine bottles. No one was talking with her. Honestly, she seemed vacant and lost. Probably the wine. How old was she, anyhow?

I asked the boys, "So, do you have any idea when the Pied Piper'll get here?"

Pindar said, "Ingall is bringing him by auto. They're expected any minute now. It's why we took our intermission. Normally, we read for at least two hours before stopping to use the toilet. Our clan is very dedicated and persistent. We don't need to rest."

I took out my pocket-watch and checked the hour. Almost a quarter after one. It felt later than that. I wondered how Nina was doing upstairs. Was she bored to death yet?

A door opened in one of the shadowed corners of the basement and a tall man in a long overcoat walked through, followed by a thin fellow in a jester costume: The Pied Piper. He held a brass flute and a vellum scroll. His face was painted in halves of white and black, with one side smiling and the other grim and dour. He wore a red and black hat adorned with bells and lacy accoutrements. His shoes looked stolen from a circus sideshow. His frilly coat was sewn with pictures of children and villages, rivers and forests and caves. A walking storybook.

Everyone cheered and that Ingall fellow looked pleased with himself for leading the Piper into the basement. I waited to get a better look at the Piper's face to see if he really did bear a resemblance to the illuminated book illustration. Our convocation speaker announced, "Seats, everyone! Our esteemed guest is here!"

We went back to our chairs and sat again, although Pindar and Quixote traded to sit closer to the pixie poet. She didn't pay any notice to that and fixed her attention on Ingall and the Pied Piper, both of whom stood under the lamp in the middle of the basement. The spotlight.

My own curiosity rose. Who was this fellow, really? He looked like a clown in that silly costume. How had someone like that managed to abduct thousands of children? It just didn't feel possible.

Ingall spoke up, "Ladies and gentlemen! Fellow poets! I am so honored to introduce a rare artist of great distinction! A poet of unsurpassable gifts! A true legend of words!" Ingall paused for dramatic effect. The moment already felt absurd. All we needed was one of Nina's zoo monkeys to ride in on a midget bicycle. "Let me give you ... the PIED PIPER!"

We all stood and applauded.

The Piper doffed his hat and offered a reverent bow. The cheers bloomed. Joy was rampant. Ingall raised his hands to calm us and everyone sat once more.

Then the Pied Piper.

His voice was raspy and hinted of accent. Eastern provinces. No surprise if that description by Harold Sketz was true.

The Piper told us, "Poetry is the art of madness and persuasion. Rhymes and riddles confuse and enlighten. The fool turns away. Truth persists despite the ignorant who fail to see the shadow behind the curtain, the dove hidden within the cape. The poetic utterance is both feather and dagger. Life is the illusion of beauty suspended on the high wire. Poetry reveals the net below. Poetry is the love and art of being. We write our own conclusions."

The Pied Piper offered another slight bow, and everyone clapped. Then he unrolled his vellum scroll and began the expected recitation.

"Rats in the cellar, now rats on the roof.
Come, Mister Piper, and offer us proof,
That you and your pipe can get rid of our rats.

Offer me gold, I'll grant you that wish.
So all of your rats will swim with the fish,
My pipe I will play to get rid of your rats.

I did as I said, and their rats were all dead,
I asked for that gold, for my purse to be fed,
Since I and my pipe put an end to their rats.

By the end of that day, no gold would they pay,
They closed all their doors and sent me away,
Though my promise I kept and got rid of their rats.

I gave them my word, and they gave me a warning,
To pack up my pipe and be gone the next morning,
No gold would I see, though I'd drowned all their rats.

So I drew out my pipe and I played a new song,
For all of their children to chase me along,
Through the woods to a cave as I'd led all the rats.

The lesson is learned as my story is told,
A debt must be paid, for promises sold,
Or loved ones might follow as I did with those rats."

At first, no one clapped. The Pied Piper had done a rather silly jig about the basement as he recited his disjointed story poem. He finished on one knee with his arms held out like a stage performer. Was he expecting a bouquet of roses?

Not from this crowd. Ingall stood and clapped. Then we all felt obligated to join him with enthusiasm for our marvelous guest. The Pied Piper bowed in each direction, and then stared at me and smiled, I thought, to let me know he knew I recognized him. And, in fact, I did. Just then. Despite the ridiculous paint on his face and his absurd costume. That nasty stealer of children. Celäenos Yeazell.

The basement door opened, and three men came through, none in costume. Overcoats. Brimmed hats. The Pied Piper laughed. Ingall went to close the basement door to upstairs. Our convocation speaker stood, angry and astonished. He told those three fellows, "You can't be here. This is invitation only."

One of the bohemians rose up, too. "Yes, you're not allowed. Please leave."

More clan poets agreed, most standing now. "Get out!"

"Go!"

"Leave!"

"This is a private clan! Go!"

I stayed in my seat. The Pied Piper kept laughing. What was so funny? He acted like a complete idiot. I didn't understand this at all. Pindar and Quixote stood shoulder to shoulder. The pixie girl retreated to one of the shadowed corners.

The Pied Piper stopped laughing just long enough to tell the convocation speaker, "You're in trouble now, my friend! You shouldn't have done that. You made them very angry! They are not in a forgiving mood!"

The speaker shouted back, "I have no idea what you're saying. You're an idiot."

The Pied Piper said, "They know what you did. Your time's up."

"What?"

One of the intruders stepped forward with a revolver now in hand and shot the convocation speaker in the head. Both of the other fellows drew revolvers, as well. One of them shot a bohemian in the back who was trying to get up the stairs. Ingall pulled out a black pistol and shot that bohemian again. The basement went berserk, screaming amid gunshots. Fear and panic. I left my chair and tried to hide in the shadows. Four more shots were fired, and I heard the voice of the Pied Piper leaning close. He was directly above me, one of those armed fellows at his side, gun pointed at my face. The Piper said, "Come with us, Mr. Brehm. You have an appointment."

Then the intruder grabbed my shoulder where I'd been shot in that trench and dragged me from the shadows toward the lower basement door and out into the night.

I was shoved into the back seat of a black Swan sedan with a powerful motor. The driver roared away from Olivette Street toward the central Metropolis. The Pied Piper sat beside me. He'd taken his silly hat off and was mopping his brow with a rag. Or perhaps wiping off some makeup. Becoming Celäenos Yeazell once again. He muttered to himself. In the front seat beside the driver, one of the fellows with a revolver spoke on a portable radiophone. The only word I heard was "Mollison." I assumed that's where I was being driven. Why?

I was frightened and angry. More killings. Persistent insanity. Death, death, death. I'd had enough of it. For some reason, I said to Yeazell, "What made you think you're a poet?"

He stopped wiping his face. "You didn't appreciate my performance?"

"No, to be honest, I thought it was ridiculous. Those stupid rhymes."

"Oh, that's a shame. I tried my best. Maybe something was lacking in my choreography. Do you think that might have been where it went wrong for you?"

I ignored his question and looked out the window as the metropolis flashed by. Streetlights and thousands of people on the evening city sidewalks. A million stars overhead. What did we know of this world apart from our madness? To be accustomed to the insanity of mass murder on a scale of great societies would ordinarily be considered unthinkable, a delusion best treated by electrical nodes and institutional therapies. When practiced by the most brilliant minds of a Republic, the unthinkable becomes habit and that habit of cruelty and moral perversion leads the simplest among us to encourage even more heinous acts. Who leads us back to the rawest semblance of virtue and goodness? After a century of despicable contortions, can anyone possibly see an escape from the endless horrors? Riding across the metropolitan night in the automobile with men whose direction was sent awry long ago, I wondered if what was decent and true still existed in the minds of men and women.

I asked Yeazell, "Are you driving me to the Mollison Institute?"

"No, Mr. Brehm, we are not."

"Then where?"

"A far less agreeable location, but possibly suitable to your recent behavior. I hear you've been a very naughty boy."

"Who told you that?"

"Your decisions have been indisputably poor, your choice of companions foolish and pretentious. History is not a classroom, Mr. Brehm. The Republic has a pattern you're far too naïve to detect. It's not really your fault. Most young people are stupid. The smarter they believe themselves to be, the stupider they become."

"Thank you."

Yeazell told me, "We didn't kill everybody back there. Maurice wanted to. He has no use for art or divergent personalities. He's a machine of death. I had to reign him in, keep him focused on the job."

"Which was?"

"That first fellow we shot organized the Mollison bombing. We had good evidence of that. He deserved to die. Dr. Boyceau Mollet was a colleague of mine once upon a time. That bomb blew his brilliant brain to bits."

"I don't know anything about that at all."

"To be determined tonight, Mr. Brehm. I should warn you, young man, there are no secrets at the Mendel Building."

I panicked. "Is that where you're taking me? Good grief, why?"

"Because you've been a bad boy, Mr. Brehm. A very bad boy. Many people are aware of your travels and nefarious dealings these past few weeks. They do not excuse your points of view as adolescent shenanigans. I cannot for the life of me begin to see why you've deliberately chosen this course for your young life. My personal opinion is that you've been duped by deranged individuals whose brains are infected by stupidity."

I looked at him in his silly costume. "I'm stupid? Is that what you're saying? I can't decide for myself what's right and wrong? Yet you're the fellow who thinks he deserves to wear a crown of gold at Désallier, right? As my father used to say, 'The height of his ambition, we know, is to be master of a puppet show.'"

Yeazell drew a sharp breath. Then he told me, "You should wear a diaper for your mouth, Mr. Brehm. These childish opinions of yours will not suit you at the Mendel Building. Sympathy there is decidedly lacking."

"Dr. Otto Paley won't be pleased to hear about this, I hope you know."

Yeazell found his ridiculous grin again. "Your envoy status, young man, has been revoked. Don't expect a pardon."

"My father has friends at the Garibaldi Building who are placed in very high positions with important connections within the Council."

"They're both dead."

"I don't believe you."

"Still dead."

Now I felt sick and scared. The Swan motor sedan roared across the night where exuberant revelry was present everywhere but in this back seat. I suppose I had no thought of rescue or absolution for whatever sins these fellows considered to be my responsibility. After all, I'd really only been a courier for the drawing and the book of fairy tales. In neither case did I know much about what I'd been carrying. I began wondering what had gone on back at Jimmy Potatoes after I'd been dragged out of there. Surely Nina had heard the gunshots. She'd have gone crazy trying to get down into the basement. Probably Ingall had locked it. He'd been the Judas who'd sold out the poetry clan to these monsters. Did Pindar and Quixote get shot? God, I hoped not. More than anyone else I'd known in the metropolis those two skinny boys exemplified the meaning of art and poetry and that vibrant culture of the heart and soul. Naturally they were naïve and silly and pretentious. Isn't that what art exists for, after all? Daring to express the sins and beauty of the world in such a way that lets somebody, somewhere, dream of another life, a better one?

Prospect Square was quiet when our motor car arrived to the garage at the Mendel Building. Only a few people strolled about. Twice that many armed guards of the Security Directorate patrolled the area. No one paid much notice to us as the black Swan auto drove by and descended to the parking lot. Celäenos Yeazell wiped off the last of his face paint and tossed the rag on the floor, then climbed out. The fellow next to the driver got out, too, and came around to my door and summoned me to join them. Frightened half to death now, I slid out. The lot was cold. Only a handful of autos parked haphazardly about. Nobody around. I was taken by the arm and guided across to a steel door and shown through to a stairwell.

Yeazell said, "Taking you downstairs to your evening's appointment, Mr. Brehm. Don't be hesitant. We have some helpful medicine waiting."

"This isn't legal."

"Of course it is."

"Says who?"

"We do."

Our voices echoed in the cold stairwell. The building felt empty. Unfortunately, I knew it wasn't. They walked me down two flights of stairs, the driver in front, followed by the fellow holding me, and Yeazell behind us. I felt almost woozy with fear. My legs were weak. I had no strength at all. If this was meant to terrify me, it worked. At the bottom of those stairs, the driver opened a door and led us into a hall lit by incandescent bulbs burning a pale electric green. The walls were blank and cement grey. A dreary construction perhaps meant to intimidate. Or just the edifice of simplicity to reflect the morally vacant acts performed down there.

I was taken to a room about midway along the hall and shown inside. A man in a white shirt and tie and black trousers was waiting for us. He looked like a doctor off-duty, or maybe a bureaucrat. There were three chairs in the room and a medical examination table. Beside the metal table was a tray with polished steel instruments and three vials of liquid and a pair of syringes. The table had leather straps.

Yeazell said, "Pay attention, Mr. Brehm. We need to get started. I want my beauty sleep." He turned to the fellow in the room. "Dr. Finster, you may begin."

"Thank you, sir."

Finster got up and walked over to me by the table. "May I have your jacket?"

"All right." I took it off and handed it to him. He passed it over to that fellow who led me into the room.

Then Finster said, "Please sit, young man. This won't be difficult."

Reluctantly, I did as I was told. What choice did I have? Both the driver and the fellow escorting me here were armed. I felt helpless, defeated.

Finster rolled up my right shirt sleeve and wrapped a blood pressure device around my arm and pumped a small rubber ball until the wrap tightened. Then he checked the gauge and took my pulse. Next, he unbuttoned my shirt and listened to my heart with a stethoscope. His expression was stern but dispassionate.

I noticed Yeazell had taken a seat in one of the chairs and was looking over a chart of some sort. Possibly a report. The other two fellows just stared at me.

"All right, Mr. Brehm," Finster said, "would you please stand up for a moment?"

I did, wondering what was next. I felt adrenaline racing through my body.

"Now, please remove all your clothing." Finster motioned to the fellow from the Swan's front seat. "Maurice? Would you help us?"

I said, "Why do I have to take off my clothes?"

Finster said, "Because I'm asking you to do so."

"I just don't understand any of this."

"Nor do you need to. Please do as I say."

Maurice looked me in the eye. "Get on with it, Brehm."

"My God, what is this?"

"Your clothes, please," Finster repeated. "All of them. You may hand them to Maurice."

I glanced at Yeazell who was still reading that report or chart, whatever it was. He was engrossed.

"Brehm!" Maurice said. "Do you want me to undress you?"

"No." I bent over to unlace my shoes. "Good grief."

All but Yeazell were watching me. I took off my shoes and socks and handed them to Maurice. His eyes were dark and ringed with shadow. His hair was oily, his skin rough and slightly mottled. Like Yeazell had mentioned in the auto, he just looked unsympathetic. No use appealing to his humanity.

I unbuttoned my shirt and handed that to him, as well. I was so nervous my buttons were a struggle. I stood still, waiting to see what came next.

"That's a very nasty wound," Dr. Finster said, brushing a finger over the bullet scar on my left shoulder.

"Glad you noticed."

"Is it painful?"

"Aches now and then."

"Don't worry," he said. "This won't agitate it."

"Thanks for the consideration."

"Trousers now, please," Finster said. "Hurry it up."

I unfastened a top button and unzipped. Then I slid them off. With my clothes off, the room felt chilly.

Finster once more. "Your drawers, too, Mr. Brehm. Don't stall."

"You want me naked?"

"Yes, I do. Take them off."

"Don't be shy, Brehm," Maurice said. "Believe me, we've seen it all."

Yeazell looked up from his reading, a vague smirk on his face. I remember hoping that one day when this was all over, somebody would kill him.

"Now, Mr. Brehm!" Finster said. "Enough of this."

I gave up and slipped off my drawers and let them fall to the floor where they were collected along with my trousers by Maurice.

I stood naked and humiliated in the cold room.

Finster said, "Now, I'm going to ask you to please lie down on the table. Maurice, will you help us?"

I climbed onto the table and laid down flat on my back, a feeling of abject helplessness. To be lying naked like that. Maurice came over and began to wrap and fasten the leather straps, one over my chest and arms, the other restraining my legs.

"Is that necessary?" I asked, feeling worse by the second.

"Just a precaution, Mr. Brehm," Finster told me. "Nothing to worry about." He addressed the Swan driver, still at the door. "Mr. Pélin?"

"Yes, sir?"

"Would you please invite Dr. Madeira to join us now?"

"Yes, sir."

He went out the door, closing it behind him.

Finster took one of the vials off the metal tray beside the table, a solution that resembled liquid gold. Next, he took a syringe and filled it from that vial. "Mr. Brehm, you'll need to relax. This will help quite a lot. It's called Oromorphium. A mild nerve agent. You'll enjoy it."

He set the syringe back onto the tray and opened a small bottle that smelled of pure alcohol. He poured a tiny amount onto a cloth and used it to clean a section of my inner arm just below my right elbow joint. Then he took the syringe and injected my vein. It stung badly and I winced. Yeazell laughed. I felt the solution flow into my arm with a warm rush. Finster stood over me, watching intently. That golden glow began to spread throughout my upper body, and I noticed a faint dizziness behind my eyes. A minute passed, and then I wasn't so afraid. I did relax and gave myself over to it.

The door opened and I watched a small lovely woman with glasses and dark hair enter the room. She wore a white lab coat and had a studious appearance. She nodded to Finster as she came over to the table. Being naked like I was, I could have felt embarrassed and self-conscious in front of her, yet I didn't. I assumed the Oromorphium had done away with that.

She offered a smile. "Hello, Mr. Brehm. I'm Dr. Madeira. We'll be working together for a little while tonight. I hope you and I can have a pleasant experience. What do you think?"

My head felt cloudy and dull. "I don't know. What are we doing?"

"Just having a nice chat, you and I. Nothing difficult at all."

"All right."

She turned to Dr. Finster. "May I have the VeraForm, please?"

"Of course."

Finster chose the vial containing a beautiful sea-blue solution. He selected a second syringe, filled it, and handed the syringe to Dr. Madeira.

She told me, "Mr. Brehm?"

"Yes?"

"May I call you 'Julian'?"

"All right."

"Thank you, Julian. This is called VeraForm. We'll be using it to facilitate the conversation you and I will be having. There's nothing unpleasant whatsoever. Its purpose is to permit an honest and delicate dialogue between us, free of inhibitions. Tempting though deception might be, you'll find it ultimately distressing and thoroughly useless. Because, Julian, as unlikely as it is, if somehow you and I fail in here, there are others in this building who prefer the direct communication of electric current to your body in methods that are both distasteful and, I must admit, obscene. So, let's you and I engage each other as friends. Shall we? You'll be truthful, won't you?"

I nodded.

"Of course you will."

Dr. Madeira set the syringe aside for a moment and took the cloth and added another touch of alcohol which she used to dab at a spot in my groin. Then she replaced that on the metal tray and pick up the syringe of blue VeraForm once again as Finster slipped a pad under my head to prop me up.

"Now, I'm sorry, Julian, but this will be a touch uncomfortable. Like a bee sting in a sensitive place. Just relax. This part will be over quickly."

I watched her lower the long syringe needle to my privates and felt her inject me just beside my testicles. The enormous pain made me gasp. She pushed it in deeply and emptied the syringe of VeraForm into my body. I held my breath against the nauseous agony of it. I felt as if I were about to vomit until she withdrew the needle and stepped back.

She smiled. "Are you alive, Julian?"

"Hmm."

"I'm terribly sorry to have you suffer that injection, but let's agree it's a necessity for our conversation."

"Mmm."

Nausea persisted but lessened by the moment. That testicle where she'd injected me still hurt. In fact, my entire groin ached. I felt sick, and yet another wave of something odd swarmed through my body and confused me. My arms and legs became numb. Dr. Madeira stared at me. The room shrunk and the lights dimmed. Or so it seemed.

"Can you hear me, Julian?" she asked, quietly.

Although I felt groggy, I found it easy to speak. "Yes."

"What is your full name?"

"Julian Charles Brehm."

"And where did you grow up?"

"Highland Park on Houghton Avenue."

"What's your roommate's name at Thayer Hall?"

"Freddy Barron."

"Have you ever been to Tamorina?"

"Yes."

"Do you know Leandro Porteus?"

"No, we've never met."

"Do you know Peter Draxler?"

I nodded. "He gave me a painting in the Dome."

VeraForm was so strange. It was as if I were listening to my own voice from across the room. I spoke without consciously forming those words. Like reflexive replies that had nothing to do with deliberate dialogue. The pleasant voice from Dr. Madeira directed what I said, and I was not only unable to resist, I had no clear sense that I wasn't. It's quite difficult to explain, but the Vera-Form seemed to work by persuading me that I was answering myself. Therefore, the entire concept of lying or creating a misdirection in the conversation was impossible, because under its influence we verbalize our interior thoughts. VeraForm persuades us into imagining we are only thinking what we tell the examiner aloud.

Dr. Madeira asked, "Do you know who planted the bomb at the Mollison Institute?"

"No, I read the headline in a newspaper on the train. Marco told me he didn't make the bomb."

"Can you tell me where to find Peter Draxler?"

"Marco says Peter lives in the undercity. He only comes up to see how we're doing. I met him in the Dome for the painting."

"What did you do with the painting, Julian, after Peter Draxler gave it to you?"

"I took it to Major Künze at Porphyry Hill with the 32nd Battalion. He bathed it in violets. Later, Samuel Protiste tried to steal it from me during the assault that blew up Major Künze. I watched two undesirables kill Protiste. The Regents have it now."

"Julian, where is the child's book of fairy tales you brought back with you from Tamorina?"

"I gave it to Harold Sketz this evening at 219 Chesterfield Avenue. He paid me fourteen credits for it. That was the agreement."

I heard the door open and close again. Someone had just left. Maurice?

"With whom was that agreement arranged?"

"The Regents."

Then I heard Dr. Finster's voice speaking inside my skull. Like a cloudy distracted dream. "Do you love our Republic, Julian? What we stand for and protect?"

"I love my family and Nina and Delia. Our Republic is a perversion. A moral atrocity."

"May we speak frankly now, Mr. Brehm?"

"Yes."

Dr. Finster asked, "Do you believe our war is justified and necessary? Do you believe that those sacrifices our soldiers endure in the Desolation have strengthened the character of this Republic?"

"No."

"Do you accept the fact of our eugenical pursuit as a moral imperative?"

"Eugenics is a moral cesspool of false and despicable ideas. It's a perversion of medical science."

"Mr. Brehm, do you understand the origin and purpose of our conflict with the undesirables?"

"To get rid of everyone we hate."

"Mr. Brehm, I want you to pay very close attention now to what I have to say. Are you listening?"

"Yes."

"Many years ago, in his early investigations with eugenics and social engineering, the great Adolphus Varane wrote: *'Progress is a phantom when such as they profit from its impediment. Roadblocks must be disrupted, dissent discontinued, all forms of nature, human and otherwise, bent to our will as a Common Good.'* Do you understand what he was attempting to express about the world and the future of our society?"

"Yes. Another obscenity."

"Later on, he wrote, *'The sorry advent of spyreosis has spawned a race so distinctly inferior and wicked that its very existence threatens our civilization. That it be exterminated as ruthlessly as possible becomes self-evident when one sees how rapidly it has evolved in the mud of that physiological quagmire. Blood, once contaminated, can never be satisfactorily purified. Avoiding that catastrophe must be universally acknowledged as a moral imperative.'* Do you agree with that statement, Mr. Brehm?"

"No. I think Varane was a criminal. He deserved to be burned up."

Dr. Madeira asked, "Julian, are you in love with Nina Rinaldi?"

"Yes, I am. Very much so."

"If it were proven that spyreosis exists in her blood, would you agree that she is unfit for our society and incompatible with your romantic intentions?"

"Proving spyreosis is like teaching a cat to tell time. Can't be done."

Yeazell laughed.

Dr. Madeira asked, "Is Nina involved with any of these bombings?"

"No."

"Does she associate herself with Marco Grenelle?"

"No, she's not friends with Marco."

"Did Nina help you bring the drawings to Porphyry Hill?"

"No. She only led me to Virgil in the mausoleum. Then she asked me to take a picture of Delia to Arturo in Tamorina."

"Did you do so?"

"Arturo wasn't there. The Regents told me he's dead and you burned his body here."

Dr. Finster asked, "Why did the Regents ask you to bring the book of fairy tales to Sumner Dawes?"

"I don't know. The Pied Piper's been stealing children out of the Desolation. Maybe someone should kill him."

"Do you know where the children are?"

"No, but Castor and Pollux probably do. You're not fooling them. They live in the undercity and they seem to be watching you. Marco says they can blow up the central metropolis if they choose to."

Dr. Madeira asked, "Did your parents know you had the drawings from Leandro Porteus?"

"No, they didn't know anything about Peter Draxler except he was accused of stealing the drawings. I kept what else I knew away from them. It wasn't safe. The Regents told me it's a drawing of a lethal chamber."

"Did Frederick Barron aid you in getting the drawing out of the city?"

"No, he helped solve Peter's code and had Angelina sew the hidden pocket into my father's jacket. Freddy's a genius at puzzles."

I kept hearing those voices badgering me and thought I was talking in my sleep, speaking to myself, thinking out loud. VeraForm must also be a mentally paralyzing hypnotic. I found it physically impossible to stop replying.

Dr. Finster asked, "Do the Regents have a plan to attack us here in the metropolis?"

"The true seat of empire resides on the palace mount, Désallier, at Laspágandélus, not in Prospect Square. The Regents intend to restore the natural order of history by exposing that false geography of the Status Imperium and the fraudulent science of spyreosis. It's how this war will end."

Dr. Madeira took a cloth to my groin and wiped carefully at my testicles. When she lifted the cloth away from me, I saw blood on it. I felt ill and my head spun.

Dr. Finster asked, "Have you met with Dr. Otto Paley since returning from Tamorina?"

"No, I've never met him at all. He signed my envoy status."

Dr. Madeira fell on the floor.

I heard Celäenos Yeazell collapse behind me.

Dr. Finster gave a strange expression, then he fell, too.

The room was still and silent.

My eyes went dark as something was put over my nose and mouth. A mask? Next, I felt someone take my arm and inject me with another needle that stung a bit. Then I heard the straps being undone and I was raised up off the table and made to stand. I didn't notice my nakedness any longer. I was just in that room. A blanket was wrapped around me and I felt myself walk again. Escorted out the door and into the drafty hall. Voices muttering softly all about. No other noise. I was led gently along the corridor but with deliberate haste. Then through a door and down a staircase. The cement steps were cold on my feet. The stairs were steep and there were many. A long descent. Then the bottom and another door and another corridor, this one darker, and a final door and darkness all around.

I was stopped and that mask of sorts was removed from my face and I breathed a dank air and noticed my thoughts becoming more precise. Someone leaned me up against a cold stone wall and the blanket fell away and I was helped to dress: drawers and trousers first, then my shirt and socks and shoes. My jacket. I tried to see where I was. My eyes were still cloudy, but I could sense a tunnel. Dark and narrow. Claustrophobic. Electric lamps encircled me. People surrounding. Not many. Perhaps a dozen?

One of them spoke to me softly and that voice was not inside my head.

"Julian?"

"Yes."

"Are you waking up?"

I nodded, reasonably confident that was true. "Yes, I think so."

"Do you remember the VeraForm?"

I did, indeed. "It was strange. Really strange."

"Are your thoughts quiet again?"

A curious question, but I understood it clearly. My thoughts *were* quieter now, and separate from my voice when I said, "I'm feeling better, yes. Thank you. Where am I?"

"You're in a tunnel under the Mendel Building. We brought you out."

Then someone stepped into the light with a handsome face I recognized. Peter Draxler.

He smiled and took my hand. "Good morning, Julian."

I squeezed his hand. "Thank you."

"Shall we go?"

"Where?"

"Away from here."

And that's where we went.

I was led underground to the basement of a rail station a mile from the Mendel Building where Farnham Avenue intersected Giardinetto Street at the empty Greek Emporium. Along our walk, one by one some of my rescuers drifted off in other directions until only Peter Draxler and two burly men were left with me.

At those rail stairs, Draxler, too, said goodbye. He told me, "You're safe for now, Julian. But you've been using up lives at a dangerous rate. I'm sorry that Samuel proved to be the scoundrel that he was. I didn't see it. The Regents did, though, so good enough. The reach of their political intelligence is profound. We owe them our lives many times over."

"I met your mother."

"So I heard."

"She's very nice."

"Thank you."

"Maybe one day you'll go see her."

"Maybe." He shrugged. "Lots still to do here besides painting lakes all day."

"I'm sure she has her point of view."

Draxler smiled. "Don't we all?"

"She told me about your father and sister. I'm sorry."

He shrugged. "That was a long while ago on this stage of horrors. Not your concern, Julian."

I felt wobbly and somewhat indistinct with my thoughts. I could tell I was too vulnerable to be on my own.

I asked, "Where am I supposed to be going now?"

Draxler told me, "A friend of yours is waiting in a motor car up on the street. He's the fellow most responsible for your rescue. Few people walk out of the Mendel Building like you just did. It requires a particular miracle and, fortunately, your friend just provided one." Draxler shook my hand again. "Goodbye, Julian."

An instant later, he left. Just that suddenly. Gone away into the dark.

Now my two guides took me up the rail station stairs to Giardinetto Street. Emerging into the fresh night air, I guessed we were about an hour or so from dawn. They led me down the block toward Farnham and a tan auto parked ahead at the curb with the motor running. When we got there, one of the fellows opened the rear door and helped me into the back seat and shut the door behind me. Then he and his partner walked across the street and separated. The auto headlights switched on and two familiar faces looked back over the front seats at me.

"Good morning," Warren Radelfinger said, with a bright smile.

"Hello, Julian," Evelyn Haskins added. "So good to see you again."

XLVII

∿

They drove me out of the city. Radelfinger worked the wheel like an auto racer or one of those frenetic taxi drivers from Cendrillon Province who learn to drive through holiday bazaars and frightening cliffside roads. They told me that we were headed to Alexanderton where Freddy and my mother and Jack McManus were waiting along with the Barron family. When I asked about Nina, Evie said, "She's back at her friend, Johara's, to see after Delia. We're supposed to telephone there when we arrive at Freddy's. It was Nina who told Freddy about Jimmy Potatoes. He telephoned to your mother and to us. Warren organized your rescue. Isn't he just the best?"

She kissed his ear.

For once I had to agree. I probably owed him my life.

Radelfinger laughed. "It wasn't so complicated as Draxler liked to think. Just an old formula I worked up in Lower School. A gas I called 'Lethereon' that has a rapid somnabulizing agent and is entirely odorless. Its dispersal rate is equivalent to air molecules in ten thousand percent acceleration and dissipates gradually with atmospheric transitions. Best of all, I found it can only be detected by witness of its experience which is nearly instantaneous. We introduced the gas into the lower floor through ventilation ducts and sent those men to rescue you once its effects had surfaced. I assume it was successful."

"Yes, thank you."

"Maybe you're wondering why you weren't also put to sleep?"

He seemed anxious to explain, so I encouraged him. "Well, I was pretty groggy from the VeraForm, and I suppose I hadn't really thought of that until you just asked. But, yes, sure. Why didn't I go out, too?"

"Well, I'm actually pretty angry at myself for not anticipating this flaw in the active chemistry of my formula, but apparently the hypno-sedative intercourse between Oromorphium and VeraForm slightly inhibits the depressive sleep agent in Lethereon such that it's not possible to produce a full loss of consciousness under those chemical conditions. Also, I had Draxler's men inject you with adrenophenotherol, which disperses the narco-hypnotic in those three agents and restores your natural consciousness. I guess it worked reasonably well since we're able to have this dialogue."

"Let's just say I recognize both your faces and am grateful for what you've done. I don't how to thank you. In the meantime, I'll work on learning to spell my own name again in the next hour or so."

Evie reached over the seat to take my hand. "We've missed you, Julian. Warren thinks you're the tops. He always says so." She kissed him again. "Don't you, honey?"

Radelfinger said, "Evie gets lonely for more company than she can tolerate with me and my toys."

"Oh, honey, that's not so at all. You're more than enough for me."

Alexanderton is about forty miles northwest of the metropolis in a pastoral region of beautiful homes, woods and fields, and a market district large enough to satisfy those who have little appetite for traveling into the city. Dr. H. Cornelius Barron's reputation and expertise in treating diseases of the heart and lungs bought him a magisterial home on hilly and cedar-shaded Rothermel Street four blocks above town. I'd only been there once for an eggs-and-cocktail brunch one summer after freshman year when Freddy had agreed to become roommates with me at Thayer Hall. Everyone seemed eager and pleasant that day except his two sisters, who were apparently harpies disguised as human females. I instantly became protective of Freddy and felt great sympathy for his having to share the house with those two. Little wonder he started drinking at fourteen.

Radelfinger rolled his tan Hanley auto up the Barrons' driveway in the early morning sunlight. Freddy bounded out of the house before we'd even left the car. He opened my door and took my arm as I wobbled out.

"Good God, Julian, you are such a wreck! How do you manage to dangle on the high-wire week after week?"

"Not on purpose, my friend."

"He's blessed with Olympian fortune," Radelfinger said, getting out of the auto with Evie. "We presume he was sufficiently informative under VeraForm to keep him alive long enough for us to get there."

"Warren stirred his magic potion and Julian's tormentors were finished," Evie added. She gave him a kiss. "He's matchless."

"That he is," I agreed.

"Your mother's here," Freddy told me. "She's beside herself. I've never seen her so angry! My mother had to slip a pinch of morpheus powder into her tea to calm her down. Father's speaking with your Mr. McManus. He's pretty upset, as well. It was quite a scene in there. You'll be the star of the show when we go in."

"I need to telephone Nina and let her know I'm here. She'll go crazy if I don't. And I want to find out what happened at Jimmy Potatoes after I left. I was afraid they'd shoot everyone. It was a madhouse once those fellows walked in with their guns."

Indoors held a lovely aroma of coffee and hot biscuits and Soulien tea brewing on the stove. Freddy announced my arrival and Mother came scurrying from the Barrons' drawing room. She had tears in her eyes. Then so did I. We'd both been put upon and our resolve tested as a family. She gave me a great hug. "Julian, my darling, you simply must stop terrifying me like this. I won't stand for it."

"I'm sorry, Mother. I know. I didn't expect this at all. I think it was a trap. Somehow they were waiting for me."

Jack McManus came down the hall from Dr. Barron's office. He agreed. "We think so, too, Julian. I have a call in at Dr. Paley's office. We've been trying to reach Dennett and Trevelyan for the past hour. No luck. Their secretaries haven't heard a word from them since sometime yesterday."

I looked at my mother, tears welling up in her lovely eyes. Then I said to them all, "That Pied Piper fellow, Celäenos Yeazell, told me they're both dead. I didn't believe him at first, but I guess now I do."

Mother gasped.

McManus frowned. "Sonsabitches."

Then Dr. Barron appeared, just as angry as you could imagine. He asked, "Have they threatened my son, too? Tell me the truth, Julian. Did they say anything about that?"

I nodded. "They asked if Freddy had helped me take the Porteus drawing out of the city. I admitted he helped solve a coded puzzle that led me to the drawing, but that was all. They seemed to know something was up."

Dr. Barron said, "I assume they used VeraForm to extract that information from you."

"Yes, sir. I'm sorry. I had no idea how it worked."

"It's insidious."

McManus added, "And illegal. We'll sue them. You can be sure of that. They'll be sorry they ever met us."

Dr. Barron glanced at Freddy, then said, "In my opinion, neither of you two boys should go back to Thayer Hall until we have assurances from the Council that you'll be safe. It's unconscionable that you would be targeted like that. What's this world coming to?"

Freddy said, "It's the Desolation, Father. Mass insanity."

The telephone rang in the drawing room. I heard Freddy's mother asking him from the kitchen to go answer it. Radelfinger and Evie followed him in there.

McManus put a hand on my shoulder. "I'm sorry about all this, son. In a way, I feel responsible. Back at your family's house that evening, I doubted your intuition about the politics of our society, those dangers we've incurred by placing the necessities of war above the rights and needs of our own people, not to mention those millions we've declared enemies. You were right, after all. We've let ourselves rot from within and we don't even see it. Eugenics as practiced by the Status Imperium has corrupted us. When college boys like yourself are taken to the Mendel Building for a session with VeraForm, we've given it all up."

"Jack, I've been saying that all along," Dr. Barron added. "The pursuit of a eugenical paradise cannot lead anywhere good. It's just nonsense to see the world as a struggle between the perfect and the flawed. Because who makes those distinctions? Who sets those lines? Spots on your apples don't of necessity make the flesh inedible. Nor does a shiny polish promise there aren't worms within. The world has never been that cut and dried. We've always needed to investigate and discuss and consider those differences between us, regardless of how great or minute they may appear. And learn to tolerate our fellow men and women, accept our neighbors as members in this wonderful fellowship of humanity."

I spoke up to say, "At Laspágandélus, a fellow by the name of Sutro told me that hatred of those who are different has driven this eugenical nonsense. It's just that simple."

Mother said, "The sheer venality of these men has not gone unnoticed by those of us not blinded from years of war and ridiculous persecutions. Charles believed we could not go on living in what he called 'the brew of discontent.' He felt that either our hearts welcomed the goodness that belongs to each of us upon our birth, or we were doomed to drown in the quagmire of our despicable acts. I used to believe in the certainty of the former, but that telephone call I received from Frederick this morning has me convinced the latter may be our fate. Unless somehow we come to our senses."

Jack McManus said to her, "Do you recall that wonderful quotation from Paul Havrincourt's, *Of Gods and Men,* that Porter Childs used to remember for us every spring assembly at Templar?"

Mother said, "Refresh my memory, Jack. I'm a bit rattled this morning."

"Well, it went like this: *'Is there a world beyond our own where no virtue goes unrewarded, no sin unpunished, whose clear blue skies and sultry evenings are recorded in the Book of Days, and all men seek perfection and immortality of good purpose?'*"

She smiled. "Yes, I do. The sentiment is quite lovely. I often wondered if there were truth in that somehow. Now, I admit I have my doubts."

"Well, Martha, we can't have doubts. I realize now that lunatic urgency I castigated Julian for is needed as much as anything these days. Those ridiculous kids saw the truth when we refused. But only we have the means to put an end to this nonsense and right the wheel of our Republic before we sail off the end of the world."

I said, "The Regents at Laspágandélus won't let that happen. You have no idea how much they know about all of this. It seems almost inconceivable to us, but I think the Status Imperium is deathly afraid of them. Like the Regents told me at their palace, everything we do is based on the concept of our eminent domain over all the provinces. Now I've learned that's not at all true. Once everyone else does, and I think they will soon enough, the game is up."

Freddy stepped out into the hall. "Julian, it's Nina."

I excused myself and went into the drawing room where Freddy held the telephone receiver for me. Evie was sitting on a sofa while Warren perused some of Dr. Barron's books. Freddy told me, "She's pretty frantic."

"Thanks." I took the receiver. "Nina?"

"Julian! Oh God, those bastards! Did they hurt you? I hope Marco kills them all!"

"No, I'm all right. Mostly. Still a bit cloudy. Try to avoid VeraForm if you can. It's a strange and nasty experience."

"It was chaos down there after you left. They killed three people. We had to break down the door. One of your poet boys was wounded but he'll live. The other went nuts. I can't stand all this. If I'd known things would be so insane, I never would've brought Delia here."

"How is she?"

"Good as can be. She's been scared for you. I think she's got a crush on my boyfriend."

"Freddy's father and our family lawyer don't want us going back to Thayer Hall until they've spoken to Dr. Paley and he tells us it's safe. I can't imagine when that might be now. Those fellows who kidnapped me didn't seem to have any regard for the law."

"What's law anymore, right? It's all out the window now. I think they're making it up as they go along at the Judas Council these days. Except obviously they needed information from you, I'm surprised they didn't just drop a bomb into the basement and kill everyone. What did you tell them?"

"Anything they asked, Nina," I said. "That's how VeraForm works. Whatever they want out of you, they get. It's pretty terrifying. Our lawyer says he'll sue, but I doubt that'll get anywhere. Might as well try suing the moon."

"Delia's home with Johara. I told her to stay there. No running off to chase cats. When can I see you? I'm at a drugstore on Kingsbury. Delia needed some ointment for a rash. I'll be back at Johara's in about an hour."

"I miss you, too," I told her. "Let me see what the plan is, and I'll telephone you there. Maybe you and Delia can come here. I'll ask Freddy." I glanced over at him and he nodded. "That might suit us both."

"All right. I love you. Be safe."

"I love you, too."

We disconnected and I handed the receiver back to Freddy, who put it back on its cradle. I asked him, "So, what do you think we should do?"

"Stay overnight. You never can tell what those fellows have planned. They won't be happy you got away."

Radelfinger added, "And they'll have terrific headaches for at least twelve hours. Lethereon raises blood pressure in the brain. It's not healthy."

I said, "Aren't you worried what they might do to you if they discover that gas was yours?"

Radelfinger shrugged. "Not much. It's untraceable. And Evie and I weren't anywhere near the Mendel Building last night. I only invented the stuff. I didn't introduce it into the vents."

"You're still on thin ice, in my opinion."

"Maybe."

Evie said, "We're not worried. Warren's got all the angles figured out and more tricks than you can imagine. He's really stupendous."

My mother came into the room with Jack McManus. She said, "Jack thinks you ought to stay here for a while. We've notified the local police about a possible situation in this neighborhood, and they've agreed to assign officers to watch this house. Dr. Barron agrees."

"We think it's the most prudent course of action as things stand this morning."

Freddy said, "I doubt the Alexanderton police department can offer much resistance to Internal Security. What's to stop them from walking right up to the door and calling us out?"

Jack McManus told us, "Although it might appear as if there are no lines the Security Protectorate can't cross these days, in fact, that's not precisely true. Profound divisions within the Judicial Council create ambiguities that mitigate unfettered illegalities. Certain actions trigger blocks pursuant to very rapid internal investigations that send heads rolling clear through the Status Imperium. Not everyone in our Republic are monsters, and those who aren't know those who are. The war has contributed to fractures in our government that have actually strengthened a perverse moral code that thirty or forty years ago appeared on the verge of fading away. Everybody seems to believe that undermining the basic structure of our Republic is dangerous and probably fatal to our entire society, whether we win the war or not. No, I don't believe Internal Security would dare pay a visit out here. And, at any rate, this situation has been fully described for Dr. Paley and his allies within the Council. There are powerful men on our side, boys. Trust me. A reckoning is coming about all of this."

Mother said, "I hope so. It's just unconscionable how those men behaved last night."

"They'll pay, Martha," Jack McManus told her. "I promise. Meanwhile, you boys should remain here. There's no good reason to leave this house until we think it's safe."

Freddy's mother came to the drawing room doorway. "Is anyone hungry?"

— · —

We ate outdoors on a garden lawn off the back terrace. Lovely flowering gardenia and lemon blossoms scented the air. Phebe Barron had cooked waffles and
Le Vau sausages, steamed potatoes and honey muffins. Freddy and I enjoyed
orange juice, while Radelfinger and Evie and the adults had coffee and steamed
tea. I thought about the Mendel Building and that room downstairs and wondered which chemicals besides VeraForm were given to Lewis Atherton during
his captivity that so damaged his brain. His confusions were strange and pro-
fuse, his psychological frailties horrific. Any society so willing and enthusiastic to torture those it deems antithetical to its own purposes must be morally
decadent and philosophically adrift. If this was how we lived now, what sort of
monsters might we become in decades ahead?

I had to keep track of time to let Nina know we'd decided to remain at the
Barrons'. Freddy had shown me a rumpus room in the basement with roll-out
beds where we'd find space for Delia and Nina and me, with a dog bed for Goliath. I'd been offered Freddy's room, but I thought Nina might prefer to keep
her little girl close once they left the anonymity of Johara's house on Meltemi
Avenue. Nobody really paid much attention to the neighborhoods there across
the eternal river. They were considered plain and bourgeois and architecturally
bland, utterly bereft of ornament and artistic appeal. Real estate values were
modest and rented rooms came cheap. Nina told me Delia ran Goliath on a
leash up and down the sidewalks all day long chasing cats and little dogs.

Drinking her tea, Mother said that she and Jack McManus would be driving back to Highland Park after he telephoned to the Garibaldi Building and
Dr. Otto Paley's office to determine whether there'd been any further news
about Dennett and Trevelyan. If they were, indeed, both dead, he assured me
that Dr. Paley's fury would set the entire Judicial Council ablaze.

Jack McManus said, "Dr. Paley has known Harold Trevelyan since Squires
Lower School. They were best pals at one time and even chased the same girl at
Freshman Glee. Paley got her and Harold took her sister. A fine arrangement
that saved a friendship. If someone in the Mendel Building has killed Trevelyan, and he discovers who's behind it, you can be sure that lights in the lethal
chamber will be lit and the gas switched on."

"He should start with Celäenos Yeazell," I said. "Maybe find out where those children are being taken."

"That's a knot to untangle. Who knows what's behind it? I'd suggest you boys stay away from that story."

Mother said, "Jack and I plan to meet Peggy at Fortunado's early this afternoon. I trust by then we'll have some assurances regarding your safety."

I kissed my mother goodbye and thanked Jack McManus for driving her out to Alexanderton and looking after my welfare. We waved his silver sedan away down the driveway to Rothermel Street. Once they'd gone, Freddy led me and Evie and Radelfinger out across the lawn to a guest cottage in the back garden under shady willows. We went inside where his mother had decorated in pleasantly colored fabrics through shades of olive and rust. A woven tan rug in the middle of the floor. Some nice sofas and chairs and standing wood lamps. Off a narrow hall was a toilet and a nice comfortable bedroom with two windows and a nightstand and dressing chair.

I asked, "Are we having a party out here? It's a little early to start drinking, don't you agree?"

Freddy smirked. "Julian, you are such a depressive. Everything for you is an obstacle to enjoyment."

"I just try to be steady, you know?"

"Well, sometimes it's better to wobble a bit, now and then."

Evie said, "Warren never wobbles. That's half his trouble."

Radelfinger kissed her shoulder. "Thanks, dear. I'm sure our friends were anxious to hear that."

Freddy raised one end of the rug exposing a trap door beneath it. The rug was attached to the trap door. "Here's my favorite wobble, kids."

We stepped back so Freddy could expose the door a little more. It was on a hinge that held it into place as he lifted the rug.

"What is this?" I asked. "Your secret life?"

He removed a square iron key from his pants pocket and stuck it into a lock on the trap and freed the door. "It's one of my hobbies. Come join me!"

A light had gone on in the cellar beneath the floor and lit the ladder of steps leading downward. Freddy told us, "Go on down. I'll follow."

Radelfinger said, "You first, Evie. I'm right behind you."

"Not on your life, darling. I'm terribly claustrophobic unless someone goes ahead of me."

I volunteered and led our little quartet into Freddy's basement paradise. There was a handle on the underside of the trap door that Freddy used to pull it shut after us. The door closed with a muffled thump. He folded a latch to lock the trap. Then Freddy crossed the room and went to a work bench and switched on more lights.

His private basement palace had a carpet and a pair of couches and some chairs, a small refrigerator and cookstove. Freddy also had a large wireless radio set on the bench. He flicked it on, and the whole contraption crackled to life.

Radelfinger rushed over. "My God, Freddy, you've been holding out on us! This is marvelous!'"

I was more than surprised myself. Here I'd always thought Freddy did nothing but drink and listen to his stupid sisters' babbling when he went home. Honestly, I had no idea my tipsy roommate was some amateur radio enthusiast. I asked, "When did you get this?"

He beamed. "Oh, I've always dabbled in one electrical recreation or another. Father has a friend in Bruguiére who's got one of these wireless set-ups and talks to people all over the world. Says it keeps him up on things he doesn't know about. Father bought this radio for consulting on cases across the provinces where the telephone exchange is spotty. He let me talk one day to some fellows in Savárus and another in Upper Siam and I got hooked. Great fun!"

"Is it legal?" Evie asked. "Please tell me it's not, so Warren won't waste his money. He'll marry one of these before me, otherwise."

"Well," Freddy said, "it requires a special operator's license from the Communications Directorate. Helps to know somebody there. Lucky for us, my father consulted on a cardiac situation with Dr. Paley several years ago and earned permission to purchase this equipment and the requisite authorization to use it with only a few restrictions."

"Which were?" I asked, curious about how extensive radio communications might be with a set like this.

"We're not allowed to cross channels with our military or any wireless signals broadcast from Prospect Square. It's incredibly difficult to do so, regardless, but Dr. Paley encouraged us to avoid temptations of any sort in that realm."

"But you could," Radelfinger said, "if you really wanted to."

"Possibly," Freddy told him. "But I'm neither curious nor stupid enough to try. My father would erase my name from the family plot if I were ever to do so, and it's already been paid for."

"Can we see it work?" I asked. "Just a simple demonstration? Maybe call someone you already know or listen in somewhere. How do you ordinarily use it?"

Freddy shrugged. "I have a couple of friends I chat with when I'm home. You know I'm not here so often any longer. I really haven't been on the wire in a while."

"Well, just choose someone," I suggested. "So we can see how it works."

"All right, I have a fellow enthusiast in Théophilia who says he's on the wireless all day and night."

"Must be married," said Radelfinger.

Evie punched his arm.

"Ow!"

"All right, let's see." Freddy fiddled with the dials and a pair of switches that made more lights come on the radio. My comprehension of any sort of electronics is non-existent, so I really had no sense of what he was doing. Radelfinger, on the other hand, acted like a boy with a new bike at Christmas. Except it wasn't his bike and he was still leaning over Freddy's shoulder.

Evie warned Freddy, "Don't you dare let Warren touch it. He's much too brilliant and rash toward restrictions on his behavior. We'll all end up on that ash heap somewhere."

Freddy picked up the microphone. "Come in, Sebti. Reply."

Static hissed from the radio.

"Come in, Sebti. Reply."

A voice buzzed back at us through the static. *"Is that you, Morley? Reply."*

We laughed. "Morley?"

He covered the microphone with one hand. "My middle name. Don't interrupt." Freddy spoke again to his friend. "Affirmative, Sebti. Reply."

"It's raining here today. Flood on the roads. Lots of wind in the fields. Reply."

"Warm and busy here. Lots of sun. Reply."

"Jealous. Reply."

"Don't be. We have rubbish in the streets. Reply."

"Sorry to hear. We have hail. You have hell. Strange weather. Reply."

"Yes. True. Have to go now. Nice chatting, Sebti. Until next time. Sign off. Reply."

"Goodbye, Morley. Sign off."

Freddy put down the microphone and began switching off the radio set. Once it was dark, he swiveled the chair back to face us. "That's how it works. Pretty simple."

I said, "You only talk about the weather?"

"No, actually he was telling me about a fresh artillery barrage outside Théophilia. Soldiers on the roads. Exchange of fire across the cornfields from mechanical rifles."

"A code!" Radelfinger said. "Oh, I love that! Very ingenious."

"Necessary," Freddy explained, "because all wireless is susceptible to over-listening from Prospect Square. We can't be too careful."

"I should think not," I agreed. "They're almost in our ear canals these days."

Evie said, "It's awfully creepy how you boys love this sort of game. Can't you ever put it down for a while and enjoy a good kiss instead?"

Radelfinger frowned. "Didn't I just kiss you, darling, not five minutes ago?"

"A good kiss, honey. Not your usual sloppy nothing. Freddy? May we go back to the house now? I'm feeling a faint coming on. It's so dark in here."

"But perfect for my demonstration, dear," Radelfinger said. "Don't you agree?"

"Oh, yes! I do!" Evie turned to us. "You absolutely must see this. Warren has the most fabulous trick to show you!"

"What sort of trick?" I asked, maybe a bit hesitant. Who knew what Radelfinger would come up with next?

"Let's see it," Freddy said. "We'll be your judges. Not that we're doubting you."

Radelfinger turned to Evie. "Dear, let me have your atomizer, please."

She opened her purse and drew one out. The glass perfume bottle attached to a rubber ball glimmered in the lamp glow. The dark liquid in the bottle was rather cloudy, an almost indistinct hue. Evie lit a cigarette as Radelfinger asked us to take a couple steps back. Once we had, he squeezed the brass lever to the rubber ball and a plume of hazy green fog issued forth. Then he took the lit cigarette from Evie. With a smile, he said, "Watch this."

495

When he pushed the burning tip of the cigarette into the expanding boundary of the faint gas, a brilliant burst of fire exploded in a flash.

"Good grief!"

"What is that?" Freddy howled. "You're completely insane! Good God!"

Radelfinger laughed. "Just a little something I've been working on. I call it 'Heliophlogistic Atomized Viridium.' I've adapted a few of Dr. Thayer's old formulas to create it. His original genius was my inspiration. I think he'd have been impressed, seeing as how his singular insights provided the gateway."

I asked the next obvious question. "But *why* did you make it? To what purpose."

He shrugged. "I really can't tell you that."

"We were sworn to secrecy," Evie told me. "Under dire threats." Then she laughed. "Not really. Warren just wants it to be a surprise. He has a demonstration planned. You'll all be invited." She kissed him. "Isn't that so, dear?"

"Of course! Any scientific discovery or achievement needs a certain protocol of unveiling. This is no different at all. Certainly, our showing will be dynamic and inspiring. The correct moment just has to be chosen for the best effect. We hope to do that soon. You'll be our special guests. Front row, if it all comes off. The five of us will celebrate together. That's my expectation."

Evie kissed him. "Warren is simply unsurpassed."

"Good enough," I said, utterly stunned by that flash of heat and light. My face owned a slight burn. I had to admit for a moment there, I was actually terrified. Radelfinger was every ounce the genius Pindar and Quixote thought Draxler was. For my money, I agreed with Evie. Radelfinger was unsurpassed.

Then a girl's voice from upstairs. *"Frederick! Mother wants you to empty out the garbage. Right now!"*

Freddy groaned. "My sisters are home. Tragedy has arrived with the noon bus. I'm afraid our holiday is over."

Back at the house, I went to use the toilet. Radelfinger and Evie had decided to go into town for a stroll and left straightaway. I planned to stay at least until hearing from Nina whom I greatly missed then, once all that earlier excitement had passed and my heart rate was returning to normal. Dr. Barron had already gone off to his morning practice with appointments expected to last half the day. Freddy's mother busied herself cleaning up after our breakfast.

Freddy himself took out the aforementioned trash after a brief but noisy scrap with his hectoring sisters. Fortunately, those statuesque twins, Henrietta and Ramona, had only come home from Saturday classes for lunch and a couple of books they required for afternoon studies. I expected them to fly away on broomsticks any minute. They really were the most dreadful girls. When the telephone rang, I thought that could be Nina calling for me and got up to go see. Ramona was there first and took the call, then hung up. As pleasantly as possible, I asked, "Who was that?"

She gave me one of her looks. "Some girl whose voice I don't know."

"You didn't ask her name?"

"Why would I?"

Henrietta came into the drawing room with a watercress sandwich on a plate of blue china. "Who called?"

Ramona told her, "Some nobody."

"Look, dear," I said, "that 'nobody' could've been my girlfriend. I've been expecting her to telephone. It's urgent."

"Then she ought to have called your house, not ours."

"Why would she do that when I'm here?"

Ramona said, "Why wouldn't she? This is our home, not a telephone exchange."

"Good grief! What's the matter with you?"

"Don't worry about it. Go upstairs and play with Freddy. We have more important things to do than take telephone calls from your girlfriend — if you even really have one, which I'm doubting more every second now."

Henrietta laughed, and both Gorgons left the room.

I was astonished that Freddy hadn't yet killed them, or himself. Giving birth to those two must've been a hideous experience for Mrs. Barron. Something had clearly gone horribly wrong. I went up to find Freddy, thinking he might be in his bedroom on the third floor under the attic.

I met him coming out of his bathroom. I said, "Put your sisters in uniform and send them to the front lines and this war would be over in a day."

"They truly are creatures from the pit of hell, aren't they?"

"The stuff of nightmares. I don't see how you survive."

"I have you as compensation from the gods, my friend. Otherwise, I'd be strapped to a wall at the Selfridge sanitarium and given electro-therapy for breakfast."

"Well, then, thank God for college."

We went into his bedroom where he had his Botany and Elemental Geology course books and notes scattered across his quilt comforter. We sat on the bed. Still waiting on Nina. The clock on Freddy's study desk told me she was already overdue to call, and I wondered even more if that telephone call Ramona had hung up on had been her.

"Nina might've telephoned a few minutes ago."

"Might have?"

"Ramona hung up without asking who it was," I told him. "Now I'm worried she won't call back. If it really was her."

"Why wouldn't she call back?"

"I don't know. Maybe she couldn't."

"You know, master, this is so far beyond what you and I are capable of handling that I wonder if we've both lost our minds."

"Well, I know I've lost mine. I can hardly think straight anymore. My decisions are ridiculous and the things I'm getting myself involved with are insane. Why did we chase around the city after Peter Draxler? What was I doing in the undercity? Why did I agree to take that train to Tamorina? Why did we go to that stupid bookstore? Why did I accept that invite to Jimmy Potatoes last night?"

"Why did you follow me into the surf at St. Etienne Shores, my friend?" Freddy replied. "It's simple. You're loyal and brave, and you want to be a big hero so all the co-eds will make our room the place to be at Regency College. *'Some are, and must be, greater than the rest.'*"

I laughed. "That's not completely true. Most of this I've done for Nina. I fell for her and she asked me to help. I wanted to please her, I guess. I'm not sure how all the rest of this happened."

"See? It all comes down to girls, Julian. Always. *'But since thou lovest, love still, and trust therein.'*"

"So you're saying I'm doomed for having fallen in love with Nina?"

"Probably, but it doesn't need to be all bad. You have all your faculties and you have me to guide you."

"In that case, I'm sure we're lost. There doesn't seem to be a map anywhere for common sense."

"Don't forget my squib books. They provide more answers than questions that may be asked."

The telephone rang again. Freddy jumped up. "My parents have a telephone in their bedroom."

He raced out into the hall.

I got up, too. I didn't care for this plan of us waiting around at the Barrons'. Were we just supposed to sit here playing cards until Dr. Paley told us we were safe to go out again?

Freddy yelled to me from down on the second floor. "Julian! It's Nina! Quick!" I came out and saw him at the door to his parents' room. "She's crying."

I hurried and he gave me the phone from a lovely nightstand. "Nina?"

She was sobbing. *"I'm at Johara's. She's dead. I found her in bed. Somebody killed her. Strangled, I think. Her neck. It's ugly."*

"And Delia?"

Nina kept sobbing as she spoke. *"She's not here. Riala's gone, too. I called Goliath and he came over from next door. He wasn't wearing a leash. Delia would never let him off his leash unless he's in the backyard. Someone must've let him out."*

I didn't know what to think, except that my escape from the Mendel Build ing must've provoked this. Dr. Madeira knew about Nina. They must've gone to get her and took Delia instead. Or they took Delia to bring Nina to her, and me to them. Something like that.

Nina cried, *"Can you come get me? We need to find Delia!"*

"How are we supposed to know where they took her?"

"They pinned a note with a number to Johara's dress. HERmes-3222. Do you know that prefix?"

"Not offhand, but Freddy can figure it out."

"You have to come get me, Julian. I can't stay here any longer. I need to find Delia."

"Is there somewhere else we can meet besides that house?" I thought Nina should leave Johara's immediately. "Away from Meltemi Avenue? Somewhere with people around?"

She was still crying. I could tell she was attempting to collect her thoughts, deciding where to send us.

Freddy was standing next to me now, listening in. He said, "I'll get Mother's auto. She never uses it."

He left the bedroom.

Nina told me, *"D'Ancona's grocery store. It's on Felcher. About six blocks from here. Always busy. I'll wait inside. Will you come now? Please? I'm so scared."*

After Nina disconnected, I telephoned to home. My thought was that Jack McManus would be there and I could tell him what had just occurred and let him know where Freddy and I were driving in case he had someone to meet us there. No one answered. Presumably they were still out. Freddy called from downstairs and I went to meet him at the Barrons' garage.

His mother owned a fancy violet Jerome convertible runabout with a tan canvas top. Freddy backed it out into the driveway, and we took off. Meltemi Avenue was about an hour away into the metropolis and west of the holy river, in Sartosé District. We took the parkway where most auto traffic was sparse and leisurely at that time of day. All sorts of leafy elms and oaks, spruce and cottonwoods gave shade and pleasure to acres of pretty woods and lawns and sidewalks. The spring air was warm and slightly breezy, the cloudless sky blue as heaven. Despite the urgency of our destination, I felt relaxed for once. Freddy was an excellent driver and his mother's auto motored along at a good pace. It had a lively engine and a nice ride. I approved.

Freddy turned on the radio and we listened to The Harley Cummings Banjo Orchestra and his new record, "Summer Moons." My father used to like that fellow's music. He'd play it on the sonograph in the late afternoon when he came back from the Garibaldi Building and listen with his favorite glass of Nouveau Monde and a couple vanilla biscuits. Such days as those he enjoyed. He told me once that we make the home of our own destiny. Somehow, I do believe that's as true as anything. Stories we tell, walks we take, people we kiss. How far do we go before somewhere ahead lies that place we call our life? It's been waiting for us all along.

Steering us through Damian Avenue toward the eternal river still a few miles on, Freddy asked, "Where do we go after we pick Nina up? Do we have a strategy?"

"I guess I hadn't given enough thought to that. Maybe Nina has some idea. I know she'll want to telephone to that number she found on Johara's body."

"I'd like to say I'm shocked they'd kill that woman, but I'm probably not, anymore. Something feels different now, a sort of frenzy in that behavior."

"I think you're right. It feels driven, somehow. A crass and wicked craziness to everything they do. Like a top spinning tighter and tighter."

"Exactly!"

"I just feel something's coming, something worse than all the rest of that insanity."

"Which means we have to wake up, Julian. We can't be so careless. I know we were clever enough to solve those Draxler puzzles and you were able to make your way out there to fairyland and all that, but now you're back, and the game's changed, I think. Warnings are off the table. They're serious now about getting what they want, whatever that might be."

Freddy slowed for a coal truck to enter the crowded roadway ahead. When he did so, I glanced in the rearview mirror and noticed a motor with two fellows in hats just behind us. Nothing special, ordinarily, except it was the same olive-green Lyman auto we'd passed back on the parkway half an hour ago. I recognized it because, when I was little, my Uncle Clement always talked about wanting to own one. He said it had the finest build and quality of workmanship, "a motor to aspire and inspire." Awkward grammar, but I was sold.

My eye on that auto behind us, I had an idea. "Freddy, take Birdwalk Drive."

"That's a detour. I thought we were in a rush."

"We'll be fine. Just do it."

A quarter mile on, Freddy veered us off on a narrow course that wound through the gardens of flowers and pretty water lily pools and lush trees of blossoms and songbirds. Ladina Park, where the immense glass and iron Crawford Aviary of exotic tropical birds dominated a great lawn of playful children and visitors from treeless provinces come to appreciate nature's springtime gaiety on a sunny afternoon.

That Lyman auto was still behind us. Not close but following. Freddy drove us onto the lawn.

"Good grief! What're you doing?"

"Taking leave of those fellows in that Lyman."

"You saw them?"

"Ten miles back," he told me. "Didn't you?"

Freddy swerved between a telephone box and a popcorn stand and ducked us into a grove of weeping willows. The Jerome was smaller than that Lyman and couldn't be matched in a race of narrow passages. We motored away and lost them beyond the aviary when Freddy steered us back into a tight alley that led through a motor lot and back out toward Van Wyck Street with the river visible now in the near distance.

"Who do you think they were?" Freddy asked. "Internal Security? Secret assassins?"

"Maybe friends of Jack McManus looking out for us."

"I hope not!" Freddy remarked. "That'd make us look stupid, don't you agree?"

"Yes, but how could we know, right? They ought to have introduced themselves, if they really were there to protect us."

"Agreed," Freddy said, motoring up onto Van Wyck in afternoon traffic. "Not our fault."

We'd slipped that shadowing Lyman somehow through our clever detour across the park and drove past the Maincy Bridge toward Alcinous Boulevard parallel to the ancient river. Ships and watercraft of all sort decorated the wide waters. Great freighters and white sail sloops, barges and fishing trawlers, skiffs and yachts passed in both directions through the eternal tributary of our vast metropolis. Motoring along busy Alcinous at midday felt vibrant and purposeful, as if we belonged to all this, a society of builders and merchants and creators. A people need not be warriors and conquerors to be great. They need only to seek goodness and moral advancement above all else. Otherwise, even the rich and exalted can delude themselves. In my travels since that blustery evening at St. Etienne Shores, I had come to realize how impossible it was to see ourselves as the despicable fiends we truly were, the kakoi to Athenian aristoi. Yet that is precisely what we had indeed become, worst of the worst, exemplars of the vilest sins imaginable, slaughterers of the innocent, irredeemably corrupt and evil.

But our days are still young. Hope rises when our hearts open and our eyes see that eventful horizon where tomorrow is not yesterday, and we can choose another way.

Traffic slowed ahead and we saw a motor smash-up near the Pisander wharf. Police autos and a firewagon were there already, sorting out detours. Freddy said, "We should get off the boulevard. Meltemi is about four miles now. If we stay along here, Nina's going to be waiting awhile."

I agreed. "Go ahead. Take Saint-Beuve to Lima and follow it out to Meltemi. It's probably quicker anyhow."

Freddy drove us up and away from the great river again and along the market streets and industrial sectors, where most of the business was on foot and he could motor more freely in the smaller Jerome runabout. We zoomed in and out of gatherings of all sorts and made better time. I'd become worried about Nina waiting by herself at that grocery store. She was clever enough to hide on her own, but I remembered that she had Goliath with her now on the leash and would not be able to dodge any pursuit as she would without him.

Once we rolled up onto Meltemi Avenue, I was tempted to have Freddy pull over to the curb in the block of Johara's house so I could take a peek indoors. That idea went away immediately upon seeing two police autos and a coroner clogging the avenue at her address.

"We can't drive past that," I told Freddy. "I don't want any chance of us being seen here. Let's go up around the block and come out beyond them."

"Done." Freddy veered us up through a series of narrow side streets, then back down onto Meltemi again past the gathering at Johara's. He accelerated us forward then toward Felcher Avenue and D'Ancona's grocery store.

The market was popular in that neighborhood, crowded indoors and out, people coming and going, milling about. Freddy parked us half a block past D'Ancona's and let me out to walk up the sidewalk alone. We thought it would be wiser if he stayed with his mother's auto in case we needed to leave in a rush. I looked about for that olive-green Lyman after considering the chance that our destination was predicted, or that Nina had been followed there from Johara's. The possible permutations in this afternoon's narrative were bewildering.

Freddy kept the motor hot as I left.

The sidewalk was busy with pedestrians of all shapes and purposes. Kids and the elderly, housewives and day laborers borrowing half an hour or so for a sandwich at the lunch counter inside the market or buying a couple of apples or cooked potatoes to take away to the job. Some walked out with cups of coffee in hand. One stocky fellow with a bad hairpiece on a fat head strolled off with a half-empty liquor bottle of tangerine Blondel and a bold smile on his ruddy face. I worked my way through that mix into the grocery store and began looking for Nina. Did they let her bring Goliath into the store? That didn't sound particularly sanitary to me, but this wasn't Highland Park.

Being a fairly small store, it was noisy and packed. Hard to get around easily. I wondered where Nina would most likely be waiting for me. Probably somewhere she had a good vantage point to see people arriving through the front doors. Or maybe she'd pretend to be shopping for fresh produce and have a bag of carrots and lettuce and spinach in one hand, Goliath on his leash in her other. I noticed tables beside the lunch counter. That would've been a good spot to be. Two tables were empty, an open paper sack of lemon tarts and a steaming mug of tea on one. Someone using the toilet? I searched for a few minutes and didn't find Nina anywhere. Worried then, I considered going back to the auto and asking Freddy's help, but that didn't feel like the smartest thing to do. We needed him to stay behind the wheel and keep the Jerome fired up.

Nina, where the hell are you?

A slender, plainly dressed woman came out of the toilet, fixing her lip paint. She had an ordinary look, suitable to the neighborhood. Probably shopped here daily. She went to her place at that table and took up her mug of tea and enjoyed a sip. Feeling both anxious and impatient, I went over to her and asked, "Excuse me, but did you happen to see a young woman in that toilet? Maybe with a little terrier on a leash?"

She smiled. "He's a lovely little dog. I have three of my own at home. They're an endless joy, let me assure you. You ought to get one."

"I'm not sure I have time for a pet these days," I replied, politely, "but I'll consider it later on. Thank you. Is she in there?"

With a sly wink after a sip of tea, she told me, "Nina took Goliath outdoors."

"Pardon?"

And a familiar voice spoke up behind me, "They're both in the truck, Julian."

Marco Grenelle gave me a nudge, a half-eaten apple in hand.

"What are you doing here?" I asked, though I shouldn't have been surprised by then. Marco seemed to be everywhere at once.

"Another rescue mission, first you, then her. You two can't seem to keep out of trouble."

"How did you know we were here?"

"Eyes, Julian." He smiled. "And ears. Let's go. She's waiting for us out back."

Marco grabbed my arm and guided us through the gang of shoppers toward the rear of the store and out a metal door to the loading lot. I saw four delivery trucks parked there, one emptying crates onto the wide platform, six burly men busying themselves unloading fresh field produce and other assorted merchandise for D'Ancona's. Marco led me past that truck to another with the tailgate shielded in canvas and the motor rumbling. He climbed up and gave me a hand getting in after him. Then I saw Nina sitting in a corner of the truck, head down, knees pulled up tightly to her chest.

Marco called out to her. "He's here. We're ready to go."

I hurried over and caught her as she stood. "Nina!"

"Oh, God, Julian!" She kissed me furiously. "We're going to get Delia. Marco promised."

"Good! I believe him."

Marco came over. "Nina, if we keep meeting like this, people are going to think we're friends."

"Well, we sure can't have that, can we?"

I asked him, "How do we find Delia?

"We have some ideas."

"That telephone number Nina has?"

"Not just that. It's another move in this game. We're putting them together as we go. We know what's urgent and what isn't."

I felt the truck lurch forward and tried to steady myself against the side panel. Marco sat down. So did Nina and I. "What about Freddy?" I asked. "He's still in the auto, waiting for us. And where's Goliath?"

Marco told me, "Meyer's riding with them both back to Frederick's home. They'll be safer there."

"Who's Meyer?"

"Thorian Meyer's one of our friends. You can trust him. He's a good shot."

Nina said, "It was my idea, dear. We can't look for Delia and worry about Goliath at the same time. It's too much."

The truck rolled out of the rear parking lot and out onto Felcher Avenue. I was tempted to have a quick peek out the back for that Lyman auto, then decided it wasn't prudent. Instead, I gave Nina a big hug and tried to relax. That was a good idea they'd had, sending Freddy back to Alexanderton with

Goliath. A big backyard would suit him. And I presumed that Meyer fellow would keep Freddy safe. Marco's people must have been everywhere about the metropolis those days, peeping through keyholes and listening in on conversations just like Internal Security. This entire mess was a spooky and incomprehensible web of intrigue and deceit and murder. How were we surviving at all?

I said to Marco, "Incidentally, where are we going?"

"Viceroy District. There's a fellow you need to meet. He'll explain some of this."

"He knows where Delia is?"

"He'll explain. It's not that simple. I already told Nina."

I looked at her eyes, worried and teary. I took her hand and she whimpered softly. That toughness I admired had faded back. Heartbreak does that sort of thing. This was the worst kind.

We rumbled along Felcher for a few miles in afternoon traffic. I smelled the river as our truck made a turn onto Alcinous where Freddy and I just been, except now we were driving north past the iron Chantilly Bridge that crossed the eternal river from west into east metropolis. Nina had the front canvas pulled aside so she and Marco and I were able see out through the driver's cab. The old bridge had ancient stone footings and cast-iron railings and the most elegant arch and towers in our Republic. Banners of viridian and gold flew from spires and lamp posts. Crowds of day-goers and hurrying bicyclists crossed in the bright warm sunlight. A festive tableau.

Four miles beyond the Chantilly, our driver chose Bardamu Avenue that ran into a busy industrial sector of the west metropolis. Canneries and storehouses, manufacturing buildings, auto repair shops, milling, trade warehouses, distributors for goods and services of all sorts. Business across the city thrived on account of these crowded blocks.

We veered off into a labyrinth of small dirty streets whose names I didn't recognize and whose purposes felt obscure to my ignorant eye. I still had no sense of where we were headed, and Marco hadn't spoken a word in half an hour. Nina seemed in a daze, lost probably to the horror of Johara's murder and Delia and Riala's disappearance. Oil smoke polluted the air as we drove down a narrow, soot-laden alley between a tall ironworks and a brick building that housed a paper manufacturer. At the end of a street called Cavell, we slowed in front of a motor garage where a pair of wooden doors were swung open and we drove inside.

Marco scrambled out the back and motioned for us to follow. Nina and I climbed down from the truck. There were perhaps a dozen autos in various states of disassembly and repair, even a flashy black Cosmopolitan, and some twenty or so fellows in work overalls laboring on and under them.

Marco got my attention. "Come along quickly. We're not supposed to be here."

He took us into a back office and out a rear door that opened into a storeroom and a ladder leading up to the dusty rafters above the warehouse and a catwalk to a dark corner of the building where a glass lamp was lit in a small room. Marco knocked and opened the door. Nina and I went in after him. Marco closed the door behind us.

An older man in cotton shirtsleeves and striped suspenders sat at a wooden desk with stacks of inventory binders surrounding him. He wore metal-framed glasses and a thin moustache and had a cigar smoldering in a glass ashtray at his elbow.

Marco told us, "This is Guterman." He nodded to the man. "Sir, here are Julian and Nina."

The man rose from his desk to shake our hands as he said, "Apparently you two have had a busy morning. That's terribly unfortunate. You're both alive, though, and that's not inconsequential these days."

Her pretty face pale and horrid, Nina said, "I'm not sure I care about being alive if something's happened to my daughter."

He told her, "I understand, honey. We intend to rectify that problem as quickly as we can."

Nina blinked as if waking up. "Do you know where she is?"

"We have a rough idea, yes. But it's not simple. There are extenuating circumstances here that are disruptive and complicated."

I asked, "Is she with the other children? And I'm not just talking about her little friend, Riala."

"Yes, I know what you mean," Guterman replied. "And we can't be sure, but that's a strong possibility."

"So where are they?"

"Why don't you have a seat and we can discuss this."

Marco took a spindle chair in a corner across the room. There was a wood stool and a woven cane office chair. I gave the cane chair to Nina and took the stool.

Guterman said, "This had been in development for quite some time, we believe. At least a couple of years."

"What has?"

"Have you ever visited the ancient Thessandrus Hippodrome?"

Both Nina and I shook our heads. "No."

"It's about two miles from here in the Viceroy District."

"I thought this was Viceroy."

"No, we're on Cavell Street, which is the west border of Hyperion District. Viceroy is west of us, where the royals played once upon a time when the holy river carried barges of gold and slaves and warriors from the east and south. Eons ago. One of their emperors built the Hippodrome as entertainment for the fortunate masses who preferred chariot races to fishing. Its scale is at least equal to the ancient Circus Maximus."

"Nobody uses it anymore," Marco said. "It's falling apart. People got hit in the head from blocks tumbling off the top."

Guterman said, "That's completely true. It was in great disrepair for decades until a restoration was commissioned by the Directorate of Imperial Architecture seven years ago. They hired engineers and antiquities experts to reconstruct the weakened edifice and bolster what had gone to rot and ruin below."

"Underground?" I asked. "Beneath the Hippodrome?"

"Yes, indeed."

Marco told me, "There's a train spur that runs into there. Not sure why."

Guterman said, "It's the original Solférino Line that brought the elite from Leucata and Sabaena Heights and families of the Judicial Council to the horse races in those halcyon days before the Great Separation and the war. The Merolino Station was once larger than Thibodeaux and offered all sorts of amusements on the royal platform for equestrian addicts. A long tunnel beginning at Montalivet brought the rail tracks under the hippodrome so those gilded people might enjoy the privilege of privacy. Apparently, it was a wonderful arrangement."

"Until it collapsed on a couple hundred of them." Marco laughed.

"That's true," Guterman agreed. "A terrible tragedy."

"Not at all," Marco said. "They were awful people who deserved to die. They voted for the Great Separation. Some of them were buried alive. Good riddance. I hope they suffered."

Nina had been sitting patiently until then. Abruptly she said, "What does this have to do with finding Delia? Somebody probably blew those people up. How does that help us get Delia back?"

"I'm getting to that, dear," Guterman told her. "It's a complicated story."

Nina said, "Well, we're not getting any younger. Hurry up."

Marco said, "That doesn't help."

"Shut up, Marco," she told him. "Nobody cares about those people anymore. I want to find Delia. How is this helping?"

She sounded increasingly panicked. I reached down to take her hand. There were tears on her lovely face again.

Guterman told her, "Honey, the tunnel was rebuilt four years ago, and construction began under the old Hippodrome presumably to bolster that ancient edifice. Yet, in fact, that was not the intention at all. As we've come to understand, under the false auspices of the Cultural Protectorate, the renowned Leandro Porteus, Vice-Chairman of the Republic Design Directorate, was supposedly commissioned to draw plans for a beautiful marketplace and theatrical arcade that would entertain crowds of horse racing enthusiasts when the Thessandrus Hippodrome was entirely restored to its former prominence and glory. This was announced to all the city newspapers and cultural notices."

"Another lie," Marco interjected.

"Yes, it was."

My turn to speak. "I happen to know those plans were for an immense lethal chamber. I saw them at Porphyry Hill. It's monstrous."

Nina asked, "So that's where they took Delia and Riala? Is that what you're telling us? A lethal chamber? Oh my God!"

Guterman shook his head. "We're not even certain the construction was completed. Nobody has been able to get underground to see. All we know for sure is that Porteus drew up the plans for that project, and a consortium of engineers and architects and theorists from the Mollison Institute were assigned to that pursuit."

"We had the names of those criminals, too," Marco said, "and caught them together in the Mollison lobby at tea time."

I said, "And blew them up? I thought you said that wasn't you?"

Marco smiled. "I said I didn't push the button. But I would have. They were asking for it."

Guterman turned to me. "Do you recall any names of those killed in that bombing?"

I said, "Only Dr. Chalybian. I remember him because of a young fellow I met at Clélius House by the name of Lewis Atherton. He was completely insane. I was told he'd been a medical intern at Mollison until he got in trouble with Internal Security over a chemical called 'clothonium.' They tortured him for one of their obscure reasons until he escaped."

Guterman said, "Actually, we sneaked Lewis out of there one night and drove him to the eastbound train at Louandre. You say he's still alive?"

"Yes, but crazy now. Utterly delusional."

Marco said, "We put that amphritrite bomb in the Mollison lobby planter to get Setchell, most of all. He was the engineer in charge of the excavation under the Hippodrome. Killing him, we thought, was our best chance to slow down whatever construction they'd been doing. Unless they'd already finished, in which case we missed our chance."

Nina said, "Since you're so good at blowing people up, Marco, why didn't you just kill them all last year? Stop it before they got going?"

Guterman answered that. "Because we didn't know what they were planning until Mr. Draxler stole those drawings. We needed to understand what was actually conceived. But by then, it was too late."

Marco added, "Doesn't matter. We killed all the principal actors in that vile drama, anyhow. Every one of them had a leading role, so we blew them all up together. It was fun, actually. They were moral vermin."

"What's that mean?" I asked Marco, whose glee for assassination felt boundless. His scars from childhood must have been profound.

"He means those people are insane," Nina told me. "They have no regard for natural life. Who are they, anyhow? Hyrtikus? Cultural Medicine? Good God! What does that even mean? Boyceau Mollet? Chemical Science?"

Guterman said, "We believe Mollet's been behind the refining and practical application of clothonium particles. You can see the threads tying each of them to this project. Setchell for the construction engineering. Chalybian, Mollet and Dr. Craigmiles for the clothonium development and Hyrtikus for political intervention with human biology. Amédée Hersam serving as intermediary to the Judicial Council for this project in terms of its social purpose within the pantheon of their despicable ideology."

Marco said, "You're right, Julian. We should've killed them all a year ago, just for the greater good of it."

"Now it's too late to prevent anything," Guterman told us. "The transport trains are running into the underground on the old Solférino Line day and night. Like clockwork. Dozens and dozens. Fully loaded."

I said, "Carrying those children I saw in Tarchon Province? There were so many."

"Tens of thousands, Julian, from all over the war provinces, everywhere east of the Fatoma. More than you can possibly imagine. Possibly eighty to one hundred thousand by now. Something like that. Just a guess. Either way, it's unheard of."

Nina said, "Delia's not across the Fatoma. Why her and Riala? That makes no sense."

Marco said, "Maybe they think she and her little friend have spyreosis."

"That's ridiculous!"

"Not to Medical Security. They probably believe we're all infected. Everyone but themselves. Then just watch. They'll turn on each other next."

"Delia's under the Hippodrome?" Nina asked. "Hidden in the dark? Is that where they've taken my daughter? We have to get her out."

"We will," Marco said. "We just haven't decided how to do that yet."

"What about the rest of them," I asked, "It can't be that easy to rescue eighty-thousand children."

"They're going to gas them all," Nina said, fear rising in her voice. "I just know it."

"Why would they?" I asked her. "What would be the good of it? You weren't out there at Kippel like I was. Those traveler people they shot and burned in that schoolhouse? If killing children was the goal, it could've been done that day. Same with the kids I saw herded out of the woods by the train that night. They shot everyone else. I'm sure they had plenty more bullets."

Guterman said, "We agree. Killing the children can't be what they have in mind. It's likely something else."

I said, "You should grab that Celäenos Yeazell fellow and ask him. It's his Pied Piper story. He organized all of this to get revenge on the Regents for not putting a golden crown on his stupid head."

"That's Yeazell's story," said Guterman, "but not the Council's. Why would they care about some grudge he has?"

"I'm sure they don't. But he probably has something they want. A new weapon, maybe?"

"But why the children?"

Nina stood up. "I don't care. I only want to get my daughter back. Just tell me how to do that."

XLVIII
∞

M arco had some thoughts to share with us. Well, two, actually. Most of his ideas were just as insane as he was, but this one made sense, somehow. First, he reminded us how the undercity was labyrinthine in its vast reaches at many depths and directions, yet, unfortunately, none of its natural cavities and corridors passed beneath the old Hippodrome. Had that not been the case, the nature of the new construction and its interruption would have easily been exposed and terminated by mole holes and earth mines. Instead, those sonic indicators that gave away its initial intrusions and waves of earth movements became immediately apparent, but no natural passage existed from the undercity to penetrate the subterranean interior of the Porteus chamber. And burrowing up from below would be obvious and deadly. Therefore, initially there didn't appear to be much that could be done about Setchell's excavations. Except that Marco had a thought, and a map of the Faubourg sewer he wanted us to see.

We were driven from Guterman's repair shop to a basement tenement apartment on Fidelity Street at the west end of Nazarene District, dingy and damp from ceaseless river trade on its lower blocks. This was one of Marco's hideouts. He showed us a cellar door that led to a muddy crawl hole and filthy sewer pit extension of the undercity. Rank and ugly, he told us, yet much better than a night with those lunatics at the Mendel Building.

"I stink to heaven," he said, "but at least I still have my mind and my freedom the next day."

I questioned that and yet had no enthusiasm for discovering which choice I'd make under those circumstances. Nina assured us she'd simply kill herself either way.

We had a good look at his little apartment with that metal cot and comforter, a small cookstove and a bar of soap in a water bucket for a sink. Rags for wash cloths. No windows. One wooden chair. A strip of worn-out canvas tarpaulin for a rug and a ratty little suitcase for keeping a change of clothes. The room smelled of sweat and mold and that not too distant wet sewer below.

"Do you really live here?" Nina asked Marco, as she took the chair. "There must be rats."

He smiled. "Only when I'm not around, which is often. I have a roommate who's here when I'm gone. Her name's Zynis and she's a thirteen-year-old Saturnian from East Fessy. She had coldpox when she was a baby and grew up along the river where her family fished for food and refuse from upstream to sell at the markets in Fremery and Slawson. The Medical Protectorate captured and gassed her whole family for persistent violation of itinerancy laws a few years ago when she was at a sea camp in Cendrillon Province with some fancy kids from Whittell. I let her stay here because Saturnian theology won't permit Zynis to go underground with the rest of us. Something to do with burial rites and afterlife cosmology."

"She prefers rats?"

"You can ask her. She'll be here shortly."

Sitting down on the cold cement floor, I asked Marco, "How often are you here?"

He chose his cot. "Not much. Only when I have to be in the Nazarene. Maybe once a month or so. We have lots of friends in this district. Nobody recognizes them because they study corporeal anonymity. They see each other with no problem, but to the rest of the city, they're invisible. You can pass one in the street and not know it. They have some excellent tricks."

"I don't follow any of that."

"You don't need to." Marco smiled. "It'll never be your life."

Nina said, "So what was it about the Faubourg sewer you wanted to show us? That thought of yours?"

Marco got up off the cot and went to his suitcase and emptied it out. He had a zippered pocket in the lining from which he drew out an old map. Lacking a desk in his drab abode, he knelt down and unfolded the map on the floor. He told us, "Everyone needs to use a toilet, right?"

Nina and I nodded. "Presumably."

"And any public building open to thousands of visitors needs a big sewer system to support those needs, correct?"

"Obviously."

"Well, until those criminals decided to build their death pit under the old hippodrome, the whole thing had been closed down for decades and left to rot and crumble, which it had. Including part of the original sewers, the oldest sections. Probably too complicated to dig out and repair. Easier to redo in another section and modernize. We're not sure it's what they've done but we're convinced that's the most logical, and those fiends are pretty logical. At least when it comes to engineering. A lot of effort's gone into this. Credits, too. Probably millions. Not that it's any special concern to them. The vault's open to anything the Council decides is of mortal concern to the Republic, especially when it funds another campaign to kill more of us."

"The sewer, Marco?" Nina prodded. "You're wandering again."

"It's dry now. Closed off to the old latrine system and redistributed throughout the earthworks. Gone back to mud and seed. But look here." He slid the map about so we could examine the westernmost part. "A hundred and fifty years ago, sewage flowed into the sea at Giedion Shores. No one cared because the coast is pretty rocky there for a couple of miles in both directions, and the nearest bathing pavilion was at Chirisco Point, almost twenty miles south. Even on a windy day, the noxious odor wouldn't carry that far."

"I'm sure it was disgusting."

"Undoubtedly, but apparently nobody was bothered because those sewer tunnels were used for almost half a century. Then the underground collapsed, and the war came, and people let the Hippodrome die away from neglect. Perfect for us."

"What does any of this have to do with Delia?" Nina asked. "Your tangents, Marco, are infuriating."

"Thank you, Nina, I'm trying my best to irritate you."

"Just get on with it," I told him. "Nina, let him finish, all right? I'm getting hungry and I want to call Mother to see if she and Jack are back at the house yet. I need to let them know where I am."

"Thank you, Julian." And Marco continued, "My point here is that those sewer tunnels of the Faubourg still exist and are passable for the six miles to Giedion Shores, which was fully dredged only another half mile down the coast for the Öersted Landing. Nobody pays any notice to the rusty old tunnels, but we can enter them after dark and make it to the perimeter of the original latrines under the Hippodrome. That's where we get to Delia and perhaps lead all those children back out to the sea. Take them away from here on boats. Maybe all the way to that Pilumnas River of yours, Julian, somewhere they can live safely again."

Nina said, "Do you actually think eighty-thousand kids are going to walk through six miles of sewer tunnels in the dark? That's ridiculous. It's impossible."

Marco frowned. "Do you have a better idea? It's not impossible. And maybe we can't get everyone out, but we can save a lot of them if we try."

I nodded. "I agree. Having been in those tunnels of the undercity, I think it's the best solution. And we can be sure of rescuing Delia that way."

Nina said, "I just think you two are crazy to imagine that would work without anyone noticing."

Marco told her, "We'll have a plan for that, too. We're not helpless. We'll have more than lanterns with us. The undercity has people with a lot of experience in these kinds of things. Believe me."

Nina asked, "How do we even know where they are right now? You said you didn't."

"That was my second thought," Marco told us. "And it's a pretty simple one. I think they're being kept in the Hippodrome. All of them. It's immense. And it's been abandoned for so many years that it's far enough removed from the closest neighborhoods of Felucia, Strathmore and Guadalquivir, none of which have much population, anyhow. If you haven't been out there in a while, you should take a taxi to have a look. It's grim. No one wants to live there who can be somewhere else. The smokestacks from those factories at Dumersan are poisoning the air and the water. Everything stinks, and no one cares because the people out there don't contribute much to our great society. Most don't even pay taxes. They can't afford it."

"So what do we do?" I asked, suddenly impatient as Nina. "What's our plan?"

Nina said, "I don't want to leave Delia there tonight. I want to go get her right now."

Marco shook his head. "You can't. We've been putting some of our people from the undercity into that sewer system all day to find the most direct tunnel to those old latrines to dig them out. They'll work fast and quietly, but it'll be another day or so. We have machines you can't imagine."

"The Protectorate'll know you're there. With that many kids, I'm sure the toilets are being used constantly."

"They won't hear a thing. The modern toilets are on the east Hippodrome and the old latrines are on the west, where no one goes at all. Like I said, it's still a ruin."

Curious now, I asked, "How do you know that, Marco? You seem pretty familiar with all of this — the Hippodrome and sewer tunnels. Those latrines you're talking about. How is that?"

"Because we figured it out last week when Zynis hopped onto one of the trains and rode it in under the Hippodrome. Even Guterman doesn't know this part, but she came out after dark with a sketch that we applied to the old architectural drawing and we made a plan from that. This is it."

Nina said, "But what about Delia? They could kill her tonight."

A door closed above us and a young girl's voice, reedy but sweet, answered from atop the basement steps. "No, she's safe for now. They all are."

The girl was a waif, small for her age. A rat's nest of brown hair. Budding breasts. Sallow-faced and pockmarked. A cruel entrée to puberty.

Marco said, "Zynis, this is Julian and Nina."

She nodded.

He asked, "Did you find Stavans?"

"He's gone to the rail depot. No more trains."

Marco told us, "We didn't want to block the tracks or explode the Montalivet tunnel because we decided it was better to keep all the children in one place, just in case, you know, they became a nuisance. No reason to give those monsters any excuse to get rid of them."

Zynis spoke to Nina, "You have a little girl?"

"Yes, sweetheart, I do. Her name's Delia."

"Is she pretty?"

"Yes, she is," Nina replied. "Just like you."

Zynis was dressed in patchwork calico and brown cotton with black button shoes. Her eyes were dark, her face diseased and grimy, her hands thin and bird-like. Filthy fingernails. Puffy pink lips. I loved her smile. It was darling in all that unfortunate mess of her.

As she came down the stairs, I asked her, "Honey, did you see where they're keeping all the children?"

She nodded. "In the field during the day and that giant room underground after dark. There's lots of them and nobody's happy. They're always crying. I hid and watched them until it was time to go. Nobody saw me."

I told Marco, "I think I need to go home and talk with my mother and our lawyer. We have to reach Dr. Paley, if possible. Describe all this or have him explain the meaning of it to us."

Nina asked, "What about Delia? Is she just supposed to wait there? My God!"

Zynis told her, "She'll be good. It's safe. That gigantic room is really warm. We'll come and get her out really quick. We're going to rescue them all. You have to trust Marco. He helps us a lot."

I said, "In any case, we can't help her from this basement. So, Nina, let's ride back to Highland Park and try to organize ourselves. We'll call Freddy. Get his advice. It's the best we can do right now."

Marco said, "Julian's right, Nina. Go with him. Truth is, our people are already in the sewer with the diggers. They'll breech the old latrine by midnight tomorrow, at the latest. I promise. Then we'll come get you and we'll go into the tunnels together, the four of us here. When we're back out again, I'll have someone drive the four of you wherever you choose. Do you have a picture of Delia?"

Nina shook her head.

"I do," I said, taking out that little photograph I'd carried to Porphyry Hill.

"May I see it?" Zynis asked. She held out her hand.

I gave it to her, and she smiled as she studied it.

Zynis told Nina, "She's beautiful."

Nina's tears welled up. "Thank you, dear."

Marco said, "When we reach the latrines, we'll send Zynis ahead to fetch Delia and her friend. She's very good with faces."

Zynis handed the picture to Nina. "It'll be no trouble at all. I'll know her forever now."

XLIX

∞

Phebe Barron's violet Jerome runabout was parked in our driveway when the taxi that Nina and I hired on Albert Street let us off. We found Freddy in the kitchen with Mother and both Jack and Peggy McManus. Freddy had a warm honey muffin on the saucer in front of him and a glass of lemonade at his elbow.

Mother came over and gave me and then Nina a good hug. She said to Nina, "Freddy told us about your daughter and that friend of yours. It's just horrific."

"Damned nonsense," Jack said, "and I told Otto Paley myself not twenty minutes ago. He's looking into it as we speak. Paley's a straight-shooter and won't tolerate insubordination. He says there's no such directive from the Council requiring the senseless murder of a young woman and child kidnapping."

Nina sat down at the table next to Freddy, who gave her a kiss on the cheek. I asked, "Did Dr. Paley address those trainloads of children from Tarchon Province and elsewhere? If anything required a directive, I should think it'd be that."

Jack said, "He wasn't at liberty to discuss it over the telephone wire, he told me, but he did suggest we meet in his office later this evening. If that suits you. I don't know him like Harold Trevelyan did, of course. I felt he was sincere in wanting to get to the bottom of all this. Some of those people on the Council are certainly duplicitous in political matters such as these. Paley doesn't seem to be that sort. In fact, he was damned furious over the disappearance of Trevelyan and Dennett. Had no answers regarding their location, or even whether they're still alive, though the idea that someone had them murdered just gave him fits. I could hear it in his voice."

Nina said, "I won't go downtown like that. I don't trust any of those people. I don't know them, and I don't want to. To me, they're all criminals."

Freddy said, "No question about that."

"Well, I disagree," I told her. "Dr. Paley was very helpful in arranging my papers to Tamorina. Without them, I doubt I'd be sitting here right now."

"That's you, Julian, not me," Nina said, that long black hair draped over half her face. "What am I to them? Your stupid bohemian girlfriend? Do you think they care at all about me? I don't."

"You mustn't feel that way, dear," Mother said. "Jack assures us that Dr. Paley was quite serious in pulling the threads on this knot."

Peggy McManus asked, "Jack, did he sound earnest in promising these two would be safe downtown? I'm afraid I'd have to agree with Nina, otherwise. This whole episode is so harrowing, who could really trust anyone, now? I doubt that I could."

Peggy was dressed as if she'd just arrived from a cocktail party: pearls and cashmere, a diamond brooch. A pretty topaz pin in her coiffed brown hair. I assumed she'd enjoyed a drink or two, yet she looked genuinely concerned for us.

Jack replied, "Well, otherwise our hands are tied. What allies do we have? Dr. Paley's placed so firmly in the upper echelon of the Council that I have great confidence in his ability to get something done here. Without him, we're fairly adrift. No one else to trust who really matters."

Nina asked my mother, "May I use the toilet, please?"

Mother said, "Certainly, dear. Let me show you."

They left the kitchen.

I said, "Maybe I should tell you what's really happening out there."

Jack and Peggy McManus both nodded. "Please do."

"Sure, Julian," Freddy said, with a wry smile. "Go ahead. Ruin their evening."

"I'll chance it."

And I related as best I could the conversation with that Guterman fellow, and then Marco's description of those loaded trains to the Thessandrus Hippodrome and little Zynis's witness of the children underground in the lethal chamber space. Their expressions were livid and dry when I was done.

Peggy said, "It just defies belief, if I need to say so. That many children?"

"Well, I believe it's true."

"Oh, I don't doubt you at all, Julian. In fact, we've both come to our senses about this war and all the nonsense our Council's been feeding us all these years." Peggy looked at her husband. "Isn't that so, Jack? We've decided to stop being fools and face up to certain realities."

Jack said, "Your father's opinions helped in opening my eyes, Julian." He nodded at Freddy. "Yours, too, young man. Not one little thing did it, but these stories you've told us, and the proof that now seems so obvious, has just pushed me into that corner where I simply cannot defend this egregious immorality pursued by the Status Imperium. Particularly in the context of your story regarding the existence of the living seat of Empire in the east. It's just astounding."

"So, what do we do?" I asked. "Can we trust anyone?"

"Dr. Paley, I believe we can trust. He really is an honorable man. You'll see that when you meet him. I can't be sure how much he knows regarding the machinations of his fellow Council members, but I do feel he has a stake in its resolution. As do we all."

Mother came back into the kitchen. She told me, "Nina is very tired and unfit to travel, even if she weren't mentally exhausted. Which she is. I gave her two drops of morphium solution in a glass of water and sent her up to your bedroom to sleep. She needs to rest her worries. For a few hours, at least."

I nodded. "All right. I guess I'll go downtown with Jack and Freddy to meet Dr. Paley."

Freddy said, "Is it safe? I don't want to go anywhere near the Mendel Building. That place creeps me out."

Jack shook his head. "Don't worry. Otto's private office is at the Nationale Club by Chapman Hall. Just off Freelings Park. He doesn't care for Prospect Square any more than the rest of us. The Internal Security Directorate has no presence by the Nationale at all. City police patrol that sector, and Otto has a great relationship with them. He sponsors their yearly retirement gala. He assured me we'll be fine."

Mother said, "You should eat some supper before you go. Let me stir up a few eggs. It'll only take a few moments."

"Thank you," Freddy said. "I'm starving."

Jack McManus checked his pocket-watch. "I suppose we have time. Otto told me that he intended to be in his office until at least nine."

Peggy said, "I'll help you, Martha. There are those leftover potatoes from your lunch at the Barron's we could fry, as well."

I got up from the table. "Let me go look in on Nina for a moment, then we can eat and go."

My bedroom window was open to the clean spring evening when I slipped in to see her. I thought she was asleep, but she spoke to me from the shadow of the streetlamps.

"Julian? Is that you?"

"Yes, dear. Freddy and I are going out for a little while. We'll be back when you wake up."

Nina's voice was groggy. "Are you getting Delia? She's awfully scared out there alone."

"We're investigating just that. Dr. Paley has a good thought that'll help us. You just need to get some rest and not worry about it for now. We won't let anything happen to her, I promise."

"I love you, Julian. You're the sweetest boy in the world. Delia adores you. Did I tell you that? She's absolutely mad about you. Is Goliath safe?"

"I love you, too, darling," I said. "Goliath is fine. Freddy has him penned in their backyard. He's happy there."

"I'm glad." Nina reached out her hand. "Come here, give me a hug."

I did, and kissed her, and tucked her back under my blanket and left the bedroom with my open window floating a lovely scent of eternal spring into the dark.

We ate those rummeled eggs and fried potatoes quickly with a pot of steaming Soulien tea and left soon afterward. Jack McManus drove with Freddy in the seat beside him. We decided it would be smart to keep me sort of hidden in the back where Jack's silver Henrouille sedan had cut-glass opera windows that obscured the rear passengers. He sped us out of Highland Park.

Dr. Otto Paley.

What did I expect? Until that evening, I'd never met any member of the esteemed Judicial Council. What were those people like? My opinions were more mixed than ever. What morality, if any, guided their official judgments? Eugenics had a clever motive for dispensing with normal human inclinations toward goodness. Why reason with compassion for the diseased whose pathetic infirmity threatens our very existence? Life supersedes the foolish indulgence of empathy and care. Let them die so that we might live. A perfect motto to ruin a society.

The Nationale Club was in the DuPont District, about a mile from Prospect Square, where elm trees bloomed along every sidewalk whose red bricks were swept each dawn and dusk, and all the impressive stone buildings seemed to be fine monuments to an aging greatness. Jack McManus parked his auto across the street at Chapman Hall. He dialed a number on his radiophone and told the person on the other receiver how we had just arrived and would be upstairs to Dr. Paley's floor in a few minutes. We got out onto the quiet sidewalk. I felt a nervous shiver being downtown again after dark. Bad memories I presumed would be mine forever.

Jack McManus led us across the street to the doorman at the Nationale Club who appeared to be expecting us. Or perhaps he was just naturally polite and enthusiastic.

"Welcome, gentlemen! May I have your names, please?"

We introduced ourselves and Jack told the doorman whom we were there to see. On hearing Dr. Paley's name, we were instantly ushered into the lobby where two more serious fellows in formal grey coats and tails greeted us. We gave our names again, and one of the fellows placed a call at the reception desk while his companion studied us with equanimity. It felt oddly disconcerting. Possibly due to the burgundy carpeted and gilt-adorned lobby being entirely empty except for the five of us.

We were shown to the main elevator and our floor chosen for us. The Nationale Club was six stories tall, and Dr. Paley's office was on the fourth. We rode the elevator up along with one of the fellows from the lobby. He stared at us floor to floor. When the doors opened, two more men in stitched grey coats were waiting.

"Welcome, gentlemen. This way, please."

We were directed down a most elegant hall of dark walnut paneling and an oriental carpet runner of woven indigo and maroon. The ceiling above was decorated in midnight-blue paint with golden stars and interlocking geometric border panels like printed mosaics. Bronze wall sconces lit our way along to where Dr. Paley's office waited. Two more gentlemen in fine coats stood flanking the door, faces expressionless yet firm.

Jack spoke up. "Attorney McManus here with Julian Brehm and Frederick Barron to meet with Dr. Otto Paley. We're expected."

"Welcome, sir." One of the gentlemen opened the door for us. "Dr. Paley is waiting inside."

It felt late at night. Probably because the building was quiet as a morgue at that hour. Paley had a nice foyer of chairs and lamps and another oriental rug with a center medallion that indicated the zodiac of Libra. Double doors led into his private office. They were open to us as we entered, and Dr. Paley was waiting beside his desk.

I'd seen chromographs and newspaper photos of the esteemed fellow. Meeting him in person was prepossessing. Dr. Paley was smaller than I'd have guessed, bald, with thick wide glasses that made him owl-eyed and keen. He wore a vested evening suit of green velvet and black, a green bow tie and a white carnation. A fine appearance.

He spoke with a voice that was utterly clear and comforting. "So pleased you're here! Much to discuss! Let's all have a seat, shall we?"

His office was lined with a pair of tall wood bookcases floor to ceiling. Mahogany chairs and a leather chesterfield. His desk was walnut and ornate, carved with flourishes and arcane decoration. Behind it was a formal portrait of Paley himself from another day, a younger version of himself, proud and smart, a man who grew to become one of the most respected personalities in our grand Republic.

Chairs had been arranged in front of Dr. Paley's desk, and Freddy and I chose those flanking Jack McManus. After closing his office doors, Dr. Paley went to his own chair behind the desk and folded his hands and began our discourse.

"May I pass on a pair of messages first?" I asked, remembering those requests from that rainy night at Porphyry Hill.

Dr. Paley nodded. "Certainly, young man."

"Well, sir, I was asked to offer the suggestion from a couple of young soldiers that if you'd improve the food in our camps out there, the war would go better."

He smiled. "A perpetual desire, indeed. Thank you. I'll include that in my paper."

Then I said, "And I was to tell you that 'Dodder' is waiting for that bout from Campion Cup."

"Oh, my! So you've met Morrie Dodd, my old fencing rival from Salius Academy. Good God, that was long ago. I can scarcely remember being that young. Were we ever?"

"He said you were quite gifted with a rapier."

"Well, that's a flatter seeing as how he was champion of our athletic league four years running, an unbeatable talent. Glad to hear he's still with us."

"Of course."

Dr. Paley rapped his knuckles on his desktop. "So, please tell me what we're to discuss tonight. I presume it's not as pleasant as memories of good old school days."

Jack McManus began. "Dr. Paley, it's come to our attention that you're holding many thousands of children captive at this moment in a lethal chamber beneath the Thessandrus Hippodrome. We understand these children have been transported by trains for weeks on end now from Tarchon and other eastern provinces involved in the war. And, as I mentioned on the telephone, concomitant to that was the apparent kidnapping this morning of two little girls from a private home on Meltemi Avenue, one of whom is the daughter of Julian's girlfriend, Nina Rinaldi. We're here to ask for your intervention in resolving these matters."

Dr. Paley looked us over. His countenance stern and troubled. "How do you know about all this? Who gave you this information?"

I said, "Nina went back to the house on Meltemi this afternoon and found her friend, Johara Ternaux, murdered in her own bed and both little girls missing. She telephoned to Freddy's home and told me what had happened. He and I borrowed his mother's auto and we drove over there to pick her up. She's asleep in my bedroom at Highland Park right now."

"Yes, all right," he nodded, "that's dreadful, of course, and I intend to look into it before leaving this office tonight, I assure you, but this story about children being held prisoner under the old Hippodrome? How did you manage to come up with that?"

Dr. Paley sounded disturbed. I wasn't sure if that was because of what we were telling him, or the fact of us knowing about it. Was he surprised or not? What was his involvement, either way?

I told him, "We know people who've seen the underground chamber there, sir. And, of course, thanks to your generous offer of those status papers that permitted my travel in Tarchon Province and along to Crown Colony, I myself witnessed many crowds of children gathered up for transport aboard those trains back to here."

"Do you imagine the Council has endorsed this situation? That we have organized and perpetrated the abduction of thousands of children?"

Jack McManus replied, "We cannot conceive of such a circumstance arising without the consent, if not explicit direction of the Council."

"We are not a monolithic organization, Mr. McManus. Each of us holds opinions that are singular to our own experience and philosophy. Even the influence of the Status Imperium has its limits on how we pursue particular policies. Debate is healthy within the Council, if not always kind and generous. When I was young and serving as Dr. Van Amringe's secretary to the Province Council, I saw men of honor and goodness argue for dominion over strategies that were intended to destroy thousands of human beings, some perceived to be guilty of moral and medical infection, some not. In the sacred halls of our Republic, decisions must forever be arrived at dispassionate of personal political opinion or theological persuasion. I've sat at that table often and have been astounded how the weight of history bends us to a will that feels too often simply irresistible."

The office was dead quiet now, the streets outside of Chapman Hall and the Nationale Club empty of traffic and night walkers. I detected a distinct consternation rising in Jack McManus beside me, something he was perhaps desperate to say. Instead, Freddy spoke up.

"Dr. Paley, my father admires you above all those on the Council. He believes your basic decency has kept this ship of state afloat longer than perhaps it ought to. He also told us this morning that eugenics is medical and philosophical nonsense. He said choosing between the perfect and the unwell is perverse because no one should be allowed to make those distinctions."

Dr. Paley replied, "Frederick, I admire your father, as well, and owe a great debt for treatments he's performed on my behalf and that of my family. For that reason alone, I cannot question his point of view regarding the question of societal eugenics except to say that decisions conceived in those years of moral disregard were certainly flawed and faulty. Knowing what we do now, I believe the course of history could have been much different and most of this disaster averted."

"Can it not be reversed," I asked. "Is that not possible? Do we have no future but that which we inspired a century ago? Are we so bound to that past we had no hand in making?"

"Mr. Brehm, such questions are exercised daily in the chambers of our Judicial Council. Unfortunately, a handful of our more astute and considerate members died in the Ferdinand Club bombing that ugly afternoon. Moderation and concern for the helpless has never been absent from our dialogue. Amédée Hersam was another sympathetic voice toward reconsideration of our eugenical directive. Unfortunately, he was blown up, too, in that Mollison attack. A great pity, let me tell you. He was a very fine man, brilliant and sensible. Dead now, as are so many others."

Jack McManus said, "Like Addison Dennett and Harold Trevelyan? I understand that you and Harold were pals at Squires back in the day. Whatever happened to those two can't be sitting well with you, sir."

Dr. Paley got up from his desk and went to the window where he stared out over Girardin Street. His hands folded together behind his back, we heard him say, "The children were not my idea, nor their disposition at any tangent to my approval. I only became aware of this most venal escapade within the Council a week ago when reports began arriving with those loaded trains in the Viceroy District. The orders were for a standard quarantine against potential spyreosis transmissions, not particularly unusual for that many arrivals from our eastern provinces. However, I do concede that my normal attempts to investigate for irregularities were shunted aside, as were Mr. Hersam's and those of our colleague, Dr. Pinard. From that point forward, our faith in the virtue of this sitting Council eroded and we were dismissed from the Determining Committee of Provincial Affairs, along with our new Vice Minister, Dart Hesse, and Dr. Gintota. We were considered anathema in these proceedings and our directives diverted elsewhere within the Internal Procedium. Such are politics."

"Quarantine?" I asked. "With all due respect, sir, I doubt anyone outside of the Council could believe that. I know my father's friends would not. I'm sure that's why they're no longer with us."

He came back from the window. His face was pale, eyes weary beneath his owlish glasses. "I have my suspicions regarding the fate of Trevelyan and Dennett. My heart weeps for their families. My own fury is unrestrained. Day by day our Republic lurches toward some unknown fate that cannot possibly be the intention of those who brought us to purpose all those centuries ago. The collecting of those vagrant children in the hollow underground of a lethal chamber beneath Thessandrus Hippodrome, one of the great landmarks of our ancient heritage, must be the apotheosis of this evil we inherited from the first summons of the Great Separation. I stand here ashamed to tell you, I've been inadequate to this moral disaster, and my guilt is indisputable."

"But what will you do now?" I asked, almost weary of handwringing and tears. "Those children, my girlfriend Nina's beautiful daughter, are suffering your inadequacy, sir. And I mean no disrespect, whatsoever. I just want to know what we can do now to maybe change the course of all this into something worth surviving."

Jack said, "You must have allies within your corner of the Council, and they must have forces capable of inflicting pain on those responsible for all this. It simply can't be left to those refugees in the undercity and out in the eastern provinces to save us from ourselves."

"Of course I do, and my intention this evening is to devise a perspective that may permit us to alter this course of disaster before it worsens. I'm thinking about those children now," Paley said, turning to me, "and your girlfriend's little daughter. Nothing's impossible. Across the great fields of our Republic, we've inflicted and received incomparable pain and sorrow. It can't stand. We know that. Winning the war can hardly be ennobling when such a victory would be so utterly disastrous to the other side. Mr. Brehm, I signed your envoy papers to let you gather information for me on where this is all leading us. Mr. McManus told me what you learned out there, and his brief report revealed the grave error we've incurred in prosecuting the war such as we have. To see how that pernicious action has led back here to my good old friend, Harold Trevelyan, well, that's the last of it for me. I promise you. There will be consequences, and they will be immediate and enduring."

Then I said something I'd been waiting to offer. "And Laspágandélus?"

"I beg your pardon?"

"The Regents at the seat of Empire."

Dr. Paley drew a deep breath. He stared at me. I heard Freddy fidget, probably horrified how, after all this, I'd brought up that fairyland.

I added, "It's the most valuable thing I learned since boarding my train at Commonwealth Station. I say that because even my mother admitted she'd never heard of it until this week."

Lowering his voice, Dr. Paley told us, "Think of Désallier as a necessary myth. Though the truth of that place is unfortunately indisputable, knowledge of it would be fatal to our Republic. Please do not refer to it again."

I did, anyhow. "It's inevitable, sir. At Laspágandélus, spyreosis is understood to be an immense criminal fraud. We have to repudiate it, too. For all the millions of lives it's stolen. I believe you know that, because repudiation is our only way back."

Shortly afterward, Dr. Paley closed his doors on us, and we were shown back down to the lobby where a message waited. The doorman handed it to me before we stepped out. Another address, with Nina's name attached.

In the silver Henrouille sedan, Jack McManus put in a call to Mother on his radiophone. All she told him was that Nina had woken from her nap and left the house like a rabbit. No word of explanation.

L

The Hotel Bremen on South Qandicha street in Calcitonia District was the polar opposite of the Nationale Club. A cramped and filthy four stories of tiny rooms and a distinctly unwelcoming lobby. Just inside the door, the air smelled putrid and the lamp above the registration desk was dim and threatening to extinguish itself. A scrawny fellow who greeted us there wore a brown cloth vest with moth holes and a thin toupée that hardly fit his narrow head.

Why were we there at ten minutes past ten in the evening? Simple. That address on the note given me by the doorman.

634 South Qandicha Street. #28. Nina

After handing our unfortunate night clerk a business card from the Hoag & Fillmore law firm on Prospect Square, Jack McManus addressed him by saying, "You have a guest upstairs in room twenty-eight. We need to have a look."

"You ain't got permission."

"Please read the card, young man."

The small fellow looked it over up and down. "So?"

"My firm is directly involved with Dr. Otto Paley, Chief Director of Internal Communications on the Judicial Council. Are you aware of him?"

"Nope." He put the card aside. "Never heard the name."

"Truly?"

"Are you deaf? I just said I ain't. What of it?"

I heard the old elevator rattling toward us from the floor up above and footsteps skipping down the wooden staircase, as well. Freddy took an old map from a metal carousel and studied it. Jack McManus had a look at his pocket-watch. The elevator opened for a fellow I didn't recognize just as Marco Grenelle came down the last step into the lobby.

Marco said, "Welcome, gents, to the good old Bremen, jewel of the western world."

"Where's Nina?" I asked straightaway, watching that other fellow at the elevator. He had his eyes on us, steely and unrelenting.

"In the undercity with some friends where she's safe. Come upstairs and I'll explain all this. It's pretty harrowing. But a lot of fun. You'll see why."

The little night clerk ignored us, preferring instead to scratch his fingernail on the guest ledger. Another nut.

Marco said, "How about you and I take the stairs, Julian. Let them have the elevator."

"Why?"

"It's quicker and I don't like elevators. I got stuck in one on Magnin Street once for five hours and had a faint. I don't trust them anymore."

"Suit yourself."

We went up the stairs to the second floor. A few of the treads were sticky and I didn't ask what from. There were people in some of the rooms. Liquor was on the guest list. I couldn't imagine what else. We beat the elevator and Marco led me down the hall to the fifth room on the left. He knocked twice in rapid succession, paused a moment, then knocked once more and went inside. I took a look down the hall as the elevator arrived, then followed Marco into the room.

Dingy would have been a flattery. Drab peeling wallpaper, soot-stained and sad. A creaky nightstand with an old iron lamp, a ratty rug in the middle of the small square room. A metal tray of vials, one sea-blue and the other brown, and a pair of syringes. A pile of leather straps. And three bodies. One facedown on the iron bed. Two on the floor. One of those was Dr. Finster.

A man walked out from behind a window curtain as Freddy and Jack McManus came into the room with that other fellow from the elevator. He gave a nod to Marco, then left. That fellow who'd come upstairs with us closed and locked the door behind him, then stood there by the wall.

Marco told us, "We killed these three with overloaded chloromorphium darts. Quieter than guns. They had Nina here for a session with VeraForm. We interrupted the game. Too bad for them."

I asked him, "How did they get her here? Why would she do this?"

"She told me she had a dream during her nap about Delia crying in the dark. Then she woke up in your bedroom and saw that telephone number and called it and the person on the other end of the line told her if she wanted to see Delia again, she needed to come to this address. When she agreed, they sent a taxicab to get her. We were expecting that and intercepted the driver at the stop sign just down the street from your house. We got the address from him and put one of our fellows behind the wheel and another in the trunk. Then we called in this destination to the taxi company while splitting the call to our own exchange and got our people here ahead of Nina's taxi. When she arrived, we killed the two men sent out to greet her, stuck the bodies in the taxi, then followed her up to this room where they were waiting with Finster and his VeraForm. Your friend was there, too."

I frowned. This whole story was astounding. The intrigue and murders. "Who's that?"

"Your Pied Piper," Marco told me. "Celäenos Yeazell. This was his game. He wanted to know what we had planned regarding his big crowd of children under the Hippodrome and figured that Nina would know. They intended to stick VeraForm into her body right here on this bed and get the whole story. Instead, we strapped him down in his birthday suit, stuffed a wet rag in his mouth, and shoved that long needle straight through his nut sack. He was not a happy boy. But we got what we wanted out of him."

"Which was what?" I asked, remembering my own experience of the needle.

"Why they took the children."

Jack McManus asked, "And what did he tell you? We've just come from Dr. Paley's office and he didn't seem to know. I believed him."

"Everybody lies these days," Freddy said. "They can't help themselves."

"Not under VeraForm, they don't," I said. "Believe me. It can't be done. I know that for a fact."

"It's the truth," Marco said, "and Yeazell did tell us what we wanted to know. They're using those children as blackmail to get our side to quit the war. Lay down our weapons and give up. Surrender the provinces. Otherwise they'll gas them all. So he said, and since it's VeraForm, I believed him."

"Who can give an order like that?" Jack asked. "It's monstrous. Nobody would go along with such a thing. It's absurd."

"Who wouldn't?" Marco replied. "To end the war?"

"Murdering thousands of children in a lethal chamber wouldn't end the war."

"Hundreds of thousands of children have already died since this war began. What's a few more? Besides, Yeazell was convinced nobody would be firing up the gas because our side wouldn't let the children die. We'd stop and let them win to save those kids. He told me they were counting on that. And he's probably right, because it sounds like that's about to happen. The warning went east by radio two nights ago, and we hear that agreements are being studied tomorrow morning at Galiñdo, Delmore, Lake Curo and Parédes del Valle. The end is coming."

I looked around. "Where's Yeazell now? Did you kill him, too?"

Marco smiled. "No, not yet. We have a cage for him in the undercity. Far down in the dark by the Potamus River. He's on his way there right now. It's a long journey. He'll have a lot of time to think about all this. Don't shed any tears for that lunatic. After Nina's session with the VeraForm, Yeazell and Finster intended to kill her in this bed with that other vial over there. It's chlorocyanide. Not a pleasant death. He'll regret even imagining that. I promise."

I heard a woman yelling from down the hall, and a motor horn out on the street. We stood quietly staring at the bodies. Marco's fellow watched by the door. The Bremen Hotel was so gruesome with its foul odor of old cigarettes and alcohol, human stink and mold. Those bodies felt part of that crude and tawdry scenario.

I asked, "When do we get Delia out of there? And those other children?"

Freddy said, "Yeah, I wouldn't trust those maniacs to stick with any bargain. How do we know they won't just kill them all anyhow for the sake of doing it? If the Council believes they're infected with a disease that could wipe us out even after the war ends? No matter how phony spyreosis is? How do we know they won't do that?"

"I agree," Jack said. "The morality of legal treaties is probably inconsequential to those who've organized all this with Yeazell. They'll pursue those actions that best fit their view of things, no matter where that might lead. If we knew the Status Imperium had no knowledge of any of this, it might be different, but we can't be certain anymore that they, too, are not a driving force here. And if that's so, we're all in big trouble, because it will mean the rule of law that has constructed and determined our Republic no longer has prominence. It's all been erased."

Marco was silent as he took a short peek out the hazy window. He was difficult to read. Probably his insanity. The flashing yellow lights of a streetcleaner lit the ceiling of our room as it rumbled by. That woman's shouting sounded closer now as a door slammed shut just when some fellow yelled back at her.

I asked Marco, "When do I get to see Nina?"

"We'll bring her back to Highland Park later tonight if you like, though she might be safer with us until morning. We could drive her up then."

"Only if that's fine with her. Let Nina choose."

"We will." He looked at us. "In the meantime, you three should go. We need to take these bodies out of here and you can't be seen when we do."

"What about that nut at the desk downstairs? He saw us already."

"Don't worry about him. That's Elden Colby, one of ours. He's harmless."

"All right. I guess I should've known that was a fake. Who hasn't heard of Otto Paley?"

Marco laughed. "No, he was serious. Elden never even knows what day of the week it is. He can't read and doesn't care to. Great card player, though. Electric memory."

LI

Freddy and I spent that Saturday night at Highland Park. He slept in Agnes's room. For my mother's sake, Jack McManus used the sofa in our basement, while Peggy stayed in our guest room upstairs next to Mother. Before turning the lights out, Jack had telephoned to a colleague who called for a police car to watch the house overnight. Favors like that were becoming much appreciated this late in the tale.

In the morning, after strawberries and waffles, Freddy drove his mother's auto back to Alexanderton so he could radio a message about the Hippodrome underground to his friend, Sebti. He had a code worked out from one of his squib books that would hide the meaning from over-listeners in the Communications Directorate. Meanwhile, Peggy McManus decided to stay with Mother for the week, and Jack arranged for security through his office. Nina arrived about an hour or so after breakfast, driven to us by a pair of Marco's people who wore a serious look. I greeted her with a kiss and a big hug on our front stoop and led her around to a bench in the back garden where we could be alone.

She cried in my arms in the shade of my mother's favorite cherry trees by the tennis court, where her fresh azalias were in spring bloom.

"I'm so scared, Julian. They wanted to kill me. When I woke from that nap, I was so confused about how to save Delia, I just telephoned to that number and did what they told me. It was so stupid. What was I thinking? How could I save Delia if I were dead? I'm such a fool."

"No, you aren't," I told her. "They had it all planned. You couldn't have known. You were tired and you were scared. They were counting on that. Those people are incredibly wicked. Nothing matters to them except getting rid of everyone they hate. Though Marco might be insane, I'm understanding his enthusiasm now for blowing those people up. I don't necessarily agree with him, but I can see how he feels that way. Kill them before they kill us. It's all so hideous."

She wiped tears from her eyes and gave me a kiss. Then she asked, "Where's Freddy? Did he go home?"

"After breakfast. He wanted to send a code to his radio pal about the Hippodrome. Did Marco tell you about Yeazell and the VeraForm?"

She nodded. "A bargain for all those children, including Delia and Riala. I don't believe them. I think they want to kill everyone. I don't know why, but I think they do."

"Maybe. Whether they do or not, those children ought to be rescued. They can't be pawns in all this. It's monstrous."

"Marco told me his diggers are getting close. He said they chose another tunnel off the main sewer that gave a simpler path for the children to follow out once the latrines are breeched."

I stood and took her hand. "Come on, darling. Let's take a walk. We need to make some decisions here today. I'm afraid of what might be coming next."

When I was younger, those wooded upper reaches of our property felt like a great magical forest whose overarching trees and shaded undergrowth concealed mysteries I was not old enough to unravel. Leafy dirt footpaths led here and there. Water ran through shallow drainage creeks. Bees labored across bushes and vines. Birds sang and dashed about the shadowy air. Feral cats hid under the brush. I used to tramp about in my youthful solitudes, creating stories of wizards and beasts. A boy's life. But there was also a book from my father's library, one of his own childhood volumes, a natural history whose illustrations I enjoyed. One colored plate in particular had me transfixed with its image of a body buried in the common ground just a few feet beneath the grassy surface and feeding the living earth above. The cycle of life unending, that enduring purpose of us. I remember embracing my fate as seed for soil, tendrils of life emerging from my brain and belly, encouraging stalks of corn and wheat and gorgeous sunflowers to grow and bloom in a newborn world. It's how I thought of death and its purpose back then. That we were not here only for our moments of joy and sharing, but also for perpetuating what was and will be. I had no fear of that when I was young. Now, hesitations engulf me and somehow death frightens when long ago it did not. Perhaps love creates and strengthens our bonds to earth and to those with whom we share it. We cannot escape what we feel. To lose this life for a greater unknown is a dreadful labor for the soul, and fear of death emanates from that. For some of us, faith in renascence or the Holy Book provides solace that allows those bonds to loosen. For me, I should still hope to summon that image of my body in the nurturing soil beneath a fruit orchard or a wild field of wheat waiting to embrace the morning sun.

—— · ——

Nina and I walked a path in the wood that led to a bench at a pretty overlook of a valley where old homes hid here and there in the shade of ancient oaks and spruce. We watched two people on horseback in the distance, then sat and held hands and kissed each other. I drew her close in my arms and gave her a gentle hug. Beautiful little Delia was in her thoughts. Mine, as well. The rescue attempt was near, I could feel it.

A cool breeze wafted across the air, scented of damp grass and leaves. Wildflowers, too. Leaning into my shoulder, Nina asked, "Julian, do you think Internal Security murdered Arturo?"

I sighed. "Yes, I do. I'm sorry, but I believe that's undeniable. He was carrying back information regarding Celäenos Yeazell and the children. They needed to kill him, and those other three couriers. I only survived because of Dr. Paley's status papers. I also realize now I was escorted on the train by that Orville Franklin fellow as protection. He probably kept me alive."

"I won't let them kill Delia. She doesn't deserve to die to satisfy their hatred of us. If anything happens to her, I'll help Marco kill them all, I swear it."

"We can't think like that. She'll be rescued tonight after dark. We'll see to it ourselves."

"Do you promise? I trust you, Julian, with her life and mine. I have ever since we met. It's been so hard for me to love anyone after Arturo left, and I wasn't sure I could, or even wanted to. Why bother? No one cares enough to share a life. Everyone's out for themselves."

"Do you really believe that?"

Nina said, "How could it be any different? Look at us! Our world. Nothing but killing, killing, killing. Who can trust anyone when all they need to do is point a finger and call you undesirable and you get shipped away or gassed or blown up. It's so hopeless and disgusting. And that fucking undercity? Good God! How do they stand it? I wasn't there twelve hours and I already wanted to kill myself. Why even bother living if it has to be like that? No wonder Marco's insane."

Tears ran on her cheeks again. I had forgotten once more how vulnerable and fearful Nina was regarding Delia and all the tragedies she'd witnessed this month from Gosney Street to Meltemi Avenue and that Hippodrome looming in her imagination. An unthinkable scenario. I said, "But Nina, you and I found each other, too, right? We fell in love, and that must be worth something, even in all this?"

I drew her close again. She kissed my ear and across that casual spring breeze, I heard her murmur, "You're worth believing in, Julian. I couldn't have any faith in love without you, but with you in my life, I do."

"Then we need to keep faith in each other, dear." I gently squeezed her hand again. "Delia needs us to be brave and resolute, so we can go into that tunnel tonight with Marco's people and rescue her. Then we can take her away from all this, maybe go somewhere far from here where there isn't any war and eugenics is a word no one's ever heard of."

Nina shook her head. "I don't think there is such a place. I wish there were."

"There has to be."

Freddy had telephoned to the house while we out on our walk. Mother said he wanted me to place a call to him, so I did. His father answered when I rang.

"Hello?"

"Yes, hello, Dr. Barron?"

"Is that you, Julian?"

"Yes, sir. My mother just told me Freddy had telephoned to us, asking me to get hold of him."

"Well, I believe he's out back in his private bunker fooling about with that old radio of mine."

"Yes, he showed it us yesterday. Very intriguing. We were impressed."

"It's nonsense unless the apparatus is used for its proper purpose. Otherwise, it could get us all into a big mess with the Communications Directorate."

"But we do have Dr. Paley on our side, isn't that so? I felt he was quite helpful and conciliatory toward all of this when we saw him last night. Without his attention and guidance, I'm not sure where we'd be. Everything is frightening now."

"We should be terrified. Your Jack McManus was supremely confident in how the world was being run until these past couple of weeks. Now he sounds like a frazzled schoolboy scared of his own shadow."

"Dennett and Trevelyan."

"No doubt. Can't trust our own eyes and ears anymore. My skeptical Frederick seems smarter by the day. I've clearly misjudged him. Phebe will never let me hear the end of it, so long as we survive the maelstrom of eugenical politics."

I asked Dr. Barron, "Do you have any sense what Freddy wanted to tell me, why he telephoned?"

"Not quite, though an hour or so ago he was trying tell us something about an armistice being discussed at DiScála in Bourgh Province. I told him that was preposterous. More rumors to distract us. I could be wrong, but I doubt it. We won't see the end of this war in our lifetimes."

"I hope that's not true, sir."

"Well, we have our opinions. I'll walk out there right now and have him telephone you."

"Thank you, sir. I'd appreciate that."

We disconnected and I went upstairs to find Nina in my bedroom. Mother and Peggy had gone out to the market to buy ingredients for Péchméja chicken and frosted strawberry cake. Jack McManus was expected to dinner. Sundays were important in our home when Father was alive. Since we'd foregone morning church services years ago, dinner together was how we established each other in our lives as family. Mother and I weren't yet willing to let go of that, particularly with Agnes away at McNeely Branson School and still angry with me over my unhappy news from the Desolation, a dishonest and unsatisfactory report, in her eyes. So be it. Nina and I, Mother, Jack and Peggy would be here for Sunday dinner, and family could have a fresh definition. I only wished Delia were there with us.

I found Nina drowsing on my pillow. She must've been exhausted from worry and fear. Crawling into bed next to her, I kissed her, and she woke and kissed me back. I got up and closed my bedroom door and locked it. Then Nina and I tossed our clothes on the floor and made love in the sheets, quietly but with that intimate fervor we feel when joining together is all that matters, the rest of the world be damned.

Then she told me about Delia as a small child, how she splashed in the tide at Deventeer-By-The-Sea, and painted shells in her classroom, and taught a neighborhood girl to ride a bicycle after she had taught herself. Nina said, "Delia had a kitten when we lived on Marsé Street in the backroom of a house that had a garden yard. She named it GuGu and kept it in a basket in our closet unless the day was sunny and no one else was home. Then she would bring GuGu out to play in the grass and dandelions. But one day, when they were out there, GuGu got away from Delia and crawled under the side fence and we had to go all the way around to the street to get to the next yard and when we did, GuGu was lost. Delia cried for days and days. I felt so inadequate to her sorrow and tried my best to get her over it, but not until we moved to Clairville and adopted Goliath did she begin to find other joys and smiles."

Nina kissed me and I hugged her close. She said, "I don't know how to be a mother. I am one, but I think I'm missing something that would make me better. I have too many conflicts. My obsessions distract me and then Delia either becomes a kind of after-thought or an annoyance. And yet, at the same time, I worry about her constantly. That's crazy, isn't it? I can't keep priorities straight. Maybe that's why I've been telling people for so long that Delia's my sister. It was just easier than being her mother. I can't really explain it very well, but that's probably why I miss Arturo now and then. Not romantically, because he was an ass and didn't love me and I knew it. No, what I mean is that I miss Delia having a father around to give her that love and attention she's needed when I can't. I've been so hopeless. And now, look, she's trapped in that fucking place and I can't even get her out."

"We will," I told her. "You know we will. Marco's plan is a good one. It'll work. I promise."

"How can you keep a promise like that? Nobody knows what's really happening there. It's impossible."

The telephone rang in my mother's room. I jumped out of bed and pulled on my trousers and ran down the hall to catch it. On the eighth ring, I grabbed the receiver. "Hello?"

"*Julian!*" Freddy's voice.

"Yes, dear. What?"

"*Sebti just told me his family took a holiday. His home is empty. Doors are unlocked. The new neighbors are in his yard.*"

"Is that important for us to know with everything else going nuts today?"

"*Of course it is, my brave roommate. That was a code. He was telling me Théophilia was just abandoned by the undesirables. They left. It's undefended. Our army just arrived to occupy it.*"

"What does that mean?"

"I think the war is over and we just won."

"Good grief, that's absurd."

"They quit because of the children. They want to save them. He said his family went to the summer home."

"What's that?"

"Across the Alban? Maybe? Or that Philateus River you told us about?"

"In the Great Chasm? It's not navigable. And how could those armies of the undesirables get across except by airship?"

"I don't know. I'm just telling you what he said."

"Well, that's very strange."

Freddy said, *"It's the armistice, Julian. Maybe the war is over."*

We decided to investigate further and telephone later that afternoon before dark when Nina and I needed to meet Marco and little Zynis at the old sewage pipe on Giedion Shores. I felt so jittery I couldn't lie back down in bed. I told Nina about my conversation with Freddy and that got her up, too. She dressed quickly and we both went back downstairs. Mother and Peggy were still out at the market, so we went into my father's office and switched on the radio set to hear any news about an armistice or conversations regarding the war. There was nothing special, so we went outdoors and sat on the front porch and looked out over Houghton Avenue and the streets below. The early afternoon air was warm, and a breeze fanned the newly green leaves and spring bloom. The earth breathed a scent of goodness and permanence. Why were we not able to embrace its beauty and fortune? Our lives are so brief, why do we trouble each other over trivialities and differences that lead us nowhere? Centuries pass and we are the same as ever, a race in search of a solution to a mystery that has no apparent resolution but whose torments to our sensibilities are ceaseless and cruel. And the wheel rolls on.

Mother and Peggy returned from shopping at two o'clock and Jack McManus drove over at four and took me and Nina into my father's office to tell us what he'd found out from his special ears in Prospect Square. His connections were far more extensive than I'd expected from just listening to Father discuss business affairs. In fact, Jack and Dennett and Trevelyan shared many of the same acquaintances in the metropolis; they just approached circumstances and situations from different angles. I suppose the simplest explanation would be to describe the Garibaldi Building as involved extensively with political commerce and McManus's firm pursuing political legalities. A vague description, perhaps, but not untrue. Therefore, just as Harold Trevelyan's professional path crossed Dr. Paley's now and then, so did Jack's intersect in specific cases. My father was apparently well aware of both. One of those many reasons I admired him and felt so intent on making him proud of me.

In the office, Jack McManus took a seat in one of Father's armchairs and had us sit on the sofa next to him. No one but Mother would dare sit behind my father's desk. Perhaps one day I would feel comfortable there, but not yet.

Jack said, "I just spoke with an associate of your father's, a man by the name of Wedemeyer who knows Dr. Paley quite well. He was out at Paley's home in East Wyck this morning for tea with a few other fellows from the Nationale, and the discussion was all about some curious diplomatic business occurring in several stations up and down the Alban River. They say it's quite unusual, for several reasons. First, no contact has been given between our two sides in almost fifty years. There seemed to be no excuse for it, given the violence of our attacks and their response. We hated them, and they hated us. Close the door. Something's changed and Wedemeyer says Dr. Paley sounded distinctly uninvolved with all that, disturbingly curious given that he is the Director of Internal Communications for the Judicial Council. If anyone should know what's being communicated out in the eastern provinces, one should think it would be Paley."

"I'd imagine so," I added. "He seems to be a smart fellow."

"With his ear in every corner," Jack agreed. "And a keen interest in maintaining that involvement, which is why this scenario is so peculiar. Wedemeyer told me that Dr. Paley appeared both fatigued and irritable at tea and seemed, he said, a bit wobbly. Very much unlike his usual indefatigable self. He and the others were quite concerned."

Nina asked, "Did your friend say anything about the children under the Hippodrome."

Jack shook his head. "No, because he doesn't know anything about that, nor did the others, and apparently Paley didn't mention it. Another curiosity.

Perhaps he was treating it as a political state secret. Who can say? It'll certainly come out."

I said, "Freddy was on Dr. Barron's basement radio this morning with a friend of his from Théophilia who's talking signs of armistice out there. He says the undesirables just abandoned the town and let our army come in and take it over. He thinks the war might be finished because of the children."

"That would be very strange," Jack said. "If I may offer my opinion?"

"Certainly."

"This war has been fought to rid the eastern provinces of that scourge we call spyreosis. It's been the driving intent for sixty years now, longer if you name the Great Separation part of this ceaseless conflict. And the goal has always been the complete eradication of the pernicious disease in everyone found possessing it. Since the other side is more than aware of this intent, why on earth would they accept an armistice that cannot possibly hold if the true aim of the war is their annihilation? It makes no sense to me whatsoever."

"Well, that's just what Freddy's pal told him by radio code."

"I don't doubt that's what he heard, nor even what his friend might be witnessing out there. I only have my suspicions about the tactics in these negotiations we've been hearing about. I take them as rumor, nothing more. For now, at least."

Nina said to me, "Are you going to tell him about tonight? Do you think we should?"

"Tell me what?" Jack asked. His face bore the concern of someone who's just heard so many unbelievable things, his brain can hardly contain them.

I told Nina, "I think we have to now, don't you? The more help, the better, and he can't help if he doesn't know."

"I agree."

"What's this you need to tell me?" Jack said. "I already feel underwater with everything since your father passed away. Your mother's been a brick. Peggy, too. I think I'm the only one chasing the narrative these days and it's left me scrambled."

I told Jack, "We're going to rescue the children tonight. Marco's people from the undercity are drilling out one of the sewer tunnels to the old latrines beneath the Hippodrome."

Nina took my hand.

I went on. "We're going to lead the children through the tunnels to Giedion Shores, then down to Öersted Landing where they'll have ships to take them away from here."

Jack seemed stunned. "Whose idea was that? It's astounding."

"I'm not sure. I don't think it was Marco's. Maybe someone in the undercity. Maybe the Regents themselves."

"And they don't think anyone'll notice eighty-thousand children walking away from the Hippodrome?"

I told him, "They'll be underground in the dark most of the time, six miles to the sea. The Öersted Landing is only another half mile from there. They believe it's possible. So do we. Right, Nina?"

She agreed. "Yes, because there's no other choice. It's the only way now."

Jack said, "What if the armistice is true and the war's really over? Perhaps none of this'll be necessary."

Nina said, "What if it isn't and they gas the children while we wait to celebrate? Do you really believe the war's over? Nobody thinks that's a risk worth taking. I'm not having it with Delia. We're getting her out of there tonight. Julian and I. We're going there after dark. Marco says he'll be waiting for us and he won't be alone. There's a lot of them from the undercity. They've been down there for a couple of days now. They're ready for this."

I telephoned to Freddy to fill him in on what Jack McManus told me about Wedemeyer and that meeting at Dr. Paley's home. Was an armistice on the horizon or not? Freddy told me he'd been on the radio with Sebti again who relayed more information from someone in Darrieux Province regarding a ceasefire at Avdeenko where the undesirables apparently walked away from their battlements in the middle of an artillery barrage and just disappeared into the forest. Freddy said the radio air was buzzing with news like that, though no one quite understood it. Nothing was clear. Those reports were intermittent and also contradictory here and there. I asked him to keep notes on the geography of these stories so we could compare them once Nina and I returned with Delia from Giedion Shores later that night. We expected it to be late, but Freddy promised he wouldn't get a wink of sleep.

—·—

I sat down to Sunday dinner with Nina and Mother and Peggy and Jack at half past six. They'd prepared the Péchméja chicken with rouge-coeur potatoes and a Moralia casserole of sauce and green vegetables. Nina and I drank a spicy hot tea to keep our spirits sharp while the others enjoyed one of Father's white Libro wines. Conversation was subdued to the occasion. Everyone knew where Nina and I were headed after sundown. Mother seemed nervous. Peggy tried keeping us in smiles with tales of her and Jack at Templar College in those days of sorority and youthful indiscretions. Nina excused herself twice to the washroom. She was scared for Delia. So was I. Whatever hope we both had for her survival would be tested in that old sewer tunnel. Just a few hours away then. I wondered how life managed to angle us into such bottlenecks of fate, those moments and circumstances where a simple choice falls to one side and what happens to us is left to chance or skill or planning, or an instant's rash decision. Had we done enough to give Delia the possibility of better days ahead? Were Marco and those friends of his from the undercity so clever and committed to this strategy that Nina and I could believe Delia and eighty thousand other children might actually be evacuated from that hellish underground in one brief night?

When Nina came back to the table a second time, Mother told us, "I've asked Jack to drive you both to Giedion Shores. I can't trust a taxicab with your lives this evening. I won't do so. Peggy agrees." She nodded to Jack's wife. "Isn't that true, dear?"

"Of course. We all do."

Jack McManus said, "Julian, there are too many pegs in this board to count them all in such a short time. While I am forced to place my faith in your scurrilous friend, Marco Grenelle, I can't say the rest of this sits particularly well with me, or Peggy and your mother."

I said, "Actually, I think we'll be fine. We're more concerned with what's occurring now in the tunnel at the latrines. Have they really been able to breech the entry there and gotten inside without being spotted? For us, that's a much bigger worry than being waylaid somehow along our route to the sea."

"Well, be that as it may," Jack told us, "I am going to drive you. It's settled."

Mother said, "My dear son, you've given me fits all month now with these adventures, and I can't stand the thought of worrying if you've even gotten to the shore to attempt that absolutely harrowing rescue. I can't imagine what your father would say about tonight, although I've no doubt he'd be exceedingly proud of your courage in even considering this. But you've simply got to promise me that you and Nina will stay as safely in the shadows as possible and come back home immediately once you've rescued that beautiful little girl."

"Actually, Mrs. Brehm," Nina said, "our idea was to go straight to Freddy's house where Delia can see Goliath again. She'll need her dog for comfort tonight. We've thought it was important enough to have that be our first destination. Delia'll sleep better that way."

Mother asked, "Do the Barrons know about this?"

I said, "I suggested it to Freddy, and he said they'll be ready for us when we arrive."

She asked, "And how do you expect to travel there from the sea? Another one of those dreadful taxis? I won't permit it, Julian."

"No, Marco promised to arrange a driver to wherever we decide to go."

"Then you'll need to telephone here the instant you're through the door."

"I promise."

And that was that. We finished our dinner. Peggy brought out the strawberry cake and I ate a small slice. Nina was too nervous for any more food and took another visit up to our bathroom to steady herself. When she came back down, we shared a half-cup of tea and gave hugs to my mother and Peggy, then took our coats. Jack McManus went outdoors to start up his motor. Streetlamps were lit now, all over Highland Park. The spring evening was pleasantly clear and cool, stars appearing gradually on a dark blue sky. That familiar breeze rustled across our front yard and through the shadowy spruce and elms. Calling out one last goodbye from the driveway, Nina and I climbed into the back of Jack's silver sedan and we headed away to the sea.

LII
∞

Black waves washed onto the cold grey sand at Giedion Shores as we walked down from a rocky bluff above. I held a small battery handtorch Jack had given me from his auto before he drove off. Wind swirled across the salt water. I saw the lights of ships and smaller boats far down the shore toward Öersted Landing. Our destination if all went well.

We looked about for the Faubourg sewer tunnel. It had to be close. Somewhere in the rocks? Decades of shorebreak had certainly disrupted the topography, but we reasoned the tunnel entrance ought to be obvious if we were in the proper location. Trouble was, Jack's handtorch wasn't powerful enough to offer much illumination beyond a dozen feet or so. Not exactly useless, but not like my father's silver ray spotlight, either. Too late now.

Nina and I wound our way down onto the sandy beach just off the rocks to get a better view of the shoreline. She saw the light before I did. Then I noticed it, too. Just a brief flash out of the dark. A cold wind gust stirred up the sand. I directed my torch toward that flash of light and saw it flash back once more. Nina and I went toward a pile of rocks just up to our right. Everything was damp in the evening sea breeze. My torch barely lit our way. Nina slipped briefly and I caught her arm. That light flashed once more and we both saw the entrance to the Faubourg and found Marco standing alone just inside the broad rusted sewer pipe, an old rucksack at his hip. Once we were close, he spoke up. "This way. Be careful. Don't cut yourselves on the edge of the pipe."

"Thanks," I said, keeping my own voice low. I spoke to Nina. "Are you here?"

"Right beside you."

Marco called out just a bit louder. "Zynis?"

That reedy young voice answered from the rocks just below us. "Here."

We hadn't noticed her at all. Just a few away. Her presence in the dark was uncanny. Like a small ghost.

Marco flashed his lamp twice back out toward the windy shore. Both up the shore and down, lights flashed back. We'd been watched all along.

He told us, "Let's go in. Something's changed."

Then we followed him and Zynis into the Faubourg sewer tunnel, completely unaware of what awaited us ahead.

The tunnel was narrow but not cramped like some of those I'd encountered in the undercity. Not so claustrophobic. Darker, though. Much darker. Harder to walk, too. Just muddy sand. Keeping a steady footing was a labor in itself.

Nina said, "It feels dirty in here. Really filthy."

Marco replied, "It's not. Nothing's been flushed through here in years."

"How can it ever be anything but polluted when tons of shit were in here. We're literally walking on tons of shit."

Marco told her, "Too late to worry about that now, honey. Buy some new shoes tomorrow if it disturbs you that much."

Nina said, "Maybe I will."

"Be my guest."

We walked for more than an hour as the geography and our footing changed and changed, sometimes narrowing where the tunnel shrunk toward us and the ceiling lowered to just atop our heads, then a section where the ground felt flat and firm and there was plenty of room for the four of us without being forced together.

But it was so incredibly dark. Marco had his lamp and I had my handtorch. The girls kept close as we lit the way onward. I asked Marco, "How are all those children expected to see where they're going without becoming terrified of the dark?"

"We have lots of people in the tunnel, Julian."

"Where are they? I haven't noticed anyone at all."

"Stop a second."

We did and waited as he took something out of his rucksack. He handed a pair of spectacles to me. "Put these on."

After I'd done so, he told me to put out my torch, and I did that, too. He switched off his own lamp and we were lost in total blackness. I literally could not see my hand in front of my own face.

Then Marco blew a whistle and the entire tunnel lit up with a spectacular ultraviolet glow. Almost surreal. I could see dozens of people, men and women, along the tunnel route, each with what appeared to be a metal candlestick of ultraviolet. The glow went so far into the tunnel, I couldn't see to the end of it. There must've been a hundred people or more lighting our path ahead. The effect was stunning, breathtaking. Bewildering. I reached for Nina beside me, found her, removed my spectacles and put them in her hand. "Put these on, dear."

A moment later, I heard her gasp.

Then Marco said, "We use ultraviolet when we want to remain invisible and anonymous. It's very effective. Nearly everyone in the undercity owns a pair of these glasses. There won't be enough for all the children, so they'll have guides if we need to use ultraviolet, but there'll be electric torches, too. Let me show you."

He blew the whistle twice.

After a few seconds, the tunnel was lit with ordinary lights, a long passage-way illuminated, again, farther than I could see, all those people with more lit candlesticks. Marco took another pair of glasses from his rucksack and handed them to me. He said, "Now you and Nina can move about the dark if you need to without drawing attention to yourselves if the wrong people are near. We've hung ultraviolet bulbs here and there. The batteries will power them for a few days. We won't need that much time."

I glanced over at Zynis and saw she was wearing those magic spectacles, as well. I wondered how her Saturnian faith interpreted this underground sewer tunnel. Perhaps the guiding principle involved depth. Or perhaps this circum-stance superseded her faith. I thought to ask her but resisted the temptation. She was here to help us rescue Delia and Riala, and as many other children as we could, not to debate that peculiar faith of her family heritage. I switched on my handtorch and we proceeded forward through the Faubourg sewer once more.

The hike became a drudgery of tricky footing and uncomfortable posture, as we needed to duck our heads and assume a single-file path where the tunnel tightened almost inexplicably. I saw what Nina meant when she argued that six miles of this would be impossible for thousands of children. Endless tears and complaints and cries of fear and fatigue. We hadn't gone more than a couple of miles ourselves and I was already exhausted. And scared, as well. What was waiting for us at the Hippodrome latrines?

I heard Marco and Zynis murmuring to each other as we trudged along. More time passed. Every step felt like the one before. My hands were filthy from rubbing the tunnel walls as I guided my way. My shoes felt grimy and wet. The sewer tunnel was unsurprisingly cold, and I was glad Nina had insisted we wear our coats, although I suspected by the end of all this, they, too, would be dirty and damp. Perhaps ruined. No matter. Anything could be replaced but lovely Delia and the other children. By now, the air felt nearly suffocating. It carried the distinctly unpleasant odor of rot and mold. Breathing became nasty and the taste of it clouded my tongue and nostrils. How much farther to go? I took out my father's watch and checked the hour. Almost eight o'clock now.

We walked on for perhaps another mile or so, when Marco stopped. He said, "There's something I need to tell you."

"What's that?" I asked.

Nina said, "Are we lost? Is that it?"

Marco told her, "No, we can't get lost down here because there's only this tunnel in and out. One way."

"Then what is it?"

Marco said, "We intercepted a couple of messages three hours ago sent to a radiograph station just outside the Hippodrome. They were coded but we have expert interpreters and they heard them clear as a bell."

"And?" Nina asked.

"The second and most important were two sentences. *'Don't let the rats breed. Exterminate them all at midnight.'* Then the communication ended, and the line was closed off. They said permanently. The circuit went dead."

"Good God!"

Marco shrugged. "Don't worry. We expected it. What did you think they planned to do with all those kids? Take them to the zoo? They're monsters. All they know is how to kill people."

"Well, then we need to hurry," Nina said, raising her voice.

"Yes, we do," Marco said. "I'm just warning you that when we get there, it'll be a madhouse, and there won't be a lot of time to waste."

"Are the kids coming out now? Why aren't we seeing any? Where are they?"

"It's not that simple. Zynis needs to go in first. She's been there and knows what to do. See how many guards there are, if any. We think they might've already left. Either way, Zynis'll get the kids' attention. Start bringing them to us so we can show them the way out." Marco gave her a pat on the head as she stopped beside him. "Isn't that so, dear? You're the key."

She nodded. "I'm the key."

"What about Delia?" Nina asked. "She has to get her out."

Covered in dust, Zynis said, "I'll find her. I memorized her face."

"Well, then let's go," Nina said, tromping on into the dark. I scrambled after her, shining the handtorch ahead of us.

We tried to hurry, slogging through the thick dirt and strange irregularities of the sewer tunnel. I tripped once and fell, aggravating my poor shoulder. Then farther on Nina did, too, and I helped her up as Marco and Zynis disappeared ahead. We rushed to catch them. No more fooling around.

Another half hour and the tunnel widened ahead. We saw tiny lights like firebugs all about and people in the shadows. Working. Voices low and chattering. Tones of urgency and organized determination. Not noisy, though. Efficient.

We arrived at the sewer beneath the old latrines. A narrow corridor had been cut through the sandstone, just wide enough to permit the huge crowd of children to escape down into the Faubourg tunnel. The machine that had carved it out rested off to one side in the dark, like some immense food grinder but without the handle. I saw the motor running, yet the iron contraption was almost entirely silent. A frictionless turbine. Only fresh dirt falling from its maw caused any sound at all. Very eerie.

The area was thick with a foul-smelling dust. Dried excrement? Dead vermin? Sweat? Probably all of that. Nina had her nose and mouth blocked already with her coat collar. I did the same. That hole into the latrine was black. Not a spotlamp pointed at it, nor anyone hovering close by. As if it were off-limits like a plague cave of sorts. Something to be avoided.

A husky fellow I didn't know came over to Marco and nodded toward Zynis. "Is she ready?"

Marco turned to Zynis, "Honey, are you all right? This is your show now."

Zynis smiled and gave them both a cute child's salute. "Yes, sir!"

"Then let's go," the fellow told Marco. "She'll crawl in first, have a look around, and the gunners'll follow on her signal."

Both Marco and Zynis nodded. Nina and I stood a few yards away, closer to that digging machine, whatever they called it. I decided if something went terribly wrong and bullets began flying, she and I might be able to use it for cover until we had a chance to run off back down the tunnel.

Marco noticed us and came over. He wore a mostly jaunty expression on his face, that constant look of emboldened certainty. I never saw it on Gosney Street, but since my stroll through the undercity, that's all he offered.

He told me, "Zynis is slipping in ahead of us because she's been everywhere throughout the Hippodrome underground on her other visits, so she's learned what's where and how to maneuver between corridors. One of our Láfhouát adepts taught her corporeal anonymity last year which makes her safer in there than any of us. When our people go in, they'll use electrocyanic darts to kill anyone guarding the children. It gives a near-instantaneous cerebral shock and poisons the heart. We'd have loved to use those fabulous myrmidon guns to rip them apart, but the noise is incredible and we can't afford to terrorize the kids. Also, no one's completely sure the structure isn't set up with earth mines, so we don't want to do anything that might send up some alarm, either. Got to do this as quickly and quietly as we can. If possible. Once Zynis shows us about, our assassins will kill everyone in there worth killing. And believe me, they'll enjoy it, too. They're very good. You won't hear a thing."

"And Delia?" Nina asked. "How do we find her?"

"Zynis just told you, she knows who Delia is and what she looks like. Zynis promised to get her first, and she always keeps her word. You can trust her."

I asked, "You don't need us in there, do you? We should wait out here, right?"

Marco shook his head. "No, in fact, you and Nina and I are going inside right after the assassins and the geographers. There'll be at least thirty of us in there guiding the children to these latrines and mapping the entire site for future reference. That first message we intercepted said that once the signal is given to release the gas — clothonium particles, we presume — they intend to use tri-nitrophlogistics on the Montalivet Tunnel line and collapse at least a quarter mile of the entire outer edifice. We guess they don't want anyone having a peek inside to discover what heinous crime against our collective humanity they performed under the historic Thessandrus Hippodrome. Nobody would possibly excuse that, even for the exalted cause of eugenics."

"Who planned all this?" I asked, out of curiosity. "The whole rescue operation? It's incredible."

"Licymnia Séché. A mother from Nédra. You don't know her. But we couldn't be here if she weren't choreographing us. No one else is smart enough."

A low air whistle peeped, and the area went utterly silent.

Marcos murmured beside us, "Put on those glasses I gave you. Lights out in thirty seconds."

Both Nina and I did as we were told. Electric lanterns and handtorches were extinguished up and down the Faubourg sewer tunnel. I switched mine off, too, grasped Nina's hand in the dark, then counted down softly to myself.

When I reached zero, everything and everyone around us flared to light in a brilliant and gorgeous ultraviolet. So many people surrounding that black gash in the latrine sub-basement. Zynis was there, a fiery glowing ultraviolet diadem flaring brightly from a tiara on her forehead. Then she crawled up into the darkness and disappeared.

Nobody else took a step. Just the opposite, in fact. Everyone remained in place like dark statues. Nina whispered in my ear, "I want to go in right now."

I felt her move but held her arm. "Don't."

We waited. All of us. I did notice several men with candle ultraviolets begin to creep toward the hole Zynis had taken. Each had some sort of apparatus on his hip. Weapons. Three women joined them, identically equipped. None murmured a single word.

Nina whispered once again, "What on earth are they waiting for? The gas to come on? Good God!"

"Shh."

"This is ridiculous."

"Just wait," I whispered. "Be patient."

"I don't want to."

Another few minutes passed. Marco eased up to the crevice and peeked inside. One of the women crept past him and climbed up into the dark hole. After another couple of minutes, she poked her head out and motioned to those carrying weapons. She backed away from the hole and they followed her up into the latrine, one after the other, quiet as cats.

We waited.

Marco came over to us. Still keeping his voice low, he said, "It's beginning. Zynis scouted the corridors around the lethal chamber and counted the guards. Our people just went inside to kill them. It won't take long."

Nina said, "You have to hurry."

Marco frowned. "We know. That's why we chose to kill everyone guarding the kids. No time to negotiate or worry over prisoners. No one really knows how many thousands of children they've got in there, but Zynis says it's too many to count. We'll just try to save as many as we can. It's the best we can do."

"But Delia!"

"Zynis'll find her. Once the guards are dead, you and Julian and I'll go in to help get her out."

I said, "This entire thing is just so insane."

Marco said, "It's how we live."

More minutes passed. Another pair of fellows with weapons hurried up into the old latrine. The only noise they made came from boots scrambling across the fresh dirt of the newly dug entrance. It was quite astonishing how they got about. Each of them.

Then the lights came on everywhere.

We heard voices from within the latrine. Echoes. Lots of them. Two of the women slid down from out of the hole. Both shook off their weapons and grabbed an armful of blankets. Another woman came out of the tunnel behind us with a medical box. She told Marco, "We're moving."

Then she chased those other two women up into the latrine, and this time we followed.

Nina bolted ahead of Marco and me up into the dirt crawlspace. Trying to catch her, I hurried up through the hole where I saw people waiting with electric torches that lit the room. Most of the stone seats in the ancient latrines were crumbling, the wall had cracks and the brick floor sagged with erratic fissures that needed repair. Past the latrines was an arched corridor of old soot-stained red bricks barely lit by more people with lanterns. I saw bodies here and there along the shadowed corridor covered up with those blankets the women had carried up to the latrine. No cause to frighten the children any more than they already had been. About a dozen yards ahead, I could hear Nina crying. Marco called for her to slow down, but she ignored him, chasing on into the black musty shadows. There were other narrow passages leading elsewhere, but they were dark and no one seemed to have gone into them. I took out Father's pocket-watch and checked the hour again. Almost ten o'clock. Good grief. Nina was right. We needed to hurry.

Far ahead, down near the end of the brick corridor, four of Marco's assassins appeared from a large door on the left, weapons held high. Alongside were those two women who'd carried in the blankets. Both held incandescent lamps. A great noise was gathering behind them in the subterranean dark. Human voices. Thousands. Chittering and humming. Tumultuous. And then masses of children began emerging from Leandro Porteus's vast lethal chamber, packed wall to wall across the stuffy corridor, flowing like a thick dark river. Marco's people held a line in front of them with the intent to slow and guide that surge of children along toward the Faubourg sewer tunnel and out of the hellish underground. They walked in measured strides: not too fast, not too slow. Purposeful. Marco and I pressed our backs against the wall as the flood of children reached us. So many orphaned kids with skins of many hues and cultural inheritances, that splintered history of us, uncountable, hundreds and hundreds of boys and girls in every imaginable fashion of clothing: rags and suits and calico and denim and cotton, shirts and skirts, coats and gloves, boots and barefoot, fat and scrawny, teary-eyed and vacant, terrified and bold and blank-faced, traumatized and angry. Some silent, some defiant and loud. Fit and lame, sick and restless. Toddlers held by teens, children holding hands, hugs and shoves. Love and hatred of us who must somehow have been responsible for the suffering they'd endured for weeks out in the provinces without their mothers and fathers, aboard those baggage trains, and there in that gigantic room, as Zynis named it, that lethal chamber from the lunatic recesses of someone's cruel and wicked imagination.

As we inched along the wall toward the death chamber, I heard Nina shouting for Delia, her voice desperate and frantic above that fantastic surge of children. I yelled to her, but she kept shoving her own desperate path forward against the crowd. There were more adult voices now in the corridor, both men and women, urging the children on.

"KEEP MOVING!"
"KEEP MOVING!"
"KEEP MOVING!"

Dozens and dozens of children were crying, others just looked dazed or sleepy or stunned or confused. A heartwrenching scene in the shadowy brick corridor of the underground, a heinous scenario played out before us. I had no words as they flowed by. What could I say? They'd been brought there to die. Were they at all aware of that monstrous fate?

I lost sight of Nina briefly by the end of the corridor near two large iron sets of doors: one off the left wall out of which the children were streaming, and another at the finish of the corridor. Those last doors were shut. She was swamped in that tidal wave of harried and frightened children. But I could hear her calling for Delia, again and again. Marco grabbed my arm and stopped me for a moment. I could barely hear him above that incessant din.

He spoke into my ear. "Julian, I need to tell you something."

"What's that?"

"The lethal chamber has electro-mechanical doors."

"What does that mean?"

"It means once they close, we can't get them open again until the system runs its cycle."

"What cycle?"

"Clothonium gas and fire. Once those doors close, that's it. No one else gets out."

"Good grief."

"I just want you to know what's going to happen there when the bell rings."

"Bell?"

"It'll ring ten times, then the doors'll close. And that'll be the end of all this."

"My God!"

"I know. Not enough time."

Another dozen yards onward, Nina emerged again near the lethal chamber, a horrid look of desperation on her tear-streaked face. Still shouting frantically for Delia. I called after her, but she was too far away to hear me above that tremendous noise of the children and their guardians. Then I lost her again.

A distant rumble shook the nightmarish corridor. I felt the stone floor sway briefly beneath my feet. Some of the children began screaming. Marco called over to me, "That's the Montalivet Tunnel. They must've just collapsed it. Part of the plan. We're sealed off. But don't worry. We're not using it anyhow."

"Why'd they blow it up?"

"Like I told you, probably to hide the evidence of all this. Next, they'll pour in tons of concrete and erase the underground completely. Pretend this never was."

"There's no end, is there?"

"Maybe not," Marco said, "but they'll pay one day. You'll see."

"If we live that long."

"Enough of us will."

One of those fellows from the undercity came out of the crowd. He told Marco, "The doors to the Montalivet are welded shut. At least an hour ago. The iron's cold."

"Is there another exit inside the chamber?"

"Nope." The fellow shook his head. "One way in, and no way out."

"So those people you killed?"

"Weren't leaving, anyhow. Probably didn't know it, either."

"Maybe the plan was to rescue them later on. After this was all over?"

"Witnesses?"

Marco frowned. "Kill them all? That wouldn't inspire much comraderie in the ranks."

The fellow shrugged. "Who cares?"

"Just wondering."

"Don't."

I smelled the lethal chamber when we were close to the end of the ancient corridor, a ghastly stink of raw sewage and filthy clothing, urine, vomit and fear. And the noise was deafening. Some of those fellows with weapons flanked the great iron doors, urging the children away from the chamber. Four others stood down at the terminus of the brick corridor, two of them frantically working a big pry bar on that other pair of iron doors that led out of this section of the underground. If the Montalivet Tunnel was crushed, I wondered where they expected to go.

Marco read my thoughts. "I think they're hoping to get some kids into that end of the tunnel once the chamber closes. Try to evacuate them in two directions to save time."

"That friend of yours said the doors are welded shut."

"Yes, he did," Marco agreed. "But they have to try something, right?"

I looked about as we approached the lethal chamber, hoping to spot Nina above the heads of the flowing children. Then we drew near enough that I could actually see inside Leandro Porteus's masterpiece of horror. That moral abyss. The smell worsened. The noise was shocking. I could not believe what I was seeing in there. What do you envision eighty-thousand children look like, stuffed literally shoulder to shoulder, acres of them in a cold, airless, almost night-dark chamber. Just a handful of dull incandescent bulbs suspended from the drab cement ceiling providing that meager illumination. No pillows or blankets. Body heat alone keeping them warm. Tattered and soiled clothing. Or no clothing at all. Hats and coats. Or no hats and no coats. Cute and homely. Curious and dull. No food I could see. Maybe a drinking fountain by the modern latrines when those welded doors were still open? A monster-show of inhumanity. What moral purpose could possibly have been sought here? What goodness in the common life of our world? And, for God's sake, how were we supposed to evacuate them all? Across the enormous lethal chamber, most were not even moving yet, a great sea of beautiful little faces, innocent hearts whose parents were lost and gone, forlorn at the last, futures denied and wasted. The impossibility of rescuing those so far from where I stood just then infected my heart, and I felt sick. Marco's people at the door worked furiously hurrying the massive crowd of children along, but the iron doors weren't nearly wide enough and the going was slow. Hardly more than shuffling. Within the chamber, the crying of innocent little kids was ceaseless and almost intolerable. Out in the cold brick corridor, a feeling of helplessness increased minute to minute. Hundreds of small children, swaying and creeping forward, packed the stone floor, wall to wall, clear down to the old latrines where life awaited. Hope in that direction. Abject despair elsewhere.

Then I saw Nina again by the door, Marco beside her. Children pushing past them. Shock on Nina's face. Worry on Marco's. Where on earth were Delia and Riala? God save them both, I thought, if they're somewhere in those distant acres across the chamber. What was fair about any of this? Who could exist in a society where the least among us were subjected to the cruelest injustice? I felt so dejected, so utterly disappointed in all of us as human beings, I almost did not want to join the fleeing mass of innocents with so many, many more certain to be left to die. I was convinced an overwhelming guilt at surviving this dreadful obscentity would be unrelenting. But then I felt a tug on my coat sleeve and turned to see tiny Zynis at my elbow. And behind her was beautiful Delia and another young girl with dirty blonde hair and a pretty face I took to be Riala.

Zynis spoke up in that thin little voice. "I found her."

And Delia, too, working on a smile through her tears, "She remembered my face."

"Because you're so pretty," Zynis told her.

Delia kissed her cheek. "I love you."

I needed to get Nina's attention. I waved and shouted. She didn't see me. I didn't want to leave Delia. I was afraid of having her carried off in the flood of children. I stood at her side and shouted again to Marco and Nina. Neither heard me, their attention focused desperately into that vast dark chamber.

Zynis gave another tug on my sleeve. She blinked and tears ran down her cheeks. She told me, "I'll bring Nina here. She's nice."

Then she was gone.

I noticed Delia and Riala were hugging each other, both crying. I could not possibly conceive of what they'd been experiencing since those awful people took them from Johara's house. They looked scared to death. I told Delia, "I want you to know that Goliath is safe. He's at my friend Freddy's house. They have a nice big backyard. He's happy. We'll go see him tonight once we leave."

Little Riala asked, "Will we see Mommy, too? She's waiting for me. I miss her so much."

I nodded. "I know you do."

Delia asked, "Where's Nina?"

A voice emerged from the din and chaos of the passing crowd. "She's right here, honey."

And Nina came up and swept Delia into her arms and gave her a kiss and a good long hug and another kiss.

I noticed Zynis holding Marco's hand. Both looked exhausted. The brick corridor was darker than just minutes before. The men who'd been laboring uselessly to pry open those iron doors had left with their tools and their hot incandescent lamps. I checked my pocket-watch. Half past ten. Still time enough.

Marco leaned close to tell me, "We need to go. There's nothing else we can do here. Some of our people are staying until the doors shut. They'll get everyone out they can. It's too bad. We just didn't have enough time."

"I understand."

"The sewer tunnel's already going to be slow with all these kids. Better to leave now. Maybe we can get around some of them."

"All right."

That sad unending flood of vagrant orphans drifted by us, their anxious guardians urging them on down the dark corridor by lamplight.

I told Nina, "Marco thinks we should go. We have to get away from here."

She nodded and hugged Delia close to her breast.

I had one final look at the lethal chamber, dark and venal and ugly. Then Marco said, "Let's go."

I put my arm around Nina, and Delia asked, "Where's Riala?"

Marco said, "She was just here. Where'd she go?"

Zynis said, "She went back to get Annie Florence."

"Who's that?" Nina asked.

"Her best doll," Delia told us. "They let Riala bring Annie Florence from her bedroom when they captured us."

"Good grief." This was just flabbergasting. "What now?"

"I'll go get her," Zynis said. "I know where she left it."

"NO!" Marco yelled. He tried to grab her arm, but Zynis escaped into the crowd.

"What should we do?" I asked Marco.

"We'll just have to wait."

Delia told Nina, "We can't leave without Riala and Zynis. I won't go."

Nina said, "We'll stay right here for them. Don't worry."

Marco told Delia, "They'll be back in a flash. Nobody can catch Zynis."

Then the bell rang.

I looked at my pocket-watch. Not even eleven o'clock.

The bell rang again.

Marco looked stunned. "It's early. We should have another hour."

The bell rang again.

Nina stared at me. "What's happening?"

The bell rang again.

"Ten bells and the doors close."

The bell rang again.

"Oh my God, Julian! We have to do something!"

The bell rang again.

Marco told her, "There's nothing we can do. Those are electro-mechanical doors. They have a cycle."

The bell rang again.

Marco went on, "Once they close, that's it."

The bell rang again.

Nina hugged Delia fiercely. I held my breath.

The bell rang again.

Screams like mass insanity echoed from the chamber door as the guardians were dragging as many kids as possible into the corridor. Two, three, four at a time, shoving them out.

The bell rang again.

Marco said, "Zynis is fast. She's counted the bells."

The massive iron doors began to slide shut. The rollers that drove them screeched and roared and I watched the smallest children being tossed out of the chamber into frantic arms flailing to grab them, child after child, as the unrelenting doors rolled and rolled and rolled and rolled, and finally slammed shut with a heavy bang that echoed down to the old latrines.

And that was it.

The exodus stopped.

Nobody moved.

The corridor went impossibly silent.

We heard a sound from within the lethal chamber not unlike the streaming hiss of a strong garden hose.

Marco murmured, "Clothonium."

Ten seconds.

Twenty seconds.

Thirty seconds.

Delia asked, "Where are they? Zynis promised they'd be right back."

The hissing stopped.

I looked at Marco. He blinked and his eyes were damp. He told Nina, "Take Delia down to the old latrines. We'll get the girls and meet you there."

Delia said, "I don't want to go."

Nina hugged her tightly. "They'll be right behind us. Come on, honey. Let's go."

"Promise?"

Nina met my hopeless gaze, then nodded. "Yes."

She took Delia by the hand and led her off into the darkness along the cracked stone wall where there were guardians waiting with electric lamps farther ahead.

Then I felt the heat emanating from those iron doors.

Marco was silent, but I saw his hands fluttering. He kept blinking tears away. The heat rose and the crowd of children began moving again, more quickly now. I noticed those last guardians carrying the smallest kids and holding onto others, leading them away from the chamber and its rising heat.

I was standing on the wall across the corridor from the iron chamber doors, and in only a few minutes the radiant heat grew too intense for me to stay there. I slid down the wall away where the temperature was more tolerable. Had I been possessed of any good sense at all, I would have left and gone after Nina and Delia. But Marco told me, "The doors'll open in five minutes. I'm going to wait. I need to see."

Unfortunately, so did I.

We both watched the last crowd of children wandering off with their guardians. Not too slowly, not too fast. Just away from where Marco and I stood in the brick shadows by the gradually dissipating heat of the lethal chamber. What had I expected to find this night under the Hippodrome? Triumph? Salvation? I'd been chasing this hideous crime since that cold mausoleum and Draxler's old copy of Virgil. Or perhaps it had been chasing me here all along.

Now that chase was over.

We heard those massive iron doors roar as the electro-mechanical cycle started its final rotation. With a noisy screech, they began to roll open. A bloom of heat expressed from within the chamber and pushed us back several feet down the wall. I held a hand over my face as my skin burned. More painful than I thought. I withdrew another few steps and waited for the cold air of the underground to ease the temperature. Marco remained still. The doors rolled slowly apart, that loud metallic shriek echoing off into the dark. I waited for the same ugly stench of burned bodies I'd experienced at Kippel to consume the narrow corridor, but there was hardly any smell at all. Only a faint and peculiar odor of smoke.

The iron doors completed their cycle and the motor stopped. The lethal chamber stood open for viewing. Pale lights switched on inside. I felt a cool draft from somewhere. Marco went forward ahead of me. He held a small camera. I could hear him breathe, almost panting. I followed him to the entrance and had my first glimpse of hell. Later on, Radelfinger told me that, once ignited, clothonium particles in a gaseous state accelerate heat so fast and with such fury that human flesh becomes ash almost instantaneously. I had no doubt. Yet the obscene science of it all felt irrelevant. What I saw in that chamber was infinitely more ghastly and heinous than any damnation imagined and rendered on canvas by Khübla, Bosch, Doré or Van Eyck. Six horrid acres of ash-blackened bodies, hardly understandable as human children any longer, almost fused together by heat and fear. But not just children. Next to the iron doors were the sooty remains of three selfless adults, presumably those who chose to save the last few infants as the tolling bell rang down.

Marco might have sought tiny Zynis in that dark crematorium, but walking without stepping on the burned and distorted corpses was impossible, so completely did their incomprehensible numbers cover the smoky cement floor of that vast chamber. Staring hopelessly across the expanse of ashen remains, those tiny bodies, I thought of our failure so intensely that a terrific nausea I ought to have experienced just then never reared up. Sadness did. Profoundly so. And, of course, horror and anger. Disgust. I won't ever forget that. Those whose souls are so perverse as to put a human mind toward conceiving and constructing a grim edifice such as that lethal chamber must be consumed, through and through, by moral rot. Then I wondered about the great architect himself, Leandro Porteus. Was this his true intent? Or a product of irresistible coercion? I had a further thought: What if, in fact, it was Porteus who had somehow facilitated Draxler's theft of those drawings? Father always spoke of him as a man of character and grace. I trusted my father's judgment. If he sensed goodness in a fellow human being, there had to be something to it. Perhaps this grotesque result of that project was not Porteus's fault, but rather our own for unraveling the truth of it too late. If that was so, then my part in this tragedy was worse than lamentable. Perhaps had Freddy and I dedicated more attention to Draxler's puzzles, I'd have reached Major Künze with the drawings sooner, and therefore the Regents and the undercity, after which this might all have been put to ruin before the flame was ever lit. An imponderable regret.

Gazing out over the blackened chamber, Marco spoke that thought he could not evade. "Why would Zynis run in there to help find a silly doll?"

Sadly, I answered, "Who loves *me*, loves my doll."

When Marco and I joined Nina by the old latrines, she'd already told Delia that her friends had died. They were both crying. We helped guide them down into the Faubourg sewer to join the sad evacuation. Six miles to the sea. A flood of survivors. Thousands of children, all weary and worn out. Hungry and thirsty, too. Pails of drinking water were offered at stations along the damp tunnel. Pieces of bread. Chocolates. Bananas, apples, oranges. Many sorts of cookies and crackers. I was touched by the simple generosity and kindness of those people from the undercity who had risked their own lives to guide these poor children to safety. I felt no complaint myself over the hours it took to march back through that long uncomfortable trek underground. Fear was gone. All my anxieties had fled. Anything that lay ahead was better than what we'd just left behind. Neither Nina nor I spoke, content simply to proceed step by step through the lamplit sewer and get Delia and ourselves out of there.

The hope was to reach the sea before dawn. Remember, we still had another half mile to walk from Giedion Shores to the Öersted Landing where we were told a large freighter was moored. I assumed many guards awaited us to prevent any further trauma as the children were led to the ship. Marco mostly kept to himself, speaking just briefly to a few of his people here and there. His demeanor had changed. No surprise. Zynis was such a little darling. Riala, too, of course, but Zynis was so brave and confident. Her spirit truly indomitable. She had saved Delia's life and lost her own. That final sacrifice provided us with more courage to see this out.

— . —

Just after four in the morning we smelled the shore and saw lights out to sea. We were tempted to cheer, but the guards near the Faubourg entrance cautioned us to be as quiet as we could. The salt air was damp and breezy. The children reached the sand ahead of us. Some went to splash in the cold tide. They were not dissuaded by anyone. Let them be silly again. As they spilled out of the sewer tunnel, the great crowd of sad orphans filled the shoreline. So many thousands. Incredible to witness. How many had we saved? Nobody seemed to have any clear idea. That head count would happen as they boarded the freighter. When Marco came out of the tunnel, I finally asked about their destination. He told me, "Champfleury."

Seven hundred miles south. A nation of Alméras, Gaoj, Calchas and Farish peoples. Mostly farmers and fishermen. I'd never been, but my late-Aunt Mae used to vacation in a lovely green cottage there by the warm sea. She told me the citizens of Champfleury were the most delightful on earth.

"Why there?" I asked.

"Because it's not here."

Nina and Delia and I walked along the dark shore with the endless column of children toward the Öersted Landing, enjoying that fresh sea breeze. Relief from the tunnels. We wouldn't go much further. Marco told me one of his people had a motor waiting for us on a pine bluff ahead. When we were close, the driver would flash his headlights twice and we'd climb a short path up through the tall muzzen grass to his auto. Then he'd drive us to Alexanderton, where Delia could have her needful reunion with Goliath. Certainly the longest and most trying night of her little life.

The freighter was old but huge. The sturdy and reliable, *Jules Grévin*. Marco told us the ship had first put to sea almost a century ago. This night, its superstructure was darkened. No lights on anywhere. The children would be guided up a gangplank and put into the ship's hold, where there were blankets and pillows, food and water enough for all. Her captain and crew had expected more survivors. We stopped on the shore to watch until the long column of brave orphans reached the ship. Both Nina and Delia wept. I kept my emotional solitude. What else was there? Then the auto lights flashed, and I found Marco wading barefoot in the sea wash and told him we were leaving. He promised his driver would park on the street outside the Barrons' home and see that we were safe for another day or so. Marco agreed to send me a note later in the day to let me know the freighter had left and the children were off to a better life.

Then Nina and Delia and I climbed the bluff.

LIII

∞

After waking to those horrors of the black chamber flooding my head, I persuaded Freddy to go back to Thayer Hall with me after breakfast to get our books and see our professors. I desperately needed a distracting respite from all that ugly mess in the Faubourg tunnel. Besides, keeping up our status as students still felt somehow valuable and worthwhile. What else could we do? Grey morning clouds and a light but cold rain greeted us. Freddy had gone into his radio basement after hearing what I had experienced under the Hippodrome and gave a coded message to his pal, Sebti. He told him, "The storeroom was completely flooded last night. Nothing left."

Sebti's reply came back, even more cryptic. *"The lighthouse went dark and is closed now."* Freddy wasn't positive what that meant.

Nina and Delia had slept together in Freddy's room, while he and I stayed out in the guest cottage to talk and use the radio. Dr. Barron had gone to his office at Umbro Plaza before we woke and Freddy's mother was on the telephone to a friend in Lakeport and couldn't be disturbed, so neither of his parents knew anything yet about the lethal chamber. I intended to reach Jack McManus from the switchboard at Thayer Hall. Just a brief notice. This was a dangerous moment. The risk for all of us was immense. I slipped a message to Nina under the bedroom door, letting her know where I'd gone, and that Freddy and I could be back by noon. I thought she and I ought to take Delia to my parents' home and stay there for awhile. My mother would insist.

Marco's driver had parked his forest-green sedan down Rothermel Street from Freddy's house. He had a cup of coffee in his hand when we went to tell him our thoughts regarding a visit to Thayer Hall. You wouldn't have seen him as anything but ordinary if you passed him on the sidewalk. Maybe the sort who delivered milk or sold you tablets in a pharmacy. Not particularly tall or muscular. Did he have a gun? I assumed so. Yet he spoke with a pleasant voice accented slightly of those farming towns out in Hengstler. A nice smile, too. Blue eyes and a plain brown leather jacket. His auto was a Model Seven, not a standout those days.

He told us, "My assignment is strictly here. But I'm also to look out for you, so we're sort of in a bind."

I said, "We understand that. Do you have any ideas?"

"Well, it's not safe to leave your girls here alone. I wouldn't."

"They can't come with us. They're both upstairs asleep."

Freddy asked, "Is it possible to ask someone else to come look after my house while we're at school?"

"It's always possible."

Rain fell gently on our street as we stood there. No other traffic. Alexanderton was a fairly quiet place at any hour.

"Should we do that?" I asked.

He took a small black device from the glove box. It had two buttons on top: one red and one green. He flicked a metal toggle switch and the green lit up. He tapped that button a few times, then the red. That light stayed lit. He waited.

I said, "I suppose it's complicated, getting someone else out here."

The driver replied, "Plenty of tricky crossroads these days. You want to keep an eye out."

His black device lit up green and flashed twice and went red again. Our driver tapped the green button about a dozen times, then red once. He told us, "Sun comes up, sun goes down. Predicability is the key. You have a nice home here."

The device flashed green another half dozen, then flashed red twice. After that, the driver flicked off the toggle switch and put his device back into the glove box. I thought about asking how his little contraption worked but restrained myself. So did Freddy, a greater feat.

The driver told us, "Someone'll be here in about fifteen minutes. Then I'll ride you to school. Please wait indoors until she arrives."

"What if anyone comes here while we're gone?"

"She won't be nice to them."

Freddy went into the kitchen for a glass of berry juice and I waited by the living room window, looking out on Rothermel's tall wet cedars. I wondered how Marco's associates were situated throughout the metropolis, how many there were and where they lived. I didn't believe they were all from the undercity.

The pale ones appeared to be from there, so sun-scarce and thin. Others looked like us, common people from neighborhoods we've walked and ridden through by evening. Tormented and pursued for decades by Internal Security and the Medical Directorate, I presumed they knew where to go, how to behave and live with a judicious anonymity until they didn't need to any longer. Did the Council fear them? I imagined so. You'd wonder who that person was with the newspaper at the bus stop, or the lovely girl selling flowers on the train platform.

Another auto drove up and parked behind our driver. A blue Zenith. Fairly up-to-date. No one got out. Freddy finished his juice and had a corn muffin in his hand as we left the house and walked down to the two motors. We wanted the plan described to us once more. The second driver was, indeed, a woman. Dark-haired. Red lipstick. Darling eyes. Just as pleasant in her appearance as our driver, yet much less ordinary. She could be one of those pretty clerks in a department store at Stahl Plaza, the ones featuring moderately expensive jewelry and perfume, or current women's fashion and handbags. A good disguise, blending in comfortably with the talked-about crowd.

Our driver got out and introduced us to the woman.

"Boys, this is Beroë."

We both said hello, which elicited a tentative smile from her. Had she killed people?

"She'll stay here until we come back from your school."

I asked her, "Were you told who's indoors just now?"

She nodded. "Your girlfriend, Nina, and her daughter, Delia, and Frederick's mother, Phebe. I'm familiar with all three."

"How so?" Freddy asked. Sort of impertinent. I doubt I'd have had the nerve. Maybe he'd added a bit of scotch to his berry juice.

Beroë looked at our driver. "Randall?"

He told us, "She acquainted herself with your girls last night in the underground. Frederick's mother has had our observation for the past week or so. His sisters, too. And yours. Both your families, in fact."

Freddy nodded.

I was stunned and impressed. How had they managed all that? Were we that important? "All right. Well, thank you both. We're very grateful."

Randall leaned inside the Zenith and said something to the woman I couldn't quite hear. She retrieved a card from her purse and handed it to him. He glanced at it and gave the card back to her. She nodded and he stepped away.

"Let's go, boys. Time for school. I think I just heard the morning bell."

I offered Beroë a smile. "Thank you, ma'am."

So did Freddy.

"Of course."

Then we followed our driver to his auto, got in and rode off to Thayer Hall.

Despite the grey morning drizzle, Regency Heights felt fresh and vibrant. Our fellow students were everywhere, like ants on a hill. I hadn't seen so many smiles since school's end last summer. No one matriculating college ought to be so happy. Academic threats weren't war, but damage to our youthful souls always felt imminent and real. We teetered daily on that precipice of a bleak tomorrow, and no one really gave a care except us. Or perhaps I was just describing myself and Freddy. I doubted any students in the Brownsill Society experienced anything like that, perpetual overachievers that they were. What might they have thought of what I'd just witnessed in the lethal chamber?

Bad became annoying.

Our room in Thayer Hall had been ransacked. Closet thrashed. Drawers spilled out. Study desks emptied onto the floor. Some of our books torn apart. Good grief.

Freddy kicked at his suitcase whose handle had been torn off. "Who did this?"

"Can you guess?"

"Fucking monsters."

I wondered what they were looking for: my old test scores, or those pathetic term papers I wrote last semester? My class notebooks for Zenas Lamberton and Dr. Pardo had been flogged and ripped. Dr. Sternwood's, too. Most of my notes for Dr. Coffeen were missing. That meant my grade for his class was dead.

"They cut my duffle," Freddy said. "Why would they do that? Bastards."

I said, "Something brought them here."

Virgil was absent from under my mattress. Nothing to learn from that. Those notes I'd scribbled with the library's Latin dictionary were gone, as well. So what?

That part of this story had been settled with the Regents at Laspágandélus. I'd love to see whomever attacked our room try their game at Désallier. Or even down in the undercity with Marco's friends. That bitterness wouldn't be easily resolved.

Freddy said, "There was nothing worth tearing through our room like this." He kicked his suitcase back into the closet and broke one of the liquor bottles there on the floor. Bourbon splashed all over. "Great!"

I grabbed a towel that had been thrown across my bed and tossed it to Freddy for the bourbon. "We ought to see if anyone heard this happening. How about if you go have a chat with Rodenbaugh while I get a telephone to Jack McManus. He needs to hear about last night."

Freddy glanced at his porcelain desk clock, lying sideways and cracked now by the window but still keeping time. "You do that. It'll make for a great conversation starter at lunch."

I tossed a sliced-up pillow back onto my bed and went downstairs to the bank of telephones. Once I got there, I remembered that I hadn't committed the number to memory, or the precise title of Jack's law firm, and therefore I couldn't give the exchange operator enough information to connect me. I thanked her, then asked if she'd please connect me to ALPine-6625.

"Yes, thank you."

I waited as it rang five times.

Then Peggy's voice. *"Hello?"*

"Hello, Mrs. McManus. It's Julian."

"Well, my gosh, how are you, dear? Your mother's been worried sick. She expected your call last night. When she hadn't heard from you, I thought she'd have a fit. What on earth happened out there?"

I told her quickly and heard several gasps on the other end of the line. Once I finished to the point of our return to the Barrons' home at dawn, she told me how Mother had just gone next door to feed our neighbor's bloodhound, but that I absolutely must call her back within the hour. *"She'll faint if you don't."*

"I promise I will. But first I really need to reach Jack. I'm at Thayer Hall this moment and Freddy and I have apparently suffered an unexpected intrusion into our room. Somebody's torn us to pieces and I'd like to get Jack's opinion. Besides hearing about our experience last night, of course. I've telephoned home because somehow I don't have the number to his office, and I couldn't recall his firm."

"It's Hoag & Fillmore on Claretie Street in Prospect Square. The number is CYPrus-7365. Jack will be thrilled to hear from you. He had his worries last night."

"Thank you. Give Mother my love. I'll call her as soon as I can."

The operator at the law firm's switchboard told me Jack McManus was away from his desk at the moment, but would telephone me at this number when he returned. Would I still be available? I told her that I would.

I sat there at the booth across from the third-floor lounge, listening to my fellow students thrilling to morning news off the radio broadcast, confirming some armistice in the eastern province of Bourgh and another in Darrieux. Idiots that they were, many in the lounge were bouncing up and down shouting, "Victory! Victory!" I tried to tune them out. If that news were true, something more terrible than war in the provinces could be next. I was sure of it.

My telephone rang and I grabbed the receiver. "Hello?"

"Julian. It's Jack."

"Yes, I've been trying to reach you. Mrs. McManus gave me this number. I hadn't really known it."

"And last night?"

I thought I ought to choose my language carefully, given that the telephone exchange at Regency College was a public service. I told him, "Almost all gone. Not enough time for the rest of them. You ought to ask Dr. Otto Paley if he can explain how this happened, who was possibly behind such a decision."

"I'd love to, Julian, but Dr. Paley died this morning on his morning walk."

"What? Are you sure? Good God!"

"It's a great shock here at Prospect Square. All anyone can talk about."

"The radio here is broadcasting armistice in several eastern provinces. Is that true?"

"We've heard the same news. Most of us are skeptical, although a couple of those disagreeable fellows on the Council are touting it up as scientific fact. They're calling it surrender. The war is over. Well, we're not holding our breath."

"When they hear what we saw, opinions may change."

"I have no doubt. That is, if anyone hears. Evidence has a strange way of disappearing from public view or is distorted in such a way as to limit its impact. Be prepared for that. Spyreosis is a nasty word. No one wants to hear it."

"I'm not concerned. What I saw was inconceivable."

"And that'll make it more difficult to accept as truth. People will always default to their own comfort and happiness at the expense of those they fear, anyhow. It's how the world goes on."

"We'll see."

"You and Freddy need to be more careful than ever now. Nina, too. We've lost a great ally in Dr. Paley."

"Our room in Thayer Hall was vandalized. Freddy and I just walked in on the mess half an hour ago. I guess that's as good a warning as any."

"For God sakes, Julian, you two need to get yourselves out of there. Call your mother and go home. I'll send one of my associates here with the firm's police out to the school. We'll start our own investigation. I've already had someone else up on Houghton Avenue this morning. Peggy felt nervous when I left."

"Marco has his own people watching us. They're with Nina at Dr. Barron's right now. Freddy and I need to go there first."

"All right, that's fine. But we need to organize this. Let's work it out over dinner tonight at your parents' home. I'll be there by six o'clock."

We disconnected and I went back upstairs to let Freddy know what our schedule needed to be for the rest of the day. He had our senior floor monitor in the room reviewing our domestic apocalypse. Sterling Rodenbaugh would not wear a medal for empathy in any known universe. Therefore, I wasn't at all disappointed when he told us that not only had nobody heard a peep behind our closed door, but that he thought none of this disaster was worth inviting the Regency police up to investigate. "After all, boys," he told us, "if you both knuckle-down in the next half hour, you can surely get this back in order, wouldn't you agree?"

"You are such an ass," Freddy said. *"Man, proud man, dressed in a little brief authority."*

In his most gratingly officious voice, Rodenbaugh told us, "I'll offer my report on this incident to Dr. Howison. But I'm sure his opinion won't differ greatly from my own."

Then he left.

Freddy threw his Botany volume at the closed door.

I told him, "I need to run over to Coffeen's office and explain why my semester was murdered in here. Then I'll come back and help clean this up."

—·—

Rain fell a little harder now as I crossed campus to Grimwood Hall under the dripping elms. Umbrellas were unfolded everywhere, mostly our comely co-eds protecting a morning hairdo. My shoes became soaked from the wet grass halfway there, my own hair damp and cold. Those identical yelps of celebration over the rumor of victory in the east echoed across the Regency lawns. Was there further news?

I hurried up the steps of Grimwood and took the only efficient elevator on campus to the third floor, where I hoped Dr. Coffeen would be in his office. He and I had a few things to discuss regarding my stolen notes and the hopelessness of passing his course without them. I intended to try begging. But I also needed to describe for him that hideous fate of the eighty-thousand children gassed and burned in the dark beneath our esteemed Thessandrus Hippodrome. I expected Dr. Coffeen to be horrified.

And he was.

As I narrated my story of the Faubourg sewer tunnels and that desperate rescue attempt at the lethal chamber, his demeanor declined, his expression soured, his hands quit fiddling with the pen and papers he'd had in front of him when I walked into Room 322 and closed the door behind me. When I finished by the cold seashore at the *Jules Grévin,* Dr. Coffeen took a piece of note paper and scribbled a number and handed it to me. "You must telephone there no later than this evening. It's of critical importance, Julian, if what you've just told me is at all true, and I assume it is."

"Every word, sir. If I should live to be a hundred, I'll never forget their faces. How could we have done that to those children?"

"It's a crime, Julian, against all we're born into this life for. A most despicable crime. An abomination, in fact. Worthy of the damned. Which is what those who've perpetrated this will most certainly suffer. If not now, then at a later sunset when all is revealed and that final accounting of our one hundred years comes due."

"Whose number is this, if I may ask?"

"It's the private home telephone of a distinguished gentleman whose knowledge and understanding of everything you've told me since returning from the far provinces is most profound, his pedigree in our Republic simply unassailable. He resides on a gardened estate somewhat west of the holy river in Solymi Province. He's been there for decades. An eminently respected individual."

"His name? Or should I not know?"

Dr. Coffeen chuckled. "I'm sorry. Of course you may. His name is Bramel Centennía Rúbotton. These days he's very reclusive, but years ago when he was out and about more frequently, particularly for gatherings at various faculty clubs around the metropolis, he used to tease everyone by claiming that he had traveled here on a balloon from Laomedonia. He may just as well have told us he'd flown down from Jupiter. A fine joke. Yet, now I believe he was simply telling us a truth, unrestrained, that by our collective disbelief cleverly concealed his genuine origins. I ought to have given you his telephone last week. I'm not sure why I did not. Perhaps I was yet a bit skeptical of your story. Now I'm not."

I smiled. "Yet you'll certainly have to flunk me."

"Why do you say that? Did I not give you a syllabus of notes when you were here last?"

"Indeed you did, sir. But that's the other reason I've come to your office this morning. When my roommate and I returned to Thayer Hall an hour ago, we found our room searched and sacked by persons unknown. My academic books were ruined, that rare edition of Virgil stolen and your syllabus missing, as well. I guess I'm doomed."

Dr. Coffen stood. "Well, you and I will need to do something about that. What if I mail my study directives to your parents' home at Highland Park? I presume that's where you'll be the rest of this week, am I right? And if you agree, I'd be pleased to put in a persuasive word to Professors Sternwood, Pardo and Lamberton. They're more reasonable than you might expect."

"Thanks, sir. I hope so. I do have Nina and her daughter to look out for until that business with the Hippodrome is resolved somehow."

"I presume you've been chasing this rumor of the war ending out in the provinces."

I got up, too. "It's not true. Or, let's just say, I'll be persuaded it is once news of the Hippodrome is revealed and explained, and those responsible are exposed in public. Otherwise, I have a feeling something very terrible is about to descend on us."

LIV

∞

I must admit, in those days of eugenics, I was much too young to see that intricately woven tapestry of our lives within a society of political diffusion and moral turpitude on a scale of millions. Too often youth is a blindfold that masquerades as clarity and insight. As I look back on those final days of who we were, I can't help but wonder if somehow it truly was 'more easy to tie knots than unloose them.' Words that go unheard become warnings unheeded. Civil discourse and the pursuit of grace and goodness is the blood that sustains the body politic. Its absence is a certain path to hell.

When Freddy and I arrived in that cold rain on Rothermel Street across from his home, our driver, Randall, asked us to remain in his auto until he had a talk with Beroë. I had assumed she was still seated in her blue Zenith sedan. In fact, as we sat there, she came out of the thick spring foliage alongside the wooden fenceline dividing Dr. Barron's property from his neighbor next door. Her clothes were rain-dampened and her hat a bit soggy. Randall crossed the street to greet her. They had a brief conversation. I noticed another motor parked somewhat erratically at the curb farther down the street. Its wipers were active on the windscreen. Beroë motioned for us to keep inside the auto. Then she and Randall went back into the wet foliage.

Freddy asked, "What do you think they're doing?"

I shrugged. "Honestly, I haven't the vaguest idea. But I need to go inside and see how Nina and Delia are doing, if they're even awake yet. Delia had a long night."

Freddy said, "Looks like Mother's up. Lights are on in the kitchen. Maybe they're all eating."

"Could be."

We sat there as the rain drummed on the roof of Randall's auto. I watched it sluice along the gutters and on down the street. That brought back the sewer tunnel in the dark and those orphaned children. Our windows began to fog, and Freddy wiped one off with a navy-blue embroidered handkerchief. Probably his father's. I couldn't quite see him at Bonté's Gentlemen's Salon.

Beroë came out of the foliage and walked down Rothermel to that auto parked along the curb with the wipers running. She got in and drove it back up the street and parked next to Freddy's house. Then she climbed out and opened the rear door. Next, Randall and another taller man in a work cap and khaki rain jacket emerged from the soaking foliage, supporting a third fellow between them as if he were lame or drunk. While Beroë watched, they carried him to the auto and pushed him into the back seat. Then they went back into the foliage. Beroë waited at the curb.

A brown Delaney coupé roared up Rothermel and was gone again, just a haze of exhaust and fog in its wake. If Beroë paid it much notice, I couldn't tell. The men came out of the foliage once more with another fellow between them. He, too, went into the back seat. Randall closed the door as the tall man went around to the driver's side, got in, gave a slight wave, then drove off.

Beroë had another short conversation with Randall. Both were staring at us across the rain-damp street. Then Randall came over and opened Freddy's door. "You can come out now. The coast is clear."

He smiled.

As we stepped out into a breezy shower, I asked, "What was that all about? Who were those men?"

"You had a pair of uninvited guests while we were away. Beroë killed them both with cyanomorphium darts."

I went cold. "Did they get into the house?"

"What about my mother?" Freddy almost went pale. "Is she all right?"

Randall nodded. "They never made it past the fence. She killed them before they set foot in your yard. Everyone's just fine. Don't worry."

"Well, we do worry," I said. "This is absolutely insane. Maybe some of you are used to it because you probably kill people all day long. But we don't, so it's all new to us. And who were those men, anyhow? Security Directorate? We're just students."

Randall gave us a look as if we'd just come from the feed store. Another day on the farm. With an expression of genuine concern, he told us, "You both look wet. I think you ought to go indoors and put on some dry clothes."

— · —

Freddy's mother had baked a chicken casserole for lunch, and he looked in on her to see if she needed his help. Fortunately, the Gorgon sisters were away at school. Good news. Plenty of drama already without those two sticking a pin in us. I went upstairs to see if Nina was awake. Peeking into Freddy's bedroom, I saw Nina and Delia cuddled together, reading from one of Freddy's old *Tales of Christoff Céleste*, a book of high seas adventure, mystery and magic. Goliath slept at the foot of the bed. I wondered how Freddy would feel about that. Knowing how he assigned priorities to his life, and how he felt about what Nina and Delia had endured this week, I suspected he'd smile. Then help his mother do the laundry.

"Hello."

They looked up in unison. "Julian!"

Delia scrambled off the bed to give me a hug. Nina came up behind her and kissed me. She asked, "Where did you boys go this morning? I went downstairs to find you, and Phebe told me you'd both left."

"You didn't see my note?" I kept one arm around Delia and kissed Nina back. "We were driven out to Thayer Hall to get our books and beg for academic mercy and indulgence from our professors."

I did intend to let her know about the assault on our room, but not with Delia listening. That lovely child deserved a bit more emotional peace and quiet just then.

Nina said, "I guess I forgot. I was so tired when I read it. Did they forgive you?"

"Mostly."

I heard Freddy call from downstairs. Lunch was served.

We ate in the dining room, where we watched the rain fall on Rothermel Street, drenching the tall cedars on the wooded slope across the way. The occasional motor car rumbled by. The sky was gloomy, a perfectly ordinary spring afternoon of showers. Mother would say, *'My flowers adore the showers in those hours before the sun.'* I always loved rainy days, so this weather was fine with me.

While we ate, Delia regaled us with stories of flood and famine on Gosney Street among the urchins like herself, and how she saw a whale one sunny morning at Deventeer-By-The-Sea while collecting seashells for a necklace she had hoped to make. Phebe Barron seemed pleasantly amused.

The doorbell rang.

Freddy excused himself to answer it.

I got up, too, and followed.

Freddy opened the front door to Beroë waiting for us on the brick stoop. Her hat and overcoat were both soggy, her pretty face-paint streaked by rain. She handed Freddy a slip of paper and told us, "This was from our companion, Dubech, who just drove off with those two unfortunates. He received it from Marco late this morning."

"Thank you."

Freddy glanced at it, then handed the paper to me. It read:

9,263 at sea

I smiled. Not every rainy-day moment was bleak.

Beroë told Freddy, "I'll be here until six o'clock. Randall will stay overnight. We have others, too. You'll be safe."

I told her, "My plan is to take Nina and Delia back to Highland Park this afternoon. Our lawyer intends on meeting us there for dinner tonight to sort some of this out."

She said, "There are two people on your street already. We'll let them know when you'll be arriving. It'll be fine. Randall will drive you there."

I hadn't thought that far ahead to plan for transportation. I was glad these people had done it for me. The extent of their organizing details through all this was stunning. I had to admit we'd be lost without them. Or dead. Yes, probably dead.

"Thank you again."

"You're welcome."

Then she walked off down the steps and back across Rothermel to her blue auto, glistening wet in the rain. We watched a green Lancer motor sedan drive slowly past the house and on down the street. Beroë kept her eye on the auto until it was out of sight at the bottom of the hill.

Freddy closed the door and we went back to the dining room.

Nina had gone into the kitchen, so I followed after her. She had the refrigerator open from which she'd had taken out a bottle of berry juice. I watched her pour a glass for Delia, still sitting at the table and gabbing away. When Nina saw me, she put away the berry juice and we kissed. Then I handed her the slip of paper. She read it and gasped. Her eyes teared up.

"That's all we saved? Julian, out of how many? My God!"

"It's still a lot, dear. We can't think of it any other way. And Delia's here. That simply has to be enough for us. We did what we could."

She hugged me and I kissed her ear and hugged her back. What else could we do?

Then, keeping my voice low, I told her about Beroë and those men she'd just killed in the thick foliage by the back fence. She grabbed my hand and took me out of the kitchen and down the hall to the toilet and shut the door behind us. For a moment there, I thought she was about to scream. "Julian, those fucking monsters just don't quit, do they? Eighty-thousand children last night weren't enough for them?"

"They don't want anyone to know about that, I guess."

"Well, everyone will certainly know soon enough!"

"Maybe."

"What does that mean? Maybe?"

I said, "Jack is worried that people simply won't believe it, especially if they think it's just propaganda from the undercity. Marco thinks they'll pour cement into that underground and cover it all up so nobody can get in there and see what they did."

"That's ridiculous! You can't hide something like that."

"Nina, if you can invent spyreosis and persuade millions of people for a hundred years that such a disease exists when it doesn't, then you can at least try to do anything you like, isn't that so? If such pronouncements come down from the Status Imperium, most people do believe them. That's how things work in our Republic. Whether they're to our advantage or not. Isn't that what you told me back on Gosney Street when we met? That I hadn't any true idea what was actually happening all across the metropolis? Well, perhaps you were right back then. I can admit it. But my eyes have been opened wider than ever these past few weeks. Threats to you and myself and your darling little girl, even to my family and Freddy's, have proven we can't trust the Council to have our interests at heart. Some of those people are truly despicable and we need to watch out."

"I hate them all," Nina told me. "I'm glad Marco kills them. He's probably insane, but so are they. I hope he blows them all up."

Once we finished with lunch, Nina took Delia upstairs to Freddy's room and put a book in front of her in bed with Goliath and closed the door. Then she came back downstairs and sat with us. In a measured voice, Phebe Barron said, "Freddy's father is expected home by four. He's had a meeting with doctors from the hospital where he intends to tell them what you saw last night. They're quite reasonable men, more astute than you might imagine regarding politics, which most doctors absolutely abhor. Once they've heard the facts, my husband expects there'll be a tremendous disruption in how our medical community perceives the Council and those decisions they make. He believes heads will roll and many aspiring autocrats will find themselves behind those cold bars at Drumont Penitentiary."

"But whose heads will roll?" Freddy asked. "Not ours, I hope."

Phebe laughed. "That is the question, isn't it, darling?"

I told her, "Nina and Delia and I are going to be driven out to Highland Park in a little while. I haven't even spoken to my mother since early last night. She's there with Peggy. People are watching her, so she's safe, but I need to go."

Nina added, "We so appreciate your hospitality, Mrs. Barron. You've been just wonderful to us. I can't thank you enough."

Phebe reached over and took Nina's hand. "Don't think anything of it, darling. Your comfort has been our pleasure. We always think of Julian as family, and now you and your lovely daughter belong to us, as well. You'll always be welcome here."

Freddy, Nina and I washed and put away the dishes for Phebe Barron, then went out back to the guest cottage and Freddy's underground lair. Rain fell harder. The grass was soaked and soggy. We had to put a metal cook pot under one of the windows that had a leak. The tap-tap-tap of the dripping water was mildly annoying.

Down in the basement, Freddy switched on his radio set and contacted his secret friend.

"Come in, Sebti. Reply."

Freddy waited a minute or so, just listening to the rain up above. Spring weather is a constant mystery. Sunny one day, cloudy the next. Rain followed by warm winds and sunshine.

"*Good morning, Morley. You have news from the storm? Reply.*"

"The floods washed what's left out to sea. Everything's fine. Reply."

"*My family has quit fighting. No more conflicts at the table. Everyone agrees. Our cousins say the same thing. Reply.*"

"My mother says there are Peeping Toms in our neighborhood. We have to keep our curtains closed. Reply."

"*Our neighbors have taken a holiday to the river. We don't know when they'll return. Reply.*"

"Good afternoon. Sign off. Reply.

"*Good afternoon. Sign off.*"

Freddy switched off the radio set and leaned back in his chair. Nina felt restless, agitated. Who wasn't? She wandered over to Dr. Barron's bookshelf and ran a finger across the dusty old spines.

I asked, "Did Sebti just tell you the war is over?"

Freddy shook his head. "He said everyone's left Théophila and no one knows if or when they'll ever be back. Only that the war is gone where he is, and people he's close to are saying it's just as true elsewhere."

"Well, it's damned confusing. I feel like we're sitting here with sacks over our heads. Something's wrong with all this."

"I agree."

Nina said, "I think I hear Delia."

She went up the basement stairs.

Freddy frowned.

I went after Nina. She'd gone outdoors into the rain and met Delia crossing the wet lawn with a book in her hand and Phebe Barron chasing behind.

"Oh, honey," Nina called to her, "what are you doing out of bed?"

Her clothes dripping wet, Delia dropped the book into a rain puddle. "I was looking for you. I thought you got lost and I wanted to help."

Nina took her up. "I'm not lost, honey. I'm right here."

"Are you sure?"

"Yes, dear, I'm sure."

Herself rainsoaked now, too, Freddy's mother told us, "The poor dear just walked right past me and out the back door without uttering a word."

Nina pressed her hand to Delia's forehead. "She has a fever."

Phebe said, "Then we need to get her up to bed."

Nina nodded and took Delia by the hand. "Let's go, honey. We have to get you out of the rain and into some dry clothes."

"Maybe a hot bath first?" Phebe suggested. "I can rustle through some of my girls' old clothing and find something to fit her."

"Thank you."

While they took Delia into the house, I went back down to see Freddy in the basement. He had his radio set wired to a broadcast from Cotelle Barbarini and was listening to a report about soldiers from the other side letting go of the town and retreating along the beach in a mile-long column. The announcer said that no one had been killed there in two days and it was agreed the war had ended.

Freddy said, "What did I tell you?"

I sat down in the chair beside him. "That may be true today, but not necessarily tomorrow. Yeazell told Marco how this armistice was based on freeing the children. Now they're dead. How do you suppose that news will be received?"

"Not well."

"No, not at all."

Freddy said, "But whoever decided to turn on the gas must've expected the betrayal would be found out. If not today or tomorrow, then eventually, right?"

"I don't believe they imagined any of those children would have left the Hippodrome alive. That's why the Montalivet tunnel was collapsed. To seal it over. Hide the crime. Like a dog having his accident in the family living room and shredding the carpet to cover it up."

"They couldn't conceive of the undercity getting into the old latrines from the Faubourg sewer?"

"Of course not," I said. "I wouldn't have believed it either if I hadn't been there and seen it with my own eyes. That digging machine they had. Just incredible. Their dedication to making the impossible real."

"I guess that's how they've stayed alive down there all these years."

"No doubt."

"Well, maybe those fellows who ordered the gassing of all those poor kids just wanted it as a distraction, a kind of red herring. What if the idea was just to get the undesirables to quit the fight and walk away? And once they did, and the armistice was agreed on, we attack?"

"That's insane. Murder eighty-thousand children and then launch some surprise attack when the other side thinks we're offering peace? If it's true, this war'll never end."

I left Freddy to his radio and went back into the house to see about Delia and decide when we should leave for Highland Park. Nina and Freddy's mother were in the bathroom upstairs attending to Delia. They had the door closed and I called to Nina from the hall outside. "Can you come out for a moment, please?"

"Just a second."

I heard her speaking to Delia, then the door opened. Nina told me, "She has a slight fever. I'm sure she caught something from being crowded into that filthy place. I'm not at all surprised. Those sonsabitches treated the children like stray dogs. Delia told me they were barely fed at all. Everyone was hungry and there was almost no water. Kids were fainting all around her. She thinks some of them died before we ever got there."

"I want us to go to Highland Park right now. Once you get Delia out of the tub and dressed. You two can have my bedroom there. Mother's very good with treating fevers of all sorts. She was a nurse for a year before she met my father."

"Well, Phebe telephoned to Freddy's father after we brought Delia inside. He's driving home now. Phebe's asked him to have a look at her before we go."

"That's a good idea."

Nina hugged me. "This is all so much, Julian. I'm afraid of going to pieces."

"You won't." I kissed her on the brow. "I refuse to let you."

I thought I ought to discuss the ride over to Highland Park with our driver, so I put on my jacket and one of Freddy's squab hats and went outdoors to the street. Both he and Beroë were parked on Rothermel, Randall farther down along the curb and on the Barrons' side of the street. They were each in their own autos. Smart, I realized. Much more difficult to kill both of them at once if it came to that. Though I couldn't see anyone sneaking up on either of them under any circumstances. How had Beroë ambushed those two men? Her skills were almost unimaginable. Better to stay under their protection than consider myself up for that sort of challenge. I'd already learned a lesson my rainy night at Porphyry Hill.

I walked down the sidewalk to Randall's motor, offering a perfunctory nod across the street to Beroë as I went. What's the protocol for acknowledging someone parked in a wet auto for your protection? I felt like a dub.

Randall's window was lowered in his Model Seven, rain leaking over the sill. He didn't appear to mind. Maybe he'd just lowered it when he noticed me coming down to see him. He had a hat on, anyhow. Kind of odd for sitting in a motor. He asked, "How can I help you?"

"Well, I think it's time we went to Highland Park, if that suits you."

"If it suits you, then it suits me. Are the girls coming out?"

"Delia's got a small fever and Dr. Barron is apparently on his way home from Umbro to have a look at her. After that, they'll dress her and we'll go."

"All right by me."

I looked up across Rothermel to the blue Zenith parked in the rain. "She said she'll be here until six o'clock. Is that so?"

"Yes, indeed. After that, she'll be replaced by someone else."

I noticed my wounded shoulder had developed a faint ache, probably from the damp cold. Maybe I'd soak it in my own bathtub once we got home. "I'll let you know when we're coming out."

"I'll be here."

He tipped his hat and I left.

Dr. H. Cornelius Barron rolled up the wet driveway about half an hour later. He met us upstairs in Freddy's room where Nina had Delia dressed but in bed under the covers. Phebe had found a pair of Ramona's old childhood flannel pajamas and cotton socks. They fit well enough for the drive to Highland Park, where my mother had bought some fresh clothes for Delia.

Dr. Barron wore a pleasant mood when he greeted Delia. "How are you feeling, young lady?"

She smiled. "Good."

"May I have a peek?"

She nodded.

Dr. Barron set his medical bag on the bed and removed a mercury thermometer and a stethoscope. He had Nina unbutton Delia's pajama top and checked her heart and lungs, then took her temperature. Delia kept her eyes on him all the while, that look each of us has when ill in the presence of our doctor, alternating between hope and worry. He smiled and checked her pulse and took out a small glass-light scope and looked into her mouth and ears and eyes. When he finished, Dr. Barron gave Delia a gentle pat on her arm. He told her, "You're going to be fine, dear." He turned to Nina. "Her temperature is just under 101°, but her lungs are clear. She probably brought some unkind bug back with her last night. It doesn't appear serious. My best guess is a touch of Quinette fever, which is plenty irritating and uncomfortable for about twenty-four hours, then more or less skips away. We'll keep an eye on her. I'll pay Delia a visit tomorrow afternoon. In the meanwhile, give her these: Taxile tablets. One for the ride, and the second with morphium powder in a teacup of warm milk at bedtime. She'll sleep like an angel in the clouds."

He looked back at Delia. "Would you like that, darling? To sleep like an angel in the clouds?"

She giggled. "Yes."

Dr. Barron turned to me. "When do you plan on leaving? If it's soon, we can give her the first Taxile now, in which case she'll likely be more comfortable in that fellow's auto. It can be a long ride at this hour."

I looked to Nina. She shrugged. "Then I suppose we'll go now."

"Good enough. Only a glass of water for the first tablet."

Freddy had just come into the bedroom. He said, "I'll get it."

The drive to Highland Park was maddeningly slow in the rain and late afternoon traffic. While Nina and Delia huddled in the back seat, I sat up front with Randall and watched the wipers on the windscreen. As we drove through Birdsall Park, I noticed gatherings of people under umbrellas along the sidewalks and near the Sadler bandshell cheering and flashing "Victory" placards. A disconcerting sight. Had they taken off work early for that? What was I missing? I asked Randall if the city radio had been broadcasting an armistice.

"They're cagey about it," he told me. "Nothing firm. No announcements from Prospect Square. Just sly hints and innuendo. Getting people stirred up."

"Saving the big fireworks for tomorrow, right?"

"I'd guess so. Make a show of it."

I took a peek over my shoulder and saw that Delia had fallen asleep in Nina's arms. I lowered my voice. "And when people hear about the Hippodrome?"

"They won't care."

"They have to."

"Nope. Those aren't their kids. If they hear anything, it'll likely be that a quarantine worked and some of the infected were so bad off they died. 'Thank goodness they weren't let out in the general population.' Something like that."

"It's obscene."

"Yes, it is."

Rain fell harder near the holy river as we made a detour around the busy parkway by Ninevité Avenue. I heard Nina whimper softly as our auto passed a group of young schoolchildren wearing yellow rain slickers and carrying colorful umbrellas. Some splashed in puddles. Lots of rainy-day smiles. I thought of a quote I recalled from somewhere: *"All hope is lost of our reception into grace."*

Traffic let up as we left the metropolis for Schuyler Province and the thick wooded highways, those bridle paths and wild gardens in full bloom drenched with spring rain. I wanted proof that our world would experience a rebirth of hope redeemed through the dismissal of eugenical thought and purpose. Let us live the life we were born for, not this madness of falsehood and terror. Let that be done and finished.

Mother had my bedroom readied for Delia when we rode up the driveway in a brief deluge. Nina quickly brought Delia indoors and put her to bed with a honey biscuit and a glass of water. A copy of Agnes's book of fairy tales from the Orient waited on my nightstand. Delia fell asleep in minutes, and Nina left her to dream.

Downstairs, my mother and Peggy sat with me in Father's office and listened to my hideous nightmare under the Hippodrome. More details than I'd given during that short morning telephone conversation I'd had with Peggy from Thayer Hall. The horrifying reality of it all. And the freighter that somehow inspired my eyes to tear up when I described those thousands of rescued children ascending the windy gangplank.

"You and Nina were very brave to risk your own lives, my darling," Mother said, her own eyes damp with fear.

"It just turned out to be so hopeless. We had no idea. But we weren't all that brave. You're describing little Zynis, who saved Delia and gave her life to rescue a doll for a little friend she'd only just met. I found that to be incomprehensible."

Peggy began crying. My mother gave her a handkerchief and held her hand.

Mother said to me, "You see, Julian, your father held that our hearts have bottomless caverns of empathy when explored by love of more than ourselves. We do things we can't have imagined, and, afterward, cannot imagine *not* having done. That dear child was born to a gift few of us will ever know."

Remembering her little salute as Zynis left Marco to enter the old latrine in that fateful last hour of her life, I told Mother and Peggy, "We're not worthy of her. None of us in this whole rotten Republic. Our persistent apathy stole her life. We should all be ashamed. I know I am."

Mother said, "Lena Redington from our Rose Club telephoned an hour ago to tell us the war is over and all debts are forgiven."

Peggy said, "We know it's nonsense, isn't that so, Martha?"

"Of course." Mother nodded. "Asking forgiveness assumes acknowledgment of guilt and I doubt anyone on the Council responsible for a lethal chamber could ever do so. Their moral fiber is too thin for that virtue. We won't ever see it. If things should come to that, those people will need to be held responsible in a most excruciating manner. Nothing less will adequately satisfy the lesson."

Nina came into the office from the kitchen where she'd brewed a hot cup of citrus tea. "Has Julian horrified you yet?"

"Indeed, he has," Mother replied. "We're so sorry for all of that. It's just unbearably dreadful."

Nina took a seat next to a side table where she set down her tea. Meanwhile, Peggy got up and told Mother, "I'm going to telephone Jack and find out when he expects to be here. I'd love to begin cooking."

My mother stood, too. "I'll help you."

Once they'd both gone, Nina said, "I just peeked in on Delia. She's asleep for now. The poor dear is so tired. No wonder she got sick. Her body just can't fight off all that trauma."

"I'm glad she was seen by Dr. Barron. That made me feel better."

Nina took a sip of tea. "He's a nice man. Delia liked him, and she's afraid of doctors."

"Who isn't?"

"What are we going to do, Julian? Will we stay here? For how long? When will it be safe for Delia to go back to school? Ever?"

"I don't know. School? I'll have to ask Marco's opinion. Maybe she'll need to go into the undercity for that. The three of us can stay here indefinitely, I think. I'm sure my mother would like that. Since Father passed away, and with Agnes off at Branson, she's been here alone. Mother's always been sociable, and having company around is good for her. I'll bet she'd love to have you help with her garden."

Nina enjoyed another sip, then put the cup down. Even with her black hair tossed and messy, her clothes rumpled, I thought she was the most beautiful girl in the world. Those cocoa-dark eyes. How had I gotten so lucky?

She told me, "I'd love to be here for a while, Julian, but I can't see myself picking carrots and tomatoes a year from now. Can't we find some place that belongs just to us? Somewhere far away from here?"

"Do you mean another country? Are you serious?"

"I don't know. I just want to be rid of all this from our lives. It's so awful, and I'm terrified for Delia. She doesn't know any better, so she never complains, but I'm sure she gets scared and wants to lay her head on a pillow of her own. Is that really asking for so much?"

"Nina, we each have our dreams of that life where everything is pleasant and wonderful. I'm not saying it isn't attainable, because what are dreams for, anyhow, if not to set us in our best direction? We may just need to be patient for a while. That's all I can say. We have to be patient."

Nina took up her tea again. "Well, if you haven't noticed, darling, I'm not a patient person."

An hour later, Jack McManus drove up and parked his silver auto at the top of the driveway. The rain had slowed to a cold drizzle and the breeze had died away. Randall's Model Seven was still parked at the curb across the street, the driver's window rolled down a few inches. I noticed he was smoking a pipe. He looked relaxed.

I met Jack in the entry hall as he was hanging up his overcoat, dripping from the rain. "Any word from downtown about the war ending?"

He hung his hat atop the brass stand. "Not a thing. No one seems to know much at all, except that their troops have apparently withdrawn from every engagement in the eastern provinces. Caesárea, for instance, hasn't seen a bullet fly in thirty-six hours, and there's been no artillery fire in either Bourgh and Elektra to the north or Pausanius down south for at least that long."

"So they say."

"Indeed. Which is precisely why we need to be skeptical of any reports these days. The Council controls these things. So far, the Status Imperium has remained silent. No one's sure why."

"The Hippodrome?"

"Maybe."

"When I went to campus, one of my professors, Dr. Coffeen, gave me a telephone number to call for a gentleman out in Solymi who supposedly knows much more about all of this than anyone else."

"Have you tried the number?"

"Not yet. I thought I'd do it after dinner."

"What did your professor say about this fellow? How does he happen to know him?"

"Only that they met years ago at faculty clubs and the gentleman told him he was from Laomedonia. Dr. Coffeen and the others assumed it was a joke. After hearing about my visit out there, now he's not so sure. I presume that's why he gave me the number."

"Well, then I agree you should telephone once we finish eating. If that man knows something about all this that can help, you need to find out."

"That's what I thought, too."

"How are Nina and Delia? Are they all right? I assume they were comfortable enough at Dr. Barron's last night."

"Delia has a fever. Freddy's father came home early to look at her. He thinks she caught something at the Hippodrome. Says she'll be fine. He gave her some tablets to help her sleep."

"That's good. I'm sure she's pretty worn out from her experience there. And Nina?"

"Irritated. Angry. Did Peggy tell you about the men who came to the Barrons' this morning?"

"What men?"

"Besides Randall across our street out there, Marco's people sent a woman to watch the Barrons' house while Freddy and I went to Thayer Hall. After we were gone, apparently two mystery villains showed up and tried to sneak into the backyard. The woman, her name's Beroë, killed them both. Then Randall and a tall fellow carried the bodies out of the yard, put them in the back seat of another motor car and drove them away."

"Good God! Maybe Security Directorate. Trying to hide the crime."

"That's what we thought."

"Let me make a telephone call, Julian. This is very serious. We need some more people up here tonight."

When I went upstairs to look in on Delia, my mother heard me in the hall and called me to her bedroom. She'd been straightening up a little and changing into something more suitable for cooking dinner. In her room, she told me, "Julian, I'd rather not have you riding off into the night to see someone you've never met, to discuss something you have no prior knowledge of. I don't believe it's safe, and worrying about you has simply worn me out."

"I haven't said a word about going anywhere, Mother. I was just asked by Dr. Coffeen to telephone that fellow. I don't know anything else at all."

Mother sat on the bed. She did look tired. Ordinarily, my mother was the busy bee of our family, buzzing about our home and her garden, the market and her clubs, those charity bureaus, without hardly taking a breath. Father used to tell me how just watching her made him feel like lying down.

"Your sister telephoned earlier. She'd like you to call her."

"When?"

"Before she goes to her dining commons, if that's possible. She's been anxious. I felt from her voice that all's not well and congenial with her new fellow out there."

"Well, why would that cause her to want to speak with me? I'm no 'Flossie Edwards, Love Counselor.' She's never chosen to even mention her romantic affections with me. Why now?"

"Darling, I'm not sure that has anything at all to do with her desire to speak with you. Just telephone as soon as you can. Don't let this be a mystery between you two. We've enough of that elsewhere these days."

"Yes, Mother. I'll do it in a few minutes. How's that?"

"Thank you, dear."

Truthfully, I had no desire to telephone Agnes. She had been so disagreeable and obstinate during our last dinner conversation, I just felt as if I needed to avoid any further conflict with her. Let my dear sister revel in those good thoughts she was enjoying of our heroic Council and all the rewards they were bestowing upon us. Her brain was so thoroughly saturated with nonsense, I didn't see any good in trying to persuade Agnes of how wrong she was. Eugenics was a societal epidemic of criminal idiocy, a false science, a medical debacle. We'd been suffering its disastrous infection for over a century now and there appeared to be no vaccine and no cure. Not only was it killing us by degrees, but people like my sister were smiling on that long stroll to the cemetery.

But because my mother asked me to, I telephoned to Agnes, anyhow.

"*McNeeley Branson School. How may I help you?*"

"Agnes Brehm, please? Tremont Hall."

"*Thank you. Connecting.*"

I waited a few moments, gathering my wits to be ready for whatever Agnes had in mind to discuss. This had been a long day so far, and I hoped her mood was at least somewhat reasonable.

"*This is Agnes.*"

"It's Jules. How are you? Mother asked me to call you."

"*Yes, thank you. She and I just spoke earlier this afternoon. She was worried about you, and since I told her I had a few things to say to you, as well, I asked her to have you call. She won't let me come home this weekend. Maybe you know why. She wouldn't tell me except to say it wasn't a good moment. Do you have any idea what that meant?*"

"Yes, in fact, she's probably right. It's best for you to stay there for a little while now."

"*Why is that? You people are always treating me like a child, and I resent it. I'm almost eighteen years old. I think I deserve better.*"

"Aggie, this has nothing to do with your age. I agree that you're not a baby any longer, and we ought to remember that."

"*Then what's so deadly that I can't go home and sleep in my own bed for a night?*"

"It's not safe here for you right now. Things have happened last night and this morning that probably caused Mother to advise you against coming here. At least for a week. I didn't know she'd made that suggestion, but I do agree with her opinion."

"*What things? And don't lie to me. I hate when people lie to me. I can't stand it.*"

"All right, I won't lie to you, but if you don't believe what I'm about to tell you, that's your choice, not mine."

"*I'm listening.*"

I told her all about the Hippodrome, and those men Beroë killed at Dr. Barron's, and the possible threat to us at Highland Park. She didn't once interrupt my story, a rare experience. Once I finished, she said, "*How do you know all this? Were you there?*"

"I just told you I was."

"*Then how come you're not dead, too?*"

"I don't understand."

"*If those children were gassed and burned up, why weren't you?*"

"Aggie, the lethal chamber was sealed to prevent the gas from escaping. That's how it works."

"*Why would anyone gas that many children? It sounds ridiculous.*"

"It was ridiculous. And obscene. You have no idea how it felt to watch it happen. I'll never get over it."

"*Well, I haven't heard anything about that on the radio, and our floor has had the news on all morning. Did you hear the war is over? That's one of the things I wanted to tell you. We won the war. So you were wrong.*"

"Wrong about what?"

"*Our Common Purpose. How the Council did what was best for us, and now we're going to be alive and safe.*"

"Aggie, don't believe everything you hear on the radio broadcasts. The war isn't over. It can't be. Not after the Hippodrome. When people find out what occurred under there, opinions about our Common Purpose won't stand."

"*Well, maybe it's not true.*"

"What's not true?"

"*What you told me. How do I know it really happened? Maybe nothing really happened at all, and you're just saying that to prove me wrong. It's obvious our Council doesn't kill children. That's just not so.*"

"Aggie, I saw it with my own eyes. My girlfriend Nina was there. And her daughter, Delia. She's only eight years old. We saved her. Otherwise she'd be dead, too. You have no idea."

"*It's cruel to tell me these awful things, Jules. Here, I just wanted us to talk and make up for that fight we had at dinner, and now you're trying to make it worse. Why do you do this to me? Do you really hate me that much?*"

I could tell she'd begun to cry. Agnes was so emotional, quick to anger, quick to tears. Quick to laugh, as well, which could make her fun to be around when she wasn't pouting or shouting.

"I don't hate you, Aggie," I told her. "You're my sister. I love you. All I'm trying to do here is explain why Mother and I don't believe it's safe for you to come home this weekend. After I told Jack McManus about those men who were killed outside Dr. Barron's yard this morning, he's decided to hire some security fellows he knows through his office to help guard our house tonight. He thinks it's prudent, and so do Mother and I."

I was loath to tell her Marco's people were probably out there at Branson already. No reason to fry her brain.

"*Why would anyone want to kill us?*"

"I'm not entirely sure, but I suspect it has something to do with what Nina and I saw at the Hippodrome last night. It only makes sense."

"*Maybe to you, Jules, but not to me.*"

"Aggie."

"*Have Mother telephone me after dinner. I want her to tell me. I don't trust you anymore.*"

She clicked off.

I met Nina coming down the stairs from my bedroom. Her lovely eyes had tears again. I asked, "How is she?"

Nina said, "I just told her that I'm her mother."

"Oh God."

"I know. Let's go somewhere we can talk."

We went down to my father's office and sat together on the sofa there.

I asked, "How did she take it? What did she say?"

"She thought I was teasing her. She laughed and called me 'Mommy,' and gave me a big hug. Then I told her I really am her mother and she became very quiet for a minute or so, then she began to cry. I don't think she grasped what I meant, how it could be true, after all these years of being her big sister and her mother having died when she was a baby. Maybe she didn't even believe me. It felt so strange saying those words to Delia."

"Why did you? Today? You thought it was best to tell her after she settled in with a new school, new friends, a new life, right?"

"What new life, Julian? We were living with Johara in a very nice house, and Delia had a wonderful best friend in Riala. Now they're both dead, and Delia was almost killed in that chamber. We're nothing again. Relying on the kindness of strangers."

"I'm a stranger? And Freddy? My mother and the Barrons? Is that really how you see us?"

"No, I don't. Oh, of course not!" She kissed me and knotted her fingers with mine. "I'm sorry I said that. It's mean and stupid. I'm just so frustrated. Delia probably hates me now for lying to her all these years, practically her entire life. Because that coward Arturo ran out on us. Nothing I do makes sense. I'm the biggest idiot."

I said, "One thing makes sense."

She wiped a tear off her nose. "What's that?"

I smiled. "You fell in love with me."

Mother and Peggy cooked beef and noodles *fraternité* with carrots and peas from her garden. Nina prepared a tray for Delia in bed upstairs with small portions of each and a glass of juice. The rest of us ate in the dining room. Once dinner was brought to the table, Jack told us how the metropolis was preparing a jubilee for tomorrow at sundown in every district across the city to declare the end of the war.

"All fighting has apparently ceased in the eastern provinces. It's been announced on radio broadcasts at each hour interval. I've never seen anything like it. Prospect Square is expected to be the epicenter of a massive rally and celebration of our glorious victory, but it looks as if every sector of the city will have its own party. The thrill of it all is undeniable, I have to admit."

Peggy had put out a scarlet carafe of Mericani wine from which each of us filled our glasses. Jack sliced up a loaf of bread from Van Houten's bakery to share around the table with olive oil and butter. Our mood was subdued and thoughtful. No one knew what to expect next. Besides Randall parked down the street, there were two other autos with security associates of Jack's at the curb on each end of our property. Some of those people in our woods, too. The necessity of them watching over us felt disconcerting. How had it all come to this?

"I presume your firm knows about the Hippodrome," I said. "You've told them, haven't you?"

"Of course I did."

"And?"

"Let me guess," Nina offered, "they didn't believe you."

Jack replied, "Oh, they believed me, all right. Not one of them wasn't sickened. At the same time, we realized there's no strategy to pursue just now, no one to chase down. All this end-of-the-war business had co-opted our revulsion at what happened down there in that chamber. At this moment, people want to revel in the wonderful, not thrash about in guilt and shame. It's the simple psychology of a long war that's spoiled so much of our society. They want to cheer again. Feel good about themselves."

"Even at the expense of eighty-thousand innocent children?"

"Even at the expense of a million, dear. That's just how it is. I don't agree with that thinking. None of us downtown do, but we feel this is just not the hour to try and catch the devil by the tail. Losing Dr. Paley this morning was a terrible blow, let me tell you. We feel severely limited with which strategies we're able to pursue. It'll change eventually, but for now that's just how it is."

"I bet they killed him," Nina said, putting down a forkful of noodles. "Why wouldn't they? Paley knew where the children were being kept. You and Julian said so."

"My goodness, dear," Mother muttered. "Just the thought of that gives me shivers."

Nina went on. "And didn't Paley tell you something about getting revenge on those people who killed his good friend, Mr. Trevelyan? They probably got him before he got them. Makes perfect sense to any of us who've experienced firsthand how they do things."

"You mean the Council?" Peggy asked. She sipped her wine. "Or the Status Imperium itself? Is that your opinion?"

I jumped in, too. "I don't think we need to speculate. Someone sent those men to the Barrons', and they weren't there to deliver groceries. Is it so great a coincidence that Dr. Paley died out on his morning walk in roughly the same hour? How exactly did he die? Has anyone said?"

Jack McManus said, "Well, the initial report suggested a stroke or a sudden heart spasm. Nothing official. I presume an autopsy is scheduled."

"I doubt it," Nina interrupted. "Just watch. They'll either put him in the ground or burn him today or tomorrow, but by the end of the week, for certain. No one wants to know what killed him. The Council won't permit it."

Mother asked, "Do you really believe that, dear? The Council murdering one of its own?"

"Why not?" Nina took a long sip of wine. "They kill everyone else, don't they?"

Peggy brought in a platter of baked custard on painted saucers for dessert. We each had one with a cup of spice tea and a hazelnut cookie. After that, Nina went upstairs to see if Delia had eaten her supper. While she was gone, Jack suggested I go make that telephone call to the gentleman from Solymi Province. He was curious what drove Dr. Coffeen to offer me the number. That name seemed familiar to him. We both agreed the connection was intriguing, with that mention of Laomedonia being the sharpest hook.

I placed the call from my father's office desk. A slight case of the jitters had my hand shaking as I put the number in front of me and took up the receiver.

"Station 9. How may I help you?"

"Could you please connect me to WINter-8100?"

"Thank you."

I got up quickly and closed the office to chatter from the dining room. When I sat back down, I heard a man's voice in the receiver.

"Good evening."

"Is this Mr. Rúbotton?"

"*Yes, it is. To whom am I speaking?*"

"Sir, my name is Julian Brehm. I was given your number this morning by Dr. Alfred Coffeen of Regency College. He suggested I telephone."

"*In which regard, please?*"

"Laomedonia, sir, above which I flew in the airship."

A studied pause.

"*And the name of said airship, if you will?*"

"Deiopcia."

"*And your name again?*"

"Julian Brehm, sir. I'm a student of Dr. Coffeen's. I've also been to Désallier."

"*Just a moment, please.*"

"Certainly."

I heard speaking in the background, voices echoing from across a large room. After a minute or so, Mr. Rúbotton again. "*Do you have an auto?*"

"No, sir, but I can be driven."

"*You must come here immediately. Is that possible?*"

"Yes, sir."

"*The address is 4 Hattier de Maistre. Gutzkow Road. It's in the west countryside, so there's no village attached. Where will you be driving from?*"

"Highland Park, sir."

"*Good, you won't need more than an hour, if that. The gate will open when you arrive. Aside from your driver, please come alone. He'll remain outdoors with the auto.*"

"Thank you, sir. We'll leave right now."

"*Excellent.*"

Rúbotton disconnected.

I went back into the dining room and told everyone where I was going. Of course, Mother had her objections, needlessly pointing out that every time I went somewhere now, it felt as if people were trying to kill me. Peggy agreed. Jack thought he ought to ride along. Peggy did not agree with that. I went upstairs to see Nina and Delia.

They were tucked into my bed together under the blankets, reading Oriental fairy tales. I told Nina about Rúbotton. She was even less enthused than the dining room crowd.

"Julian, you just can't go off like this in the middle of the night. It's completely insane."

Delia said, "Don't go. Stay here with us. The stories are really good."

I said, "I won't be long. He told me it's less than an hour away. I think I ought to go. Something's important there. I just have that feeling. I've already chased down so many rabbit holes this month, I need to know."

Nina said, "You're trying to be the key to a lock for a door that has a secret behind it that maybe you don't want to see. I'm not sure I would. Too many puzzles."

"But I do want to see. That's the point here."

"I'd want to," Delia said. "I like solving puzzles. They're fun."

"And you're very clever, too, honey." Nina pinched her cheek, then said to me, "How do you know it's even safe? You don't, do you?"

"I'll have Randall drive me. Those people are smarter than I am. Smarter than any of us. They've had a lot of practice. Like Marco said: They're very good at this. I trust him."

"With your life and ours?"

"We already have. At the Barrons' this morning. Remember?"

I gave her a kiss and Delia a hug and went back downstairs to say goodbye. Mother advised me to keep the windows rolled up. Jack asked me to take notes.

Then I left.

LV

Out in the auto, I climbed into the back seat and gave Randall the address. He studied it for a few moments, then took that odd black gadget from his glovebox once again and flicked it on. He tapped the green button maybe a dozen times, then the red. I watched his windshield wipers work against the rain by the glow of our streetlamps. His auto felt cold and damp. That he had sat out here alone hour after hour in the rain astounded me.

The gadget gave off a few flashes on the green button, then red. Randall switched it off and put it back into the glovebox. He started the engine. "Let's go."

This time I couldn't resist. "What is that thing and how does it work?"

"A magic box. Works pretty well."

That's all he said.

I let it drop.

He drove us out of Highland Park and took the highway west from Shreve to Mirebalais Hills, where the rain picked up and a wet wind threw spring leaves across the windshield as we roared on. I wondered how long I was expected to wander in this labyrinth of mysteries. Our vast Republic was neurotic and disproportionate in its duty to citizens across our varied provinces near and far. The war was more than disruptive and cruel to those without high leather offices at Prospect Square. Our imperious disgrace infiltrated the souls of so many people, young and old, among hundreds of disparate cultural origins and persuasions, how did we possibly expect to purge the epic disease of eugenical dogma that had been systematically inculcated across the decades throughout this nation of individuals? Was it even reasonable to imagine anymore? Because, when wars end, then what? Do all wounds truly heal? Does every pain and resentment die away in its own moment? Mr. Sutro suggested that generations must pass before such memories as our war against the unfortunates may vanish, even though vanish they will. And perhaps that's true. Who would deny that hope? Yet what of us now? Was there truly light ahead? Where in this dark troubled labyrinth were those candles lit?

— · —

The rainy countryside west of the metropolis was pitch dark. Our road narrowed and the pavement roughened. The Model Seven had a poor suspension, so the ride was harsh. I also felt cold air and water leaking in from the side windows above the fitting.

I asked Randall, "Do you know this area?"

"Sure."

"How so?"

"My Uncle Enoch worked as a shepherd out here when I was a boy until he caught a flu from some chickens and coughed to death. His boss found him out in the field getting picked at by the crows."

"That's awful."

"We thought so."

I looked out the window into the night rain. Little to see but fields and trees. Some houselights in the distance.

I asked, "Do you know where we are exactly?"

"Nope."

"But we're not lost, are we?"

"Nope," he said. "This is somewhere on Pennoyer Road. We go along here far enough, and we'll hit Gaston. Then we're close and I sort of know where to go from there. Mostly."

"Is this Solymi Province?"

"Four miles back."

"I couldn't tell."

"It's dark."

I sat back in the seat and kept my mouth shut for a while then. My healing shoulder ached from sitting at an uncomfortable angle. I adjusted. I wished Jack had come along. Someone to talk to. Not Nina. If she were here, I'd be scared for both of us. That wouldn't do. Delia needed her too much. Maybe Freddy? He could be pretty entertaining. We'd have some laughs. But, no, I guessed for this I was better off with Randall.

I watched the road ahead.

More rainy miles of country fields.

Too dark to see much.

We drove on for a while. Straightaways and easy hills, A few bumps here and there, then a hard right onto another long road of gentle curves. Trees and fences.

Randall spoke up. "Now this is Gutzkow. We're probably two miles away."

I saw lights ahead. "Is that it?"

"No."

"Are you sure?"

"I'm sure."

He slowed our auto. Rain fell harder, so I couldn't see clearly. We rolled on farther. Those lights flickered in the downpour. Randall brought us to a stop and switched off his headlamps. He just sat behind the wheel, watching. Rain tattered on our roof. A couple of minutes passed. Then I asked, "What are we doing?"

"Waiting."

"For what?"

He didn't answer.

I thought I saw dim pinpricks of light scattering on the road ahead. Then darkness once again. More rain.

Another few minutes.

Randall got his black gadget out of the glovebox, switched it on, and tapped the green button rapidly. Then the red. A couple of moments passed, and his green button flashed, and the red. He put the gadget away and closed the glovebox.

Then he turned on his headlamps and put the auto in gear, and we rolled forward up the road, briefly flooded now from the cloudburst.

As we approached those lights, I saw two black motors, one on each side of the wet road, forming a makeshift auto cordon. There were several people in dark slickers by each motor as we rolled up. Randall put our auto in neutral, set the brake, and got out into the rain. A man and a woman came over to speak with him. They led him over to the black motors and Randall had a peek into each of them and shook his head. Then he nodded to the man and woman and came back to our auto and climbed in behind the wheel and closed the door.

He told me, "You had a welcome party."

"Pardon?"

"You're a popular boy these days."

"What happened?"

"Four men waiting for you. Two in each motor. Probably Internal Security. We drive up, they kill us both. Then hurry home and dry off. Kiss the wife. Play with the kiddies. Have a nightcap. Go to bed. Pleasant dreams."

Randall put his auto in gear again and we rolled slowly between the pair of black motors. I eased my window down to have a look into one of them as we passed. Blood on broken glass. Head facedown on the steering wheel. I couldn't see the other fellow. Randall gave a nod and a smile to the people standing there out in the rain. Then we went on by.

Up the road, we passed two more autos parked by the ditch, lights off. There Randall told me, "We had our people dressed up in those motors as if driving to a dinner party in Pewell. They passed through the roadblock and stopped up here just out of sight and put off their lights. Then they snuck back through the ditch in the dark and waited until our auto came along and shot all four of those fellows. Just for us."

"I appreciate that."

"You ought to."

A few minutes later, we were turning onto Hattie de Maistre, a narrow gravel lane bordered by thick blackthorn hedges. The addresses there were far apart owing to the size of each property, certainly many acres apiece. Rúbotton's estate was almost a mile up the lane, difficult to locate in the dark rainfall. His gate had a brick arch at its entrance but just a single lamp lit above the address number. We missed it at first before Randall put the auto in reverse. As Rúbotton had promised, the iron gate swung open for us and up the gravel driveway we went.

A stately mansion. Four elegant stories of brick and stone. Mansard roof and dormers. Palladian arches and carved columns. Tall Georgian sash windows. Iron castings on the rain-drenched porte-cochère we drove in under. Randall kept the motor running as I got out. He expected to wait until I returned. I thanked him and went up to the door and rang the bell. I heard footsteps approaching across the foyer.

When the door opened, I was greeted by a curiously short fellow in a fancy plaid vest and crimson trousers. He was dark-skinned and wore a jockey's cap and a pencil-thin moustache above a pleasant smile.

He bowed slightly as he stepped aside to let me in. "Welcome, sir."

A curious accent, as well. From the sea? Parthenian?

The foyer was large but warm. The floor was polished marble and echoed under my footfall. That little fellow led me across the way to a reading parlor, where I smelled a fire roaring on the hearth and aromatic pipe tobacco wafting about. My host was waiting for me by a large walnut desk, a leather-bound book in his hand. He was much older than my father. White hair, gaunt, frail. Wrinkled. Yet firm, too.

He smiled at me. "Welcome, Julian." We shook hands. "I'm Bramel Rúbotton."

A kind voice. Relaxed. Confident.

"Thank you, sir."

"Sorry to drag you out on such an unfortunate evening. Our weather has been atrocious all day long."

"I guess we can't choose, can we?"

"No, we can't. Not yet."

He gestured to a pair of leather chairs with side tables nearer the fireplace. Each had a decanter of scotch and a glass tumbler. "Would you care to sit, Julian? We have many things to discuss tonight of great importance."

"Thank you, sir. Dr. Coffeen thought I should meet you."

"Yes, I was just on the telephone with Alfred when your auto arrived. I let him know you'd found me."

The room was framed in walnut and burgundy silk curtains. Oriental rugs covered most of the floor. Bookshelves with volumes of all sorts filled the walls. The air smelled of dusty leather and tobacco.

Rúbotton said, "I trust your family is safe at home? And your attorney, Mr. McManus, and his lovely wife?"

Rúbotton filled his tumbler with scotch. No need to feel fuzzy, I left mine alone for the moment. I told him, "There are people looking after them, yes. I hope they're safe there."

"I'm sure they are. And you, too. That driver of yours is a clever fellow. I've heard excellent reports."

"Well, we just had an incident on the road a few minutes ago," I said, wondering how extensive his information about all this really was. Did everyone have those little black boxes? "Four men were shot. Randall said they had a trap set to kill me."

Rúbotton frowned. "Good Lord! You weren't injured, were you?"

"No, not at all."

"We weren't intended to meet. That's the base cause of it. Killing you was the simplest solution. Not that it's important any longer. Neither was anyone supposed to know about the children beneath our Thessandrus Hippodrome. And those who did, weren't to hear that those children are now deceased. It's an unparalleled crime, even for this age of slaughter and mayhem."

"Nothing I witnessed in the Desolation could match it. Now I'm hearing the war is over, and nobody will care what happened in that chamber. I expect they'll say it was necessary to protect us all from the contagion of spyreosis. We'll fire off those skyrockets tomorrow across the metropolis and pretend this was only a bad dream. A sixty-year nightmare."

"Well, we do care, Julian. Very much. This has certainly been a long nightmare, but it hasn't been any sort of dream at all. Millions of kind and innocent human beings have lost their lives for the cruel and foolish indulgence of a very few whose science and philosophy served their own obscure social prejudice. The fact is, Julian, the war is, indeed, about to end, but not how they could have ever conceived. It's why I've summoned you."

"On the ride up here, I thought about Laomedonia."

"A wonderful memory," Rúbotton said. "Where I was born, ninety-one years ago. I've never been back. Is it still beautiful?"

"I only saw it by airship and at night, but my eyes were entranced. Why did you leave?"

"Why am I here?"

"Yes."

"May I be truthful on this dreary evening?"

"I hope so."

Rúbotton sipped from his tumbler. "What drew me here was your corrupt society. The ugliness of that which you pronounced as moral virtue. To study this once exalted Republic in its inevitable decline and dissolution. I was urged by the Regents to see this for myself, your cruel perversion of Socrates' thoughts on selective breeding. In fact, my life was perfectly wonderful at Laomedonia. I had a family who loved me and a faithful dog to help hunt rabbits in the Salérien Woods. Once upon a time, I was even adored by the loveliest girl. Zohrina Valéra was her name. We studied together at the Mignard Institute and played like children in the fields of Mnestheus. My youthful world was a vivid landscape of beautiful things. I was blissfully ignorant and unaware of yours. Isn't that how it is when we're young? We're so thoroughly absorbed in discovering ourselves that those horizons beyond us are far away. Too distant to bother considering."

Quoting my father, I interjected, "We grow out of that when we begin wearing long pants."

He tipped his glass to me. "That's the ideal, of course, isn't it? The clock strikes a certain hour, and we assume maturity."

"Or my understanding of it. I'm not so sure how to recognize that boundary. Let's just say that a month ago I knew more than I do now."

Rúbotton smiled. "A sign of maturity. Good for you."

"I've had unavoidable lessons. For instance, my father just passed away. I only found out when I stepped through the door from my adventure in the east. I was completely unprepared."

"Of course you were. We can only guess."

"I realize that now."

He drank again from his tumbler. The room felt warmer, sitting close to the fireplace as we were. His library of old books towered over me. My presence there felt odd and somehow disconcerting. Why was I there? What was so urgent that Randall had to race us through the rain and nearly into a fatal ambush on that dark road?

"Years ago, I taught at Regency College in Practical Philosophy and Disseminated Literature. Nobody knew my origins in Laomedonia and Illium. The Regents provided papers that confirmed an unassailable background from a town and a college we called Tábdolliére in those rural wooded hills above the southern sea. A hard life and instructive for defining one's purpose in the world. I would be the son of a smithy and a midwife. I would have no brothers or sisters. I had traveled alone to the metropolis for a future I could not anticipate otherwise. I was welcomed and accepted wherever I went. I won their trust and admiration with elaborate tales of exotic empires and thrones of gold. They thought my stories were simple flights of fancy, when in truth I was only telling the embroidered history of Laspágandélus and our dear Désallier. The distinction mattered not at all since your own history became equally fanciful and false. But I arrived as an investigator, not an emissary. The Regents had sent me to discover whether eugenics had truly invigorated and restored your factitious society. I walked the streets of your economically segregated districts and saw no enlightenment, nor true revitalization. Only a pernicious apathy. Beggars still begged. The poor were yet vanquished by the wealthy. Common fishmongers were common as ever. Children still played barefoot in the filth of stone tenements in sad Calcitonia and the tawdry East Catalan. Lies about social education and progress told in the offices of lawyers and politicals and professorial smoking clubs proliferated as always. Farms were factories for the preferred. The holy river was arterial and fluid to the ruling class and the wealthy, those fortunate born, not from strenuous achievement, but of simple advantage. The rest of your grand eugenical society persisted in squalor and hopelessness. Had spyreosis been medical fact rather than fiction, it might be said to have infected your entire Republic west of the broad Fatoma."

Rúbotton drank his tumbler empty and poured himself another. His eyes were glassy and dark, his bearing more imperious than ever. I felt like an autumn freshman in my first lecture at Thayer Hall. I had no rejoinder, no basis upon which to contradict one word of his. Yet I offered this perhaps impertinent question. "What did you expect to find here, after all? Some Olympian utopia? A race of supermen? That eugenical nonsense."

"No, in fact, I generally thought I'd find a metropolis of disconnected human beings who had sacrificed their moral conscience on that dry faceless wheel of prejudice and profit. My expectations were met quite rapidly. After just a few months, I decided your fresh eugenical society was a wretched mess of rampant hypocrisy. Within three years, I watched you go to war. A sad rejection of all your Great Separation was promised to have accomplished, that Common Purpose of a better world."

I began to wonder about the purpose of this lecture. Again, why *was* I there? I asked, "So, why did you stay, sir? As my father used to say, '*The dawn of childhood marks the future man.*'"

He enjoyed a further sip of scotch, then smiled. "Because by then I'd been elected to the Status Imperium, and I helped direct the war."

Rúbotton held his tumbler and stared at me, unblinking. What sort of response had he anticipated? I asked, "Why would you do that?"

"Well, do you understand the structure and position of the Status Imperium? How it functions?"

"It's our seat of government, our ruling firmament. The heads of state, as it were."

After another sip of scotch, he nodded. "Julian, the Status Imperium exists as a five-headed overlord to the Republic. Five people, each appointed individually by the one who retires so as to retain a manner of exclusivity and distinction between each person philosophically. There are five members so that no vote or decision can be deadlocked. None of the five know the identity of more than one of the others. No names, only numbers. During my tenure, I was Four. We inhabit five exclusive chambers with discreet entrances in the uppermost floors of the Parrish-Lavinian Tower at Zinsser Court. There are dozens of such chambers and offices in the Tower, and our purposes there at any given hour are obscured to observers by false titles. By design, we may appoint our own successors. In the case of unexpected death, three of the four remaining members vote for someone on the outside to choose the anonymous successor. Such identity is mandated to remain secret. Should one reveal his or her position in the Status Imperium, that person is immediately removed and replaced through the procedure I've just explained. Any individual in the Status Imperium is, therefore, able to walk freely about the metropolis as if invisible."

"And each is drawn from the Judicial Council, isn't that true?"

My lesson in the basic Civics of the Republic, third year of Upper School where my grades were named as Sustaining, but not Excelsior.

"No, that is not true. Rarely has a member of the Status Imperium ever served on the Council. It's thought to be politically and philosophically unwise. The intention was always for those two bodies to be kept entirely separate. The Judicial Council supervises the state and organizes its operations across many social, scientific and economic determinations. Security and education, too. That's its directive and purpose. I was never a member, nor had I any desire to be one, although I was socially familiar with many, many of its individuals. And I still am, as much as one can ever be close to those people, particularly these days. Egos and ideology can make personalities nearly impenetrable during a moral crusade, or a war. No, I was elected to succeed a woman by the name of Felícia Péronneau, great-granddaughter of the architect who designed and oversaw the construction of National Cathedral. She plucked me off the streets, so to speak, because of a lecture she recalled I'd given one night at Torelli Hall on the cross-pollination of provincial cultures within the districts of our metropolis and how they serve to the betterment of our fractured society. She apparently enjoyed how calmly I fended off a myriad of vicious responses to my presentation. Incidentally, have you ever wondered why we've never had a Caesar or some such authoritarian personality as our head of state, rather than these archaic bureaucratic constructions?"

I shrugged. "I suppose I've never really thought about it, although I can see how that could be of great appeal to certain groups of our populace. Some people do prefer to hear a single voice guiding them, that's true. A fellow who thinks he's God, or some such delusion. So I've heard in classes on the history of cultures."

Rúbotton drank more scotch and I began to wonder how he was still conscious. "Well, you only need to understand our own history to find your answer. We were established here as part of that empire to the east, and the Status Imperium was created by Queen Isabella Nouille to oversee these western provinces. That singular head of state, then, was always her, and the Status Imperium served at her desire. Once the Republic was declared, we lived with a form of government that was familiar and effective, and we've never seen or felt the need to alter it. Truthfully, there have been individuals who considered themselves ideologically superior in concept to the Status Imperium and have sought to overturn centuries of that body's stability. Each has failed into a hasty grave."

I was feeling impatient then. Mostly from fatigue and worry. Who was Bramel Rúbotton, anyhow?

I said, "I still don't follow why you'd take responsibility for a war that has ruined this society. Why would you do that?"

"I'll explain it, if you promise to listen, please."

"I do."

"Julian, my boy, societies grow tired and lazy, consumed by boredom that leads finally to dull markets and mortal disputes. A threat to the common welfare is generally a panacea to the certain morbidity of a dying state. Forty years earlier, the Great Separation invigorated your troubled world by naming the undesirables as the root of societal decline and dissatisfaction. That popular virus drew your wrath again. Promoted by a restless Council and an unhappy populace, the First Directive was launched in the early spring, a glorious season that year. The most beautiful wildflowers in bloom across the fields of Trivánder Province and the loveliest sunsets we could ever recall. I conceived the tactics that brought us across the Whitestone frontier and over the Fatoma River in those three overwhelming waves using hydrocyanic gas and radioactive shells that killed two hundred thousand survivors of the Great Separation. By autumn, we'd killed more than a million people, men and women and children of all ages and origins and forced everyone else off into the hinterlands. There was no great standing army to resist us. They were helpless and so they died. We offered no pity and felt no remorse. Our weapons and training were much superior. They were mostly farmers, orchard keepers, schoolteachers, merchants: unprepared and unable to defend what they had evolved and constructed in those years since the trains left them off in that most fearsome purge."

He offered a feeble smile. "Isn't that awful?"

"Pointlessly cruel, if I may."

"But you're wrong, Julian. There was certainly a point to it, a critical strategy on my part. When a million people are caused to die, there must be a discernible reason, wouldn't you agree? A purpose to their deaths, however wicked and tawdry."

"If you say so."

"Well, I do. You see, Julian, we chased them throughout the winter and into that following spring, when I directed Dr. Christian Bernadotte to order the breeching of the great Florian Border. A most critical move. We were able to kill more than one hundred thousand people that first day of the assault. A great success. They were driven far into the east through Darrieux, Solomon and St. Marta provinces toward Fabian, Tarchon and Caesárea, Ephyrae and Cisterna to the south, Bourgh, Tyghe and Elektra in the north. We were winning stupendous victories, as I'd expected we would. The war was thrilling. Everyone was happy and pleased with my decisions."

I began to wonder if Rúbotton was a worse maniac than Grover Colborne or that energetic Colonel Watson at Porphyry Hill. Why boast about the death of millions? I said, "I wouldn't brag about that in the undercity. They have different memories."

"I'm sure they do, but that's not the end of my story. You see, Julian, I also gave the order a year later that sent our elite Xanthus Brigade into the Cortina ravine where they were completely annihilated. Every man lost. Our enemy used phenotheric earth mines and mobile incinerators. We had never seen them before. The effect was ghastly. Then I directed General Justus Fín Bec to assault the Maurreau stronghold at Duvros that cost the entire Layton Brigade, as well. No survivors. More strange weapons. Indefensible. Bodies violently dissected and left unrecognizable. Horrifying. Terrible losses in both campaigns. Utter disasters. From that, I relinquished my seat in the Status Imperium to Dr. Fenestros Risso, a surgeon from Treppel with a reputation for distinct moral reflection. Afterward, I retired to this estate to await my letters from Désallier."

I heard footsteps and a voice echo from the foyer.

"Uncle, he doesn't have all night. Would you please tell him why you did it?"

I looked over my shoulder and saw Warren Radelfinger coming into the reading room, his hair and jacket askew.

I got up. "Warren?"

"Sorry, Julian. The old man likes to tell his stories. He'll get to the point eventually, but not until he's worn you down. My father warned me about him when I was in diapers. By the way, Evie sends her regards from upstairs where she's had far too much to drink. She will not be joining us."

Rúbotton said, "'*Patience is bitter, but its fruit is sweet.*' Your dear father, Warren, had less patience than a mouse on a stove top. Your friend Julian needs to know why I've brought him out here on this rainy evening from a comfortable living room and the arms of his own lovely girlfriend."

"Tell him, old man, before he's completely convinced that you're a monster." Warren chose another chair and brought it over to us. "You do think he's a monster, now, don't you, Julian? Be truthful."

"It's all so hideous."

Rúbotton told me, "Warren is my grandnephew on Sister Brunetta's side. A troublesome child, if I'm to be honest. Ever snooping into things. A wasteful mind, too."

Warren smiled as he grabbed the decanter of scotch and my empty tumbler. "I'm his favorite. He just can't bring himself to admit it."

"I do admit that you are unique, my boy, and that's the tale of it."

Warren filled his tumbler and had a drink. "Well, then, have your tale with Julian and finish it up. We need to explain why he's here."

I agreed. "I do want to get back home, but I also need to hear what this is all about."

Rúbotton said, "There are secrets, Julian, circulating throughout the Judicial Council, all twenty-four members, like malignant air. That's forever been true. And the institutionalized anonymity of the Status Imperium both contributes to, and ameliorates this, and always has. Dialogue among members of the Council is vibrant and transparent, while the Status Imperium is opaque and discrete, best understood when one realizes their identities are withheld from everyone, including each other. Decisions within the Status Imperium are indicated through undefined message channels. Debate is non-existent, conflicts deliberately intended to be explored within the Council."

"An eccentric version of imperial democracy," Warren added. "No sane person would accept that nowadays."

"Yet, it is accepted," Rúbotton pointed out. "Whether reluctantly or not."

Warren said, "Clearly the central rot of our Republic, I'd add."

Rúbotton gave his grandnephew a withering glance, then took another sip of scotch.

I said, "I'm not quite following what this has to do with what you did back then. It sounds as if you were playing both hands of the game."

"Tell him, Uncle. Shame yourself. It's late, anyhow. Nothing matters anymore."

Rúbotton told me, "On my schedule and watch, by the insistence of a Council majority, the Status Imperium voted to uphold the essential directive of the eugenical crusade and exterminate in the eastern provinces every survivor of the Great Separation in order to protect the sanctity, health and well-being of what they perceived to be their own perfect and untainted society."

Warren interjected, "Institutionalized lunacy."

Rúbotton told me, "The simplest explanation of my decisions in those years is this: I directed and permitted the extinction of millions in order to save tens of millions. Perhaps, ultimately, hundreds of millions. The blackest ledger in human history. A scale of unequal weight that hoped to allow this ancient civilization of ours to live on. Morality is a convenience in those circumstances, the purest social necessity that by force was briefly shunted aside so that its purposeful glory might endure later on. My intention and desire had been to inspire a revolt from our enemy, a bitter defense of life and humanity, a desperate fight for existence. I'd flattered myself that all of it was logical and pure, good and right. Once I realized how decisively the Regents had intervened, my own horror was complete. Two rabid armies falling onto each other, decade after decade, across an eternity of fields. I'd instigated an endless war that by its own device forgave the repugnant and let these interminable shadows descend upon all of us."

"Those beautiful children in the Thessandrus Hippodrome," I said, "were gassed and burned to ash because of your own devious experiment in geo-political engineering. Is that right?"

Rúbotton nodded. "Undeniably."

Warren said, "And now, Uncle? Please? Tell him what's about to follow that catastrophe. Tell him what happens when the great firmament falls."

"Your own cleverness, Warren, is not exempt from our folly, I hope you realize. Your part is integral to this disaster."

Warren told him, "*We* are integral, Uncle, you and I. Inseparable in the execution of this last act."

I sat up. "What do you mean? What's about to happen? What can possibly be worse than the Hippodrome? What is it? We've lost so much already. So many people."

Rúbotton said, "My grandnephew is both layabout and genius. His young blood was circulated through the Mignard Institute during Lower School, and his ideas, even as a raw child, were inventive and unorthodox."

Warren explained, "I taught a mouse to dance and light candles on a birthday cake. I don't quite recall how I managed that, but I'm sure it was a very clever scheme no one had thought of attempting before me."

"Revenge, Julian," Rúbotton said, "not worse than the Hippodrome, although this will certainly eclipse that horrid crime. Not worse, my boy, but *because* of the Hippodrome."

"Late this morning at Veuillot Fields," Warren told me, "the undesirables who quit the battle to end the war in retreat were surrounded and massacred. More than a thousand killed and left for the crows. The same villainy occured three hours ago in the Pimodan Woods, hundreds ambushed and annihilated."

Rúbotton added, "By order of the Judicial Council. Well, specifically, three people. Widsalia Rose Grummond, Dr. Benson Agard and Loye Sargentich. I've determined these three are also responsible for the massacre of those children in the lethal chamber. On their own direction and absent of any debate or consultation within the Judicial Council. In fact, I have irrefutable proof. They are eugenicists and degenerate sociopaths, all three, and wield together enormous power and influence over policies and prosecution of directives from above. I am also certain that one of them is romantically involved with a member of the Status Imperium. It's forbidden, of course, but that very fact encourages tremendous political and philosophical possibilities and potential for the final ruin of this state and society."

"Not that any of it matters now," Warren added. "The die was cast with the betrayal of that cruel bargain under the Hippodrome. These latest venalities only promise that no second thoughts will be entertained from this evening forward."

Rúbotton said, "As it happens, I've invited that trio of lunatics to enjoy cocktails with me on the roof of the Girardin Hotel tomorrow at sundown, and they've each accepted. We'll have our toasts above Prospect Square and enjoy the celebrations before we all say goodbye."

I stood up and walked over to Rúbotton's desk. I felt nervous now, incredibly agitated by that conversation. What on earth were they talking about? Why this obfuscation? These code words. I said, "Is it impossible for you to speak plainly? I still have no idea what you two are talking about."

Warren took a drink of scotch and looked at Rúbotton, who nodded in return. Then he said, "Julian, do you remember my little demonstration in Freddy's radio hole with Evie's atomizer and that burning cigarette?"

"Of course. It was frightening."

"Well, the Regents invited me to develop that magic gas for just this moment they'd hoped would never arrive. But now it has, and tomorrow a greater demonstration will be performed in the atmosphere for millions to enjoy. At least momentarily."

Rúbotton told me, "Every story has a conclusion, Julian. It's logical and necessary. Only love endures forever, and there's insufficient love in this narrative to permit it to continue. Therefore, it will end tomorrow at sunset above the holy river, Livorna, when the Regents will order the metropolis destroyed."

Warren finished his drink. "And God save us all."

LVI
∾

I listened to rain dripping from the eaves outside my bedroom window as I lay beside Nina on the far end of midnight in those final hours of all this. Across the hall, Delia slept peacefully in Agnes's bed with a tiny lamp lit on a nightstand and Goliath at her feet.

The house was quiet. Mother and Peggy had long since gone to bed by the hour I returned from Rúbotton's estate. Nina and Delia, too. Jack McManus was awake and reading legal briefs in Father's office, a glass of bourbon on the desk beside him. He'd waited up for me. I was glad because of what I needed to tell him. First, though, I telephoned to the Barrons' house and Freddy answered. I let him know I had news but was unable to share it on the porous metropolitan exchange. We agreed that he would drive his mother's auto over here before breakfast. He had news to tell me from a coded radio dialogue with Sebti earlier in the evening. He assured me what he'd heard was shocking. As if much of anything could shock either of us then. When I asked if Beroë was still parked out front of his home, Freddy told me how she'd been there off and on most of the afternoon until two more autos came to watch the house, relieving her of night duty. Rain fell steadily, and he said Rothermel Street had flooded at the bottom when the creek overflowed just after dusk.

After that conversation, I told Jack about the attack Radelfinger and Rúbotton had promised for tomorrow.

"That was a joke, right?"

"No, I don't think so. Not by the expression on their faces. You wouldn't have thought so if you'd been there."

"Well, I don't believe it's possible to blow up the entire city. That's an army's pipe dream."

"Not blow up. Just burn. You didn't see Radelfinger's show in Freddy's basement. It was astonishing. That gas, how it burst into flame."

"Clothonium?"

"No, this was something else Radelfinger came up with. Another of his special brews. Clothonium, as I understand it, would have killed all of us in the basement before he had a chance to ignite it. This is different."

"For Christsakes, Julian, my office is downtown. And the Garibaldi Building."

"Yes, and the Mollison Institute and Hollerith Plaza. The Mansurette Library and Dunham Gardens. Well, all our parks and museums and theaters. Department stores. Banking districts and the Stock Exchange. The cathedrals. The Dome. The wharves all along the riverfront. All our colleges. The Éspezel and Flammarion Hospitals and the Organic Medicine Institute. Dr. Paley's Nationale Club and, of course, Prospect Square and the Mendel Building. No great loss there."

"But district neighborhoods, Julian. Millions of people! Why would they want to do that?"

"Why?" This entire scenario of our Republic infuriated me now and I finally understood how narcissistic we truly were. "Jack, we've been killing millions of them for decades now. That first year of the war when they had no defense? Good grief! How many died? Even the Great Separation? And how about those eighty-thousand children we just gassed and burned? Each of them was born like us into this world to live and be happy. Didn't they have people who loved them? Didn't they laugh and play with favorite toys and darling pets and other children who became friends? Didn't they see something new every day? And weren't they tucked into bed each night to dream and dream of wonderful tomorrows? And don't you guess they were scared and lonely in those train cars and in that underground up to that moment we ended their young lives? It's sickening to admit, but we've been earning this for a very long time. I suppose for our persecuted enemy, the bill is due and tomorrow they're coming to collect."

Jack grabbed a bottle of my father's bourbon and went down into the basement where he'd made himself comfortable these past couple of nights. He was infuriated and disgusted. Scared, too. No more lawyer's bravado.

As I went about the house turning off lights before I retired upstairs to be in bed with Nina, I heard a soft knocking at the backyard kitchen door. It startled me, at first. Then I thought it was probably Randall, maybe asking for a glass of water or a biscuit and a cup of coffee. But when I nudged the curtain aside, I saw Marco there, soaking wet.

I let him in.

He draped his jacket over one of the chairs at the kitchen table and sat down. His hair was drenched and dripping, so I got a towel for him.

"Been raining for hours," Marco said, drying off. "My little apartment in the Nazarene's flooded. I had to take a cot in a storeroom at Kaufmann & Frankel. That print shop on Boegle?"

"What are you doing out here?"

"You saw Bramel Rúbotton tonight."

"Yes, I did. Nothing like hearing about the end of the world. Warren Radelfinger was there, too. Inventor of our doom. Did you know his lineage? How does someone keep a secret like that?"

"Survival, Julian. Basic instinct. This whole business had been one big secret since Adolphus Varane decided to be God and the Status Imperium agreed to worship at the altar of eugenical persecution and murder. Since then, no one's been healthy, and no one's been safe." He glanced about the kitchen. "Is there anything to eat?"

"Sure."

I fixed him a meat and lettuce sandwich and heated up a cup of lemon tea. Marco had a strange air about him that ran a needle-thin tightrope of heroism and insanity. I wondered how much came by his own volition and how much was someone else's instigation. Marco was erratic but faithful. Terrific as an ally, brutal and merciless otherwise. He had kept me alive. Nina and Delia, too.

"You ought to eat more," I told him, noticing how frail he looked. "Health is a virtue."

Marco chewed off a bite of his sandwich. "There's a barge scheduled for departure tomorrow from the Gillihan wharf. We haven't heard yet which one, but you, Nina and Delia need to meet Warren Radelfinger and Evelyn Haskins on the docks no later than five o'clock. Freddy Barron, too, if he's willing."

"Why?"

"To leave the city. It won't be safe for you after sundown tomorrow. Not for any of us. We can barricade the undercity, but you're not mentally fit to live down there. Neither is Nina. Delia would do fine, but Nina won't let go of her, so you three have to travel together."

"Why Freddy?"

"His name's come up on a ledger, same as yours and Nina's. If we didn't have our people watching his home tonight, he'd probably be dead already."

Marco ate the sandwich as if he hadn't seen any food in a week.

"I thought the war was over. Why do they care about us?"

Marco stopped chewing long enough to smile. "They're mad at you, Julian. Didn't you know that? You got all the way out to Porphyry Hill and back without taking a bullet in the head. Someone even shot you and you're still alive. That's just impossible. And you helped the kids escape from the Hippodrome. Well, enough of them at least to spoil the fun."

"Internal Security knows about that?"

"They found the Faubourg sewer and sent their dogs in after some of our people who'd been photographing the chamber for our records."

"Good grief."

Marco shrugged. "Not a shock. We assumed they'd figure it all out eventually. We killed the dogs and their agents at the shore, then packed up our equipment and left."

"No wonder they hate you."

"It's pretty mutual, but you can see why you have to get out of the city tomorrow. Lots of trouble arriving. Loose ends being tied up and resolved. The end-of-war celebrations are expected to involve most of the metropolis. Did Rúbotton tell you he intends to be down in Prospect Square at sunset?"

"Yes, but why would he do that? He told me what's coming."

"Rúbotton's one of those old-time fellows who has a peculiar sense of duty. I think he's nuts, but, apparently, he insists on seeing this out, whatever that means. Don't worry about him. We think there might be a million people in the streets, so we can sneak you through to the wharf fairly easily. We hope."

"Is Randall driving us?"

Marco had a drink of tea. "Yes, with two other fellows ahead and behind. Keeping anyone marking your auto from getting too close. You'll be safe."

"And what are your plans?"

He smiled. "I have somebody to visit out in Bonestell."

LVII

The sky was cloudy with a faint drizzling mist in the morning as the house began to wake up. I was out of bed late, after nine. Nina had gone to see about Delia, who had a cough, and I dressed to go downstairs, where Mother and Peggy were preparing breakfast. Jack McManus was on my father's office telephone, his voice urgent and irritated. He didn't appear to have slept all that well. I needed to reach Freddy to let him know I was awake and that he ought to bring his overnight pack just in case. With Jack occupying the telephone, and Nina upstairs with Delia, I decided to go outdoors and have a word with Randall about our plans for later in the day and see if he needed anything just then. What did he eat, anyhow? He never acted hungry. His Model Seven was still parked at the curb just down Houghton Avenue from our home. Another auto was farther down the sidewalk at the Stadtmuller's and a third was just visible up Houghton by Dame Hackett's where the avenue dipped away from us.

Randall gave me a nod as I crossed over the damp pavement to have a word. He got out and opened the back door for me. I slid in behind his seat and pulled the door shut. For politeness sake, I asked if he was hungry.

"Nope, just had my breakfast." He held up a mug of coffee.

"You sure you wouldn't like anything else? My mother's preparing eggs, waffles and fruit cups for us right now. It'd be no trouble at all to prepare a plate for you. Knowing her, she'd be very pleased to do so."

"I'm fine, thank you."

"Did you see Marco last night?"

Randall nodded. "Wouldn't get in the auto. Made me roll down this window. Got my clothes wet. Not all that considerate. If he wants to be pals, that little fellow needs to try harder. That's all I have to say on the subject."

"But did he tell you the plan for today?"

"He said his idea, if that's what you mean."

"Well, does it work? Can you drive us?"

"Not down onto the wharf. We've been listening to the city radio all morning. A lot of crowds and shouting. It'll be worse later on. Biggest holiday ever. End of war jubilee. Streets are closed all over. We won't get within three miles of the river. Can't be done."

"Well, what can we do?"

"We're studying on it, checking our maps. We'll come up with something. Don't worry."

Uncertain what sort of information was being traded about among Marco's people, I was hesitant to say much. But I asked Randall, "Do you know anything about today? Have you heard any rumors?"

He said, "There's a reckoning."

"What do you think about that?"

"It's overdue. Has been for a long while now."

I watched the drizzling rain increase a little on the windscreen. The auto interior was cold. Off to the east, though, I saw blue skies breaking through the morning clouds. On another occasion, I might have expected a nicer day by afternoon.

More curious than I ought to have been, I said, "May I ask you a question?"

"Sure."

"You don't have to answer if I'm being too rude, but where are you from? Your dialect. That story about your uncle. It's interesting. I've heard so much these past few weeks. I'm curious about these ties between so many of you."

"Well, I can admit that I grew up by a little town called Chickering. That's down in Henius Province on the western shore of the Fatoma River. Both of my folks were born there and their folks, too. Lots of families in and about Chickering since anyone can remember. Farms with good soil. Plenty of fishing business on the river. Home orchards and deep wells. Normal people with big hearts. Generous and kind, as I recall. Looked for the best in each other and took that to be the truth. My father worked a tannery, my mother kept us clean and fed and did some seamstress work and taught piano part of the morning. I had two brothers and three sisters. I was the oldest. Chickering had three schools, two Lower and one Upper. Mine was called Montella Union and had a view of the river that I found distracting to my lessons, so I did not perform to the peak of my abilities."

Randall gave me a smile.

I said, "That sounds familiar."

"We do share our humanity in unexpected ways."

"I suppose we do. But why are you here? Why are you doing this?"

"Well, that's my story. You see, Chickering was not on the hub of any great industry or commerce, so maybe we lacked the foresight to see much past sunrise and sunset. Now, I won't say our people were unintelligent. That would be misleading you as to the nature of our community, person to person. My father's skills were more than I could comprehend in those days, and I've yet to hear anyone grace the keys of a piano as did my mother. But there was a fellow who had a house in a willow grove by the river who was a thinker like none other. His name was John Partridge, and he was held to be the smartest man in that part of the country. He was a widower with a pretty little girl called Cammeline I used to see around town with a jump rope and a kitten in a straw basket. People admired him, so it had to be John Partridge who stood up in the town square one evening and told us about events in the metropolis and a war on the horizon and that we would not be ignored. He scared Chickering and people were unhappy about that and told him to go away, and he did. Partridge sold his house and bought a boat and went off downriver, and life went back to normal for another half year or so until someone reported soldiers in the fields ten miles away and we heard the Roesch and Burnaby families were shot to death and their homes set on fire. Smoke carried for miles. Terrible rumors, too. Why had the soldiers come to us? We knew all about the Great Separation, but we had no refugees in Chickering. None of us were infected. No one in town could even spell 'spyreosis.' We had hunting rifles and my father had a shotgun and the men vowed to defend our town. Then we heard cannons and the wheat fields caught fire and a dark gas came down upon us like this rain outside my auto. I can yet remember that nasty odor, sour and mean. People were yelling and choking and falling over, black water pouring out of their mouths and noses. Mother wrapped us up in cotton blankets and ran us to the river and hid us under a boat she'd flipped over. Being stubborn, I crawled out into the reeds to look for my father, so he'd know where we were when he came to rescue us. Nothing but shooting and explosions and fire all over. Most of Chickering was burning up, houses and schools and stores. And then I saw our men coming to the river with hands over their heads, and my father was with them. And the soldiers made them kneel by the water. Then they shot them all. Killed every last one of them. I saw my father get shot in the head when I was nine years old. My mother kept us under the boat until dark, then had us flip it back over again and we floated off down that river where John Partridge had gone with the good sense we ought to have had when he told us what was coming."

"Good God."

"I know something's on the way, son, and I say whatever it might be, it's well deserved. Chickering was nobody's enemy. I don't believe there were true enemies anywhere. Never have been. Just a desire of some people to kill others. Now maybe it's a payback."

"Do you think that's fair? Not everyone's guilty."

"Doesn't matter anymore. Nobody'll be judging."

Nina was getting dressed in my bedroom when I went upstairs. Delia was listening to a station broadcasting Délessért folk music on Agnes's radio set. Nina and I kissed and held each other for a few minutes. I'd been so distracted by everything that I'd forgotten about loving and being loved, forever the best part of life.

"Delia's feeling better," Nina told me, after one last warm kiss. "Her fever broke this morning and she was so hungry I had to go downstairs and warm up a couple of honey muffins. After she ate, she remembered about Riala and Zynis and cried for a while. She and I are going to take Goliath for a walk in a few minutes. Do you want to come with us?"

"It's raining out."

"Your mother showed me umbrellas we can use."

"There's something else, too."

"What's that?"

I told her about Bramel Rúbotton and Radelfinger's demonstration above the metropolis, and then what Marco had told me last night. Nina's eyes watered and she sat back down on the bed. Her breathing was ragged. She gasped and I sat beside her and took her hand. She said, "Julian, we have to leave. That's all there is to it."

"That's the plan. A ship at five o'clock. Randall's supposed to drive us into the metropolis. He says we can't get to the wharf by auto because of the crowds closing certain streets, but they're working up some alternative route for us."

"We can't tell Delia until it's time to go. She'll be scared again."

"We won't," I said. "We'll just get into the auto and go. Maybe we'll just say we're off to see the boats on the river, all those flags and streamers and such. People out celebrating."

"Maybe."

"She's very adaptable, Nina. She's strong and smart. It'll work out. Believe me."

I heard my mother call from the bottom of the stairs, so I gave Nina a kiss and went down to see what she needed.

"Freddy telephoned while you were outdoors," Mother told me as I followed her back into the kitchen. "He says he'll be over here within the hour."

"He didn't ask me to call him back?"

"Not that I understood. He's probably in Phebe's auto already."

"All right, thanks, Mother. Will we be eating soon? Nina wants to take a walk with Delia and Goliath. Is there time for that?"

"Better they do it after we eat. Peggy's got everything on platters. We don't want the food to get cold."

I nodded. "I'll tell Nina."

Jack McManus came into the kitchen. "Julian, may I borrow you for a moment?"

"Not too long, Jack," Mother warned. "We're just about to eat."

He and I went back into my father's office, where he showed me a telegram. He said, "I just received this from downtown. Go ahead, read it."

The telegram said:

THE WAR IS OVER. NO CONCERN. CHAMPAGNE AT FOUR.

Jack had just that look.

I said, "Well, there's no persuading them if that's what they want to believe. It's hard to deny. But when the proof arrives, it'll be too late to change their minds."

"Maybe so, but I intend to go down there and have my say, anyhow. If I can get any of them out of there, it'll be worthwhile."

"That's crazy. What if you get stuck and can't get yourself out? I've heard the crowds are expected to be enormous, particularly at Prospect Square. A million people in the streets. It'll be the epicenter of foolishness. Honestly, you'd be insane to go."

"Probably, but I'll feel like a goddamned coward if I don't. Those are friends of mine, not just colleagues."

"Did you tell Peggy? She won't vote for this once she knows what we know."

Jack said, "We won't tell her, Julian. Not just yet. I mean that, too. Do not say a word to her. Peggy's my wife and she deserves to know, but that's my responsibility, not yours. I'll telephone from the office, let her know when I'm on my way back."

"It's not a good idea."

"It's settled, Julian. Go eat some breakfast."

Then he left.

While my mother and Peggy and I set the dining table for breakfast, Nina brought a tray of waffles and strawberries upstairs to eat with Delia. She also took a bowl of Whipple dry meal for Goliath that Mother had bought at the market. Nina and Delia drank berry juice and we had hot tea downstairs with our own breakfast. I refused the temptation to tell Mother and Peggy anything about what was to happen in the metropolis. Highland Park was safe. They'd be safe. Alexanderton would be safe. Lots of places would be safe. Perhaps people celebrating our victory inside the Dome of Eternity would even be safe. But no one else would outside in the greater city at sunset.

I began to feel agitated and tired. I hadn't slept well. My dreams had been lucid and erratic. Half a dozen times during the night I'd awakened and reached for Nina, believing that she'd taken Delia and gone back to Gosney Street to a house that no longer existed. I had another dream where Lewis and Marco and I were playing *Qantara* and asking me questions I tried to answer with a squib book whose pages were blank. I woke with a night sweat and worried that I'd caught a plague and passed it to Nina, and then realized that was a dream, too, and I was fine and so was she, breathing so gently I had to put my ear to her mouth to be sure she was alive. Those dreams were fluid and frightening and when morning lit the bedroom curtains, I resolved to stay awake. And so I did.

We ate a leisurely breakfast, Mother and Peggy chatting about garden clubs and charity districts, ideal travel destinations in late summer. Nina and Delia came downstairs with their plates after an hour or so and went into the kitchen to wash and put them away. Goliath followed, wagging his tail, anxious for fresh air, I imagined. Instead of a stroll up along the Houghton sidewalk, they agreed to run about in the back garden by the tennis court and spring fruit trees where the amusements were plenty and we knew they'd be safe. The rain had softened but they had umbrellas just in case.

Freddy arrived just after they went outdoors.

He was frantic and made me chase him down into the basement where nobody in the house could hear a word we said.

Freddy pulled a sheet of paper out of his pocket and unfolded it on my father's billiard table. A list of towns in the eastern provinces. He told me this was what he got from Sebti on the radio last night and again this morning, just before he drove here.

"And, by the way, I had some old black Royale motor following me most of the drive here until I saw it go into a ditch along Levison Road. Just rolled over. Then another auto pulled up next to it, had a look, and drove off just like that. Scared the hell out of me."

"They want to kill us, Freddy," I said. "Marco told me so last night. There's some ledger and all our names are on it."

"See? Didn't I tell you back when we were fooling around with those Draxler puzzles? This was all too dangerous for us get involved with. We were idiots. And now look, we're target practice. What are we supposed to do?"

"We're leaving this afternoon on some ship from the Gillihan docks. It'll take us out of the city. You, me, Nina, Delia, Warren Radelfinger and Evie."

"Warren? Why?"

I told Freddy about my excursion last night to Rúbotton's estate and Radelfinger's gas and the end of the world as we knew it. He sat down on the sofa and put his head in his hands. He said, "What is all this, Julian?"

"Maybe some of the insanity of the Desolation is finally coming home."

"If that's true, Julian, then you brought it with you. It's your fault. Everything was going along well enough until you played Romeo with Nina and got us into that game with Draxler. None of this would've happened otherwise. If my family gets killed, Julian, I'm blaming you."

"Freddy, you're talking like Agnes now. As if closing our eyes prevents bad things. It doesn't. We just don't see them until it's too late. Wasn't it you who told me that death wasn't the result of our eugenics war, but the very reason for it? I know you didn't get that from your squib books. You've always known this insanity would catch up to us eventually, one way or another, whether we involved ourselves directly or not. It's our fate that's had it be now and in this way."

Freddy refused to look at me. "If you think so, Julian."

"Well, I do, in fact, and I am also aware that without us, perhaps all of those children would've died in that lethal chamber. Every single one of them. We might feel put upon with these maniacs chasing around, trying to kill us, but it's really only what's been happening all about the Republic for the past sixty years. Why should we be so privileged as not to have it on our own doorstep?"

"I don't care."

"I'm sorry, roommate, but it's too late for that."

I let him stew there in his own pity for a few minutes while I looked over that paper he'd spread flat on the billiard table. As I did, I thought about my father in this room where he'd died and wondered what he would've thought about all this. *Gone glimmering through the dreams of things that were.* He used to refer to the Council and the Status Imperium with a variation on another favorite quotation of his: *'Julian, some men seek to achieve fame by building palaces, but it does not yet appear what they, or we, shall be.'* Then he would retire to his office and close the door. Older now and more experienced in this world than even last week when my father was alive, had I another chance I might have knocked and gone in to ask him what that meant for those of us who had no ambition to make the Republic a private playground of victims and puppets. I'd like to think he would've approved of what I've done in all this insanity, how I've handled myself, those choices I've made, the moral and ethical responsibilities I've acknowledged and assumed. And why not? Who I am, for better or not, came from his instruction and guidance; I owe my father more than I could ever imagine.

Freddy finally got up and with a flat voice pointed to the paper. "You see this list here?" He directed my attention to towns whose names I didn't know: Engleston, Fournel, Escholiér, Geffroy, Châtelet Heights, Noack, Mellerio, Raysacc, Mandorla, Cotelleville, Vrooman, Greisberg.

"Yes? What about it?"

"Sebti radioed last night to say that each town in Bourgh Province on the northwestern shores of the Alban River is haunted by ghosts."

"What does that mean?"

"The code wasn't clear. Maybe it wasn't a code at all. Next, he said, *Nobody knows his neighbors anymore.* Then this morning, he said, *Crown Colony is given to a Book of Days.*"

"Well, I don't follow any of that."

"Neither do I, but after I signed off from Sebti, I caught a radio frequency from Rodenberg that kept broadcasting this same message over and over: *A war ends with freedom, not death. A war ends with freedom, not death. A war ends with freedom, not death.*"

"Who was broadcasting that message?"

Freddy shook his head. "I don't know."

He was quiet for a minute then, just staring at the paper of names. So did I. Something was happening we weren't privy to, something momentous beyond our notice and private conversations.

Freddy said, "I'm sorry for what I said, Julian. It was ridiculous and idiotic. I don't blame you for anything. I never have and I never will. We're guilty of our mutual enthusiasms. You and I are like a pair of twin Pandoras. We couldn't resist our natural curiosity to open this box, but I agree it needed to be opened. And I'm glad we did it together."

I smiled. "So am I. We trust each other. Without you, I'd be lost in this maze of death and deceit."

"Both of us."

"Marco's people are protecting our families. I do trust them, too. They haven't needed to help us, yet they have."

I told him about those autos on the rainy road to Rúbotton's, the bodies and blood.

"Good God, Julian!"

"I know, but my point is that Randall and those people out there in the rain saved my life and knew how to do it. We're pretty helpless, Freddy. Fortunately, they're not."

Freddy folded up his paper and we shot a few rounds of billiards to kill time. Then we threw some darts, where he beat me again and again as ever. Finally, we went upstairs, and out into the back garden to see after Nina and Delia. Rain fell more like mist then, so we ignored umbrellas and found those two under Mother's ivy-draped gazebo by the tennis court. The damp spring earth breathed a ripe and beautiful scent, sifting with our jasmine and gardenia. The wet grass soaked my shoes, but I paid little care. That eager morning air was more than fair compensation.

Freddy gave a wave. "Hello, Nina."

"Hello, Freddy." Her cascading black hair dripped like damp seaweed. My lovely siren. I presumed they'd left off Mother's umbrellas, as well.

I asked pretty Delia, whose hair was also wet, "How's Goliath?"

She grinned. "He loves to run. We chased him around the swimming pool, and Nina slipped on the grass and almost fell in. I laughed so hard."

Nina rolled her eyes. "Thank you, dear, for the consideration."

Delia told Freddy, "Nina's not my sister anymore. She's my mom now."

"So I heard. She's a great mom, I'll bet."

Delia smiled at us. "Well, I'm still training her. So we'll see how she does."

"She's very bossy," Nina added. "I may not survive."

Delia told her, "You just need to pay better attention. That's what good moms do."

"Thank you, dear. I'll work at it."

"I know you will. That's why I love you."

Nina looked at me, her dark eyes moist. "When do you think we should leave? Delia and I are packed already. Your mother made us all sandwiches. They're in my suitcase."

I told her, "Our appointment at the wharf is for five o'clock. Ordinarily we'd have plenty of time, but if Randall can't get us close, we'll have to walk and there's no telling how far that could be. If the crowds really are thick and crazy, we might need an extra hour or more. Who knows? Depends where he lets us off. He told me they're still working on that."

"Then we should leave soon."

"I think so."

Nina asked Freddy, "You're coming with us, right? You can't stay here. Not with those maniacs running all over the place. You have to come along."

Freddy gave a shrug. "So it appears. I'll have to telephone my parents. Tell them where I'm going."

"No, you can't," I corrected him. "That's not safe. Electric ears?"

He frowned. "You're right. My mistake."

"It's just all ridiculous," Nina said. "We can't behave like normal people because those lunatics are so completely insane, they won't let us."

Delia took Goliath's leash and led him off across the wet grass court toward Mother's old greenhouse. Nina called after her, "Don't go too far, dear."

She yelled back, "I won't."

Nina sighed. "This is so much for her."

"I can't imagine."

Freddy said, "Eight years old? I was gluing walnuts to my forehead at that age and pretending I was a demon to scare my sisters."

I laughed. "And look where that got you. Locked in a toy chest."

"A dreadful accident of birth, those two. Very quaint original devils in flesh, they are."

"I presume you brought your overnight bag?"

"Fortunately."

"Well, I'll need to go in and pack," I told them. "Why don't you two wait out here with Delia until she's ready to come back indoors." I thought that would be soon since a light rain began to fall again. "Meanwhile, I'll go see what Randall has in mind."

I went around to the gate on the side of the house and walked out to Houghton again. Randall was still in his auto, smoking one of those old wood diable pipes from Batelière. My father had one he'd inherited from my Grandfather Karl. He gave it up when Mother insisted his tobacco smoke from that pipe and his oriental Porter cigars was ruining our furniture.

I asked Randall if he had reached any conclusion regarding our itinerary.

He told me, "Upper Graeff Street is the closest we can safely get you to for that walk down to the Gillihan wharf. It's too steep for most people, so we figure the crowds'll be thinner there. At least half the way. Better yet is that we can get a decent look at our route, judge what'll be safe and what won't."

"Do you think anyone'll be waiting for us?"

"We expect it."

"So, how do we get by without someone shooting us?"

"Our people will be there first," Randall said, as the rain picked up. I wished I'd grabbed an umbrella. "A few of them are already setting up in place. We've done this before. The advantage is ours because we know where we're heading. They won't until we arrive."

"I believe you."

"It'll be a little hectic, but we'll get you to the boat."

"Rúbotton said five o'clock." I took out my pocket-watch and checked the hour. "It's almost two now."

"We know."

"Well, thanks for all you're doing. It's much appreciated."

Randall nodded, then rolled up his window and I went back across the rainy street and indoors again.

Up in my bedroom, I saw Nina's small suitcase. She was ready to go. I wondered how often she'd packed herself and Delia up for another move. House after house after house. How must it feel never to belong? Like sad vagrants. I dug my own overnight satchel out of the closet and stuffed in a needful change of clothes and my bathroom toiletries. Without any sense of what Marco's intention was, I had no real idea where that ship would be taking us. But I trusted him. Nina wouldn't, but I did. We just had to go. Far from here. Somewhere Nina and Delia could lie down and rest at last. And let me be with them. The future is considered a blessing because the past is gone, and the present reveals itself moment to moment. We can plan and we can hope, but do we ever truly know?

Rain pattered on the roof as Mother leaned her head inside my room. "Julian, may I borrow you for a moment."

"Of course."

I got up and followed down the hall to her bedroom. Peggy was waiting there on the chair at the vanity. She held a handkerchief and her eyes were teary.

My mother said, "I see your bags are packed, so I presume you'll be leaving. Isn't that right?"

I nodded.

She went on. "Well, you simply must tell me where you're going. I've had so much trauma over you these past few weeks, I couldn't stand the worry of wondering over your health and safety."

I looked at Peggy. I sensed that she and Mother already suspected part of what I was about to say. It was neither right nor fair to exclude them. On the other hand, what I needed to tell them would be more upsetting than anything they'd ever heard.

I told them, anyhow.

And Mother sat on the bed when I finished. Her face was drawn and pale.

Peggy wept.

I felt like going into a closet and closing the door.

"It can't be true," Peggy said. "Jack would've told me this morning. He'd be here so we could stay together."

I said, "He made me promise not to say a word. It's my fault."

Mother said, "My dear, you cannot be expected to keep that sort of promise. It's entirely unreasonable when it involves others besides yourself and Jack. That story you just told us is very unsettling, and I don't know that I'll be able to sleep for a month if it's a fact. I'll need to telephone Agnes immediately."

"Please don't. She's safe where she is, Mother," I said. "Branson is miles and miles from the metropolis. So long as she stays put, she'll be fine. Same here with you two, and the Barrons over in Alexanderton. We're very far away."

"And where do you and Nina think you're going? That little girl had a fever and ought to remain in bed for another day or so. It's not wise to pack her up and go off to who knows where."

"Nina told me Delia's fever broke this morning, and she's feeling better. Goliath needed to go outdoors, so they're in the garden with Freddy. We'll be in Randall's auto within the hour. There's a ship waiting for us at the Gillihan wharf to sail us out of the city. Marco wouldn't say where, but he did tell me that Freddy and Nina and I are on some sort of death list and we need to go now while we still can."

Peggy bolted from her chair, telling us, "I have to call Jack this instant."

She ran off to the downstairs.

We heard her telephone the exchange, then Mother got up and closed her bedroom door.

She came back to the bed and had me sit beside her.

As I did, she told me, "Julian, when your father and I were younger, much before you and Agnes, he used to say, *'I am not now that which I have been, but to be loved needs only to be known today.'* He had that certain gleam in his eye that gave our world all the light we ever sought. His goodness, and my faith in his goodness, lent honesty to our purpose, which was to love each other without reservation or fear. Our life was blessed by that simple truth. You and Agnes became the fulfillment of our promise to one another, and, as these years have gone by, we saw how kind and good and gracious life can be. In fact, our devotion to the Bureau of Perpetual Benefactors, and my precious garden, have proven that, season upon season. Now your father's gone, and you've told me there's a ship at anchor on the eternal river waiting to take you away to another destiny because the darkest heart of our society is about to be erased. My dear, it's almost too much to bear."

For a few moments, I watched the rain through her bedroom window. It fell softly but continued as if never to end. Days and days of spring rain and bloom. Sunshine and shadow. Clouds and blue skies.

I took her hand. "I'm sorry, Mother. It's not fair. None of this. I wish it weren't true and that I could be here with you. When I traveled into the Desolation, I missed you and Father so much, I could hardly stand it. Isn't that how it goes? We can't know what we adore until we've lost it? Well, I've always adored our home, our family, this house and yard, our street, the woods. It's part of who I am, whom I'll always be. I went far away, Mother, farther than I'd ever dreamed, but I returned because I needed to. And no matter where we go this afternoon, how far that ship sails us to sea, after all this is over and settled, I promise I'll be back. You have to trust me and look after Agnes, regardless of her mood, which we both know can be a dreadful trial."

Mother laughed at that, even as tears welled up in her eyes. A gust of wind shook the leafy elm branches outside her window.

She told me, "Your sister has a singular outlook, Julian. Ever challenged 'to gather up her face in a smile.' But she'll come around. She can be a dear when she chooses. I have faith in you both. So, please do come back, my baby boy, and make my heart sing once more."

I gave my mother that promise and one last kiss, then left to gather my companions.

LVIII
∾

I n those final hours of that world, I helped Randall put our luggage into the trunk of his Model Seven. We had to shift some of his stuff around to fit, two canvas bags and a small leather case whose contents I didn't inquire about. Needful items, I assumed. Perhaps to protect us. Nina, Freddy and Delia sat in back, Goliath on Delia's lap. I took my place up front with Randall, who fiddled with his black device, punching those green and red buttons just before we rolled forward down Houghton Avenue. Ahead of us was a mystery, while behind was all we'd known and loved. The rain-grey sky appeared to be offering patches of blue on the horizon toward the great river, a hopeful sign.

Randall drove evenly, unhurried but at a constant rate. I watched one of those autos that had parked all night down Houghton running about a quarter of mile on and noticed another behind us. Our escorts. We each felt that tension of uneasiness. Freddy, in particular, was uncharacteristically quiet. He was seated directly behind me and tapped his foot on the seatback in a nervous rhythm. Meanwhile, Nina whispered with Delia, who was doing her utmost to keep Goliath calm by petting him. There was traffic, but it wasn't so awful as we'd feared. The expressway looked empty as if this were Sunday morning. I presumed our populace was elsewhere celebrating that great victory over the undesirables who'd spoiled so much of our potential these past decades. Could we ever forgive them? Probably not. Why bother? We'd won the war. If we were fortunate now, perhaps soon they would all just die off and let the earth consume their diseased corpses. Let our wonderful Republic be blessed once again with light and happiness.

Half an hour down the highway, I asked Randall, "When we arrive on Graeff Street, will we be met straightaway by our guides? Will they be waiting for us at the curb, so to speak?"

The thought of us entering the vast city crowds on our own terrified me. What if we became separated? More than a million people expected in those streets? How could we ever find each other?

"Some you'll see, most you won't."

"But we'll be safe when we step out onto sidewalk, right? We won't be swallowed up?"

"You'll be fine."

"Are you coming with us?"

"Yes, I am. That's my assignment."

"Good. I trust you."

"Scared?"

"Yes."

"That's smart," Randall told me. "It'll keep you healthy."

I took out Father's pocket-watch and checked the hour. Almost three o'clock. I wasn't entirely sure whether we were ahead or behind schedule. Given the uncertainty of the crowds, that was probably unknowable just then. We'd likely have a better idea the closer we got to the metropolis.

Rain still fell, but intermittently. The roads were wet. Grass and leaves flurried in the damp breeze as we roared along.

Freddy leaned forward over the seatback to say, "Should we stop at Thayer Hall in case there's something we need from our room?"

I laughed. "Your bourbon?"

"Not only that."

"No," Randall told him. "It's not protected, and we have a schedule."

"I just thought it could be worthwhile to have a quick look. Who knows what we might've forgotten?"

"Nope." Randall shook his head as we overtook a slow delivery truck on the Moffitt Parkway. "It's too late for any of that. Like I said, we're on a schedule. No detours."

An hour closer then, traffic began to thicken on the outskirts of the city. Those districts of Maillard and Gotha were not densely populated like the Catalan or Calcitonia and Sartosé. More like Viceroy but without the coal soot and garbage. Neighborhoods were nice and groomed, not quite affluent, but pleasant and clean. Too far from industrial frenzy to be harmed by ugliness and urban distress. Another few miles on and that spring rain gradually eased off and we saw people out walking without umbrellas or winter coats and galoshes. None were tooting any horns, though, and I wondered how invested they were in the celebrations ahead. Maybe they hadn't heard the war was over. Or maybe they didn't care.

We drove past riders on horseback under the elegant spruce trees lining Tureille Park and descended toward the great metropolis.

Then we saw hundreds of people crowding along the sidewalks and exiting city bus lines and taxi cabs, waving flags of Imperial viridian and gold. Noisy and exuberant. Rude in vituperative descriptions of our Common Foe, those hideous monsters we'd vanquished at last. Traffic slowed to a depressing crawl, and I became anxious we'd miss our appointment at the holy river. And if we did? What precisely was coming? I'd seen Radelfinger's demonstration, but what did that mean for the metropolis? Was there to be some giant atomizer to spritz his horrid gas over the city? How was that monstrous cloud to be distributed? Or was it just a boast, a threatening nightmare? I had no idea, but I was terrified of witnessing its awful potential trapped with everyone else in the labyrinthine streets of the central metropolis.

Freddy's foot was tapping at my seatback more firmly now. Goliath growled at Delia as she squeezed him tightly. Nina began petting him. Randall paid no attention to us at all. My own stomach clenched as we drove slowly down Eurytheseus Street that brought us at last into sight of Prospect Square and the Dome of Eternity. We were more than a mile and a half away, but now the fearsome reality of this concluding adventure was arriving, and we could do nothing to evade it. The crowds were flowing over the sidewalks, barricading dozens of shops and businesses and apartment buildings whose stairs and stoops were packed with people preparing to depart for the jubilee. Our Model Seven repeatedly came to a stop as celebrants crossed the wide street in front of us, apathetic to the threat of oncoming trucks and motorcars. Here and there, ecstatic passersby banged on our auto and waved. Randall just stared ahead. If he had concerns, he didn't show it.

"This is so crazy," Nina said from the back seat, sheltering Delia with one arm. "How can we even hope get to the river through all the traffic?"

"I presume we won't stay on this street." I asked Randall, "Isn't that right? We'll make a turn somewhere and get off here?"

"Vanderbelt."

"How far is that?"

"Another quarter mile and up the hill past Pitzler to the old iron bridge and over the river to Graeff."

"Our escort knows?"

"Yes, they do."

Looking toward the central metropolis, I saw hundreds of brightly hued flags aloft on the great grey monuments and government buildings at Prospect Square and atop the Dome of Eternity, east of the immortal river. A day unlike any other in memory. The relief of exhaustion and terror of our perpetual war finally ending had apparently given birth in our populace this immense urge to express a joy that no one could possibly have anticipated even a month before. The war was over. The war was over. Just muttering those words felt absurd and ridiculous. A magical chant of unimaginable hope come true in these fantastical hours. Was that the emotion we were experiencing? The war was over. The war was over. But how could it be true?

Freddy said, "I wish I'd brought a bottle. Then I'd feel more like celebrating. Otherwise, this is all insane."

"I'm surprised you hadn't stuffed one in your jacket," I told him. "It's not like you to leave home without a good jolt on hand."

He gave my seatback a good thump. "It's in my bag and my bag's in the trunk. I feel destitute. Corn flakes and apple juice are no way to start the day."

With the last of the morning rain gone, Freddy rolled down his window and stuck his head out into the fresh air and drew a deep breath.

"Roll it up," Randall told him. "Now!"

"What for? It's stuffy in here."

"You'll get us shot, and we'll all be dead before you know it."

"Freddy," I told my poor liquor-addicted roommate, "do as he says. We're getting close. Don't mess us up."

"Sorry." He quickly rolled up his window. "I'm feeling a touch claustrophobic. You know how that is?"

"I'm sympathetic, yes. I'd just rather be claustrophobic than dead."

"Touché."

Randall hit the brakes on our auto. Traffic in front of us rolled ahead, but we weren't moving. A motor horn wailed behind us. Then another. I saw what Randall had his eye on. Two tall fellows in long charcoal-grey raincoats across the street were winding through the noisy sidewalk crowds in our direction. Just a dozen yards away.

Nina asked, "Why are we stopped?"

I held my breath.

Randall stayed put with both hands on the steering wheel.

Those fellows were closer now, eyes on us but pretending not to. I was used to that look. Did we have a plan? If Randall had a gun, he wasn't holding it. What if those fellows began shooting?

Nina asked, "Aren't we going to go? Delia's getting anxious. So am I."

Freddy's attention was on our side of the street where a fellow was approaching from a narrow basement-stairs crowded with youths shouting nonsense into the afternoon air. This fellow held a gun in his fist and was looking straight at me.

Six feet from our auto, he stumbled and fell to the cement.

Back across the street, a woman in an olive-green dress and a man in a grey business suit and hat blocked the path of one of those two other serious fellows. The woman dropped her purse. The man beside her stuck his hand into the fellow's raincoat and grabbed him behind the neck and led him to the brick wall defining the sidewalk. Three other men in brown work clothes and caps grabbed the second fellow and shoved him through the front door of a busy florist.

The fellow on the sidewalk just outside my door laid there quiet as a rock.

Randall put our auto in gear and drove us forward again.

The anxious motor horns behind us kept at it, but Randall paid no notice.

Two blocks on, we turned up Vanderbelt Avenue and rose to the top of Pierides Hill with fine brick and stone houses and a pair of stately hotels and the holy river, Livorna, in plain view, reborn in the fresh sun. I thought maybe we'd lost our escort motors in the crowds and traffic on Eurytheseus, and I was wrong. I saw that tan Salius sedan which had led us into the city still ahead now as we descended to the old bridge. And looking out the rear window, I did locate the other auto, that black Métro, as well, trailing just two motors behind us. So our little caravan was intact.

The ninety-year-old Halderson Bridge was narrow and worsened by pedestrians crowding off the walkway into our path as our auto crawled along with dozens of others. People were marching and dancing and darting across the old iron span singing, "Hail Republic," and waving handheld imperial flags.

The mass of celebrants extended ahead farther than the shoreline and on up Vanderbelt Avenue. I wondered where our ship was and took a long look downriver to the huge industrial wharves where so many barges and freighters, cargo ships, coal vessels, tugs, paddle wheelers, schooners, pleasure craft, flatboats, skiffs and big commercial fishing trawlers were moored. By the middle of the bridge, a spring wind whipped up from the cold river and tossed at the hats and flags. Some flew away over the water. I felt our auto buffeted by gusts. Goliath moaned in the back seat and Delia spoke to him softly. Nina mentioned something about needing to pee and I wasn't sure to whom she was referring.

Leaning over the seatback again, Freddy said, "Do you know this old bridge collapsed in a monster windstorm fifty years ago?"

Randall said, "That's a myth."

"I read about it in a magazine at my father's office. One of those historical journals," Freddy told him. "Fell into the river with some trucks. Lots of people drowned."

"Nope, not so."

"What makes you sure about that?" Freddy asked. "Were you there?"

"Not old enough yet," Randall replied, "but I worked here when I was your age reinforcing the trestle. Part of it, that day you're talking about, had failed from a garbage scow that struck a pylon and almost tipped the bridge. Some fellows had overloaded a delivery truck and it fell into the river where the railing broke off. A couple of them drowned. One of them didn't. That's where your story comes from. The germ of it."

"Well, that doesn't sound like the same thing."

"It's not, because yours isn't fact."

I watched the tan Salius arrive at the far shore and stop at a rail crossing that ran parallel to the holy river. A freight train with thirty loaded cars chugged slowly past, stalling all of us yet on the bridge. Two men climbed out from the back seat of the Salius and stood by the road watching our approach and the autos ahead and behind us and the throng of pedestrians crossing, as well.

I looked back along the bridge to that black Métro sedan escorting us across and saw the same story, two men out of the back seat now on the road watching us and the surrounding motorcars and people. Were they being cautious or was this another set-up? I felt scared again. Nina had quit murmuring with Delia.

Her face was blank, her dark eyes glassy. I tried smiling at her, but she didn't respond. I assumed she was either tired or terrified. I was both.

The train went by without anyone shooting at us or throwing a bomb.

I watched the lead auto head up the hill.

Randall drove us safely across the bridge and over the rail tracks. I let the air out of my lungs as we motored after the Salius sedan. Vanderbelt Avenue was terrifically steep in this block and there weren't as many pedestrians on the sidewalk. Most of the bridge celebrants were navigating the lower slope of Mulhouse Heights on Aitken Lane that walked parallel to the train route. They'd surely come out near the bottom of Graeff Street, intersecting our intended route. Where we ascended, rows of identical two-floor framehouses leaned against the hill and took the afternoon sun bleached in whitewash and yellow. These were plain homes belonging to working-class citizens whose wages were not dependant upon political maneuvers. Regency College admitted the children of these ordinary people with enrollment stipends that gave them just advantage enough to attend classes with the rest of us and become more than those eugenic elitists at Prospect Square ever expected from day-laboring backgrounds. In fact, the progress of these young scholars proved the falsehood of eugenical insistence on the well-born and fortunate of prime social status. Top marks on semester reports paid little notice to street addresses and last names in the society columns and country club registers. One succeeded or not according to each hour of study. Egalitarian philosophies of academics and personal industry flourished day after day in our venerable institution, and most of us felt proud of it. As Dr. Coffeen instructed one morning when reminding our class that we should not have expected less of our classmates from the middle neighborhoods and ought not therefore raise a glass too high in cheering them forward: "*Who well deserves needs not another's praise.*"

Yet, apparently, these unassuming citizens, too, were intended to burn with everyone else at sundown.

Isn't that what Rúbotton had promised last night?

What Randall had called a reckoning?

Apparently neither mercy nor vengeance needed a pedigree.

— · —

Our autos crested the hill and rolled another two blocks to Graeff Street, then made a left-hand turn and parked ahead on the downsloping curb by a grocery market and across from a billiard hall. Randall got out after both Salius and Métro sedans emptied. Eight of them. Seven men and one woman. Jackets and hats. The woman and one of the men went down the sidewalk about fifty yards ahead to mingle with the crowds. Two fellows went for a look inside the grocery store. Another crossed the street to the billiard hall and stood by the wall there, hands in his pockets.

Randall came around to the curbside of the Model Seven and opened our doors, front and back. "Let's go."

I slid out first. Then Freddy, Delia with Goliath, and Nina last. The rain had gone, but the air was still cold and breezy. Clouds drifted above. Randall opened the trunk and let us grab our luggage. I took both mine and Nina's, while Delia led Goliath to a short tree planted by the curb and let him piss in the dirt.

Nina said, "We need to pee, too."

Randall frowned at her a moment. Then he went back up the sidewalk to those fellows from the black Métro and had word with them. When Randall came back to us, he said, "One of these fellows'll take you into the market. You can use the toilet there."

His partner came down the sidewalk and escorted Nina and Delia indoors. They left Goliath on the leash tied to the tree.

I asked Randall, "How far down the street are we supposed to go?"

"Haven't decided yet. We'll play it by ear depending on the crowds."

"It looks like thousands at the bottom."

It did, too. Not more than scattered pedestrians up here, but down there, lots and lots of people collecting from the lower streets that led to Prospect Square and the vast city parks. You wouldn't ordinarily have expected that many to be on foot, but it was obvious now that motor traffic of any sort, whether autos or busses, was hopeless. Walking was necessary, whether appreciated or not.

Freddy said, "I'm glad it's downhill. I haven't done my daily constitutional since Upper School when our bus left us off at the bottom of Rothermel. Do you know how far that is? I begged my mother to drive down and get me, but she refused. It's still a sore point between us."

I saw a couple men on the threshold of the billiard hall watching us as Nina and Delia came out of the market. Probably it was Nina they had that happy eye for. Randall's fellow standing on the wall beside the door didn't appear overly concerned and he'd been listening to their chatter.

Delia held a ripe apple in one hand and a fruit cookie in the other. She put the apple in her coat pocket and ate the cookie as she untied Goliath's leash from the tree. She told Nina, "It's good. You should've got one."

"I'll just share yours, dear."

Delia smiled. "No, thanks."

Randall took that black device out of his jacket pocket and switched it on. Then he tapped the green button a few times and hit the red button. He nodded to the fellow across the street by the billiard hall. The green button flashed twice and went to red and Randall switched it off. He told me to give Nina her suitcase.

I said, "I can carry it. No trouble at all."

He shook his head. "Nope, everyone needs to keep one hand free."

I shrugged and gave Nina her suitcase and we started down the street.

That fellow by the billiards kept to his side. The two others from the Métro followed twenty yards or so behind. The one who'd gone into the market with Nina and Delia stayed with us. Those three men and the woman from the tan Salius sedan spread out and walked down the sidewalk at our pace. I felt so vulnerable out of the auto and in plain sight now. Randall kept behind us, and the market fellow led. People were gathering in their own little crowds as we proceeded, chattering loudly, paying us little notice. Everyone knew where the celebrations were waiting. From Graeff Street to the Dome was at least a half-hour walk without foot traffic ahead. Today with so many people blocking the routes, I thought it could take an hour or more. Fortunately, we weren't going that far. Another couple of long blocks and I began to hear the din of celebrations. Goliath strained at Delia's leash. Nina helped her tighten it. I searched our fellow pedestrians for signs of impending murder. Would I even recognize my assassin before he stuck a gun in my ear? Probably not. I hoped to God that Randall's people would.

Wind flurried and kicked at those scrawny trees planted along the sidewalk. I felt a chill that was both spring weather and relentless fear. Freddy walked as if in a daze. I wondered if he'd somehow sneaked a jolt off his bottle while we were waiting for Nina and Delia to come out of the market. I knew that look.

Nina grabbed Delia's apple and ate a chunk out of it and handed it back. She smiled and gave Delia a pat on her head.

Dodging in and out of more people, we made steady progress down the sidewalk. The houses we passed had windows open to the afternoon air, and I could hear the radio broadcasts spilling out of the upper rooms with music and commentary on the end of the war. Some people sat in window balconies and waved to us as we went by. Others called out to friends and neighbors passing down the hill. Four blocks from the bottom, we saw the crowds funneling in from adjoining streets, so dense and exuberant there seemed to be no easy path through them, wherever we were intending to go. Randall's fellows slowed us. Then again. And again, until we were hardly walking at all, barely shuffling forward.

"What are we doing?" Nina asked. "We have to hurry."

I saw Randall tapping his device.

Down the sidewalk, that man and woman directly ahead of us stopped completely. So did the fellow on the other side of the street. He had one of those devices and was busy tapping his own message. Randall put his back into a pocket. He told me, "Detour."

Ahead of us between a pharmacist and a petite-ville pawnshop was a narrow alley, basically a gap between buildings. The two on our sidewalk went into it and the man from across the street came over to join them. When we got there, those three were already halfway through the alley. Our fellow from the market entered just ahead of us. The passage was so tight we were only really able to file through one after another. I went in ahead of Nina, Delia and Goliath. Randall behind me, Freddy was on his heels. Our last escorts delayed entering the alley until we were most of the way through. I did feel claustrophobic except for the grey sky visible high overhead. The buildings were so close to each other that most of the noise from Graeff Street was muffled.

We came out into a vacant lot of grass and rocks and scattered trash. A muddy path led across. We were alone in the field that sloped almost to the dooryard of houses at the bottom and up to another row of homes a hundred yards or so above where some people sitting out on porches were looking down at us. All of Randall's people were in the lot now, paused here and there along the weedy path. I felt exposed out in the open like that and wanted us to get on across the grass to the shelter of those thick trees ahead.

But then I saw why we'd stopped.

From that empty lot, unobstructed by all the buildings in that neighborhood, we had a fantastic view of the central metropolis and what must have been more than a million people completely filling the streets and plazas and city park lawns. The most enormous crowds I had ever seen in my life. Almost indescribably immense. We could see the entire length and width of Prospect Square from the Dome of Eternity and Ehrenhardt Boulevard past Dardanus Way bisecting Immanuel Fields and the Montclos Gardens to Lourdes Memorial Cemetery. Even at our fortunate vantage point, we could not find a square yard unoccupied by our citizenry. No streets, sidewalks or patches of grass were absent of human beings. Just a ceaseless mass of celebrants, miles long. As if everyone on earth had come into the central metropolis that grey afternoon. Imperial flags and banners aloft. Kites, too, flown in the windy air about the parks. Streamers hurled from rooftops of our grand structures. Flocks of birds sailing by the hundreds to and fro above that gargantuan sea of humanity gathered to worship at the fount of victory. And, of course, I saw the holy river, Livorna, too, flooded with a carnival flotilla of flag-draped vessels, both grand and humble, almost clogging the cold wide tributary between the busy wharves on both shores. And although more than a mile away, we could hear the cascading echo of bells ringing from the National and Archimbault Cathedrals at each end of Ehrenhardt Boulevard, ringing together in a great melodic and syncopated rhythm for summoning the patriotic to join the great celebration of the end of war and our conquering of evil.

Were all those people truly going to die at sundown?

Was Jack in that roaring crowd somewhere? I hoped not.

Freddy spoke up to say exactly what I'd just been thinking, "I'm not going down there. Not a chance."

I said, "I don't think that's the plan."

Nina added, "It's insane, if it is. I'd rather sit here all day with Delia, take our chances in the dark, find our way out of the city. Go somewhere else."

Fiddling with his black device, Randall told us, "We won't be anywhere close to that mess. There's another route we have figured."

"How's that?" I asked. "Those crowds are everywhere between us and the river."

"Not everywhere."

Looking down over the dense streets and neighborhoods that flanked the river, all I saw were thousands and thousands of people. Impossible to get through. Absolutely impenetrable. A ridiculous hope.

Then I saw a fellow on a flat rooftop about a quarter mile below us. He had telescopic binoculars on a tripod, and he was not studying the great crowds. He was looking at us.

Our escorts up ahead crossed the lot into a stand of mulberry trees on the other end. Three in the lead passed under the shadow of low branches, while one remained out in the grass providing cover.

"Start walking," Randall told us, "but don't run. We just stopped for a look-see and now we're getting on again. Nothing to pay any undo attention toward. Ignore that fellow on the roof. He won't be there long."

The path from that weedy lot led through the mulberry shade to an old stone staircase and iron railing that went down a stepped path between the embankment of lush spring weeds and falling ivy and a dense wooded ravine. The man and woman led our descent. I gripped the railing as I followed Randall, Freddy just off my shoulder, Nina helping Delia guide Goliath just behind Freddy. Our remaining escorts kept up the rear. No one spoke a word.

About fifty yards from the shady bottom where it was possible to see people walking by on the lane, the man and woman stopped at a cement platform next to a concrete structure, just a big cement block, really, but with a rusted iron door on the side. The woman rapped at it with her knuckles, and the door opened with a nasty creak. She and the fellow with her went in ahead of us. Still a few steps away, I could already see it was dark. Freddy was about to have a fit. For once I was glad he'd brought a bottle.

At the door with Randall, I asked, "What is this?"

"One of the first electric light stations. Skaife Generator #9. Shut off and closed down decades ago for that big hydroelectric plant at Rotrou Point."

He went through the door. I had a look back at Freddy, who was just sticking that bottle of bourbon back into his satchel. He smiled and followed me into the shadows where Randall was waiting. No electrical machinery left at all, but a flurry of voices echoed out of a hole in the floor where a storm drain cover was slid aside, and an iron ladder led downward. Staring down into the opening, Freddy asked Randall, "Is this absolutely necessary?"

"Yes."

I told Freddy, "I'll go first."

There was a fellow waiting at the bottom of the ladder, and I lowered my bag to him. Not that far down. Maybe a dozen rungs into a dank underground. Randall helped Delia with Goliath and that fellow went up the ladder to take hold of her and she came down with her little terrier, leash and all. Then Nina and Freddy. And Randall with the rest of our escorts. The iron door above rang shut, and the last fellow above the ladder dragged the drain cover over the hole and sealed us off.

"Where do we go now?" I asked Randall.

A string of dim lights began switching on along a cramped service passage, grimy and wet. Another day, another rough-hewn tunnel. I was learning to live like a rat. Our guides went ahead. Randall told me, "We're about half a mile from the river here. Easy walk. Keep your shoes dry if you can."

"How do they know this place?"

"Back in the day, some fellows from the undercity began melting the grid from this old station. Has a sweet spot in some hearts now." He offered a rare smile. "Come on, let's go to your boat."

Randall led us along again, his work boots splashing through shallow puddles here and there. I kept close as I could. Nina held Delia's hand as her pretty little daughter led poor Goliath by the leash. Somewhere close behind us, I heard Freddy pop the cork on his bottle of bourbon. He must've been terrified. No need. The tunnel wasn't that long. Nothing like the Faubourg sewer. After only a short while, we reached the end under the sagging floor of a derelict fishing shack. Another short ladder and a wooden trap door in a crawl space behind the wall of a cook stove brought us out of the tunnel, and a folding cabinet bed with a filthy mattress opened into the shack. All pretty clever and secretive. Something to admire on another day.

As our escorts climbed up from the underground, one of them dressed like a vagrant went out the door to the river.

With Randall looking stoic as ever, I asked, "Now what?"

"Got to choose your ship."

"Marco told me it's a barge."

"We put that out in the air last night. Fishing a bit. You never know who's listening."

"So, it's not a barge?"

"Might be. Just depends."

Delia tugged at Goliath's leash. "Can we go out now? He's very anxious to see the fish."

Nina looked at Randall, who shook his head. He told Delia, "We need to be just a little patient, dear."

Delia said, "I'm patient. He isn't. I think he wants to swim."

The shack had a single window facing the river with a curtain drawn against the glass. I asked Randall, "May I have a look out?"

He shook his head again. "Better not to."

This entire operation was too complicated to unravel. Threats just seemed to be all around us. I could hear people marching in ragged groups along the riverfront and horns booming out on the water. People seemed delirious. Firesticks banged sharply every so often. Probably kids lighting them off. Cheers and laughter echoed everywhere.

Why were we here, really? Jammed together in this rundown shack, waiting to make a run to some ship that was supposed to sail us away. Why did we need to do that? I'd already given that book to Sketz. We'd already seen those children burned up. Dr. Paley was dead. The war was over. Revenge?

I asked Randall, "They actually want to kill us? Even now?"

"Yes, they do."

"Does it really matter that much, whatever we've done?"

"They think so."

Behind us at a small table in a corner of the shack by the black cook stove, some of his people were huddled around their black devices, tapping green buttons. The woman was smiling with a man we hadn't seen before.

Randall checked his own device. The green flashed rapidly for a few moments, then went red.

The derelict shack smelled like soot and mold. That stove didn't look as if anyone used it anymore. I wondered what kept this shack from being torn down. Apparently, somebody had a stake in its survival.

Freddy took his bottle out and had another slug of bourbon. His eyes had gone bloodshot. A couple of Randall's fellows stared at him like he was defective.

Nina reached into Delia's pocket for that apple and had another bite. She winked at me and smiled. I went over and gave her a kiss, then held her hand after she replaced Delia's apple. She murmured, "I've never felt so helpless."

"Me neither."

Putting her back to Delia, she whispered, "Are we going to survive? God, I'm so nervous."

"Yes, we are."

A short knock at the door.

Randall went to the curtain and nudged it aside. Then he opened the door and a fellow I hadn't seen before came in and Randall closed the door behind him. Those two joined the other group by the stove, where they gathered together away from us. I snuck my own peek out the window. Lots of people were walking by in the direction of the Hesperien Pier, still about a mile away. Constructed in antiquity, that section of the great wharf had a broad stone staircase that led up from the river into the metropolis directly in line with the Dome of Eternity. I presumed it's where everyone was heading. I hoped that wasn't us.

I checked my pocket-watch. Good grief! Almost five o'clock. Time had fled. We were about to be late. Would that ship leave without us? If it did, what then? Weren't we too important to abandon? When I'd first met Freddy during freshman year, he liked to quote a pal of his from Upper School at Haehnlan Academy who boasted how he and his fellow classmates were each, *"Well born and wealthy, wanting no support."*

I also knew a girl who liked to brag as she went about, *"I have youth and a little beauty. What else matters? We don't live forever."*

Her name was Grace and she had little of that, but boys enjoyed her laughter and her luscious bosom and that led her onward. Born fortunate? In scolding some of my youthful indiscretions, Father used to tell me, *"Some of us find virtue too painful an endeavor."* I lent myself often to his instructions and rarely failed when I did. It's easy enough to say we're lucky to be alive when threats are trivial, and life lies mostly ahead. Few of us endure this lovely and dangerous world alone. In moments of desperate trial and fear, we either look inward for guidance or toward a guiding hand to offer that direction we hadn't otherwise thought to seek.

—.—

Randall came over to tell us it was time to go. "We found your boat."

"Where?" I asked, anxious to get this over with.

"Down the shore about half a mile on the wharf. A barge called, *Triton's Abundance.*"

"With all those people?"

"Can't be helped."

Nina said, "How could that be safe? We don't want to get killed out there."

"You'll be fine. I promise."

More little firesticks were popping outdoors. That made me more jittery than ever. When one hit off, I felt a jolt from Nina. She was scared as I was. Freddy just stood over by the wall, gazing at nothing. Delia fidgeted with Goliath's leash.

A couple of Randall's men came over by the door. One of them had a peek out the window. He said, "Looks good."

Randall told me, "All right, let's go."

He opened the door and stepped outside and was shot in the chest.

The fellow at the window had a pistol out and shot the other fellow by the door.

Nina screamed and I jerked her back away from the window. Delia dove to the floor with her arms around Goliath. By the stove, two men shot each other, and the woman shot one of them and then shot the fellow at the window. The man who'd been with her along the sidewalk went to the door and fired six shots outside. Randall was flat on his back in the doorway, blood spreading across on his upper chest. He was coughing and more blood bubbled from his lips. Three of the men back at the stove came forward and stepped over Randall and went outdoors, guns in hand. One of them fired another shot. The woman went to see about Randall. Freddy was tucked up next to the cabinet bed.

More firesticks popped down at the waterfront. With the curtain pulled aside, I saw a gang of boys race past. I heard Nina telling me something, but my ears had gone deaf from the gunfire and I couldn't make out much of it. Delia was crying, though, and so was Nina. One of the men who'd gone outdoors came back in and said something to the woman with the gun. Then he went back out again. She grabbed my arm and spoke directly into my face. "We have to go right now. They know we're here. Get your friends."

"You shot each other."

"We just fixed that."

"I don't trust you people."

"Not asking you to, but we need to go, or you'll die here in five minutes."

I went over and grabbed Freddy, then back to Nina and helped Delia to her feet. The woman had already gone outdoors. Randall had stopped breathing, wet blood soaking his mouth and chest. More death, more tears.

One of those fellows who'd been back at the stove went over to the cabinet bed and closed it up. Then he stood by the door and waited for us for collect ourselves and go.

We stepped out into a swirling breeze from across the river, cold and damp. Fish-tainted water and wet rot of sludge and moss carried that familiar scent of the ancient tributary. A stink of oil, too, and that ugly odor of smokestacks urging black clouds into the late afternoon air. Ship horns burst across the day. More firesticks popped. We avoided Randall's body and saw three more dead men just off from the old shack, one of them with a bullet-hole in his left eye.

Upriver were wooden piers for fishing boats and skiffs tied off and bobbing on the current. Downriver was the great wharf and the big ships and those thousands of celebrants, crowding the miles of boardwalk and old rusted and windworn buildings, warehouses and shops and barns, fishmongers, crab shacks and marine industry.

Her hair fluttering in the draft, I heard the woman ask one of the fellows beside her, "Where now?"

"The barge." He fastened the buttons on his jacket and pointed downriver. "It's at the Gillihan wharf, ready to go. They're waiting for us."

Two of the men behind me came up and went past us, keeping a dozen feet apart. One stayed off my shoulder closer to the grassy river tide while the woman and the other fellow flanked us as we headed toward the wharf.

I had no idea how we were expected to manage those crowds. I'd trusted Randall with our lives. I didn't know any of these people. None of us did. How could we? That shooting. What was it? A trap? An ambush? A betrayal? All of that? How were we supposed to know if our side won? According to Rúbotton and Radelfinger, something was coming at the end of this day to put a period on our story. Did these people dragging us along even understand that?

I wondered if I ought to tell them, or at least ask what they knew, if anything. For the sake of Nina, Delia and Freddy?

More firesticks popping. The roar of that crowd in the central metropolis was audible now, even above ship horns and delirious cheers and the constant shouting of everyone up ahead on the wharf, packed impossibly wall to pier. Entering that crowd now felt insane. Just ahead of us was a broad wooden staircase leading from the riverbank up onto the plank boardwalk. Kids were hanging off its railing, some playing in the sandy shadows beneath. I checked my pocket-watch as we approached. Almost half past five. So late now. I became terrified that we'd be stuck somewhere on the wharf when time ran out, whatever that entailed. I wished I'd asked Radelfinger to clarify what he meant by a "demonstration in the atmosphere."

Gulls circled overhead, screeching on the cloudy grey afternoon draft. One of the fellows in the lead went up the stairs. The other stood at the bottom with those kids and watched the crowd around us. When we were only a few strides from the steps, I heard a voice shout out on the wind.

"Hold up!"

I saw that ever-present specter, Marco Grenelle, approaching rapidly with a young woman wearing a dark red bandanna and another older fellow just behind them both.

Nina called to him before I did, "What are you doing here? We're supposed to be on the ship by now. We're already late."

Marco ignored her, instead addressing the woman and the man flanking us. "Where are you taking everyone? What's the plan?"

The woman answered first. "The barge, *Triton's Abundance*. That's where we were told to go."

"Who said to go there?"

The fellow beside her spoke up, "Randall got a message. He told us. That's the plan. They're waiting."

"I bet they are."

By now, those fellows who were trailing our little party came up and formed a cordon around us, shielding our group off from people passing toward the boardwalk. What was Marco doing there? Who was that girl with him and that older man? Nina looked frantic as she slipped her arm around Delia, who was struggling with Goliath on his leash. Freddy was still vague.

Marco asked the others, "Did any of you get that message?"

They just stared at him, watching.

He rephrased the question. "Did any of you actually hear Randall say you were to go to the barge?"

The fellow with the woman replied, "He told me personally and I was supposed to pass it on to everyone else while he got these kids together."

"He said the plan was to take everyone to the barge?"

"Yes, he did."

"But Randall got shot, so now you're in charge of getting them there?"

"Mirés agreed." He nodded to the woman. "Didn't you, honey?"

The woman said, "If that's what Randall told you, sure."

"Well, he did."

Another round of firesticks went off under the boardwalk, scaring the gulls. A beautiful white yacht packed with cheering revelers joined the flotilla swelling toward the Hesperien Pier where celebrations were ecstatic, and that penultimate hour of jubilee was arriving.

Marco took a pistol from his pocket and shot the fellow in the head who had just promised to take us to the barge. A mist of blood. Then he quickly bent over the body and took one of those black devices from a back trouser pocket and stuck it into his own jacket.

He told the woman, "Cohn lied. He sent that message to Randall himself. They turned him. Internal Security is on the barge right now waiting to kill you all. *Triton's Abundance* was not the plan, but it's why Randall's dead." He told the other people. "Let's go. Back the other way. Leave the body."

Those kids under the stairs were wailing and scrambling away to the water or up onto boardwalk, where people were coming to see what had happened.

Then Marco said to us, "I'm sorry about all of this. The Protectorate infiltrated our group this morning. Just a few of them, but that would've been enough to get you killed, and more of us, too."

Still in shock, I asked, "What's the real plan?"

"A fishing trawler back up the river past that shack you came out of. We'll be on the water in five minutes. I promise."

— · —

At the end of a narrow pier a quarter of a mile upriver, we met Warren Radelfinger and Evelyn Haskins bundled up in warm clothing, travel bags in hand. Greetings and hugs. Then we hurried onto the boat. The trawler was plenty large enough to fit all of us and our luggage. The woman named Mirés came onboard with Marco and his two companions, that girl and her fellow holding a hunting rifle now.

Then we were out on the immortal river amid the flags and horns and cheers, one of hundreds of vessels plying the wide waters of our greatest tributary. Marco had gone straight into the wheelhouse to have a talk with our pilot, a fellow he called, "Le Soleil." Whether that was his name or a reputation, I didn't get. Either way, the old fellow was guiding us cleverly through the cold current in the general direction of the Hesperien Pier, but maneuvering closer to the far side of the river at Marco's insistence.

The girl who'd come onboard with him sat at the stern with that fellow and his hunting rifle. Mirés took her solitary place amidships and gazed out across the waters. The rest of us sat together next to the forward superstructure and wondered what was about to occur. First, though, Freddy dug out his bottle of bourbon, down by half, and offered it to Radelfinger, who politely declined. Evie, however, accepted enthusiastically.

She tipped the bottle into her mouth, then said, "Warren swore there'd be refreshments onboard. There aren't even any fish. If I can't eat, I simply have to drink."

I took that opportunity to ask Radelfinger, "What should we expect now?"

"Evie will be drunk in ten minutes and absolutely ruin everything. She can't help herself."

She kicked at him. "That's not at all true. Why, I'm twice the fun once I'm in the bag. You know that better than anyone, darling."

She passed the bottle back to Freddy, who'd apparently gone mute from all the alcohol. Or he'd swallowed his own tongue.

I kept my focus on Radelfinger. "You know what I mean."

He smiled. "I'd rather not spoil the surprise, Julian. It'll be more than you could ever dream of. I promise you that. My great-uncle is probably into his third cocktail on the Girardin rooftop about now. I'm sure his guests are at least that far along. The doors are bolted up top, and they have great seats for the spectacle."

A fresh motor boat dressed in colored flags sped past us, tooting its horn. It was transporting a gaggle of pretty girls dressed in white sailor suits at the stern who were shouting something into the chilly wind that sounded awfully like an obscenity. We were all being drowned out by celebrations on the water, droning megaphones from the embankments, and even more so by the roar of millions within the central metropolis and those nearby districts on both sides of the eternal river. I thought it must have been absolutely deafening throughout Prospect Square and Immanuel Fields and miles along Ehrenhardt Boulevard.

Nina spoke up to tell me, "Delia's tired. I think she's still a little sick. Her forehead's warm again."

"I'll see if I can find her a blanket."

I got up and went into the wheelhouse to ask.

Those grey clouds to the east were offering intimate suggestions of sunlight over the river now as the day was ending. I stared out at all the traffic on the river and the wharf whose crowded boardwalk was so thick and hectic there'd be nowhere to go when the hour struck.

The Hesperien Pier was directly off our starboard now across the river, filled with people and their flags and horns and streamers and firesticks. I saw that barge we'd been expected to board, moored between a coal vessel and a large freighter, men visible on the barge's port bow with binoculars. Too far away to threaten us now.

Marco stood beside the pilot at the helm. I called to him, "Delia needs a blanket. She's a little feverish."

The pilot said something to Marco, who told me, "There's a locker just below deck. Blankets are in there. Water, too, with food in a trunk. You'll see it."

"Thanks."

"It's ten minutes to six o'clock," Marco said. "The hour of Jubilee is almost upon us."

I corrected him. "The hour of Judgment."

I took a ladder below deck and retrieved that thick wool blanket and brought it up for Nina to wrap around Delia. They both looked pale and tired. Goliath was curled up at Nina's feet. Freddy's attention was focused on the Hesperien Pier that was becoming gradually distant.

Radelfinger came over and grabbed my arm. For once, his persistent insouciance appeared to have fled. He told me, "We can't be here, Julian, when the show begins. We won't survive."

"Did you tell Marco that?"

"I thought so, but I'm assuming now he didn't quite get the gist of this. He seemed to think it's just some bomb we're setting off."

I shrugged. "He likes bombs."

"It's not a bomb, Julian. Not at all. Believe me, we can't be this close when it happens."

"Well, where, then?"

He stared at me, abject fear in his eyes. "A lot farther downriver. At least three miles away."

A brisk wind tugged at Delia's blanket and Nina's lovely black hair. I saw whitecaps on the water in the wake of vessels maneuvering quick and slow through the cold current. I decided to try Marco once more, see if we weren't using all the trawler's horsepower.

I went back into the wheelhouse and interrupted his conversation with the pilot. "Warren says we need to go faster."

Marco looked annoyed now. "This isn't a speedboat, Julian."

"He just told me we'll be dead if we don't."

Marco leaned over and told the pilot what I'd just said, and I saw the old fellow stiffen at the wheel. Then he studied his gauges and did something with a lever that gave the engine a bigger roar. Our trawler sped up.

But it really was too late.

That hour of Jubilee had arrived.

At six o'clock, every church and cathedral in the greater metropolis rang its bells in a cacophony of celebration for the end of our endless war. Skyrockets lit off in the atmosphere with brilliant showers of sparks and smoke. Firesticks popped by the thousands. Vast swarms of pigeons fled the Dome of Eternity and hundreds of peaked rooftops across the city. A crescendo of cheering and ecstasy swept across the water from both riverbanks.

Then Nina was shouting my name. I left the wheelhouse to see what she needed.

I found her and Freddy, Radelfinger and Evie, Marco's people at the stern and Mirés amidships, their eyes on those grey clouds to the east where a copper sky lit the sunset horizon and the heralds of world's end had just arrived.

Five gigantic airships of improbable scale and proportion descended slowly from the clouds a mile apart, each greater in length and width than the immense Thessandrus Hippodrome. Cathedral bells yet rang and rang and rang, but those myriad firesticks quit and the megaphones and ship horns and ecstatic cheering ceased. As if a great hush settled over the earth and water, all attention drawn now to the heavens. Not *Deiopeia*, whose purpose was wonder and elegance. I almost thought the great airships, graceful and shameless, would bring relief to us, some needful intervention in our sordid affairs, even as those long shadows fell across a dozen vital districts of our grand metropolis.

Radelfinger had left Evie at the railing and rushed into the wheelhouse, where I could hear him yelling frantically at Marco and our river pilot. Freddy stood mumbling to himself. Nina cowered with Delia whose eyes were shut. I watched the giant airships slow and draw nearer to our world. Cathedral bells finally stopped ringing. River craft of all sorts drifted now almost aimlessly on the bitter current. We found a quicker path as the trawler's engine roared louder still. Radelfinger took a spot just outside the wheelhouse and watched as all five airships hung suspended like dark fingers of God above our city and the immortal river.

I noticed Nina staring at me. We both tried to smile. What was there to say? Goodbye?

Our trawler was at least a couple miles now downriver from the Hesperien Pier. Not far enough. I looked at Radelfinger. He was nodding, counting to himself. What did he know? This was his creation, wasn't it? His responsibility? Or ours for a century of persecution and murderous apathy to any sort of goodness and morality? Now and then, enlightenment comes too late and we suffer the consequence of that. Sadly, this appeared to be ours.

As we watched, each of those immense airships released from its belly a vast cloud of emerald-green gas, Radelfinger's celestial atomizer borne to earth, sparkling through that last sunlight of the day. The gas cascaded into the atmosphere, blooming out across the air as it fell ever so gently toward us. Undeniably beautiful and carrying a divine scent of honeysuckle. One final breath of a lovely but unattainable garden. I saw the green clouds from each airship shroud the metropolis from the Catalan and the hills of Simoni District to Beuiliss, Sartosé, Cristel, Honoré, Treppel, Calcitonia, even over Regency Heights. The great central airship hovered a thousand feet above Prospect Square and the Mollison Institute, where that descending gas cloud had just begun to grace the gilded spires of our Dome of Eternity. Next, the paralyzed silence devolved into panic and screams, a million people suddenly afraid the green cloud was poison gas.

Evie yelled something incomprehensible to Radelfinger, who shouted back, "For Christsakes, darling, I just don't know!"

Our trawler took us farther away downriver. Both embankments were alive with fear now. The wharf became a massed scattershot of humanity, thousands of people diving into the cold water to evade that airborne death as the gas drifted toward the western shore and slowly settled onto the ceaseless ripples of the holy river, Livorna.

We'd escaped the cloud, but few others did. Those great freighters and barges and coal ships, pier-bound vessels by the hundreds, were hidden in that hazy green fog. The huge Hesperien Pier was almost invisible. We heard urgent foghorns blasting as desperate boats behind us began colliding in the current.

Radelfinger trained a spyglass on the central airship. Evie was at his side, her arms firmly about his waist. Nina and Delia cuddled low to the deck with Goliath. Freddy held his hands high above his head like some supplicant even he wouldn't recognize. Those others who had come onboard with Marco were gathered together at the stern, just watching the gas clouds unfurl over the fading metropolis.

Then sundown.

And the giant airships began to lift away from us toward the dark clouds.

Higher and higher above our world.

At perhaps two thousand feet, each airship cast off a golden flare.

We watched the flares drop like shooting stars, falling to earth from that clouded firmament.

Down.

Down.

Down.

Until each glowing flare touched that green cloud of gas, and Radelfinger shouted, "Close your eyes!"

The flash of light and heat was astonishing. For a moment, our entire universe disappeared. No great bang or wrenching explosion. Utterly soundless. Just a gust of wind. A hot dry summer wind.

We were far enough away to be alive and remember what we saw after.

Fire.

Incineration.

Everywhere.

Burning flags atop burning buildings.

Birds by the thousands ablaze and tumbling from the sky.

Radio antennaes melting.

Gas tanks exploding.

Glass windows evaporating.

Trees bursting into enormous fiery torches.

Vessels on the eternal river enflamed like funeral pyres.

People, wherever we looked, burning alive.

By the tens of thousands.

Across the blazing wharf and all along the river embankments.

Human candles aboard every vessel.

Incandescent people floundering hopelessly in the cold water and through the wet reeds and grass and fiery brush.

Ghastly screams.

Endless tribulations of pain and torment and witness of death.

My imagination sparked hellish scenes of Prospect Square and Immanuel Fields and Regency Heights, the Mollison Institute and Nationale Club, the Hotel Bremen, Bronzeville Square, Gosney Street, Meltemi Avenue and Jimmy Potatoes utterly engulfed in that holocaust of flame and horror. Perhaps the flames were visible even from Highland Park, Alexanderton, and Hattier de Maistre.

I do admit I wished somehow to see the Mendel Building on fire, burning embers rising from those who had pulled the lever to the lethal chamber for that gas and brilliant heat that ended the lives of brave Zynis, Riala and those other eighty-thousand beautiful children.

— · —

Hell, Death and the Devil come short of me.

We navigated far away downriver.
    From the echoing screams.
    And still felt the heat for miles.
    Night fell.
    The airships were gone.
    Every corner of the metropolis burned and burned.
    Death had at last become legion for them, too.

LVIV
∾

A skiff intercepted our trawler off Adorciés Point to rendezvous with Marco and his pals and bring them back to the undercity, where there were many decisions to consider. Nina and Delia huddled with Evie below deck while I waited with Radelfinger and Marco and Freddy, who'd sobered up and stared wordlessly toward that fiery glow on the night horizon upriver.

Marco told me, "*The end of all things is the beginning of others.* That's what my mother used to say. Is there any truth in that, Julian? Or is it just talk?"

"Lots of truth, Marco. Too much truth."

He said, "The undercity has always been more sanctuary for us than prison, though unfortunately some haven't quite seen it that way. I think tonight they will."

As Marco's companions were transferring one by one to the wooden skiff, I asked him, "Where are we being taken?"

"Out to sea where you'll meet the steamship, *Ardea Purthdnos*. You'll go south to Trecéirea, roughly three days voyage from here. Castor and Pollux tell me it's wonderful. You'll be happy there."

"I'll miss my family. So will Freddy."

"You'll be able to come back one day. Just not for a while. You'll know when."

I watched Mirés take her seat at the bow of the skiff. She was bundled up. That fellow with the rifle eased in beside her.

I said to Marco, "I should thank you for saving our lives."

He offered his hand, and I took it. Maybe he was insane, yet he was also brave and rational where it happened to matter most. I hoped he'd survive.

As he boarded the skiff, Marco told me, "One day this'll be a story we'll want to remember to tell. Opinions will vary, details may change. But it'll only be a story."

The night was cold and damp and windy. Side by side, Freddy, Radelfinger and I watched until the skiff vanished into the dark. Then we went down below deck.

A great dark sea awaited.

INFINITE RICHES

The war did end. In shame and sorrow. Almost two million people died in the metropolis, where the fires raged for more than a month. Smoke sailed across continents and out to sea for thousands of miles. I'd smelled it myself occasionally when the wind drifted west and south.

Trecéirea had a mild climate and a most cheerful and pleasant populace. The town where Nina and I settled with Delia and Freddy was called Musset. It was a small fishing village with pretty painted houses and crushed-stone streets. We lived in a green two-story house at the top of a lush tree-shaded lane a couple of blocks from the shore where Delia could walk Goliath to the beach and gather seashells for her bedroom collection. Our rooms were upstairs, and Freddy took his on the bottom floor off the kitchen facing a dooryard of orange and lemon trees. No one explained how we were able to be there, but we supposed it had been arranged for us. We were appreciative and had no complaints, except Freddy feeling desperately bored every so often on those afternoons when a subtropical squall kept us all indoors and he had no new games to play or fresh puzzles to unravel. I finagled a job teaching composition and preliminary Latin at Delia's Iasius Mare School in the next village, and Nina began working half-days at a shop that sells pottery and ancient oils.

Radelfinger and Evie traveled up into the mountains to live in a very old house Rúbotton had owned. Warren claimed a wonderful playroom to occupy himself with odd inventions. Evie writes poetry and samples local intoxications. We've promised to visit one day but have yet to do so.

I learned to sail with Nina whose father once fished at sea. We have a boat that feels safe if we keep close enough to shore that we could swim to safety if all went wrong. Freddy refused to tempt that theory. His explanation for avoiding our adventures was to tell us, *"I'm not a fan of fish or dolphins, thank you."*

Freddy lived in our house at Musset for a year until his chance arrived to voyage back home by ship and auto to Alexanderton. He's there now in his old bedroom and his radio basement. We know a fellow in the village with a micro-radio set of his own, and once a month or so he lets us have a conversation with Freddy across the deep waters. My old roommate tells us he's happy, so we are, too.

Two years after Freddy left, I felt safe enough to go back, as well, to see my mother and discover the fate of all I'd ever known. I found her healthy and in high spirits. Her garden flourished as ever and reflected her constancy. My bedroom remained as I'd last seen it. That pleased me no end because it meant she still considered me her "baby boy." Agnes had gone off to live in Rosborough with that church fellow from McNeeley Branson. They hoped to marry one day but had no firm plans. Mother let me know that Agnes had calmed down and was growing into a fine young woman. I had expected Mother to be lonely in the absence of my father and Agnes and myself. Truth is, I worried about her. But she told me that after Jack McManus died in the fires, Peggy had decided to come live with her and share the advantage and convenience of companionship. It was a nice arrangement that suited them both and complimented their spirits. I was better than satisfied. When we visited my mother a year later, her heart had even more to sing about.

Regency College had suffered grievous damage. Our floor at Thayer Hall had been hollowed out by fire. Hundreds of students and professors had perished. Of mine, though, only Dr. Sternwood had been killed. Pardo, Lamberton and Dr. Coffeen had survived. No one had a word regarding Walker Bailey or Percy McDonnell, and I had no idea how to investigate the fate of Pindar and Quixote, though I supposed poetry was undying. After wandering about campus for a couple of hours, I hired a taxi from Regency Heights to Immanuel Fields to see the central metropolis. Three years had erased much of the damage and the basic geography and structure of the city remained, but what had been lost was stunning. Vegetation was primitive. Trees were young and spindly. Flower beds sparse and common. The city sidewalks were more spacious and less vibrant. Fewer smiles, fewer confrontations. Diminished crowds on street corners. Façades of most great buildings bore the scars of intense flash and fire. Stately banks and offices, tall department stores reflected that moment of trauma all throughout the metropolis. Bitter layers of soot reigned as the pre-dominant decoration on century-old stone and marble. I hated to imagine how the poorer districts had fared, but suffering need not be eternal. So I hoped.

Eventually curious about all of it, I found myself at a reading table inside the Mansurette Library on Hollerith Plaza. Reports and discourse about the Republic since the war ended was fairly erratic and inconsistent at Musset. Had Crown Colony truly been incinerated? Was the undercity now free and open for trade and transit? Only rumors and scattered news. We were made aware, though, how the Regents and emissaries of Laspágandélus had traveled to the metropolis, and, under the eternal stars within the Dome of Eternity, formally dissolved the Status Imperium and appointed a new governing Judicial Coun-cil whose morality and edicts of reform and re-education finally reversed the obscenity of eugenics throughout our Republic. The truest victory. Aurora begets apologue. A public study and evaluation of spyreosis within the restored Organic Medicine Institute rescinded each chapter of scientific confirmation for a bug that was categorically proven to be nonexistent, and the professional medical journals thoroughly demonstrated this correction. In the stacks of photographic records, I also managed to locate the observance of a solemn ceremony I'd been given notice of by mail one morning at Musset. It offered a collection of dignitaries from Regency College and the Mignard Institute gath-ered on the Marcellus Shore. There, in a portrait of that esteemed crowd, I saw Dr. Coffeen posed hand-in-hand at the water's edge with Mr. Sutro.

Our first month at Musset, I married Antonina Terésa Rinaldi in a lovely grove of hyacinth and clover. Freddy stood up as my best man and Delia graced Nina's hand as her maid of honor. A Eumelius priest performed the ceremony at sun-rise on a day of clear blue skies and infinite riches. A year later, Nina gave birth in our own bed to a most beautiful boy we named Nicolaus Charles, for the victory of all peoples who refuse to deny that life is solely concerned with love.

As I write this, eight years after meeting each other one afternoon outside that shaded gallery at Thayer Hall, Nina has brought spice wine and bread, citrus juice and ginger cookies to the shore where we are sitting on a wool blanket I retrieved from my father's closet. The day is warm, a pretty sea breeze is rustling in the olive trees behind us. I'm studying a book this morning on horticulture, and Nina teases me for knowing nothing about fruit trees that I claim we can graft and grow for our morning bowls. We scrap and kiss and hug, and finally lie contentedly together in the late summer sun, all the while watching Delia wade through the blue water with Nicolaus, teaching her little brother day by day how to find all the best of everything there is in this world.

ACKNOWLEDGEMENTS

∞

Our first readers inspire us to do our best work. They are indispensable. Here are mine, and I thank them for inspiring me to continue on:

Annie Dahlgren, Erin Dougherty, Marianne Dougherty, Debra Drexler, Wylene Dunbar, Cheri Flanigan, Karen Ford, Venilde Jeronimo, Christine Casey Logsdon, Carol Shelley, Anne-Lise Spitzer, David Stanford, Simon Van Booy, Buddy Winston, George Zaffle.

Of course, Gary Groth and Eric Reynolds for inviting me once again into print. As ever, I'm very grateful.